# of love & life

Three novels selected and condensed
by Reader's Digest

The Reader's Digest Association Limited, London

CONTENTS

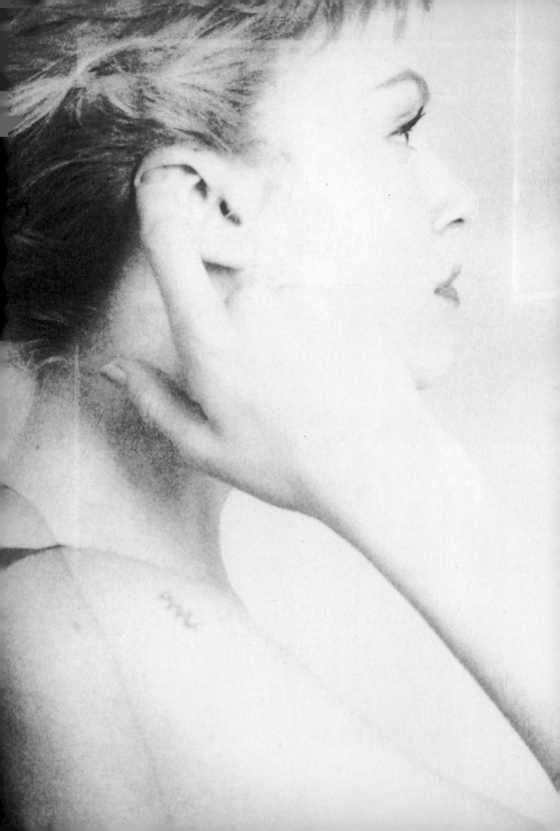

ANYBODY OUT THERE?

MARIAN KEYES

Anna Walsh, PR girl extraordinaire at Candy Grrrl Cosmetics, had the perfect life in New York—until fate intervened and tipped her world upside down.

Now, as she lies on her parents' sofa in Dublin, all she wants is to be reunited with her husband, Aidan. But he seems to be so distant, so impossible to reach . . .

PART ONE

1

MUM FLUNG OPEN the sitting-room door and announced, 'Morning, Anna, time for your tablets.'

She tried to march in briskly, like nurses she'd seen on hospital dramas, but there was so much furniture in the room that instead she had to wrestle her way towards me.

When I'd arrived in Ireland eight weeks earlier, I couldn't climb the stairs because of my dislocated kneecap, so my parents had moved a bed downstairs into the Good Front Room. Make no mistake, this was a huge honour: under normal circumstances we were only let in to this room at Christmas. The rest of the year, all familial leisure activities—television-watching, chocolate-eating, bickering—took place in the cramped converted garage, which went by the grand title of Television Room.

But when my bed was installed in the GFR there was nowhere for the other fixtures—tasselled couches, tasselled armchairs—to go. The room now looked like one of those discount furniture stores where millions of couches are squashed in together.

'Right, Missy.' Mum consulted a sheet of paper, an hour-by-hour schedule of all my medication: antibiotics, anti-inflammatories, anti-depressants, sleeping pills, high-impact vitamins, and painkillers that induced a very pleasant floaty feeling.

All the different packets and jars stood on a small carved table—several china dogs had been shifted to make way for them and now sat on the floor looking reproachfully at me—and Mum began sorting through them, popping out capsules and shaking pills from bottles.

My bed had been thoughtfully placed in the window bay so that I could look out at passing life. Except that I couldn't: there was a net curtain in place that was as immovable as a metal wall. Not *physically* immovable, you understand, but socially immovable: in Dublin suburbia, brazenly lifting your nets to have a good look at 'passing life' is a social gaffe akin to painting the front of your house tartan. Besides, there *was* no passing life. Except . . . actually, through the gauzy barrier, I'd begun to notice that most days an elderly woman stopped to let her dog wee at our gatepost. Sometimes I thought the dog, a cute black and white terrier, didn't even want to wee, but it seemed as if the woman was insisting.

'OK, Missy.' Mum had never called me 'Missy' before all of this. 'Take these.' She tipped a handful of pills into my mouth and passed me a glass of water.

'Dear Jesus,' a voice said. It was my sister Helen, home from a night's work. She stood in the doorway of the sitting room, looked round at all the tassels and asked, 'How can you stand it?'

Helen is the youngest of the five of us and still lives in the parental home, even though she's twenty-nine. But why would she move out, she often asks, when she's got a rent-free gig, cable telly and a built-in chauffeur (Dad)?

'Hi, honey, you're home,' Mum said. 'How was work?'

After several career changes, Helen—and I'm not making this up, I wish I was—is a private investigator. Mind you, it sounds far more dangerous and exciting than it is. She mostly does white-collar crime and 'domestics'. She spends a lot of time sitting in wet hedges with a long-range lens, trying to get photographic evidence of adulterers leaving their love nest. She could stay in her warm, dry car but then she tends to fall asleep and miss her mark.

'Mum, my throat is killing me. War-crime sore. I'm going to bed.'

Helen, on account of all the time she spends in damp hedges, gets a lot of sore throats.

'I'll bring you up some ice cream in a minute, pet,' Mum said. 'Tell me, I'm dying to know, did you get your mark?'

'Yes, I got him. Ding-dong! Right, I'm off to bed.' Instead she stretched out on one of the many couches. 'The man spotted me in the hedge, taking his picture.'

Mum's hand went to her mouth, the way a person's would on telly, if they wanted to indicate anxiety.

'Nothing to worry about,' Helen said. 'We had a little chat. He asked for my phone number. Cackhead,' she added with blistering scorn.

That's the thing about Helen: she's very beautiful. Men, even those she's spying on for their wives, fall for her. Despite me being three years older than her, she and I look extremely similar: we're short with long dark hair and almost identical faces. But, unlike me, Helen's got some magic pull. When men meet the two of us, you can see their confusion. You can actually see them thinking: They look the same, but this Helen has bewitched me like a drug, whereas that Anna is just so-what . . . Not that it does the men in question any good. Helen boasts that she's never been in love and I believe her. She's unbothered by sentimentality and has contempt for everyone and everything.

Even Luke, Rachel's boyfriend—well, fiancé now. Luke is so dark and sexy and testosteroney that I dread being alone with him. I mean, he's a lovely person, really, really lovely, but just, you know . . . all man. Everyone is sexually attracted to him. Not Helen, though.

All of a sudden Mum seized my arm—luckily, my unbroken one—and hissed, in a voice throbbing with excitement, 'Look! It's Jolly Girl, Angela Kilfeather. With her Jolly Girl girlfriend! She must be visiting!'

(Helen once worked with an Indian man who mistranslated 'gays' as 'Jolly Boys'. It caught on so much that nearly everyone I know—including all my gay friends—now refers to gay men as 'Jolly Boys'. And always said in an Indian accent. The logical conclusion is that lesbians are 'Jolly Girls', also said in an Indian accent.)

Mum placed one eye up against the gap between the wall and the net curtain. 'I can't see, give me your binoculars,' she ordered Helen, who produced them from her rucksack with alacrity—but only for her own personal use. A small but fierce struggle ensued. 'She'll be GONE,' Mum begged. 'Let me see.' She was trying to grab the binoculars from Helen and they wrestled like children, only stopping when they bumped against my hand, the one with the missing fingernails, and my shriek of pain restored them to decorum.

After she'd washed me, Mum took the bandages off my face, like she did every day, then bundled me up in a blanket. I sat in the matchbox of a back garden, watching the grass grow and airing my cuts.

But the doctor had said that exposure to direct sunlight was strictly *verboten*, so even though there was scant chance of that in Ireland in April, I wore a stupid-looking wide-brimmed hat which Mum had worn to my sister Claire's wedding; luckily there was no one there to see me.

The sky was blue, the day was quite warm and all was pleasant. I listened to Helen coughing intermittently in an upstairs bedroom and dreamily watched the pretty flowers sway to the left in the light breeze, then back to the right, then to the left again—the painkillers made me super-dopey and serene and it was only when the salt water of my tears ran into my cuts and made them sting that I discovered I was crying.

I wanted to go back to New York. For the last few days I'd been thinking about it. Not just considering it, but gripped by a powerful compulsion and unable to understand why I hadn't gone before now. The problem was, though, that Mum and the rest of them would go mad when I told them. I could already hear their arguments—I must stay in Dublin where my roots were, where I was loved, where they could 'take care of me'.

At the thought of how long and loud they'd protest, I was grabbed by another panicky seizure: I *had* to return to New York. I had to get back to my job. I had to get back to my friends. And, although there was no way I could tell anyone this, because they would have sent for the men in the white coats, I had to get back to Aidan.

I closed my eyes and started to drift, but suddenly, like a grinding of gears in my head, I was plunged into a memory of noise and pain and darkness. I snapped my eyes open. This had started over the past few days: the painkillers were wearing off faster and ragged chinks were appearing in the blanket of mellowness they dropped on me and the horror would rush in, like water from a burst dam.

I struggled to my feet and went inside where I watched *Home and Away*, had lunch (half a cheese scone, five satsuma segments, two Maltesers, eight pills), then Mum dressed my wounds again before my walk. She loved this bit, busying about with her surgical scissors, briskly cutting lengths of cotton wool and white sticky tape. Nurse Walsh tending to the sick. I closed my eyes. The touch of her fingertips on my face was soothing.

'The smaller ones on my forehead have started to itch, that's a good sign, isn't it?'

'Let's see.' She moved my fringe aside to take a closer look. 'These really are healing well,' she said, like she knew what she was talking about. 'I think we can probably leave the bandages off these. And maybe the one on your chin.' (A perfect circle of flesh had been removed from the very centre of my chin. It will come in handy when I want to do Kirk Douglas impersonations.) 'But no scratching, Missy! These sutures are far better than stitches. It's only this one, really,' she said, gently stroking antiseptic gel onto the deep, puckered gash that ran the length of my right cheek, then pausing to let me flinch with pain. This wound wasn't held together by sutures; instead it had dramatic Frankenstein-style stitches that looked like they'd been done with a darning needle. Of all the marks on my face this was the only one that wouldn't eventually disappear.

'But that's what plastic surgeons are for,' I said, parroting what the doctor had told us.

'That's right,' Mum agreed. But her voice sounded faraway and strangled. Quickly, I opened my eyes. She was hunched in on herself and muttered something that might have been, 'Your poor little face.'

'Mum, don't cry!'

'I'm not.'

'Good.'

'Anyway, I think I hear Margaret.' She rubbed her face with a tissue and went outside to laugh at Maggie's new car.

Maggie had arrived for our daily walk. The second eldest of the five of us, she is the maverick of the Walsh family, our dirty secret, our white sheep. Maggie had 'rebelled' by living a quiet, well-ordered life with a quiet, well-ordered man called Garv, who, for years, my family *hated*. They objected to his reliability, his decency and most of all his jumpers. (Too similar to Dad's, was the consensus.) However, relations have softened in recent years, especially since the children came along: JJ is now three and Holly is five months.

I will admit to having entertained some jumper-based prejudice myself, of which I'm now ashamed because about four years ago Garv helped me to change my life. I'd reached a nasty little crossroads and Garv got me a job in the actuarial firm where he worked. *Then* he encouraged me to get a qualification, so I got a diploma in public relations. I know it's not as impressive as a masters degree in astrophysics, but if I hadn't got it, I would never have ended up in my current job—The Best Job In The World™. And I would never have met Aidan.

Now I hobbled to the front door, where Maggie was unloading children from her new car, a wide-bodied people-carrier, which Mum was insisting looked like it had elephantitis. Dad was also out there, trying to provide a foil for Mum's contempt; he was demonstrating what a fine car it was by walking round it and kicking all four tyres.

'Look at the quality on it,' he declared and kicked a tyre again to underscore his point.

'Look at the little piggy eyes on it!'

'They're not eyes, Mum, they're lights,' Maggie said, unbuckling something and emerging with baby Holly under her arm.

'Could you not have a Maserati?' Mum asked.

'Not fast enough.'

Mum watched *Top Gear* and had developed a sudden, late-in-life longing for a fast, sexy car.

Maggie's torso disappeared into the car again and, after more unbuckling, she emerged with three-year-old JJ under her other arm.

Maggie, like Claire (the sister older than her) and Rachel (the sister younger than her), is tall and strong. The three of them come from an identical gene pool to Mum's. Helen and I, a pair of short-arses, look astonishingly different to them and I don't know where we get it from. Dad isn't small, it's just the meekness that makes him seem that way.

Maggie has embraced motherhood with a passion—not just the actual mothering, but the look. One of the best things about having children, she says, is not having the time to worry about what she looks like, and she boasts that she has totally given up on shopping. Other than her hair, which is shoulder-length and a lovely chestnut colour (artificial—clearly she hasn't given up completely), she looks more mumsy than Mum.

'Look at that hickey oul' skirt on her,' Mum murmured. 'People will think we're sisters.'

'I heard that,' Maggie called. 'And I don't care.'

'Your car looks like a rhino,' was Mum's parting shot.

'A minute ago it was an elephant. Dad, can you open out the buggy, please.'

Then JJ spotted me and became incoherent with delight. Maybe it was just the novelty value, but I was currently his favourite auntie. He squirmed out of Maggie's grip and rushed up the drive like a cannon-ball. He was always flinging himself at me, and even though three days earlier he had accidentally headbutted my dislocated knee, which was just out of plaster, I still forgave him.

I would have forgiven him anything: he was an absolute scream. Being around him definitely lifted my mood but I tried not to show it too much because the rest of them might have started with the well-meaning platitudes—that I was young, that I would eventually have a child of my own, etc. etc.—and I wasn't ready to hear them.

I took JJ into the house to collect his 'walk hat'. When Mum had been searching out a wide-brimmed, sun-deflecting hat for me, she'd come across a cache of dreadful hats she'd worn to weddings over the years, and for some reason JJ had fallen in love with a flat, glazed straw hat with a cluster of cherries dangling from the brim. JJ insisted it was 'a cowboy hat' but, really, nothing could have been further from the truth. Already, at the age of three, he was displaying a pleasing strain of eccentricity.

When we were all ready, the cavalcade moved forward: me leaning on Dad with my unbroken arm, Maggie pushing baby Holly in the buggy and JJ, the marshal, leading the party. Mum refused to join us on our daily constitutional, on the grounds that if she came there would be so many of us that 'People would be looking'.

As we neared the green—it wasn't far, it just felt that way because my knee was so sore that even JJ, a child of three, could go faster than me—one of the local lads spotted us and alerted his four or five pals.

'Howya, Frankenstein,' Alec called, when we were near enough to hear.

'Howya,' I replied with dignity.

It had upset me the first time they'd said it. Especially when they'd offered me money to lift my bandages and show them my cuts. At the time tears had flooded my eyes and, shocked at how cruel people could be, I'd turned round to go straight back home. Then I'd heard Maggie ask, 'How much? How much to see the worst one?'

A brief consultation had ensued. 'A euro.'

'Give it to me,' Maggie had ordered. The oldest one had handed the coin over, looking at her nervously.

Maggie'd checked that it was real, then she'd said to me, 'Ten per cent for me, the rest for you. OK. Show them.'

So I'd shown them—obviously not for the money but because I realised I had no reason to feel ashamed. After that they always called me Frankenstein, but not in an unkind way.

Today they noticed that Mum had left off some of the bandages. 'You're getting better.' They sounded disappointed. 'The only good one left is the one on your cheek. And you're walking faster. You're nearly as fast as JJ now.'

For half an hour or so we sat on the bench taking the air. In the few weeks we'd been doing this daily walk, we'd been having unIrishly dry weather, at least in the daytime. It was only in the evenings, when Helen was sitting in hedges with her long-range lens, that it rained.

The reverie was broken when Holly started screeching. According to Maggie, her nappy needed to be changed so we all trooped back to the house. While Maggie was off dealing with baby wipes and nappy bags, JJ got a rust-coloured lipliner from my (extremely large) make-up bag, held it to his face and said, 'Like you.'

'What's like me?'

'Like you,' he repeated, touching some of my cuts, then pointing at his own face with the pencil. *Ah!* He wanted me to draw scars on him.

'Only a few.' I wasn't at all sure this was something that should be encouraged, so I coloured in some half-hearted cuts on his forehead, then held a hand-mirror in front of him. 'Look.'

He liked the look of himself so much, he yelled, 'More!'

'Just one more.'

He kept checking himself in the mirror and demanding more and more injuries, then Maggie came back and I saw the look on her face. 'Oh God. Maggie, I'm sorry. I got carried away.'

But with a funny little jump, I realised she wasn't angry about JJ looking like a patchwork quilt—it was because she'd seen my make-up bag and got The Look.

It's been the oddest thing. Despite all the horror and grief of the recent past, most days some member of my family would come and sit on my bed and ask to see the contents of my make-up bag.

Maggie walked towards me like a sleepwalker, with her hand outstretched. 'Can I see?'

'Help yourself. And my washbag is on the floor here. There's good stuff in there too.'

As if in a trance, Maggie was removing lipstick after lipstick from the bag. 'Some of them haven't even been opened,' she said. 'How come Helen and Mum haven't stolen them?'

'Because they already have them. Just before . . . you know . . . everything, I'd sent a consignment of the new summer products.'

'They never told me about the new stuff,' Maggie said sadly. 'And I only live a mile away.'

'Oh. Maybe it's because they think you wouldn't be interested in make-up. When I go back to New York, I'll send things directly to you.'

'Will you? Thanks.' Then, a sharp look. 'You're going back? When? You can't go anywhere. You need the security of your family . . .' But she was distracted by the lipsticks. She continued taking things out, opening them, trying them on the back of her hand, then closing them neatly. When she'd examined everything she sighed heavily. 'I might as well see your washbag now.'

'Help yourself. There's a lovely vetiver shower gel.' Then I thought for a second. 'No, wait, I think Dad took it.'

She sifted through the shower gels and exfoliators and body lotions, uncapping and sniffing and rubbing, and said, 'You really *do* have the best job in the world.'

My job and how I got it

I work in New York City as a beauty PR. I am assistant vice-president for Public Relations for Candy Grrrl, one of the hottest cosmetic brands on the planet. (You've probably heard of them; and if you haven't, it means someone, somewhere, isn't doing their job properly. I hope it's not me.) I have access to a dizzying array of free products. I am not just permitted to wear Candy Grrrl products, I am obliged to. We all have to take on the personality of the brands we represent. *'Live it,'* Ariella urged me, when I got the job. 'Live it, Anna. You are a Candy Grrrl girl, twenty-four seven, you are always on duty.'

What makes it all exponentially fabulous is that it's not just Candy Grrrl stuff I get. The agency I work for, McArthur on the Park (founded and still owned by Ariella McArthur), represents thirteen other beauty brands, each more delicious than the previous.

Besides free products, there are other perks. Because McArthur on the Park has the Perry K account, I get my hair cut and coloured for free at Perry K. (Just one thing, though: at the risk of seeming ungrateful, it *seems* caring, but I've no choice about the haircuts. I *have* to have them and I get no input: whatever is on the catwalks is what I get given. McArthur owns my soul, which is bad enough. But to own my hair . . .)

Anyway, people often ask me, their faces distorted with jealousy, 'How do you get a job like yours?'

Well, I'll tell you.

With my diploma in PR, I got a job in the Dublin press office of a low-rent cosmetic company. It was crappy money and backbreaking work—mostly stuffing envelopes for mail shots—and I didn't even have the compensation of free make-up. But I had some idea of how PR could be, the fun and creativity you could have in the right place, and I'd always had a hankering for New York . . .

I didn't want to go on my own so all I had to do was convince my best friend, Jacqui Staniforth, that she too had a hankering for New York. But I didn't give much for my chances. For years, Jacqui had been like me—entirely without a career plan. She'd spent most of her life working in the hotel trade, doing everything from bar work to front-of-house, then somehow, through no fault of her own, she had become a VIP concierge at one of Dublin's five-star hotels. When showbiz types came to town, it was her job to provide whatever they wanted. No one, especially Jacqui, could figure out how it had happened. She had no qualifications, all she had going for her was that she was chatty, practical and unimpressed by eejits, even famous ones.

Her looks might have had something to do with her success: she often describes herself as a blonde daddy longlegs and, in all fairness, she is very *hingey*. She is so tall and thin that all her joints—knees, hips, elbows, shoulders—look like they've been loosened with a wrench, and when she walks you can almost believe that some invisible puppet-master is moving her by strings. Because of this, women aren't threatened by her. But thanks to her good humour, her dirty laugh and her incredible stamina, when it comes to staying up late and partying, men are comfortable with her.

The visiting celebs often bought her expensive presents. Like the professional she is, she never—well, rarely—got off with the male celebs in her charge, but occasionally she got off with their friends. Usually they were horrible; she seemed to prefer them that way. I don't think I had ever liked any of her boyfriends.

The night I met her to make my pitch she showed up, her usual shiny, happy, hingey self, in a Versace coat, a Dior something, a Chloé something else, and my heart sank. Why would anyone leave a job like this? But it just goes to show.

Before I even mentioned New York, she confessed that she was sick of overpaid stars and their silly requests. She'd had it with celebrity, she said. She wanted a complete change. This was the perfect time to take the US work-permit application forms from my bag. Two months later, we were waving Ireland goodbye.

When we arrived in New York, we stayed with Rachel and Luke for the first few days, but this turned out to be not such a great idea: Jacqui broke out in a sweat every time she looked at Luke, so much so that she nearly had to start taking rehydration salts.

Because Luke is so good-looking people go a bit funny around him. They think that there has to be more to him than there is. But basically, he's just an ordinary, decent bloke, who's got the life he wants, with the woman he wants. He has a gang of lookalike pals—although none is as physically devastating as him—collectively known as the Real Men. Their idea of a big night out is the air-guitar-playing championship—there is such a thing, honestly—and although they are all gifted amateurs, one of them, Shake, showed real promise and got as far as the regional final.

Jacqui and I set about looking for work. Within a week she'd got a job in a five-star Manhattan hotel, in an almost identical post to the one she'd left behind in Dublin.

'I really wanted to do something different,' she said to Rachel, Luke and me when she came home after her first day. 'I don't know how this happened.'

Well, it was obvious: clearly she was more in thrall to that glittering, celeb-tastic world than she'd realised. But you couldn't say that to her. Jacqui has no time for introspection: things are what they are. She is almost the only person I know who has never seen a therapist.

Anyway, just before Jacqui went into muscle spasm from mineral depletion from looking at Luke, we found a place of our own. A studio (i.e. one room) in a crumbling block on the Lower East Side. It was shockingly small and expensive and the shower was in the kitchenette, but at least we were in Manhattan. We weren't planning on spending much time at home—it was simply for sleeping in and having an address; a tiny foothold in the naked city.

Right away, I registered with several ritzy employment agencies. I went for a couple of interviews but got no solid offers and I was just starting to worry when, one Tuesday morning, I got a call to hotfoot it round to McArthur on the Park. Apparently, the previous incumbent had had to 'go to Arizona' (NYC-speak for 'go into rehab') in a big, fat hurry and they urgently needed a temp because they were preparing for a major pitch.

I knew about Ariella McArthur because she was—aren't they always?—a PR legend: fiftyish, big-haired, big-shouldered, controlling, impatient. She was rumoured to sleep only four hours a night (but I later discovered she disseminated that rumour herself).

So I put on my suit and showed up, to discover that the office suites really were on Central Park (thirty-eighth floor—the view from Ariella's office is amazing, but as you're only ever invited into her inner sanctum to be bollocked, it's hard to savour it).

Everyone was running around hysterically and no one really spoke to me, just shrieked orders to photocopy stuff and to glue things to other things. Despite such shoddy treatment, I was dazzled by the brands McArthur represented and the top-end campaigns they'd run, and I found myself thinking: I'd give anything to work here.

I must have glued the right things together, because they told me to come back the following day, the day of the actual pitch, when they were all even more twitchy.

At 3 p.m., Ariella and seven of her top people took up positions around the boardroom table. I was there too, but only in case anyone needed anything—water, coffee, their forehead mopping. I could make eye contact if necessary, but not speak.

As we waited, I overheard Ariella say in a low urgent voice to Franklin, her second-in-command, 'If I do not get this account I will kill.'

For those who don't know the Candy Grrrl story—and because I've lived and breathed it for so long, I sometimes forget there are people who don't—Candy Grrrl originated with the make-up artist Candace Biggly. She began mixing her own products and turned out to be so good at it that the models she was making-up got all excited. Word began to filter down from The Most Fabulous On High that Candace Biggly's stuff was something special.

Then came the name. Countless people, including my own mother, have told me how 'Candy Grrrl' was Kate Moss's pet name for Candace. I'm sorry if this disappoints you, but it's not true. Candace and her husband, George (a creep), paid an expensive advertising agency to come up with it (also, the growling-girl logo), but the Kate story has entered popular folklore and what's the harm in letting it stay there?

Stealthily, the Candy Grrrl name began to appear in beauty pages. Then a small store opened in the Lower East Side and women made pilgrimages all the way downtown. Another store opened, this time in LA, followed by one in London and two in Tokyo, then the inevitable happened: Candy Grrrl was bought by the Devereaux Corporation for an undisclosed eight-figure sum. Suddenly CG went mainstream and exploded onto counters in all the big department stores. However, Candace and George weren't 'comfortable' with the in-house public-relations service Devereaux were providing so they invited some of New York's biggest agencies to pitch for the business.

'They're late,' Franklin said, fingering a little mother-of-pearl pillbox.

Then, with a surprising lack of fanfare, in came Candace, looking nothing like a Candace—brown unstyled hair, black leggings and, strangely, not a scrap of make-up. George, on the other hand, could be considered good-looking and charismatic—he certainly thought so.

Ariella began a gracious welcome, but George cut right across her, demanding 'ideas'.

'If you got the Candy Grrrl account, what would you do?' He pointed a finger at Franklin.

Franklin stammered something about celebrity endorsement, but before he'd finished George had moved on to the next person. He worked his way round the table and got the usual cookie-cutter PR ideas: celebrity endorsement; feature coverage; flying all the major beauty editors somewhere fabulous.

When he got to me, Ariella desperately tried to tell him that I was a nothing, a nobody, just one step up from a robot, but George insisted. 'She works for you, right? What's your name? Anna? Tell me your ideas.'

Ariella was in the horrors. More so when I said, 'I saw these great alarm clocks in a store in SoHo at the weekend'—

Ariella put a hand to her throat like a Victorian lady planning to swoon.

—'They're a mirror image of a regular alarm clock. All the numbers are back-to-front and the hands go in the wrong direction, they actually turn backwards. So if you want to see the right time, you've got to look at the clock in the mirror. I was thinking it would be perfect to promote your Time-Reversal Day Cream. We could do a shoutline like, "Look in the mirror: you're reversing time." Depending on costings we could even do an on-counter giveaway.' (Note to the girl who wants to get ahead: Never say 'cost'; always say 'costings'. I've no idea why, but if you say 'cost' you will not be taken seriously. However, liberal use of the word 'costings' allies you with the big boys.)

'Wow,' George said. He sat back and looked round the table. 'Wow. That is great! The most original thing I've heard here today. Simple but very wow! Very Candy Grrrl.' He and Candace exchanged a look.

The high-tension mood around the table shifted. Some people relaxed but some others got even more tense. (I say 'some others' but I mean Lauryn, more of whom later). The thing is, though, I hadn't planned to have a great idea, it just happened. The only thing I will say is that I'd stopped at Saks on the way home the night before, picked up a CG brochure and learned about their products.

Lauryn tinkled. 'Well, isn't that the thing! I saw those alarm clocks—'

'Shut up, Lauryn.' Ariella cut Lauryn off with terrifying finality, and that was that.

It was my finest hour. Ariella got the account and I got the job.

2

DINNER CHEZ WALSH was from the local Indian takeaway and I did well: half an onion bhaji, one prawn, one chunk of chicken and approximately thirty-five grains of rice, followed by nine pills and two Rolos.

Mealtimes had become battles of will, where Mum and Dad forced cheer into their voices, suggesting another forkful of rice, another chocolate, another vitamin E capsule. I did my best—I felt empty but never hungry—but whatever I ate, it just wasn't enough for them.

Exhausted by the Madras-based tussle, I retreated to my room. Something was rising to the surface: I needed to talk to Aidan. I spoke to him in my head a lot, but now I wanted more: I had to hear his voice. Why hadn't this happened before?

I checked on Mum, Dad and Helen, who were deeply ensconced in the kind of TV detective drama they're hoping will be made out of their lives. They waved me in and began elaborate shifting along the couch to make room, but I said, 'No, I'm fine, I'm just going to—'

'Grand! Good girl.'

I could have said anything: 'I'm just going to set the house on fire', and I'd have got the same response. They were in a profoundly unreachable state, and would remain that way for the next hour or so. I closed the door firmly, lifted the phone from the hall and took it into my room.

My heart was banging in my chest and I was hopeful—excited, in fact. So where should I try him? Not at work because someone else might pick up. His cellphone was the best idea. I didn't know what had happened to it, it might have been disconnected, but when I hit the number I'd called a thousand times, there was a click and then I heard his voice. Not his real voice, just his message, but it was enough to stop me breathing.

'Hi, this is Aidan. I can't take your call right now, but leave a message and I'll get back to you as soon as I can.'

'Aidan,' I heard my voice say. I sounded quavery. 'It's me. Are you OK? Will you really get back to me as soon as you can? Please do.' What else? 'I love you, baby, I hope you know that.'

I disconnected, feeling shaky, dizzy, elated; I'd heard his voice. But within seconds I'd crashed. Leaving messages on his cellphone wasn't enough. I could try emailing him. But that wouldn't be enough either. I had to go back to New York to try to find him. There was a chance he mightn't be there but I had to give it a go.

Quietly, I replaced the phone in the hall. If they found out what I'd been up to, there was no way they'd let me leave.

How I met Aidan

The August before last, Candy Grrrl were preparing to launch a new skin-care range called Future Face. Constantly on the quest for new and innovative ways to love-bomb beauty editors, I had a middle-of-the-night, light-bulb-over-the-head moment and thought I would buy each editor a 'future' investment thing to tie with the 'future' theme of the launch. I hadn't the first clue about them except what I'd heard about people pulling down millions of dollars working in Wall Street. And I couldn't get an appointment with a Wall Street futures analyst. I tried several and got stonewalled over and over. By then I was sorry I'd ever started but I'd made the mistake of boasting about the idea, so I was forced to work my way through less and less famous banks until finally I found a stockbroker in a Midtown bank who agreed to see me and only then because I'd sent Nita, his assistant, tons of free stuff.

So along I went, taking the rare opportunity to strip myself of kooky accoutrements. Let me explain—all McArthur publicists have to take on the personality of the brand they represent. As Candy Grrrl's profile was a little wild and wacky, a little kooky, I had to dress accordingly. But kookiness is a young woman's game and I was thirty-one and burnt out on matching pink with orange. I was thrilled to have the chance to dress soberly. My hair was gloriously denuded of all stupid slides and accessories and I was wearing a navy skirt suit (admittedly dotted with silver stars but it was the most conservative thing I had) and I was clopping along the eighteenth floor looking for Mr Roger Coaster's office, when I rounded a corner and several things happened at once.

There was a man and we bumped into each other with such force that my bag tumbled from my grasp, sending all kinds of embarrassing things skittering across the floor (including the fake glasses I'd brought to look intelligent).

Quickly, we bent down to retrieve stuff, simultaneously reached for the glasses and bumped our heads with a medium-to-loud crack. We both exclaimed, 'Sorry!' He made an attempt to rub my bruised forehead and in the process spilt scalding coffee on the back of my hand. Naturally, I couldn't shriek in agony because I was in a public place. The best I could do was shake my hand vigorously to make the pain go away and while I was doing that and marvelling that the coffee hadn't done more damage, we realised that the front of my white shirt looked like a Jackson Pollock painting.

'You know what?' the man said. 'With a little work, we could get a real routine going here.'

We straightened up and, despite the fact that he'd burnt my hand and ruined my shirt, I liked the look of him.

'May I?' He indicated my burnt hand but didn't touch it—sexual harassment lawsuits are so rife in New York that men often won't get into an elevator with a lone woman, just in case he gets landed with a witness-free accusation of trying to see up her skirt.

'Please.' I thrust my hand at him. Apart from the red scald marks it was a hand to be proud of. I'd rarely seen it looking better. I'd been moisturising regularly with Candy Grrrl's Hands Up, our super-hydrating hand-cream, my acrylic nails had been filled and were painted in Candy Wrapper (silver) and I'd just been de-gorilla'd, an event that always makes me feel joyous and skippy and carefree. I have quite hairy arms—God knows, this is not easy to talk about—but some of my arm-hairs kind of . . . extend to the backs of my hands.

In New York, waxing is as necessary to survival as breathing and you are only really acceptable in polite company if you're almost entirely bald. You can have head hair, eyelashes and two sliverettes of eyebrows, but that's *it*. Everything else must go.

'I am so sorry,' the man said.

'A mere flesh wound,' I said. 'Don't apologise, it was just a terrible, terrible, *terrible* accident. Forget it.'

'But you're burnt. Will you ever play the violin again?'

Then I noticed his forehead: it looked like an egg was trying to push out through his skin.

'Oh God, you've a lump.'

'I do?' He shifted the light brown hair that fell across his forehead. His right eyebrow was split in two by a tiny, silvery thread of a scar. I noticed it, because so is mine. Tenderly, he rubbed the lump.

'Ouch,' I said, wincing on his behalf. 'One of the finest brains of our time.'

'On the verge of breakthrough research. Lost for ever.' He pronounced 'for ever' as 'for evah', like he was from Boston. Then he looked at my temporary ID badge. 'You're a visitor here?' ('visit-ah') 'Would you like me to show you to the bathroom?'

'I'm fine.'

'What about your shirt?'

'I'll pretend it's a fashion statement. Really, I'm fine.'

'You are? You promise?'

I promised, he asked if I was sure, I promised again, I asked if he was OK, he said he was, then he went off with what remained of his coffee and I felt deflated as I carried on my way and found Mr Coaster's office.

I tried to get Nita to explain to Mr Coaster why I was spattered with coffee but she had zero interest. 'Yeah, go on in,' she said irritably, waving her hand in the direction of a closed door.

I knocked and took myself and my dirty shirt inside.

Mr Coaster was a short, big-swinging-dick super-flirt. As soon as I introduced myself, he gave me an overly twinkly grin and said, 'Hey! Is that an accent I hear?'

'Mmm.' I gave the photo of him and—who I can only presume were—his wife and two children, a hard stare.

'British? Irish?'

'Irish.' I gave the photo another meaningful eye-flick. 'Now, Mr Coaster, about these futures.'

'*Now, Misthur Coasther, about dese fewchurs.* I love it! Keep talking!'

'Hahaha.' I laughed politely, while thinking, Fuckhead.

It was a little while before I managed to get him to take me seriously and then it was only a matter of seconds before I discovered that 'futures' were more of a conceptual thing, that I couldn't just waltz out of the door with a handful of gorgeous futures, take them back to the office, wrap them in handwoven boxes and have them messengered over to ten of the city's most powerful beauty editors. I'd have to come up with some other bright idea.

But I wasn't as disappointed as I should have been because I was thinking about the guy I'd bumped into. There had been *something*. And not just the synchronicity of our his'n'hers scars. But once I'd walked out of this building the chances were that I would never see him again. Not unless I did something about it.

First, I'd have to find him, and this bank was a big place. And if I did manage to locate him, then what should I do? Mr Coaster was explaining expansively and I was nodding and smiling but I was far away inside my head, riveted by indecision.

Then, like a switch had been flicked, I fixed on a plan of action. 'Mr Coaster, sir,' I interrupted politely. 'On my way in here I bumped into a gentleman, which resulted in him spilling his coffee. I'd like the opportunity to apologise before I leave. I didn't get his name but I can describe him.' I spoke quickly. 'He's tall, at least I think he is, although I'm so short everyone looks tall to me. Even you.'

Mr Coaster's expression went very stony. He cut in on me. ''Fraid I can't help.' And with lightning speed, I found myself outside his office.

Nita was studying herself in a compact.

'Nita, can you help me? I'm looking for a man.'

'Welcome to New York City.' She didn't even look up from the mirror. 'Eight-minute dating. Like speed-dating, but slower. I got four matches last time.'

'Not just any man. He works here. He's quite tall and . . . and . . .' There was no other way around this, I had to say it. 'And, um, beautiful. He sounds like he might be from Boston.'

Suddenly, I had her interest. She jerked her head up. 'Aidan Maddox. In IT. Further along this floor. Make a left, then another, two rights, then you'll see his pod.'

'Thank you. Just one other thing. Is he married?'

'Aidan Maddox? No, he's not married.' She gave a little chuckle that said, *And he's never likely to be either.*

I found him and stood by his cubicle, looking at his back, willing him to turn round. 'Hey,' I said, affably.

He swivelled round quickly. 'Hey,' he said. 'It's you. How's your hand?'

I extended it for him to have a look. 'I called my lawyer, the writ is on its way. Would you like to go for a drink sometime?'

He looked like he'd been hit by a train. 'You're asking me out for a drink?'

'Yes,' I said firmly. 'Yes, I am.'

After a pause, he said, sounding perplexed, 'But what if I said no?'

'What's the worst that can happen? You've already scalded me with boiling coffee.'

He looked at me with an expression curiously akin to despair and the silence stretched too long. My confidence burst with a bang and suddenly I was desperate to leave.

'Do you have a card?' he asked.

'Sure!' I knew a rejection when I heard one.

I fumbled in my wallet and passed over a neon pink rectangle with 'Candy Grrrl' in red wet-look type, followed in smaller writing by 'Anna Walsh, Public Relations Superstar'. In the top right-hand corner was the famous growling-girl logo.

We both looked at it. Suddenly, I saw it through his eyes.

'Cute,' he said. Once again he sounded confused.

'Yes, it really gives the impression of gravitas,' I said. 'Well, er, bye.'

'Yeah, OK, bye,' he replied. Still sounding baffled.

And off I went.

So, you win some, you lose some. It's a New York thing: you meet, you connect, then you never see each other again. It's very nice. Usually.

But I didn't want my encounter with this Aidan to be a one-off, and for the following days I was a little expectant in every ringing-phone and incoming-email situation, but *nada*.

How Aidan and I met for the second time

A barrel-chested man slung a hamlike arm round my neck, swung a tiny plastic bag of white powder at my face and said, 'Hey, Morticia, want some coke?'

I extricated myself and said politely, 'No thank you.'

'Aw, c'mon,' he said, a little too loudly. 'It's a party.'

I looked for the door. This was dreadful. You'd think that if you took a ritzy loft overlooking the Hudson, added a professional sound system, a ton of drink and a load of people, you'd have a great shindig on your hands.

But something wasn't working. And I blamed Kent, the guy throwing the party. He was a banker and the place was overrun with hordes of his identikit pals, and the thing about these guys was they didn't need anything to boost their confidence, they were bad enough *au naturel*, without adding cocaine to the mix.

Everyone looked florid and somehow desperate, as if the crucial thing was to be having a good time.

'I'm Drew Holmes.' The man swung the bag of coke at me again. 'Try it, it's great, you'll love it.'

'The eighties will never die,' I said. 'No, thank you. Really.'

'Too wild for you, huh?'

'That's right, too wild.' I looked around for Jacqui. This was all her fault—she worked with Kent's brother. But all I saw were lots of shouty meatheads with saucer-like pupils, and trashy-looking girls necking vodka straight from the bottle.

'Tell me about yourself, Morticia.' Drew Holmes was still at my side. 'What do you do?'

I didn't even hide my sigh. Here we go again. This party was lousy with incessant bloody networkers, and—at their request, I might add—I'd already explained my job to two other guys and neither of them had listened to a word.

'I test-drive orthopaedic shoes.'

'Well!' Deep breath before he launched into it. 'I'm with blah bank, blah, blah . . . tons of money . . . I, me, myself, being fabulous, blah, promotion, blah, bonus, workhardplayhard, me, mine, belonging to me, my expensive apartment, my expensive car, my expensive vacations, my expensive skis, me, me, me, me, MEEEEE . . .'

Just then a canapé—it was going very fast but I believe it was a miniburger—caught him on the side of the head and as he sought the perpetrator, his eyes bulging with rage, I slipped away.

I decided I was leaving. Why had I come in the first place? Well, why does anyone go to the party of someone they don't know? To meet men, of course. And funnily enough, whatever the hell was going on with the planets, for the previous couple of weeks I'd been *overrun* with men.

Jacqui and I had gone to the eight-minute speed-dating that Nita at Roger Coaster's office had told me about and I'd got three matches: a handsome, interesting architect, a red-haired baker from Queens and a young, cute bartender. Each had submitted a request for a date and I'd agreed to all three.

But before you start thinking a) that I'm a three-timing slut, or b) that the whole thing was a recipe for disaster, let me explain the rules of

Dating in New York City, especially the whole exclusive/non-exclusive end of things. What I was currently doing was Dating Non-exclusively—a perfectly acceptable state of affairs.

How it is in Ireland, is people just drift into relationships. You start by going for a couple of drinks, then on another night you might go to a film, then you run into each other at a party given by a mutual friend and at some stage you start sleeping together—probably this night, in fact. It's all very casual and drifty, but although no one ever says anything about exclusiveness or non-exclusiveness, *he's definitely your boyfriend*. So if you discovered the man you'd been sharing fireside nights and videos with for the last few months having a nice dinner with a woman who wasn't a) you or b) a female relation of his, you'd be perfectly within your rights to pour a glass of wine over him and to tell the other woman that she's 'welcome to him'.

But not in New York. In NYC you'd think: There's one of the men I've been seeing non-exclusively, having dinner with a woman he's also seeing non-exclusively. How civilised we all are . . . However, it's an ill wind and during this time of non-exclusivity you can ride rings around yourself; you can sleep with a different man every night should you so wish and no one can call you a six-timing tramp. Not that I'd touch any of the overgrown frat-boys at this party, no matter how accommodating the system.

I battled through the crowded room. Where the hell was Jacqui? Panic flickered as my path was blocked by another man with yet another butch name. In fact, now that I think about it, it might *actually* have been Butch. He pulled at my dress and said peevishly, 'What's with all the clothes?'

I was wearing a black wrap-around jersey dress and black boots, which seemed not unreasonable attire for a party.

'What's with the Addams family thing you've got going on?'

I was wondering whether to tell him I was an elephant voice coach or the inventor of the inverted comma, when a voice cut in on us and said, 'Don't you know Anna Walsh?'

Butch said, 'Say what?'

Say what, is right. I turned round. It was Him. The guy, the one who'd spilt coffee on me, the one I'd asked out for a drink and who'd blown me off. He was wearing a beanie and a wide-shouldered working-man's jacket and he'd brought the cold night in with him, refreshing the air.

'Yeah, Anna Walsh. She's a . . .' He looked at me and shrugged enquiringly, 'A magician?'

'Magician's girl,' I corrected. 'I passed all my magician exams but the assistant's clothes are a lot cooler.'

'Neat,' Butch said, but I wasn't looking at him, I was looking at Aidan Maddox, who had remembered my name, even though it was weeks since we'd met. There was a twinkle in his eyes that hadn't been there the last time.

'She disappears,' Aidan said, 'but then, as if by magic, she reappears.'

He'd taken my number but he hadn't called and now he was hitting me with some of the corniest lines I'd heard in a long while. I looked at him in cold inquisition.

His face gave nothing away but I didn't stop looking at him. Nor he at me. What seemed like ages later someone asked, 'Where do you go?'

'Hmmm?' The someone was Butch. I was surprised to find him still there. 'Go? When?'

'When you get magically disappeared? Hey presto!' He winked brightly.

'Oh! I'm just out back, having a cigarette.' I turned back to Aidan and when his eyes met mine again, the shock of our connection made my skin flame.

'Neat,' Butch said. 'And when you get sawn in half, how does that work?'

'False legs,' Aidan said. His eyes didn't leave my face.

I could actually feel poor Butch's smile trickle away. 'You guys know each other?' Aidan and I looked at Butch, then back at each other. Did we? 'Yes.'

Even if I hadn't known that something was happening with me and Aidan, the way Butch treated us was a sign: he backed off. 'You kids have fun,' he said, a little subdued.

Then Aidan and I were left on our own.

'Enjoying the party?' he asked.

'No,' I said. 'I hate it.'

'Yeah.' He scanned the room. 'What's not to hate?'

Just then, a short, dark man butted his way between us and asked, 'Wherja get to, buddy? You just took off.'

A look passed over Aidan's face: were we ever going to be left alone? Then he smiled and said, 'Anna, meet my best buddy, Leon. Leon works with Kent, the birthday boy. And this is Leon's wife, Dana.'

Dana was about a foot taller than Leon. She had long legs, a big chest, a fall of thick multi-toned hair and radiant, evenly tanned skin.

'Hey,' she said.

'Hey,' I replied.

Anxiously, Leon asked me, 'It's a sucky party, right?'

'Um . . .'

'You're with the good guys.' Aidan said. 'Tell it like it is.'

'OK. It's super-sucky.'

'Jeez.' Dana sighed. 'Let's mingle,' she said to Leon. 'Sooner we start, sooner we can leave. Excuse us.'

'Bail just as soon as you can't stand it,' Leon told Aidan, then we were alone again.

Aidan said, 'Anna, can we get out of here?'

Can we get out of here? I looked at him, annoyed at his presumption. I was thirty-one years old. I didn't just 'get out of here' with strange men.

I said, 'Let me just tell Jacqui I'm leaving.' I found her in the kitchen, showing a cluster of people how to make a proper Manhattan, and told her I was off. But before I could leave, I had to retrieve my coat from beneath a couple having sex in Kent's bedroom.

'Which coat is it?' Aidan asked. 'This one? Excuse us, buddy. Just need to get this—'

He tugged and the coat moved an inch, then another, then with a final yank it slithered free and we were out of the door. On a high from our escape we belted down several flights of stairs and ran right out into the street. It was early October, the days were still bright but the nights were chilly. Aidan helped me on with my coat, a midnight-blue velvet duster, painted with a silvery cityscape.

'I like your look.' Aidan stood back to check me out properly. 'Yeah.'

I liked his too. With the hat and the jacket and the big boots it was very Working-Man Chic. Not that I was going to tell him. And good thing Jacqui wasn't there to hear Aidan, because remarking on my clothes was classic Feathery Stroker acting-out. (Details on Feathery Strokers to follow.)

'Just a point I'd like to clear up,' I said, a little snippily. 'I didn't "disappear". I went *away*. Because you didn't want to go for a drink with me, remember?'

'I did want to. I wanted you from the very moment you headbutted me, I just wasn't sure I could have you.'

'Excuse me, you headbutted *me*. What sort of not sure?'

'Every sort.'

No wiser. Leave it alone. For a while anyway.

Two blocks away we found a bar, with red walls and a pool table, and at Aidan's request I told him all about my life as a magician's girl.

'We're called Marvellous Marvo and Gizelda. Gizelda is my stage name and we're *huge* in the Midwest. I sew all my own costumes, six hundred sequins per outfit, and I go into a meditative state when I'm doing it. Marvo is actually my dad and his real name is Frank. Now tell me about you.'

'No, you tell me.'

I thought about it for a while. 'OK. You're the son of a deposed East European despot, who stole millions from his people.' I smiled, a little cruelly. 'The money is hidden and the two of you are looking for it.' He looked progressively more anxious as his identity worsened. Then I took pity and redeemed him. 'But the reason you want to find the money is to return it to your impoverished people.'

'Thank you,' he said. 'Anything else?'

'You've a good relationship with your first wife, an Italian tennis player. In fact, you were an excellent tennis player yourself, you could have gone professional, until RSI put paid to it.'

'Speaking of which, how's your burnt hand?'

'Good. And I'm happy to see you've recovered from the coma I put you in. Any side-effects?'

'Evidently not. Judging from how this Saturday night has turned out, I seem to be smah-tah than evah.'

That Boston accent again. I found it devastatingly sexy.

'Say it again.'

'What?'

'Smarter.'

He shrugged, willing to please. 'Smah-tah.'

A rush of physical desire, similar to but worse than hunger, overtook me. I'd want to keep an eye on that.

'Game of pool?' I suggested.

After twenty minutes of potting balls, I beat Aidan.

'You're good,' he said.

'You let me win.' I poked him in the stomach with my pool cue. 'Don't do it again.'

He opened his mouth to protest and I pushed the cue a bit further. Nice hard stomach muscles. We held a look for several seconds, then in silence returned our cues to the rack.

When the bar closed at 4 a.m., Aidan offered to walk me home, but it was too far. By about forty blocks.

'We're not in Kansas any more, Toto,' I said.

'OK, we'll get a cab. I'll drop you off.'

In the back seat, listening to the driver yelling in Russian on his cellphone, Aidan and I didn't speak. I took a quick look at him, the lights and angular shadows of the city moving across his face, making it impossible to see his expression.

We pulled up at my crumbling stoop. 'I live here.'

Privacy would have been nice for our awkward what-happens-now conversation but we had to sit in the cab, because if we got out without having paid the cab-driver might have shot us.

'Look . . . I guess you're seeing other guys,' Aidan said.

'I guess I am.'

'Can you put me on your roster?'

I thought about it. 'I could do that.'

I didn't ask if he was seeing other women; it was none of my business (that's what you had to say anyway).

'Can I have your number?' he asked.

'I already gave you my number,' I said, and got out of the cab. If he wanted to see me that badly, he'd find me.

While I waited to see if Aidan Maddox would find my number and ring me, I got on with my life. I had my hands full of speed-dating dates.

However, Harris, the interesting architect, turned out to be a little too interesting when he suggested that, for our first date, we had a pedicure together. Nearly everyone shrieked that it was adorable, that it was original. But I had my misgivings. As for Jacqui, who had no time for that feather-strokery sort of nonsense, she threatened to walk past the salon and shame me; luckily, she was working that evening and, when the time came and I was sitting beside Harris, the two of us up to our ankles in little pools of soapy water, I'd never been so glad. Two women bowed before us, tending to our feet. All I could see were the tops of their heads, and I was too ashamed to carry on a relaxed conversation in their abject, silent presence. Harris, however, seemed perfectly comfortable, asking away about my job, telling me all about his. Then he produced a cocktail shaker and two glasses, poured me a drink and raised his glass.

'To toe-sucking,' he said.

Oh, no. Oh, dear me, no. So he had a foot thing. Which was fine. Fine. Not for me to judge. Just don't include me in it.

Not that he planned to. As soon as we'd finished and paid, he said to me, quite nicely, 'We didn't click. Have a good life.' Then he strode away on his freshly buffed feet.

Bloodied but unbowed, I prepared for my date the following evening with Greg, the baker from Queens. Although it was October and far from warm, he'd suggested a picnic in the park. We were meeting straight after work because Greg went to bed very early on account of having to get up in the middle of the night to make bread. Also, after seven thirty, it would bee too dark to actually see each other and what we were eating.

At the park, I saw Greg waiting with a rug over one arm, a wicker picnic basket on the other and—with a thrill of horror—some sort of Panama hat on his head.

It's a terrible thing to say but he was a lot fatter than I remembered from the speed-dating. That night we'd been sitting down with a table between us and I only really saw his face and chest. At full height, he was . . . he was . . . diamond-shaped. His stomach was massive and—although it kills me to say it because I hate it when men say this about women—he had a ginormous arse. But, curiously, his legs weren't too bad and sloped down to a pair of neat little ankles.

He spread out the rug on the grass, then tapped his basket and said, 'Anna, I promise you a feast of the senses.'

Already I was afraid.

Reclining on the rug, Greg opened his basket, took out a loaf, then closed the lid quickly, but not before I'd seen that all that was in there was loads of bread.

'This is my sourdough,' he said. 'Made to my own recipe.'

He tore a bit off, in a real bon viveur's way, and approached. I could see the way this was going: he was planning a seduction via bread— once I'd tried his creations, I'd go all swoony and fall in love with him. I was dealing with a man who'd seen *Chocolat* once too often.

'Close your eyes and open your mouth.' Oh, cripes, he was going to feed me!

But he didn't even let me eat the damn thing. He rubbed it round inside my mouth and said, 'Feel the roughness of the crust on your tongue. Take your time,' he urged. 'Savour it.'

Over the course of ninety long, chilly minutes, Greg made me lick bread, smell bread, watch bread and caress bread. The only thing he didn't make me do was listen to it.

'We live in carb-phobic times,' Jacqui later remarked. 'Does he know anything?'

Bloody and, at this stage, quite bowed, I was in no mood when, the following day, the cute bartender rang me at work and said, 'Got a great idea for our date.'

I listened in silence.

'I'm part of a project where we build houses for some poor folks in Pennsylvania—they provide the materials, we provide the labour.'

A pause for me to praise him. I didn't. So, sounding confused, he continued, 'Going down this weekend. Be great if you'd come along. We could get to know each other and do some good for our fellow man.'

Altruism: the latest fashion. Weariness washed over me.

'Thank you for asking,' I said. 'But I just don't think it's for me.'

'Whatever. Got plenty of other chicks.'

'I don't doubt it. I wish you well.'

I slammed the phone down and turned to my friend, Teenie, who sat close by. She is Korean and kooky to the bones. 'You know what? I've had it with New York men. They're lunatics! No wonder they have to go to speed-dating, even in a city where women are desperate for a date. Whoever heard of going on a date and building a house?'

The phone rang, interrupting my rant; I took a deep breath and said, 'Candy Grrrl publicity, Anna Walsh speaking.'

'Hey, Anna Walsh, it's Aidan Maddox speaking.'

'Oh, right.'

'What have I done?'

'Are you calling to ask me out?'

'Yes.'

'Bad timing. I've just sworn off New York men. I've had the weirdest week, with the weirdest dates. I don't think I can take another one.'

'Oh, that's OK. I'm from Boston. So how about we go for one drink? Is that unweird enough?'

'Depends. Where are we having it? The surface of the moon?'

'I was thinking more of a bar.'

'OK. One drink.'

'And if, by the end of the drink, it's not working out for you, just say you've got to go because there's a leak in your apartment and the plumber is coming. How does that sound?'

'OK. Just one drink. And what will your get-out clause be?' I asked.

'I don't need one.'

3

I WOKE UP in the narrow bed in the sofa-filled front room and spent several dopey minutes trying to look out of the window. Here came the elderly woman and her dog; I watched sleepily. Then less sleepily. I half sat up: I wasn't imagining it. That poor dog did not want to do its business but the woman was insistent. The dog kept trying to get up and leave but the woman wouldn't let it. 'Here!' I couldn't hear it, but I could see her say it. Odd.

Then in came Mum and I partook of a hearty breakfast—half a slice of toast, eleven grapes, eight pills and a record-breaking sixty Rice Krispies—because I needed to convince her how well I was getting. While she was washing me—a miserable business with towelling cloths and a bowl of scummy lukewarm water—I went for it.

'Mum, I've decided to go back to New York.'

'Don't be ridiculous.' And continued rinsing me.

'My scars are healing, my knee can take weight, the bruises are gone.'

It was strange, really; I had myriad injuries, but none had been serious. Although my face had been black and blue, none of the bones had been broken. I could have been crushed like an eggshell and spent the rest of my life looking like a cubist painting (as Helen had put it). I knew I'd been lucky.

'And look how fast my fingernails are growing.' I wiggled my hand at her; I'd lost two fingernails and the pain had been far worse than my broken arm. Now my fingers barely hurt.

'You've a broken arm, Missy. Broken in three places.'

'But they were clean breaks and it doesn't hurt any more. I'd say it's nearly better.'

'Oh, you're a bone surgeon now, are you?'

'No, I'm a beauty PR and they won't keep my job open for ever.' I let that thought settle with her, then I whispered, 'No more free make-up.'

But not even that worked. 'You're going nowhere, Missy.'

However, I'd picked my time well: that very afternoon I had my weekly hospital check-up and if the professionals said I was getting better, Mum wouldn't have a leg to stand on.

After lots of hanging around, an X-ray was taken of my arm. As I'd thought, it was healing fast and well; the sling could be removed and the plaster could come off in a couple of weeks.

Then on to the skin specialist, who said I was doing so well that the stitches could be taken out of my cheek and even I hadn't expected that. It hurt more than I'd thought it would and an angry, red, puckered line ran from the corner of my eye to the corner of my mouth, but now that my face was no longer being held together by navy-blue thread, I looked far, far more normal.

'What about plastic surgery?' Mum asked.

'Eventually,' he said. 'But not for a while. It's always hard to tell how well these things will heal.'

Then on to Dr Chowdhury to have my internal organs poked and prodded. According to him, all the bruising and swelling had subsided.

'She's talking about going back to New York,' Mum burst out. 'Tell her she's not well enough to travel.'

'But she was well enough to travel home,' Dr Chowdhury said, with undeniable truth.

Mum and I drove home in grim silence. At least, Mum did. My silence was happy.

'What about your gammy knee?' Mum said, suddenly animated. 'How can you go to New York if you can't climb a step?'

'I'll make you a deal,' I said. 'If I can walk to the top of the stairs on it, I'm well enough to go back.'

She agreed because she thought I hadn't a hope of doing it. But she had no idea how determined I was to leave. I would do it. And I did do it—even though it took over ten minutes and left me covered in sweat.

'See?' I gasped, sitting down on the landing. 'I'm all better. Arm, face, innards, knee—better!'

'Anna,' she said, and I didn't like her tone, it was so sombre, 'there's more wrong with you than just physical injuries.'

I processed that. 'Mum, I know. But I have to go back. I *have* to. I'm not saying I'll stay there for ever. I might arrive back home very quickly, but I've no choice. I must go back.'

Something in my voice convinced her because she seemed to deflate. 'It's the modern way, I suppose,' she said. 'Getting closure.'

'Rachel will be in New York to help me,' I reassured her.

'And maybe you'd think about going for that counselling stuff.'

'Counselling?' I wondered if I was hearing right. Mum totally disapproved of any kind of psychotherapy.

'Yes, counselling. Rachel might be able to recommend someone.'

Several years ago, while Rachel had first been living in New York, she'd developed a fondness for the devil's dandruff. (Cocaine.) Things got very messy and after a dramatic suicide attempt, she landed in an expensive Irish rehab. A year or so after that she went to college, got a degree in psychology, then an MA in addiction studies and she now works in a rehab place in New York.

'Mmm,' I said, musingly, as if I was considering it, but I wasn't. Talking about what had happened wouldn't change a single thing.

'Come on, we'd better tell your father what's happening. He might cry, but ignore him.'

Poor Dad. In a houseful of strong women, his opinion counted for nothing. We found him watching golf on the telly.

'We've a bit of news. Anna's going back to New York for a while,' Mum said.

He looked up, startled and upset. 'Why?'

'To get closure.'

'What's that?'

'I don't really know,' Mum admitted.

'Isn't it a bit soon to be leaving? What about the broken arm? And the gammy knee?'

'All on the mend. And the sooner she gets this closure, the sooner she'll be back to us,' Mum said.

Then it was time to tell Helen and she was quite distraught. 'But I thought we could go into business together, you and me. We could be private investigators. Think of the laugh we'd have.'

Think of the laugh *she*'d have, snuggled up in her nice, warm, dry bed while I loitered in damp shrubbery doing her job for her.

'I'm more use to you as a beauty PR,' I said, and she seemed to buy that.

So they sent for Rachel to bring me back.

Mum fought her way over to my bed. 'Rachel'll be here on Saturday morning.' Two days away. 'And the two of you'll be flying back to New York on Monday. If you're still sure that's what you want.'

'It is. Is Luke coming over with her?'

'No. And thank God for that,' Mum added heartily, lying down beside me.

'I thought you liked him.'

'I do like him. Especially since he's agreed to marry her.'

'I think it might have been since *she* agreed to marry *him*.'

Rachel and Luke had been living together for so long that even Mum had given up hoping that Rachel would 'stop making a show of us all'. Then, just over two months ago, to everyone's great surprise, they announced their engagement. Initially, the news plunged Mum into despair because she concluded the only reason they were getting married was because Rachel was pregnant. But Rachel wasn't pregnant; they were getting married simply because they wanted to. And I'm very glad they went public when they did, because if they had waited even a few days longer they'd have felt that, out of deference to me and my circumstances, they couldn't. But the date was set, the hotel was booked—and if Rachel and Luke backed out now, they knew I'd feel even worse.

'So if you like Luke, what's the problem?'

'I just wonder . . .'

'What?'

'I wonder, does he wear underpants?'

'Jesus,' I said, faintly.

She was staring at the ceiling, locked in some Luke-centric reverie, when Dad stuck his head round the door and said to Mum, 'Phone.'

She gave a little jump, then heaved herself off the bed, and when she returned she was clearly troubled.

'That was Claire. She's coming from London on Saturday afternoon.'

'Is it a problem?'

'She's coming because she wants to see Rachel in person to beg her not to get married to Luke.'

'Ah.' Just like she'd begged me not to marry Aidan. Maybe she'd had a nerve doing such a thing but, as it happened, I'd had my doubts. I'd known Aidan was a risk—although not in the way it turned out.

Claire, the first-born, recently turned forty. Despite this, she remains a strong-willed, upbeat type. Back in the distant past, her life had a little hiccup, when her husband, patronising James, left her on the same day she gave birth to their first child. This meant that she had the stuffing knocked out of her for—ooh, close on half an hour, then she got over it. She met another bloke, Adam, and she had the good sense to make sure he was younger than her and easy to scare into submission. Mind you, she also had the good sense to make sure he was a dark, handsome hunk with lovely broad shoulders. As well as Kate, the 'abandoned child', Adam and Claire have two other children.

'I'm not having Claire mess up this wedding on me,' Mum said.

'It's not her fault.' After her own union went so disastrously wrong, Claire began to deride marriage as 'a load of bollocks'. She went on about women being treated like serfs and that the 'giving away' bit reduced us to nothing but chattels.

'I want this wedding to go ahead,' Mum said.

'You'll have to get a stupid-looking hat. Yet another one.'

'A stupid-looking hat is the least of my worries.'

When Rachel arrived on Saturday morning, the first thing Mum said to her was, 'Look radiant, for the love of God. Claire is coming to tell you not to get married.'

'She isn't?' Rachel was amused. 'I don't believe it. She did that to you too, Anna, didn't she?' Then, realising she'd put her foot in it, she jerked as if someone had just rammed a poker up her bum. Quickly, she changed the subject. 'How radiant do you want me to look?'

Mum and Helen surveyed Rachel doubtfully. Rachel's look was the low-key, sleek, New York downtime one.

'Do something with your hair,' Helen suggested, and obediently Rachel unclasped a clip on top of her head and a load of heavy dark hair tumbled down her back.

'Why, Miss Walsh, you're beautiful,' Mum said sourly. 'Comb it! Comb it! And smile a lot.'

The thing was that Rachel usually is radiant. She has an air about her, a sort of throbbing stillness, with the faintest suggestion of a secret dirty streak.

Then Mum clocked The Ring. How had she not noticed until now? 'Right, let's see it.' Rachel eased the sapphire ring off and, after a scrabble between Helen and Mum, Mum got it. 'By Janey,' she said fiercely, clenching her hand into a fist and punching the air. 'I've waited a long time for this day.'

Then she examined the ring in great detail, holding it up to the light and squinting, like she was a gem expert. 'How much was it?'

'Never you mind.'

'It's meant to be a month's salary,' Mum said. 'At *least*. Anything less and he's taking you for a fool. Right! Time for us all to make our wish. Let Anna go first.'

Mum gave me the ring and Rachel said, 'You know the rules: turn it three times towards your heart. You can't wish for a man or money, but you can wish for a rich mother-in-law.' Again, as she realised what she'd said, she went poker-up-the-bum frozen.

'It's OK,' I said. 'It's OK. We can't go on tiptoeing around it.'

'Really?'

I nodded.

'You sure?'

I nodded again.

'OK, let's see your make-up bag.'

For a while, squashed between Rachel, Helen and Mum, all of us strewn with cosmetics, everything seemed normal.

Then we pretended to be Claire.

'Marriage is just a form of ownership,' Mum said, doing Claire's soapbox voice.

'She can't help it,' Rachel said. 'Her abandonment and humiliation traumatised her.'

'Shut up,' Helen said. 'You're ruining the fun. Chattels! That's all we are, chattels!'

Even I joined in: 'I thought getting married was all about wearing a really lovely dress and being the centre of attention.'

'I hadn't thought through *any* of the gender-political implications,' we all (even Rachel) chorused.

We laughed and laughed and even though I was aware that at any moment I might descend into uncontrollable weeping, I managed to keep laughing.

4

FOR OUR ONE-DRINK DATE, Aidan and I went to Lana's Place, a quiet, upmarket bar, with concealed lighting and muted tones.

'This OK?' Aidan asked, as we sat down. 'Not too weird?'

'So far,' I said. 'Unless it's one of those places where the bar staff tap-dance at nine o'clock every night.'

'Jesus.' He clutched his head. 'I never thought to check.'

When the waitress took our order, she asked, 'Should I open a tab?'

'No,' I said. 'I might have to leave in a hurry . . . If you turn out to be a weirdo,' I added, after she'd gone.

'I won't be. I'm not.'

I didn't really think he would be. He was different from the speed-dating guys. But it doesn't do to be too trusting.

'We have matching scars,' he said.

'Hmm?'

'Scars. On our right eyebrows. One each. Isn't that . . . special?'

He was smiling: I wasn't to take this too seriously.

'How d'you get yours?' he asked.

'Playing on the stairs in my mother's high heels.'

'Aged what? Six? Eight?'

'Twenty-seven. No. Five and a half. I was doing a big Hollywood musical-style thing, and I fell down the stairs and at the bottom I hit my forehead on the corner of the convection heater.'

'Convection heater?'

'Must be an Irish thing. I needed three stitches. How did you get yours?'

'Day I was born. Accident with a midwife and a pair of scissors. I also got three stitches. Now tell me what you do when you're not being a magician's assistant.'

'You want the real me?'

'If that's OK. And if you could speak quickly, I'd appreciate it. Just in case you decide to leave.'

So I told him all about my life. About Jacqui, Rachel, Luke, the Real Men, Shake's air-guitar prowess, Nell, the upstairs neighbour I'd recently met, and Nell's strange friend. I told him about work, how I loved my products and how Lauryn Pike, my manager, had stolen my promo idea for some orange and arnica night-cream and passed it off as her own.

'I hate her already,' he said. 'Is your wine OK?'

'Fine.'

'Just that you're drinking it kind of slowly.'

'Not as slowly as you're drinking that beer of yours.'

Three times the waitress asked, 'You guys OK for drinks?' and three times she was sent away.

After I'd brought Aidan up to speed on my life, he told me about his. About his upbringing in Boston, how he and Leon had lived next door to each other and how unusual it was in their neighbourhood for a Jewish boy and an Irish-American boy to be best friends. He told me about his younger brother, Kevin, and how competitive they'd been as kids. 'Only two years between us, everything was a battle.' He told me about his job, his roomie, Marty, about his lifelong love of the Boston Red Sox; and at some stage in the story, I finished my glass of wine.

'Just hang on while I finish my beer,' he said and, with admirable restraint, he made the last inch last a full hour. Finally, he couldn't avoid being done and he looked regretfully at his empty glass. 'OK, that's the one drink you signed up for. How's the plumbing in your apartment?'

I thought about it for a moment. 'Perfect.'

'**W**ell?' Jacqui asked, when I got in. 'Nutjob?'

'No. Normal.'

'Vrizzzon?'

I thought about it. 'Yes.' There certainly had been a frisson.

'Snog?'

'Kind of.' He had kissed me on the mouth. Just a brief impression of heat and firmness and then he was gone, leaving me wanting more.

'Like him?'

'Yes.'

'Oh, really?' Suddenly interested. 'I'd better take a look at him.'

I set my jaw and held her look. 'He is not a Feathery Stroker.'

'I'll be the judge of that.'

Jacqui's Feathery Stroker test is a horribly cruel assessment that she brings to bear on all men. It originated with some man she had slept with years ago. All night long he'd run his hands up and down her body in the lightest, feathery way, up her back, along her thighs, across her stomach and before they had sex he asked her gently if she was sure. Lots of women would have loved this: he was gentle, attentive and respectful. But for Jacqui it was the greatest turn-off of her life. 'He kept stroking me,' she said afterwards, wincing with revulsion. 'In this awful feathery way, like he'd read a book about how to give women what they want. Bloody Feathery Stroker. I wanted to rip my skin off.'

And so the phrase came about. It suggested an effeminate quality that instantly stripped a man of all sex appeal. Jacqui's criteria were wide and merciless—and distressingly random. Here are some examples. Men who didn't eat red meat were Feathery Strokers. Men who noticed your shoes and handbags were Feathery Strokers. (Or Jolly Boys.) Men who said pornography was exploitation of women were Feathery Strokers. (Or liars.) All academics with beards were Feathery Strokers. Men who stayed friends with their ex-girlfriends were Feathery Strokers. Men who did Pilates were Feathery Strokers. Men who said, 'I have to take care of myself right now,' were *screaming* Feathery Strokers. (Even I'd go along with that.)

It was only when I realised how anxious I was that Jacqui might dismiss Aidan as a Feathery Stroker that I saw how much I liked him. It wasn't that Jacqui's opinions affected me, it just makes things a bit awkward if your friend despises your boyfriend. Not that Aidan was my boyfriend . . .

I'd never seen a Feathery Stroker being decategorised: once a Feathery Stroker, always a Feathery Stroker. Jacqui was like the Roman Emperor in *Gladiator,* the thumb went up or the thumb went down, the fate of a man was decided in an instant and there was no going back.

'So when are you seeing this possible Feathery Stroker again?' she asked.

'I said I'd give him a call when I was in the mood,' I said airily.

However, he rang me two days later, said his nerves couldn't take the waiting for me to ring and would I meet him for dinner that evening. Certainly not, I replied, he was a stalker and I had a life. Mind you, I could do the following night if he wanted . . .

Four nights after that dinner, we went to a jazz thing, but it wasn't too bad; the musicians took breaks after every second song—or so it seemed—so there were plenty of opportunities to talk.

In the meantime I went on a date with a friend of Teenie (to the Cirque du Soleil, a terrible night), then I met this other bloke called Trent but he was going out of town, so we arranged a date for when he got back. In theory, I was open to all offers, but the man I saw the most of was Aidan. Non-exclusively, of course.

We never strayed into serious territory. I had questions—like why he hadn't rung me when I'd first given him my card or why he'd said he'd wanted me but didn't think he could have me. But I didn't ask them because I didn't want to know. Or rather, I didn't want to know yet.

On around our fourth or fifth date, he took a breath. 'Don't be scared but Leon and Dana want to meet you, like, properly. What do you think?'

I thought I'd rather remove my kidneys with a blunt spoon.

'We'll see,' I said. 'Funnily enough, Jacqui wants to meet you too.'

He had a little think. 'OK.'

'Really? You don't have to. I told her I wouldn't ask because it might scare you away.'

'No, let's go for it. What's she like? Will I like her?'

'Probably not.'

'What?'

'Because,' I said, 'you know when two people are meeting for the first time and the other person—me—really wants them to like each other and says, "You'll love each other"? Their expectations are too high, so they end up being disappointed and hate each other. The key here is to lower expectations. So, no, you won't like her at all.'

'The three of us will have dinner!' Jacqui declared.

We would not. What if she and Aidan didn't hit it off? Two to three hours making light conversation while forcing food down tense throats—aaarrrgh! A quick post-work drink would do; nice and easy and, above all, short. I decided on Logan Hall, a big, rackety Midtown bar, noisy enough to cover up any dips in conversation.

On the designated night, I arrived first and got a booth on the balcony. Jacqui was next to arrive, and eight minutes later Aidan hadn't yet appeared.

'He's late.' Jacqui sounded approving.

'There he is.' He was downstairs, pushing his way through the throng, looking a little lost. 'We're here,' I called.

He looked up, saw me, smiled like he really meant it, and mouthed, 'Hey'.

'Christ, he's gorgeous.' Jacqui sounded astonished, then recovered herself. 'Which counts for nothing. You could have the best-looking man in the world but if he won't eat the bar nuts because he's got a Feathery Stroker fear of germs, it's curtains.'

'He'll eat the nuts,' I said shortly, then stopped because here he was. He kissed me, slid in beside me and nodded hello to Jacqui.

'Can I get you guys a drink?' A waitress was flinging down cocktail napkins, then placed a bowl of mixed nuts mid-table.

'A saketini for me,' I said.

'Make it two,' said Jacqui.

'Sir?' The waitress looked at Aidan.

'I've no mind of my own,' he said. 'Better make it three.'

I wondered what Jacqui would conclude from that. Were mixed drinks too girly?

'Have a nut.' Jacqui offered him the bowl.

'Hey, thanks.'

I smirked at Jacqui.

It was a great night. We all got on so well that we stayed for a second drink, then Aidan insisted on picking up the bill. Again, this worried me. Would a non-Feathery Stroker have insisted we split it three ways?

'Thank you,' I said. 'You didn't have to do that.'

'Yes, thanks,' Jacqui said and I held my breath. If he said stuff about it being a pleasure to be out with two such lovely ladies, we were sunk.

But he just said, 'Welcome,' and surely this would count in his favour in the final Feathery Stroker shake-down?

'Better go to the ladies' room,' Jacqui said, 'before the great migration home.'

'Good idea.' I followed her and asked, 'Well? Feathery Stroker?'

'*Him?*' she exclaimed. 'Definitely not.'

'Good.' I was pleased—delighted even—that Aidan had passed with such flying non-Feathery Stroker colours.

With warm admiration, she added, 'I bet he's a hard dog to keep on the porch,' and my smile wobbled just a little.

On Saturday afternoon, a taxi drew up outside chez Walsh. The door opened and a high-heeled spindly sandal appeared, followed by a tanned leg (slightly orange and streaky around the ankle), a short frayed denim skirt, a straining T-shirt that said MY BOYFRIEND IS OUT OF TOWN, and a fall of vanilla-striped hair. Claire had arrived.

'She's forty,' Helen said, in alarm. 'She looks like a tramp. She was never that bad before.'

'This is much more like it. Better than that bloody Margaret,' Mum said, heading to the front door and welcoming Claire by calling out at the taxi, 'Mutton dressed as lamb! Good girl, yourself.'

Grinning, Claire swung up the drive, displaying six inches of thigh that was only slightly cellulitey, and into Mum's embrace.

'I've never seen you looking so well,' Mum declared. 'Where did you get that T-shirt? Listen, would you have a word with Margaret—she's your younger sister and she looks older than me. She's bad for my image.'

'The state of you,' Helen said scornfully. 'Dressed like trailer trash— at forty!'

'And you know what they say about forty?' Claire put her hand on Helen's shoulder.

'Your arse hits the floor?'

'Life begins!' Claire yelled right into her face. 'Life *begins* at forty. And forty is the new thirty. And you're only as young as the person you're feeling.' She pivoted on her narrow heel and, with a dazzling smile, gathered me into her arms. 'Anna, how are you feeling, love?'

Worn out, actually. Claire had been home only a matter of minutes and already the shouting and the insults had plunged me right back into my childhood. I'm just not like the rest of them. All four of my sisters are noisy and volatile—they'd be the first to admit it—they love a good row. Or a bad row. Any kind of row, really—they've always seen bickering as a perfectly legitimate means of communication. I spent my childhood watching them like a mouse watches a cat, curled up small and quiet, hoping that if they didn't realise I was there, they couldn't start a fight with me.

'You look loads better,' Claire said, then began surveying the hall, looking for Rachel. 'Where is she?'

'Hiding.'

'I'm not fucking hiding. I'm meditating.' Rachel's voice came from somewhere above us. We all looked up. She was lying on her belly on the landing, her nose poking through the banisters. 'You could have saved yourself the journey because I'm definitely marrying him and how do you reconcile your feminist principles with a skirt that short?'

'I'm not dressing for men, I'm dressing for me.'

'Yeah,' Mum sneered.

Eventually, Rachel snapped out of the childish state we all seemed to have reverted to (especially Mum) and became all wise and serene again and agreed to give Claire her ear. Helen, Mum and I asked if we could be in on it, but Rachel said she'd prefer it if we weren't and Helen lowered her eyes and said, 'Obviously, we respect that.' Then the minute the pair of them closeted themselves in a bedroom, the three of us raced upstairs (well, they raced and I hobbled) and listened at the door, but, apart from the occasional raised voice, 'Chattels!' 'Objects!' and Rachel doing her super-irritating 'I understand' murmur, it quickly got boring.

Claire, having failed in her attempt to talk Rachel out of getting married, departed in high dudgeon on Sunday evening.

That night, Dad came to talk to me—as best he could. 'Ready for the oul' journey tomorrow?'

'Ready, Dad.'

'Well, um . . . good luck when you get back and keep up the oul' walking,' he said stoutly. 'It helps the oul' knee.'

The number of times he said 'oul' was an indication of how mortified he was: the 'oul' index was at an all-time high. Dad would lie down and die for me and all his family, but he would not, could not, talk about emotions.

'Maybe when you get back, take up an oul' hobby,' he suggested. 'Keeps the oul' mind off things. Golf, maybe. And that'd be good for the oul' knee too, of course.'

'Thanks, Dad, I'll think about it.'

5

AFTER JACQUI HAD DECREED that Aidan would be a hard dog to keep on the porch, she told him, 'You pass. You can come out with us whenever you like.'

'Er, thank you.'

'In fact, tomorrow night it's Nell's strange friend's birthday. The Outhouse in Mulberry Street. Come along.'

'Um, OK.' He looked at me. 'OK?'

'OK.'

The love-in between Jacqui and Aidan continued the following night, when, in the heaving bar, Jacqui indicated an Adonis leaning against a wall. 'Look. He's gorgeous. Think he's waiting for someone?'

'Ask him,' Aidan suggested.

'I can't just go over and ask him.'

'Want me to go?'

Her eyes nearly fell out of her head. She clutched him. 'Would you?'

'Sure.'

Sadly, Adonis turned out to be called Burt and up close he had an immobile kind of face and no interest in Jacqui, but even so Jacqui thought Aidan was the cat's pyjamas.

Great stuff. Everyone getting on well. However, because Aidan had come out with my friends twice, I was obliged to meet Leon and Dana and I was not looking forward to being judged and found wanting. But we had an unexpectedly (unexpected on my part, anyway) nice time.

Then, a few days later, the Real Men had a Hallowe'en party, where they (the Real Men) dressed up as themselves. I was standing around wondering whether Aidan was going to show when someone appeared in front of me, wearing a sheet over their head and going, 'Woooooooh!'

'Right back at you,' I said.

Then the person lifted the sheet and exclaimed, 'Hey, Anna, it's me!'

It was Aidan. We shrieked with surprise and delight. (Not that it was that surprising to see each other, but anyway.) I launched myself at him and he grabbed me, his arms around my back, our legs tangled together, and a jolt of want leapt from me. He felt it too because his eyes changed, instantly becoming serious. We held the gaze for a timeless moment, then Nell's strange friend stuck a pitchfork in Aidan's bum and broke the spell.

At this stage I'd seen Aidan about seven or eight times and not once had he tried to jump me. Every date we'd gone on, we'd had just one kiss. One kiss was as good as it got.

Aidan rang the day after Hallowe'en and said, 'Last night was fun.'

'Glad you enjoyed it. Listen, on Saturday night, Shake's in the local heat of the air-guitar championship. We're all going along to laugh. Like to come?'

A pause. 'Anna, can we . . . talk?'

Oh, Christ.

'Don't get me wrong. I really like Jacqui and Rachel and Luke and Shake and Leon and Dana and Nell and Nell's strange friend. But I'd like to see you, just the two of us?'

'When?'

'Soon as possible? Tonight?'

A funny feeling started fluttering in the pit of my stomach. It increased when Aidan said, 'There's a nice little Italian on West 85th.'

There was more than a nice little Italian on West 85th. Aidan lived on West 85th.

'Eight o'clock?' he suggested.

'OK.'

We got through our food super-speedily. An hour and a half after we'd arrived, we were at the coffee stage. How had that happened?

Because our minds weren't on our food, that's how. I was very, very nervous—although I shouldn't have been. Shortly after we'd come to New York, Jacqui and I had done a class in seduction techniques, so, in theory, I could pull one or two sexual tricks out of the box, like when you take your bra off, you should wave it above your head like you're trying to lasso a runaway steer. And yet when Aidan twirled my hair round one of his fingers and said, 'Come back to my place. See who won *The Apprentice* before you embark on your long journey downtown,' all the little hairs on the back of my neck stood to attention.

After he had let us into his apartment, I stood in the hall, listening. 'Where's Marty tonight?'

'Out.'

'Out? How out?'

A hesitation. 'Very out.'

'Hmmm.' I pushed a door and walked into a bedroom. I took in the neat, crisp bed linen, the candles dotted about, the meadow-fresh smell. 'This yours?'

'Um, yes.' He followed me in.

'And it always looks this good?'

Pause. 'No.'

I flicked my eyes at him and we laughed nervously. I moved round his room, picking things up and putting them down. The candles on his nightstand were Candy Grrrl ones. 'Oh, Aidan, I could have got you these for free.'

'Anna?' he said softly. He was right beside me. I hadn't heard him approach. I looked up. 'Fuck the candles,' he said.

He slid his hand along my neck, under my hairline, sending electric shivers down my back, brought his face to mine and kissed me, and I was overwhelmed by his nearness, the roughness of his hair, the heat of his body through the thin cotton of his shirt. I moved my thumb along the leanness of his jawline, my fingers down the line of his spine. His shirt buttons had opened and there was his stomach, flat, muscled, a line of dark hair, leading downwards . . .

Leaning over me, his shoulders flexing, he unwrapped me like I was a present. 'Anna, you're so beautiful,' he said. 'You're so beautiful.'

He kissed me everywhere, from my eyelids to the backs of my knees. All my training went by the board. I'd really meant to twirl my bra above my head but in the heat of the moment I forgot. I'd other stuff on my mind, the heat and the need building, exquisite pleasure radiating outwards and inwards.

For a long time afterwards, neither of us spoke. Slick with sweat and knocked out by pleasure, we were flattened against the sheets. I was having little conversations with myself in my head: *That was amazing. That was incredible.* But I said nothing.

'Anna?'

'Mmm?'

He rolled over on top of me and said, 'That was one of the best things that has ever happened to me.'

But it wasn't just good sex. I felt like I knew him. I felt like he loved me. We went to sleep spooned together, his arm tight round my stomach, my hand resting on his hip.

I woke to the sound of a cup clattering beside my ear. 'Coffee,' he said. 'Time to get up.'

I pulled myself out of my blissful slumber and tried to sit up.

'You're already dressed,' I said, surprised.

'Yeah.' He wouldn't meet my eye. He sat on the foot of the bed, pulling on his socks, and suddenly I was wide awake.

I'd been here before. I sipped my coffee and said, 'You haven't forgotten tomorrow night? Shake's air-guitar stuff? You're still coming?'

Without turning to look at me, he mumbled into his knees, 'I won't be around this weekend.'

I forgot to breathe. I felt as if I'd been slapped.

'Gotta go to Boston,' he went on. 'Stuff to sort out.'

'Whatever.'

'Whatever?' He turned round. He looked surprised.

'Yes, Aidan, whatever. You sleep with me, you go weird on me and now, all of a sudden, you're not around this weekend. Whatever.'

His face drained of colour. 'Anna, yeah, look . . . I guess there's no right time for this.' Something bad was coming.

'What?' I asked, sharply.

'Well, how would you feel about, you know, you and me being exclusive?'

'Being *exclusive*?' Being exclusive was nearly like getting engaged.

'Yeah, just you and me. I don't know if you're seeing other guys . . .'

I shrugged. Neither did I. And there was a much more important question: 'You still seeing other girls?'

A pause. 'That's why I need to go to Boston.'

6

ON THE FLIGHT from Dublin to New York, my injuries caused a few nudges, but nothing like the stir they'd caused on the outward journey.

Once we'd landed and got our luggage and gone outside, I had a bit of a freaker about getting into a taxi. I was literally trembling with fear, but Rachel said, 'This is New York City—you'll need to use cabs all the time. You're going to have to get back on the horse at some stage. Why not do it now while I'm here to take care of you?'

I had no real choice: I either got in the cab or got the plane back to Ireland. With knees that felt watery with dread, I got in.

On the drive Rachel talked about things—stuff that had nothing to do with anything, but was diverting all the same. It kept me calm.

Then we crossed the bridge into Manhattan. I was almost surprised to find that it was still there, still going on with its business, still being Manhattan, regardless of what had happened to me.

Then we were in my neighbourhood, the so-called Mid-Village. (Between the charm of the West Village and the edginess of the East Village, Mid-Village was a realtors' term to try to give character to a place that didn't really have much.) And then we were outside our apartment building and the shock of seeing it made my stomach lurch.

Even though Rachel carried my luggage, it was a bit of a challenge climbing up the three flights of stairs with my bad knee, but as soon as I put my key in the lock—and Rachel insisted that it was I who opened the door and not her—I sensed someone else in the apartment and I almost jackknifed with relief: he was still there. *Oh, thank God.* Only to discover that the person was Jacqui. Thoughtfully, she'd come along so I wouldn't be upset by arriving back to an empty place, but my disappointment was so acute that I had to check every room, just in case.

Not that there were many rooms to check. There was the living room with a cramped kitchen annex carved out of it, a half-bath (i.e. a shower and no bath) and at the back our gloomy bedroom with its sliver of glass looking into the lightwell (funds hadn't stretched to a proper window). But we'd made it cosy: a lovely big bed with a carved headboard, a couch wide enough for us to lie on side by side, and vital accessories like scented candles and a widescreen TV.

I hobbled from room to room, I even looked behind the shower curtain, but he wasn't there. At least the photos of him were still on the walls; some 'thoughtful' soul hadn't taken it upon themselves to get rid of them.

Rachel and Jacqui pretended nothing strange was happening, then Jacqui smiled and I stared at her in shock. 'What happened to your teeth?'

'Present from Lionel 9.' Some rap star. 'He decided at four in the morning to get his teeth gold-plated. I found a dentist willing to do it. Lionel was so grateful he gave me the gift of two gold incisors. I hate them,' she said. 'I look like a bling Dracula. But I can't get them removed until he's left town.'

Rachel clapped her hands together in a parody of good humour and declared, 'Food! It's important to eat. What'll we have?'

'Pizza?' Jacqui asked me.

'I don't mind. I'm not the one with gold-plated teeth.' I gave her the Andretti's leaflet. 'Will you order?'

'Better if you do,' Rachel said.

I looked at her bleakly.

'Sorry,' she said awkwardly. 'But it is.'

'When I order they never bring the salad.'

'If that's how it has to be . . .'

So I rang Andretti's and, as I predicted, they forgot the salad. 'I told you,' I said, with weary triumph. 'I did warn you.'

As soon as we'd finished eating, Jacqui produced a twelve-inch-high heap of envelopes. 'Your mail.'

I took the bundle, put it in the closet and closed the door tight. I'd look at it sometime.

'Er . . . don't you want to open it?'

'Not right now.'

A tricky silence.

'I've just got here,' I said defensively. 'Give me a chance.'

It was strange to see the two of them united against me. It's not that they didn't like each other—not exactly—but Rachel's motto was, 'The unexamined life isn't worth living,' while Jacqui's was, 'We're not here for a long time, we're here for a good time.' They had never bitched to me about the other but, if they were to, Rachel would say that Jacqui was too shallow and Jacqui would say that Rachel needed to lighten up.

After further silence, I said, 'So! Jacqui, what's happening with you? Are you over Buzz yet?'

Buzz was Jacqui's ex-boyfriend. He had a year-round tan and tons of confidence and money. He was also incredibly cruel. Jacqui used to keep saying what a bastard he was and that she'd had it with him—no, she'd *really* had it with him this time. But she always gave him one more chance. Then he'd broken up with her on New Year's Eve and she'd been devastated.

Jacqui never got a chance to answer me. As if I hadn't spoken, Rachel said, 'There are lots of messages on your machine. We thought you might like someone here when you're listening to them.'

'Why not?' I said. 'Hit it.'

There were thirty-seven messages. All kinds of people had come out of the woodwork.

'Anna, Anna, Anna . . .'

'Who is *that*?'

'. . . It's Amber. I just heard . . .'

'Amber Penrose? It's for ever since I heard from her. Delete!'

'Anna,' someone whispered, 'I've just heard and I can't bel—'

'Yeah, yeah, yeah. Delete!'

Rachel muttered something. I caught the word 'denial'. 'At least write down their names.'

'I don't have a pen.'

'Here.' She passed me a pen and a notebook which had magically materialised on her person, and obediently I wrote down the names of everyone who had called, and the trade-off was that I didn't have to listen to their full commiserations.

Then Jacqui and Rachel made me switch on my computer and retrieve all my emails: there were eighty-three. I scanned the sender's addresses; I was only interested in getting an email from one person and it wasn't there.

'Read them.'

'No need. I'll get round to them. Now look, girls, I'm sorry. I need my sleep. I've got work in the morning.'

'What!' Rachel yelped. 'Don't be so insane. There's no *way* you're well enough either physically or emotionally to return to work. You're in total denial about what's happened to you.'

'Rachel,' I said, 'thank you for all your kindness, but the only way this will be OK is if I carry on as normal.'

'Don't go to work.'

'I have to. I've already told them to expect me.'

A face-off ensued. Rachel was very strong-willed but, at that moment, so was I. I sensed her start to buckle so I seized my advantage. 'Luke will be wondering where you are.'

I began edging them towards the exit but, I swear to God, I'd thought they'd never leave. At the door, Rachel cleared her throat. 'Anna, I can't know exactly the hell you're going through, but when I admitted I was an addict I felt like my life was over. How I got through it was by deciding: I won't think about for ever, I won't even think about next week, I'll just think about getting through today.'

'Thank you, yes, lovely.' *Get out.*

'I put that toy dog in your bed,' Jacqui said. 'To keep you company.'

'Dogly? Thank you.'

As soon as I was sure they were really gone and wouldn't be leaping back through the door to check on me, I did what I'd been dying to do for hours—I rang Aidan's cellphone. It went straight to his message service but, even so, it was such a relief to hear his voice that my stomach turned to water.

'Aidan,' I said. 'Baby, I'm back in New York. Back in our apartment, so you know where to find me. I hope you're OK. I love you.'

Then I wrote him an email.

To: Aidan_maddox@yahoo.com
From: Magiciansgirl1@yahoo.com
Subject: I'm back

Dear Aidan,
It feels funny writing to you like this. I don't think I've ever written you a proper letter before. Hundreds and hundreds of little emails, yes, to ask who was bringing dinner home and what time would we meet and that sort of thing, but never like this.

I'm back in our apartment, but maybe you know that. Rachel and Jacqui came over—Jacqui got a present of two gold teeth from a client—and we had takeout pizzas from Andretti's. They forgot the salad, as always.

Please be OK, please don't be frightened, please come and see me or get in touch somehow.

I love you.
Anna

I read back over what I'd written. Was it light enough? I didn't want him to know how worried I was, because whatever he was going through was bound to be difficult enough without me making it worse.

Decisively, I hit SEND with my index finger and a red-hot shock shot from my regrowing nail up my arm. Christ, I'd have to go easy on the grand-gesture-style typing using the two fingers with the banjaxed nails. The pain made me queasy and momentarily it distracted me from the sudden wave of feeling that washed over me. Something like rage or sadness at not being able to protect Aidan—but it was so fleeting it was gone before I could grasp it.

In the bedroom, tucked into Aidan's side of the bed was Dogly, the toy he'd had since he was a baby. He had long, swingy ears, syrupy eyes, an eager, adoring expression, and his caramel-coloured fur was so thick it was more like a sheep's fleece. Not in the first flush of youth— Aidan was thirty-five, after all—but not bad for his age. 'He had some work done,' Aidan said once. 'Eyes lifted, collagen injection to plump out his tail, a little liposuction on his ears.'

'Well, Dogly,' I said. 'This is a bit of a disaster.'

It was time to take my last batch of pills for the day, and for once I was grateful for the mood-altering stuff—the antidepressants, painkillers and sleeping tablets. Coming back to New York was harder than I had expected and I needed all the help I could get.

But even filled with enough mellowing stuff to knock out an elephant, I didn't want to get into bed. Then, suddenly, I felt I'd had an electric shock: I noticed his grey sweatshirt on our bedroom chair. It was if he'd just pulled it off and flung it there. Cautiously, I picked it up and sniffed it and enough of his smell still lingered to make me dizzy. I buried my face in it and the intensity of his presence and absence made me choke.

It didn't have the special lovely smell of his neck, but it was enough to get me into bed. I closed my eyes and the pills pulled me into an undertow of sleep. But in that halfway state that precedes unconsciousness, I caught a glimpse of the enormity of what had happened. I was back in New York, he wasn't here and I was alone.

The first thing I did when I woke was switch on the computer, checking my email, hoping for a reply from him. The indicator said there were five messages and I stopped breathing, my heart pounding with desperate hope. But from Aidan, *nada*.

Disconsolate, I trudged off to shower and was shocked to find that I could barely wet my body, never mind my hair. Have you ever tried to have a shower without getting one arm wet? For the past eight or nine weeks everything had been done for me, so much so that I hadn't noticed how incapacitated I was.

I reached for my shower gel and a memory hit me like a blow: it was No Rough Stuff, the new Candy Grrrl exfoliator. That last day, all those weeks ago, I'd been test-driving it, and when I got out of the shower, I'd asked Aidan, 'Do I smell nice?'

Obediently he'd sniffed me. 'Great. Although you smelt ever nicer ten minutes ago.'

'But ten minutes ago I only smelt like me.'

'Exactly.'

I had to hold tightly to the sink until the feeling passed, clenching with my one good hand, my knuckles turning bone-white.

Time to get dressed. My already low heart dipped a little lower and Dogly watched sympathetically. It was the kookiness, hanger after hanger of it, plus rack after rack of colourful shoes and bags—and, worst of all, the hats. I was facing my thirty-third birthday, far too old for this. What I needed was a promotion, because the further up the feeding scale you went, the more you were allowed to wear suits.

To: Aidan_maddox@yahoo.com
From: Magiciansgirl1@yahoo.com
Subject: Kooky girl goes back to work

Today's outfit—black suede boots, pink fishnets, black crepe-de-Chine vintage dress with white polka dots, pink three-quarter-length coat (also vintage) and butterfly bag. Silly hat? I hear you ask—oh, but of course: a black beret at an angle. All in all, a little subdued, but I should get away with it today.
    I would really like to hear from you.
    Your girl, Anna

He always got a kick out of my work uniform. The irony was that he tried to subvert his conservative suits with funky ties and socks— Warhol prints, pink roses, cartoon superheroes—and I was desperate to be sombre and tailored.

I left another quick message on his cell, and finally left the apartment. Out on the street, I found I was shaking. I wasn't used to going to work on my own; we always got the subway together, he got off at 34th Street, I carried on up to 59th.

I began walking towards the subway, then stopped as I considered what it would be like down there. Steps up and down everywhere, and my knee was already aching, far worse than it had done in Dublin. I'd taken only half of my usual dose of painkillers because I didn't want to start nodding off in meetings, and it was a shock to discover how much pain the painkillers had actually been killing.

But how else was I going to get to work? I shrank from getting into a cab. I'd coped with taking one from the airport because Rachel had been with me, but I was petrified at the thought of being in one alone.

Then, after standing on the sidewalk for an indeterminate time and getting curious looks from passers-by, I watched myself hail a cab and, in a dreamlike state, get in. Could I really be doing this? The fear was profound; saucer-eyed, I watched all the other cars, flinching and shrinking whenever any of them came too close, as if my scrutiny alone would prevent them from driving into me. Suddenly, with a bang to my chest that nearly stopped my heart, I saw Aidan. He was sitting on a bus which had paused at an intersection. It was only a sidelong view, but it was definitely him. All the city noise retreated, leaving only a muzzy, staticy buzzing, and as I clawed for cash and reached for the door handle, the bus surged forward. In a panic, I twisted round and stared out of the back window.

'Sir!' I said to the cab-driver, but we were moving also and already too far gone. It was too late to turn and the traffic going back down-town was stuck solid.

'Yeah?'

'Nothing.'

I was trembling violently: the shock of seeing him. It didn't make sense for him to be on that bus—he was going completely the wrong way, if he was going to work. It couldn't have been him. It must have been someone who looked like him.

But what if it *was* him and this had been my one chance to see him?

The security guards couldn't believe I was back. No employee of McArthur on the Park had ever taken such a long time off work before.

'Hey, Morty, Irish Anna's back.'

'She is? Irish Anna, we thought they'd sacked your ass. And whatcha *do* to your face?'

Delicately they high-fived my bandaged right hand, and I joined the throngs of people streaming to the banks of elevators. I squashed into the crammed metal box, everyone holding their coffee and avoiding each other's eyes.

On the thirty-eighth floor, the elevator doors opened with a silent swish. I struggled to the front and popped out like a pinball. An unseen voice said, 'Welcome back, Anna.' I nearly jumped out of my skin. It was Lauryn Pike, my manager, and she looked like she'd been standing there all night, waiting. Tentatively, she extended her hand, as though she was thinking of touching me, then thought better of it. I was glad.

'You look great!' she said. 'Really rested. So! Ready to go, yeah?'

I looked terrible but if she acknowledged that, she might have to make allowances for me. Lauryn is scrawny skinny, always cold, has a nasty brown cardigan that she is always dragging and wrapping about her in an attempt to get warm. She burns with a manic intensity and has very poppy eyes. If I was a magazine beauty editor and I saw Lauryn coming to pitch me a Candy Grrrl piece, I'd hide under my desk until she'd gone. Despite that, Lauryn gets *loads* of coverage.

All of a sudden, I was gripped by terrible fear that I wouldn't be able to handle being back at work, but I said, 'I'm good to go, Lauryn.'

'Good! Because we have, like, a *lot* happening right now.'

'Just bring me up to speed.'

'Sure. And you let me know, Anna, if you can't cope.' She didn't mean this in a kind way. She meant for me to let her know if she needed to sack me. 'And when will that . . . thing . . . on your face be better?' They hate physical imperfection round here. 'And your arm? When will it be out of the cast?' Then she noticed my bandaged fingers. 'What's that all about?'

'Missing nails.'

'Jesus H,' she said. 'I'm gonna throw up.'

She sat down and breathed deeply but didn't throw up. In order to throw up, it's necessary to have something in your stomach.

'You gotta do something about them. Go see someone. Fix them. Today.'

'Yes, but . . . OK.'

A flash of silver caught my attention—it was Teenie! Wearing a silver boiler suit tucked into orange vinyl knee-boots. Today her hair was blue. To match her glittery blue lips. Teenie is my favourite of all the McArthur staff. She'd even rung me in Ireland.

'Anna!' she said. 'You're back! Ooh, your hair is pretty. It's gotten so long.' Together we discreetly sidled away from Lauryn, and Teenie said quietly, 'Sweetie, how're you doing?'

'OK.'

'You are?' She quirked a blue, glittery eyebrow at me.

I slid a glance at Lauryn; she was far enough away not to hear. 'OK, maybe not exactly. But, Teenie, the only way I'll get through this is if we pretend everything is the way it always was.'

'Lunch?'

'Can't. Lauryn says I've got to get my nails fixed.'

'What's up with them?'

'They're missing. But they are growing back as fast as they can.'

'Eew.'

'Yes, well,' I said, going back to my desk. Here, things felt familiar yet very different. The temp—or temps—had rearranged my stuff, and someone had put my photo of Aidan in a drawer. I took it out and banged it down angrily on the spot where it always stood.

'Oh, my gosh, Anna, you're back!' It was Brooke Edison. Brooke is twenty-two and loaded and lives with Mommy and Daddy in a triplex on the UES (Upper East Side). She'd been hired as the Candy Grrrl junior, the person who did the heavy lifting, like stuffing envelopes with samples for the magazines. But she's always having to leave work early or come in late because she's attending charity benefits or having dinner with the chairman of the Guggenheim. Ariella keeps her on the staff because she knows *everyone*—people are always being her god-mother or her dad's best friend or her old piano teacher.

She did her private-girls'-school-in-Europe walk over to my desk, swinging her thick, glossy, naturally beautiful hair, which glowed with privileged-rich-person's health. Her skin is fantastic and she never wears make-up, which would be a sacking offence for me and Teenie, but not for her. Same with her clothes: Brooke isn't even remotely kooky and no one says a thing. Today she wore wide-cut trousers in beige cashmere and a dinky little fawn sweater, also in cashmere.

She extended her hand (with short, neat, clear-glossed nails), didn't even flicker as she scanned my scar and said with genuine-sounding sincerity, 'Anna, I am so sorry about what happened.'

'Thank you.'

Then she left, she didn't labour it—an awkward situation, handled just right. Brooke always gets everything just right. She is the most appropriate-aware person I have ever met.

'OK, people,' Lauryn called. 'Now that Anna has finished her conversations, could you all possibly spare me a few moments of your time for a Candy Grrrl briefing?' (Said sarcastically.)

All day long, everyone was looking at me—but never directly. When I met girls from other brands in the corridors or the washrooms they gave me slanting, sidelong glances and as soon as I left I knew they were whispering about me.

Mid-morning, Franklin took me into Ariella's inner sanctum so I could thank her for keeping my job open. In her trademark powder-blue power-suit, Ariella acknowledged my gratitude by nodding slowly, her eyes half closed. There was nothing more disconcerting than Ariella in her *Capo di tutti capi* mode. 'Maybe sometime you can do something for me.' Either she had a permanent sore throat or she deliberately put on a hoarse Don Corleone-style mumble. 'I need a favour, I can count on you?'

I work very hard for you, I wanted to say. Before all this happened, I got more coverage than any of your other publicists and I intend that that will be the case again. You didn't pay me for one second while I was away and it's not like I took off on a whim.

'Of course, Ariella.'

'And get a haircut.'

She nodded at Franklin in his immaculate suit: the signal to take me away.

Out in the hallway, he did his sympathetic face. 'So how ya doing, girlfriend?'

Franklin is my boss. In fact, his is my boss's boss. (Lauryn reports to him.)

'OK.' There was no point in saying any more. He has zero interest in anyone else's problems. He patted me on the shoulder and pulled the shutters down on his face. 'You'll be OK, kiddo.'

I'd have to be.

'And you heard Ariella. Get a haircut. Go see someone at Perry K.'

Just what I needed: ridiculous high-maintenance hair when barely one of my hands was operational.

At lunchtime I tried to get my nails done, but when I took off the bandages and revealed them to the manicurist she went green and said they were far too short for acrylic ones to be fitted. When I returned with the bad news Lauryn behaved as if I was lying.

'The girl told me to come back in a month,' I protested weakly. 'I'll get them done then.'

'What-ev-er. Eye Eye Captain—I want your thoughts on the campaign by the weekend.'

When Lauryn said she wanted 'my thoughts', she actually meant that she wanted a fully realised campaign, complete with press releases, spreadsheets, budgeting and a signed contract from Scarlett Johansson saying she was so thrilled to be the new face of Candy Grrrl that she'd do it for free.

'I'll see what I can do.' I dashed to my desk and started speed-reading through the Eye Eye Captain data.

It wasn't until late afternoon that I checked my emails. Unlike my home email, my work stuff had been opened and answered. I scrolled back through them. A lot were from beauty editors asking for products. Then my heart nearly jumped out of my mouth. This was what I'd been waiting for. In bold black type—meaning it was new and unread—was an email from Aidan.

To: AnnaW@CandyGrrrl.com
From: Aidan_maddox@yahoo.com
Subject: Tonight

Just tried to call, but you're on the line. Wanted to catch you before I left. See you tonight. Nothing to report, just wanted to tell you that I love you and will love you for ever and ever, no matter what happens.
  A xxxxxxxx

I read it again. What did it mean? He was coming to see me tonight? Then I noticed the date: February 16 and today was April 20. This wasn't new. This must have arrived after I'd left to meet him that evening nine weeks ago. And because it was obviously personal, the temp hadn't opened it and had left it for me to read. All the adrenaline racing through my poor, hopeful body pulled up in a big jerk and I went home in disgust.

The first time I met the Maddoxes

'What are you doing for Thanksgiving?' Aidan had asked.
'Dunno.' Hadn't given it much thought.
'Want to come to Boston and spend it with my family?'
'Um, OK, thanks. If you're sure.'
A low-key response, but I knew that this was a big deal. In the unwritten New York dating rules I was jumping the gun by at least seven weeks. It was forbidden—indeed, up until now it had been thought technically *impossible*—to move directly from a declaration of exclusivity to meeting his family. It was most unorthodox. Highly irregular. No good would come of it, my friends all prophesied, shaking their heads despondently.

I didn't need their doom and gloom. I had my own worries: Aidan had told me about Janie.

It should have been the subject of a late-night confessional, but circumstances dictated that it was a morning bean-spilling—the morning after we'd first slept together and he'd gone weird on me. It had made me late for work but I didn't care. I had to know.

Here's the gist: Aidan and Janie had gone out with each other for about a hundred and sixty-eight years. They'd been brought up a couple of miles from each other in Boston and had been an item since high school. They went away to different colleges and the relationship ceased by mutual consent but, when they arrived back in Boston three years later, everything kicked off again. All through their twenties they were a loved-up couple and they became part of each other's families, Janie joining the Maddoxes on their summer vacations in Cape Cod and Aidan going along with the Janies to their place in Bar Harbor. Over the years, Aidan and Janie tried dating other people, but they always returned to each other.

Time passed and they moved into apartments—but not together— and the marriage hints from their families were starting to get a little heavy when, about eighteen months before I met him, Aidan's firm transferred him to work 'in the city'.

It was a bit of a shock all round but Aidan and Janie kept reminding each other that New York was a mere hour's flight away, they'd see each other every weekend and, in the meantime, Aidan would look for another job back in Boston and Janie would apply for jobs in NYC. So off Aidan goes, promising to be true.

'You can guess what happened,' he said.

Actually, I was still trying to figure it out. That first night when he'd asked me to put him on my roster, he'd given the impression that he was available—albeit in a non-exclusive way.

'You've barely paid off the taxi in Manhattan when you're trawling the bars, looking for takers?'

He laughed a little sadly. 'Not exactly. But, yes, I slept with other women.'

In his defence he refused to blame the exquisite-looking, brazen NYC ladies who'd done classes, learning how to twirl their bras over their heads.

'No one to blame but me,' he said miserably. 'I wanted to flagellate myself with shame. Don't laugh, but I went to confession.'

'Oh. Are you, like . . . a practising Catholic?'

He shook his head. 'A recovering Catholic. But I felt so shitty I would've tried anything.'

I didn't know what to say.

'Janie deserved so much better,' he said. 'She's a great human being, a very good person. She sees the positive in every situation.'

Oh God. I was going head-to-head with a living saint.

'That first day we met, when I spilt coffee on you, I'd just made a fresh resolution that I was going to be totally faithful to Janie.'

So that was why he'd given off waves of despair when I'd asked him out.

'So what happened?' I asked, angrily. 'Am I another of your guilty slips? Will it be another trip to the confession box?'

'No. No, no, no, no, not at all! About a month later, when I was in Boston, Janie said we should take some time out. She hinted that she knew about the other women. Said we'd been messing around for too long, it was make or break time. We should see other people, get stuff out of our systems, then see where it left me and her.'

'And?'

'I'd shredded your card. I was so scared I was going to call you. But I couldn't stop thinking about you. I'd remembered your name and where you worked, but I thought it was too late to call.

'You know, I nearly didn't go to that party that night and when I saw you there, talking to that meathead, *that* made me believe in God. Seeing you, it was like . . . like getting hit with a baseball bat . . .' He looked like he was going to puke. 'I don't want to scare you, Anna, but I've never felt this way about anyone else, ever.'

I said nothing. I felt so guilty. But I couldn't help also feeling . . . a little . . . flattered.

'I wanted to talk to Janie before I talked to you. I didn't know if you'd be, like, interested in being exclusive—I hate that stupid phrase—but it's over for me and Janie. I just feel bad that you know before she does.'

Tell me about it.

And shallow girl that I am, I wanted to know what Janie looked like. I had to clamp my lips together extremely tightly to stop myself asking, but it didn't work and little sounds escaped. *Mwahdoz zhee mlook mlike.*

'Wha—Oh! What does she look like?' His face went suddenly blank. 'Um, you know, nice, she's got'—he made a rotating gesture with his hand—'hair, curly hair.' He paused. 'Well, she used to. Maybe lately it's been straight.'

OK, he hadn't a clue what she looked like. He'd been with her for so long that he didn't look at her properly any more. Nevertheless, a powerful intuition was warning me that I should not underestimate this woman and the strength of Aidan's attachment. They'd shared fifteen years of history and, like a boomerang, he kept returning to her.

He went to Boston and all weekend I felt mildly queasy; contradictory thoughts chased each other in a never-ending circle. At the air-guitar competition, Shake accused me of not paying attention when he'd been on, and he was right: I'd been staring into space wondering how Janie was taking it.

On the Sunday evening Aidan showed up on my doorstep. 'She took it pretty good.'

'Really?' I asked hopefully.

'She kind of hinted . . . you know . . . that maybe she might have met someone else too.'

This was balm—for half a second. You know how thick men can be; no doubt Janie had done what she could to save face but right at that moment she was probably running a hot bath and getting the cutthroat razor out of the bathroom closet.

As the plane, full of Thanksgiving returnees, touched down in Logan I asked Aidan, 'Tell me again, how many girls other than Janie have you brought home for Thanksgiving?'

He thought for ages, counting stuff out on his fingers and whispering numbers under his breath, and eventually said, 'None!'

It had become a familiar routine over the previous four weeks, but now that I had actually arrived in Boston I felt sick. 'Aidan, it's no joke. I shouldn't have come. Everyone will hate me for not being Janie. The streets will be lined by angry Bostonians stoning the car.'

'It'll be fine.' He squeezed my fingers. 'They'll love you.'

His mom, Dianne, picked us up from the airport and instead of pelting me with gravel she gave me a hug and said, 'Welcome to Boston.'

She was lovely—a bit scatty, driving erratically and blathering away. Finally we fetched up in some suburb that wasn't a million miles different from the one I came from.

The house too seemed familiar, with horrible swirly carpets and awful soft furnishings. I felt right at home.

I dropped my bag on the hall floor and almost the first thing I saw was a photo on the wall of a younger-looking Aidan with his two arms around a girl, hugging the back of her body to the front of his. Right away I knew it was Janie. I felt a little shaky even before I'd absorbed that she was beautiful, with dark, long corkscrew curls.

But clearly it had been taken a long time ago, judging by how bright-eyed and innocent Aidan looked.

Someone shouted, 'Dad, they're here,' then a door opened and a young man appeared: dark hair, very smiley, *extremely* cute. 'Hi, I'm Kevin, the younger brother.'

'And I'm Anna—'

'Oh, yeah, we know *all* about you.' He dazzled me with a smile. 'Wow. Any more like you at home?'

'Yes.' I considered Helen. 'But you'd probably be terrified of her.'

He didn't realise I wasn't joking and he laughed.

Next to appear was Mr Maddox, a lanky bloke with a vague, wavery voice. He shook hands with me but said little. I didn't take it personally:

Aidan had warned me that when he did talk, it was usually about the Democratic Party.

Kevin insisted on carrying my bag to my bedroom, a room that could have been twinned with the spare room in my parents' house.

Then I saw it. On the dressing table: another picture of Aidan and Janie. A 'motion' shot, they were turned towards each other and it had been taken half a second before they kissed.

Again I felt queasy and, after eyeballing it for a few minutes, I laid it face-downwards. A light knock on the door made me jump guiltily and Dianne breezed in. 'Fresh towels!' Instantly, she noticed the toppled picture. 'Oh, Anna! It's stood there for years, so long I don't even see it any more. That was so tactless of me.'

She picked it up, left the room with it and returned empty-handed. 'Sorry about that,' she said. 'Truly.' She seemed sincerely sorry to have upset me. 'Whenever you're ready for dinner, come on down.'

The dinner was the whole Thanksgiving nine yards: a massive turkey and millions of spuds and vegetables and wine and champagne and crystal glasses and candles. The atmosphere was very friendly, everyone was chatting away, and even Old Man Maddox made a joke and although it was about the Democratic Pah-dy and I didn't understand it, I laughed obligingly.

In the middle of swallowing a mouthful of turkey, I spotted yet another picture that I'd missed earlier and once again my gullet shut down briefly. I took a swig of wine to assist things along and Old Man Maddox asked, 'Janie, dear, can you pass the roast potatoes?'

Who?

I looked from side to side but as the dish of spuds was in front of me and Old Man Maddox was looking my way, I concluded that it must be me he was talking to. Obediently, I shunted the bowl along and Kevin gave me a comforting wink, while Aidan and Dianne looked horrified and mouthed, 'Sorry.'

But two seconds later, Dianne said, 'Oh, Aidan, we met Janie's dad at the hahd-ware stoh. He says to tell you he finally finished the shed and to come by to see it. How long ago was it that you guys stah-ted on it?'

Then Old Man Maddox piped up. 'You might like to know what he was doing at the hahd-ware stoh?' he asked Aidan. He'd suddenly gone all bright-eyed and amused. 'Buying paint, that's what. White paint, by the way. For their place in Bah Hah-ba. We still can't figure what came over you two guys, painting the place pink.'

Flushed with amusement, he looked from Aidan to me, then panic flickered behind his eyes. *She's not Janie.*

The following day we went to the mall because there's only so much sitting around your new boyfriend's parents' house, living in fear of hearing further reminiscences about his ex-girlfriend, you can do.

But once we were in the mall I cheered up because when I'm away from home, even shops that are normally beneath me suddenly become exciting. Aidan bought me a souvenir of Boston—a snow-dome—then said, 'Guess we'd better go back.'

So we got in the cah and had just left the pahking lot, when it happened. Even before Aidan made a funny, involuntary noise, I'd noticed the jaw-clenching tension suddenly emanating from him.

I looked out of the window, my eyes scudding from side to side, desperate to see what he'd seen. A woman was walking towards us. But we were moving quite fast, we'd already passed her and my intuition was yelling, *Look round, look round, quickly.*

I whipped my head over my shoulder. The woman was walking away from us. She was quite tall and her hair was straight and dark and hung to her shoulders. Her bag was nice, I'd seen them in Zara. I kept watching until she disappeared into the lot.

I turned back and settled myself firmly against the seat. 'That was Janie, wasn't it?' If he lied to me at that moment, there would be no future for us.

He nodded, a little grimly. 'Yes, that was Janie.'

We were very quiet on the flight home. The visit had been a terrible mistake, a risk worth taking but one that hadn't worked out. Aidan was a great guy in lots of ways but he had too much baggage and too much unfinished business. He belonged in Boston with Janie and I admitted to myself that, no matter what, he would always return to her and she would always take him back. They had too much history, too much in common.

He was grey-green with tension and in the cab from the airport he held my hand so tight he hurt my fingers. He was trying to figure out a way to tell me it was over, but there was no need, I knew exactly what was going on.

The cab dropped me at my apartment and I kissed Aidan on the cheek and said, 'Take care of yourself.'

As I clambered out of the cab he called after me, 'Anna?'

'Yes?'

'Anna, will you marry me?'

I stared at him for a long, long moment, then said, 'Get a grip on yourself,' and slammed the car door.

7

I STARED AT MY SCREEN and took a swig of coffee. No, the coffee didn't help—the line was still atrocious and I deleted it. I was trying to write a press release for Eye Eye Captain, our new eye treatments, and was attempting a play on mutiny, salt water, piracy and other ship-based stuff. But it so wasn't working.

I'd seen Aidan again on the way to work. This time he was walking along Fifth Avenue in a jacket that I didn't recognise. He'd found time to buy new clothes but not to call me? Once again, the taxi was moving too fast, so I didn't get the driver to stop. But now I desperately wished that I had and the regret was interfering with my concentration.

I typed 'Eye Eye Captain' then had absolutely nothing further to say. God, I really needed to get it together. I was Assistant VP for Public Relations and I had responsibilities.

I was actually scared. This was my third day back at work and I felt like I was in a dream. My head wouldn't think, my body was in pain, everything felt like the world had tilted off its axis.

Forty minutes later I printed out my crappy press release and went to Lauryn's desk, ready to play the humiliation game. The responsibility for Candy Grrrl's publicity was shared out between me and Lauryn like this: *I* did the work and came up with the ideas, while *she* made my life a misery, was paid fifty per cent more than me and got all the credit.

I had a second-tier duty: badgering beauty editors, taking them out to lunch, telling them how lovely Candy Grrrl products were and persuading them to give us a four-line soundbite and a photo on their beauty news page. The inches of magazine coverage I generated were measured, then compared with how much would have had to be spent in advertising to get the same space. My target this year was twelve per cent higher than the previous year's, but I'd lost two months' worth of badgering while I'd been in Ireland. It was going to be hard to make it up.

I gave Lauryn my Eye Eye Captain press release. A one-second glance was all it took.

'This is shit.' She threw it back at me.

That was fine. I always had to present her with at least two attempts;

she would trash my first offering, then trash the second, then she usually accepted the first.

Unpleasant perhaps, but it was nice to know where I stood.

I didn't leave work until seven thirty, and when I got home there was an email from my mother.

To: Magiciansgirl1@yahoo.com
From: Thewalshes1@eircom.net
Subject: The woman and her dog

Dear Anna,

I hope you are keeping well. Just remember you can come home whenever you want and we will mind you. I am writing in connection with the woman and the dog who was 'doing his business' at our front gate. I will admit that we all thought you were imagining things, as a result of the tablets you are on. But myself and Helen have watched her over the last few mornings and it has become clear that she is indeed urging her dog to 'pee' at our front gate and I just wanted to keep you 'in the loop' as they say. As yet we haven't identified her. As you know, she is an old woman and all old women look the same to me.

Your loving mother,
Mum

Less than a week after he first asked me to marry him, Aidan did it again, this time with a ring made by a jeweller I'd once said I liked. In white gold with a delicate band and seven diamonds in a star setting. I was freaked out.

'Snap out of it,' I said to him. 'Take it down a notch or two. We had one bad weekend. You're overreacting.'

I hurried home to Jacqui and related what had happened.

'A ring?' she exclaimed. 'You're getting married!'

'I'm not getting married. Why should I?'

'Duh . . . because he asked you?' Testily, she said, 'So why won't you marry the guy?'

Incoherently, I splutter, 'Reason a) I barely know him and I've spent so much of my life being impulsive, I've used it all up. Reason b) Aidan has too much baggage and I don't want a fixer-upper. Reason c) As you yourself, Jacqui Staniforth, said—and I bet you're right—he's probably a hard dog to keep on the porch. What if he's unfaithful to me?'

'Actually, it's none of the above,' Jacqui said. 'It's reason d) Because you're a late starter. Which means,' she said, loudly, 'that while every other single woman of our age would be *delighted* to marry anyone, even a three-eyed dwarf who has to shave his nose, you're still naive enough to think you shouldn't go round marrying the first man who asks you. But basically, Anna Walsh, you haven't a *clue* how lucky you are!'

I waited for her to finish shouting.

'Sorry,' she said, her colour high, her breathing louder than usual. 'But you do love him, Anna,' she accused. 'And he loves you. I know it's been quick, but it's serious.'

The next time Aidan produced the ring I said, 'Why do you want to marry me?'

He sighed. 'I can list the reasons but it still won't convey anything like enough: you smell good, you're brave, you like Dogly, you're funny, you're smart, you're really, really cute-looking, I like the way you say "curly-wurly", I like how your head works . . .' He spread his hands in a gesture of helplessness. 'But it's much, much more than that.'

'What's the difference between how you feel about me and how you felt about Janie?'

'I'm not dissing Janie because she's a great person, but there's no comparison . . .' He snapped his fingers. 'OK, got it! Have you ever had, like, a really bad toothache? One of those screaming ones where it's like electricity crackling up into your head and ears? Yeah? OK, convert that same intensity into love and that's how I feel about you.'

'And Janie?'

'Janie? Janie is like when you bump your head on a low ceiling. Bad but not unbearable. Am I making any sense?'

'Strangely, yes.'

On paper so many of the boxes were ticked. The problem was Janie. I couldn't forgive Aidan for dumping her.

'In all the time I was with Janie,' Aidan said, 'I never asked her to marry me. And she never asked me either.'

'I don't care,' I said. 'All this marriage stuff is doing my head in.'

'What are you so scared of?'

'Oh, you know, all the obvious reasons: I'll never be able to sleep with anyone else ever again, I don't want to be part of a smug couple who finish each other's sentences.'

But my real fear was that it mightn't work out, that he might run off with someone else—or, more likely, go back to Janie. When you love someone as much as I suspected I loved Aidan, there was so much further to fall.

'I'm afraid that it might all go horribly wrong,' I admitted. 'That we'd end up hating each other and losing our trust in love. I couldn't bear it. Then I'd become an over-made-up lush with big hair who drinks Martinis for breakfast and tries to sleep with the pool boy.'

'Anna, it won't go wrong, I promise. This is good stuff, you and me, as good as it gets. You know that.'

Sometimes I did. Which meant that—like the urge I got on the top of a tall building, to just jump off—my biggest fear of all was that I might say yes.

'OK, if you won't marry me will you come on a vacation with me?'

'I don't know,' I said. 'I'll have to ask Jacqui.'

'Kill or cure,' was Jacqui's conclusion. 'It could be a total disaster, trapped in a foreign country with nothing to say to each other. I'd say, go for it.'

I said I'd go so long as he didn't once ask me to marry him. 'Done,' he said.

I went to Ireland for Christmas and when I got back, Aidan and I went to Mexico for six days.

After the cold and drear of a New York winter, the white sands and blue skies were so dazzling it almost hurt to look at them. But the best bit of all was having Aidan on tap twenty-four hours a day. First thing in the morning, last thing at night, at all points in between . . .

To make sure we got out of bed once in a while, we checked out the dusty local town and decided to do a beginners' scuba-diving course, which was run by two ex-pat Californian stoners. It was dirt cheap and, with the benefit of hindsight, maybe we should have been concerned by that.

But we didn't give a damn, we were having a great time, crouched in the tiny practice pool with nine other beginners. On day three, we were taken out for our first dive in the sea, and although we were only twelve feet beneath the waves, we were transported to another world. A world of peace, where all you can hear is the sound of your own breathing, and everything moves with slow grace. The water was as clear as glass and sunrays filtered all the way to the bottom, to highlight the white sand on the ocean floor.

Aidan and I were mesmerised. Holding hands we slowly flapped past delicate coral and fish of every imaginable colour. Shoals of them in for-mation, moving silently past us, heading for somewhere else. Aidan pointed and I followed his finger. Sharks. Three of them, hanging around at the edge of the reef, looking mean and moody, like they were wearing leather jackets. Reef sharks aren't dangerous. Usually. All the same, my heart beat a little faster.

Then, for a laugh, we took out our mouthpieces and used each other's spare 'octopus' air tube, becoming one unit, the way lovers in films set in the 1930s link arms and drink champagne from each other's glass.

The last day was the big banana, the grand finale. They were taking all of us to deeper waters, which involved decompressing on our ascent. We'd been practising in shallower waters, but this time it would be for real. But on the boat taking us out, events turned pear-shaped: Aidan had developed a cold, and although he was pretending he was in the full of his health, the instructor noticed and nixed Aidan's dive.

'You won't be able to equalise the pressure in your ears. Sorry, man, you can't go.'

Because Aidan wasn't coming, I got 'buddied' with a man who'd been reading *Codependent No More* on the beach. He'd come on holiday on his own and had been buddied with the instructor for every other dive.

Final instructions were called to us before we jumped off the side of the boat, then we splashed down into that silent other world. Mr Codependent wouldn't hold my hand, but that was fine because I didn't want to hold his either. Swimming along, we'd been near the ocean floor for several minutes—it's hard to keep track of time down there—when I realised that on my last two inhales, no air had come out of my tube. I took another suck just to make sure and no, nothing was happening. I tried my octopus arm—my spare tube—and felt the first tickle of fear when nothing came out of that either. My indicator said I still had twenty-five minutes of air left, but nothing was coming out.

I stopped Mr Codependent and signalled No Air. It was only when I went to grab his octopus and take a lovely mouthful of oxygen that I noticed there wasn't one! No extra air tube! Even in my shock, I knew what had happened: he'd detached it in order to demonstrate his lack of codependence.

Well, that was just tough because, seeing as he'd abandoned his spare tube somewhere, he'd have to give me a go of his own mouthpiece. I pointed and signalled Give It to Me but, as he went to take it out of his mouth, he panicked. Even through his mask, I could see it. Codependent was too scared to leave himself without air for even a few seconds. One hand guarding his air tube, he jabbed towards the surface with the other: Go Up. To my horror, he started swimming away from me, still protecting his air supply.

The others had gone on ahead, I could see them disappearing into the distance. There was no one to help me. *This isn't happening. Please, God, let this not be happening.* I was forty-five feet beneath the surface and I had no air. Surface, I thought. I've got to get to the surface.

Diving upwards, my legs kicking, my lungs bursting, I raced up, up, up, breaking all the rules, thinking, I'm going to die.

Every fifteen feet I was supposed to hang around decompressing for two minutes. Never mind two minutes, I didn't have two *seconds*. I kicked past a surprised shoal of clown fish, praying to break the surface. My blood roared in my ears and images flitted into my head.

Just when I thought my head was going to burst, I broke the blue line that separates the two worlds. The noise and the glare hit me, a wave slapped me in the ear and I was tearing the mask off my face, gulping in glorious oxygen.

The next thing I remember, I was lying on the deck of the boat, still heaving desperately for air, and Aidan was bending over me. His expression was a mixture of horror and relief. I made a monumental effort and managed to speak. 'OK,' I gasped. 'I'll marry you.'

8

IN THE DARKNESS, I woke with a bump, my heart beating fast and hard. The light was switched on before I knew I had done it and I was super-alert and awake. I'd nodded off on the couch in my work clothes because I'd kept postponing the moment when I had to go to bed.

Something had woken me. What had I heard? The sound of a key in the door? Or had the front door actually opened and closed? All I knew was, I wasn't alone. You can tell when someone else is in your space, it feels different.

It had to be Aidan. He'd come back. And although I was excited, I was also a bit freaked. Out of the corner of my eye, over by the window, I saw something move, something fast and shadowy. I whipped my head round but there was nothing there.

I stood up. There was nobody in the living room, nobody in the kitchenette, so I'd better check the bedroom. As I pushed open the door, I was sweating. I reached for the light switch, almost paralysed with terror that a hand might grab mine in the dark. What was that tall narrow shape over by the closet? Then I hit the switch and the room flooded with light and the dark, ominous shape revealed itself as nothing more malign than our bookshelf.

Hearing my own gaspy breathing, I turned on the bathroom light and pulled back the wave-patterned shower curtain with a violent swish. No one there either.

So what had woken me?

I realised I could smell him. The tiny space was filled with him. The panic was back and my eyes scudded around looking for—what? I was afraid to look in the mirror, in case I saw someone else looking at me. It was then that I saw that his washbag had slipped off the shelf onto the tiles. Things had tumbled out and a bottle of something had broken. I crouched down; it wasn't Aidan I could smell, it was just his aftershave.

I went to get a brush to clean up the broken glass but in the kitchenette another smell awaited me, something sweet and powdery and oppressive. Nervously, I sniffed the air. I recognised the scent. It was lilies, a smell I hate—so heavy and musty, like death.

I looked around fearfully. Where was it coming from? There were no fresh flowers in the apartment. But the air was thick and cloying.

After I'd tidied the broken bottle away, I was afraid to go back to sleep so I switched on the TV. Eventually, I drifted back into a half-sleep, where I dreamt I was awake and Aidan opened the door and walked in.

'Aidan, you came back! I knew you would.'

'I can't stay long, baby,' he said. 'But I've something important to tell you.'

'I know. So tell me, I can take it.'

'Pay the rent, it's overdue.'

'That's it?'

'That's it.'

'But I thought . . .'

'The demand is in the closet with all the other mail. I'm sorry, I know you don't want to open any of it, but just find that one. Don't lose our apartment. Be a hero, baby.'

'**A**nna, where are you?' It was Rachel.

'Work.'

'It's ten past eight on a Friday night! It's your first week back, you should be building up slowly.'

'I know, but I've so much to do and it's taking me for ever to do it.'

Spending half the previous night in front of the television instead of being asleep hadn't helped. I'd been exhausted all day. Lauryn was piling stuff on me and Franklin was on at me to get my hair cut.

Rachel said, 'Some of the Real Men are calling round to play Scrabble. It might be an easy way for you to start meeting people again. Could you face it?'

Could I? I didn't want to be alone. Mind you, I didn't really want to be with anyone else either. Paradox as that was, it made sense; I simply wanted to be with Aidan.

In the four days I'd been in New York, I'd never had so many invitations. Everyone had been fantastic, but, as yet, the only people I'd been able to call were Jacqui and Rachel (who came as a job lot with Luke). There were loads of people I still had to get back to: Leon and Dana; Ornesto, our Jolly Boy upstairs neighbour; Aidan's mother. Anyway, all in good time . . .

I switched off my PC and jumped in a cab on 58th Street—it was getting slightly easier to be in cabs. En route, I called Jacqui and invited her along.

'Scrabble with the Real Men? I'd rather set myself on fire.'

Apart from Luke, Jacqui had no time for the rest of the Real Men.

Luke let me in. Although his rocker-type hair is a lot shorter now than when he first met Rachel, he still wears his jeans just that smidgeon too tight. My eyes are always drawn inexorably to his crotch. I have no control over it. A bit like the way everyone had started addressing all conversation to my scar instead of to me.

'Come on in,' he invited my scar. 'Rachel's just having a quick shower.'

'Grand,' I said, to his crotch.

Rachel and Luke's apartment was a rent-controlled place in the East Village. Massive by New York standards, which meant you could stand in the middle of the living room and not be able to touch all four walls. They'd lived there for nearly five years, and it was very cosy and comfortable. Lamps cast pools of soft light and the air smelt of the cut flowers in a bowl on the coffee table.

'Beer, wine, water?' Luke asked.

'Water,' I told his crotch. I was afraid that if I started drinking I would never stop.

The buzzer went. 'It's Joey,' Luke said. Joey is his best friend. 'You sure you'll be OK around him?'

I tried to tell Luke's face, I really did, but my eyes just slid downwards. 'No problem.'

Seconds later, Joey strode in, closed the door behind him with some fancy foot rotation, grabbed a straight-backed chair, twirled it round, pulled it to him and planted himself in it, facing into the chairback, all without splitting his jeans.

'Hey, Anna, sorry about your . . . you know . . . it's rough.'

He gave my scar a long, brazen stare then sat—there's no other word for it—brooding. Joey is always like that. His habitual humour is one of dissatisfaction with the world. Lots of people, after meeting him for the first time, say, with sudden venom, 'What the fuck was up with that Joey bloke?'

He can be actively and gratuitously obnoxious. Like, if someone gets a radical new haircut, Joey is most likely to say, 'Sue. You'd get millions.'

Other times he says nothing at all. Just sits in a group of people watching everyone with narrowed eyes, his mouth set in a grim line. As a result of this, a lot of women find him attractive. I always know that they've crossed the line from thinking he's a grumpy fucker to fancying him, when they say, 'I've never noticed it before, but Joey looks a bit like Jon Bon Jovi, doesn't he?'

Rachel says he 'has anger issues'. Other people, who don't know about things like anger issues, say, 'That Joey chap would want to learn some manners.'

A few minutes later saw the arrival of Gaz and Shake, the air-guitar champ. They did their best not to stare at my scar. Gaz, a beer-bellied, balding sweetie—not the brightest, but never mind—pulled me to his squashy tummy in a tight hug. 'It's a bad scene, Anna, man.'

'Yeah,' Shake said, shaking back the shaggy head of hair of which he is justifiably proud, with the action that gave him his name. 'It sucks.' Then he too embraced me while not actually looking at me.

I stood and endured it. It had to be done. Now that I was back, sooner or later I would meet everyone I knew and the first encounter would always be like this.

Rachel emerged from the bathroom, in a steamy cloud of lavender. As the lads got stuck into their Scrabble and beer, we curled on the couch in a softly lit corner and Rachel gave me a hand massage on my non-gammy hand.

I was just starting to doze off when the buzzer went again. To my surprise it was Jacqui. She burst into the apartment, full of shine and sparkle and chat: she'd had her gold-plated teeth restored to normality, someone had given her a Louis Vuitton something and she was on her way to a private view.

'Hi.' She waved at the Real Men at the table. 'I can't stay long. But as the private view is only two blocks down I thought I'd drop in and say hi.'

'How honoured are we?' Joey drawled. He was doing something with a matchstick in his teeth.

Jacqui rolled her eyes. 'Joey, you brighten every room you leave.' She came over to me and Rachel. 'Why is he always so horrible?'

'He doesn't like himself very much,' Rachel said. 'And he turns that dislike outwards.'

'I don't get it. Why can't he just be normal? Well, I'm sorry I came. Have a good night,' she called over to the table. 'Everyone except Joey.'

She left and the Scrabble kicked off again, but about half an hour later I was seized by a strange panic: suddenly, I couldn't be with these people any longer.

'I think I'll be off now,' I said, trying to keep the urgency from my voice.

Luke and Rachel watched me anxiously. 'I'll come down and put you in a cab,' Rachel said.

'No, you're not dressed, I'll do it,' Luke said.

'No, please, I'm fine.' I looked longingly at the door. If I didn't leave soon, I'd burst.

'If you're sure.'

'I'm sure.'

'What are you doing tomorrow?' Rachel asked.

'Going shopping with Jacqui.' I raced through the words.

'Want to go to a movie in the evening?'

'Fine, yes, fine,' I said, my breath constricted. 'See you tomorrow, then.'

And then the door was being opened and I was free. My pulse rate slowed down, my breathing became easier. I stood on the sidewalk and felt the panic abate. Then it built back up again as I thought: God, how bad is it that I can't even be with my own sister? And now I have to go back to my empty apartment.

I started walking. I hobbled a wandering, circuitous route, but eventually I reached my building, because there was no place else for me to go. At the bottom of the steps, as I was wasting a few more seconds hunting in my bag for my keys, someone yelled, 'Babycakes. Wait up.'

It was Ornesto, our upstairs neighbour, coming down the street in a bright-red pimpy suit. *Shite.*

He caught me up and said accusingly, 'I've been calling you. I have left you, like, eight trillion messages.'

'I know, Ornesto, I'm sorry, I'm just a little weird—'

'Whooh! Would you look at that face! Whoo-ee, Babycakes, that is *bad.*' He practically ran his nose along my scar, then pulled me to him in a painful embrace. Luckily Ornesto is very self-obsessed and it didn't tale long for his attention to snap back to him. 'I'm home for a New York minute, then I'm going right back out to look for'—he paused to yell—'HOT MEN! Come and talk to me while I get changed into my party frock.'

'OK.'

In Ornesto's Thai-themed apartment, right beside a gold Buddha there was a photo stuck to the wall with a kitchen knife. It was of a man's face and the knife went right through his open laughing mouth. Ornesto noticed me looking. 'Omygod, you totally missed it all. His name is Bradley. You would not believe what that man did to me.'

Ornesto has bad luck with men. They are always cheating on him.

'He beat me up.'

He displayed his black eye proudly. All I could see was slight purplish bruising beside his eyebrow. I sucked in my breath sympathetically. 'That's terrible.'

'But the good news is that I've started taking singing lessons!' Ornesto—unexpectedly, perhaps—is a veterinary nurse. 'My voice coach says I have a real gift. Says he never saw anyone get the breathing right so fast!'

'Lovely,' I said vaguely.

I looked around; I could smell something . . . Then I noticed it on his table. A big bunch of flowers. Lilies.

'You have lilies?' I said.

'Yeah, trying to be good to myself, you know?'

'When did you get them?'

He thought about it. 'Right about yesterday. Something wrong?'

'No.' But I was wondering if it had been Ornesto's lilies I had smelt last night. The smell could have come through the air vent into my kitchen. Was that what had happened? Had it been nothing at all to do with Aidan?

'**A**re we really getting married?' I asked Aidan.

'Sure.'

'Then let's do it soon,' I said. 'Three months' time. Start of April?'

'Where will we do it?' Aidan asked. 'New York? Dublin? Boston?'

'None of the above,' I said. 'Let's go to County Clare. West coast of Ireland,' I explained. 'We went there for our holidays every summer. My dad's from there. It's lovely.'

'OK. Is there a hotel? Give them a call.'

So I rang the local hotel in Knockavoy and my stomach flipped alarmingly when they said they could fit us in. I hung up the phone and backed away.

'Christ,' I said to Aidan. 'I've just booked our wedding.'

Then everything happened very fast. I decided to leave the menu to Mum. 'Work away, Mum,' I said magnanimously. 'The catering is your area.' But minefields lay in the most innocent-looking of landscapes—I made the mistake of suggesting that we should have a vegetarian option and that set her off: she didn't believe in vegetarianism.

'Grand, grand, whatever,' I said. 'They can eat the bread rolls.'

I was far, far more worried about the bridesmaid issue. I really felt I couldn't cope with all four of my sisters arguing over colour and style. After a big summit it was decreed that I would have *no* bridesmaids but that Claire's three children would be flower girls. Even Luka, her son.

Then there was the dress. I had a vision in my head of what I wanted—a bias-cut satin sheath—but couldn't find it anywhere. In the end it was designed and made by a contact of Dana's, a woman who ordinarily made curtains.

And, of course, there was the invitation list.

'OK with you if I invite Janie?' Aidan asked.

It was a tricky one. Naturally, I didn't want her there if her heart was broken but it would be nice if we could meet and be civilised.

'Sure. You've got to invite her.'

So he did, but we got a nice letter back, thanking us for the invitation but saying that, as the wedding was in Ireland, she wouldn't be able to attend.

I didn't know whether I felt relieved or not. Anyway, she wasn't coming and that was that.

But it wasn't.

Because when I went on to our wedding list website, I saw that someone called Janie Sorensen had bought us a present. For a minute I thought, Who on earth is Janie Sorensen? Then I thought, It's *Janie*! Aidan's Janie. What had she bought us? I clicked like mad to get the details and saw that Janie had bought us a set of kitchen knives. Really sharp, pointy ones. Fair enough, we'd put them on our list, but why couldn't she have chosen a couple of fluffy cushions?

Later I tentatively put it to Aidan and he laughed and said, 'That's typical of her sense of humour. But nothing to be scared of.'

There was more to come. Less than a couple of weeks later, on a Friday night, I was round at Aidan's place, and he was opening his mail, when something in one of the envelopes shocked him. I felt it across the room.

'What?' I asked, staring at the letter in his hand.

He paused, looked up and said, 'Janie's getting married.'

'What?'

'Janie's getting married. Two months after us.'

I was carefully watching his reaction. He was smiling as he said, 'This is great. Just great.'

'Who's she marrying?'

'Someone called Howard Wicks. Never heard of the guy.'

'Are we invited?'

'No. They're doing it in Fiji. Just close family. She always said that if she got married she'd do it in Fiji.' He read through the letter again and said, 'I'm really happy for her.'

'Do they have a present list?' I asked.

'I don't know,' he said, 'but if they do we could send her a nice big machete.'

Despite delegating as much as we could, organising the wedding meant three horribly stressful months. But it was all worth it. On a bright, blustery blue spring day, in a church on a hill, Aidan and I got married. The daffodils were out, throngs of shocking yellow, bobbing in the brisk breeze. The foamy sea sparkled in the distance.

In the photos taken outside the church, men in shiny shoes and women in pastel frocks are smiling. We all look beautiful and very happy.

All week, I put in twelve or thirteen hours a day at work, and some-how enough time passed so that it got to be Friday evening. But no sooner had I let myself in and put down my keys, than I saw, like a big guilt-making, accusing thing, the flashing light on my answering machine. I kept my feet planted where I stood and leaned the top half of my body over to look: three messages. I looked at Dogly's kindly face and said, 'I bet they're all from Leon.'

I'd have to ring him back soon; it was only a matter of time before he arrived in person at the apartment—or set Dana on me. But I just couldn't bear to, not yet anyway.

Instead, I turned on the computer—and my heart lifted when I saw that there was a new email! I held my breath and waited, frozen with hope. But it was from Mum.

To: Magiciansgirl1@yahoo.com
From: Thewalshes1@eircom.net
Subject: Woman and dog

I am still keeping you 'in the loop' as they say. This morning I 'lay in wait' for the old woman and her dog. She normally comes at ten past nine, so I was ready for her. As soon as she appeared, I pretended to be putting out the bins which I though was a good 'ruse', even though bin day is Monday and it is your father's job anyway.

'Nice morning for it,' I said, meaning, 'Nice morning for making your dog do its wees at an innocent stranger's gate.' Right away, your woman pulls at the lead and says, 'Hurry up, Zoë.' Now we have a clue. What a name for a dog! Then something terrible happened: the woman gave me a 'look'. Our eyes met and, as you know, Anna, I am not a fanciful woman, but I knew I was in the presence of evil.

Your loving mother,
Mum

PS In a couple of weeks' time myself and your father are going away to 'The Algarve' for a fortnight. It will be nice. While we're gone, Helen will be staying with 'Maggie' and 'Garv', as you all insist on calling them. This means it will be hard to keep 'tabs' on the old woman, but seeing as she gave me such a dirty look, this is probably no harm.

Across the room, the flashing light of the answering machine continued to accuse me. I wished I could delete the bloody messages without having listened to them, but the machine wouldn't let me, so I hit PLAY, then legged it to the bathroom, hearing as I went, 'Anna, it's Leon. I know this is hard for you, but I need to see you . . .'

To drown out his voice I ran the water with such Niagaraesque force that I drenched the front of my dress. Eventually I guessed that he'd finished what he had to say and I tiptoed from the bathroom and hit Delete.

'All messages deleted,' the machine said.

'Thank you,' I replied.

9

IT FINALLY HAPPENED. Aidan finally showed up.

Two and a half weeks after I'd come back from Ireland, I was at work, sitting at my desk, labouring at a quarterly spreadsheet, when he just walked in. The joy at seeing him was like the warmth of the midday sun—I was *thrilled*.

'About time,' I exclaimed.

He sat on a corner of the desk and his smile nearly split his face in two. He looked delighted and shy simultaneously. 'Happy to see me?' he asked.

'Jesus Christ, Aidan, I'm *so* happy! I can't believe this. I was afraid I'd never see you again.' He was wearing the same clothes he'd been wearing the first day we'd met. 'But how did you manage it?'

'What do you mean? I just walked in here.'

'But Aidan'—because I'd just remembered—'you're dead.'

I woke with a jump. I was on the couch. Lights from the street lit the room with a purplish glow and there was some racket outside: people shouting and the boomy bass-line of a flashy limo, which pulsed below me until the traffic lights changed and it moved on.

I closed my eyes and went straight back into the same dream.

Aidan wasn't smiling any longer, he was upset and confused and I asked him, 'No one told you you were dead?'

'No.'

'That's what I've been afraid of. And where have you been?'

'Hanging around. I saw you in Ireland and everything.'

'You did? Why didn't you say anything?'

'You were with your family, I didn't want to butt in.'

'But you're family now. You're my family.'

The next time I woke it was 5 a.m. The morning beyond the blinds was already citrus-bright but the streets were silent. I needed to talk to Rachel. She was the only one who could help me.

'Sorry to wake you.'

'Are you OK?' She tried hard to stifle a yawn.

'Can you meet me?'

''Course. How about Jenni's?' It was some twenty-four-hour coffee place. 'See you there in thirty minutes.'

I pulled on some clothes and ran out of the door; I couldn't stay in the apartment a moment longer. Once outside I hailed a taxi. Along the way I saw Aidan walking along 14th Street, only this time I knew it wasn't him.

I arrived at Jenni's far too early, and ordered a latte, tried to eavesdrop on the intense conversation that was taking place between a foursome of gaunt, good-looking men dressed in black.

Then Rachel arrived. 'It's a while since I've been here,' she commented. She sat down and ordered a green tea. 'Anna, are you OK? Has something happened?'

'I dreamt about Aidan last night.'

'That's normal, one of the things that's meant to happen. Like seeing him everywhere. So what did you dream?'

'I dreamt that he was dead.'

Pause. 'That's because he is, Anna.'

'I know that. But I don't want him to be dead.'

Rachel's eyes filled with tears. 'Of course you don't! He was your husband, the man—'

'Rachel, please don't say "was". I hate all this past-tense stuff. And it's not about me, it's him I'm worried about. I'm so afraid he'll freak out when he discovers what's happened.' Suddenly I couldn't bear it. 'Rachel, Aidan's going to hate being dead. We had so many plans. We weren't going to die until we were eighty. And he worried about me, he wanted to take care of me. How's he going to handle having died?'

'Er . . . um, let's see.' This had never happened before: Rachel looked blank. Then I realised she was in shock. 'Anna, this is too big for me. You need someone who specialises in this. A grief counsellor.'

'Rachel, I just want to talk to him. That's all I want. I can't bear to think of him trapped someplace awful and not being able to contact me. I mean, where is he? Where did he go?'

Her eyes got bigger and bigger as the dismay on her face worsened. 'Anna, I really think—'

The men in black were leaving and as they passed our table one of them clocked Rachel and did a double take.

He had a lean face, tormented brown eyes and long dark hair. He wouldn't have looked out of place in the Red Hot Chili Peppers.

'Hey!' he said. 'I've met you? The meetings in St Mark's Place? It's Rachel, right? I'm Angelo. So how're you doing? Still conflicted?'

'No,' Rachel said snippily, giving off strong This Is So Inappropriate vibes.

'So? You gonna marry the guy?'

'Yes.' More snippiness. But she couldn't resist sticking out her hand for him to admire her engagement ring.

'Wow. Getting married. Well, congratulations.'

Then he looked at me. A look of deep compassion. 'Oh, little girl,' he said. 'It's bad, hey?'

'Were you listening to our conversation?' Rachel snapped.

'No. But it's sorta obvious.' To me he said, 'Just take it a day at a time.'

'She's not an addict. She's my sister.'

'No reason for her not to take it one day at a time.'

I went to work, thinking: Aidan is dead, Aidan has died. I hadn't actually realised it until now. I mean, I knew he'd died but I'd never believed it was permanent.

I moved through the corridors like a ghost and when Franklin called, 'Morning, Anna, how're you doing?' I felt like answering, 'Good, except my husband died and we were married less than a year. Yes, I know you know all about it, but I've just realised.'

But there was no point saying anything. It was old news for everyone else; they'd long moved on.

We'd been on our way out for dinner, just him and me, and what was unendurable was that this was something we rarely did. We were more likely to snuggle on the couch and ring for take-outs.

If we'd stayed at home that night, he'd still be alive. In fact, we almost didn't go. He'd booked a table at Tamarind but I'd asked him to cancel it because we'd eaten out just two nights earlier for Valentine's Day. But it seemed to mean so much to him to go that I gave in.

So I was waiting on the street for him to pick me up when, alerted by honks, I saw a yellow cab lurching across three lanes of traffic and heading in my direction. Sure enough, there was Aidan, making a scared face and flashing seven fingers at me.

'Seven?' I mouthed. 'Good work.' Seven out of ten. Nutter alert. Our personal scoring system for mental cab-drivers.

With a shudder, the cab stopped beside me, I hopped in and before my door was even closed we screeched back into the heavy traffic. I was flung against Aidan and he managed to kiss me before I was thrown back in the opposite direction.

He shook his head in admiration and said in an undertone, 'It's good, this one, Anna, it's good stuff. We haven't had one of these in a while.'

Without warning, we zigged across and were thrown, with force, against the right-hand door. I clutched Aidan. He was laughing and that made me happy. He'd been a bit low for a day or two: a few nights earlier he'd had a call—work—that had wrecked his buzz.

Funnily enough, the accident wasn't the fault of our seven-out-of-ten driver. We were totally unaware of the events playing out on the junction of the cross-street: a woman doing an unexpected dash across the road, an Armenian cab-driver swerving to avoid hitting her, and his front wheel connecting with a pool of oil. With brutal impact, another cab had ploughed into the side of ours and its front bumper was trying to get into our back seat—the sort of thing that happens in a nightmare. My head was full of grinding and breaking, then we were spinning backwards in the road, like we were on an evil merry-go-round.

The shock was—still is—indescribable, and the impact broke Aidan's pelvis, six of his ribs and mortally injured his liver, kidneys, pancreas and spleen. I saw it all in slow motion: the shattered glass filling the air like silver rain, the tearing metal, the short gush of blood from Aidan's mouth and the look of surprise in his eyes. I didn't know he was dying, I didn't know that in twenty minutes' time he'd be dead, I just thought we should be angry that some asshole had side-rammed us.

Out in the street people were screaming, someone yelled, 'Jesus, Jesus *Christ*!' Whirling past me were people's legs and feet. I noticed a pair of red spindly-heeled boots. Red boots are such a statement, I thought hazily. I still remember them so clearly I could pick them out in an identification line-up.

I was really lucky, everyone said later. 'Lucky' because Aidan took all the impact. By the time the other driver had had his momentum broken by Aidan's body, he was nearly all out of steam, with barely enough force left to break my right arm and dislocate my knee. Obviously, there was collateral damage—the metal in our ceiling buckled and gouged a deep furrow in my face and the tearing metal in the door ripped off two of my nails—but I didn't die.

Our driver hadn't a scratch. When the never-ending backwards-spinning stopped, he got out of the cab and looked in at us through the hole where his window used to be, then backed away and bent over. From the sounds he was making, I realised he was throwing up.

'Ambulance is coming, buddy,' a man's voice said and I didn't know if I had really heard it or if it was just in my head. For a short time, things were oddly peaceful.

Aidan and I looked at each other in a can-you-believe-this? way and he said, 'Baby, are you OK?'

'Yes, are you?'

'Yeah.' But his voice was weird, kind of gurgly.

On the front of his shirt and tie was a sticky, dark red bloodstain and I was distressed because it was such a nice tie, one of his favourites. 'You're not to worry about the tie,' I said. 'We'll get you another one.'

'Does anything hurt?' he asked.

'No.' At the time, I felt nothing. Good old shock, the great protector, gets us through the unbearable. 'How about you?'

'A little.' That was when I knew it was a lot.

From far away, I heard sirens; they got nearer and louder, then they were right up beside us and, abruptly, mid-shriek, they stopped.

Aidan was taken out of the mangled car, then we were in the ambulance and things seemed to speed up. We were in the hospital and on separate gurneys and running through corridors.

'What is your relationship to this patient?' I was asked. 'His wife? His friend?'

'Both,' Aidan answered, in the gurgly voice.

When they rushed him off to theatre, I still didn't know he was dying. 'Make him be OK,' I told the surgeon, a short, tanned man.

'I'm sorry,' he said. 'He's probably not going to make it.'

My mouth fell open. Excuse me? Half an hour earlier we'd been on our way to have dinner. And now this suntanned man was telling me that he was 'probably not going to make it'.

And he didn't. He died very quickly, barely ten minutes in.

By then the pain had started in my hand and arm and face and knee. I was in such a fog of agony that I could barely remember my name, so trying to understand that Aidan had just died was like trying to imagine a totally new colour.

I spent two days in the hospital and all I can remember is a non-stop stream of people. Aidan's parents and Kevin flew in from Boston. Mum, Dad, Helen and Maggie came from Ireland. Dana and Leon—who cried so much he got given drugs too—Jacqui, Rachel, Luke, Ornesto, Teenie, Franklin, Marty, people from Aidan's work and two policemen, who took a statement from me.

Then we were on a plane to Boston, then we were at the funeral, which was like our wedding, but a nightmare version of it. Being pushed up the aisle in a wheelchair, seeing faces I hadn't seen for ages, felt like a dream where a disparate collection of people are inexplicably gathered together.

Then I was on a flight, then I was home in Ireland sleeping in the living room, then I was back in New York, and I was only just facing what had really happened.

PART TWO

1

Extract from *Never Coming Back* by Dorothea K. Lincoln

About a week after my husband died, I was in my sun room . . . when, in through the open window, flew a butterfly. It was incorrigibly beautiful, intricately patterned in red, blue and white. As I watched in wonder, it flitted around the room, alighting on the stereo, a pot plant . . . and my husband's old chair.

As the World Turns was on the TV, but the butterfly hovered over the remote. It seemed to be telling me something—could it be that it wanted the channel changed? 'Well, OK, buddy,' I said. 'I can try.'

I flicked through several channels and when I got to Fox Sports, the beautiful creature landed on my hand, as if gently telling me to stop. Then it sat on my shoulder and watched half an hour of the US Open Golf; the room was filled with a deep, deep peace. When Ernie Els went to three under par, the butterfly stirred, flitted to the window, hovered on the sill for a moment, as if saying goodbye, and finally flew away. There was no doubt in my mind that this had been a visit from my late husband. He'd been telling me that he was still with me, that he always would be . . .

I put down the book, sat up, looked around my living room and thought, Where's my butterfly?

It was about four or five weeks since my early-morning conversation at Jenni's with Rachel and not much had changed. I had a nice little daily routine going: I'd wake at the crack of dawn, ring Aidan on his cellphone, go to work for at least ten hours, come home, ring Aidan again, construct elaborate fantasies in which he hadn't died, cry for a few hours, then doze off on the couch, wake up and do it all again. I got through each day and the only thing that kept me going was the hope that tomorrow would be easier. But it wasn't. I had hoped that by returning to New York and being immersed in normal stuff, like work and friends, the nightmare would disperse. But it hadn't.

This morning, like every morning, I'd woken horribly early. There was always a split second when I wondered what the terribleness was. Then I'd remember.

I lay down again, a dull, persistent ache in my bones, what I imagined rheumatism or arthritis would feel like. When the pains had first started, I'd thought that maybe I was suffering side-effects of the accident. But my doctor said that what I was feeling was 'the physical pain of grief'. That this was 'normal'. Which came as a shock. I'd known to expect emotional pain but the physical pain was a new one on me.

I popped a couple of painkillers, switched on the telly, but when I couldn't find anything to catch my interest, I flicked through *Never Coming Back*. Great title, by the way, I thought. Cheery. Bound to perk up the spirits of the recently bereaved.

It was one of a deluge of books—arriving in the post from Claire in London, being left outside my door by Ornesto, handed over in person by Rachel, Teenie, Marty, Nell, even Nell's strange friend—and even though I could barely concentrate long enough to read a paragraph, I'd noticed the butterfly motif was a common one. But no butterflies for me.

Funnily enough, I wasn't that keen on butterflies. It was a hard thing to admit because everyone loves butterflies and not liking them is akin to saying you don't like Michael Palin or dolphins or strawberries. But to me, butterflies were slightly sneaky; all they were, were moths in embroidered jackets. Nevertheless, since I'd started reading these books, I'd been looking everywhere for butterflies or doves or strange cats that hadn't been around before. I was desperate for any sign that Aidan was still with me. I mean, he had to be *somewhere*. His personality or spirit or whatever you want to call it—it couldn't just be snuffed out. All the things that were unique to him, that made him a one-off human being—they couldn't just be *gone*. He was so full of—yes, life, that he must be somewhere. It was just a question of finding him.

I still saw him in the street but now I accepted that it wasn't him. I still emailed him and rang his cellphone but I understood I wouldn't hear back from him. But some days I'd forget he was dead. I mean, literally just for a moment or two. And then I'd be overwhelmed with horror that he'd been removed from this earth, from this being-alive business and gone to a place where I could never track him down.

Until now, I'd always thought that the worst thing that could happen to you was that someone you loved abruptly disappeared. But this was worse. If he'd been imprisoned or kidnapped or even done a runner, I'd have hope that he might eventually come back.

And my *guilt* was unendurable. His story had been cut off so brutally and prematurely, while I was still here, still alive and well and working and with everything to play for. His body had taken the full impact of the crash so I felt that he had died in order for me to live, and it was the most appalling feeling. Like I'd cheated him out of the rest of his life.

At the funeral, the priest had said a lot of guff about how Aidan had gone to 'a better place'. When my grandparents died I'd been too young or hadn't cared enough to wonder if they'd really gone to heaven. Now I was being forced to think about an afterlife, and the absence of any certainty was terrifying.

In my teenage years, I'd yearned for a connection with some sort of spiritual being. Not with the Catholic god I'd been brought up with, but with the vague, all-purpose god of dreamcatchers and chakras and fringy skirts. I taught myself to read tarot cards and I wasn't bad at it. I liked to believe that that was because I was quite psychic but, looking back, it was just because I'd learned what the symbols meant.

I'd knocked off the tarot cards some years back, but I'd never stopped believing in a vague 'something'. But now that it mattered, I found I didn't know what I believed. I didn't believe Aidan was in heaven. I didn't believe in heaven at all. I didn't even believe in God. I didn't not believe in God either. There was nothing to cling on to.

I looked at my watch. I had to get up and get ready for work. I forced myself to have a shower, then picked up the phone to ring Aidan's mobile . . . and that's when it happened. Instead of hearing his message, there was a funny beeping noise. Had I called the wrong number? Already, I had a presentiment of doom. Holding my breath, praying for everything to be OK, I waited for his voice but all I got was the funny beeping noise again.

His cellphone had been cut off.

Because I hadn't paid the bill. With the exception of the rent on the apartment, I hadn't paid any bills.

I felt so dizzy that I thought I might faint. 'Now how am I meant to get in touch with you?' I asked the room.

The urge to talk to him was suddenly so huge that my body couldn't contain it. In the space of a second I was drenched in sweat and I had to run to the bathroom to vomit. Ten, maybe fifteen minutes passed, with me resting my head against the porcelain, too light-headed to get up.

I needed to talk to him. I would have given everything I possessed, I would have been prepared to die myself, just to talk to him.

I had a second shower, got dressed—in a swirly patterned Pucci dress and jacket from Goodwill—and was so late for work that I called and told Lauryn I would go straight to my ten o'clock appointment. I was sourcing promo items for You Glow Girl! (A highlighter. Nothing more to be said about it.) and I was thinking of buying the beauty editors lamps (thereby picking up on the 'glow' theme).

My ten o'clock was with a wholesaler in West 41st Street who imported unusual lamps, ones that looked like halos—you clip them onto your mirror and your reflection looks like an angel.

The cab dropped me on the wrong side of the street, and as I was waiting to cross over I saw a man I knew and automatically nodded hello. Then I realised that I couldn't remember where I knew him from and was afraid I'd Recognised a Famous Person. Rachel had once done that: stopped Susan Sarandon in the street and interrogated her as to where she'd seen her before.

But the mystery man was stopping to talk to me.

'Hey, little girl,' he said. 'How're you doing?'

'Good.' I nodded desperately.

'You're Rachel's sister? I'm Angelo. We met one morning in Jenni's.'

How could I have forgotten him? He was so unusual-looking, with his gaunt, drawn face, dark, deep-set eyes, long hair and Red Hot Chili Pepper-style magnetism.

'Things any better?' he asked.

'No. I feel very bad. Especially today.'

'You wanna go for coffee?'

'I can't. I have a meeting.'

'Take my number. Call me if you ever want to talk.'

'Thank you, but I'm not an addict.'

'That's OK. I won't hold it against you.'

He scribbled something on a torn piece of paper. Limply, I accepted it and said, 'My name is Anna.'

'Anna,' he repeated. 'You take care. Great clothes, by the way.'

'Bye,' I said and let the scrap of paper fall into the bottom of my bag.

I went to my meeting with Mr Fancy Lights but I was off form and left without having agreed anything.

Back out on the street, I was strolling along, scanning the traffic for a cab, when a guy handed me a leaflet. Normally, I stick them straight in the first bin I see because, in this neck of the woods, they're always fliers for 'designer' sales to catch the tourists. But something made me look at this one: *Discover your future. Receive answers from the other side. From a medium with the true gift of the second sight. Call Morna.*

At the bottom was a phone number and suddenly I was seized with an excitement close to frenzy. I moved out of the flow of bodies into a doorway, pulled my cellphone out of my bag and, with fingers that trembled with hope, rang the number. A woman answered.

'Is that Morna?' I asked.

'Yes.'

'I'd like to have a reading.'

'Can you come now? I have a free appointment.'

'Sure! Yes! Absolutely!' Who cared about work!

Morna directed me to an apartment two streets away. Nearly in tears from excitement, hope, desperation, I found it and rang her bell.

A voice called through the door, 'Who is it?'

'My name is Anna. I rang a few minutes ago.'

There came the rattle of chains and locks being undone and finally the door was opened. In my state of overblown hope, I'd pictured Morna wearing flowy, beaded layers, with heavy kohl around wise old eyes, living in a dimly lit apartment full of red velvet throws and fringy lamps. But this was an ordinary woman, probably in her mid-thirties, in a dark blue track suit. Her hair could have done with a wash and I couldn't see how wise and old her eyes looked because she avoided eye contact. Her apartment was also a disappointment: children's toys were scattered on the floor and there was a very strong smell of toast.

Morna directed me to a stool at the breakfast bar and said, 'Fifty dollars for fifteen minutes.'

It was a lot but I was so hyped up that I just said, 'OK.'

My breath was coming in short, tight gasps and I thought Morna would notice my frantic state and treat me accordingly. But she just clambered on to a stool on the opposite side of the breakfast bar and handed me a pack of tarot cards. 'Cut them.'

I paused. 'Instead of a card reading, can you try to contact . . . someone who has died.'

'That's extra.'

'How much?'

She studied me. 'Fifty?'

I hesitated. It wasn't the money, it was the sudden, unpleasant suspicion that I was being had. That this woman wasn't really a medium.

'Forty,' she said, confirming my suspicion.

'It's not the money,' I said, on the verge of tears. Hope had spilt over into disappointment. 'If you're not a medium, please tell me.'

'Sure, I'm a medium.'

'You get in contact with people who have died?' I stressed.

'Yeah. You want to go ahead?'

What was to be lost? I nodded.

'OK, let's see what we've got.' She pressed her fingers to her temples. 'You're Irish, right?'

'Right.'

'I have someone here.'

My excitement spiked.

'Your grandma.'

My excitement plummeted.

'She says her name is . . . Mary?'

I shook my head. No granny called Mary.

'Bridget?'

Another shake of the head.

'Bridie? Maggie? Ann? Maeve? Kathleen? Sinead?'

'Don't worry about the name,' I said. 'What else are you getting?'

'OK, they don't give me the correct name, but she's definitely your grandma. I can see her clearly. She's a little bitty thing, dancing around, in boots and a flowery apron over a dirndl skirt. She's got grey hair in a bun at the back of her neck and small round glasses.'

'I don't think that's my granny,' I said. 'I think that's the granny from the *Beverly Hillbillies*.' I didn't mean to be snide; I just had too much desperation and hope swilling around in me and all this time-wasting was doing me in.

Morna looked at me, alert to my sarcasm. 'So who do you want to talk to?'

I took a big, shuddery breath, which became a sob. 'My husband. My husband died.' The tears were suddenly sluicing down my face. 'I want to talk to him.'

Morna pressed her fingers to her temples again. 'I'm sorry,' she said. 'I'm getting nothing. But there's a reason for that. Someone has put something bad on you, this is why these bad things are happening to you.'

What? 'You mean like a curse?'

'A curse is a strong word—but yeah, I guess like a curse. But don't worry, baby'—for the first time, she smiled—'I can take it away.'

'You can? Thank you. Oh my God, thank you.' Briefly, I thought I might faint with gratitude. 'Can you take it away now?'

'Yeah, we can do it now. But you've got to understand that removing a curse as big as the one on you will cost money.'

'Oh? How much?'

'A thousand dollars.'

A thousand dollars? That jolted me back to reality.

'You've got to do this, Anna. Your life will only get worse if you don't deal with this.'

'My life will definitely get worse if I throw away a thousand dollars.'

'OK, five hundred,' Morna said. 'Three? OK, two hundred dollars and I can remove this curse.'

'How come you can do it for two hundred dollars now and it was a thousand dollars a minute ago?'

'Because, baby, I'm afraid for you. You need this removed, like *now*, or something really terrible will happen to you.'

For a second she got me again. What could happen? The worst thing I could ever think of had already happened. But what if there *was* a curse on me? If it was why Aidan had died . . . Suspended between fear and scepticism, my thoughts were seesawing back and forth when we were interrupted by the sounds of children banging on a door and calling, 'Mom, can we come out yet?'

I snapped back to sanity and couldn't leave that place quick enough. My anger was so immense that on the way down I kicked the elevator wall. I was raging with Morna and raging with myself for being so stupid. Back on the street, I powered all the way to Central Park, fuelled by hot, sour fury. By the time I reached the office, I'd calmed down. I understood what had happened: I'd had back luck. I'd met a charlatan, someone who preyed on vulnerable people.

Somewhere out there is a real psychic who'll put me in touch with you. All I have to do is find them.

2

To: Magiciansgirl1@yahoo.com
From: Thewalshes1@eircom.net
Subject: Number twos!

Dear Anna,
I hope you are keeping well. Listen, it's gone to hell here altogether, with the old woman and her dog. Since we came back from the Algarve there hadn't been sight nor sound of her and would you blame us for thinking we had 'shaken' her. But she was back with a vengeance this morning. She came early and made her dog do a 'number two'. Your father is not a man who is easily stirred to action but this has stirred him. He says we are going to get to the bottom of this. This will involve Helen and her 'skills'.
    Your loving mother,
    Mum

PS We had the post-holiday blues anyway, especially since your father's sunburn became infected, and because of this dog business we are now very 'low'.
PPS If you see Rachel will you tell her that Baked Alaska is a beautiful dessert. The waiters light it with sparklers and turn off the lights and when they did it on our last night in Portugal, tears came to my eyes.

I assumed the Baked Alaska was wedding-related. Rachel wasn't getting married until next March and already she and Mum were sniping at each other. And no way was I getting involved; wedding-menu crossfire could be very messy.

However, I almost brought it up that evening, because Rachel appeared unexpectedly at my apartment.

'Hello,' I said cautiously. I should have expected this: I'd given her the slip all weekend.

'Anna, I'm worried about you, you've got to stop working so hard.'

This was a regular gripe of Rachel's. She insisted I was using work as an excuse not to see her, or anyone. And she was right. What could I say? I could hardly tell her the truth, which was that I'd spent most of Saturday and Sunday on the Internet, looking up psychics and asking Aidan for some sort of sign to indicate which one I should use.

'It was an emergency.'

'You work with cosmetics, how can it be an emergency? Anyway! I came to talk to you in person,' she said, 'because I don't seem to be getting through to you on the phone. And I mean getting through in an emotional sense, by the way, not getting through in a telephonic sense.'

Like I'd think anything else. 'I know, I know. So tell me, Rachel, how are the wedding plans?' If she badgered me too much, I'd say, 'Two words, Rachel. Baked Alaska.'

'Christ,' she said. 'Wedding plans. Don't ask.' Resentfully, she exclaimed, 'Luke and I just wanted a small wedding. With people we liked. With people we *knew*. Mum wants to invite half of Ireland.'

'Maybe they won't come. Maybe it'll be too far.'

'Why do you think we're getting married in New York?' She laughed darkly. 'Anyway, don't think you'll distract me. I'm here because I'm concerned about you. Have you any Diet Coke?'

'I don't know. Look in the fridge.'

'Thank you.' She stopped moving and cocked her ear to listen. 'What's that racket?'

In a nearby apartment someone bellowed, 'Goooooo-aaaaaald-fin*gah*!' at the top of their voice.

'It's Ornesto. He's practising.'

'Practising what? Scaring the living bejaysus out of people?'

'Singing. He's taking lessons. His teacher says he's got a gift.'

'Heeeza maaaan, maaaan wida Midas*torch*!'

'Does he do this a lot?'

'Most nights.'

'Doesn't it keep you awake?' Rachel is really rather neurotic about sleep. There was no point telling her I hardly slept anyway.

'Any luck with the Diet Coke?'

'No. there's almost nothing in here. Anna, you need to see a therapist. I know a lovely grief counsellor. She won't tell me anything that you say, I promise.'

'I'll go,' I said.

'You will? Great!'

'I'll go when I'm a bit better.'

'Oh, for God's sake. This is exactly what I'm talking about! I see you putting in all those hours at work, trying to forget—'

'No, I'm not trying to forget!' That was an awful thought. 'I'm trying'—how could I put it?—'I'm trying to get far enough down the line so that I can remember.' I stopped, then continued, 'So that I can remember without the pain killing me.'

And the days *were* stacking up. And weeks. And months. It was now almost the middle of June and he'd died in February, but I still felt like I'd just woken from a horrible dream, that I was suspended in that stunned, paralysed state between sleep and reality where I was grasping for, but couldn't get a handle on, normality.

'Golden words he will pour in your *ea-ah*!'

'Oh God, he's off again. I don't know how you cope, I really don't.'

I shrugged. I quite liked it. It was a bit of company without me having to actually see him. Ornesto kept knocking on my door but I never answered, and when we met in the hallway I told him I was taking a lot of sleeping tablets, which was why I didn't hear him. It was better to lie: he was so easily wounded.

'But his *lies* can't *dis-guise* what you *fea-ah*! It's the kissssss of *death*! From Missss-tah . . . Gold-*fingah*!'

'Look, would you like me to give you ear-plugs?'

'It's OK, thanks.'

'This heart is COLD. HELOVESONLYGOLD, HELOVESONLY-GOOOLLLLLL DDDDDD!'

'God, I won't stay. Let's get together for dinner some night this week.'

'I'm meeting Leon and Dana on Wednesday night,' I said quickly, seeing her to the door.

'Good girl, very good. I won't be around at the weekend, I'm going on retreat, but let's get together Thursday night. Yes?'

She made me nod, yes.

'Goodbye.'

I went back to the sitting room and lay on the couch, while upstairs Ornesto continued belting out the tunes.

Outside Diego's, Leon and Dana were emerging from one cab while I was paying off another. Perfect timing. That used to happen a lot when I was with Aidan and the four of us were meeting up.

Then Leon saw me and his face lit up. 'Hey, Anna!'

Leon and Aidan had been friends since childhood but with Dana and me in the mix, we'd been a perfect fit. The four of us used to go away on weekends together, had spent a week in the Hamptons last summer and had gone skiing in Utah in January.

We used to see each other for dinner about once a week—Leon is a man who is fond of his food and he gets excited about new restaurants.

For some reason, after I'd come back from Dublin, it had taken me longer to face Leon than anyone else. I was afraid of seeing the extent of his grief because then I would see my own. The problem was that Leon had been as desperate to see me as I was desperate not to see him. I'd kept ducking him, but I'd caved in a few weeks back and agreed to meet.

'We'll get a table at Clinton's Fresh Foods,' he'd declared.

I'd been horrified at the idea of trying to recreate one of our four-some nights.

'Why don't I just call over to your apartment?' I'd said.

He'd managed to badger me into going over to them a few more times to hold his hand while he cried and reminisced. Tonight, however, in an attempt to move on, we were going out. Only to Diego's, though. It was a small neighbourhood place.

Dana fingered through the cosmetics and halfheartedly thanked me. The problem was that Candy Grrrl wasn't expensive enough for her.

'Can we go in?' Leon asked. 'I'm starved.'

'You're always starving.'

Diego himself was at the front desk and delighted to see us. 'Hey, you guys! Been a while.' He made his eyes super-sparkly to pretend he hadn't noticed my scar. 'Table for four?'

'Four,' Leon said, pointing at our usual table. 'We always sit there.'

Diego started picking up menus.

'Three,' Dana and I said together.

'Four,' Leon repeated. There was this dreadful pause, then his face buckled. 'I guess it's only three.'

At the table all Leon could do was cry. 'Sorry, Anna,' he kept saying, looking up through hands wet with tears. 'I'm so sorry.'

In subdued tones Diego asked, 'Can I get you guys a drink?'

'A Pepsi,' Leon sniffed. 'With a twist of lime, not lemon.'

'Glass of Chardonnay,' Dana said.

'Me too.'

When Diego came back with the drinks, he murmured, 'Would you like me to take the menus away?'

Leon's hand shot out to flatten the menus against the table. 'I guess we have to eat.'

'OK.' Diego retreated. 'Just holler when you're ready.'

Without replying, Leon picked up his menu and studied it. We could hear him crying behind it.

He managed to pull himself together long enough to order the venison, but broke down as he told Diego, 'But hold the capers.'

'They give him gas,' Dana said.

Once the food was ordered, Leon was able to relax and *really* get into the crying.

'He was my best friend, the best buddy a guy could have,' he wept.

'She knows,' Dana said. 'She was married to him, remember?'

'I'm sorry, Anna, I know it's bad for you too . . .'

'It's OK.' I don't know how I managed it, but I didn't let myself think that it was Aidan he was crying about. He was just crying and it was nothing to do with me.

'I'd give everything I have to wind the clock back. Just to see him again, you know?' Leon looked at us questioningly, his face wet with tears. 'Just to talk to him?'

That reminded me that I needed a medium. 'Hey,' I said. 'Do either of you know any reputable mediums?'

Momentarily, the tears paused in their journey down Leon's cheeks. 'A medium? To talk to Aidan? Oh, you must miss him so baaad.' And he was off again.

'Anna, mediums are *bullshit!*' Dana exclaimed. 'They take your money and take advantage. You need to see a grief counsellor.'

'I see mine three times a week,' Leon stopped crying long enough to tell me. 'He says I'm doing good.' Then he sobbed for the rest of the meal, pausing only to order bitter-chocolate pie with vanilla ice cream.

There were pages and pages of testimonials on the Internet. *But,* I asked Aidan, *how can I trust any of them? The mediums might have written them themselves.* Dispirited, I checked my emails. Only one, from Helen.

To: Magiciansgirl1@yahoo.com
From: Lucky_Star_Pl@yahoo.ie
Subject: Job!

Anna, I've got a job! Proper job. In crime. Ding-dong! All kicked off yesterday.

In office, nothing to do, feet up on desk, thinking if looked like real
PI, something might happen, instead of 'case of mystery dog poo'.
Next thing—as if by magic—car pulled up outside, parked on double
yellows.

No tinted windows, but back seats had pink ruched curtains, like
Austrian blinds but smaller. Two bozos got out. Big, burly, leather
jackets, bulges in chest pockets, meant to say guns! but bet were just
cheese baguettes.

In the pair of boyos comes and one says: 'Are you Helen Walsh?'

Me: 'Too right I am!'

Haven't time at moment to tell you everything—but it's all going on.
Criminals, guns, extortion, 'muscle', tons of money—and they want
ME on board! Stand by for long, thrilling email.

It all sounded more than just a little far-fetched. I went back to
Googling random stuff like, 'Talking to the dead' and 'Non-swizzy mediums', which was when I hit gold: *The Church of Spiritualist Communication.*

I clicked on the site—it seemed to be an actual, legitimate church
that believed you could channel the dead! They had a few branches in
the New York area. Most were upstate or in the outer boroughs but
there was one in Manhattan on 10th and 45th. According to the website there was a service on Sunday at two o'clock.

I looked at my watch: quarter to three. No, no, no! I'd just missed
this week's. I could have howled. Anyway, I told myself, breathing
deeply and talking myself down, I'd go there next week.

At the idea of really speaking to Aidan, I felt giddy with hope. So
much so that I thought I could face the world. For the first time since
he died, I actually wanted to see people.

I tried Jacqui's cellphone because she was always out, but it went to
voicemail. On the offchance, I tried her apartment and she answered.

'I can't believe you're at home,' I said.

'I'm in bed.' Her voice sounded choked.

'Are you sick?'

'No, I'm crying.'

'Why?'

'I ran into Buzz last night in SoHo House. He was with some girl who
looked like a model. He tried to introduce me to her but he couldn't
remember my name.'

'Of course he could,' I said. 'That's typical Buzz game-playing. He
was just trying to undermine you.'

'Was he?'

'Yes! By pretending that although he'd been your boyfriend for a
year, you're so insignificant he can't even remember your name.'

'Whatever. Anyway, I'm having a duvet day, with my blinds down.'

'But it's a beautiful sunny afternoon. You shouldn't be hiding at home.'

She laughed. 'That's my line.'

'Come on, let's go to the park,' I said.

'No.'

'Please.'

'OK.'

The park was jammers with people. I found a spot on the grass and a few minutes later Jacqui came gangling along. She was in a really short denim dress, her blonde hair was in a ponytail and her red-rimmed eyes were hidden behind massive Gucci shades. She looked great.

'He's a horrible, horrible man,' I said by way of introduction.

'But it's more than six months since we broke up. How come I'm so upset? I hadn't even thought about him for ages.'

Wearily, she stretched out on the grass, her face towards the sun.

'For your next boyfriend you wouldn't consider a Feathery Stroker, would you?' I asked.

'Couldn't. I'd puke.'

'But all these non-Feathery Strokers,' I said helplessly, 'are terrible.'

She shrugged. 'I like what I like. Anyway, I'll never have another boyfriend. I'm going to get a dog instead. I saw these really cute ones called Labrodoodles. They're a cross between Labradors and poodles and, Anna, they're the cutest things. They're small but shaggy, and they've got Labrador faces. They're the perfect town dog, everyone's getting one.'

'Don't get a dog,' I said. 'It's only one step away from getting forty cats. Don't lose faith. Please.'

'Too late. I have. Buzz let me down too often. I don't think I'll ever be able to trust a man again.' Putting on an over-earnest tone she said, 'He damaged me.' She started to laugh. 'Listen to me! I sound like Rachel. Ah, let's cheer ourselves up. Let's get ice cream.'

'OK.'

Jacqui never ceases to amaze me. If I could have only a hundredth of her bounce-backability, I'd be a very different person.

To: Magiciansgirl1@yahoo.com
From: Lucky_Star_PI@yahoo.ie
Subject: Job!

So, like I said, two burly bozos came into office and one says: 'Are you Helen Walsh?'

Me: Too right I am!

Bozo Number One: A certain gentleman of our acquaintance would like a word. We have instructions to bring you to him. Get in the car.

Me (laughing head off): I'm not getting in a car with two men I've never met before.

Bozo Number One (throws wad of money on table): Now will you get in the car?

Me: Depends. Where are we going?

Him: We're going to see Mr Big.

Me (excited): Mr Big? From *Sex and the City*?

Him (wearily): That bleedin show has caused trouble for local crime lords around the world. The name Mr Big is meant to inspire dread and terror and instead everyone thinks of this well-dressed debonair man. We have to go through the bleedin *Sex and the City* scenario every time we get a new job. Get in the car.

Me: Not until you tell me exactly where we're going. And just because I'm small don't think you can push me around. I can do Tae Kwan Do. (Well, been for one lesson with Mum.)

Him: Oh, can you? Where do you go? Wicklow Street? I teach there; funny, I haven't seen you there before. Anyway, we're going to a pool hall in Gardiner Street where the most powerful man in Dublin crime wants to talk to you.

Well, who could resist invitation like that?

I stopped reading. Was this for real? It sounded like a screenplay. I emailed her: Helen, this email you've sent me? Is it real? Did any of it actually happen?

She replied immediately: True as God. All of it.

OK, I thought—still not entirely convinced—and carried on reading.

Sat in front of car beside Bozo Number One. Bozo Number Two had to go in back with shame of Austrian blinds.

Me: Mr Bozo Number one, do you have a name?

Bozo Number One: Colin.

Me: Does Bozo Number Two have a name?

Him: No. Bozo will do.

Eventually pulled up outside dingy pool hall with orange lighting. Inside, small, neat man is sitting in booth. Trimmed bristly moustache.

He (looking up): Helen Walsh? Sit down. Would you like a drink?

Me: I'll have a Grasshopper. (Don't even like Grasshoppers, hate crème de menthe. Just wanted to be awkward.)

Him: Kenneth, get my friend here a Grasshopper.

Kenneth (the barman): A glass of what?

Mr Big: A glass of nothing. A GRASShopper. Right, Miss Walsh, down to business. Anything that's said here goes no further. I'm telling you this in total confidence. Right?

Me: Mmmm. (Because minute I got home was going to tell Mum and now telling you.)

Me (indicating Colin): What about him?

Mr Big: Colin's all right. Me and Colin have no secrets. Right, the thing is . . .

Next thing, he dipped his head, put hand in front of eyes like he was going to cry. I flashed excited look at Colin, who looked concerned.

Colin: Boss, are you OK . . . would you prefer to do this another time?

Mr Big (sniffing loudly): No, no, I'm all right. Ms Walsh, I want you to know that I'm fond of my wife, Detta. But lately she's been . . . How can I put it? . . . distant, and a little vulture whispered in my ear that she might be spending a bit too much time with Racey O'Grady. Racey and meself have jogged along together nicely for the last few years. He has his department and I have mine. One of my lines of work is offering protection. (For moment thought he meant bodyguarding, then realised he meant extortion.) But twice in the last six weeks, I've met with contractors to conclude our usual business and they say they're already covered. Now this is very interesting to me, Miss Walsh, because very few people even know these schemes are going ahead. Most of them haven't even got planning approval yet.

Me: And you think Racey is the one muscling in on your . . . er . . . patch? What do you think is going on?

Him: A less paranoid man than me might think Detta is picking my brains, taking her findings to Racey. All I want you to do is bring me proof of her and Racey together. I can't tail her and she knows all the lads and the cars. That's why I'm going against a lot of advice and bringing in an outsider.

Me: How did you hear of me? (Thinking I must be legend in Dublin private investigating.)

Him: Yellow pages.

Me (disappointed): Oh, right.

Him: Now the thing about Detta is, she has class. Detta comes from Dublin crime aristocracy. Her father, Chinner Skinner, was the man who opened Ireland's doors to heroin. We all owe him a debt of gratitude. What I'm saying is, Detta's no fool. Have you a gun?

Me: No gun. (I'm thinking, Don't know about this.)

Him (insistent): My treat.

Me (thinking better to just play along for a while): OK. But why would I need a gun?

Him: Because someone might shoot you.

Me: Like who?

Him: Like my wife. Like her boyfriend, Racey O'Grady. Like her boyfriend's mother—she's the one to watch out for. Tessie O'Grady. Misses nothing.

Then Mr 'Big' stood up. Even smaller than I'd expected.

Mr Big: I've a meeting now. Colin here will drop stuff round to you later. The gun, more money, photos of Detta, Racey, all that. Just one more thing, Ms Walsh. If you fuck this up, I'll be annoyed. And the last time someone annoyed me—when was it? Last Friday?—I crucified him on that pool table.

Anna, he was looking at me funny. Like I say, it's a good job I don't believe in fear.

And on that compelling note, it ended. Frantically, I keyed down to see if there was any more, but there wasn't. No matter how much she insisted every word of it was true, I knew it was wildly exaggerated. But she was so funny and full of life that a little of it had rubbed off on me.

3

I CHECKED MY WATCH again. Only four minutes since the last time I'd checked. How could that be? It felt like at least fifteen minutes.

I was pacing, actually *pacing* with nervy excitement, waiting for it to be time to leave for the spiritualist church place, for their Sunday service.

Eventually, I left home miles too early, got the subway to 42nd and Seventh and walked across town. The closer I got to the Hudson, the more bleak and warehousey and seagully the landscape became. This part of New York was a world away from Fifth Avenue. It was always colder here and the air was different, sharper.

The further west I walked, the more my anxiety burgeoned: there couldn't be a church here. *What should I do?* I asked Aidan. *Keep walking?* I felt even worse when I found the building—it certainly didn't look like a church. It looked like a converted warehouse. Not terribly converted either. But in the lobby, a sign on the wall listed the Church of Spiritualist Communication as being on the fifth floor.

Some people passed by me, on their way to the elevator and, full of sudden happiness, I ran and squeezed in with them. They were three women about the same age as me: one had a bag that I'd have sworn was a Marc Jacobs, then I noticed that another had her nails painted with—I almost gasped—Candy Grrrl Chick-chickachicka (pale yellow). Of all the brands in all the world? What were the chances? I took this as a Sign.

'What floor?' Marc Jacobs bag asked me. She was nearest to the button panel.

'Fifth,' I said.

'Same as us.' She smiled.

I smiled back.

Obviously, talking to the dead of a Sunday afternoon was more commonplace than I had realised.

I followed the trio out of the elevator, down a bare-floored corridor and into a room full of other women. Everyone started saying 'hi' to each other, and an exotically attired creature approached me. She had long dark hair, bare shoulders, a long, fringy skirt (I had a moment of teenage flashback) and tons of filigree-style gold jewellery, around her neck, around her waist, up her wrists and arms and fingers.

'Hi,' she said. 'Belly-dancing?'

'Excuse me?'

'You're here to learn to belly-dance?'

It was only then I noticed that the other women in the room were also wearing long, bell-infested skirts, little belly tops and spangledy slippers, and that my three elevator-mates were changing out of their ordinary clothes into jangly fringy things.

'No, I'm here for the Church of Spiritualist Communication.'

Now that was a conversation stopper if ever I encountered one. The entire room became one discordant jangle as everyone whipped round to look at me.

'Not here,' the chief lady said. 'Probably down the hall.'

Under the gaze of the filigreed girls, I retreated. Out in the corridor, I checked the number on the door. It was 506, the talking-to-dead-people was in room 514.

I carried on down the corridor, passing rooms on both sides. In one, several elderly women were singing 'If I Were a Rich Man', in another four people were clustered around what looked like a script and in yet another, a man with a rich baritone was singing about the windy city being mighty purty, while someone accompanied him on a clapped-out piano. The whole place reeked of amateur dramatics.

I *had* to be at the wrong address. I consulted my piece of paper again. It said room 514—and there *was* a room 514. Right at the end of the hallway. It looked nothing like a church, just a bare room with a circle of ten or eleven hard chairs on a dusty, splintery floor.

Uncertainly, I wondered if I should leave. But hope intervened. Hope and desperation. In fairness, I *was* early. And I'd come all this way. I might as well see if anyone else showed up.

I sat on a bench in the corridor and passed the time by watching the proceedings in the room across the way.

Eight buff young men—two rows of four—were stamping and clattering across the bare boards, singing that they were going to wash some man right out of their hair, while an older man yelled dance cues.

'Excuse me,' a voice said, 'are you here for the spiritualism?'

I whipped my head round. A young guy, probably early twenties, was looking eagerly at me. I saw him clock my scar.

'Yes,' I said cautiously.

'Great! It's always great to see a new face. I'm Nicholas.'

'Anna.'

He extended a hand. 'The other guys should be here soon.'

This Nicholas was lean and wiry—his jeans were hanging off him—with dark sticky-up hair and a T-shirt saying BE UNAFRAID. BE VERY UNAFRAID. Several woven bracelets were twined round his wrist, and he wore at least three chunky silver rings and had a tattoo on his forearm.

He looked perfectly normal but that was the thing about New York: lunacy appeared in all shapes and sizes. It specialised in Stealth Nutters.

He nodded at the *South Pacific* lads being put through their paces. 'Fame costs,' he said. 'And right here's where you start paying.'

He *looked* normal. He *sounded* normal. And all of a sudden I asked myself why *shouldn't* he be normal?

'Nicholas, you've been to . . . this . . . before?'

'Yeah.'

'And the person who does the channelling'—

'Leisl.'

—'Leisl. Does she really communicate with . . . the spirit world?'

'Yeah.' He sounded surprised. 'She really does. My dad died two years ago and, via Leisl, I've spoken to him more in the last two years than I did my entire life. We get on a lot better now that he's dead.'

'My husband died,' I splurged. 'I really want to talk to him. I went to someone who said she was a psychic, but she was just a swizzer. She said there was a curse on me and she could take it away for a thousand dollars.'

'Oh, man, you've got to be careful.' He shook his head ruefully. 'There are a lot of hustlers out there. All Leisl asks for is enough money to cover the rent. And here's the lady herself.'

Leisl was a short, bow-legged woman, laden with shopping bags. Her curly hair was lopsided: When Perms Go Bad.

Nicholas introduced me. 'This is Anna, her husband bought it.'

Leisl immediately put down her bags and gathered me into a tight hug, pulling my face into her neck so that I was breathing into an impenetrable thicket of hair. 'You'll be OK, sweetheart.'

'Thank you,' I mumbled, close to tears from her kindness.

She released me, and said, 'And here's Mackenzie.'

I turned to see a girl walking down the corridor like she was walking down a catwalk. A Park Avenue Princess, with blown-out hair, a Dior bag and wedge sandals.

'She's coming here?' I asked.

'Comes every week.'

My spirits rose. Mackenzie should be able to afford the best medium money could buy, but she chose to come here. It *must* be good.

Behind Mackenzie lumbered a hulking, eight-foot-nine bloke, in an undertaker's suit and a green-white face. 'That's Undead Fred,' Nicholas whispered. 'Come on, let's help set up the room.'

Leisl had put some spooky-sounding cello music on a tapedeck and was lighting candles when people started flooding in.

There was a round-faced, frumpy girl, who was probably younger than me but looked like she had totally given up, an older gentleman named Juan, small and dapper with pomaded hair, and a selection of older women with nervous tics and elasticated waistbands.

When another man walked in, carrying a kitbag, Nicholas grabbed me and said, 'Here's Mitch. His wife bought it. You guys must have loads in common. C'mon and meet him.'

He shunted me across the room. 'Mitch, this is Anna. Her husband died—when? Few months back?'

Mitch and I locked eyes and it was like I'd touched an electric fence, there was such a *bzzzzz* of connection. He understood; the only one who did. I saw right through his eyes and all the way down into his bleak, abandoned soul and recognised what I saw.

Everyone was sitting down and holding hands with the people beside them. I counted only twelve of us, including Leisl, but with the candles flickering in the dark room and groany cello noises in the background, the mood felt right.

Leisl did a little intro, welcoming me, and saying stuff about deep breaths and centring ourselves and hoping that 'Spirit' would deliver what everyone needed. Then we were allowed to stop holding hands.

Silence fell. And continued. And continued.

When Leisl finally spoke, I jumped.

'I have a tall man here.' My eyes snapped open and I wanted to put my hand up, like I was at school. It's for me! It's for me!

'A very tall, broad, dark-haired man.' My heart sank. Not for me.

'Sounds like my mom,' Undead Fred said, in a slow, gargly voice.

Leisl did a quick recalculation. 'Fred, I'm sorry, yes, it is your mom. She's telling me to ask you to be careful getting on the subway. She says that you don't pay attention, that you could slip.'

After a period of silence, Fred asked, 'That it?'

'That's it.'

'Thanks, Mom.'

'I've got Nicholas's dad now.' Leisl faced Nicholas. 'He's telling me— I'm sorry, these are his words, not mine—that he's pissed with you.'

'So what's new?' Nicholas grinned.

'There's a situation in work that you have issues with?'

Nicholas nodded.

'Your dad says you're blaming the other guy, but you've got to look at where you're responsible for what's happened.'

Nicholas stretched out, extended his arms above his head, scratched his chest thoughtfully. 'Maybe, yeah, he's probably right. Bummer. Thanks, Dad.'

More silence followed, then the young frumpy girl's mother told her that everything was going to work out for the best; Juan, the pomadey guy, got told to live in the now; and Mitch's wife said she was happy to see he'd been smiling a bit more this week.

All meaningless, vaguely spiritual-sounding platitudes. Comforting stuff, but obviously not coming from 'the other side'.

It's all bollocks, I thought bitterly, which was just when Leisl said, 'Anna, I'm getting something for you.'

Sensation burnt through me. *Thank you, Aidan, thank you, thank you.*

'It's a woman.' *Shite.* 'An older woman, she's talking very loudly at me.' Leisl looked a little distressed. 'And she's banging a stick on the ground for attention.'

Christ! It sounded like Granny Maguire! That was exactly what she used to do.

Leisl said, 'She says it's about your dog.'

It took a moment for me to stammer, 'I don't have a dog.'

Mackenzie piped up, excited. 'I have a dog. This must be for me.'

'OK,' Leisl turned to Mackenzie. 'Spirit says he needs more exercise, he's getting fat.'

'But I walk him every day. I would *never* have a fat dog.'

Leisl looked doubtful and cast a glance around the room. 'Anyone else with a fat dog?'

No takers.

'Time's up,' Leisl said, then people were putting crumpled dollar bills into a bowl, and getting to their feet and blowing out the candles.

In the corridor, I was devastated with disappointment and couldn't hide it.

'Well?' Nicholas asked.

Rigidly, I moved my head from side to side. No.

'No,' he admitted sadly. 'I guess it didn't happen for you.'

Leisl came racing out and grabbed me. 'I'm so sorry, sweetie, I really wanted something good to come through for you, but I've no control over these things.'

'What if we tried . . . would you be available for an individual reading?'

But, sorrowfully, Leisl shook her head. 'One-on-ones don't work for me. I need the energy of the group.' For that alone, I respected her. Almost trusted her.

'But sometimes I get messages at unexpected times. If anything comes through for you, I'll be sure to pass it along.'

'Thank y—'

I ran out of words because, without warning, her body went rigid and her eyes glazed over. 'Oh, wow, I'm getting something for you now. How about that?'

My knees turned to water.

'I'm seeing a little blond boy,' she said. 'Wearing a hat. He's your son? No, not your son, your . . . nephew?'

'My nephew, JJ. But he's alive.'

'I know, but he's important to you.'

Thanks for telling me something I already know.

'He'll become more important to you.'

What did that mean? That Maggie was going to die and I was going to have to marry Garv and be a stepmother to JJ and Holly?

'Sorry, sweetie, I don't know what it means, I just pass on the message.' And off she went down the corridor.

'What was that?' Nicholas asked.

'My nephew, she said.'

'Not your dead husband?'

'No.'

'OK, let's get Mitch over here. He'll tell you about Neris Hemming,' Nicholas promised. 'She's often on TV shows and she even helped the cops find a murdered girl. She's so good she spoke in Mitch's wife's voice. Mitch!' he called. 'Mitch, c'mere buddy.'

Mitch came over.

'OK,' Nicholas told me. 'Tell him everything.'

I swallowed. 'My husband died and I came here today hoping to get in touch with him. I wanted to have a conversation with him. Find out where he is.' My throat thickened. 'Check if he's OK.'

Mitch understood completely, I could see it.

'I told her about you going to Neris Hemming,' Nicholas said. 'She connected with your wife, she actually started speaking in her voice, didn't she?'

Mitch gave a little smile at Nicholas's enthusiasm. 'She didn't speak in her voice, but, yeah, I was really talking to Trish. I've gone to lots of psychics and she's the only one who did it for me.'

My heart was beating fast and my mouth was dry. 'Do you have a number for her?'

'Sure.' He produced an organiser. 'But she's very busy. You'll probably have to wait, like, a long time to see her.'

'That's OK.'

'And it'll cost you. It's two thousand dollars for thirty minutes.'

I was shocked: two thousand dollars was an horrific amount. My finances were in a shambles. Aidan hadn't had life insurance, and the rent on our apartment was so extortionate that paying Aidan's share as well as my own was eating up nearly every cent of my salary. However, I was more than happy to go into debt for this Neris Hemming.

Mitch was staring at his organiser, looking confused. 'It's not here. I keep doing that, like, I keep losing stuff . . .'

So did I. I felt another jolt of connection with this Mitch.

'I can get the number,' he said. 'How about I give it to you next week?'

'Can you take my number? Could you call when you find it?'

'Sure.' He took my card.

'Can I ask you something?' I said. 'Why do you come here after seeing someone so good?'

He stared into the distance, considering. 'After talking to Trish via Neris, I was able to let a lot of stuff go. And Leisl is good, in her own way. She doesn't hit gold every week but her averages are pretty high. And the people here understand how it is for me—everyone else in my life, they think I should be over it by now. So coming here, I can be myself.' He tucked my card in his wallet. 'I'll call you.'

'Please do,' I said.

Because I wouldn't be coming back.

But later on, at home, I was filled with a terrible need to talk to Aidan.

Typing furiously, I looked up Neris Hemming on the internet. She had her own site, bearing literally hundreds of grateful testimonials. There were also details of her forthcoming twenty-seven-city tour: she was playing thousand-seater venues in places like Cleveland, Ohio, and Portland, Oregon, but, to my bitter disappointment, she wasn't coming to New York.

The nearest city was Raleigh, North Carolina. I'll go, I thought, with sudden determination. I'll take a day off work and fly down. Then I discovered that it was booked out and another wave of wretchedness hit me.

I had to arrange a personal reading with her, but I clicked on every single link until it became clear that there was no way of contacting her via the site. I needed that phone number from Mitch.

4

MONDAY MORNING. Which meant the Monday Morning Meeting. Walking to the boardroom, Teenie linked her arm through mine. She looked almost normal today, wearing a silver Barbarella-style shift dress and long silver and grey sneakers that laced right up to her knee.

'Step right up,' she said. 'Get your humiliation here!'

'Be degraded in front of your peers,' I said.

Easy for us to laugh, we were doing OK.

I was getting good newspaper coverage. No great coups, but at the Monday Morning Meetings I always had a couple of things to show and tell after each weekend. Maybe the beauty editors felt sorry for me with my scarred face and my dead husband.

Normally, when the MMM is over, there's a feeling that the week can only get better. But not today. Today was Day Zero for Eye Eye Captain. Today was the day that 150 Eye Eye Captain kits would be assembled and packaged ready to be couriered out to all the magazines and newspapers the following day: a one-stop eye-care skin-kit. Three different products, each of which worked in tandem to enhance the efficacy of the others (or so they said). There was Pack Your Bags (a cooling gel to zap puffiness and under-eye bags), Light Up Your Life (a light-deflecting concealer pen to banish dark circles) and Iron Out The Kinks (a whipped-mousse wrinkle-killer).

Just one tiny problem: the trio of products hadn't arrived from the manufacturers in Indianapolis. They were on their way. Oh, they were definitely coming. They'd be with us by eleven. But eleven came and passed. Lauryn made an hysterical phone call and got a guarantee that the driver was in Pennsylvania and would definitely be with us by one.

It was after five by the time the big cardboard boxes were being hefted into the boardroom. No one was meeting anyone else's eyes because we were all thinking the same thing: Who was going to stay late—very late—and do it?

Brooke was going to a benefit, saving something or other: whales, Venice, three-legged elephants. Teenie had college (and it wasn't her job anyway) and there was more chance of Lauryn eating a three-course meal. It had to be me. Just me.

Everyone was so used to me working late that they didn't even ask if I'd any plans but, as it happened, I was meant to be seeing Rachel. I'd given her the slip over the weekend, citing pressures of work. And now I really *had* to work—the girl who'd cried overtime.

'Does anyone mind if I make a quick call? Just to cancel my sister?'

I sounded so sarcastic that startled looks were exchanged. Now and again, unexpected spurts of anger, so red-hot they almost scalded me, were shooting up through me and carrying rage-soaked words out of my mouth.

'Er, no, go right ahead,' Lauryn said.

Teenie helped me slit the boxes open and pile the products along the boardroom table and Brooke, in all fairness to her, had already put 150 press releases into 150 padded envelopes.

And then everyone was gone. The building was quiet, nothing but the hum of computers. I took a look at all the stuff on the boardroom table and was stabbed with self-pity.

I bet you're really pissed off with the way they're treating me.

I began by lining the inside of all the padded envelopes with sheets of silver lamé. This took until after eight; I was slower than I'd normally be because of my nails. Then I became a human conveyor belt. At one end of the table I stuck a printed label on the padded envelope, then I moved on to pick a Pack Your Bags from one pile, a Light Up Your Life from the next and Iron Out The Kinks from the third, let them tumble into the padded envelope, picked up a handful of tiny silver stars, scattered them in on top, sealed the envelope, chucked it in the corner and returned to the start.

I kind of got a rhythm going. Label, pick-pick-pick, tumble, stars, seal, throw. Label, pick-pick-pick, tumble, stars, seal, throw.

It was very soothing and I had been crying for a long time before I noticed. Tears ran down my face without any input from me; it was very peaceful. I cried the entire way through the job and although my tears blurred the ink on *Femme*'s address label, no other harm was done. By the time I had finished, it was midnight. But all 150 packages were waiting to be couriered in the morning.

Another email arrived from Helen.

To: Magiciansgirl1@yahoo.com
From: Lucky_Star_Pl@yahoo.ie
Subject: Job!

First day of surveillance on Detta Big. Stuck in hedge in back garden of her big detached house in Stillorgan, binoculars trained on her bedroom.

She's about fifty, roundy bum, big knockers, leathery cleavage. Shoulder-length blondey curly hair, Carmen heated rollers end-product. Wearing high heels and cream knitted (bouclé?) skirt and jumper.

At ten to ten, she put on coat. We were going out. By-passed car, big silver Beemer, and walked to local church. She was going to Mass! I sat at back, just grateful not to be in hedge.

Afterwards, she went to newsagent, bought *Herald*, *Take A Break*, twenty Benson & Hedges and packet of mints (Extra Strong). Then went home again and I resumed vigil in hedge. She put kettle on, made tea, sat in front of telly, smoking and staring into space. One o'clock, she got up and I thought, please, let's be going out. But she was just making a bowl of soup and toast, then went back to sitting in front of telly. About four o'clock, she got up. But she wasn't going out—she was doing the hoovering. Really going for it.

After hoovering frenzy, Detta went back to the kitchen, put the kettle on, made tea. Hope tomorrow's going to be bit more exciting.

And an email from Mum . . .

To: Magiciansgirl1@yahoo.com
From: Thewalshes1@eircom.net
Subject: Organised crime

Dear Anna,

We're in a bad way. Helen no longer cares about our 'domestic' issue (i.e. the dog poo). She is too caught up in her new job. She is 'lording' it over us because she is associating with known criminals.

She says that the one she's surveilling, the wife of the 'crime lord', has lovely clothes for an elderly person. Could that be true? And that she does her cleaning herself!

I tried using her camera but it is a 'digital' one and neither myself nor your father could figure it out. How are we to catch the old woman in the act? She was back again on Monday, up to her old tricks. If you are talking to Helen, would you try persuading her to help out? I know you are 'bereaved', but she might listen to you.

Your loving mother,
Mum

All week, I was on tenterhooks waiting for the Mitch bloke to call with Neris Hemming's number, but the days passed and I heard nothing. So I made a plan: if he hadn't rung by Sunday I'd go back to that place. Then I remembered that it was the holiday weekend, July 4—what if he'd gone away?

It had been a bad week at work. I'd been ferociously narky, and I kept bumping into things; I'd knocked a cup of coffee into Lauryn's desk drawer and I'd made a whiteboard topple over at a briefing session.

But these accidents were as nothing compared to the Eye Eye Captain disaster: because I'd cried all over the *Femme* address label and made it too blurry to be read, their package had been returned to us by the couriers on Tuesday afternoon, and we'd missed the print slot. Lauryn was still thin-lipped with fury.

On Friday evening, when I walked into my local newsagent's to get supplies for an evening of crying, I finally realised why I'd been so narky: I was roasting. The little shop was like an oven.

'It's so hot!' I said to the man.

I wasn't expecting a reply because I didn't think he spoke English but he said, 'Hot! Yes! For many days a heatwave!'

Many days? What did he mean? 'What . . . when did this heatwave start?'

'Thursday.'

'Thursday?' That wasn't so bad.

'Tuesday.'

'Tuesday?' Said in high alarm.

Disturbed, I slowly made my way home with my bag of sweets. This heatwave business was not good. I'd been so locked inside myself that I hadn't noticed it.

After my regulation-issue three hours' sleep, I woke on Saturday morning with sweat trickling into my hair. So it was true: we were in the thick of a heatwave and it was summer. Panic seized me.

I don't want it to be summer. Summer is too far away from when you died.

I'd thought I'd wanted enough time to pass so I could think of him without the pain killing me, but now that it was July I wanted it to be February for ever.

Time was a great healer, people said. But I didn't want to heal, because if I did I'd be abandoning him.

Flattened by the sweltering heat, I was too hot to move. The air-conditioner needed to be set up, but it was the size of a telly. Last autumn, Aidan had put it away on a high shelf in the living room. The horror washed over me. *You're not here to take it down.*

Ornesto would have to help me get it down. I knew he was home because for the last ten minutes he'd been singing 'Diamonds are Forever' at the top of his lungs.

He opened the door in gold lamé dungaree shorts and flowery Birkenstocks.

'You look lovely,' I said.

'Come in,' he invited. 'Let's sing a song.'

I shook my head. 'I need a man to lift my air-conditioner down from a high shelf and carry it over to the window.'

Ornesto opened his eyes wide. 'Well, you know what? Let's get Bubba from upstairs to help us.'

'Bubba?'

'Or something. He's a big guy. With bad clothes. He won't care if he sweats all over them. C'mon.' Ornesto led the way upstairs and knocked on number ten's door.

A deep voice called suspiciously, 'Who is it?'

Ornesto and I looked at each other and got an unexpected fit of the giggles. 'Anna,' I called, in a strangled voice. 'Anna from number six.' I nudged Ornesto.

'And Ornesto from number eight.'

'Whaddya want? To invite me to a garden party?' Pronounced 'goo-ah-d'n paw-dee'. New York humour, see. That gave us the excuse to laugh.

'No, sir,' I said. 'I was wondering if you could help me move my air-conditioner.'

The door moved back and a saggy, fifty-something man in his vest stood there. 'You need a bit of muscle?'

'Er, yes.'

'Long time since a woman said that to me. Lemme get my keys.'

The three of us trooped down the stairs and into my apartment where I pointed out the AC high up on the shelf.

'Shouldn't be a problem,' Bubba said. He climbed up on a chair, which Ornesto made a big show of holding steady.

Then the AC was down and was hefted over to the window, plugged in, and—like a miracle—mercifully cold air was blowing into the apartment. The gratitude!

I thanked the man effusively and asked, 'Would you like a beer, sir?'

'Eugene.' He stuck out his hand.

'Anna.'

'A beer would be appreciated.'

Luckily, I had one. One. Literally. God knows how long it had been there.

As Eugene leaned against the kitchen counter and sucked down his possibly-out-of-date beer, he asked, 'What happened to the guy who lived here? He move out or something?'

A stricken hiatus followed. Ornesto and I looked at each other.

'No,' I said. 'He was my husband.'

I paused. I couldn't bring myself to say the D word: it was taboo. Everyone sympathised with the 'tragedy' or my 'sad loss' but no one would say 'death', which often filled me with a terrible compulsion to say loudly, "Actually, Aidan *died*. He's *dead*. Dead, dead, dead, dead, dead, dead, dead, dead, dead, dead, dead, dead, dead, dead, DEAD. There now! It's only a word—nothing to be frightened of!' But I never said anything; it wasn't their fault. We get no lessons in dealing with death, even though it happens to everyone.

I took a deep breath and flung the D word into the middle of the floor. 'He died.'

'Aw, I'm so sorry, kid,' Eugene said. 'My wife died too. I've been a widower for nearly five years.'

Oh my God. I'd never thought of it like that before. 'I'm a widow.' I started to laugh. I laughed and laughed until tears ran down my face. But it was the wrong sort of laughter and the boys were clearly aghast.

Eugene gathered me to him, then Ornesto put his arms around the two of us, a strange, well-meaning group hug. 'It gets better, you know,' Eugene promised me. 'It really does get better.'

Still no word from Mitch by Sunday morning and I bowed to the inevitable and got ready to go to the spiritualist church place. Once again I got there miles too early and I sat on the bench to wait. Like the previous week, Nicholas was the next to arrive. Today his T-shirt said DEATH BEFORE DISHONOUR.

'You came back! This is the best!'

I was so touched that I hadn't the heart to tell him that the second I got the number from Mitch, I was off.

'Does Mitch come every week?' I asked.

'Most weeks. All of us come most weeks.'

Eagerly, he sat down beside me, when down the corridor came Leisl. She lit up like Times Square when she saw me. 'Anna! I'm so happy you came back. I really hope you'll get a better message this week.'

Steffi, the young frumpy girl, was next and she smiled shyly and said she was glad to see me, as did Carmela, one of the older elasticated-waist ladies, then dazzling Mackenzie. Even Undead Fred expressed pleasure at my presence.

I felt a huge rush of warmth and gratitude to them . . . but where was Mitch?

Down the corridor they came: Pomadey Juan, a few more elasticated waists—everyone was here except Mitch.

The room was set up and the candles were flickering and we were all taking our places in the circle of chairs and there was still no sign. I was wondering whether I should ask Nicholas if he had a number for Mitch when the door opened.

It was him.

'Just in time,' Leisl said.

'Yeah, I'm sorry.' He did a quick scan of the circle and his glance landed on me. 'Anna, I'm sorry I didn't call. I lost your card. I'm a mess,' he said. 'But I've got the number here.'

He handed me a piece of white paper and I unfolded it and gazed at the number written on it. Ten precious digits that would lead me to Aidan. Right, I could go now!

But I stayed where I was. They'd all been so nice that I felt it would be rude to leave. And now that I was there and the groany cello music was going full blast, I began to hope that something might happen. The first message was for Mitch.

'Trish is here,' Leisl said, her eyes closed. 'She looks like an angel today. So pretty, I wish you could see her. Mitch, she's asking me to tell you that things will get better. She says she'll always be with you, but you've got to start moving on.'

Mitch looked as bleak as any person could look. 'How?'

'It'll happen, if you're open to it.'

'Yeah, well, I'm not open to it,' Mitch said. 'Trish,' he said, and it was shocking hearing him address her directly, 'I'm not moving on, because I don't want to leave you behind.'

Silence fell and we all shifted a little uncomfortably. After a while,

Leisl said, 'I'm getting a man'—my stomach nearly jumped out of my mouth. But it jumped straight back in again when Leisl said, —'called Frazer. Mean anything to anyone?'

'Me!' Mackenzie said, at the same time as Leisl said, 'Mackenzie, it's for you. He says he's your uncle. He says there is no missing will.'

'But there's gotta be a will!'

Leisl shook her head. 'He seems totally sure.'

'But if there's no will, what am I going to do for money?'

'He says get a job.' Pause for Leisl to listen to the voice in her head. 'Or marry a rich guy. That's outrageous!' Leisl added.

Mackenzie's tanned face was flushed. 'Tell him from me he's a drunken asshole who knows nothing. Get me Great-Aunt Morag!' she ordered, as if Leisl was a personal assistant.

I felt very sorry for Leisl—having to pass on stuff that people didn't want to hear.

'He's gone,' Leisl said. 'And no one else is coming through.'

'This is bullshit!' Mackenzie exclaimed.

'Ssshh,' Pomadey Juan said. 'A little respect.'

Mackenzie put her hand to her mouth. 'I'm so sorry.' Then she dropped her voice to a whisper. 'Sorry. Sorry, Leisl.'

Leisl was sitting very still. She hadn't opened her eyes in a while and the mood in the room was very uncomfortable. 'Today has been very strange,' she said. 'This is usually a very loving place. There's a lot of angry energy here today. I think we should stop.'

Nothing had come through for me, but curiously I didn't mind. I wanted to talk to Mitch. Out in the corridor afterwards I cornered him.

'Thank you so much for this.' I indicated the piece of paper. 'Do you mind . . . can I ask you a bit about your reading with Neris? Like, what convinced you she was for real?'

'There was some personal stuff that no one else could have known about. Trish and me, we had special names for each other.' He smiled, half embarrassed. 'And Neris told me them.'

That sounded convincing.

'Did Trish say where she was?' My obsession: where was Aidan?

'She said she couldn't describe it in a way that I'd understand. She said it was not so much a question of where she was and more a question of *what* she had become. But that she was always with me. I asked her if she was scared, and she said no. She said she was sad for me, but that she was happy where she was. She said she knew it was hard but that I had to try to stop thinking of her as a life interrupted. It was a life completed.'

'What happened . . . to Trish?'

'How did she die? An aneurism. One Friday night she came home from work, same as usual—she was a teacher. An English teacher. About seven o'clock she said she was feeling dizzy and nauseous, by eight she was in a coma and by one thirty a.m. in the ICU, she was dead.' He paused. Like Aidan, Trish had died young and suddenly. No wonder I'd felt such a tangible connection with Mitch.

'Nothing anyone could have done. Nothing that would have showed up in any tests. I still can't believe it.' He sounded baffled. 'It happened so quickly. Too quickly to believe it, you know?'

I knew. 'How long ago did it happen?'

'Nearly ten months. It'll be ten months on Tuesday. Anyway.' He swung his kitbag on his shoulder. 'I'm going to hit the gym.'

He looked like he went to the gym a lot. Maybe it was his way of coping.

'Best of luck with Neris,' he said. 'See you next week.'

I called Neris Hemming's number as soon as I got home, but a recorded message told me that their office hours were Monday to Friday, nine until six. I slammed down the phone far too hard and in one of those sudden uprisings of acid rage, I shrieked, 'Oh, Aidan!'

A storm of tears overtook me and I convulsed with frustration, my powerlessness and my terrible, terrible need.

A few minutes later, I wiped my face and said humbly, 'I'm sorry.'

I repeated, 'I'm sorry,' to every photo of Aidan in the apartment. It wasn't his fault that Neris Hemming's office took Sundays off. And this was a holiday weekend, so they probably wouldn't be in tomorrow either. I'd ring from work on Tuesday, I decided. I was so terrified of losing the number that I wrote it in several—hopefully unexpected—places, just in case someone ever broke into my apartment and decided to steal all the Neris Hemming numbers.

Now what?

I braced myself to ring Aidan's parents; Dianne had called while I was out. Somehow—and I'd no idea how it had happened because it was the last thing I wanted—we'd got into a routine where she rang me every weekend. I dialled their number, screwed my eyes up tight and beseeched, over and over, in my head, *Don't be in, don't be in, oh, please don't be in*, but—damn—Dianne picked up. She sighed, 'Oh, Anna.'

'How are you, Dianne?'

'I'm pretty bad, Anna, pretty low. I was thinking about Thanksgiving.'

'But it's only July.'

'I don't want to do it this year. I was thinking of just getting the hell out, going on vacation on my own, to a place where they don't have Thanksgiving. It's a time for family. And I can't bear it.'

'How's Mr Maddox?' I could never think of him as having a first name.

'Coping in his usual way. Buried in his work. I'd get more emotional support from a three-year-old.' She laughed, in a scary way.

I was pretty sure I knew what was coming next. 'I'd better go, Dianne. You take care. We'll talk about the ashes some other time.' We still hadn't sorted that out.

'Yeah,' she said wearily. 'Whatever.'

Done for another week! Oh, the relief! Feeling light and free, I rang Mum, who answered the phone with a gaspy 'Hello'.

'It's me, Anna.'

'Anna, pet! What's happened?'

'Nothing. I'm just calling for a chat.'

'A chat?'

'Yes. What's wrong with that?'

'Because everyone knows we watch *Midsomer Murders* at this time on a Sunday night. *No one* rings.'

'Sorry, I didn't know. OK, I'll call back.'

Via a series of cunning lies—I told Rachel I was going to Teenie's, I told Teenie I was spending the day with Jacqui and I told Jacqui that I was hanging out with Rachel—I managed to avoid having to attend any holiday rooftop barbecues and firework displays on Monday and had a pleasant enough time, sitting downwind of my air-conditioner and watching reruns of *The Dukes of Hazzard, Quantum Leap* and *MASH*.

'**N**eris Hemming's office.'

'Oh my God, I can't believe I'm finally through!' I was so overwhelmed I couldn't stop talking. 'I'm at work and I've been ringing for *hours* and kept getting your message—'

'Can I have your name, honey?'

'Anna Walsh.'

I knew it was crazy but I'd fantasised that when she heard my name she'd go, 'Oh, yeah, Anna Walsh,' then shuffle through some papers on her desk, containing messages from the dead, and say, 'Yes, there's a message for you from a guy called Aidan Maddox. He said to say he's sorry he died so unexpectedly like that, but he's hovering around you all the time and can't wait to talk to you.'

'A-n-n-a W-a-l-s-h.' Keys clicked as she inputted me.

'You're not Neris, are you?'

'No, I'm her assistant. Number and email, please.'

I called them out, she read them back to me, then she said, 'OK, we'll be in touch.' But I didn't want the call to end; I needed *something*.

'You see, my husband died.' Tears began to pour down my face and I ducked my head so that Lauryn wouldn't see.

'Sure, honey, I know. Like I said, we'll be in touch.'

'Yes, but—'

'Great talking to you.'

She was gone—and here came Franklin, clapping his hands together, rounding up his girls for the Monday Morning Meeting, even though it was Tuesday.

I was still getting pretty good newspaper coverage. So it was a bit of a shock when Ariella said, from the head of the table, 'What's going on with you, Anna?'

Shit. However, all those long hours I'd been putting in paid off and I was able to give a decent answer. 'The biggest project I'm working on at the moment is Candy Grrrl going to Super Saturday in the Hamptons.'

Super Saturday was a high-profile, celebrity-ridden charity fund-raiser. Members of the public (but it was the Hampton public, so it was very select, really) had to pay to get in—a lot, like several hundred dollars—but once you were in you got to buy designer clothes for next to nothing; there were giveaways, treatments, raffles and a sensational goody bag when you left.

'Our stand is twice as big as it was last year, we're giving away Candy Grrrl beach-bags and, best of all, I've persuaded Candace to come and do make-overs. Getting her in person should be a huge draw.'

Ariella couldn't find anything to criticise in that, so she turned on Wendell, who organised PR for Visage, the Devereaux Corporation's upmarket cosmetic range. 'You're doing Super Saturday too, yeah? You got a world-famous make-up artist coming along?'

'Dr De Groot will be attending,' Wendell said.

Dr De Groot was skin-care scientist for Visage. He was the oddest-looking man I'd ever met—he was actually frightening—and he definitely took his work home. We reckoned he practised chemical peels and restylane injections of himself. I know I was a fine one to talk with my mutilated face but, really, anyone who met him would never use Visage again.

'The phantom of the opera?' Ariella said. 'Try to get him to wear a bag on his head.'

Wendell nodded efficiently. 'Done.'

Ariella seemed to sag. There was no one to yell at; we were all too efficient today. 'Go on,' she nodded at us all. 'Get out of here, I'm busy.'

When I got home that evening, an email was waiting and, all of a sudden, the sun came out from behind the clouds.

To: Magiciansgirl1@yahoo.com
From: Psychic_Productions@yahoo.com
Subject: Neris Hemming

We have noted your request for a one-on-one reading with Neris Hemming. Due to her busy schedule, Ms Hemming is fully booked for several months. When a vacancy becomes available her office will contact you to arrange a half-hour phone reading. The cost for Ms Hemming's time will be $2500. We accept all major credit cards.

Cripes, it had gone up a lot since Mitch had talked to her. Not that it mattered. If only I could talk to her *now*.

To: Psychic_Productions@yahoo.com
From: Magiciansgirl1@yahoo.com
Subject: Several months?

How long is several months?

To: Magiciansgirl1@yahoo.com
From: Psychic_Productions@yahoo.com
Subject: Re: Several months?

Between ten and twelve weeks, usually, but this is not a guarantee, simply an estimate. Please note this in any legal action.

What? People *sued* because they didn't get to talk to Neris in the promised time? There was also an attachment full of exemption clauses. It was couched in convoluted legalese, but the gist was that if you didn't get to hear what you wanted from Neris, no way could you hold her responsible; and although she could cancel for any reason she liked, if you weren't there at you're appointed slot, you'd forfeit your money.

There was also an email from Helen:

To: Magiciansgirl1@yahoo.com
From: Lucky_Star_Pl@yahoo.ie
Subject: Tedi-arse

Break in routine! Detta drove to Donnybrook in personality-free Beemer and went to war-crime dress shop. You know the type—small boutiques for rich old bats. Have 'exotic' names like 'Monique's' and 'Lucrezia's' and warcrime old assistants who say, 'These stinky expensive warcrime items are just in from Italy—goooooooooorgeous, aren't they?' And, 'This yellow would be lovely on you, Annette, really brings out your teeth.'

Didn't go in, just hovered outside like homeless person because a) place was too small and Detta would have spotted me, and b) once you're through door of shop like that, if you try to leave without buying anything, they shoot you in the back with sniper's rifle.

5

FRIDAY, JULY 9, my birthday; I was thirty-three. Rachel wanted to make sure that my first birthday without Aidan was a lovely affair: a lovely restaurant and lovely presents with lovely people who loved me. I'd begged her to reconsider. I'd reminded her how difficult I found any social event and one that had me at its epicentre would be close to unendurable, but she was immovable.

I was late getting home from work. I had ten minutes before Jacqui came to pick me up and I wasn't remotely ready. I didn't even have a clue where to start. Teeth, I decided. I'd brush my teeth. But when I picked up my toothbrush, a dreadful pain, like a streak of electricity zipping through me, shot up my arm, through my ribs and down through my legs. I still had the arthritis/rheumatism-style aches, but in the last few days they'd been joined by these shooting electric jolts.

My bell rang. Jacqui was early. 'Ah fuck!' I flung my toothbrush into the sink.

Jacqui looked me over and said, 'Oh, good, you're ready.'

Actually, I was still in my work clothes (pink ballerina-style skirt, pink vest, fishnet cut-offs and ballet slippers embroidered with flowers) but as my work clothes looked more like party clothes than most people's party clothes, I decided I'd do.

As the cab moved through the Friday-night traffic, I thought only of Aidan. *I'm on my way to meet you. You'll be here tonight, you'll have come straight from work to the restaurant. You'll be wearing your blue suit and*

you'll have taken off your tie and when Jacqui and I walk in you'll wink at me
to show that you know I have to be mannerly and say hello to everyone else
first. We'll speak politely to everyone there but you'll do something small and
intimate, something only I'll know about—maybe you'll pass by me and
quickly circle your thumb over the palm of my hand or . . .

Jacqui had said something and resentment flared momentarily. I
loved being in my own head so much, it was getting harder and harder
being with other people.

'Sorry. What?'

'We're here,' she repeated.

'So we are,' I said, in surprise.

Flanked by Jacqui, like I was a prisoner on day release, I walked into
La Vie en Seine, where a crowd awaited: Rachel, Luke, Joey, Gaz, Shake,
Teenie, Leon, Dana, Dana's sister Natalie, Aidan's old room-mate Marty,
Nell, but not Nell's strange friend, thank God. They were standing
around, drinking champagne from flutes, and when they saw me a little
cheer went up and someone said, over-jovially, 'Here's the birthday girl!'
Someone else handed me a flute, which I tried to down in one go.

Everyone was smiling and looking at me—people were always either
super-cheery or super-solicitous, no one could be normal—and I
couldn't think of a single thing to say. This was worse, far worse, than
I'd anticipated.

'Let's take our places,' Rachel said.

At the table, the insides of my cheeks were hurting from holding a
smile. I picked up another glass of champagne—I wasn't sure it was
mine, but I couldn't stop myself. Up until now I'd stayed away from
heavy drinking because I was afraid I might like it too much. It looked
as if I'd been right.

As I wiped sticky champagne dregs from my chin, I realised a waiter
was standing patiently beside me, waiting to hand me a menu. 'Oh
God, sorry, thank you,' I murmured.

Jacqui was telling me how hard it was to get hold of a Labrodoodle,
they were in very short supply and were being sold on the black
market. I was trying to pay attention but Joey was diagonally opposite
her and he was singing 'Uptown Girl', changing the real words for snide
ones about Jacqui. He was being very unpleasant—nothing unusual
there—but he was really putting an extraordinary amount of work into
it. Then I understood—oh my God . . . he fancied Jacqui. When had
that started?

My nerve endings were so raw that finally I had to say, 'Joey, could
you stop?'

'Wha—Oh, sorry, man. It's the voice, yeah?' Joey said. 'Tone deaf, always was.'

My attention was caught by a young, beautiful woman at the next table. She was very New York—sleek and coordinated with shiny, blown-out hair. She was smiling and talking animatedly to the dull-looking man with her, her manicured hands flashing to emphasise what she was saying. I watched her shirtfront rise and fall as she took a breath. And another. And another. And another. Breathing. Staying alive. One day something would happen and her chest wouldn't rise and fall. She'd be dead. I thought of all that life-stuff going on beneath the skin, her heart pumping, her blood flowing, and what makes it stop . . .

Slowly, I realised that everyone was staring at me.

'Are you OK, Anna?' Rachel asked.

' . . . um . . .'

'It's just that you were staring at that woman.'

Oh my God, I was out of control. What should I say? 'Yes . . . wondering if she's had Botox.'

Everyone turned to look.

'Course she has.'

Then I felt wretched. Not just because I was sure the woman hadn't had Botox—she was so animated—but because I wasn't fit to be let out.

Gaz squeezed my shoulder. 'Have a proper drink.' And I decided I would. Something strong. When my Martini arrived, Gaz said, encouragingly, 'You're OK. You're doing great.'

'D'you know something, Gaz?' I gulped from the glass and heat flooded my system. 'I don't think I am. I have this . . . sensation . . . that I'm looking at the world through the wrong end of a telescope. It feels like my lens on the world has been interfered with so that everyone looks much further away, do you know what I mean?' I took another deep gulp of my Martini. 'The only time I feel half-normal is when I'm at work, but that's because it's not the real me. Can I tell you what I was thinking when I was looking at that beautiful woman? I was thinking that one day we'll all be dead, Gaz. And it mightn't be in forty years' time or whatever you're counting on. Gaz, you could go like that.' I tried to snap my fingers, but couldn't manage it. 'I don't mean to be morbid, Gaz, saying you could drop dead any minute, but it's the truth. I mean, look at Aidan, he's dead and he was younger than you, Gaz, by a couple of years.'

I have a vague memory of his desperate face, but I couldn't do a thing to stop myself. 'I'm thirty-three, Gaz, thirty-three today and my husband is dead and I'll have another Martini because if you can't have a Martini when your husband is dead, when can you have one?'

I continued in this vein for some time. I half noticed a glance being exchanged between Gaz and Rachel, but it was only when Rachel got to her feet and said, over-cheerily, 'Anna, I'm coming over to you. I haven't had a proper chat with you all night,' that I realised people were almost paying bribes in order not to sit beside me.

'I'm so sorry, Gaz,' I grasped his hand.

'Hey. Nothing to be sorry about.' Tenderly he kissed the top of my head, but then he nearly broke into a run. Seconds later he was sitting at the bar, knocking back an amber-coloured liquid. I knew, without having to be told, that it was a Jack Daniel's.

I woke on Saturday morning with a horrible hangover. I was trembly, tearful and in terrible pain. I was also swollen-tongued with thirst. Images of the previous night flashed through my head and I cringed with mortification. Drunk as I'd been last night, I had picked up on the mood around the table. She's as bad as she ever was, they'd all been thinking. Worse, even. Funny, you'd think that after five months she'd have got it together a bit . . .

Maybe after five months I *should* have got it together a bit. Leon had improved noticeably. He was a lot cheerier and he could be in my company without crying. Mind you, he had Dana, he hadn't lost everything.

Another image from the previous night popped up: me talking to Shake about the next air-guitar championship heats.

'Play,' I'd urged him. 'Play your heart out, Shake. Because you could be dead tomorrow. Later tonight, even.'

He and his hair had been nodding along with me but he'd recoiled speedily when I mentioned the possible imminence of his death.

Rachel had kept moving me along, from person to person, before I wrecked anyone's buzz too much. But I suspected I'd engendered a bit of a panic because after the dinner, as we'd stood outside deciding where to go next, the Real Men were drunkenly punching the air and hollering that the night was young and that they were going to play Scrabble till the sun came up. They were all in a howling-at-the-moon, grab-life-by-the-balls frenzy.

'I spooked them,' I said out loud. 'Aidan, I spooked them.' And suddenly it seemed funny and comforting. He and I were in it together. 'We spooked them.'

God only knew what they'd got up to: I hadn't stayed around to watch. With my arms filled with gift-wrapped scented candles—everyone bar none had given me one as a birthday present—I'd peeled away quietly, light-headed with gratitude at escaping a big 'the bereaved woman is leaving early' scene.

It was too soon to ring anyone to find out what I'd missed so I went back to sleep—a rare, rare event (I might try these hangovers more often)—and when I woke again I felt better. I switched on the computer. Incoming email from Mum.

To: Magiciansgirl1@yahoo.com
From: Thewalshes1@eircom.net
Subject: Many Happy Returns of the day!

Dear Anna,
 I hope you are keeping well and enjoyed your birthday 'celebration'. I am remembering this time thirty-three years ago. Another girl, we said. We wish you were here. We had a cake in your honour. A chocolate Victoria Sandwich. There was a sale of work for the upkeep of the Protestant church and, although I don't like to encourage them, I cannot deny they are 'dab hands' at cake-making 'et al'.
 Your loving mother,
 Mum

PS If you see Rachel, will you tell her that none of my sisters—NONE of them—have heard of sugar-snap peas.
PPS Is it true that Joey fancies Jacqui? A little bird (Luke) tells me there was a bit of a 'vrizzon' at your birthday party last night. Is it true that Joey stole one of her Scrabble A's and put it down his pants and told her that if she wanted it back she knew where to find it? I didn't know if Luke was just 'having me on'.
PPPS Was it just in his trousers pants or in his underpants pants?

Oh my God. Aidan, what did we miss?
I sat staring at the screen and after a while I rang Rachel.
'Mum's sent me an email.'
'Oh, yes? If this is to do with sugar-snap peas—'
'No. About Joey and—'
'Joey was outrageous! He kept writing words like "sex" and "hot" on the board, then looking meaningfully at Jacqui. Since when did he start fancying her?'
'I don't know. I haven't a clue! It's too weird. Mum says he put one of Jacqui's A's down his jocks.'
'No, he didn't.'
'So why did she think—?'
'It was one of her J's. Which is worth eight points.'
'And what happened?'

'He told her that if she wanted it back, she knew what she had to do. So all credit to her, she rolled up her sleeve, fished around and got it back out again.'

To: Thewalshes1@eircom.net
From: Magiciansgirl1@yahoo.com
Subject: Scrabble down the pants?

No, Joey did not steal one of Jacqui's Scrabble A's and put it down his pants and tell her that if she wanted it back, she knew where to find it. He stole one of her Scrabble Js and put it down his pants and told her that if she wanted it back, she knew where to find it.
    Love,
    Anna

PS It was his underpants pants, not just his trousers pants, and she did retrieve it.

To: Magiciansgirl1@yahoo.com
From: Thewalshes1@eircom.net
Subject: Re: Scrabble down the pants?

Your father is upset. He read your last email by mistake, thinking it was for him. (Although who ever writes to him?) He says he'll never be able to look Jacqui in the eye again. He is not himself, what with this weather and all this dog business.
    Your loving mother,
    Mum

PS So she actually delved in and got it back out? She's tougher than she looks, so she is. I'd be able for it, as in 'a former life' I was used to handling turkey 'giblets', but not everyone would have the stomach for it.
PPS I have thought of a 'pun'. Jacqui 'scrabbled' around in Joey's jocks.

I reached for the phone. I *had* to talk to Jacqui. This was unbelievable—her and Joey? But her machine picked up. The frustration!

'Where are you? In bed with Joey? Surely to God not? Ring me!'

I left the same message on her cellphone, and paced around, chewing my nails, trying to kill time. Which was when I made a discovery—I had ten nails to chew. Somehow, while I hadn't been paying attention, the two missing ones had grown back.

At five past five in the afternoon, Jacqui finally surfaced.

'Where are you?' I asked.

'In bed.' She sounded sleepy and sexy.

'Whose bed?'

'Mine.'

'Are you alone?'

She laughed, then said, 'Yeah.'

'Have you been alone all night?'

'Yes.'

'And all day?'

'Yes.'

Casually, I said, 'Last night was fun?'

'Yeah.'

Then super-*super*-casually, I said, 'Have you ever thought Joey looks a bit like Jon Bon Jovi?' To which she roared with laughter.

But, interestingly, didn't reply.

'I'm coming over to you,' she said.

Wearing white cut-offs (Donna Karan), a tiny white T-shirt (Armani), displaying long, tanned legs and arms, and with an aqua metallic Balenciaga bag slung over her shoulder, she arrived. Her hair was tangled and bed-heady and her mascara and eye-stuff was smudged so that her eyes were dark and come-hither. She looked, if it's possible, like a really sexy ironing-board.

I told her as much. Because if I didn't say it, she would.

She shrugged off my praise. 'I look OK in clothes but when you see me in my bra and knickers for the first time, you might get a bit of a fright.'

'Who's going to be seeing you in your bra and knickers for the first time?'

'No one.'

'No one at all?'

'No.'

'OK. Let's go for a pizza.'

'Great idea.' Little hesitation. 'But first I've got to drop by Rachel and Luke's. I left something there last night.'

I stared at her steadily. 'What? Your sanity?'

'No.' She sounded a little annoyed. 'My cellphone.'

I murmured an apology.

But when we arrived at Rachel and Luke's, lo and behold, who happened to be sprawled on their sofa, moodily kicking the brick wall with his boots? Only Joey.

'Did you know he was going to be here?' I asked Jacqui.

'No.'

At the sight of Jacqui, Joey sat bolt upright and agitatedly brushed his hair back. 'Hey! Jacqui! You left your cellphone here last night. I called you. Did you get my message? I said I'd swing by with it.'

I looked at Jacqui. So she *had* known he was here. But she wouldn't look at me.

'Here it is.' Joey leapt up and retrieved it from a shelf.

It was quite entertaining, seeing him trying to be nice.

'Thanks.' Jacqui took the phone and barely looked at Joey. 'Anna and I are going for a pizza. Everyone's welcome to join us.'

'And after the pizza,' I asked, 'will we be playing Scrabble?'

At the word 'Scrabble', something funny happened, as if there had been a power surge in the room. Between Jacqui and Joey there was a vrizzon, a definite vrizzon.

'No Scrabble tonight,' Rachel said, dousing the mood. 'I need my sleep.'

'**A**idan? The spiritual place? Should I go today?'

No voice answered. Nothing happened. He just continued to smile from the photo frame, frozen in a long-ago moment.

'OK,' I said. 'Let's do a deal.' I tore out a page from a magazine and scrunched it up. 'I'll throw this ball of paper at the bin over there and if I miss, I'll stay at home. If I get it in, I'll go.'

I closed my eyes and threw, then opened them to see the scrunched-up page lying in the bottom of the bin.

'Right,' I said. 'Looks like you want me to go.'

When I got there, Nicholas was already waiting in the corridor. This week his T-shirt said DOG IS MY CO-PILOT. He was reading a book. Gradually, all the regulars arrived and we all went into the room: Leisl started. Great-Aunt Morag came through for Mackenzie and reiterated that there wasn't a will. Nicholas's dad advised him on his job—he seemed like such a nice man, he really did. So concerned. Pomadey Juan's wife told him to eat properly.

By the end of the hour, once again no one had come through for me but, still on a high from my Neris Hemming contact, I didn't mind.

I said goodbye to everyone and went towards the elevator, joining forces with some of the belly-dancing posse; then behind me someone called my name. I turned round: it was Mitch.

'Hey, Anna, do you have to be someplace now?'

I shook my head.

'Want to do something?'

'Like what?'

'I dunno. Get a coffee?'

'I don't want to get a coffee,' I said. It had started to make me feel nauseous. I feared I was going to have to start drinking herbal teas and run the risk of turning into one of those aggressively calm people who drink peppermint and camomile infusions. 'Let's go to the zoo.' I had no idea why I'd said this.

'The zoo?'

'Yes.'

'The place with animals?'

'Yes. There's one in Central Park.'

'OK.'

The zoo was busy, with loved-up couples twined around each other and straggling family groups with strollers and toddlers and ice creams. We started with the Rainforest which was mostly monkeys. There was quite a selection—winging from trees and scratching themselves and staring grumpily at nothing.

As we watched, one with a bright red bottom fell off a branch and two more came along to taunt and make high-pitched laughing sounds, which pleased the crowd enormously. They surged forward with their cameras and I got separated from Mitch. It was only when I was looking around for him that I discovered I didn't really know what he looked like.

'I'm over here,' I heard him say and I turned and found myself looking into those bleak eyes. I tried to file a couple of other details about him: he had very short hair and a dark blue T-shirt, and he was a bit older than me, late thirties probably.

'We move on?' he asked.

Suited me. I didn't have the concentration span to linger on anything. We found ourselves in the Polar Circle.

'Trish loved polar bears,' he said, 'even though I kept telling her they were vicious guys.' He stared at them. 'Cute-looking, though. What's your favourite animal?'

He caught me on the hop; I wasn't sure I even had a favourite animal.

'Penguins,' I said. They'd do. 'I mean, they try so hard. It must be tough being a penguin—you can't fly, you can barely walk.'

'But you can swim.'

'Oh, yes. You know, I'd forgotten that.'

'What was Aidan's favourite animal?'

'Elephants. But there are no elephants here. You have to go to the Bronx for that.'

We arrived at the sea lions' pool just as feeding-time was about to begin. A large crowd of people, mostly family groups, were waiting, the air electric with anticipation.

When three men in Wellingtons and red overalls appeared with buckets of fish, the atmosphere became almost hysterical. 'Here they come, here they come!' Bodies pushed towards the barrier, the air filled with the clicks of a hundred cameras and children were lifted up for a better look. 'There's one, there's one!'

An enormous, shiny, grey-black force erupted out of the water, stretching up for his fish, then bellyflopped back into the pool, sending a huge wash across to the sides. Mitch and I watch impassively, like we were cardboard cut-outs of ourselves.

We waited until the fourth sea lion had eaten a fish, then Mitch looked at me. 'Keep moving?'

'Sure.'

We walked away from the people who were still starry-eyed and in thrall.

'What's next?' he asked.

I consulted our map. It was penguins. I'd have to pretend that I was thrilled to see them. I enthused as best I could, then Mitch suggested we walk on. We'd spoken very little. I wasn't uncomfortable with it, but I knew next to nothing about him, except that his wife had died.

'Do you have a job?' I asked. It came out a bit bald.

'Yeah,' he said. 'I design and install home-entertainment systems. I can tell you more if you want to hear it. It's kinda technical.'

'No, it's OK, thank you—I couldn't pay attention long enough to understand. Hey, we've missed the Temperate Territory—butterflies, snow monkeys, red pandas, ducks.'

'Ducks?'

'Yes, ducks. We can't possibly miss them. Come on.'

We retraced our steps, halfheartedly admired the Temperate Territory animals, and suddenly things started to look familiar; we were back where we started.

'Is that it?' Mitch asked. 'Are we done?' Like it was a chore.

'Looks like it.'

'OK, I'm going to hit the gym.' He shouldered his kitbag. 'See you next Sunday?'

'OK.'

I waited until he was good and gone. Even though I'd spent the last couple of hours with him, I was suffering from fear of the False Goodbye Syndrome: when you don't know someone that well, and then you unexpectedly bump into each other a few minutes later, at the bus stop or the subway station or trying to hail a cab. I don't know why but it's always mortifying and the easy conversation that you'd been having only a few minutes earlier has dissipated entirely and the mood is tense and strained.

Then when the train or taxi or bus comes, you say goodbye once more and you try to make a laugh of it by saying gaily, 'Goodbye, *again*,' but it's nothing like as nice as the previous time and you feel as if you've ended on a bad note. Like a soufflé, a goodbye can't be reheated.

While I waited until it was super-safe to leave, I wondered about Mitch. What had he been like before? What would he be like in the future? I knew I wasn't seeing the real him; at the moment all he was was his bereavement. Like me.

I looked at my watch. Mitch had been gone ten minutes. I could chance it. On the street, I did a few furtive look-arounds and there was no sign of him. I hailed a cab and when I reached my apartment I was feeling quite good. That was most of Sunday taken care of.

That night I got an email from Helen:

To: Magiciansgirl1@yahoo.com
From: Lucky_Star_PI@yahoo.ie
Subject: Tedi-arse

Another break in routine! Detta had lunch in restaurant with 'the girls': three other women, all about same age as her, maybe also married to crime lords? Chanel handbags, really war-crime quilted ones with gold chain handles. Again, had to hang around in street like homeless person, watching through window, and this time someone tried to buy methadone from me. No sign of Racey O'Grady, though.

On way out, banshee shrieks of laughter, but not from Detta. Smiling absently and sort of staring into space. Took couple of pics on mobile, in case they're of any interest to Harry Big. This is so boring, but I'll tell you something, Anna, am getting paid bloody fortune.

A week later, all the gang were there, sitting in a line on the benches in the corridor. Very quickly, the spiritualist church place had become part of my Sunday routine. I liked the people who went; they were very kind, and to them I wasn't Anna with her Catastrophe—well, maybe I was—but they'd all had catastrophes too. I was no different.

Nicholas saw me. 'Cool! Here's Miss Annie.' Today, his T-shirt said WINONA IS INNOCENT.

Mitch was slouched back against the wall and he shifted forward to get a look at me. 'Hey, peanut.' He stretched out his leg to touch me with his foot. 'How was your week?'

'Oh, you know,' I said. 'How was yours?'

"Bout the same.'

We took our places in the circle of chairs, the cello groaning started up and several people got messages, but yet again nothing for me.

Then Leisl slowly said, 'Anna . . . I'm seeing the little blond boy again. I'm getting the initial J. He really wants to talk to you.'

'But he's alive! He can talk to me any time he wants!'

Afterwards, I cornered Leisl. 'Why would I be getting messages from my nephew, who's still alive? And not from Aidan?'

'I can't answer that, Anna.' Her eyes, underneath her frizzy fringe, were so kind.

'There isn't some sort of waiting period after someone has died before they start being channelled, is there?'

'Not that I know of,' she said. 'Have you tried EVP? Electronic voice phenomenon?'

'What's that?'

'Recording the voices of the dead.'

'If this is a joke . . .'

'Not a joke!' All the others knew about EVP. A flurry of voices said, 'That's a good idea, Anna. You should try it.'

Defensively, I asked, 'How do you do it?'

'You need a quiet room,' Leisl said. 'And a regular tape recorder. Use a new tape. Set it to record, leave the room, come back one hour later and pick up your messages!'

'It's got to be done after sunset on the night of a full moon,' Mackenzie said.

'Preferably during a thunderstorm,' said Nicholas, 'because of the gravitational effect.'

'Nicholas, I'm really in no mood for any of your bonkers beliefs.'

'No,' several voices insisted. 'It's not one of his bonkers beliefs!'

'There's actually a scientific basis for this,' Nicholas said. 'The dead live in etheric wavelengths which operate at much higher frequencies than ours. So we can hear them on tape when we can't hear them talking directly to us.'

'Have you tried it? Has your dad spoken to you?'

'Oh, sure. It was kinda hard to hear him, though. You might have to speed the tape up or slow it down a lot when you're listening back. I'll email you all the instructions,' Nicholas said.

I asked Mitch, 'Have you tried it?'

'No, but only because I spoke to Trish via Neris Hemming.'

'When's the next full moon?' Mackenzie asked.

'Just missed it,' Nicholas said. 'But there's another in less than four weeks. You can do it then.'

'OK. Thanks. See you all next week.'

I started walking away, wondering if Mitch would follow.

He caught me up before I reached the elevator. 'Hey, Anna, do you have to be someplace now?'

'No.'

'Wanna do something?'

'Like what?' I was interested to see what he came up with.

'How about the Museum of Modern Art?'

Why not. Being with Mitch had many of the advantages of being alone, but without the actual aloneness. Speedily, we moved from painting to painting and we barely spoke. At times we were even in different rooms, but were linked by an invisible thread.

When we'd seen everything, Mitch checked his watch.

'Look at that!' He sounded pleased and almost smiled. 'That took two hours. The day is nearly done. Have a good week, Anna. See you next Sunday.'

6

A COUPLE OF NIGHTS LATER, by accident, I saw Neris Hemming on telly! It was a profile, a half-hour special. Probably in her late thirties, with shoulder-length bubble curls and wearing a blue pinafore dress, she was curled in an armchair, talking to an invisible interviewer.

'I was always able to see and hear "other" people,' she said, in a soft voice. 'I always had friends that no one else could see. And I knew that stuff was going to happen before it did, you know? My mom used to get so mad at me.'

'But something happened to change your mom's mind,' the invisible interviewer prompted. 'Can you tell us about it?'

Neris closed her eyes in order to remember. 'It was an ordinary morning. I'd just gotten out of the shower and was drying myself off with my towel when everything went sort of misty and I wasn't in my bathroom any more. I was in a different place. I was in the open air, on a highway. I could see and feel the hot tar under my feet. About thirty feet away from me, a huge truck was on fire and the heat was intense. Lots of cars were on fire too and the worst bit was that bodies were scattered on the highway. It was horrible. And suddenly I was back in my bathroom again, still holding my towel.

'I didn't know what was happening to me. I thought I was losing my mind. I was so scared. I called up my mom and told her what I'd experienced and she was real worried.'

'She didn't believe you?'

'No way! She thought I was cracking up. She wanted to get me to the hospital. Later, that evening, I turned on the TV. The news channel had a report on a horrible accident that had just happened on the interstate and it was totally what I'd seen. A big truck carrying chemicals had exploded, other cars had caught on fire, a bunch of people were dead . . . I couldn't believe it. Next thing the phone rings. It was my mom, and she said, "Neris, we've got to talk."'

I knew all of this, I'd read it in her books, but it was fascinating to hear it from her own mouth.

I also knew what happened next. Her mom decided to stop telling her she was a nutjob and instead started booking gigs for her. All her family worked for her now.

'People tell me that they'd love to be psychic,' Neris said. 'But, you know what, it's a tough road. I call it a blessed curse.'

Then the screen cut to coverage of one of her live shows. Neris was standing on a huge stage, just her, looking very little. 'I have a . . . I'm getting something for . . . do we have someone here tonight called Vanessa?'

A camera panned over rows and rows of audience and, somewhere near the back, a heavy-set lady put her hand up and got to her feet. She mouthed something and Neris said, 'Wait a minute, honey, until the mic gets to you.'

A runner was pushing her way between the seats. When the heavy-set woman was holding the mic, Neris said, 'Can you tell us your name? You're Vanessa?'

'I'm Vanessa.'

'Vanessa, Scottie wants to say hi to you. Does that mean anything?'

Tears started to pour down Vanessa's face and she mumbled something.

'Say again, honey.'

'He was my son.'

'That's right, honey, and he wants you to know he didn't suffer.' Neris put her hand to her ear and said, 'He's telling me to tell you, you were right about the bike. Mean anything?'

'Yeah.' Vanessa's head was bowed. 'I told him he drove that thing too fast.'

'Well, he knows that now. He's telling me to say, Mom, you were right. So, Mom, you get the last word here.'

Somehow, Vanessa was smiling through her tears.

Back to Neris in the armchair, and she was saying, 'The people who come to my shows, nearly all of them are looking to hear from their loved ones who have passed over. These folks are in bad psychic pain and I have a responsibility to them. But sometimes,' and she gave a little laugh here, 'if lots of spirit voices are all trying to get through at the same time, I have to say, "Calm down, guys. Take a ticket, get in line!"'

I was mesmerised. She made it all sound so ordinary, so possible. And I was touched by her humility. If anyone could put me in contact with Aidan, it was this woman.

Impulsively, I rang Jacqui. 'How's Narky Joey?' I asked.

'Oh, fine, fine. I can look at him, acknowledge that he does bear a resemblance to Jon Bon Jovi, but I don't fancy him in the slightest.'

'Thank God!' Suddenly, I got a mad rush of fondness and really wanted to see her. 'Would you like to do something later?' I asked. 'Watch a video or something?'

'Oh, I can't tonight.'

I waited for her to tell me why she couldn't. When she didn't, I said. 'What are you doing?'

'Playing poker.'

'Poker?'

'Yeah.'

'Where?'

'Gaz's apartment.'

'Gaz's apartment? You mean Gaz *and Joey's* apartment?'

Grudgingly, she conceded that yes, she supposed Joey did share an apartment with Gaz.

'Well, can I come?' I asked.

I mean, I thought she'd be delighted. She'd been badgering me for months to get out more.

The things was, though, that Gaz wasn't there. Only Joey was in and he didn't look one bit happy to see me. I mean, he never did. But this was a different sort of displeasure.

'Where's Gaz?' I asked.

'Out.'

I looked at Jacqui but she wouldn't meet my eyes.

'The place looks lovely,' I said. 'Beautiful candles. Ylang-ylang, I see—*very* sensual. And what are those flowers called?'

'Birds of paradise,' Joey mumbled.

'Gorgeous. Can I have one of these strawberries?'

Narky pause. 'Go ahead.'

'Delicious! Ripe and juicy. Try one, Jacqui. Come here, let me feed one to you. What's this scarf for, Joey? Is it a *blindfold*?'

He made some angry I-haven't-a-clue gesture.

'Look, I'm off,' I said.

'Stay,' Jacqui said. She looked at Joey. 'We're only playing poker.'

'Yeah, stay,' Joey said, about as halfheartedly as anyone could.

'Please stay,' Jacqui said. 'Really, Anna, it's great to see you out and about.'

'But . . . are you sure?'

'Yes.'

'Maybe I should. Like, can you even *play* poker with just two people?'

'Well, there's three of us now,' Joey said sourly.

'True. Although do you mind if we don't play poker?' I asked. 'I just don't get it. Let's play a proper game. Let's play rummy.'

After a long silence, Joey said, 'Rummy it is.'

We sat at the table and Joey flung seven cards at each of us. I bowed my head and stared hard. Then I asked, 'Would it be OK if we turned on a light? It's just I can't see my cards.'

With short, jerky movements, Joey leapt up, hit a switch with venom and threw himself back into his chair.

'Thank you,' I murmured. In the brightness of the overhead light, all the flowers and candles and strawberries and chocolates suddenly looked a little shamefaced.

'I suppose you want the music off too so you can concentrate,' he said.

'No, I *like* Ravel's *Boléro*, actually.'

I was sorry to be ruining the seduction scene but I hadn't realised I'd be intruding. Jacqui had more or less said that Gaz would be there. And both she and Joey had insisted that I stay, even though neither of them had meant it.

I looked up from my—admittedly excellent—hand of cards and caught Joey openly watching Jacqui. He was like a cat with a fluff-ball, he was mesmerised. She was harder to read; she wasn't staring at him the way he was at her, but she wasn't her usual outgoing self. And her mind certainly wasn't on her cards because I kept winning. 'Rummy!' I said gleefully, the first couple of times. Then it got embarrassing, then a little boring.

As an evening it was not a success and it drew to an early close.

'At least poor Gaz can come home from wherever Joey banished him to,' I said, as Jacqui and I waited for the elevator.

'We're just friends,' she said, defensively.

To: Magiciansgirl1@yahoo.com
From: Lucky_Star_Pl@yahoo.ie
Subject: Great news

Two weeks off from Detta Big. She's going to Marbella with 'the girls' (collective age three thousand and seven if that crowd I saw her having lunch with are anything to go by). But I'm not off the hook. I have to keep an eye on Racey O'Grady. Make sure he stays in the country.

To: Magiciansgirl1@yahoo.com
From: Thewalshes1@eircom.net
Subject: Photos!

Dear Anna,
   I hope you are keeping well. Well, finally we have photos of the woman and Zoë the dog! Helen is a good girl and hid in the hedge and 'fired off a roll'. She wanted to shout, 'We're on to you, Missis,' but I told her not to.
   I will be taking the best pictures to Mass next Sunday and will ask people if they recognise either the woman or Zoë. God help poor Zoë, it's not her fault, dogs have no sense of right and wrong. Human beings have a conscience, that's what separates us from the animals. Although Helen says the difference is that animals can't wear high heels. Either way, I must admit the whole business has me baffled. Obviously, the old woman has some sort of 'grudge' against us.
   Your loving mother,
   Mum

To: Magiciansgirl1@yahoo.com
From: Lucky_Star_Pl@yahoo.ie
Subject: Racey O'Grady

Racey O'Grady lives in Dalkey, respectable neighbourhood.
Surprised. Thought all crime lords would live near each other, so they could pop in and out of each other's houses all day, borrowing cups of bullets and saying they had to nip down to shops for minute, so would

other person keep an eye on their hostage, and so on. Racey—vay keen on privacy—big house, electronic gates, high walls, spikes on top.

I parked down road and not one person went in or out all day. Then at five o'clock the gates opened and out comes Racey. Looks well in flesh. Tanned, bright blue eyes, pep in step. Far, far better than Mr Big.

He was carrying kitbag. I was convinced it was full of saws, pliers and other torture tools, but he was just going to gym. Followed him (on foot) to Killiney Castle health club where they wouldn't let me in because I wasn't member so I said was thinking of becoming member and would they give me tour. OK, they said, and when they showed me the gym there was Racey, his blue veiny legs going hell for leather on the stairmaster. Innocence itself. Ages later he left, I followed him back, sat in car for another hour, then thought, Fuck this for a game of skittles, he's obviously not going to Marbella this evening, I'm going home.

On the train, Mitch and I rocked shoulder to shoulder in silence. We were returning from Coney Island amusement park, where we'd partaken of the rides a little too grimly. But that was fine. We weren't there to enjoy ourselves, simply to pass the time.

The train rounded a particularly sharp corner and we both nearly fell out of our seats. When we'd straightened up again, I suddenly asked, 'What were you like before?'

'Before . . .?'

'Yes, what kind of person were you?'

'What am I like now?'

'Very quiet. you don't say much.'

'I guess I talked more.' He thought about it. 'Yeah, conversations. I had opinions, I liked to talk. A lot.' He sounded surprised. 'Issues of the day, movies, whatever.'

'Did you smile?'

'I don't smile now? OK. Yeah, I smiled. And laughed. What were you like?'

'I don't know. Happier. Sunnier. Hopeful. Not terrified. I liked being around people.'

We sighed and lapsed back into silence.

Eventually, I spoke. 'Do you think we'll ever go back to being who we were?'

He thought about it. 'I don't want to. It would be like Trish had never happened.'

'I know what you mean. But, Mitch, are we going to be like this, for ever?'

'Like what?'

'Like . . . *ghosts*? Like we died too, but someone forgot to tell us.'
'We'll get better.' After a pause, he added, 'We'll be better but different.'
'How do you know?'
He smiled. 'Because I know.'
'OK.'
'Did you notice I smiled just there?'
'Did you? Do it again.'
He arranged his face in an ultra-brite smile. 'How's that?'
'A bit game-show host. *Wheel of Fortune*.'
'Practice. That's all I need.'

To: Magiciansgirl1@yahoo.com
From: Thewalshes1@eircom.net
Subject: Latest update

No one at Mass recognised the old woman in the photo. I am going to bring it to golf and bridge and if I still don't get a 'result' I am going to ring RTE and see if I can get it on *Crimewatch*. Or *Crimeline*. Or *Crimetime*. Or whatever they're calling it these days. Can you think of any more?
   Your loving mother,
   Mum

7

ALL SET FOR TONIGHT?' Nicholas asked. 'The full moon?'
   'Yes,' I said, quietly, bringing the phone close to my face. I was at work and although it was unlikely that anyone would guess that I was discussing recording my dead husband's voice, I wasn't taking any chances.
   'You know not to start until after sunset?'
   'Yes. I know everything.' Nicholas had emailed me a vast quantity of information on electronic voice phenomenon.
   'Well, take this to the bank! Weather channel says there's an eighty per cent chance of thunderstorms this afternoon. That's going to totally up the chances of Aidan talking to you.'
   'Really?' My insides clenched with excitement.

'Yes, really. Good luck. Call me.'

I was agitated and fidgety. I couldn't work, all I could do was pace and stare out of the window. Late afternoon, the sky got darker and darker and I willed it on, and when the first rumble of thunder rolled over Manhattan I let out a sigh of relief. Seconds later the sky cracked with lightning and the heavens opened. Listening to the hiss of torrential rain drenching the city, I was trembling with anticipation. When my phone rang, I could barely talk. 'Candy Grrrl publicity. Anna Walsh speaking.'

It was Nicholas again. 'Can you believe it?' he exclaimed.

'A full moon *and* a thunderstorm,' I said numbly. 'What are the chances of the two happening together?'

The next phone call was from Mitch. 'Good luck tonight.'

'Can you believe the two happening together?' I asked.

'No. It's got to be a sign. Call me later if you want to talk.'

Every cab and car service in Manhattan had been commandeered and I got drenched running from the subway to my apartment. I was elated. I paced the floor, drying my hair with a towel and wondering what time could be officially considered 'after sunset'. The sun might have been scared off by the thunder and lightning but mightn't have actually *set*.

Waiting to talk to Aidan was killing me but I forced myself to hold out until after ten; under normal non-stormy circumstances, the sun would have definitely set by then.

I put the tape recorder in the bedroom because it was far quieter than the front room, which faced onto the street. The rumbles of thunder had stopped but the rain was still tumbling from the sky. I took a deep breath and spoke into the mic. 'Aidan, please talk to me. I'm . . . um . . . going to leave for a while, and when I come back I'm really hoping to hear a message from you.'

Then I tiptoed out and sat in the front room, jiggling my foot, watching the clock. I'd give it an hour.

When the time was up, I tiptoed back in; the tape had come to an end. I rewound it, then hit PLAY, all the time praying, *Please, Aidan, please, Aidan, please have left a message.*

I jumped when I heard my own voice at the start, but after that came nothing. My ears were straining to hear anything, anything at all. But all there was was the hiss of silence.

Suddenly, a high-pitched shriek came from the tape; faint, but definitely audible. I recoiled with fright. Oh my God. Oh my God, was that Aidan? Why had he screamed?

My heart was thumping as fast as an express train. I put my ear close to the speaker; there were other sounds too. A muzzy jumble, but undeniably the sound of a voice. I caught a word that might have been 'men' then a ghostly 'oooooooh'.

I couldn't believe it. It was happening. Aidan had contacted me. All I had to do was listen hard enough to hear what he had to say. *Thank you, sweetheart. Oh, thank you, thank you, thank you.* Every one of my muscles tensed, desperate to hear something that made sense. I was still getting only a sound or a word here and there when, out of nowhere, I caught an entire sentence. There was no doubt as to what it was. I heard each word with crystal clarity.

It was, 'Ab-so-lut-lee sooooaaak-ing WET!'

It was Ornesto. Upstairs. Singing 'It's Raining Men'. As soon as I knew what it was, all the other muzzy sounds instantly fell into place.

For a moment I felt nothing. Nothing at all.

I sat in the dark room for I couldn't tell you how long, then I went through to the living room and automatically switched on the telly.

To: Psychic_Productions@yahoo.com
From: Magiciansgirl1@yahoo.com
Subject: Neris Hemming

I contacted you on July 6 so that I could speak to my husband, Aidan, who died. You confirmed that I would have an appointment with Neris Hemming in ten to twelve weeks. It has been over five weeks and I was wondering if it would be possible to have my appointment moved to an earlier date? Or even if you could tell me what date it'll be on, it would probably make things a little easier to bear.
   Thank you in advance for your help,
   Anna Walsh

To: Magiciansgirl1@yahoo.com
From: Psychic_Productions@yahoo.com
Subject: Re: Neris Hemming

It is not possible to move your appointment to an earlier date. At the moment it is not possible to confirm your appointment date. You will be contacted approximately two weeks before the date. Thank you for your interest in Neris Hemming.

'Let's do something on Saturday night,' Jacqui suggested.
   'What? No two-personed poker matches lined up?'
   'Stop.' She giggled.
   'You just giggled.'

'No, I didn't.'

'Jacqui, you did.'

She thought about it. 'Shit. Anyway, let's do something on Saturday night.'

'Can't. I'm doing Super Saturday in the Hamptons.'

'Oh! You lucky, lucky bitch.'

That's what everyone said when they heard I was going.

'The dirt-cheap designer clothes!' Jacqui said. 'The freebies! The parties afterwards!'

But I was working at it. *Working.* And it was very different when you were working.

In the Friday-afternoon haze, Teenie and I sat on the Long Island Expressway in bumper-to-bumper traffic. The car was crammed with boxes and boxes of products. We had to bring it all ourselves because if we trusted it to couriers there was a very real chance that it wouldn't arrive on time.

It was after nine by the time we got to the Harbor Inn. First, we had to check Candace and George's suite, to ensure that it was sufficiently fabulous and that champagne, a fruit basket, exotic flowers and handmade chocolates were awaiting their arrival. Then Teenie and I had a late dinner and retired for a few hours' sleep.

The following morning we were at the exhibition centre by seven. Shortly after seven thirty Brooke arrived; she'd been in the neighbourhood since Wednesday, staying with her parents in their mansion.

'Hey, you guys!' she said. 'How can I help?'

Funnily enough, she meant it. Within seconds she was balanced on a stepladder, suspending the six-foot-by-ten-foot backdrops from the ceiling. Then she figured out how to click together the separate pieces of the black lacquer display table. Say what you like about rich people with a sense of entitlement, but Brooke is extaordinarily practical and obliging.

Meanwhile, Teenie and I were unpacking box after box of products. We were promoting Protection Racket, our new sun-cream range. It came in what looked like old-fashioned perfume bottles. The highest protection factor, thirty, was a deep burgundy colour and the range went through several progressively lighter pinks, down to the lowest factor—four—in baby pink. They were gorgeous.

We also had hundreds of Candy Grrrl T-shirts and beach-bags to give away, countless goody bags of trial sizes, plus every item of cosmetics we carried, for Candace to do her make-overs.

Just as we'd got the last lip gloss slotted into place on the display table, Lauryn arrived.

'Hey,' she said, her poppy eyes moving in a restless quest to find something to criticise. Disappointed, she could find nothing wrong.

By ten o'clock, the place was thronged. There was a lot of interest in Protection Racket but the question everyone asked was, 'Will it make my skin look pink?'

'Oh, no,' we said, again and again and again. 'The colour disappears on the skin. The colour disappears on the skin.'

Trade was brisk in the giveaway beach-bags (not so brisk in the T-shirts, but never mind) and all three of us conducted dozens of mini-consultations: skin type, favourite colours etc., before pressing a load of suitable trial sizes on the woman in question.

We were smiling, smiling, smiling and I was getting a horrible crampy feeling in my mouth, when Teenie said, 'Shit! It's nearly twelve. Where's the line of women crazy to meet Candace?'

Candace was due at noon. We had advertised in the local press and it had been announced every fifteen minutes on the tannoy system, but so far no one had shown.

'We gotta start badgering people,' Teenie said. She loved the word 'badger'. 'If we don't have a long line, our ass is grass.'

'It's OK. Here they come.'

I looked. Four women were approaching the stand. But, instinctively, I knew they hadn't come for a Candy Grrrl make-over. They all had excellent cheekbones, jaw-length bobs and were dressed in sun-bleached shades of stone and sand. They looked like they'd stepped straight out of a Ralph Lauren ad and they turned out to be Brooke's mother, Brooke's two older sisters and Brooke's sister-in-law.

Then, through the crowds, I saw someone I knew, but for a moment I couldn't remember where I knew her from. Then it clicked: it was Mackenzie! Wearing faded blue jeans and a white shirt, quite different from the glam rig-outs she'd worn to the spiritualist place every Sunday, but definitely her. I hadn't seen her for three or four weeks now.

'Anna!' she said. 'You look adorable! All that pink!'

It was strange, I barely knew her, but she felt like my long-lost sister. I flung myself into her arms and we hugged tightly.

Naturally, being posh, Mackenzie knew Brooke's family, the Edisons, so there was a flurry of kisses and enquiries after parents and uncles.

'How do you two guys know each other?' Lauryn asked. She had suddenly reappeared and her eyes were bulging with suspicion and roving from me to Mackenzie.

Mackenzie's eyes flashed a desperate signal. *Don't tell them, please don't tell them.*

Don't worry, I flashed back. *I'm saying nothing.*

We were saved from a mortifying 'How do we know each other, Anna?' 'I don't know, Mackenzie, how *do* we know each other?' schtick by the arrival of Queen Candace and King George.

Candace—dressed in downbeat black—thought the Edison women and Mackenzie were the crowd waiting to be made over by her.

'Well, hey,' she almost smiled. 'Better get started.' She picked the obvious Alpha female and extended her hand. 'Candace Biggly.'

'Martha Edison.'

'Well, Martha, would you care to take a seat for your make-over?' Candace indicated the silver and pink vinyl stool. 'You other ladies will just have to wait.'

'Make-over?' Mrs Edison sounded aghast. 'But I only use soap and water on my skin.'

Confused, Candace looked at an Edison sister, then at another one, then at the sister-in-law.

'Soap and water,' they parroted, shrinking away. 'Yes, soap and water. Bye, Brooke, see you at the Save the Moose picnic.'

'Mackenzie,' I said brightly. 'How about you?'

'Hey, why not?' Obligingly, she got up on the stool and introduced herself to Candace as 'Mackenzie McIntyre Hamilton'.

George said to Candace, 'OK, babes, seeing as you're all set, I'll just take a stroll.'

'Start rounding up a crowd,' Lauryn hissed.

But it proved impossible: a high proportion of passers-by were planning to attend the Save the Moose picnic and didn't want to look over-made-up for it.

Candace strung out Mackenzie's make-over for as long as possible, but finally Mackenzie descended from the stool and I cornered her.

'Will I see you soon?' I asked, without moving my lips.

She shook her head. 'I don't think so,' she said very, very quietly. 'I'm trying something different.'

'The rich-husband route?'

'Yeah. But I miss you guys. How's Nicholas?'

'Um, good.'

'What did his T-shirt say last week?'

'Jimmy Carter for President.'

She laughed out loud. 'Vintage. God, he's just adorable. A little cutie. Is it just me or is he kinda . . . *hot*?'

'I'm not really the person to ask.'

'Sure. Sorry.' She sighed, quite sadly. 'Well, tell Nicholas I said hey. Tell everyone I said hey.'

She left and I resumed my badgering of the crowd. Still no takers, which was bad enough, but then someone said, 'I totally broke out when I tried Candy Grrrl's day-cream,' and—horror of horrors—Candace heard.

She dashed down her blusher brush and said, 'I've got better things to do with my time than try the hard sell on these assholes. I've got an annual turnover of thirty-four million dollars.'

I feared client melt-down. Anxiously, I looked around for George. Lauryn, naturally, had also disappeared.

'I want ice cream,' Candace said petulantly.

'I'll go and get you some. Teenie and Brooke will stay with you.'

'I'm sorry, but I have to leave now,' Brooke said. 'I've pledged to sell raffle tickets at the moose benefit.'

'OK, well, thanks, Brooke, you've been a total star today.'

I dived into the throng, desperately seeking ice cream. Fifteen frustrating minutes later I returned, triumphantly bearing an Eskimo bar and three other assorted ice creams.

Grumpily, Candace accepted the Eskimo bar and sat slumped on the high stool, her chin on her chest, tucking in.

This was the moment, of course, that Ariella, visiting friends in East Hampton for the weekend, did a drop-by. It didn't look good. Mercifully, Ariella couldn't linger. She was on her way to the Save the Caribou cook-out.

'Is that different to the Save the Moose picnic?' Teenie asked.

'Totally,' she snapped.

Then they were all gone and it was just Teenie and me.

'So what's up with the moose anyway?' Teenie asked. 'I didn't even know it was endangered. Or the caribou.'

I shrugged. 'Maybe they've run out of stuff to save.'

'**A**nna, it's me, you're mother. It's urgent—'

I grabbed the phone. Something was wrong with someone. Dad? JJ?

'What?' I asked. 'What's urgent?'

'What's the story with Jacqui and Joey?'

I had to wait for my racing heart to slow down. 'That's why you're ringing? Because of Jacqui and Joey?'

'Yes. What's going on?'

'You know. He fancies her. And she fancies him.'

'No! She's slept with him. Over the weekend, while you were in those Hamptons.'

Jacqui hadn't told me. In a little voice, I said, 'I didn't know.'

Fake-cheerily, Mum said hastily, 'Sure it's only Monday morning, she'll tell you soon. And, God knows, who *hasn't* slept with Joey?'

'I haven't.'

'And neither,' she sighed heavily, 'have I. But just about everyone else has. Was it a one-night stand?'

'How the hell do I know?'

'No, it's a joke. A whole night? Does Joey do that kind of commitment?' Mum said.

'Good one.' Then I said, 'Well, I can't help you. I don't know what's going on. Ask Rachel.'

'I can't. We're not talking.'

'What now?'

'The invitations. I want nice silver italics on nice white paper.'

'And what does she want?'

'Twigs and twine and shells and woven papyrus stuff. Would you have a word with her?'

'No.'

A startled silence came from Mum's end, then I explained, 'I'm the daughter who's been recently bereaved, remember?'

'Sorry, pet. Sorry. I was mixing you up with Claire for a minute.'

It was only after she hung up that I wondered how she knew about Jacqui. Luke, I presumed.

Straight away, I rang Jacqui, but she wasn't picking up either of her phones. I left messages for her to call me *immediately*, then went to work, bursting with curiosity.

She didn't call all morning. Mid-afternoon, I was just about to ring her once more when a shadow fell over my desk. It was Franklin. Very quietly, he said, 'Ariella wants to see you. Her office.'

Oh God, I was sacked. I was so sacked.

Franklin walked me in and I was surprised to discover several people already there: Wendell from Visage, Mary-Jane, coordinator of the other seven brands, and Lois, one of Mary-Jane's 'girls'. Lois worked on Essence, one of our more worthy, touchy-feely brands.

Was this going to be a job-lot sacking?

Five chairs were set in a semicircle around Ariella's desk.

'Siddown,' she Don Corleoned. 'OK, the good news is that you're not fired. Yet.'

We all laughed far too loud and long.

'Settle down, kids, it wasn't that funny. First thing you've got to know is, this is super-confidential. What you hear here today, you do not discuss outside this room, with anyone, anywhere, anytime, anyhow. Got it?'

Got it. But I was intrigued.

'Formula 12?' Airella asked. 'Heard of it?'

I nodded. I knew a bit. It had been formulated by some explorer who had been down in the Amazon Basin. When the local lads there got wounded, an ointment would be made up of ground roots and plants; the explorer had noticed how quickly the wounds healed and how residual scarring was minimal. He tried to make the ointment himself, but didn't get it right until the twelfth attempt, hence the name. It had been regarded as medicinal and he'd been trying to get approval from the Food and Drugs Administration.

Ariella took up the story. 'So while he's waiting for FDA approval, Professor Redfern—that's the guy's name—had an idea: skincare. Using the same formula, in a modified form, he's created a day-cream.' She handed out documents to each of the five of us. 'And the trials have been phenomenal. It's all there.'

The funny thing about Ariella is that when she has to talk for any length of time, she stops the Don Corleone carry-on. Clearly it is just an affectation to scare people.

'It's been bought by Devereaux. The company is going huge on it. It's going to be the hottest brand on the planet.' She half smiled, moving eye contact from one of us to the next. 'McArthur on the Park . . . is pitching for their publicity.'

She took a moment to let us say wow and how fabulous that was.

'I want each of you three'—she pointed at me, Wendell and Lois, in turn—'to come up with a pitch. Three individual pitches.'

Another momentous pause. In fairness, that *was* fabulous. A pitch of my own. For a totally new brand.

'If they're good enough, we pitch all three to them. If they go with your pitch, maybe you get to head up the account.'

Oh. Now, that *would* be amazing. A promotion. Although what would a Formula 12 girl have to wear? Stuff inspired by the Amazon Basin?

'How much time do we have?' Wendell asked.

'Two weeks today, you three pitch to me. That gives us time to nix any glitches before the real thing. Not that I want any glitches.' Ariella was suddenly low and menacing. 'Another thing, you do all of this in your own time. Coming in here every day, you carry on like normal, giving one thousand per cent to your current brands. But you can forget about having a life of your own for the next coupla weeks.'

I was in luck. I had no life of my own anyway.

'And, like I said, *no one must know.*'

She switched to regal mode. 'Anna, Lois, Wendell, you don't need me to tell you what an honour this is. Do you?' Energetically, we shook our heads. No, indeed we did not. 'Do you know how many people I have working for me?' No, we didn't, but plenty, for sure. 'I spent a lot of time with Franklin and Mary-Jane assessing every single one of my staff and, out of all of them, I picked you three.'

'Thank you, Ariella,' we murmured.

As Franklin walked me back to my desk, Lauryn looked up with eager interest. 'Did you get fired?'

'No.'

'Oh. So what did she want to see you for?'

'Nothing.'

'What's in the file?'

'Nothing.'

Already I was sorry to be one of the chosen ones.

I opened the Formula 12 file and tried reading the information. Lots of it was scientific data about the biological qualities of the plants and the properties they contained and why they worked the way they did. If we got the account it would be my job to reduce all this information to understandable, bite-sized pieces for beauty editors' consumption.

The file contained a photo of Professor Redfern, who looked nice and explorery. Suntanned and wrinkled around the eyes and wearing a hat and one of those sleeveless khaki gilets that seem to be mandatory for explorer blokes. Beardy? But of course. Not unattractive, if you like that sort. Promotable? Possibly. Maybe we would present him as an Indiana Jones *du jour*.

Finally, there was a little jar of the magic cream itself. It was a nasty-ish mustard-yellow with dark-coloured flecks—a bit like 'real' vanilla ice cream. Most face creams were either white or palest pink, but the mustard-yellow wasn't necessarily a bad thing; it might make it seem more 'authentic'.

I rubbed a thin layer over my face, and a few minutes later my scar started to tingle. I rushed to the mirror and almost expected to see the puckered skin bubbling and expanding, but no, nothing unusual was happening. My face looked the same as it always did.

Before I went to bed, I tried Jacqui one more time. I'd got used to her not answering, so I was very surprised when she picked up.

'Hey-Illloooo.' She sounded all breathy and gaspy.
'It's me. What's up with you and Narky Joey?'
'We've been in bed since Friday night. He's just left.'
'So do you fancy him?'
'Anna, I'm mad about him.'

I swear to God, I thought I could see an improvement in my scar the very next morning. I couldn't be sure, but I took a photo of it just to be on the safe side. If Formula 12 could effect a visible improvement after one go, what would it be like after fourteen? It might come in very handy for my pitch.

I couldn't decide which way to go with it, but obviously I didn't want to overlap with Wendell or Lois. I could guess what Wendell would propose because I knew her style: Wendell threw money at things. Every beauty editor in New York would be off to Brazil on a private plane if Wendell had anything to do with it.

Lois was a lesser-known quantity. She might go on about the natural ingredients and that sort of thing.

So, if the Brazilianness and the naturalness aspects of Formula 12 were already annexed, where did that leave me? Nothing was coming. No starbursts of inspiration. I stared at the little yellow jar and wondered.

To: Magiciansgirl1@yahoo.com
From: Lucky_Star_Pl@yahoo.ie
Subject: Result!

Finally got shots of Detta Big at Racey O'Grady's house. Took loads of pics of her talking into gate intercom, driving in, parking, getting out of car, ringing front-door bell, going inside . . .

Printed them off at high speed, then rang Colin and told him to collect me. I never meet Harry anywhere except the snooker hall, but am not allowed to make own way there.

Harry drinking milk. I put envelope of photos in front of him.
Me: There's your proof. Now give me my money and let me off this boring job.
Harry (opens envelope, shuffles through pics): You're still on the job.
Me: Why?
Him: I like having you around the place.
Me: Well, I'm sick of this job. I want out.
Him: You're very fond of your mother, aren't you?
Me (surprised): No, I'm not.

Where did he get that mad idea from?

Me: Are you threatening me?

Him: Yes.

Me: Well, you'll have to try a bit harder than threatening my mother.

Him: So who are you fond of?

Me: No one.

Him: You've got to be fond of someone.

Me: I'm not. My sister Rachel says there's something wrong with me, like I've a bit missing.

Him (Puts head in hands. Sign that he is thinking. Looks up): I need better proof than this. I need proof of them together, if you get me?

Me: Do you mean them riding each other?

Him (wincing): In my day women used to have some decorum. But I'll double what I'm paying you. How does that sound?

Me (desperate): It's not about the money. Look, Harry, this job has got to get more exciting. I'm losing the will to live.

Him: Stop calling me Harry. Show a little respect.

Me: Actually, Harry, I was thinking about the whole Mr Big thing. I've been trying lateral thinking. How does Mr Fear grab you?

Him (nodding slowly): I like it.

Me: Will we try it for a while, see if it catches on?

Him: OK. (To Colin) D'you get that? We're going to run with Mr Fear for a while. Put the word out to the lads.

Me (because I want to get off this job): Harry, you have photographic proof of your wife with another crime lord. Why would they be meeting if they weren't up to something dodgy?

Him: Lots of reasons. Racey's mammy, Tessie O'Grady, was great friends with Detta's da. Detta could just be being friendly, like.

Me: So Detta and Racey are old friends! Why am I surveilling old friends? (I'm thinking, He's cracked. Cracked and mad.)

Him: No, *they're* not old friends. Their ma and da were old friends.

Me: But still a perfectly innocent reason for them to meet up. (Fuck's sake.)

PS: Didn't entirely mean it when said I wasn't fond of anyone. Quite fond of you.

PPS: Not just saying that because your husband died.

I couldn't come up with a pitch for Formula 12. For the first time ever, all my inspiration had deserted me.

Franklin asked how it was coming along.

'Good,' I said.

'So tell me.'

'I'd rather not,' I said. 'It's not fully there yet.'

By Sunday I'd still drawn a blank, so at Leisl's I jokingly asked the gang for help.

'If anyone comes through for any of you today, will you ask them what I should do for my pitch?'

'What've you done so far?' Nicholas asked.

'Nothing. I've come up with nothing.'

'Isn't that telling you something?' Nicholas asked.

'Telling me what?'

'To do nothing.'

'And get sacked? I don't think so.'

'How do you get the goose out of the bottle?'

'*What* goose?'

'It's a Buddhist thing. There's a goose trapped in a bottle—how do you get it out?'

'Break the bottle,' Mitch said.

'That's one way.' Nicholas looked at me. 'Any other suggestions?'

'I give up,' I said. 'Tell me.'

'This isn't a riddle. There isn't a straight answer.'

'What? So the goose stays in the bottle?'

'Not necessarily. If you wait long enough the goose will be thin enough to slip out of the bottle. Or if he gets fed, he'll grow and break the bottle himself. But all *you* have to do is nothing.'

'I don't know,' I said. 'I was hoping for more practical advice.'

To: Magiciansgirl1@yahoo.com
From: Thewalshes1@eircom.net
Subject: 'Results!'

Dear Anna,

I hope you are keeping well. We have finally 'nailed' the old woman. I 'hit paydirt' at bridge. Dodie McDevitt identified her from the photos. Funnily enough, it was Zoë the dog she recognised first. She said, 'That's Zoë O'Shea, as sure as eggs.'

When she said 'Zoë' I thought I might topple off my chair. 'Yes!' I said. 'Zoë, Zoë! Who owns her?'

'Nan O'Shea,' says she.

Dodie was even able to give me her address—Springhill Drive, which is not that far away, although it is a long way to make a small dog walk every day. I am not sure what to do now. I might have to 'beard' her in her 'den'. But whatever happens I will keep you 'in the loop'.

Your loving mother,
Mum

The Formula 12 pitch was all I could think about but I hadn't come up with a single idea. I had never experienced a block like it. In the past I had always managed to pull the rabbit out of the hat. But, to my horror, still nothing came and I had only six days left . . . five days . . . four days . . . three days . . . two days . . . one day . . .

The morning of the pitch to Ariella, I wore my only sober suit, the one I'd worn the first time I met Aidan, when he'd spilt coffee on me. It might help my eleventh-hour inspiration to be taken seriously. I almost died of shock when I saw Wendell. She was wearing a yellow suit. *Yellow*. With feathers. She looked like Big Bird. She must be pitching some carnival-type theme. Quickly, I looked over at Lois, who was wearing a sleeveless khaki gilet with loads of pockets, just like Professor Redfern's. Her pitch must be going the explorer route.

At five to ten, Franklin gave us the nod and led Wendell and me to the boardroom. Coming from the opposite direction were Mary-Jane and Lois. Wendell and Lois had storyboards tucked under their arms. I had none.

'Siddown, siddown,' Ariella said, from the head of the table. 'Now, *amaze* me.'

Wendell went first and what she proposed was no great surprise. She wanted to showcase the Brazilianness of Formula 12 by flying twelve super-selected beauty editors to Rio for Mardi Gras. She revealed her first storyboard, which was a photograph of a small executive jet.

'This is similar to the plane we would fly them in,' she said. 'Then we're gonna put each editor in a suite in a five-star hotel in Rio—so many to choose from.'

Here she unveiled her second card—a photograph of the Rio Hilton. Her third card was a picture of a large hotel room. 'Then we'll get them fitted out in fabulous carnival costumes.'

More cards were produced. Pictures of lithe tanned women in skimpy yellow bikinis and massive spangly, feathered headdresses. 'This will be a trip they will never forget. The coverage will be *beyond*.'

I smiled encouragingly and felt it would be mean-spirited to mention that Rio was thousands of miles from the Amazon Basin and that there wouldn't be a Mardi Gras for at least another six months.

Lois was next and, as I'd suspected, her pitch was a little po-faced. She proposed to take the beauty editors—twelve of them, just like Wendell—with Professor Redfern, to meet the indigenous people who invented Formula 12. 'We fly to Rio, where we take a light aircraft to the jungle.' She unveiled her first visual: a photo of a plane. It looked very similar to Wendell's plane. They probably downloaded them from the same executive-jet site.

'After landing in the jungle'—a photo of thick jungle was thrust before us—'we will then trek for half a day. The editors can see the actual plants that go to make up the product.' A picture of a plant was produced for our inspection.

'Trekking in a jungle?' Ariella said. 'What if they get bitten by an anaconda and we have a freaking lawsuit on our hands?'

'We'll have guides,' Lois said, speedily producing a picture of a half-naked, smiling, black-toothed man.

'Nice,' Franklin murmured.

'Everyone will get appropriate clothing. Like this.' Lois pointed to her gilet. 'It'll be totally safe. This will be great, something very different.'

I agreed with that. It was good. Better in a way than Wendell's, although Wendell's was safer.

And then it was my turn. I took a deep breath and held up the little jar between my thumb and index finger.

'Formula 12.' I swivelled so that everyone could see the jar. 'The most revolutionary advance in skincare since Crème de la Mer. How best to promote it? Well, I'll tell you.' I stopped talking, looked each person in the eye and announced, 'We do . . . nothing.'

That got their attention: I'd lost it. Horror sat on Franklin's face: he'd allowed me to keep my pitch secret until now and Ariella would kill him. Of course, Wendell and Lois were thrilled—half of the opposition dispatched without them having to do a thing. Just before Ariella got off her chair, I opened my mouth again.

'Well, not *quite* nothing.' I twinkled. At least I tried to. 'I'm thinking: a whispering campaign. Every time I have lunch with an editor, I drop hints that there's a new skin-care product coming. Something off the map. But if they ask me questions, I clam up, say that it's top secret, beg them to say nothing about it to anyone . . . but that when they get it, they'll be amazed.'

Everyone was watching me very carefully.

'These plants and roots that make up Formula 12 are very rare. I plan to give one jar—one tiny jar—to, say, the beauty editor at *Harpers*. The *only* beauty editor in the United States to get it. Literally. And I don't mail it. I don't even messenger it. I bring it, in person, to her. Not to her office but to some neutral venue. Almost like we're doing something illegal.' Now I had them. 'She gets it if she promises me a full page. And if she can't do it, I go to someone else. *Vogue*, probably. And the jar should be made out of a semi-precious stone, like amber or tourmaline. I'm thinking this tiny, heavy thing that fits in the palm of my hand. Weighty, you know? Like a little bomb of super-powered stuff.'

Ariella inclined her head in a small gesture of approval.

'And there's more,' I said. 'Read my lips. No. Celebrity. Endorsement.'

Franklin blanched. Celebrity endorsement was his life.

'Nobody gets this stuff for free. If Madonna wants it, Madonna pays for it—'

'Hey, not Madonna,' Franklin objected.

'Even Madonna.'

'This is crazy,' he muttered.

'And no advertising,' I said. 'Formula 12 should be a word-of-mouth phenomenon, so that people feel they're in on a big secret. By the time it finally goes on sale—in one outlet in the United States—the waiting list is already full. Women will be queuing outside the store before it's even opened. Jars of Formula 12 will be changing hands on the black market. It'll be the most elite thing in New York. Which means the most elite thing in the world. Money can't buy it. Contacts can't swing it. You just have to wait your turn—and women will wait because it's worth waiting for.

'Nine months later we do it all again with the serum, and six months after that with the base. Then we've got the eye-cream, the lip balm, the body repair, the body wash and the exfoliator all to come.'

Ariella gave another of those almost invisible nods. This was the equivalent to her jumping on her desk, shrieking, '*Go Anna!*'

'But that's not all,' I said, striving for a wry tone.

'Oh, yes?'

'I've got an added extra.' I paused, made them wait, then pointed to my scar. 'As you may have noticed, I am the lucky owner of a badly scarred face.'

I let them have their embarrassed little chuckle.

'In the two short weeks since I started using Formula 12 there's been a huge improvement.' I took a photo of my scar just before I started using it. It was actually after the first night, but never mind. 'The difference is already visible. I believe in this product. I genuinely do.' Well, I'd give it a go. 'When I pitch to beauty editors, I will be visible proof that Formula 12 is amazing.'

'Yes!' Ariella was impressed with this proposal. 'And if the results aren't dramatic enough, we can always send you for plastic surgery.'

'Hey, Nicholas,' I called down the corridor. 'Thanks for your funny Buddhist-goose advice. It got me the gig.'

I got close enough to see him colouring with pride. 'You really did nothing? Oh, wow. That's so cool. So tell me.'

'OK.' But I was distracted by his T-shirt. Today's said THE GEEK SHALL INHERIT THE EARTH. 'Nicholas, I've never seen you with the same T-shirt twice. Do you wear a different T-shirt with a different message every day of your life.'

He grinned. 'Hey, you'll just have to meet me in the week to find out!'

The mood turned suddenly awkward and a blush inched its way up his face. 'Oh, wow, sorry, Anna.' He bowed his head. 'Flirting with you. Totally inappropriate.'

'Were you? Look, don't worry . . .'

'I mean, you and Mitch . . .'

'What! Mitch? Oh my God, no, Nicholas. It's not like that with Mitch. Not at all!'

Do you mind me spending so much time with Mitch? You know it's just as friends, don't you? You know we're just helping each other?

I'd been so thrown by Nicholas's comment that, after the channelling, I told Mitch I couldn't go on today's outing. I felt filthy with guilt and I couldn't escape fast enough; I set off walking in the direction of home. Though I'd have preferred not to face it, I saw how easy it would be to get the wrong idea about him and me. Why hadn't I told Rachel or Jacqui about him? I mean, *I* knew the truth and Mitch knew the truth—but did Aidan?

Aidan, if you mind, just show me and I'll never see him again. Give me a sign. Anything at all. OK, I'll make it easy for you—I'm going to keep walking down this street and if you're angry about Mitch, how about . . . how about . . . making a flowerpot fall from a window ledge right into my path.

I walked and walked but nothing landed on or near me and I was hot and tired. Eventually I hailed a cab. The driver, a young Indian man, was on his mobile. I gave my address and slumped back into the seat.

8

JOEY IN LOVE was compelling viewing. A dinner had been organised for no other reason than everyone wanted to see the unlikely combination of Jacqui and Joey together.

In all, twenty-three of us came along to Haiku in the Lower East Side one Thursday night. Joey and Jacqui were twined around each other in the centre of a long booth, and there was a bit of unseemly jostling from the rest of us to get the seats nearest to them.

It was strange: Joey hadn't started smiling or anything—he still looked narky—but when he was tracing the curve of Jacqui's face with his finger, or staring into her eyes, his narkiness looked quite nice. Quite sexy, actually. Intense, Heathcliffy, although his hair wasn't dark enough. It might be if he stopped using Sun-In (he denied it vigorously though we all knew), but he was very attached to his goldeny-brown lowlights.

'This is going to be good,' Teenie said, with glee.

And it was. All through the dinner, Joey and Jacqui were constantly whispering and giggling and feeding each other.

'It's adorable.' Brooke clasped her hands, her eyes ashine. 'True love can happen with anyone. Like, who says he has to work in Wall Street! He could be, like, just a plumber, or a construction worker.' Her gaze fastened on Shake, on his tight, tight jeans and his grand head of hair, and took on a sudden, acquisitive gleam.

The arrival of fantastic news!

To: Magiciansgirl1@yahoo.com
From: Psychic_Productions@yahoo.com
Subject: Re: Neris Hemming

Your phone interview with Neris Hemming is scheduled for 8.30 a.m. on Wednesday, October 6. The number to call will be sent to you closer to the date. The cost of Ms Hemming's time is $2500. Please forward your credit-card details. Also note that you must not call the number until 8.30 a.m. and that you must finish exactly on nine.

I rang Mitch to tell him. I was so excited. In just over two weeks' time I'd be talking to Aidan.

I couldn't wait. I couldn't wait. I couldn't wait.

Franklin leaned over my desk, flicked a furtive look at Lauryn and said, 'Anna, we've finally got a confirmation date from Devereaux for the Formula 12 pitch.'

He smiled happily, and suddenly, with a cold trickle down my spine, I knew what was going to happen. Even before he spoke the words, I knew exactly what he was going to say. 'Wednesday of next week, October 6, nine a.m.'

Electric pains shot up and down my legs. Wednesday, October 6 was the morning of my conversation with Neris Hemming. This was like a cosmic joke. I couldn't be at the pitch. I had to tell him. But I was afraid. *Say it, go on, say it.*

'I'm sorry, Franklin.' My voice sounded shaky. 'It won't be possible for me to be there. I have an appointment.'

His eyes turned to chips of ice.

'It's, um, medical.'

'So reschedule. We need you at this pitch,' Franklin said.

'I can be here by nine thirty.'

'I don't think you're hearing me. We need you at this pitch.' Then he turned his back on me and walked away.

With shaking fingers, I emailed Neris Hemming's people to see if my interview with Neris could be rejigged to the following day. A speedy reply told me that if I missed this window, I'd have to go to the back of the queue and wait the mandatory ten to twelve weeks.

And I couldn't! I just couldn't! I was so desperate to talk to Aidan and I'd waited so long, been so patient.

But if I didn't make the pitch, I'd be sacked. And my job was pivotal to me. It kept me going. It gave me a reason to get up in the morning and it took my mind off things. Not to mention that I got paid for it, which was vital as I was up to my eyes in debt. I'd moved two and a half grand into a separate account as soon as I'd heard from Neris Hemming's people, so at least that was safe. Other than that I was just making the minimum card payments every month. For as long as I was earning money I could keep the show on the road, but even a couple of wageless weeks could mean everything collapsing.

I tried to think of other ways around the dilemma: I could call Neris on my cellphone from the coffee shop near work, then be at work just after nine. Except I couldn't; I wouldn't be able to properly savour my conversation with Aidan.

Things clicked into place; I'd made my decision. Not that there had every really been any doubt. I would talk to Neris and blow off the pitch.

I made my way to Franklin's desk.

'Can I have a word?'

Coldly, he nodded.

'Franklin, I can't be at the pitch. But someone else could do mine. Lauryn could.'

Exasperated, he said. We need *you*, you're the one with the scar. Lauryn hasn't got a scar.' He was silent for a moment, and I'm sure he was considering whether he *could* scar Lauryn. He must have decided that, darn, he couldn't, because he asked, 'What's got you so sick?'

'It's, um, gynaecological.' I thought it would be safe saying that to him, what with him being a man. It had always worked in other jobs— telling a man boss I had period pains, when I just wanted the afternoon off to go shopping. Usually they couldn't get rid of me quickly enough. Instead, Franklin leapt up from behind his desk, grabbed me and wove speedily through the desks.

'Where are we going?'

'To see Mommy.'

Shite, shite, shite.

'She says she can't make the pitch,' Franklin said, very loudly. 'She says she's got a medical appointment. She says it's gynaecological.'

'Gynaecological?' Ariella said. 'She's having an abortion?' She looked at me in powder-blue shoulder-padded fury.

'No. Oh my God, no, not at all. It's um, my . . . cervix.'

'Is it cancer?' She tilted her head enquiringly and held my look for a long, long moment. 'Do you have cancer?' The message was clear: if I had cancer, she'd allow me to miss the pitch. Nothing less would do.

'Pre-cancerous,' I choked out, dying with shame at what I was saying.

Suddenly, Ariella went scary calm. Her voice dropped to her sore-throat whisper. 'Anna, have I not been good to you? Have I not taken care of you? Put clothes on your back? Did I not keep your job open for you when your husband bought the farm? Took you back although you have a scar on your face that would scare even Dr De Groot?'

As she said the final, damning line, I said it too, in my head.

And this is how you repay me?

Over the next two weeks, Wendell and I were put through myriad run-throughs of the pitch so that we were word-perfect. (It had been decided to drop Lois's idea in case of accidents.) Ariella and Franklin cross-examined us on costings, timings, customer profile, competitors—every conceivable question we might be asked.

I went along with it even though I knew I wouldn't be there.

But I'd co-opted Teenie; we'd gone for lunch and I'd sworn her to secrecy. 'The pitch on Wednesday? I can't make it.'

'Wha—?'

'You do my pitch. Cover yourself in glory.'

'But . . . I mean, like, you can't be . . . Ariella will go *crazy*.'

'Yes, and then she'll need someone to do my pitch. Make sure it's you.'

On the eve of the pitch, Wendell and I were put through our paces one final time. At about six thirty, Ariella called it a day.

'See you tomorrow, Anna,' Franklin said meaningfully.

'Bright and early,' I said.

I hadn't decided if I would come in after the phone call with Neris, or if I would simply never come back. Just in case, I took my framed photo of Aidan off my desk and put it in my bag.

9

IT FELT LIKE the night before the most important day of my life. I couldn't settle to anything.

Aidan, what if you don't come through? How will I cope?

When the phone rang I jumped. It was Kevin, Aidan's brother. I let the machine pick up. 'Anna,' he said, 'I gotta talk to you, this is urgent. Call me.'

I barely registered it.

Sometime later my buzzer went. I ignored it but it rang again. On the third go, I answered. It was Jacqui. 'You'll never guess,' she said.

'So tell me.'

'I'm pregnant.'

I stared at her and she stared back at me. 'Are you jealous?' she asked. Just like that.

'Yes,' I said. Just like that.

'I'm sorry. And I don't even want to be effing pregnant. Do you know when it happened? The first night. When you were in the Hamptons. Can you believe it? I'm only six weeks pregnant but they count from your last period, so I'm officially eight weeks.'

'Does Narky Joey know?'

She shook her head. 'No, and when I tell him, he'll break up with me.'

'But he's mad about you.'

She shook her head. 'Dopamine. When men think they're in love, it's only because their brain is producing too much dopamine. It usually goes away after the first year. But if I tell him I'm pregnant, I bet it'll go away immediately. Narky Joey doesn't want responsibility.'

'Talk to him about it, it might all be OK.'

'Maybe.' Pause. 'I've been thinking. Being pregnant isn't the horrible disaster it would have been five years ago, or even three years. Back then, I'd no security. But now . . . I have an apartment, a well-paid job, and I sort of like the idea of having a baby around the place.'

'Um, Jacqui, having a baby is a huge life-changing event. You mightn't even be able to *do* your well-paid job. Are you sure you've really thought this through?'

'Oh, yeah! It'll cry a lot, I'll be skint.' She paused. 'But it'll be fun! Let's hope I get a girl baby, their clothes are much nicer.' Then she burst into tears.

'Thank God,' I said. 'That's the first normal thing you've done.'

After she left, I tried but never got properly to sleep. I just skimmed the surface and was fully awake again by 5 a.m. I watched the clock count down to eight thirty, when I would finally get to talk to Aidan. To pass the time, I got my emails.

To: Magiciansgirl1@yahoo.com
From: Lucky_Star_Pl@yahoo.ie
Subject: Full frontals

You're not going to believe what happened. This morning in post, got A4 envelope, full of photos of Racey and Detta together. Nothing left to imagination. You'd need a strong stomach. So they were at it all along! Harry was right, I was wrong. But why is someone sending me pictures of them?

To: Magiciansgirl1@yahoo.com
From: Thewalshes1@eircom.net
Subject: All is revealed

You'll never guess who Nan O'Shea is. Go on, have a go. You'll never get it. I'll give you a hint. It's is all your father's fault. Something I should have known all along. Go on, guess. I'm not going to tell you yet. Wait'll you hear thought—you'll never believe it!
Your loving mother,
Mum

To get her off my back, I dashed off an absent-minded reply.

To: Thewalshes1@eircom.net
From: Magiciansgirl1@yahoo.com
Subject: Re: All is revealed

I don't know. I give up. Is she an old girlfriend of Dad's?

I'd waited so long to talk to Aidan that I'd started to believe that 8.30 would never come. But it did. I looked at the two hands on the clock:

they were in the magic formation, the time had finally arrived. I picked up the phone and punched the numbers.

It rang four times, then a woman's voice said hello and I was shaking so much I could hardly speak to say, 'Hello, is that Neris?'

'Yeees?' Said cautiously.

'Hello, it's Anna Walsh, calling from New York for my reading.'

'Um.' She sounded perplexed. 'Do you have an appointment?'

'Yes! Yes! I've paid and everything.'

'I'm sorry, honey. I've got construction works in here, running all over the place. I told the office. No way can I concentrate on a reading.'

Shock robbed me of speech. This couldn't be happening. 'You mean you're not going to channel for me?'

'Not right now, honey.'

'But I've been desperate for this day to come—'

'I know, honey. So call the office. Let's reschedule.'

'But I had to wait three months for this appointment and—'

'I'll tell them to prioritise you.'

'There's no chance we could do something quick just now, is there?'

'No, there sure is not.' Her breezy tone stayed breezy but with a steely addition. 'Call the office. Y'all take care now.'

And she was gone.

I stared at the phone, then a tangle of outrage, disappointment and thwarted hope erupted together. I was overwhelmed by an entire reservoir of white-hot fury—not with Neris but with Aidan.

'Why won't you talk to me?' I screeched. 'Why are you blanking me at every fucking turn?' I was pulling at my hair. 'And why did you have to die? You should have tried harder, you lazy, useless *bastard*. If you'd loved me enough, you'd have held on to your life instead of just giving in.'

I hit Redial and got the engaged tone and that just made me worse.

'Why won't you talk to me?' I shrieked. 'You had a *choice*, you could have *stayed*, but you didn't care about me enough, you didn't love me enough, you were more concerned with *yourself*.'

Eventually, I ran out of words and over and over again I shrieked into my hands, tearing my throat raw as I tried to get the rage out of me.

I couldn't stay in the apartment. In a haze of red, I made for the door. Outside I stood on the street and found I had nowhere to go except work. I didn't give a damn about the pitch but, as is the way with these things, I got a cab immediately, there was almost no traffic, and every light was green. I'd never got to work so quickly in my life.

I took my time ambling from the elevator to my desk, where Franklin, Teenie and Lauryn were in a head-to-head. Franklin was the colour of chalk. Then he turned and saw me and I almost laughed when I saw his expression. He was too relieved to be angry. 'You're here.'

'Yeah. Teenie, I'm so sorry to mess you around like this.'

'No way,' she said. 'It's your pitch.' She gave me a little kiss. 'Way to go.'

'**H**ere she is!'

Triumphantly, he displayed me to Ariella, who said, 'Cutting it a little fine, no?'

'I told you, I had an appointment.'

Glances were exchanged: what was going on with me? But then word came that the Devereaux people were on their way up to the boardroom and everyone stapled on their happy faces.

Wendell—in her yellow Big Bird rig-out—went first and gave a pretty dazzling display. Then it was my turn. I watched myself do my pitch, almost as if I was standing outside my body: I was full of adrenaline, my voice was louder than usual and I laughed a little too bitterly when I pointed out my scar, but nothing else untoward happened.

I answered their tricky questions with perfect ease—I was word-perfect after the hours of practice. Then it was all over and hands were being shaken and they were gone. As soon as the elevator doors closed behind them, I walked out of the boardroom, leaving Ariella and Franklin staring after me in bewilderment.

Back at my desk, Teenie said, 'How'd it go?'

'She couldn't do it. She had the contractors in.'

'Excuse me?'

'Oh, the pitch. Fine, fine.'

'Are you OK?'

'Fine.'

'Right. Messages for you. Jacqui rang. She's breaking the news to Narky Joey tonight. Then Kevin rang. You've gotta call him. It's urgent.'

With sudden curiosity, I switched on my cellphone; there were two messages from Kevin. Why did he want me to call him?

And all at once, I knew why. Kevin wanted to talk to me for the very same reason that Aidan wouldn't in those couple of days before the accident. Uneasiness, which had existed at the back of my mind for months, abruptly moved to the forefront. I'd hoped this would never happen. But, whatever this was, it was coming to a head; I was powerless to stop it.

I had to talk to Leon.

I called him at work. 'Leon, can I see you?'

'Great! How's Friday sound?'

'No, Leon. I need to see you now.'

'But it's ten thirty. I'm at work.'

'Fake something. A meeting. A sore tooth. Just for an hour, Leon. Please. Can you be in Dom's Diner in twenty?'

'OK.'

I announced to the desks around me: 'I'm going out in ten minutes, I'm taking an early lunch.'

Lauryn didn't even answer. She didn't care. I'd messed up so badly by almost missing the pitch that I was probably going to be sacked anyway.

To: Magiciansgirl1@yahoo.com
From: Thewalshes1@eircom.net
Subject: All is revealed

Dear Anna,

How did you know? Was it a lucky guess? Or did Helen tell you? Yes, Nan O'Shea is the woman your father 'dumped' for me. She has carried a grudge all these years. Who would have thought that someone would feel so strongly about your father?

It all came out when I made your father come over with me to her house to 'front her out'. We rang the bell and the front door was opened very forcefully, then your woman spots your father.

She said. 'Jack?' And he said, 'Nan?' And I said, 'You know this woman?'

Your father said, 'What's going on, Nan?' And she said, 'I'm sorry, Jack.'

I said, 'You'd bloody well want to be, you raving lunatic,' and your father said, 'Sssh, sssh, she's upset.'

She brought us in for a cup of tea and your father was all chat, sitting down and accepting Hobnobs, but I remained 'standoffish'.

Anyway, it seems she had been heartbroken when your father 'kicked her to the kerb' and had never forgotten him.

I asked your father why he hadn't recognised the name and he said he didn't know. Then I asked Nan O'Shea why she had started pestering us only recently and warned her not to say that she didn't know either. She said she had lived 'away' for many years. It turned out that she has been living in Cork since 1962. She has recently 'retired' and moved to Dublin.

Your father was all pallsy and when we were leaving Nan O'Shea said, 'Maybe you'll drop in for a cup of tea once in a while, Jack.'

'No,' I said. 'He certainly won't. Come on, Jack, home.'

So that's the end of that. How are things with you?

Your loving mother,

Mum

Leon was already there. I slid into the brown vinyl booth opposite him and said, 'Leon, I know this is hard for you and if you have to cry, feel free. I'm going to ask you some questions and I'm begging you to be honest with me. Even if you think you're going to hurt me.'

He nodded anxiously.

'That night that Aidan died, he was about to tell me something important.'

'What was it?'

'I don't know. He died, remember?'

'Sorry, I thought you meant . . . So how do you know he was going to tell you big stuff?'

'He'd booked a table for us at Tamarind.'

'What's funny about that?'

'It's funny because Aidan and I hardly ever went out for dinner, just the two of us. And we'd already been for a fancy romantic Valentine's Night dinner two nights before. And, looking back, something had upset him. He'd had a call on his cell—he said it was work, but I don't think it was because he was very subdued after it.'

'Work stuff can do that to a guy.'

'I don't know, Leon, it seemed bigger than that. I mean, he tried his best, especially on Valentine's Night . . . The next thing is he'd booked a table at Tamarind and I said I didn't understand why we were going out for dinner again so soon, but he said please, so I said OK. I remember thinking that if it was important to him that we go out to talk—because obviously we weren't just going for the food—then I would do it.'

'But you never got there.'

'No. And I sort of forgot about it. I mean . . . there was too much stuff going on. Leon, you were his best friend. Was Aidan cheating on me?'

Leon looked appalled. 'No way! He was crazy about you.'

'But would he have told you?'

'Absolutely. And I'd have guessed it anyhow,' Leon said. 'We were tight, you know. He was my best buddy.' His voice broke. 'The best buddy a guy could have.'

Automatically, I reached into my handbag and passed him a tissue. Leon spread it over his face and choked into it, while I asked myself if I believed him. Yes, I decided. I believed him. So what was going on?

When I got back to the office, there was a series of frantic messages from Kevin on my voicemail, the last one saying, 'I'm coming to see you in New York tomorrow morning. I can't get there before then. Anna, if any woman you don't know calls you, don't talk to her.'

Oh my God. Leon was wrong and I'd been right. This was what I'd been waiting for. I felt sick. But calm. I could have rung Kevin and found out everything, but I didn't want to. I needed a little longer to remember my life with Aidan the way I'd thought it had been.

'**A**nna, Anna!' I was brought back to the present by Franklin. 'Ariella's office, right now.'

'Oh-kay.' I trailed along slowly and sat down without Ariella telling me to. She flashed a look at Franklin, who was standing behind me.

Go on then, sack me. Get on with it.

Ariella cleared her throat. 'Anna, we have some news for you. Devereaux are going with our pitch.'

'Hey, that's just great,' I said super-perkily. 'Wendell's or mine?'

'Yours.'

'But you want to fire me. So fire me.'

'We can't fire you. They loved you. The head guy, Leonard Daly, thought you were, I quote, "a great kid, very courageous", and a natural to do a whispering campaign. He said you had believability.'

'That's too bad.'

'Why? You're not quitting?'

I thought about it. 'Not if you don't want me to. Do you?'

Go on, say it.

'No.'

'No what?'

'No, we don't want you to quit.'

'Ten grand more, two assistants and charcoal suits. Take it or leave it.'

Ariella swallowed. 'OK to the money, OK to the assistants, but I can't green-light charcoal suits. Formula 12 is Brazilian, we need carnival colours.'

'Charcoal suits or I'm gone.'

'Orange.'

'Charcoal.'

'OK, charcoal.'

It was an interesting lesson in power. The only time you truly have it is when you genuinely don't care whether you have it or not.

'Right,' I said. 'I'm giving myself the rest of the day off.'

To: Lucky_Star_Pl@yahoo.ie
From: Magiciansgirl1@yahoo.com
Subject: Are you OK?

What's happening?

A short time later, I got a reply.

To: Magiciansgirl1@yahoo.com
From: Lucky_Star_Pl@yahoo.ie
Subject: Wow!

Back at my office a note had been shoved under door. It said, 'Do you
want to know who sent the nudie pictures of Detta and Racey? Do you
want to know what's really going on? (Course I bloody well did!)
It said to show up at 10 p.m., at address on docks. It was a warehouse.
(Why can't these things ever take place in nice comfortable bar?)
Turned on the radio. A shooting incident in Dalkey was main news story.
A man in his fifties (Harry Fear) had 'shot several times at another man'
(Racey). Target had escaped injury and gunman had 'evaded capture'.
Police warning people 'not to approach him'.

This was ridiculous. She was out of her mind to be involved in all this.

To: Lucky_Star_Pl@yahoo.ie
From: Magiciansgirl1@yahoo.com
Subject: Re: Wow!

Helen do NOT go to that warehouse place. You are way out of your
depth. I want you to promise me you won't go.
Anna

To: Magiciansgirl1@yahoo.com
From: Lucky_Star_Pl@yahoo.ie
Subject: Re: Wow!

Ah feck. I promise.

I settled down to wait. In a way, it felt like a rerun of the previous
night, but back then I'd been full of hope and now I was weighed down
with foreboding. Kevin rang and once again I didn't pick up. He said
he'd be arriving on the 7 a.m. shuttle from Boston. Tomorrow I would
know everything.

Then Jacqui showed up; she'd broken the news to Narky Joey. The
fact that she was here did not bode well.

She shook her head. 'Dopamine wipe-out. He doesn't want to know.'

'Oh, no!'

'Yeah, he doesn't want to know.'

'Like he didn't have anything to do with it! Was he horrible?'

'Not horrible. Just the old non-dopamine Narky Joey. I mean, I knew
he wasn't going to go for it, but I was hoping, you know . . .'

I nodded. She sank onto the couch and had a good old sob. After a
while, she began to laugh even though she was still crying. 'You know

something, Anna, you'll have to be my birthing partner. We'll have to go to the antenatal classes together and all the other man-and-woman couples will think we're a pair of Jolly Girls!'

'You're a trooper,' I said.

'I'm a gobshite, and I can't even drown my sorrows. Stick on *Dirty Dancing* there, would you? Sappy movies are all that's available to me for the next seven months. Who's the message from?'

I was on the floor, searching for the DVD. 'What?'

'Your message light, it's flashing.'

'Oh, it's Kevin, he's coming to town tomorrow.' It was amazing how normal I sounded. I couldn't tell Jacqui what was going on; she had enough on her plate.

After she left, I went to bed, went to sleep—sort of—then got up around seven thirty feeling like I was going to be executed. I washed and got dressed as usual. My mouth was as dry as cotton wool so I had a glass of water but it came right back up again.

I didn't know what to do. Until Kevin arrived, everything was on hold. I made a bargain with myself: if I could find an episode of *Starsky and Hutch* on the telly, I'd watch that. And if I couldn't? Well, then I'd go to work.

Strange as it sounds, not one episode was on and, well, a bargain is a bargain. I forced myself towards the door and slowly descended the stairs. In the front porch, the mailman was just leaving. It was the first time this year that it felt like autumn; leaves were skittering past outside and there was a chill in the air.

I wasn't going to bother opening my mailbox. What did I care if I'd got post? But something told me to unlock the box. Then, right off, something else told me to walk away.

But it was too late. I was unlocking it and there, waiting in my mailbox, was one handwritten letter, addressed to me.

There was no return address on the envelope, which was a little weird. Already, I was slightly uneasy. The sensible woman would not open this. The sensible woman would throw it in the bin and walk away. But, apart from a short period between the ages of twenty-nine and thirty, when had I ever been sensible?

So I opened it.

It was a card, a watercolour of a bowl of droopy-looking flowers. And flimsy enough that I could feel that there was something inside: a photograph. A photograph of Aidan. Why was I being sent this? I already had loads of similar ones. Then I saw that I was wrong. It wasn't him. And, suddenly, I understood everything.

PART THREE

I

I WOKE UP in the wrong room. In the wrong bed. With the wrong man.

Apart from one small lamp, the room was in darkness. I listened to the sound of his breathing but I couldn't look at him. I had to get out of there. I slid from between the sheets, determined not to wake him.

'Hey,' he said. He hadn't been asleep. He leaned up on his elbow. 'Where are you going?'

'Home. Why aren't you asleep?'

'I'm watching you to see that you're OK.'

With my back to him, I foraged on the floor for my clothes, trying to hide my nakedness.

'Anna, stay until the morning.'

'I want to go home.' I couldn't find my bra.

He got out of bed and I recoiled; I didn't want him to touch me. 'Just going out front,' he said. 'Giving you some privacy.'

He left the bedroom. I could look only at his legs, and even then just from the knees down.

When he came back I was dressed. He handed me a cup of coffee and said, 'Let me call you a cab.'

'OK.' I still couldn't look at him. The previous day was coming back to me, in all its horribleness. I had lain, naked, on his bed and screeched, 'Come on!' I had wanted him to drive out my rage, my loss, my despair. I had wanted him to drive out my dead husband so I wouldn't feel the pain any more.

The sun was coming up and everything was early-morning quiet as I went home in the cab. I let myself into my silent apartment, snapped on a light, and once again got the envelope out of my bag and looked at the photograph of the little boy who was the image of Aidan but who wasn't Aidan.

The previous day, as I'd stood on my front step, examining the picture of the toddler in the Red Sox cap, it was the scar through the eyebrow that had given the game away. Aidan had got his the day he was born; a tiny nick in his just-new skin that had never healed. The boy in the picture had two perfect eyebrows, no scar. Then I'd seen the date on the photo. This little boy had been born only eighteen months ago.

A letter had come with the photo; the flimsy card opened out to become a big sheet of writing paper. I scanned for the name at the end and—surprise, surprise—who was it, but Janie.

The red mist had descended and I felt I was going crazy. She had had him for all those years. Now she had a son by him. And I had nothing.

Immediately, I'd known what I was going to do.

My fingers trembling in the chilly morning, I rang Mitch. But someone who wasn't Mitch said, 'Mitch's phone.'

'May I speak to Mitch, please?'

'Not right now.' The person chuckled. 'He's suspended from a twenty-foot ceiling, doing micro-electronics. Minute he's finished, I'll get him to call you.'

I cut the call and agitatedly kicked the front step, thinking, Who, who, who? It couldn't be any of the Real Men. Then I got it. It wasn't meant to be Mitch. It was meant to be Nicholas.

I called him at work: got his voicemail. I called him on his cell: got his voicemail. I couldn't believe it. I needed this. Why were all these obstacles being put in my way?

In the middle of the rage I remembered something. Hands shaking, I grabbed my handbag and tipped the contents all over the step, searching for that little bit of paper. And there it was. A small curling strip of paper. My lifesaver: Angelo's number. Angelo, who I'd met with Rachel in Jenni's one morning.

It wasn't meant to be Nicholas, it was meant to be Angelo.

But I got a no-show from Angelo's number, too. I left my name and cellphone number, hung up, scooped everything back into my bag and sat down. I couldn't think of anyone else.

Then, like salvation, the phone rang. One of them ringing back! Which one? 'Hello?'

But it was Kevin. 'Anna, I'm here at JFK. We've got to talk.'

'It's OK, Kevin. I know all about it.'

'Shit. I wanted to tell you gently.'

'Where are you staying?'

'The Benjamin.'

'Go straight to your hotel. I'll see you there.'

So it wasn't meant to be Mitch, Nicholas or Angelo. It was meant to be Kevin.

I hailed a cab and climbed in. 'Benjamin Hotel. East 50th.' Then I got the envelope out again and studied the photo, which had been taken only four days earlier, and tried to figure out the sequence of events. When had I first met Aidan? When did we go exclusive? What age exactly was this child? He looked like he was eighteen months but he could be big for his age, or small. If he was only, say, sixteen months, what implications did that have? Would it be worse if he was twenty months? What if he'd been a preemie? But I couldn't nail the time line. I'd nearly have it hooked and then it would all slide way again.

When my cellphone rang, I almost didn't hear it.

'Hi,' a voice said. 'This is Angelo. You called me?'

'Angelo! Yes. I'm Anna, Rachel's sister, we met—'

'Sure, I remember you. How you doing?'

'Very, very badly.'

'Would you like to meet for coffee?'

'Where are you right now?'

'In my apartment. Sixteenth, between three and four.'

I looked out of the window, managed to focus on street numbers long enough to see that we were on fourteenth.

'I'm in a cab, two blocks away,' I said. 'Can I drop by?'

It wasn't meant to be Kevin. It was meant to be Angelo.

My buzzer jolted me awake—every cell in my body got such a fright I thought I was going to have a seizure. I'd lain down, with the photograph of the little boy on my chest, and I must have dozed off.

On shaky legs, I got to my feet and the buzzer went again. It had just gone 8 a.m. This early in the morning, it could only be one person: Rachel.

Angelo had called her the day before, when it became clear that he had a total lunatic on his hands. She had showed up with Luke and I'd given a garbled account of the photo and letter, which they had insisted on seeing. They had tried to take me home but I had refused to leave and eventually they went away again. I guessed that Angelo had let Rachel know that I'd gone home.

It *was* Rachel. 'Hi,' she said. 'How are you?'

'As good as can be expected, considering that my dead husband was unfaithful to me.'

'He wasn't unfaithful, Anna. Read the letter. Where is it? In your bag? Get it out.'

Under her watchful gaze, I reluctantly unfolded the letter and tried to read it, but the words were jumping all over the place. With a sharp rustle, I thrust it at her. 'You read it.'

'OK. And listen carefully.'

Dear Anna,

I don't even know how to start this letter. Start at the beginning, I guess. This is from Janie, Janie Wicks (née Sorensen), Aidan's ex-girlfriend. We met briefly at Aidan's funeral.

I don't know how much you know of what's been going on, so I'll just tell it all. It's hard to write this without drawing a bad picture of me, but here goes. After Aidan left Boston to work in New York, he came home a lot on the weekends, but the in-between bits were not good and after I guess about sixteen months, I met someone else (Howie, the man I'm married to now). I didn't tell Aidan about Howie (or Howie about Aidan), but I said to Aidan that he and I should take time out and date non-exclusively, just to see.

So for a while I was dating (and sleeping with) both Howie and Aidan— whenever he was home from New York. Then I found I was pregnant. The problem was, I didn't know if the father was Aidan or Howie. (Take it from me, I know how trashy that sounds.)

I wanted to talk to Aidan about it, but the next time he came home to Boston, it was to break up with me. He'd met someone else (you), he was crazy about you and wanted to marry you, he was sorry to break up with me like this, we'd always be friends; you can imagine the script. So I had a choice to make: do I tell him I'm pregnant or do I take a chance and hope that the child is Howie's? So I took that chance and Howie and I got married. Jack didn't look like Howie when he was born, but he didn't look much like Aidan either, so I decided there was no problem.

But when Jack got a little older, he started to look lots like Aidan. I was just sick with worry. Then my mom noticed and called me on it. I admitted the truth to her and she made me see I had a moral obligation to tell Aidan he had a son and the Maddoxes that they had a grandson.

Anyways, first I told Howie. He moved out for a while, but now he's back and we're trying to work things out. Then I called Aidan and, like anyone being hit with that sort of news, he went into a total tailspin. He was freaked out that you might think he'd cheated on you. But just to make it way clear: this happened before he and you were exclusive. (Like, at least eight weeks before.)

I emailed him some photos of Jack so he could see the similarity for himself. But, like a day or so later, Aidan got in the accident and I don't know if he ever got to tell you about Jack. If all this comes out of the blue, I am truly sorry.

I was ready to tell the Maddoxes about Jack when I heard about the accident and then I didn't know what to do and my mom said Dianne and Fielding Maddox were not doing so good and I ought to wait until they were improved. Lots of times I wanted to call you and check to see if you knew about Jack and also just to let you know that I miss Aidan too. He was a great guy, the best. But I sorta felt I couldn't talk to you about Jack until I'd told Fielding and

Dianne and I felt it would be wrong to just talk to you about Aidan and not tell you about Jack. Does that make sense?

Anyways, on Tuesday I bumped into Kevin Maddox. I hadn't seen him in the longest time and I was really happy to see him. But then Kevin looked in the stroller and he was staring at Jack like he was looking at a ghost. He started yelling, 'This is Aidan's son! Aidan had a son! Mom has a grandson! Who knows? Does Anna know? How come no one told me?' Then he began crying.

I said, 'Kevin, let's go get a coffee and I'll tell you everything,' but he took off, yelling that he was going to call you and tell you everything. So I guess you've had a least one manic phone call from Kevin. I wanted to call you too, but I thought it would be better if I wrote it all down.

This might be way, way too soon, but would you like to meet Jack? I could bring him to New York if you didn't want to come to Boston.

Once again, I apologise for any distress I might have caused by telling you this. I felt you have a right to know, and that seeing a part of Aidan living on might make your loss a little easier to bear.

Yours sincerely,

Janie

'So you see,' Rachel said. 'He wasn't unfaithful.'

'I don't care,' I said. 'I still hate him.'

Rachel brought me up to speed on everything that had been happening in my life while I'd been absent without leave.

'You still have a job. I spoke to that Franklin guy. I told him you weren't well.'

'Oh God.' The Formula 12 campaign made it a terrible time for me to be 'not well'. 'Did he start hyperventilating?'

'Yeah, a bit. But then he suggested that you take the rest of the week off. Try to get it together, he said.'

'Thank you, Rachel, thank you very much for dealing with it. For taking care of me.' My gratitude was immense. If she hadn't spoken to Franklin, I'd probably never have dared to reappear at work. Then I thought of something else. 'Christ! Kevin!' Was he still in his hotel, waiting for me to show up?

'It's all taken care of. I spoke to him, told him the story. He's gone back to Boston. Give him a ring.'

'What time is it?' I looked at the clock. 'Twenty past eight. Is that too early?'

'No. I think he's keen to hear from you. He was very worried.'

I winced with shame and picked up the phone. A sleepy voice answered, 'Kevin here.'

'Kevin, it's me, Anna. I'm really so sorry to abandon you like I did. I went bonkers.'

'It's OK,' he said. 'I went crazy too when I found out.' He paused. 'We went to see Jack last night, Mom, Dad and me, and he is such a cute little guy. We're going to see him again today. Why don't you come?'

'No.'

'How about this weekend?'

'No.'

'Oh. OK, Anna, you take your time. Take all the time you need. But he really is the cutest. And funny, you know? And he has this bear—'

'Sorry, Kevin, I've got to go. Bye.'

I hung up and Rachel said, 'You might want to apologise to Angelo.' Angelo! 'Oh, Christ. I was pure mental. He wouldn't have sex with me.'

'Of course he wouldn't. What kind of man did you take him for?'

'Just a man man. Speaking of which, has Joey gone back to Jacqui?'

'No. And I think you'll find he's not going to.'

All I can remember from that time was that my bones ached worse than ever. Even my hands and feet hurt. I removed every photo of Aidan, even the one in my wallet, and dispatched them all to the dusty Siberia of Under the Bed. I wanted no reminders of him.

The only person I wanted to be with was Jacqui, who couldn't stop crying.

'It's just hormones,' she kept saying, between bouts of sobbing. 'It's not Joey. I'm absolutely fine about him.'

When I wasn't with Jacqui, I went shopping and shelled out a fortune on two charcoal suits, black high-heeled shoes, sheer hose and a Chloé handbag. Every time I signed for another purchase I thought of the two and half grand that I'd paid Neris Hemming and I flinched. I should pursue her, try to get the money back, but I wanted to forget I'd ever heard of her. And there was no way I wanted to reschedule; I knew it was all nonsense. Talking to the dead? Don't be so silly.

In the evenings, for some strange masochistic reason, I watched baseball on the telly. The World Series was on: the Red Sox playing the St Louis Cardinals. The Red Sox hadn't won since 1919, but I knew with a cold, unwavering certainty that this year they were going to end their losing streak. They were going to win because that asshole had been stupid enough to die and miss it. The pundits, the newspapers and the Red Sox fans were in an ecstasy of anxiety: they were so close but what if they didn't win?

I never doubted that they would and, just as I had predicted, they did and I was the only person in the world who wasn't surprised.

'You stupid fucker,' I told him. 'If you hadn't died, you could have seen this.'

And that, I decided would be the last time I spoke to Aidan.

Wearing my most expensive charcoal suit, I returned to work.

'I'm good to go,' I told Franklin.

He hustled me straight into Ariella's office. She brought me up to speed on Formula 12: the Devereaux execs wanted a day-by-day schedule of my whispering campaign: when could they expect the brand to break; the jeweller needed to speak to me about my vision for the amber pot; the marketing team wanted my input on label design . . .

'You've got a lot of work ahead of you.'

'I'll set up meetings right away.'

'There's just one thing . . .' Ariella said. 'Your clothes.'

'We agreed charcoal,' I said. 'Charcoal or I walk.'

'Your plan is a whispering campaign, right? Rumours of an amazing new product but no details yet, right? Which means you've got to be a Candy Grrrl girl in Candy Grrrl clothes until Formula 12 breaks.'

Openly I glared at her; she was right. 'For how long?' I asked.

She shrugged happily. 'It's your campaign. How long until you build a buzz? Coupla months anyway.'

I would rather have chopped my hand off than make the call. But for as long as I didn't apologise to Angelo, the shame would be with me.

'Angelo, it's Anna, Rachel's sis—'

'Hey, little girl, how're you doing?'

'Angelo, I'm so sorry. It was a terrible way to treat you. I'm so embarrassed. I could die.'

'Hey, you were in shock. I've been there. And worse. I swear to you.'

'Well, thank you for not . . . you know, taking advantage of me.'

'Aw, come on. I'd have been a pretty poor excuse for a man if I had.'

'Thank you for not saying that if things were different that you would have . . . you know . . . taken me up on my offer.'

'Bummer.'

'What?'

'Cos that's just what I was thinking.'

At work, I began living a double life. To most people I was still a Candy Grrrl, purveying my goofy products. But I was also an undercover Formula 12 girl, who had intense meetings with Devereaux, thrashing out publicity plans and fine-tuning packaging. Any left-over time I had, I spent with Jacqui, reading baby books.

I never cried and I never got tired: a pilot light of bitterness fuelled me. I didn't reschedule with Neris Hemming and, abruptly, I stopped going to Leisl at the Church of Spiritual Communication.

The first Sunday, Mitch rang. 'We missed you today, peanut.'

'I think I'm going to give it a miss for a while.'

'How'd it go with Neris Hemming?'

'Bad, and I don't want to talk about it.'

Silence. 'They say anger is good. Another phase in the grieving process.'

'I'm not angry.' Well, I was, but not for the reasons he thought.

'So when am I going to see you?'

'I've got a lot on at work right now . . .'

'Sure! I totally understand. But let's stay in touch.'

'Yes,' I lied. 'Let's.'

Then Nicholas called and we had a similar conversation, and for months afterwards they both rang regularly, but I never spoke to them and never returned their calls. Eventually, they stopped ringing and I was relieved; that part of my life was over.

I'd closed up like a flower at night, a bitter little bud, sealed tight.

But I was far from being unprofessional—on the contrary, I was probably more professional than I'd ever been before. And it appeared to be paying off because just before Thanksgiving, the first tantalising reference to Formula 12 appeared in the press, described as a 'Quantum Leap in Skincare'.

'**A**nna, this new "quantum leap" skincare? What do you now about it?'

My phone was ringing off the hook: beauty journos, their curiosity piqued.

'What have you heard about it?' I asked.

'That it's like nothing we've ever seen before.'

'Yes, I heard that too.'

All through December the buzz around Formula 12 built. Amid the craziness of Christmas drinks and parties and shopping, the whispers intensified.

The time had almost arrived. I'd decided that *Harpers* was the magazine we were going for and I set up a lunch with their beauty editor, Blythe Crisp, for early in the new year. 'A very special lunch,' I promised her.

'End of January,' I told Devereaux. 'That's when we break it.'

The nurse moved the scanner over Jacqui's gel-covered bump and said, 'Looks like you're having a little girl.'

'Cool!' Jacqui punched the air from her prone position. 'A girl! What'll we call her, Anna?'

'Joella? Jodi? Joanne? Jo?'

In a sappy voice Jacqui said, 'So Narky Joey will know how much I stiiilll love him. Or better still—how about Nark-Ann? Or Narkella?'

'Narkella!' The thought of calling the little girl Narkella struck us as so funny that we collapsed into convulsions, clutching each other and apologising weakly to the nurse for our unseemly behaviour. I couldn't remember the last time I'd had a belly-laugh like it and it felt great.

In the cab home, I said, 'What if Rachel and Luke ask about the scan?'

'What do you—oh, you mean they might tell Joey?'

'Mmm.'

She thought about it, then said, almost impatiently, 'I suppose he'll have to know at some stage that I'm having a girl. Tell them what you like. Tell them all about Narkella.'

'Grand. Fine. I just didn't want to do the wrong thing . . .' I let a little time elapse, then said, 'In all fairness, though, Jacqui, no stupid names. Call your baby something normal.'

'Like what?'

'I dunno. Jacqui. Rachel. No Honey, Sugar, Treacle—'

'Treacle! That's so cute. We could spell it with a k. And an i and an l. Treakil. Ikkil Treakil!'

'Jacqui, no, that's terrible, please . . .'

2

'WHERE'S THE INVITATION?' Mum shrieked.

In the dining room, over the remains of our Christmas dinner, I exchanged perplexed looks with Rachel, Helen and Dad. A moment ago Mum had been in the kitchen on the phone to Auntie Imelda.

She flung open the dining-room door and paused at the threshold, breathing heavily. In her hand she held the twig-and-papyrus wedding invitation. Her eyes sought Rachel's.

'You're not getting married in a church,' she said, thickly.

'No,' Rachel said calmly. 'Like it says on the invitation, Luke and I are having a blessing in a Quaker hall.'

'You made me think it was a church and I have to find out from my own sister that you're not getting married in a church.'

'I never said it was a church. You simply chose to assume it.'

'And who'll be carrying out this so-called'—she almost spat the word—'blessing?'

'It's a friend of mine, a minister.'

Mum's fury set the tone for what remained of the Christmas period. 'It's a joke,' she raged. 'It's not a wedding, it's a travesty. A "blessing" no less! Well, she can count me out.'

But Dad was secretly thrilled because he thought that if it wasn't a 'proper' wedding he wouldn't have to make a speech. Rachel, too, was serene and unflappable.

'Aren't you upset?' I asked. 'Do you mind getting married without Mum and Dad being there?'

'She'll be there. Do you honestly think she'd miss it?'

I hunkered down and hid in soppy films and chocolate biscuits and counted the days until I got back to New York. I'd never been that keen on Christmas, but I was finding this one particularly tough.

Janie had sent me a Christmas card—a photo of 'little Jack' in a Santa hat—she *kept* writing and sending photos and saying we could meet whenever I wanted. The Maddoxes were also badgering me to meet 'little Jack' and I was still stonewalling them. I would never meet him.

'**C**hopper's taken off,' the man with the walkie-talkie said. 'Blythe Crisp on board. ETA twenty-seven after twelve.'

To create the necessary air of drama around Formula 12, I was having Blythe Crisp helicoptered from the roof of the *Harpers* building to a 120-foot yacht moored in New York harbour.

Even though the weather was freezing—it was January 4—and the water was choppy, I thought the yacht was a nice touch, it smacked a little of drug-smuggling.

'Is that it?' I thought I could hear a helicopter.

Walkie-talkie man checked his big, black, waterproof, nuclear-bomb-proof watch. 'Right on time.'

Inside a minute, a bone-dry Blythe was click-clicking down the parquet hallway in high leather boots to where I was waiting in the main salon, champagne already poured. 'Anna, my God, what's all this about? The chopper, this . . . boat?'

'Confidentiality. I couldn't risk our conversation being overheard.'

'Why? What's going on?'

'Sit down, Blythe. Champagne? Gummi Bears?' I'd done my research; she loved Gummi Bears. 'OK, I've got something for you but I want it in the March issue.' The March issue was due out at the end of January.

She shook her head. 'Oh, Anna, it's too late, we've put March to bed. It's about to go to the printers.'

'Let me show you what this is about.' I clapped my hands and a white-gloved waiter brought in a small, heavy box on a tray and presented it to her.

Wide-eyed, Blythe took it, opened it up, stared into it for a long moment and whispered, 'Oh my God, this is it. The super-cream of super-creams. I'll just go wake March up.'

After the chopper had whisked her back uptown I rang Leonard Daly at Devereaux. 'It's a go.'

'Take the rest of the day off.' A joke, of course. I had tons to do and now that Formula 12 was about to officially exist, I had to set up our office. I wanted to locate the Formula 12 camp of desks as far away from Lauryn as possible; she was not at all happy that I'd landed another job. She was even less happy that I was taking Teenie with me. My other assistant was a bright young spark called Hannah.

On January 29, the March issue of *Harpers* hit the stands and immediately I emerged, a beautiful Formula 12 butterfly from my Candy Grrrl chrysalis, and paraded around in my charcoal suits for all to see.

As soon as January clicked over into February, the anniversary of Aidan's death began to loom like a big shadow. As the days passed, I had moments of real panic, a genuine expectation that something terrible might happen.

On February 16, I went to work as normal but, with super-real recall, I relived every second of the same day the previous year. By mid-afternoon I'd had enough. I invented an interview, left work, went home and commenced a vigil, counting down the minutes and seconds to the exact time of Aidan's death.

The seconds ticked away and I remembered the moment of impact from the other cab, then us waiting in the wrecked car, the arrival of the ambulance, the race to the hospital, Aidan being rushed into theatre . . .

Closer and closer I got to the time he died, and I have to admit that I was desperately—crazily—hoping that, when the clock reached the exact second he'd left his body, a portal would open between his world and mine and that he might appear to me, maybe even speak. But nothing happened. Straight-backed, I sat staring at nothing and wondered: Now what happens?

The phone rang, that's what. Mum rang from Ireland and made sympathetic noises. 'How are you sleeping these days?' she asked.

'Not so good. I never get more than a couple of unbroken hours.'

'God love you. Well, I've good news. Me, your father and Helen are coming to New York on March 1.'

'So soon? That's more than two weeks before the wedding.' *Oh God.* 'Where are you staying?' I asked.

'We'll farm ourselves out. We'll spend the first week with you.'

'With me? But my apartment is tiny.'

'It's not that small.'

That wasn't what she'd said the first time she'd seen it.

'And we'll hardly be there. We'll be out all day shopping.'

'But where will you all sleep? I asked.

'Me and Dad will sleep in your bed. Helen can sleep on the couch.'

'But what about me? Where will I sleep?'

'Aren't you just after telling me that you hardly sleep at all? So it doesn't matter, does it? Have you an armchair or something?'

'Yes, but . . .'

'Ha, ha, I'm only having you on! As if we'd stay in your place; there isn't room to swing a mouse, never mind a cat. We're staying in the Gramercy Lodge.'

'The Gramercy Lodge? But didn't Dad get food poisoning the last time you stayed there?'

'He did, I suppose. But it's handy.'

'Handy for what? Catching food poisoning?'

'You don't catch food poisoning.'

'Fine, fine, whatever.' Old dogs, new tricks.

A couple of days later I woke up and felt . . . different.

I didn't know what it was. I lay under my duvet and wondered. The light outside had altered: pale lemon, springlike, after the grey drear of winter. Was that it? I wasn't sure. Then I noticed that for the first morning in over a year I hadn't been woken by aches in my bones. But it wasn't that either, and suddenly I knew what the difference was: today was the day that I'd completed the long journey from my head to my heart—finally, I understood that Aidan wouldn't be coming back.

I'd heard the old wives' tale that we need to live through an entire year without the person, to experience every part of our lives without them, and it's only when that's done that we begin to understand.

For so long I'd tried to make myself believe that he would come back, that somehow he'd manage it because he loved me so much. Even when I was so angry over little Jack that I'd stopped talking to him, I'd still held out hope. Now I knew, really knew: Aidan wouldn't be coming back.

For the first time in a long time I cried. After months of being frozen to my very centre, warm tears began to flow.

To Magiciansgirl1@yahoo.com
From: Psychic_Productions@yahoo.com
Subject: Re: Neris Hemming

Your rescheduled appointment with Neris Hemming will take place on March 22 at 2.30 p.m. Thank you for your interest in Neris.

'I'm not interested,' I told the screen. Two seconds later, I put the date and time in my organiser. I hated myself for it, but I couldn't help it.

'**A**nna! Hey, Anna!'

I was hurrying along 55th Street, on my way to a lunch with the beauty editor of *Ladies' Lounge*, when I heard my name being called. I turned round. Someone was running towards me: a man. As he got closer, I thought I recognised him but I couldn't be sure. I was pretty sure I knew him . . . Then I saw that it was Nicholas!

Before I knew what was happening, he'd scooped me up and we were hugging each other. I was surprised by how warmly I felt towards him.

He put me down and we smiled into each other's faces.

'Wow, Anna, you look great,' he said. 'Sorta sexy and scary.'

'Thanks. Look, Nicholas, I'm sorry I never called you back. I was going through a really bad time.'

'That's OK. I understand. Truly.'

I felt a little embarrassed asking, 'Do you still go to Leisl's?'

He shook his head. 'Last time I was there was about four months ago. None of the old gang go any more. Not even Undead Fred.'

'Wow. OK.' This was something I had to ask. 'Nicholas, you know when Leisl used to channel your dad? Do you think she really did? Do you really think you were talking to him?'

He thought about it. 'Yeah. Maybe. I don't know. But I guess that, at the time, I needed to go and hear what I heard. It got me through.' He'd changed since I'd last seen him. He looked more like a grown-up.

'It's good to see you,' I blurted.

He smiled. 'And it's good to see you. Why don't you call me sometime. We could do something. Maybe we could catch a movie.'

3

'WHICH ONE OF YOU stole my Multiple Orgasm?' Mum opened her bed-room door and shrieked down the hotel corridor. 'Claire, Helen, give me my Multiple Orgasm!'

A middle-aged couple, wearing practical sightseeing clothes, were just leaving their bedroom. Mum saw them and, without missing a beat, said, 'Lovely morning.'

They looked scandalised and hurried towards the lifts.

'Calm down,' I said, from inside the room.

'Calm down? My daughter's getting married today, even if it isn't in a church, and one of you has stolen my Multiple Orgasm. And what's your father doing in the bathroom, he's been in there for days. Go down to Claire's room and see did she steal my lipstick.'

Claire and family and Maggie and family were also staying in the Gramercy Lodge. Everyone was on the same floor.

'Go on,' Mum urged. 'Get me a lipstick.'

Out in the corridor, JJ was kicking a fire extinguisher. He was wearing a wide-brimmed yellow hat, part of Maggie's wedding ensemble, I deduced. I watched his assault on the fire extinguisher and wondered about what Leisl had said: why was JJ so important to me? Why would he become 'more important'? Then it hit me: Leisl had said 'a blond-haired little boy in a hat' and 'the initial J'; little Jack fitted that description just as much as JJ did. Maybe Aidan—through Leisl— had been trying to tell me about him? I was suddenly covered in goosebumps.

So had Leisl really been channelling Aidan? I supposed I'd never know.

'What have you done with my good hat?' Maggie had rushed out into the corridor. 'Give it to me and stop kicking that thing.'

From Maggie's room came the sound of baby Holly singing.

Then Claire and Kate, her twelve-year-old daughter, appeared wearing similar clothes: knicker-skimmingly short skirts, tottery high heels and lots of glitter. By contrast, Claire's six-year-old daughter, Francesca, wore old-fashioned buckle shoes and a puff-sleeved smock trimmed with broderie anglaise. She was like a china doll.

'You're gorgeous,' I told her.

'Thank you,' she said. 'They tried to make me wear all that shiny stuff but this is my look.'

'Has anyone an iron?' Maggie asked. 'I need to iron Garv's shirt.'

'Give it to me,' Claire said. 'Adam will do it.'

'He's more like an indentured houseboy than a man!' Helen's voice shouted from a nearby bedroom. 'How can you respect him.'

Outside the Quaker hall everyone was milling about, looking their shiny best. Through the throng I spotted Angelo, all in black. I'd known he was going to be there; he and Rachel had become quite pally since the terrible day I'd showed up at his apartment. I gave him a smile and positioned myself in the thick of my sisters and nieces. I didn't want to talk to him.

'I'm opening a book on how late they're going to be.' Helen was circulating and gathering money.

'Rachel won't be late,' Mum said. 'She doesn't believe in it. She says it's disrespectful. Put me down for right on time.'

'That'll be ten dollars.'

'Ten! Oh, here's Mr and Mrs Luke! Marjorie! Brian!' Mum grabbed Dad by the sleeve and sailed forward to greet them. 'Lovely day for it!'

They'd met a few times in the past but they didn't know each other well. Wreathed in bright, brittle smiles, both sets of parents circled each other warily.

Someone called out, 'Don't tell me this is the happy couple!' Everyone stormed the door and crowded, with unseemly haste, into seats. The hall was festooned with spring flowers, and their scent filled the air.

Moments later, Luke marched up the aisle to the front of the hall. His collar-skimming hair was glossy and neat and although he was wearing a suit, his trousers seemed tighter than necessary.

'Do you think he gets them taken in specially?' Mum whispered. 'Or does he just buy them that way?'

'Dunno.'

She gave me a sharp look. 'Are you all right?'

'Yes.'

This was the first wedding I'd been to since Aidan died. I'd never admitted it but I'd been dreading this.

Up the aisle came Dad and Rachel. Rachel was wearing a pale yellow sheath dress and carrying a small posy of flowers. A thousand camera flashes lit her way.

'Your father's tie is crooked,' Mum hissed at me.

Dad delivered Rachel to Luke, then shoved his way into our row and the service began: someone read a poem about loyalty, someone else sang a song about forgiveness, then the minister spoke about how he'd first met Rachel and Luke and how suited they were to each other.

'Rachel and Luke have written their own vows,' the minister said.

'They would.' Mum elbowed me to share the joke, but I was remembering mine. 'For richer, for poorer, for better or worse, in sickness and in health.' I thought I was going to choke when I remembered, 'All the days of our lives.' It felt like a hand round my throat. *I miss you, Aidan Maddox. I miss you so much. But I wouldn't have forgone my time with you. The pain is worth it.*

I pawed around in my little handbag for a tissue; Helen pressed one into my hand.

Up on the little dais, Luke and Rachel held hands and Rachel said, 'I am responsible for my own happiness, but I surrender it to you, it is my gift to you.'

'Before I met you,' Luke said, 'been a long time, a long, lonely time.'

Dad was baffled. 'Is it not all a bit . . . what's the word you say?'

'Feathery strokery,' Jacqui whispered loudly behind us.

'That's right, feathery strokery.' Then he realised it was Jacqui who'd spoken and, mortified, he stared at the floor. He still wasn't over the Scrabble email.

Would you look at the way Narky Joey keeps staring over at Jacqui,' Mum said.

Everyone snapped their heads round. Joey was at one of three tables crammed with Real Men. Undeniably, he was staring at Jacqui, who was at the 'Single People' table.

'Mind you,' Mum admitted reluctantly, 'she's looking very well for an unmarried woman who's nearly eight months pregnant.'

Seated among our peculiar cousins, Jacqui positively glowed. Most pregnant women I know got eczema and varicose veins, Jacqui looked better than she ever had before.

'Cripes!' Mum yelped, as something hit her in the chest. A yellow hat. Maggie's.

JJ and Claire's son, Luka, were playing frisbee with it.

'Best thing for it,' Mum said. 'It's rotten. She looks more like the mother of the bride than I do.' She twirled the hat back to Luka, then looked down at her plate. 'Oh, these must be the famed sugar-snap peas. Well, I won't be touching them.' She shoved them onto her side plate. 'Look,' she hissed. 'Joey's still staring at her.'

'At her bazoomas.' This from twelve-year-old Kate.

Mum looked at her sourly. 'You're your mother's daughter and no mistake. Go back to the children's table. Go on! Your poor Auntie Margaret is over there trying to control the lot of you.'

'I'm going to tell her what you said about her hat.'

'Don't bother your barney. I'll tell her myself.'

Kate sloped off.

'Where's Dad?' I asked.

'Powdering his nose.'

'Again? What's up with him?'

'His stomach is sick. He's nervous about his speech.'

'He's got food poisoning!' Helen declared. 'Hasn't he?'

'No, he has not!'

'Yes he has.'

'Anna, there's some man, over there, who keeps sneaking looks at you,' Claire said.

'The one who looks like he's out of the Red Hot Chili Peppers?' Mum said. 'I've noticed him too.'

'Givvus a look,' Helen said. 'The one in black? With the long hair?' She drawled, 'He looks like a bad, bad man.'

'Funny that,' I said. 'Because he's a very good one.'

Francesca collared me. 'Auntie Anna, I'll dance with you because your husband died and you've no one to dance with.' She took my hand. 'And Kate will dance with Jacqui because she's having a baby and she doesn't have a boyfriend.'

'Um, thank you.'

'Hold on,' Mum said. 'I'm coming for a bop too.'

'Don't say bop!' Helen said, in anguish. 'That's a terrible word.'

'Dad?' I asked. 'Will you dance?'

Carefully, he shook his head, his face as white as the tablecloth.

'Maybe we should get him a doctor,' I said quietly. 'Food poisoning can be dangerous.'

'He's not poisoned, it's just nerves. Hit the floor!'

We merged forces with Jacqui and Kate, all of us holding hands. Helen joined us, then Claire, then Maggie and baby Holly, then Rachel. We were a girl-circle, our party dresses swinging, everyone happy and smiling and laughing and beautiful. Someone handed me baby Holly and we twirled together, my sisters' hands helping to spin me. Swirling, whirling past their radiant faces, I remembered something I hadn't known I'd forgotten: Aidan wasn't the only person I loved; I loved other people too. I loved my sisters, I loved my mother, I loved my dad, I loved my nieces, I loved my nephews, I loved Jacqui. At the moment I loved everybody.

4

'NERIS HEMMING HERE.'

'Hello, it's Anna Walsh. I'm calling for my reading.' I was curious. Curious but not hopeful. OK, maybe a bit hopeful.

Silence whistled on the line, then she spoke. 'Anna, I'm getting . . . yes, I've got a man here with me. A young man, taken before his time.'

When I'd originally made the booking, I'd told the reservations person that my husband had died. Who was to say that she hadn't passed this information to Neris?

'You loved him very much, didn't you, honey?'

Why else would I be trying to contact him? My eyes welled up.

'Didn't you, honey?' she repeated, when I remained silent.

'Yes,' I choked. I was ashamed of crying when I was being so crudely manipulated.

'He's telling me he loved you very much too. He was your husband, right?'

'Yes.' Damn I shouldn't have told her.

'And he passed on after an . . . illness?'

'An accident.'

'Yes, an accident, in which he became very ill, which caused him to pass on.' Said firmly.

'How do I know it's really him?'

'Because he says so . . . He's remembering a vacation you took by the ocean? I'm getting a picture of a blue, blue sea, a blue sky, barely a cloud in it, a white beach. A little rum.' She chuckled. 'Sounds about right?'

'Yes.' I thought of our time in Mexico. But who hasn't had a vacation by the ocean? And tequila, rum, they were both holiday drinks.

'And, oh! He's interrupting me. He says, don't mourn him any longer. He's gone to a better place. He didn't want to leave you, but he had to, and even though you can't see him, he's always with you.'

'OK,' I said dully.

'Have you any questions?'

'Yes, actually. There was something he wanted to tell me. What was it?'

'Don't mourn him any longer, he's gone to a better place—'

'No, it was something he wanted to tell me *before* he died.'

'That was what he wanted to tell you.' Her voice was steely.

'How could he have wanted to tell me, before he died, that he was gone to a better place?'

'He had a premonition.'

'No, he didn't. You're just saying stuff that could apply to anyone.'

She blurted out, 'He used to make you breakfast.' She sounded—what? Surprised?

I was surprised too—because it was true! I'd once remarked that I loved porridge and the following morning I found Aidan standing at our stove, stirring something in a saucepan. 'Oatmeal,' he'd said. 'Or porridge, if you prefer.'

'I'm right, yeah? He made you breakfast every morning?'

'Yes.' I was meek.

'He really loved you, honey.'

He did. I remembered what I'd forgotten: he used to tell me sixty times a day how much he loved me. He'd hide love notes in my handbag.

'What did he make me for breakfast?' If she could answer that, I'd believe in her.

Confidently she said, 'Eggs.'

'No.'

Pause. 'Granola?'

'No, forget it. Here's an easier one. What was his name?'

After a silence she said, 'I'm getting the letter L.'

'Nope.'

'M?'

'Nope.'

'B?'

'Nope.'

'A?'

'OK. Yes.'

'Adam?'

'That's my sister's boyfriend's name.'

'Yes, of course it is! He's here with me and is telling me—'

'He's not dead.' He's alive, in London. Probably ironing something.

'Oh. OK. Aaron?'

'Nope. You'll never get it.'

'Tell me.'

'No.'

'It's driving me crazy!'

'Good.' Then I hung up.

Mitch looked like a different person. Even his face was a different colour. Six, seven, eight months ago, I hadn't known that he looked grey and rigid. It was only now that he'd lost that terrible stiffness and had become animated that I noticed.

He spotted me and broke into a massive smile. A real dazzler, the likes of which I'd never seen him do before. 'Anna. Hey, you look great!' His voice was louder than it used to be.

'Thank you.'

I'd called him after my reading with Neris Hemming; there were a couple of questions I wanted answers to. He'd professed himself delighted to hear from me and suggested we meet for dinner.

'Right this way.' He led me into the restaurant.

'For two?' the desk-girl asked.

Mitch smiled and said, 'We'd prefer a booth.'

'So does everybody.'

'I guess they do,' he acknowledged, smiling. 'But see what you can do.'

'I'll go see,' the girl said grudgingly. 'But you might have to wait.'

'That's OK.' He smiled again. He was flirting with her!

I noticed something else. 'You don't have your kitbag! This is the first time I've seen you without it.'

'Really?' He barely seemed to remember. 'Oh, yeah,' he said slowly. 'That's right. Back then, I just about lived in the gym.'

'And you've spoken more in the last five minutes than in all the months I knew you.'

'I didn't talk?'

'No.'

The girl was back. 'Gotcha a booth.'

'For real? Thank you so much,' Mitch said, sincerely.

She coloured. 'My pleasure.'

So the real Mitch was a charmer. My speedy reassessment of him continued apace.

After we'd ordered, I said, 'I have to ask you a question.'

'So ask it.'

'When you spoke to Neris Hemming, did you really believe she was channelling Trish?'

'Yeah.' He seemed embarrassed. 'At the time, I was out of my mind. I needed to believe.' He shrugged. 'Maybe she channelled Trish, maybe she didn't. All I know is, it probably stopped me from going over the edge.'

'Do you remember you told me that she guessed your nicknames? Yours and Trish's for each other? What were they?'

An embarrassed little laugh. 'Mitchie and Trixie.'

Mitchie and Trixie? 'I could have guessed that for free.'

'Yeah. Well, like I said, it did what it needed to do at the time.'

'Do you still try to, you know, contact Trish?'

He shook his head. 'I still talk to her and have pictures of her everywhere, but I know she's gone and, for whatever reason, I'm still here. Same goes for you. I don't know if you'll ever contact Aidan, but, the way I see it is, you're alive. You've got a life to live.'

'Maybe. Anyway, I'm not going to any more psychics,' I said.

'Glad to hear it. Hey, are you free Sunday afternoon? I've got a billion great places for us to go to. How about the Planetarium, they do simulated spacecraft rides? Or bingo, we could go to bingo?'

Bingo. I liked the sound of that.

'Jacqui? Jacqui?'

'I'm down here,' she called. 'In the kitchen.'

I followed her voice and found her on her hands and knees with a basin of soapy water. 'What on earth . . .?'

'I'm scrubbing the kitchen floor.'

'But you're forty weeks pregnant, you're due to have a baby any minute.'

'I just got the urge,' she said brightly.

I watched her doubtfully. 'Other than the fact that you seem to have lost your mind, how are you?' I asked.

'Funny you should ask, I've been having twinges all day. In my back.'

'Braxton Hicks,' I said firmly.

'Not Braxton Hicks,' she said. 'Braxton Hicks go away when you do something physical.'

It was her hand that I noticed first: it was clenched so tightly that the skin over the bones went white. then I saw that her face was contorted and her body was arching and twisting.

In horror, I ran to her. 'Twinges like that?'

'No.' She shook her head, her face bright red. 'Nothing like as bad.'

I grabbed one of the helpful leaflets we'd been given and read. 'Did it "begin in the back and move forward in a wavelike motion"?'

'Yes!'

'Oh shit, that sounds like a contraction all right.' Suddenly I was terrified. 'You're going to have a baby!'

Something caught my eye: a pool of water was spreading across the clean kitchen floor. Had she knocked over a basin of soapy water?

'Anna,' Jacqui whispered, 'I think my waters just broke.'

She was right. The water was coming from under Jacqui's skirt. She really *was* going to have a baby. I focused enough to ring the hospital.

'I'm Jacqui Staniforth's birthing partner. Her waters have just broken and she's in labour.'

'How far apart are the contractions?'

'I don't know. She's only had one. But it was terrible.'

'Time the contractions and when they're five minutes apart, come in.'

I hung up. 'We've to time them. Where's the stopwatch?'

'With all the other labour stuff.'

I wished we didn't have to keep saying the word 'labour'. I found the stopwatch, rejoined her on the kitchen floor and said, 'Right. Any time you like. Go on, give us a contraction.'

We collapsed into nervous giggles. When they had subsided, I looked at Jacqui. 'Just out of curiosity, is there any particular reason we're sitting on the wet floor?'

'No, I suppose not.'

We got to our feet and Jacqui changed her clothes and had two more contractions. Ten minutes apart, we established. I rang the hospital back. 'They're ten minutes apart.'

'Keep timing them and come in when they're five minutes apart.'

'But what should we do until then? She's in terrible pain.'

'Rub her back, have her take a hot bath, walk around.'

So I rubbed Jacqui's back and we watched *Moonstruck* and said all the words, and paused it during every contraction so that Jacqui wouldn't miss anything.

By 1 a.m., the contractions were seven minutes apart.

'I'm getting in the bath,' Jacqui said. 'It might help with the pain.'

I sat in the bathroom with her and put on some relaxing music. For forty-five minutes the contractions were seven minutes apart. Would we ever reach the magic figure of five minutes?

'I think you need to do some walking,' I said. 'It might speed things up.'

The dark streets were quiet. With our arms linked, we walked. 'Tell me lovely things,' Jacqui said.

'Like what?'

'Tell me about when you fell in love with Aidan.'

Instantly, I was pierced by feelings so mixed-up I couldn't put names on them. Sadness was there and maybe some bitterness. And there was something else, something nicer.

'Please,' Jacqui said. 'I'm in labour and I've no boyfriend.'

Reluctantly, I said, 'OK. In the beginning I used to say it out loud. I used to say, "I love Aidan Maddox and Aidan Maddox loves me." I had to hear myself say it because it was so fabulous that I couldn't believe it.'

'How many times a day did he tell you he loved you?'

'Sixty.'

'No, seriously.'

'Yes, seriously. Sixty. He said he couldn't sleep easy until I'd been told sixty times.'

'Wow. Hold on.' She grabbed tight onto some railings and moaned and gasped her way through another contraction. Then she straightened up and said, 'Tell me five lovely things about him. Go on,' she urged.

Grudgingly, I said, 'He always gave a dollar to bums.'

'Tell me a more interesting one.'

'I can't remember.'

'Yes, you can.'

Well, yes, I could, but this was harder to talk about. My throat felt tight and achy. 'You know how I get cold sores on my chin? Well, there was one night and we were in bed, and the light was off and we were just going to sleep, when the tingling on my chin started. If I didn't put my special ointment on it immediately I'd look like a leper by the morning. But I hadn't filled my prescription. So Aidan got up, got dressed and went out to find a twenty-four-hour drugstore. And it was December and snowing and so cold . . .' All of a sudden, I was in convulsions, crying. So bad I had to lean over some railings, just like Jacqui had in the throes of a contraction. I sobbed so much I started to choke.

Jacqui rubbed my back and when the storm of crying passed, she patted my hand and murmured, 'Good girl, three more.'

I'd thought because I'd got so upset, she'd let me off the hook. 'He used to come shopping for clothes with me, even though he was mortified in girls' shops.'

'Yes. True.'

'He did excellent Humphrey Bogart impersonations.'

'That's right, he did! It wasn't just the voice; he was able to do something brilliant with his upper lip so he actually looked like him.'

'Yes, he sort of made it stick to his upper teeth!'

'OK, I've got one,' Jacqui said. 'Do you remember when you moved in with him and, as consolation, he helped me to move to my new place? He hired a van and drove it and lifted all my boxes and stuff. He even helped me clean the new place, and you got me by the throat and said, "If you say he's a Feathery Stroker for this, I'll hate you." And I said to you, "That guy hasn't a Feathery Strokery bone in his body. He must really love you."'

'I remember.'

She sighed, then she said, 'You were so lucky.'

'Yes,' I said, 'I was.' I didn't feel any rush of bitterness.

'Incoming contraction!' Jacqui crouched down on the front steps of a brownstone as the spasm gripped her.

'Breathe,' I instructed. 'Visualise. Oh, Christ, come back!' Jacqui had toppled off the step and rolled onto the sidewalk. From the corner of my eye I noticed that we'd attracted the attention of a cruising black and white. It pulled in and two cops, walkie-talkies crackling, got out and walked over. One looked like he lived on Krispy Kreme doughnuts, but the other was was tall and handsome.

'What's going on?' Doughnut boy demanded.

'She's in labour.'

Both men watched Jacqui as she writhed about on the sidewalk.

'Shouldn't she be in the hospital?' the handsome one asked.

'Not until her contractions are five minutes apart,' I said.

'Does it hurt?' Doughnut boy asked, anxiously.

'She's in labour!' Handsome said. 'Sure it hurts!'

'How would you know?' Jacqui shouted up. 'You . . . you . . . *man!*'

'Jacqui?' Handsome said in surprise. 'Is that you?'

'Karl?' Jacqui rolled onto her back and smiled graciously up at him. 'Good to see you again. How've you been?'

'Good. Good. And you?'

'Five minutes!' I said, staring at my stopwatch. 'They're five minutes apart. Come on!'

By the time we got to the labour and delivery suite at the hospital, the contractions were four minutes apart. I helped Jacqui into a horrible gown, then a nurse appeared.

'Oh, thank God,' Jacqui said. 'Quick, quick, the epidural!'

The nurse examined Jacqui and shook her head. 'It's too soon for an epidural. You're not dilated enough. It will slow down the labour.'

'But I must be! I've been in labour for hours. I'm in agony.'

The nurse gave a patronising smile that said: Millions of women do this every day. 'The midwife is on her way.'

'Don't fob me off, she can't give me an epidural, only the man can. Oh God, here we go again,' Jacqui whimpered.

Time passed nightmarishly slowly. At some stage I noticed it was ten in the morning so I rang work and left a message with Teenie, telling her what was happening.

Soon afterwards, the midwife had a fiddle up Jacqui's 'canal'. 'You should be ready to start pushing,' she said.

Jacqui huffed and puffed frantically, then the curtains swished aside dramatically, and who was standing there? Only Narky Joey.

'What's he doing here?' Jacqui yelled.

'I love you.'

'Close the curtains, asshole!'

'Yeah, sorry.' He pulled the curtains closed behind him. 'I love you, Jacqui. I'm sorry, sorrier than I've ever been about anything.'

'I don't care! Get out. I'm in agony and this is all your fault.'

'Jacqui, push!'

'Jacqui, I love you!'

'Shut up, Joey, I'm *trying* to push,' Jacqui screeched. 'And it makes no difference if you love me because I'm never having sex again.'

The nurse reappeared. 'What's happening now?'

'Please, oh, please, lovely nurse, can I have my epidural now?' Jacqui begged.

The nurse had a quick feel, then shook her head. 'It's too late.'

'*What?* How can that be? Last time it was too soon, this time it's too late!'

'Give her the goddamned epidural,' Joey said.

'You shut up.' From Jacqui.

'Keep pushing,' the midwife said.

'Jacqui.' I was staring in high alarm. 'Something's happening!'

'What?'

'It's the head,' the midwife said.

More and more of the head appeared. When you see it happening with your own two eyes, it's nothing short of miraculous.

And then its face appeared.

'It's a baby,' I yelped. 'It's a baby!'

'What were you expecting?' Jacqui gasped. 'A handbag?'

Then the shoulders appeared and, with a gentle tug, the baby slithered out. The midwife counted ten fingers, ten toes, then said, 'Congratulations, Jacqui, you've got a beautiful baby girl.'

Narky Joey was in floods. It was hilarious.

The midwife swaddled the baby in a blanket, then handed her to Jacqui, who cooed, 'Welcome to the world, Treakil Pompom Vuitton Staniforth.'

It was a beautiful moment.

'Can I see her?' Joey asked.

'Not yet. Give her to Anna,' Jacqui ordered.

Into my arms was placed a tiny scrunched-faced mewing bundle, a new person. A new life. Her doll-sized shrimp fingers stretched up at me, and in my heart the last shard of bitterness with Aidan melted and

I recognised the feeling I hadn't been able to name earlier. It was love.

I handed Treakil to Joey.

'I'll leave you three to get to know each other,' I said.

'Why? Where are you going?'

'Boston.'

When we touched down at Logan Airport I was the first off the plane. Dry-mouthed with anticipation, I followed the signs for Arrivals. I clip-clopped along the linoleum floors, breathing hard. My grown-up ladies' handbag bounced against my side. The only thing to mar my sophisti-cated image was Dogly, whose head was sticking out of my bag. His ears were swinging enthusiastically and he looked like he was checking out everything we passed. Dogly was going back to his Boston roots. I'd miss him but it was the right thing to do.

Then I was passing through the automatic glass doors and I looked beyond the barrier, searching for a blond-haired two-year-old. And there he was, a sturdy little boy, in a grey sweatshirt, blue jeans and a Red Sox cap, holding hands with the dark-haired woman beside him. I felt, rather than saw, her smile.

Then Jack looked up, saw me and, even though he couldn't have known who I was, he smiled too, showing his little white milk teeth.

I recognised him immediately. How could I not? He looked exactly like his daddy.

Epilogue

JACQUI AND JOEY and Treakil are a modern-day family unit—Joey babysits Treakil when Jacqui goes out with Handsome Karl, the cop. She's reconsidering her ban on Feathery Strokery men, especially as Handsome Karl—who really is very handsome—is as besotted with Treakil as he is with Jacqui. However, there's no denying there's still a vrizzon between herself and Narky Joey, so who knows . . .

Rachel and Luke are the same as ever: a pair of happy Feathery Strokers. Helen is working on a new case: it's all very exciting. Harry Fear was never arrested for trying to shoot Racey O' Grady and Racey didn't finger him. Apparently they are both running their respective empires, just like they've always done, and it's business as usual in Dublin crime. Mum and Dad are well. There has been no recurrence of the dog-poo situation.

Almost every Sunday I go to bingo with Mitch. It's great fun, especially since it transpires that the new Mitch—or is it the old Mitch?—is highly competitive. He dances when he wins and sulks when he doesn't.

Leon and Dana are expecting a baby. Dana complains that every symptom of pregnancy is 'had-i-aaassss', and Leon is thrilled because he has more things than ever to worry about.

I meet Nicholas regularly. I brought him to Treakil's 'Welcome to the world, baby girl' party and everyone declared that he was 'Adorable!'; the Real Men seem to have adopted him as a mascot.

The other day I came home after doing Pilates. It was a warm afternoon and I curled up on a corner of the couch, which was in a pool of sunshine. I started to feel sleepy, to drift, and the membrane between being awake and asleep was so barely there that when I passed into a dream, I dreamt that I was awake. I dreamt I was on the couch, in my front room, just like I really was.

It was no surprise to suddenly find Aidan there beside me. It was such a great, great comfort to see him and to feel his presence. He took my hands and I looked into his face, so familiar, so beloved.

'How are you?' he asked.

'OK, better than I was. I met little Jack.'

'What did you think of him?'

'He's a cutie, a total sweetheart. That's what you were going to tell me, isn't it? The day you died?'

'Yeah. Janie told me a few days before. I was so worried about you, how you were going to feel.'

'Well, I feel OK now. I really like Janie—and Howie, actually. And I see a lot of Kevin and your parents. I go to Boston to see them, or they come here.'

'It's weird how stuff turns out, isn't it?'

'Yes.'

We sat in silence and I couldn't think of anything more important to say than, 'I love you.'

'I love you, Anna. I'll always love you.'

'I'll always love you too, baby.'

'I know. But it's OK to love other people too. And when you do I'll be happy for you.'

'You won't be jealous?'

'No. And you won't have lost me. I'll still be with you.'

'Will you visit me again?'

'Not like this. But look for the signs.'

'What signs?'

'You'll see them if you look for them.'

'I can't imagine loving anyone except you.'

'But you will.'

'How do you know?'

'Because I'm privy to that sort of info now.'

'Oh. So do you know who it is?'

He hesitated. 'I shouldn't really . . .'

'Oh, go on,' I cajoled. 'What's the point of you visiting from the dead if you don't give me some juice?'

'I can't give you his exact identity—but I can tell you, you know him already.'

He kissed me on the lips, placed his hand on my head, like a benediction, and left. Then I woke up, and moving from sleeping to waking seemed like nothing at all. Deep, joy-filled calm sat in and around me and I could still feel the weight and warmth of his hand on my head.

He'd really been here. I was certain of it.

I sat without moving, and felt the miracle of my breath moving in and out, in and out, in the circle of life.

And then I saw it: a butterfly. This one was beautiful, blue and yellow and white, decked out in lacy patterns, and I took it all back about butterflies only being moths in expensive embroidered jackets.

It flitted around the room, landing on our wedding photo (I'd restored all pictures of Aidan to their rightful places), the Red Sox banner, everything that had meaning for Aidan and me. Mesmerised, I watched the show.

It touched down on the remote control and fluttered its wings very fast so that it looked like it was guffawing. Then, with a touch I could barely feel, it landed on my face, on my eyebrows, my cheeks, beside my mouth. It was kissing me. Eventually it moved to the window and sat on the glass, waiting. Time to go. For now.

I opened the window and the noise rushed in; there was a great big world out there. For five or six seconds, the butterfly hovered on the sill and then off it flew, small and brave and living its life.

All about Marian Keyes

She was born in the West of Ireland in 1963

I was a month overdue and I often wonder what my life would have been like if I'd been born on time. How being a dynamic sunny Leo, instead of a critical, crap-in-bed Virgo would have been. But we will never know.

She was brought up in Dublin and spent her twenties in London

When I left school I went to college, got a law degree, then put it to good use by going to London and getting a job as a waitress. Eventually I upped and got respectable and got a job in an accounts office, where I worked (I use the term oh-so-loosely) for a long, long, long time. I thought I'd be there for ever, that I'd end up a a a desiccated, bad-tempered old bag who lived with a one-bar heater and forty cats. That small boys would throw stones at me. What I certainly had no notion of doing was becoming a writer.

She started writing in 1993 and her first book *Watermelon* was published in Ireland in 1995

I decided to send my short stories off to a publishers. So that they'd take me seriously, I enclosed a letter saying I'd written part of a novel. Which I hadn't. I had no intention of so doing, either. I was much more into the instant gratification of short stories. But they wrote back and said, send the novel, and for once in my self-destructive life I didn't shoot myself in the foot. I wrote four chapters of my first novel *Watermelon* in a week, and was offered a three-book contract on the strength of it.

Since then she has become a publishing phenomenon

In November 1996 I was finally able to give up my day job and become—allegedly anyway—a full-time writer. Except that almost from the moment all my time was free to write with, I began to try and distract myself and do anything but write. I'm up and down the stairs, checking to see if the post has come. (Even after it already has.) I pray for the phone to ring. I make appointments for root-canal treatment and toy with the notion of scrubbing the kitchen floor. Anything other than switch on the computer. Of course, once I start it's not so bad, I always find.

Her books are an unusual blend of comedy and darkness and cover subjects like depression and addiction

OK, so a book about someone with depression doesn't exactly sound like a laugh a minute, but in my experience the best comedy is rooted in darkness. All five of my books are different but share a common theme of people who are in The Bad Place, and who achieve some form of redemption. I've been in The Bad Place myself many's the time, which wasn't very pleasant while it was happening but has since come in very handy for writing about it.

Her Top Ten Favourites . . .

Favourite thing about being a writer?
Meeting my readers.

Favourite thing to snack on while writing?
Apples and Percy Pigs (strawberry flavour jelly-style candy—they're fabulous!).

Favourite item in her closet?
Blue suede Paul Smith coat.

Favourite purchase she's made recently?
My ice-green Balenciaga handbag. I love it so much I want to sleep with it.

Favourite items always to be found in her handbag?
Murray Mints. 68 lipsticks. 14 pens (all leaking). Torn pieces of paper with mysterious phone numbers on them. YSL Touche Eclat. Kleenex patterned with shoes—too pretty to use. Just for Today card.

Favourite authors?
Impossible!—too many—current favourites include Val McDermid, Carolyn Pankhurst, Philip Roth.

Favourite movie?
Raising Arizona and *Roman Holiday*.

Favourite place she'd like to travel to?
Cambodia and Laos.

Favourite thing about being married?
Having a best pal always around.

Favourite guilty pleasure?
Driving fast.

Taken from: www.mariankeyes.com

ANGELS FALL
NORA ROBERTS

Two years ago Reece Gilmore was the sole survivor of a brutal killing spree that left her emotionally scarred. Unable to settle, she now prefers to keep moving as she fights the panic attacks and nightmares that haunt her. When she arrives in the sleepy town of Angel's Fist, she doesn't intend to stay. But, as Reece knows all too well, life isn't predictible . . .

Chapter One

REECE GILMORE SMOKED through the tough knuckles of Angel's Fist in an overheating Chevy Cavalier. She had $243 and change in her pocket, which might be enough to cure the Chevy, fuel it and herself. If luck was on her side, and the car wasn't seriously ill, she'd have enough to pay for a room for the night.

Then, even by the most optimistic calculations, she'd be broke.

She took the plumes of steam puffing out of the hood as a sign it was time to stop travelling for a while and find a job. No worries, no problem, she told herself. The little Wyoming town huddled around the cold blue waters of a lake was as good as anywhere else. Maybe better. It had the openness she needed—all that sky with the snow-dipped peaks of the Tetons rising into it like sober, and somehow aloof, gods.

She'd been meandering her way towards them, through the peaks and plains for hours. She hadn't had a clue where she'd end up when she started out before dawn, but she'd bypassed Cody, zipped through Dubois, and though she'd toyed with veering into Jackson, she dipped south instead.

So something must have been pulling her to this spot.

Over the past eight months, she'd developed a strong belief in following those signs, those impulses. A peculiar slant of sunlight down a back road, a weather vane pointing south. If she liked the look of the light or the weather vane, she'd follow, until she found what seemed like the right place. She might settle in for a few weeks, or, like she had in South Dakota, a few months. Pick up some work, scout the area, then move on when those signs pointed in a new direction.

There was a freedom in the system she'd developed, and often—more often now—a lessening of the constant hum of anxiety in the back of her mind. These past months of living with herself, essentially by herself, had done more to smooth her out than the full year of therapy.

To be fair, she supposed that the therapy had given her the base to face herself every single day. Every night. And all the hours between.

And here was another fresh start, another blank slate in the bunched fingers of Angel's Fist.

If nothing else, she'd take a few days to enjoy the lake, the mountains, and pick up enough money to get back on the road again. A place like this—the signpost said population 623—probably ran to tourism, exploiting the scenery and the proximity to the national park. There'd be at least one hotel, probably a couple of B and B's, all needing someone to fetch and carry and clean.

But her first priority was a mechanic.

She eased her way round the long, wide lake. Patches of snow made dull white pools in the shade. The trees were still their wintering brown, but there were a few boats on the water. She could see a couple of guys in windbreakers and caps in a white canoe, rowing right through the reflection of the mountains.

Across from the lake she noted a gift shop, a little gallery. Bank, post office, sheriff's office. She angled away from the lake to pull the labouring car up to what looked like a big barn of a general store. There were a couple of men in flannel shirts sitting out front in stout chairs that gave them a good view of the lake. They nodded to her as she cut the engine and stepped out, then the one on the right tapped the brim of his blue cap that bore the name of the store—Mac's Mercantile and Grocery. 'Looks like you got some trouble there, young lady.'

'Sure does. Do you know anyone who can give me a hand with it?'

He pushed out of the chair. He was burly in build, ruddy in face, with lines fanning out from the corners of friendly brown eyes. 'Why don't we just pop the hood and take a look-see?'

'Appreciate it.' When she released the latch, he tossed the hood up and stepped back from the clouds of smoke. 'It started up on me about ten miles east, I guess. I wasn't paying enough attention. Got caught up in the scenery.'

'Easy to do. You heading into the park?'

'I was. More or less. I think the car had other ideas.'

His companion came over, and both men looked under the hood with knowing frowns. 'Got yourself a split radiator hose,' he told her. 'Gonna need to replace that.'

Didn't sound so bad, not too bad. Not too expensive. 'Anywhere in town I can make that happen?'

'Lynt's Garage. Why don't I give him a call for you?'

'Lifesaver.' She offered her hand, a gesture that had come to be much easier with strangers. 'I'm Reece Gilmore.'

'Mac Drubber. This here's Carl Sampson.'

'Back East, aren't you?' Carl asked. He looked a fit fifty-something to Reece, and with some Native American blood mixed in.

'Yeah. Boston area. I really appreciate the help.'

'Nothing but a phone call,' Mac said. 'You can come on in out of the breeze if you want, or take a walk around. Might take Lynt a few to get here.'

'I wouldn't mind a walk, if that's OK. Maybe you could tell me a good place to stay in town. Nothing fancy.'

'Got the Lakeview Hotel just down a ways. The Teton House, other side of the lake's some homier. More a B and B. Cabins on the lake rent by the week or month.'

She didn't think in months any longer. A day was enough of a challenge. And *homier* sounded too intimate. 'Maybe I'll walk down and take a look at the hotel.'

'It's a long walk. Could give you a ride on down.'

'I've been driving all day. I could use the stretch. But thanks, Mr Drubber.'

'No problem.' He stood another moment as she wandered down the wooden sidewalk. 'Pretty thing,' he commented.

'No meat on her.' Carl shook his head. 'Women today starve off all the curves.'

She hadn't starved them off, and was, in fact, making a concerted effort to gain back the weight that had fallen off in the past couple of years. She wouldn't have agreed with Mac's *pretty thing*. Not any more. Once she'd thought of herself that way, as a pretty woman—stylish, sexy when she wanted to be. But her face seemed too hard now, the cheekbones too prominent, the hollows too deep. The restless nights were fewer, but when they came, they left her dark eyes heavily shadowed and cast a pallor, pasty and grey, over her skin.

She wanted to recognise herself again.

She let herself stroll, her worn-out Keds nearly soundless on the sidewalk. She'd learned not to hurry—had taught herself not to push, not to rush, but to take things as they came. The cool breeze blew across her face, wound through the long brown hair she'd tied back in a tail. She liked the feel of it, the smell of it, clean and fresh, and the hard

202 | Nora Roberts

light that poured over the Tetons and sparkled on the water.

She could see some of the cabins Mac had spoken of, through the bare branches of the willows and the cottonwoods. They squatted behind the trees, made of log and glass, with wide porches and, she assumed, stunning views. It might be nice to sit on one of those porches and study the lake or the mountains. To have that room around, and the quiet.

One day maybe, she thought. But not today.

She stopped to admire green spears of daffodils in a half whiskey barrel next to the entrance of a restaurant. They trembled a bit in the chilly breeze, but they made her think of spring. Everything was new in spring. Maybe this spring, she'd be new, too.

She shifted her eyes up to the wide front window of the restaurant. More diner than restaurant, she corrected. Counter service, two- and four-tops, booths, all in faded red and white. Kitchen open to the counter, waitresses bustling around with trays and coffeepots.

Lunch crowd, she realised, then caught sight of the sign in the window.

COOK WANTED
ENQUIRE WITHIN

Signs, she thought again, taking a careful study of the set-up. Open kitchen, that was key. Diner food, she could handle that in her sleep. Or would have been able to, once.

Maybe it was time to find out, time to take another step forward. If she couldn't handle it, she'd know.

The hotel was probably hiring, in anticipation of the summer season. Or Mr Drubber might need another clerk at his store. But the sign was right there, and her steps had brought her to this spot. She took a long, long breath in, then opened the door.

Fried onions, grilling meat, strong coffee, a jukebox on country and a buzz of chatter. Clean red floors, scrubbed white counter. Photographs on the walls—black-and-whites of the lake, of the mountains.

She was still gathering her courage when one of the waitresses swung by her. 'Afternoon. If you're looking for lunch you've got your choice of a table or the counter.'

'Actually, I'm looking for the manager. Or owner. Ah, about the sign in the window. The position of cook.'

The waitress stopped, balancing a tray. 'You're a cook?'

There'd been a time Reece would have sniffed at the term good-naturedly, but she'd have sniffed nonetheless. 'Yes.'

'That's handy.' The waitress cocked her head and gave Reece a sunny smile out of a pretty face. 'Why don't you go and sit at the counter. I'll see if Joanie can get out for a minute. How about some coffee?'

'Tea, if you don't mind.'

'Coming up.'

Didn't have to take the job, Reece reminded herself as she slid onto a chrome-and-leather stool and rubbed her damp palms on her jeans. Even if it was offered, she didn't have to take it. She could stick with cleaning hotel rooms.

The waitress walked back to the grill and tapped a short sturdy woman on the shoulder, leaned in. After a moment, the woman shot a glance over her shoulder, met Reece's eyes, then nodded. The waitress came back with a white cup of hot water, with a Lipton tea bag in the saucer.

'Joanie'll be right along. You want to order some lunch? Meat loaf's the special today. Comes with mashed potatoes, green beans and a biscuit.'

'No, thanks, no, tea's fine.' Nerves bounced in her belly. Panic wanted to come, that smothering wet weight in the chest.

She should just go, Reece thought. Go right now and walk back to her car. Get the hose fixed and head out. Signs be damned.

Joanie had a fluff of blonde hair on her head, a white butcher's apron splattered with grease stains tied round her middle and high-topped red Converse sneakers on her feet. She measured Reece out of steely eyes that were more grey than blue. 'You cook?'

'Yes.'

'For a living, or just to put something in your mouth?'

'It's what I did back in Boston—for a living.' Fighting nerves, Reece ripped open the cover on the tea bag.

Joanie had a soft mouth, almost a Cupid's bow, in contrast to those hard eyes. 'Boston.' In an absent move, she tucked a dishrag in the belt of her apron. 'Long ways.'

'Yes.'

'I don't know as I want some East Coast cook who can't keep her mouth shut for five minutes.'

Reece's mouth opened in surprise, then closed again on the barest curve of a smile. 'I'm an awful chatterbox when I'm nervous.'

'What're you doing around here?'

'Travelling. My car broke down. I need a job.'

'Got references?'

Her heart tightened. 'I can get them.'

Joanie sniffed, frowned back towards the kitchen. 'Go on back, put on an apron. Next order up's a steak sandwich, med-well, onion roll, fried onions and mushrooms, fries and coleslaw. Dick don't drop dead after eating what you cook, you probably got the job.'

'All right.' Reece pushed off the stool and, keeping her breath slow and even, went through the swinging door at the end of the counter.

She didn't notice, but Joanie did, that she'd torn the tea bag cover into tiny pieces.

It was a simple set-up. Large grill, restaurant-style stove, refrigerator, freezer. Holding bins, sinks, work counters, double fryer. As she tied on an apron, Joanie set out the ingredients she'd need.

'Thanks.' Reece scrubbed her hands, then got to work.

Don't think, she told herself. Just let it come. She set the steak sizzling on the grill while she chopped onions and mushrooms. She put precut potatoes in the fry basket, set the timer. Her hands didn't shake, though her chest stayed tight.

Joanie tugged the next order from the clip on the round. 'Bowl of three-bean soup—that kettle there—goes with crackers.'

Reece simply nodded, tossed the mushrooms and onions on the grill, then filled the second order while they fried.

'Order up!' Joanie called out, and yanked another ticket. 'Reuben, club san, two side salads.'

Reece moved from order to order. The atmosphere, the orders might be different, but the rhythm was the same. She plated the original order, handed it to Joanie for inspection.

'Put it in line,' she was told. 'Start the next ticket.'

'I need to—'

'Get that next ticket. I'm going to go have a smoke.'

Reece worked another ninety minutes before it slowed enough to step back from the heat and guzzle down a bottle of water. Joanie was sitting at the counter, drinking coffee.

'Nobody died,' she said.

'Whew. Is it always that busy?'

'Saturday lunch crowd. We do OK. You get eight dollars an hour to start. You still look good in two weeks, I bump in another buck an hour. That's you and me and a part-timer on the grill, seven days a week. We open at six-thirty so that means first shift is here at six. You can order breakfast all day, lunch menu from eleven to closing, dinner, five to ten. You get two days off. I don't pay any overtime, so you go over forty hours, we take it off your next week's hours. Any problem with that?'

'No.'

'You get all the coffee, water or tea you want. You pay for food. Not that it looks like you'll be packing it away while my back's turned. You're skinny as a stick.'

'I guess I am.'

'Last shift cook cleans the grill, the stove, does the lock down—'

'I can't do that,' Reece interrupted. 'I can't close for you. I can open, I can work any shift you want, but I can't close for you. I'm sorry.'

Joanie raised her eyebrows, sipped down the last of her coffee. 'Afraid of the dark, little girl?'

'Yes, I am. If closing's part of the job description, I'll have to find another job.'

'We'll work that out. Your car's fixed, sitting up at Mac's.' Joanie smiled. 'Word travels, and I've got my ear to the ground. You're looking for a place, there's a room over the diner I can rent you.'

'Thanks, but I think I'm going to try the hotel for now. We'll both give it a couple of weeks, see how it goes.'

'Itchy feet.'

'Itchy something.'

'Your choice.' With a shrug, Joanie got up. 'You go on, get your car, get settled. Be back at four.'

A little dazed, Reece walked out. She was back in a kitchen, and it had been all right. She'd been OK. Now that she'd got through it, she felt a little light-headed, but that was normal, wasn't it? A normal reaction to snagging a job doing what she hadn't been able to do for nearly two years.

She took her time walking back to her car, letting it all sink in.

When she walked into the mercantile, Mac was ringing up a sale at the counter. The place was what she'd expected: a little bit of everything—produce and meat, dry goods, hardware, housewares, fishing gear, ammo. When he finished, she approached.

'Car should run for you now,' Mac told her.

'So I hear, and thanks. How do I pay?'

'Lynt left a bill here for you. Paying cash, you can just leave it here. I'll be seeing him later.'

'Cash is good.' She took the bill, noted with relief it was less than she'd expected. 'I got a job.'

'That so? Quick work.'

'At the diner. I don't even know the name of it.'

'That'd be Angel Food. Locals just call it Joanie's.'

'Joanie's then. Hope you come in sometime. I'm a good cook.'

'I bet you are. Here's your change.'

'Thanks. Thanks for everything.'

'You tell Brenda on the hotel desk you want the monthly rate. You tell her you're working at Joanie's.'

'I will. I'll tell her.' She wanted to take out an ad announcing it in the local paper. 'Thanks, Mr Drubber.'

The hotel was five storeys of pale yellow stucco that boasted views of the lake. There was, she was told, high-speed Internet for a daily fee, room service and a self-service laundry in the basement.

Reece negotiated a weekly rate on a single—a week was long enough—on the second floor. Anything below the second was too accessible for her peace of mind, and anything above the second made her feel trapped. With her wallet now effectively empty, she carted her duffle and laptop up two flights rather than use the elevator.

Checking the locks twice, she opened the windows, then just stood looking at the sparkle of the water, the glide of boats, and the rise of the mountains that cupped this little section of valley.

This was her place today, she thought. She'd find out if it was her place tomorrow. Turning back to the room, she noted the door that adjoined the neighbouring guest room. She checked the locks, then dragged the single dresser in front of it. That was better.

She wouldn't unpack, not exactly, but take the essentials and set them out. Some toiletries, the cellphone charger. She left the bathroom door open while she took a quick shower, did the multiplication tables out loud to keep herself steady. She changed into fresh clothes.

New job, she reminded herself and took the time to dry her hair, to put on make-up. Not so pale today, she decided, not so hollow-eyed.

After checking her watch, she tucked her phone, her keys, driver's licence and three dollars of what she had left in her pockets. Grabbing her jacket, she headed for the door.

Before she opened it, Reece checked the peephole, scanned the empty hall. She checked her locks twice, and pressed a piece of sticky tape over the door below eye level, before she walked to the stairs.

She jogged down, counting as she went. After a quick debate, she left her car parked. Walking would save her petrol money. Couple of blocks, that was all. Still, she fingered her key chain, and the panic button on it.

Her palm was clammy when she reached for the door of Joanie's, but she opened it. And she went inside.

The same waitress she'd spoken to during the lunch shift spotted her, wiggled her fingers in a come-over motion. Reece stopped by the booth where she was filling the condiment caddy.

'Joanie's back in the storeroom. She said I should give you a quick orientation when you came in. I'm Linda-Gail.'

'Reece.'

'First warning. Joanie doesn't tolerate idle hands. She catches you loitering, she'll jump straight down your back.' Her bright blue eyes twinkled. Her blonde hair was in smooth French braids and she had on jeans, a red shirt with white piping, turquoise earrings. She looked, Reece thought, like a western milkmaid.

'I like to work.'

'You will, believe me, this being Saturday night. You'll have two other wait staff working—Bebe and Juanita. Beck'll bus, and Pete's the dishwasher. You need a break, you tell Joanie. There's a place in the back for your coat and bag. No bag?'

'No, I didn't bring it.'

'Come on then, I'll show you round. Joanie's got the forms you need to fill out in the back. I guess you've done this kind of work before, the way you jumped in with both feet today.'

'Yeah. I have.'

'Rest rooms. We clean the bathrooms on rotation. You've got a couple of weeks before you have that pleasure.'

'Can't wait.'

Linda-Gail grinned. 'You got family around here?'

'No. I'm from back East.' Didn't want to talk about that, didn't want to think about that. 'Who handles the drinks?'

'Waiting staff. We serve wine and beer but mostly people drink over at Clancy's. Anything else you want to know, just give me a holler. Welcome aboard.'

'Thanks.'

Reece moved into the kitchen, took an apron. A good, wide solid ledge, she told herself. A good place to stand until it was time to move again.

Chapter 2

LINDA-GAIL WAS RIGHT, they were busy. Locals, hikers, a scatter of tourists, people from a nearby campground who wanted an indoor meal. Reece and Joanie worked with little conversation while the fryers pumped out steam and the grill spewed heat.

At some point, Joanie stuck a bowl under her nose. 'Eat.'

'Oh, thanks, but—'

'You got something against my soup?'

'No.'

'Sit down at the counter and eat. It's slowed down some and you've got a break coming. I'll put it on your tab.'

'OK, thanks.' The fact was, now that she thought about it, she realised she was starving. A good sign, Reece decided as she took a seat at the end of the counter.

It gave her a view of the diner, and the door.

Linda-Gail slid a plate over to her with a sourdough roll and two pats of butter. 'Joanie said you need the carbs. Want tea with that?'

'Perfect. I can get it.'

'I'm in the mode. You're quick,' she added as she brought over a cup. After a glance over her shoulder, she leaned closer. 'Quicker than Joanie. And you plate food pretty. Some of the customers commented on it.'

'Oh. I didn't mean to change anything.'

'Nobody's complaining.' Linda-Gail's smile showed off dimples in her cheeks. 'Kind of jumpy, aren't you?'

'I guess I am.' Reece sampled the soup. The broth had a subtle bite. 'No wonder this place stays busy. This soup's good.'

Linda-Gail glanced towards the kitchen again. 'Some of us have a bet going. Bebe thinks you're in trouble with the law. She watches a lot of TV, that one. Juanita thinks you're running from an abusive husband. Me, I think you just got your heart broken. Any of us hit?'

'No, sorry.' There was a twinge of anxiety, but she reminded herself that restaurants were full of little dramas and gossip. 'I'm just at a loose end, just travelling.'

'Something in there,' Linda-Gail said. 'To my eye you got heartbreak written all over you. And speaking of heartbreakers, here comes Tall, Dark and Handsome now.'

He was tall, Reece thought as she followed Linda-Gail's gaze. A couple of inches over six feet. She'd give him dark, too, with the shaggy jet hair and olive complexion. But she wasn't sold on handsome. There was something rough about his scruff of beard over rawboned features, about the hard line of his mouth and the way his eyes tracked the room. And there was nothing slick about the battered leather jacket or worn-down boots.

Not the cowboy type, she decided, but he looked strong, and maybe just a little mean.

'Name's Brody,' Linda-Gail said. 'He's a writer, and he's had *three* books published. Mysteries.' Linda-Gail watched out of the corner of her eye as Brody strode to an empty booth. 'Word is he used to work for a big newspaper in Chicago and got fired. He rents a cabin on the lake, keeps to himself, mostly. But he comes in here three times a week for dinner. Tips twenty per cent. How do I look?'

'Terrific.'

Linda-Gail wandered towards the booth, drawing her pad out of her pocket. From where she sat, Reece could hear her cheerful greeting.

While she ate, she watched the waitress flirt, and when Linda-Gail turned away, she shot Reece an exaggeratedly dreamy look. Brody shifted his gaze, locked in on Reece's face.

The full-on stare made her stomach jump. Even when she quickly averted her eyes she could feel his on her, deliberately probing. For the first time since she'd begun her shift, she felt exposed and vulnerable.

Pushing off the stool, she carried her dishes to the kitchen.

He ordered the elk chops and whiled away the wait time with a bottle of Coors and a paperback. Someone had paid for Emmylou Harris on the jukebox. Brody wondered about the brunette and her sudden, frozen stillness. She had a fragile look about her, the sort that could turn on a dime to brittle. He wondered why.

From his vantage point he could see that she worked steadily, in that professional cook's way that made it seem she had an extra pair of hands somewhere. Since she was more interesting than his book, he continued to watch her while he nursed his beer.

Not attached to anyone from town, he decided. He'd lived there the best part of a year and if anyone's long-lost daughter, sister, niece, third cousin twice removed was due to breeze in, he'd have got wind. She didn't look like a drifter to him. More like a runner, he mused. There was a wariness in her eyes, a readiness to leap and dash at a moment's notice.

And when she moved to set a finished order in line, those eyes flicked in his direction—just a flick, then the door opened, and her gaze shifted. Her smile flashed and everything about her changed, went lighter, softer so that he saw there was more—at least the potential for more—than fragile beauty tucked away in there.

When he looked over to see what had caused that smile, he saw Mac Drubber shooting her a grin and a wave. Maybe he'd been wrong about the local connection.

Mac slid in the booth across from him. 'How's it going?'

'Can't complain.'

'Got a hankering to eat something I don't have to fry up myself. What looks good tonight?' He waited a beat. 'Besides the new cook?'

'I ordered the chops. Don't see you in here on Saturday nights, Mac.

You're a creature of habit, Wednesday spaghetti special.'

'I wanted to see how the girl was doing. Limped into town today with a broken radiator hose.'

'Is that so?'

'Next thing you know, she's working here. Got herself a room at the hotel. Name's Reece Gilmore.' He stopped when Linda-Gail brought Brody's food.

'Hi there, Mr Drubber, what can I get you tonight?'

Mac leaned over to take a closer look at Brody's plate. 'That looks pretty good.'

'Brody, get you anything else?'

'Take another beer.'

'Coming right up. Mr Drubber?'

'I'll take a Coke, and the same thing my friend's having.'

Brody cut into one of the chops, sampled. Cut another bite. 'If she's putting up at the hotel, she may not stay long.'

'Booked a week.' Mac liked knowing what went on in town, and who it went on with. 'Truth is, Brody, I don't think the girl has much money. Paid cash for the radiator hose, and the hotel, I hear.'

No credit cards. Brody wondered if the woman was running under the radar. 'Could be she doesn't want to leave a trail.'

'You got a suspicious mind. She's got an honest face.'

'And you have a romantic bent. Speaking of romance.' Brody cocked his head towards the door.

The man who came in wore Levi's and a chambray shirt under a black barn coat, accented with snakeskin boots and a stone-grey Stetson that screamed cowboy. Sandy, sun-streaked hair curled under his hat. He had a smooth, even-featured face set off by light blue eyes that, everyone knew, he used as often as possible to charm the ladies.

'Lo's coming 'round to see if the new girl's worth his time.' Mac shook his head. 'You can't help liking Lo, but I hope she's got more sense.'

Part of the entertainment Brody had enjoyed in the Fist in the past year was watching Lo knock over women like tenpins. 'Ten bucks says he sweet-talks her before the end of the week.'

Mac's brows knitted in disapproval.

'I'm going to take that bet, just so it costs you.'

In the kitchen, Joanie was flipping a pair of burgers. 'You see the one just sat down at the counter?' she said to Reece.

'The one who looks like he just rode in off the trail?'

'That would be William Butler. Goes by the nickname Lo. That's short for Lothario. Now on most Saturday nights, Lo would have himself a hot date. But tonight he's come in here to get a look at you.'

'Not much to see,' replied Reece.

'You're new, you're female, young and, as far as it goes, unattached. To give him his due, Lo doesn't poach on married women. Just letting you know how it is.'

'Got it. But don't worry. I'm not looking for a man—temporarily or permanently.'

Joanie put the burgers on a plate, and was just dumping fries and beans on too, when Lo sauntered into the kitchen. 'William.'

'Ma.' He bent, kissed the top of her head.

Ma, Reece thought, her stomach sinking.

Lo sent Reece a slow, easy smile. 'Heard you were classing up the place. Friends call me Lo.'

'Reece. Nice to meet you.'

'You go ahead and clock out,' Joanie told her. 'Be here by six sharp tomorrow.'

'All right. Sure.' She started to untie her apron.

'I'll drive you down to the hotel,' Lo said. 'Make sure you get there safe.'

'Oh, no, don't bother.' Reece glanced towards his mother, hoping for some help from that quarter, but Joanie had already turned away to shut down the fryers. 'It's not far. I'm fine, and I'd like a walk anyway.'

'Fine, I'll walk you. Got a coat?'

Argue, she decided, and it was rude. 'All right.' She got her denim jacket. 'Joanie, see you at six.'

Reece mumbled her goodbyes, started towards the door. She could feel the writer—Brody—staring holes in her back.

Lo opened the door for her. 'You're not letting my ma work you too hard now, are you?'

'I like to work.'

He stepped out after her. 'I bet you were busy tonight. Why don't I buy you a drink so you can unwind a little.'

'Thanks, but I've got the early shift tomorrow.'

'Supposed to be a pretty day.' His voice was as lazy as his gait. 'Why don't I pick you up when you get off? I'll show you around. No better guide in Angel's Fist, I can promise you.'

He had a great smile, she had to admit, and a look in his eyes that was as seductive as a hand stroking along the skin. And he was the boss's son.

'That's awfully nice of you, but I'd better pass, and take tomorrow to settle in a little.'

'Rain check, then. That's a sight, isn't it?' Above the ragged shadows of the mountain, hung a full, white moon. 'Take you on a ride up the river. Nothing better than the Tetons on horseback.'

'I don't ride.'

'I can teach you. That's what I do, mostly, out of the Circle K. Guest ranch. Can promise you a day you'll write home about.'

'I'm sure you would. I'll think about it. Here's my stop.'

'I'll walk you up.'

'You don't have to do that. I'm—'

'My mother taught me to walk a lady right to her door.'

He opened the door to the hotel.

'Evening, Tom,' he called out to the clerk on night duty.

'Lo. Ma'am.' And Reece saw the ghost of a smirk on his face.

When Lo turned towards the elevator, Reece stopped. 'I'm just on the second floor. I'm going to walk up.'

'An exercise nut, are you? Must be why you stay so slim.' But he changed direction smoothly, then pulled open the door to the stairs.

'I appreciate you going to all this trouble.' She ordered herself not to panic because the stairwell seemed so much smaller with him beside her. She was relieved when they stepped out into the hall on two.

'I'm right here.' She dug out her key card, automatically glancing down to make sure the tape across the door was secured.

Before she could slide the key card into the lock, he took it from her, did the small chore himself. He opened the door, then handed the key back to her. 'Left all your lights on,' he commented. 'TV running.'

'Oh. I guess I did. Overanxious to start work. Thanks for the escort.'

'My pleasure. We're going to get you on a horse right soon. You'll see.'

She managed a smile. 'I'll think about it. Thanks again. Good night.'

She eased through the doorway, shut the door. Flipped the deadbolt, then hooked the safety chain. Moving to the far side of the bed, she sat where she could look out of the window, at all that open space, until she no longer had to work to keep her breath even.

Steadier, she went back to check the peep before she pushed a chair against the door. Once she'd checked the locks again, she got ready for bed, then bargained with herself over how many lights she could leave burning through the night. She set her flashlight by the bed. There could be a power failure, caused by a fire. Someone could fall asleep smoking in bed, or some kid could be playing with matches.

The little tickle in her chest made her think longingly of the sleeping pills in her bathroom kit. Those and the antidepressants, the antianxiety medications, were just a security blanket she reminded herself. It had been months since she'd taken a sleeping pill, and tonight she was tired enough to sleep without help. Besides, if there was a fire, she'd be groggy and slow. End up burning to death or dying of smoke inhalation.

'Just stop it, Reece. Stop it now. You've got to get up early and perform basic functions like a normal human being.'

She made one more round of the locks before getting into bed. She lay very still, listening to her heart thud, listening for sounds from the hallway, from the next room. Safe, she told herself. She was perfectly safe. No one was going to break into her room to murder her in her sleep.

But she kept the TV on low to lull her to sleep.

The pain was so shocking, so vicious, she couldn't scream over it. It crushed her lungs, pounded her head, slamming, slamming down. She tried to gasp for air, but the pain was too much, and the fear was beyond even the pain.

They were out there, outside in the dark. She could hear them, hear the glass shattering, the explosions. The screaming.

Ginny? Ginny?

No, no, don't cry out, don't make a sound. Better to die here in the dark than for them to find her. But they were coming for her.

The sudden light was blinding. Wild screams burst in her head. 'We've got a live one.'

She slapped and kicked weakly at hands that reached for her.

And woke in a sweat, gripping the flashlight like a weapon.

Was someone there? Someone at the door? At the window?

She sat shivering, shaking, ears straining for any sound.

An hour later, when the clock radio alarm beeped, she was still sitting up in bed, every light in the room burning.

After the gut-shot of panic, it was hard to face the kitchen, the people, the pretence of being normal. But not only was she essentially broke, she'd given her word. Six o'clock sharp. Her only other choice was to retreat, and all the months she'd been inching forward would be wiped away. One phone call, she knew, and she'd be rescued.

And she'd be done.

She took it a step at a time. Getting dressed, leaving the room. Stepping outside in the chilly predawn.

Stay calm, she ordered herself, reciting snatches of poetry in her head. The distraction got her to the door of Angel Food.

The lights burned bright inside. She could see movement—Joanie, already in the kitchen. She had to knock on the door, Reece told herself. Knock, put a smile on her face, wave. Once she pushed herself inside, she'd drown this anxiety in the work. But her arm felt like lead and refused to move.

'Problem with the door?'

She jolted, swung round. Linda-Gail was slamming the driver's door of a sturdy little compact. 'No. No. I was just—'

'You don't look as if you got much sleep last night.' The bright blue eyes were aloof. 'Surprised you showed up at all. Lo's got a reputation.'

'Lo? I don't—Oh!' Shock jumped right over the nerves. 'We didn't . . . I didn't . . . Linda-Gail, I met him for like ten minutes.'

Linda-Gail flushed. 'Sorry. I shouldn't have jumped on you just because you left together.'

'He walked me back to the hotel, suggested maybe a trail ride. He gets a ten on the cute-factor scale, and another ten on behaviour and manners. I didn't realise you two had a thing.'

'A thing? Me and Lo?' Linda-Gail made a dismissive sound. 'We don't.' She shrugged as she opened the door.

'Wondered if you two were going to stand out there and gab all day. I'm not paying you to gossip.'

'It's five after six, for God's sake, Joanie. Dock me. Oh, speaking of pay, here's your share of last night's tips, Reece.'

'My share? I didn't wait any tables.'

Linda-Gail pushed the envelope into Reece's hands. 'Shop policy, the cook gets ten per cent.'

'Thanks.' Reece stuffed the envelope in her pocket.

'If you're finished passing the time now?' Joanie folded her arms. 'Get those breakfast set-ups going, Linda-Gail. Reece, you think you're ready to get your skinny ass back here and work?'

'Yes, ma'am. Oh, and just to clear the air,' she added as she rounded the counter for an apron, 'your son's very charming, but I slept alone last night.'

'Boy must be slipping. Can you make huevos rancheros?'

'I can.'

'They're popular on Sundays. So are flapjacks. You start frying up bacon and sausage. Early crowd'll be right along.'

Shortly before noon, Joanie pushed a plate holding scrambled eggs and rashers of bacon into Reece's hand. 'Go on, sit down and eat.'

'There's enough for two people here.'

'Yeah, if both of them are anorexic. Go sit in my office.'

She'd seen the office. 'I've got a problem with small spaces.'

'Afraid of the dark, and claustrophobic. You're a bundle of phobias. Sit out at the counter, then. You've got twenty.'

She did what she was told. A moment later, Linda-Gail put a cup of tea beside her. 'Hey, Doc.' Linda-Gail sent a good-morning smile to the man who slid onto the stool beside Reece. 'Usual?'

'Sunday cholesterol special, Linda-Gail. My day to walk on the wild side.'

'Doc's here, Joanie,' she called back, without bothering with a ticket. 'Doc, this is Reece, our new cook. Reece, meet Doc Wallace. He'll treat anything that ails you. But don't let him pull you into a poker game. He's a slick one.'

'Now, now, how am I going to fleece the newcomers if you talk like that?' He gave Reece a nod. 'Heard Joanie got herself somebody who knew what they were doing in the kitchen. How's it going?'

'So far, so good. I like the work.'

'Best Sunday breakfast in Wyoming.' He settled back with the coffee Linda-Gail put in front of him. 'You go right on and eat that while it's hot.'

He'd been the town doctor for nearly thirty years, he told her. He'd come as a young man, looking for adventure. 'Fell in love with the place. Raised three kids here. Lost my wife two years back to breast cancer. It's a hard, hard thing.'

'I'm so sorry.'

'Here you go, Doc.' Linda-Gail set a plate in front of him. A stack of pancakes, an omelette, a thick slice of ham, and a trio of link sausages. Reece goggled at it. He looked fit, she thought, in his sensible cardigan and wire-rimmed glasses. Yet he tucked into the enormous breakfast like a long-haul trucker.

'You got family back East?' he asked her.

'Yes, my grandmother in Boston.'

'That where you learned to cook?'

She couldn't take her eyes off the way the food was disappearing. 'Yes, where I started. I went to the New England Culinary Institute in Vermont, then a year in Paris at the Cordon Bleu.'

'Culinary Institute.' Doc wiggled his eyebrows. 'And Paris. Fancy.'

'Sorry?' She realised abruptly she had said more about her background in two minutes than she normally did to anyone in two weeks. 'More intense, actually. I'd better get back to work. Nice meeting you.'

Reece worked through the lunch shift, and with the rest of the afternoon and evening in front of her decided to take a long walk. She could circle the lake, maybe explore some of the forests and streams. She could take pictures and email them to her grandmother and, between the fresh air, the exercise, tire herself out.

She changed into her hiking boots, outfitted her backpack precisely as her guidebook recommended for hikes under ten miles. She'd take time every day she could manage it, she decided, fanning out from the town, into the park. She was better outdoors, always better in the open.

She set out at an easy pace. That, at least, was one of the advantages of her life now. She could do what she chose to do at her own speed. And in the past eight months, she'd seen and done more than in the previous twenty-eight years. Maybe she was a little bit crazy, and she was certainly neurotic, phobic and slightly paranoid, but there were pockets of herself she'd managed to fill again.

She'd never be what she'd once been—the bustling, ambitious urbanite. But she'd discovered she liked whatever she was forming into. Now, she paid more attention to details that had once blurred by. She could stop where she was, right now, and watch a heron rise, silent, from the lake, watch the ripples fan out until they reached the paddles plied by a boy in a red kayak.

She remembered her camera too late to capture the heron, but she captured the boy and his red boat, in the dazzling reflection of mountains that spanned the blue water.

She'd attach little notes to each photo, she thought as she started to walk again. Reece knew she'd left worry behind in Boston, but all she could do was send chatty emails, make a phone call now and then to let her grandmother know where and how she was.

There were houses and cabins scattered round the lake, and someone, Reece noted, was having a Sunday barbecue. A dog paddled out into the water after a blue ball, while a girl called encouragement. Reece veered from the lakefront and strolled into the evergreens.

Cooler here, she thought as she followed a little stream through pockets of snow and ice. When she found animal tracks, she was thrilled and started to dig out her guidebook.

The rustle had her freezing, cautiously looking around. She stared at the mule deer in shock. I must be upwind, she thought. Or was it downwind? Reaching slowly for her camera, she managed a full-on shot, then made the mistake of laughing in delight. The sound had the deer bounding away. She couldn't hear the dog barking any longer, or any rumble from cars on the main road. Just the breeze moving through the trees.

'Maybe I should live in a forest. Find myself a little cabin, grow some vegetables,' she considered. 'I could start my own business. Cook all day, sell the products over the Internet. Never leave the house. And end up adding agoraphobia to my list.' No, she'd live in the forest—that part was good—but she'd work in town. Maybe even—

She let out a yelp and stumbled back.

It was one thing to run into a mule deer and another entirely to come across a man lying in a hammock, with a paperback splayed over his chest, watching her.

Her face was pale, the eyes huge and startled, and a deep, rich Spanish brown.

'Lost?'

'No. Yes. No.' She looked around as if she'd dropped in from another planet. 'I was taking a walk, I didn't realise. I must be trespassing.'

'You must be. You want to wait while I go get my gun?'

'Not really. Um. That's your cabin, I guess. It's nice.' She studied the simple log structure, the long porch with its single chair, single table. 'Private,' she added. 'I'm sorry.'

'I'm not. I like it private.'

'I meant . . . well, you know what I meant.' She took a deep breath, twisting and untwisting the cap on her bottle of water. 'You're doing it again. Staring at me. It's rude.'

He lifted an eyebrow, then reached down, unerringly hooked a bottle of beer. 'Who decides what's rude in any given culture?'

'Well, I'll let you get back to your reading.'

She took a step back, and he debated whether to ask her if she wanted a beer. Since it would have been an almost unprecedented gesture, he'd already decided against it when a sharp sound blasted the air.

She hit the dirt, throwing her arms up to cover her head.

His first reaction was amusement. *City girl.* But he saw, when she neither moved nor made a sound, it was more than that. He swung his legs off the hammock, then crouched down. 'Backfire,' he said, easily. 'Carl Sampson's truck. It's a wreck on wheels.'

'Backfire,' she murmured over and over as she trembled.

'Yeah, that's right.' He put a hand on her arm to steady her, and she tightened up.

'Don't. Don't touch me. Don't. I just need a minute.'

'OK.' He got up to retrieve the water bottle that had gone flying when she dropped to the ground. 'You want this? Your water?'

'Yes. Thanks.' She took the bottle, but her shaking fingers couldn't manage the cap. Saying nothing, Brody took it from her, unscrewed the cap, handed it back. 'I'm fine. Just startled me. I thought it was a gunshot.'

'You'll hear that, too, in hunting season, and people around here target shoot. It's the Wild, Wild West, Slim.'

Some colour had come back into her face, but in Brody's judgment, it was pure embarrassment. Even when she pushed herself to her feet, her breath remained choppy. 'Enjoy the rest of your day.'

'Plan to.' A nice guy, he thought, would insist she sit down.

She kept walking, then slowed to glance over her shoulder. 'I'm Reece, by the way.'

'I know.'

'Oh. Well. See you around.'

Hard to avoid it, Brody thought, as she walked away. Spooky woman with those big doe-in-the-thicket eyes. Pretty though, and she'd probably edge up to sexy with another ten pounds on her. But it was the spooky that intrigued him. He could never resist trying to figure out what made people tick. And in Reece Gilmore's case, he figured whatever ticked inside her had a lot of very short fuses.

Reece kept her eyes on the lake—the ripples, the swans, the boats. Why couldn't she have been alone in the woods when the stupid truck backfired? Of course, if she had been, she might still be curled up there now, whimpering. At least Brody had been matter-of-fact about it. Here's your water, pull yourself together. It was so much easier to handle that than the strokes and pats and there-theres.

When she finally reached the hotel, the girl on the desk shot Reece a smile, asked how she had enjoyed her hike. Reece knew she answered, but all the words seemed tinny and false.

She wanted her room.

She got up the stairs, found the key, then just leaned back against the door when she was inside. Once she'd checked the locks—twice—she curled on the bed, fully dressed, still wearing her boots. And closing her eyes, she gave in to the exhaustion of pretending to be normal.

Chapter 3

A SPRING STORM DROPPED eight inches of wet, heavy snow. Some of the locals ploughed through it on snowmobiles while Lynt, with weather-scored face, took breaks from his snowploughing duties to refill his Thermos with Joanie's coffee and complain about the wind.

Reece had experienced it herself on her walk to work that morning. It blew like wrath down the canyon, across the lake. It beat at the diner windows. When the power died, Joanie yanked on her coat and boots to trudge outside and fire up her generator.

It didn't stop people from coming in. Lynt turned off his plough to settle in with a bowl of buffalo stew. Carl Sampson chowed down on meat loaf and huckleberry pie. Others came and went. They all wanted food and company. Human contact and something warm in the stomach to remind them that they weren't alone. While she grilled, fried and chopped, Reece too felt steadier for the hum of voices.

But there wouldn't be voices and contact once she finished her shift. Thinking of her hotel room, she fought her way down to the mercantile on her break for spare flashlight batteries. Just in case.

'Winter's got to take her last slap,' Mac told her as he rang up the batteries. 'How you doing down at Joanie's?'

'Generator's going, so we're still in business.'

'The power should be back up in a couple of hours. And the storm's already passing.'

Reece glanced towards the windows. 'Is it?'

'Time the power's back, she'll be done. You'll see.'

In just over an hour, Mac's predictions proved on target. The wind tapered down to an irritable mutter. Before another hour had passed, the jukebox—which Joanie refused to run on the generator—whined back on, hiccupped, then offered up Dolly Parton.

Reece mixed up vats of stew according to Joanie's recipes, grilled pounds and pounds of meat and poultry and fish. At the end of every shift, she counted up her tip money, then tucked it in an envelope she kept zipped in her duffle bag.

Three days after the storm, she was ladling up stew when Lo strolled back. He made a small production out of sniffing the air. 'Something sure smells good.'

'Tortilla soup.' She had finally convinced Joanie to let her prepare one of her own recipes. 'And it is good. Do you want a bowl?' She handed him the one she'd just prepared. 'Your mother's in her office if you want to see her.'

'I'll catch her before I head out. Came in to see you.'

'Oh?' She filled the next bowl, sprinkled on the grated cheese, the fried tortilla strips. She thought wistfully how much better it would have been with fresh cilantro as she set it on a plate with a hard roll and two pats of butter. 'Order up,' she called out, then took the next ticket.

Maybe she could talk Joanie into adding cilantro, and a few other fresh herbs, to the produce order. If she could just—

'Hey, where'd you go?' Lo demanded. 'Can I come, too?'

'What? Sorry, did you say something? I get caught up when I'm cooking.'

'Guess you do. Damn! This *is* good.' He spooned up more soup.

'Thanks. Make sure to tell the boss.'

'I'll do that. So, Reece, I checked the schedule. You're off tonight.'

'Mmm-hmm.' She nodded at Pete as the bantamweight dishwasher came in from his break.

'Thought you might want to take in a movie.'

'I didn't know there was a movie theatre in town.'

'There isn't. I've got the best DVD collection in western Wyoming. Make a hell of a bowl of popcorn, too.'

'That's a nice offer, Lo, but I've got a lot of things to catch up on tonight. You want a roll with that soup?'

'Maybe.' He edged a little closer. 'You know, honey, you're going to break my heart if you keep turning me down.'

She flipped the grill orders, then got him a roll and a plate. She glanced at him. 'You want the truth? I like you. I'd prefer to keep liking you. You're my boss's son, and that makes you the next thing to the boss in my line-up. I don't sleep with the boss, so I'm not going to sleep with you.'

'Didn't ask you to sleep with me yet,' he pointed out.

'Just saving us both time.'

He ate in a slow and thoughtful way. 'Bet I could change your mind, you give me half a chance.'

'That's why you're not getting one.'

She finished the orders, put them up. 'Now go sit at the counter and finish your soup.'

He grinned at her. 'Bossy women are a weakness of mine.'

But he strolled out when she started on the next ticket.

When the fryer buzzed, she let the potatoes drain in the baskets and started to make sandwiches. Joanie came in, handed her a cheque. 'Payday.'

'Thanks.' Reece made a decision on the spot. 'I wonder if when you have a chance you could show me the apartment. If it's still available.'

'Haven't seen anybody move in, have you? My office.' Joanie headed out.

Reece followed. Inside, Joanie opened a shallow wall cabinet. There was an army of labelled keys on hooks. She took one out, passed it to Reece. 'Go on up, take a look. Stairs out the back.'

'All right. I'll be back in ten.'

She climbed the rickety open stairs and unlocked the door. It was essentially one room with an alcove where an iron day bed was nestled, and a short counter that separated a little kitchen. The walls were an industrial beige. There was a tiled bathroom with an old cast-iron claw-foot tub. The main room held a sagging plaid sofa, a faded blue armchair and a couple of tables holding lamps that had obviously been flea market bargains.

She was smiling even before she turned to walk to the windows. A trio of them faced the mountains, and seemed to open up the world.

Shadows shifted over the snow-laced peaks as the clouds gathered and parted, and she thought she saw a faint glimmer that might have been an alpine lake. The town with its slushy streets spread below her. Standing where she was she felt a part of it, yet safe and separate.

'I could be happy here,' she murmured. 'I could be OK.'

She'd have to buy some things. Towels, sheets, kitchen supplies. She thought of the pay cheque in her pocket, the tip money. She could manage the essentials. And it could be fun. The first time she'd bought her own things in nearly a year.

Big step, she thought, then immediately began to second-guess herself. Was it too big a step, too soon? What if she had to leave? What if she got fired? What if—

She heard footsteps on the stairs outside, and the bubble of fear opened in her chest. She grabbed one of the tacky table lamps in her hand. When Joanie opened the door, Reece set it down as if she had been examining it.

'Ugly, but it gives decent light,' Joanie said, and left it at that.

'Sorry, I took longer than I meant to. I'll go right down.'

'No rush. We're slow, and Beck's on the grill. Long as it's nothing complicated, he can handle things. You want the place?'

'Yes, if I can manage the rent. You never said what—'

In her stained apron and thick-soled shoes, Joanie took a quick pass around the room. Then she named a monthly figure that was slightly less than the hotel rate.

'I'd rather we do it by the week. I like to pay as I go.'

'Doesn't matter to me. You can move in today if you want.'

'Tomorrow. I need to get some things. Thanks, Joanie. I appreciate it.'

'No need for gratitude. You do the job and you don't cause trouble. You got that raise coming. Don't ask questions, either. Now I figure that's because you don't want questions back.' Joanie's hand patted her apron pocket where Reece knew she kept a pack of cigarettes. 'Let's get this said. Anybody with two licks of sense can see it just by looking at you. I guess you've got what they like to call "issues".'

'Is that what they call them?' Reece murmured.

'The way I see it, if you're working through them or just standing still, it's your business. But you don't let it get in the way of your job, so that's mine. You're a better cook than I ever had behind the grill. I figure on making use of that, especially if I figure you're not going to go rabbiting off and leave me flat. And if you're still here in a couple of months, you'll get another raise.'

'I won't leave you flat. If I need to go, I'll tell you beforehand.'

'Fair enough. Now I'm going to ask you straight out, and I'll know if you're lying. You got the law after you?'

'No.' Reece let out a weak laugh. 'Hell, no.'

'Didn't figure you did, but you might as well know people in the Fist like to speculate, passes the time.' She waited a beat. 'It might help if someone comes looking for you, you tell me whether you want them to find you.'

'There's only my grandmother, and she knows where I am.'

'All right, then. You've got the key. I got a duplicate in my office. But you're late with the rent, I'll take it out of your pay. No excuses. I've heard them all.'

With her pay and tip money, Reece headed to the mercantile. Basics, she reminded herself. Essentials and no more.

But God, it was a kick to be shopping for more than new socks or a pair of jeans. The idea of it lightened her steps. She breezed in with a quick jingle of the bell that hung over the door.

There were other shoppers, and some she recognised from the diner. Steak sandwich, extra onions for the man in the plaid jacket. The woman and the little boy—fried chicken for him, Cobb salad for her. She lifted a hand at Mac Drubber and found a comfort in his acknowledging nod. It was nice to recognise and be recognised. And here she was looking at packaged sheet sets. Maybe the pale blue, with its pattern of tiny violets. Yellow towels for some sunshine in the bathroom.

She took the first haul to the counter.

'Got yourself a place, did you?'

'Yes. The apartment over Joanie's,' she told Mac.

'That's fine. You want me to start an account for you?'

In her current mood it was tempting. 'That's all right. I just need a few things for the kitchen, and I'm set.'

She did the maths in her head as she selected what was absolutely necessary. A good cast-iron skillet, a decent pot. Even as she calculated, she glanced over each time the little bell jingled. So she saw Brody come in.

Same battered leather jacket, same down-at-the-heels boots. He looked like he might have shaved. But that look in his eyes, something that said he'd seen it all already and didn't miss it, was still there as he headed to the grocery section.

She pushed her trolley to the counter. 'That should do it, Mr Drubber.'

'No charge on the teakettle. It's a housewarming gift.'

'Oh, you don't have to do that.'

'My store, my rules.' He wagged a finger at her. 'Be a minute here, Brody.'

'No problem.' Brody set a quart of milk and a pound of coffee on the counter. Nodded to Reece. 'How's it going?'

'Fine, thanks.'

'Reece is moving into the apartment over Joanie's.'

'That so?'

'I get this rung and boxed, you give her a hand hauling it over there, Brody.'

'Oh, no. No, that's OK. I can manage.'

'You can't cart all this stuff on your own,' Mac insisted. 'Got your car outside, don't you, Brody?'

There was a ghost of a smile around Brody's mouth. 'Sure.'

'Heading on down to Joanie's for dinner anyway, right?'

'That's the plan. Put my stuff on account, Mac.' Brody stacked his purchases on top of one of the boxes Mac had already packed, hefted it. Before the rest was finished, he was back for box number two.

Trapped, Reece lifted the last one. 'Thanks, Mr Drubber.'

'You enjoy your new place,' he called out as she followed Brody to the door.

'You don't have to do this. Seriously,' she began the minute they were outside. 'He put you on the spot.'

'Yeah, he did.' Brody loaded the second box into the bed of a black Yukon, then reached for the one Reece carried. 'Get in.'

'I don't want—'

'I've got your stuff.' He rounded the hood. 'You can ride with it, or you can walk.'

She got inside, opening the window so she didn't feel closed in. Since the radio was blasting out Red Hot Chili Peppers, she didn't have to pretend to make polite conversation.

He parked on the street, then dragged out a box. She pulled one from the other side. 'The entrance is around back.' Her voice was clipped, surprising her. She couldn't remember the last time she'd been seriously annoyed with anyone other than herself.

She propped the box against the wall in order to deal with the key.

Brody simply shifted the box he held to one arm, took the key, unlocked the door.

A fresh wave of resentment washed over her. This was *her* place now. And here he was striding across the floor to dump her box of precious new possessions on the counter. Then he was striding out again, without one comment. On a huff of breath, Reece set her box down. She dashed to the door and out, hoping to catch him and take the last load herself.

But he was already starting back.

'I'll take it from here. Thanks.'

'I've got it. What's in here? Bricks?'

'It's probably the cast-iron skillet. I can get it, really.'

He simply ignored her and climbed the steps. 'Why the hell did you lock the door when we were coming right back?'

'Habit.' She turned the key, but before she could reach for the box, he'd pushed by to take it in himself.

'Well, thanks.' She stood beside the open door, knowing it was rude. 'Sorry for the imposition.'

'Uh-huh.' He turned a circle. 'Could use some fresh paint,' he commented. 'And some heat. You'll freeze those bird bones of yours in here.'

'No point in turning up the heat until I move in tomorrow. I don't want to hold you up.'

He aimed those eyes at her. 'You're not worried about holding me up, you just want me out.' For the first time, he gave her a quick, genuine smile. 'You're more interesting when you've got a little bite to you. What's the special tonight?'

'Fried chicken, parsley potatoes, peas and carrots.'

'Sounds good.' He strolled to the door, stopped directly in front of her, watched her body brace. 'See you around.'

Spring thaw meant mud. Trails and paths went soft and thick with it, and caked boots left it streaked over the streets and sidewalks. At Joanie's, the locals who knew her wrath scraped off the worst of it before coming in. Tourists were in short supply. But there were those who came for the lake, and for the river, paddling their canoes and kayaks. Angel's Fist settled down to the quiet interlude between its winter and summer booms.

With only a scattering of after-dinner customers, Linda-Gail took counter duty. She dumped a piece of apple pie in front of Lo, topped off his coffee. 'Been seeing a lot of you the last couple of weeks.'

'Coffee's good, pie's better.' He forked up a huge bite, then grinned. 'View's not bad.'

Linda-Gail glanced over her shoulder to where Reece worked the grill.

'Heard you struck out there, slugger.'

'Early innings yet. Got any more of the story on her?'

'Her story, I figure. Her business.'

He snorted over his pie. 'Come on, Linda-Gail.'

She struggled to stay aloof, but damn it, she and Lo had loved talking the talk since they were kids. 'Keeps to herself, doesn't shirk the work, comes in on time.' With a shrug Linda-Gail leaned on the counter. 'Doesn't get any mail, from what I'm told. But she did get a phone for upstairs. And . . .'

He leaned in so their faces were close. 'Keep going.'

'Well, Brenda told me while Reece was at the hotel she moved the dresser in front of the door to the next room. If you ask me, she's afraid of something, or someone. Hasn't used a credit card, not one time, and she never used the phone in the hotel except for her computer, as dial-up's cheap.'

'Sounds like she could use a friend.'

'That's some euphemism, Lo.'

'I can be a friend. You and me, we're friends.'

'Is that what we are?'

Something shifted in his eyes, over his face. He slid his hand over the counter towards hers. 'Linda-Gail—'

But she looked away from him, drew back and put on her waitress smile. 'Hey, Sheriff.'

'Linda-Gail. Lo.' Sheriff Richard Mardson slid onto a stool. He was a big man with a long reach, who kept the peace by reason when he could, by steely-eyed force when he couldn't.

He was already reaching for the sugar when Linda-Gail poured him out a cup of coffee. 'You two wrangling again?'

'Just talking,' Lo told him. 'About Ma's newest cook.'

'She sure can work that grill. Linda-Gail, why don't you have her do me a chicken-fried steak.' He had clear blue eyes, blond hair he wore in a brush cut. 'You after that skinny girl, Lo?'

'Made a few tentative moves in that direction.'

'You need to settle down with the love of a good woman.'

'I do. Every chance I get. The new cook's got an air of mystery. Some people think she's on the run.'

'If she is, it isn't from the law. I do my job,' Rick said. His level gaze shifted towards the kitchen. 'Most likely took off from her husband, boyfriend, who tuned her up regular.'

'I don't get that. A man who hits a woman isn't a man.'

Rick drank his coffee. 'There are all kinds of men in the world.'

Once she finished her shift, Reece settled in upstairs with the journal she kept on her laptop. She had the heat at a conservative sixty and wore a sweater and two pairs of socks. She calculated the savings would offset the lights burning day and night. She was tired, but the apartment felt good to her, safe and spare and tidy. Safer yet when she braced one of the two stools Joanie had given her for the counter under the doorknob.

Slow again today. Nearly everyone who came in was a local. It's too late to ski or snowboard, though I hear there's snow above us. Down here it's all mud and brown grass.

I have tomorrow off. A full day off. I'll take one of the easy trails up the canyon, go as far as I can, watch the river. I want to see the white water. Maybe someone will be rafting. I'll pack a little lunch and take my time.

The kitchen was brightly lit, and Reece hummed as she scrubbed down the stove. It was her last night at Maneo's, so she intended to leave her work space sparkling. She had the entire week off, and then she'd start as head chef for Oasis. Head chef for one of the trendiest restaurants in Boston. She'd supervise a staff of fifteen, put her own signature dishes up against the very best in the business. The pressure would be insane.

She couldn't wait.

She'd trained Marco herself, and between him and Tony Maneo, they'd do fine. She knew Tony and his wife, Lisa, were happy for her. In fact, she had good reason to know—since her prep cook, Ginny, couldn't keep a secret—that there was a party being set up right now to celebrate her new position, and to say goodbye. She was going to miss this place, miss the people, but it was time for this next step.

Stepping back from the stove, she nodded in approval, then carried the cleaning supplies to the little utility closet. The crash from outside the kitchen had her rolling her eyes. But the screams spun her round. When gunfire exploded, she froze. Even as she fumbled for her cellphone, the swinging door slammed open. She saw the gun, saw nothing but the gun.

Then she was flung backwards into the closet, punched by a hot, unspeakable pain in her chest.

The scream ripped out of Reece as she lurched up in bed, pressing a hand high on her chest. She could feel it, that shock, where the bullet had struck. But when she looked at her hand, there was only the scar.

'It's all right. I'm all right. Just a dream.' But she trembled all over as she grabbed her flashlight and got up to check the door, the windows.

No one was there, not a soul moved on the street below. The cabins and houses were dark. No one was coming to finish what they'd begun two years before. They didn't know where she was. She was alive—just an accident of fate, just the luck of the draw, she thought as she rubbed her fingertips over the scar the bullet had left behind.

She was alive, and it was almost dawn of another day. She stood, watching the light in the east streak the sky with pink and gold, then spread over the glass of the lake until the water glowed like a quiet fire.

By the time she'd stocked her backpack, it felt like it weighed fifty pounds. It was eight miles, up and back, but it was a good, clear day and she was going to take advantage of it.

She'd barely got ten feet when she was hailed.

'Doing a little exploring this morning?' Mac asked her. He wore a flannel shirt tucked into jeans and a US navy watch cap.

'I thought I'd hike a bit of Little Angel Trail.'

His brows came together. 'Going on your own?'

'It's an easy trail, according to my guidebook. I've got a map. Don't worry, Mr Drubber. I won't be going far.'

She shifted her pack, then set out to skirt the lake and take the trail through the woods towards the wall of the canyon. When the trail forked, she took the fork marked for Little Angel Canyon. The incline was slow, but it was steady through the damp air sheltered by conifers. Huge boulders sat among pools of melting snow and mud.

The trail rose gently at first, up the moraine, tracking the slope through a stand of firs, then dropping to a deep, unexpected gulch. The mountains speared up, snow-breasted pinnacles shining in sunlight, and the trail angled steeply. When she'd hiked the first mile, she stopped to rest and drink. She could still see the glint of Angel Lake to the southeast. The breakfast shift would be peaking now, she thought, with the diner full of clatter and conversation. But here she was alone with the light wind wafting through the trees.

She continued on. The trail cut through the still-sleeping meadows, switchbacked over the steeps. Huffing her way along the slope, she heard the first rumble that was the river. When the trail forked again, she looked wistfully at the signpost. Her leg muscles were in shock, and she'd probably gone seriously overboard with the supplies in her pack, but she'd hiked Little Angel Trail halfway.

She climbed up the muddy slope. When she made it round the next switchback, she had her first look at the brilliant ribbon of the river. It carved through the canyon with a steady murmur of power. Here and there huddles of rock were stacked on its verge as if the river had simply flung them out.

She got out her camera, already knowing a snapshot wouldn't capture the view. Then she saw a pair of bright blue kayaks and, delighted, framed them for scale. She watched the kayakers paddle, heard the dim sound of voices, then pulled out her binoculars. A man and a boy.

Her binoculars round her neck, Reece followed the trail.

The height was enthralling. As her body pushed itself forward she felt the burn of muscles, the giddiness of adventure, and no tingle of worry or anxiety. What she felt, she realised, was utterly human. Small and mortal and full of wonder. Even with the chill on her face, the sweat of effort dampened her back. She trudged up and up, panting.

And stopped short, skidding a little, when she saw Brody perched on a wide, rocky ledge. He barely spared her a glance. 'Should've known it was you. You make enough noise to start an avalanche.'

'What are you doing up here?'

'Minding my own business.' He picked up the notebook on his lap. 'You? Other than tromping along gasping "Ain't No Mountain High Enough"?'

'I was not.' Oh, please, she was not. 'I'm hiking the trail. It's my day off. You're writing up here?'

'Researching. I'm killing someone up here later. Fictionally. Good spot for it, this time of year. Nobody on the trails—or nearly nobody. He lures her up, shoves her over.' Brody leaned out a little, looking down. 'Long, nasty drop. Terrible accident, terrible tragedy.'

Despite herself, she was intrigued. 'Why does he do it?'

He only shrugged, broad shoulders in a denim shirt. 'Mostly because he can.'

'There were kayakers on the river. They might see.'

'That's why they call it fiction. Kayakers,' he mumbled and scribbled something on his pad. 'Maybe. What would they see? Body dropping. Scream echoes. Splat.'

'Oh, well. I'll leave you to it.'

Since his response was nothing but an absent grunt, she continued on, a little irritated. He had a good spot to take in the view, which would've been *her* spot. But she'd find her own. Just a little higher up.

She knew she was hitting the wall of her endurance. Stopping, she braced her hands on her thighs and caught her breath. One more switchback, she decided, just one more, then she'd unpack her lunch and enjoy an hour with the river.

She was rewarded for that last struggle of effort with a view of white water. It churned and slapped at the rock, then spilled down in a short, foaming waterfall. The roar of it filled the canyon, and rolled over her own laugh of delight. She'd made it after all. With relief she unshouldered her pack, before sitting down on a boulder. She unpacked her lunch and pleased herself by eating ravenously.

Top of the world, that's how she felt. Calm and energised at once, and absolutely happy. She bit into an apple so crisp it shocked her senses as a hawk soared overhead.

She lifted her binoculars to follow the hawk's flight, then skimmed them down to track the powerful surge of the river. With hope, she began to scout the rocks, the stands of willow and cottonwood, back into the pines for wildlife. A bear might come fishing or a moose come to drink.

If she hadn't been searching the rough shoreline, she would have missed them.

They stood between the trees and the rocks. The man had his back to her. The woman faced the river, hands on her hips.

Even with binoculars, distance made it impossible to see them clearly, but she saw the spill of dark hair over a red jacket, under a red cap. Reece wondered what they were doing. Debating a place to put into the river, she mused. But she skimmed the glasses along and didn't see a canoe or kayak. Camping, then, though she couldn't spot any gear.

With a shrug, she went back to watching them. 'Having an argument,' she murmured. 'That's what it looks like to me.'

There was something aggressive and angry in the woman's stance, and she jabbed her finger at the man. He made a gesture like an umpire calling a batter safe at the plate, and this time she slapped him, shoved both hands against his chest, then slapped him again.

Reece started to lower the glasses, but her hand froze, and her heart jolted. The man's arm reared back. She couldn't tell if it was a punch or a slap, but the woman went sprawling.

'No, no, don't,' she murmured. 'You both have to stop.'

Instead, the woman leapt up, charged. Before she could land whatever blow she intended, she was thrust back again, landing hard.

The man walked over, seemed to reach down as if to offer her a hand up. The woman's nose was bleeding, but her mouth was working fast.

It got worse, horribly worse when he straddled the woman, jerked her head by the hair and slammed it to the ground. Leaping to her feet, Reece stared through the glasses. His hands closed over the woman's throat.

Boots beat against the ground; the body bucked and arched. And when it went still, harsh sobs ripped out of Reece's chest.

She turned, stumbling, going down hard on both knees. Then she shoved herself to her feet, and ran.

It was a blur, slithering down the path at a crazed speed. Her heart rammed into her throat while she stumbled and slid round the sharp switchbacks. The face of the woman in the red jacket became another face, one with staring, baby-doll eyes.

Ginny. It wasn't Ginny. It wasn't Boston. It wasn't a dream.

Still it all mixed and merged in her mind until she heard the screams and the gunshots. Until the world began to spin.

She slammed hard into Brody, struggled wildly against his hold.

'Stop it. What are you, crazy? Suicidal?' He shoved her back against the rock face, bracing her when her knees gave way. 'Shut it down, now! Hysteria doesn't help. What was it? Bear?'

'He killed her, he killed her. I saw, I saw it. It wasn't Ginny. He killed her, across the river.'

'Breathe.' He angled his head down until her eyes met his. 'I said breathe. OK, again. One more time.'

'OK, OK. I'm OK.' She sucked air in, pushed it out. 'Please help me. Please. They were across the river, and I saw them, with these.' She lifted her binoculars. 'He killed her, and I saw it.'

'Show me.'

She closed her eyes. 'Up the trail. I don't know how far.'

She didn't want to go back, didn't want to see it again, but he had her arm and was leading her.

'I stopped to eat at the little falls,' she said. 'There was a hawk. I got my binoculars. I thought . . . I was scanning the rocks, and I saw two people.'

'What did they look like?'

'I couldn't see very well. But she had long hair. Dark hair, and she had a red jacket and cap. She had sunglasses on. His back was to me.'

'What was he wearing?'

'Um. A dark jacket, and an orange cap. Like hunters wear. He had sunglasses, too. I didn't see his face. There, there's my pack. I left everything and ran. Over there. It was over there.' She pointed. 'In front of the trees. They're gone now, but I saw them. I have to sit down.'

When she lowered herself to the rock, shivering, he said nothing, but took the binoculars. He saw no one. 'What exactly did you see?'

'They were arguing. She slapped him, then she shoved him back and slapped him again. He knocked her down, but she got up and went after him. That's when he hit her again. I saw blood on her face. I think I saw blood on her face. Oh God, oh God.'

Brody flicked a glance in Reece's direction. 'You're not going to get hysterical again. You're going to tell me what you saw.'

'He got down, and he grabbed her by the hair and he slammed her head down, I think. It looked like he strangled her.' Reece rubbed the back of her hand over her mouth, prayed she wouldn't be sick. 'Her feet were beating the ground, and then they weren't.'

'It's a long distance. You're sure about this?'

She looked up then, her eyes swollen and exhausted. 'Have you ever seen someone killed?'

'No.'

She pushed herself up, reached for her pack. 'I have. He took her somewhere, carried her body away, but he killed her. And he's getting away. We have to get help.'

'Give me your pack.'

'I can carry my own pack.'

He pulled it away from her, sent her a pitying look. 'Carry mine, it's lighter.' He shrugged out of it, held it out to her.

She put it on, and, of course, he was right. It was considerably lighter. She'd brought too much, but she'd just wanted to be sure . . .

'Cellphone! I'm an idiot.'

'No signal,' he said as she dug into her pocket.

Though she kept walking, she tried it anyway. 'You'd make it faster alone. You should go ahead.'

'No. Who'd you see killed before?'

'I can't talk about it. How long will it take to get back?'

'Until we get there. And don't start that are-we-there-yet crap.'

She nearly smiled. He was so brusque, so brisk, he pushed her fear away. His stride ate up the ground as she tried to keep up with him.

Chapter 4

THEY WALKED IN SILENCE. Her body felt numb, her mind hazed.

'Brody?'

'Still right here.'

'Will you go with me to the police?'

He stopped to drink, then offered her the water bottle. His green eyes were cool and calm. 'We'll call from my place. It's closer than going all the way into town.'

'Thanks.'

Relieved, grateful, Reece continued to put one foot in front of the other. To keep centred, she ran through recipes in her head, seeing herself measuring, preparing.

'Sounds pretty good.' Brody jerked her out of the visual.

'What?'

'Whatever you're making in there.' He tapped a finger to his temple. 'Grilled shrimp?'

No point, she decided, absolutely no point in being embarrassed. 'Brined grilled shrimp. I didn't know I was talking to myself. It's a problem I have.'

'I don't see a problem, except now I'm hungry, and shrimp's not in big supply around here.'

'I just need to think about something else. Anything else. I just need—oh boy, oh crap.' Her chest went tight and her breath short. As her head went light, she bent from the waist. 'Can't breathe. Can't.'

'Yes, you can. You are. But if you breathe like that you're going to hyperventilate. No way I'm carrying you back, so cut it out.' He hauled her up. Their eyes locked. 'Cut it out. Finish cooking the shrimp.'

'OK. Um. Add half the garlic oil to the bowl of grilled shrimp, toss. Transfer to a platter, garnish with lemon wedges and divided bay leaves, and serve with grilled ciabatta bread and the rest of the garlic oil.'

'If I get my hands on some shrimp, you can pay me back for this and make me a plate of that. Are you planning on fancying up Joanie's?'

'No. It's not my place.'

'Did you have your own place? Restaurant?'

'I worked in one. I never had my own. Never wanted my own. I just wanted to . . .' She'd nearly said create, but decided it sounded too pompous. 'To cook.'

'Wanted?'

'Want. Maybe. I don't know what I want.' But she did, and as they walked through the cool forest, she decided just to say it. 'I want to be normal again, to stop being afraid. I want to be who I was two years ago, and I never will be. So I'm trying to find out who I'm going to be for the rest of my life.'

'The rest is a long time.'

He dug for his cellphone. The woman was a bundle of mystery wrapped in nerves but he didn't think she was as fragile as she believed herself to be. 'Should get a signal from here,' he said and punched in some numbers.

'Rick, it's Brody. I'm with Reece Gilmore, just about a quarter-mile from my place on Little Angel Trail. I need you to meet us at my cabin. Yeah, she witnessed a murder. That's what I said. She can fill you in on that. We're nearly there.'

He shoved the phone back in his pocket. 'I'm going to give you some advice. You're going to need to stay calm. You want to get hysterical again, cry, faint, better wait till you're out of my cabin because I don't want to handle it. Be thorough, be clear and get it done.'

'If I start to lose it, will you stop me?' She actually felt his scowl before she glanced up to see it. 'I mean interrupt me, or knock over a lamp. Don't worry, I'll pay for it. Anything to give me a minute to pull myself back?'

'Maybe.'

'I can smell the lake. You can just see it through the trees. I feel better when I see water. Maybe I should live on an island, except I think that might be too much water. I have to babble for a minute. You don't have to listen.'

'I've got ears,' he reminded her, then veered off to take the easiest route to his cabin.

He approached it from the rear where it was tucked in the trees and sagebrush. Her mouth went dry as he opened the back door. He hadn't locked it. Anyone could come in.

Screwing up her courage, she stepped into the small kitchen. Brody went immediately to the coffeemaker, filling the tank, measuring the grounds. He flipped it onto brew, then reached in a cupboard for mugs.

'Um, do you have any tea?'

'Oh sure. Let me just find my tea cosy.'

'I'll take that as a no. I don't drink coffee; it makes me jittery. More jittery,' she amended when he cocked a brow at her. 'Water'd be fine. Do you leave the front door unlocked, too?'

'No point in locks out here. If somebody wanted in, they'd just kick the door down.' When she actually paled, he angled his head. 'What? You want me to go check under the bed?'

She simply turned away from him to unshoulder his pack. 'I bet you've never been afraid a day in your life.'

Got a rise out of her, he thought, and preferred the edge of insult and anger in her tone than the shakes and quivers. 'Michael Myers.'

Confused, she turned back. 'Who? Shrek?'

'Hell, Slim, that's Mike Myers. Michael Myers. The creepy guy in the mask in *Halloween*. I saw it when I was about ten. Scared the living daylights out of me. Michael Myers lived in my bedroom closet for years.'

Her shoulders relaxed a little. 'How'd you get rid of him?'

'I snuck a girl into my room when I was sixteen. Couple of hours in the dark with her, I never gave Michael Myers another thought.'

'Sex as exorcism?'

'Worked for me.' He moved to the refrigerator, got her out a bottle of water. 'Let me know if you want to try it.'

'I'll do that.' Sheer reflex had her catching the bottle of water. But her shoulders went to stone with the brisk knock on the front door.

'That'll be the sheriff. Want to do this in here?'

She looked at the manhole-cover-sized table. 'Here's good.'

When he went to answer, she twisted the top off the bottle and gulped down cold, cold water. Calm, she reminded herself.

Rick came in, nodded at her. 'Reece. Got some trouble, I hear.'

'Yes.'

'Let's sit down, so you can tell me about it.'

She sat, and she began, struggling to relay the details without bogging it down. Brody set a mug in front of Rick, leaned against the counter, saying nothing. As she spoke, the sheriff took notes.

'OK, you think you could identify either one of them?'

'Her, maybe. Maybe. But his back was to me.'

Rick swivelled to look at Brody. 'You hiked back up to where she'd been. You see anything?'

'No. You want the spot, I'll get a map, show you where.'

'Appreciate that, Brody. Reece,' Rick continued when Brody walked out, 'did you see any boat, truck? Anything like that?'

'I didn't. I guess I looked for a boat, sort of, but I didn't see one. I thought they must've been camping, but I didn't see any equipment. I just saw them.'

'Tell me everything you can about him. Whatever comes to mind,' he prompted. 'You never know what you're going to remember.'

'He was white—I'm pretty sure. He had gloves on, black or brown. It all happened so fast. He had a dark jacket and one of those orange hunting caps.'

'OK, that's a good start. How about his hair?'

'I don't think I noticed.' She wanted to shiver. It had been like this before. The questions she simply couldn't answer. 'The hat covered it, I guess. I don't think it was long.'

Brody came back in with a map of the area. He laid the map on the table, pointed with his finger. 'Here.'

'You sure about that?'

'I am.'

'OK, then.' Rick pushed to his feet. 'I'm going out there right now, see what there is to see. Don't you worry, Reece, we're going to take care of this. I'll get back to you. Meanwhile, anything comes to you, anything at all, I want to hear about it. OK?'

'Yes. Yes, OK. Thanks.'

Nodding to Brody, Rick picked up his hat and headed out.

'Well.' Reece let out a long sigh. 'Do you think he can? Is he capable?'

'I haven't seen anything to make me think otherwise. It's mostly drunk and disorderlies around here, a few domestic disputes, lost or injured hikers or boaters. He seems to handle them.'

'But murder. Murder's different.'

'Maybe, but he's the guy in charge. You gave your statement. Nothing else to do. I'll drive you home.'

She got up. 'You don't have to bother. I can walk.'

'Don't be stupid.' He hauled up her pack and headed out of the kitchen towards the front. Reece dragged on her jacket and followed him through the casual disorder of the living area and out of the front door.

'I've put you to a lot of trouble today,' she began.

'Damn right you have. Get in.'

She stopped and gratitude warred with insult, outrage and exhaustion. Gratitude lost. 'You're a rude, insensitive son of a bitch.'

He leaned back on his car. 'And your point is?'

'A woman was murdered today. Strangled to death. Do you *get* that? She was alive, now she's dead. I just had to stand and watch. Do nothing, just like before. I watched him kill her, and you were the only one I could tell. Instead of being sympathetic, you've been snippy and dismissive. So go to hell. I'd rather walk back up that trail than ride with you in your stupid, macho SUV. Give me my damn pack.'

He stayed just as he was. 'About time. I wondered if you had anything approaching a normal temper in there. Feel better?'

She hated that she did. That his carelessness had revved her up until she'd spewed out a great deal of her anxiety and her dread. 'You can still go to hell.'

'I'm hoping for a reserved seat. But meanwhile, get in. You've had a crappy day.' He pulled the door open. 'And guys are physiologically incapable of snippiness. Next time use *callous*. That works.'

She climbed in. 'You're an irritating, confusing man.'

'That works, too.'

He slammed the door, then strode to the driver's side. Tossing her pack in the back seat, he got behind the wheel.

'Did people find you irritating, confusing and callous when you got fired in Chicago?' she asked him.

'I didn't get fired.'

'You didn't punch your boss and get fired from the *Tribune?* That's what I heard.'

'I punched what could loosely be called a colleague for cribbing my notes on a story, and since the editor took his word over mine, I quit.'

'To write books. And writers are allowed to be surly and solitary and eccentric?'

'Maybe. Suits me anyway.'

'To the ground,' she replied, and made him laugh.

The sound surprised her enough to have her look over. He was still grinning as they rounded the lake. 'There you go, Slim. Already know you've got spine. Nice to know you've got teeth to go with it.'

But when he pulled up in front of Angel Food, and she glanced up at her own window, she felt her spine loosen, and her teeth wanted to chatter. Still, she got out. And stood on the sidewalk wavering between pride and panic.

'Problem?' He pulled out her pack.

'No. Yes. Damn it. Look, you've come this far. Could you walk up with me, for a minute?'

'To make sure Michael Myers isn't waiting for you?'

'Close enough. Feel free to take back the compliment—if that's what it was—about me having a spine.'

He only tossed the backpack over his shoulder and started round the building to her steps. Once she'd dug out her key and unlocked the door, he opened it himself to walk in ahead of her.

'What the hell do you do in here?' he said.

'What? Excuse me?'

'No TV,' he pointed out, 'no stereo.'

'I just moved in, really. I don't spend a lot of time here.'

He poked around, and she didn't stop him. There wasn't much to see. The neatly made day bed, the couch, the bar stools.

'Nice laptop.' He tapped a finger on it.

'You said you were hungry.'

He glanced up from her computer, and it struck him how the near-empty room made her seem so alone. 'Did I?'

'Before. If you are, I could make you a meal. We could call it payback for today, and call it even.'

She said it lightly, but he was good at reading people and this one wasn't ready to be alone. And he was hungry. 'What kind of meal?'

'Ah.' She pushed a hand through her hair, glanced towards the kitchen. 'I could do some chicken and rice quickly.'

'Fine. Got beer?'

'No. Sorry. I have wine. A nice white. It's chilled.'

'Good enough.'

She got out the wine first, and a corkscrew, then took a pack of skinless chicken breasts out of the freezer to thaw in the microwave. While she took her coat, and the one he'd tossed over a stool, to the day bed, Brody opened the wine.

'I only have regular tumblers.' She crossed back to open a cupboard. 'Actually, the wine was mostly for cooking.'

'You're serving me cooking wine. Well, *slàinte*.'

'It's a good wine,' she said with some aggravation. 'I wouldn't cook with anything I wouldn't drink. It's a nice Pinot Grigio. So *salute* is more appropriate.'

He poured some into the tumbler he gave her, then some into a second one. He sampled, nodded. 'OK, where'd you study cooking?'

She turned away. 'A couple of places.'

'One being Paris.'

She took out garlic, green onion. 'Why ask if Doc Wallace already told you?'

'Actually, it was Mac, who got it from Doc. You haven't picked up the small-town rhythm yet.'

'I guess not.' She took out a pot to boil water for the rice.

Brody took his wine, settled on a stool and watched her.

Competence, he thought. The nerves that seemed to hum around her otherwise didn't show when she was in this element. What she needed was to eat what she prepared until she put on a solid ten pounds. Pounds he was speculating she lost after whatever had sent her running from Boston. Again, he wondered who she'd seen killed. And why. And how.

She did something, quick and easy, with some crackers, cream cheese, olives and paprika, then arranged them on a saucer. 'First course.' She offered him a hint of a smile.

He polished off half the crackers, while she handled three pans—the chicken she'd sliced with some chopped garlic, the rice and stir-fried peppers, the mushrooms and broccoli. 'How do you know how to have it all ready at the same time?'

Her face was relaxed, a little rosy from the heat. 'How do you know when to end a chapter and go on to the next?'

'Good point. You look good when you cook.'

'I cook better than I look.' Shutting down the heat, she plated the meal, then set his in front of him before she sat beside him. And for the first time, picked up her wine.

She half toasted him, sipped. 'Well? How is it?'

He took his first bite, sat back as if to consider. 'You've got a face on you,' he began. 'Fascinating in its way, and a lot of it's about those big, dark eyes. But,' he continued as she seemed to draw back a little, 'maybe you do cook better than you look.'

The way her grin flashed in appreciation made him think otherwise, but he continued to eat and to enjoy the meal, and her company more than he'd expected.

'So, you know what's buzzing around downstairs about now?' he asked.

'In Joanie's?'

'That's right. People see my car out front, don't see me in there. Somebody says something, somebody else says, "I saw him go up with Reece. Been up there some time now."'

'Oh.' She blew out a breath. 'Oh well, it doesn't matter.' Then she sat up a little straighter.

'You don't care what people think or say about you?'

'Sometimes I do, too much. Sometimes I don't care at all. I sure as hell don't care that you lost a bet with Mac Drubber over me with Lo.'

His eyes lit with amusement. 'I underestimated you.'

'Maybe if people think we have something going, Lo will stop trying to go out with me. So I guess I owe you another one.'

'I guess you do. Do I get another dinner out of it?'

'I . . . well, I suppose. If you want.'

'When's your next night off?'

'Ah . . .' How'd she managed to box herself in so neatly? 'Tuesday. I have the early shift, off at three.'

'Great. I'll come by at seven. That work for you?'

'Seven. Sure. Sure.'

Now what? she wondered. She just couldn't think of any small talk. Once she'd been good at this, she thought. She'd enjoyed dating, liked sitting with a man over a meal, talking, laughing. But her brain just wouldn't walk down that road.

'He'll be here when he gets here.'

She met Brody's eyes. 'If I'm that transparent, I'm going to have to install some shades.'

'It's only natural to have it stuck in your head. You let it go while you were cooking. The sheriff will find something.'

She jumped at the sound of footsteps outside.

'Probably him now,' Brody said easily and slid off the stool to answer the door himself.

'**B**rody.' Rick removed his hat. 'Reece.' His gaze skimmed over the counter. 'Sorry to interrupt your dinner.'

'We're finished. It's not important.' Though her knees shook, Reece slid off the stool to stand. 'Did you find her?'

'Mind if I have a seat?'

How could she have forgotten the ritual when cops came to call? Ask them to come in, to sit down, offer them coffee. 'Please.' Reece gestured to the sofa. 'Can I get you something?'

'I'm just fine, thanks.' After settling on the sofa, Rick set his hat on his lap and waited for Reece to sit. She knew before he spoke, saw his carefully neutral expression. 'I didn't find anything.'

And still, she shook her head. 'But—'

'Let's just take it slow,' Rick interrupted. 'Why don't you go over what you saw for me again?'

'Oh God.' Reece rubbed her hands hard over her face. Yes, of course. Another part of the ritual. 'All right.'

She recited it all, everything she remembered. 'He must have thrown the body in the river, or buried it, or—'

'We'll look into that. Brody, you sure about the location?'

'I showed you the map. Right near the little rapids.'

'Other side of the river,' Rick said to Reece, his tone as neutral as his face. 'That kind of distance, you could've been off. There wasn't any sign of struggle in that area. There wasn't any I could find when I branched out from there.'

'He must've covered it up.'

'Could be. I'm going back in the morning, once it's light. Meanwhile, I'm going to make some calls, see if any female tourists or residents are missing.'

'There are some cabins around that area,' Brody said.

'I went by a couple of the closest ones. Got my own, Joanie's got a couple. Mostly rental places out there, didn't see any sign they were being used. I'm checking on that, too. We'll get to the bottom of this, Reece. I don't want you to worry. Brody? You want to take a ride out there with me in the morning?'

'Sure, I can do that.'

'Let's get this checked out before the word spreads. I'll come by about seven thirty.' Rick pushed to his feet. 'Reece, you try to enjoy the rest of your evening. Put this out of your mind for a while. Nothing more you can do.' Rick settled his hat on his head and went out.

'He doesn't believe me,' Reece said.

'I didn't hear him say that.'

Helpless anger bubbled up. 'Yes, you did, under it.'

Brody set his wine down. 'Why wouldn't he believe you?'

'Because he didn't find anything. Because no one else saw it. Because I've only been in town a couple of weeks. Because, because.'

'I've got all that same information and I believe you.'

Her eyes stung. She gripped her hands together hard in her lap. 'Thanks.'

'I'm going to head home. You might take the sheriff's advice and put this out of your mind for a while. Take a pill, go to bed.'

'How do you know I have any pills to take?'

His lips curved, just a little. 'Take a sleeping pill and tune out. I'll tell you what's what—one way or another—tomorrow.'

'Fine. Thanks.' She got up to walk over and open the door herself. 'Good night.'

Satisfied he'd left her annoyed rather than depressed, he strolled out without another word.

Rick let himself into the sheriff's office, switched on the lights. He hung up his hat, his coat, then went back to the small break room to brew a short pot of coffee. While it brewed, he called home. As he expected, his oldest girl answered on the first ring. 'Hey, Daddy! Can I wear mascara to the Spring Fling? Just a little, *everybody* else does. Please?'

He pressed his fingers to his eyes. Not yet thirteen and already it was mascara and dances. 'What did your mother say?'

'She said she'd think about it. Daddy—'

'Then we'll discuss it tomorrow. Put your mama on now.'

'*Mom!* Daddy's going to talk about mascara tomorrow.'

'Thanks for the bulletin,' Debbie Mardson chuckled into the receiver. 'I was hoping you were on your way home.'

'Stuck here at the office awhile. Why the hell does that girl have to wear mascara? She's got your eyes, longest lashes in Wyoming.' He could see them, that long sweep, the bluebonnet eyes.

'Same reasons I do—it's a basic female tool.'

'And you're going to let her?'

'I'm considering.'

He rubbed the back of his neck. 'Next thing she'll be wanting a tattoo. It's the end of the world.'

'I think we can hold back the tattoo awhile yet. You want to call before you leave? I could have your dinner warmed up.'

'May be late. I picked up a meat-loaf sandwich at Joanie's. Don't worry about it. Kiss the girls for me. Love you.'

'Love you back. Bye.'

He sat for a time in the quiet, drinking his coffee, eating his sand-wich, going over Reece's statement, winding his way—again—through the details. With a shake of his head, he booted up his computer.

It was time to find out more about Reece Gilmore than she had no criminal record and came from Boston.

At seven thirty in the morning while Reece was struggling to concen-trate on buttermilk pancakes and eggs over easy, Brody armed himself with a Thermos of coffee and climbed into Rick's car.

'Morning. Appreciate you going out with me, Brody.'

'No problem. I'll think of it as research.'

Rick's smile came and went. 'Guess you could say we've got a mys-tery on our hands. How long again did you say it was from the time Reece said she saw this until you got back there with her?'

'I don't know how long it took her to run down. I was heading up the trail. Ten minutes, at a guess. Five minutes, I'd say, before we headed back, fifteen to where she'd stopped.'

'And her state of mind when you saw her?'

'Like you'd expect when a woman sees another woman strangled.'

'All right now, Brody. I have to look at this differently. I want to know if she was coherent, if she was clear.'

'After the first couple of minutes, yeah. You take into consideration that she was alone, shocked, scared and helpless while she watched it happen.'

'Through binoculars, across the Snake River.' Rick held up a hand. 'I have to factor in the lack of evidence. Maybe she saw a couple of people having an argument.'

He'd given it a lot of thought the night before. Gone over the details himself, point by point. And he remembered her face—clammy and pale, her eyes huge, glassy and deep. 'I believe she saw exactly what she said she did.'

Rick puffed out his cheeks. 'Are you two involved?'

'In what?'

Rick snorted out a laugh. 'I gotta like you, Brody. You're smart. Are you two personally involved?'

'What difference does it make?'

'Information always makes a difference in an investigation.'

'Then why don't you just ask me if I'm sleeping with her?'

'Well now, that was an attempt to be sensitive and subtle. But all right, then. Are you sleeping with her?'

'No.'

'All right, then,' he repeated with the faintest of smirks.

They drove awhile in silence until Rick pulled off the road. Brody slung a small pack over his shoulder. They moved through sagebrush and forest, where the soft dirt held tracks Brody recognised as deer, bear—and, he assumed, Rick's boots from the day before.

'No human tracks leading to the river,' Rick pointed out. 'Mine from yesterday. 'Course they could have come in from another angle, but I took a good look around. You got a body to deal with, you have to get rid of it. Throw it into the river, might be first instinct, first panic reaction. Or you'd bury it. There'd damn well be signs of that, Brody. I'm going to ask you again, could you have given me the wrong location?'

'No.'

The ground was moist from the thaw. The low rumble of the rapids came through the cottonwoods and the sunlight grew stronger until Brody could see it reflected off the water. Beyond was the canyon, and the spot high up on the other side where he'd stood with Reece.

'That's where she was sitting when she saw it happen.' Shielding his eyes with his hand, Brody pointed to the rocks.

'I've got to say, Brody, that's a hell of a long way.' Rick took out his field glasses. 'Get some glare that time of day.'

'Rick, we've had a friendly relationship the past year, so I'm asking you straight out why you don't believe her.'

'Let's just take it a step at a time. She's up there, sees this happening down here, runs back down the trail, where she runs into you. Meanwhile, what's this guy doing with the dead woman? Throws her in, she's going to wash up. And she'd have been spotted by now, more than likely.' Rick bit off a sigh. 'Have you seen any signs anyone's been tromping in and out of here, dragging off a body, burying one?'

'No, I haven't. Not yet.'

'Now you and me we'll take a walk around like I already did yesterday. I can't see anything to indicate there was anyone here passing the time of day, much less knocking a woman to the ground and strangling her.'

The logic of it was indisputable. And still. 'He covered his tracks.'

'Assuming he saw Reece up there, he managed to clear out in thirty minutes? Give it forty and it still doesn't hold for me.'

'You think she's lying? Made it up? What's the point?'

'I don't think she's lying. There's more to this, Brody.' Rick shoved back his hat, gave his brow a troubled rub. 'Let's do that walk around, and I'm going to tell you. I expect you can keep what I tell you to yourself. I figure you're one of the few people in the Fist who can do that.'

They walked, eyes on the ground or studying the brush. 'I did some checking up on her,' Rick said. 'Reece was involved with something a few years ago.'

Brody spoke carefully. 'Involved with what?'

'Spree killing at the restaurant where she worked in Boston. She was the only survivor. She was shot twice.'

'What?'

'Left for dead in some kind of storage closet until the cops found her. Coma after surgery, patchy memory after. And her mental state wasn't much better.'

Nothing Brody had imagined came close. 'How could it have been?'

'What I'm saying is she had a breakdown. Did some months in a psychiatric hospital.' Rick stopped, gave a long, slow scan, then changed direction. 'I recollect it made the national news. I'm surprised you didn't hear, Brody. Being a big-city reporter.'

Brody calculated the timing. 'I took what we'll call a moratorium from the news for a couple of months after I left the *Trib*.'

'Well, I guess the media business of it would have petered out in that length of time. But I gotta say, it was a hell of a thing for Reece to come back from, and it could be she's not all the way back even now.'

'So she, what, hallucinated a murder? Screw that, Rick.'

'Might've fallen asleep, just nodded off and had a bad dream. It's a long way up that trail for a novice, and she'd have been tired, could've been light-headed on top of it. Joanie says the girl hardly eats unless she shoves a plate at her. Got some nerves, too. Dragged the dresser in front of the door of the adjoining room in her hotel. Never unpacked.'

'Overly cautious isn't crazy.'

'Now, Brody, I never said crazy. Likely she's still emotionally fragile. That's how I'm seeing it because, when it comes down to it, that's all I have to see. I'm not calling in State at this point. Nothing for them to do here. I'll make enquiries into missing persons. Can't do more than that.'

'Is that what you're going to tell her?'

Rick took off his hat, raked fingers through his hair. 'You seeing what I'm seeing here? If you've got the time I'd like you to go with me while I check out the other cabins. I checked Joanie's and my own, being the closest ones.'

'I've got time. But why me instead of one of the deputies?'

'You were with her.' Face set, Rick settled his hat back on his head. 'We'll call you a secondary witness.'

'Covering your ass, Rick?'

'You want to call it that,' Rick said without rancour.

'You just don't believe her.'

'At this point, Brody?' Rick looked across the river, up to the rocks. 'No, I surely don't.'

When the breakfast rush was over, Reece dived straight into the prep for the soup of the day. She simmered beans, cubed leftover ham, diced onions. Joanie's didn't run to fresh herbs, so she made do with dried.

Better with fresh basil and rosemary. And how was she supposed to cook with garlic powder? And wasn't there anywhere around here that had tomatoes this time of year with some *taste*?

'Sure are full of complaints.' Joanie walked over to the pot, sniffed. 'Looks good enough to me.'

Talking to myself again, Reece realised. 'Sorry. It's fine; it'll be fine. I'm just in a mood.'

'I could see that for myself all morning. You want cordon bleu you should've aimed your car towards Jackson Hole.'

'It's fine. I'm sorry.'

'Didn't ask for the first apology, and the second's just annoying. You want something we don't have, you make a list. I'll think about ordering it. Maybe.'

'OK.'

'Doesn't look to me as if a day off did you much good.'

'No, it didn't.'

'Mac said you hiked up Little Angel Trail. Saw you come back with Brody.'

'We ran into each other.'

'The way your hands are shaking you're going to end up slicing your hand instead of those carrots.'

Reece set the knife down, turned. 'Joanie, I saw—' She broke off when Brody came into the diner. 'Can I take my break?'

Joanie watched the way Brody paused and waited. 'Go ahead.'

Reece moved fast. Her heart slammed against her ribs. And her hand reached out for Brody's. 'Did you find—'

'Let's go outside.'

She only nodded, which was just as well since he was already pulling her to the door. 'Did you find her?' Reece repeated. 'Tell me. Do we know who she is?'

He kept walking, his hand firm on her arm, until they were at the steps to her apartment. 'We didn't find anything.'

'But . . . Oh God, he must have thrown her in the river.' She'd visualised that countless times through the night.

'I didn't say anyone, Reece. I said anything.'

'He must have . . .' She caught herself. 'I don't understand.'

'We covered the ground where you said you'd seen them, the five closest cabins are empty, and there's no sign they've been otherwise. There weren't any tracks.'

She hugged her arms. 'That's just not possible. They were there. They argued, they fought, he killed her. I *saw* it.'

'Didn't say otherwise. I'm telling you there's nothing out there to support that.'

'He'll get away with it. He'll just walk away and live his life. I'm the only one who saw, and I couldn't do anything.'

'Does the world always revolve around you?'

She looked up then, torn between shock and misery. 'And how the hell would you feel? I guess you'd just shrug it off, go have a beer and stretch out in the hammock.'

'Little early yet for a beer. Sheriff's going to check on missing persons. He's going out to the guest ranch, the B and B's, campgrounds.'

'Why didn't he come back to talk to me? Because he doesn't think I saw anything,' she said before he could answer. The sick dread started in her belly. 'I want to go out there, see for myself.'

'Up to you.'

'I don't know how to get there. And maybe you're the last person I want to ask for a favour, but you know what? You're also the only person I'm absolutely sure didn't kill that woman. I'm off at three.' She strode off. 'You can pick me up here.'

Chapter 5

REECE PUT THE SOUP to simmer, and since her blood was up, started a list of what she considered essential items for any kitchen. Five-star restaurant, small-town diner, what did it matter? Food was food, and why the hell shouldn't it be perfectly prepared? She handled a few orders for people who, for reasons that escaped her, wanted a buffalo burger before noon.

'Reece.' Joanie's voice was cool. 'My office a minute.'

Reece followed Joanie into the little office.

'Close that door.' Joanie yanked her cigarettes out of her pocket. 'I just got a call from my boy. Seems the sheriff's been out to the ranch, looking for some woman who might've gone missing. Rick says maybe somebody saw something happen to this woman, maybe that person was up on Little Angel and thought something happened across the river. Not being a fool, I figure somebody who maybe saw something would be you.'

'The sheriff asked me not to say until he'd investigated . . . I saw a man strangle a woman, and I was too far away to help. And now they can't find anything. It's like it never happened.'

Joanie blew out a quick stream of smoke. 'What woman?'

'I don't know. I didn't see her that well. I saw . . . I saw . . .'

'Don't you go hysterical on me.' Joanie kept her voice firm.

'OK. All right.' Reece rubbed away the tears that had started. 'I was the only one who saw what he did to her. I was the only one who saw anything.'

Her boots drumming into the ground.

High-topped black Nikes outside the storeroom door.

His black jacket and orange hunter's cap.

Dark grey hoodie, big, black gun.

'I was the only one who saw anything,' she repeated. 'And I didn't see enough. Brody was on the trail further down. He didn't see. I didn't imagine it.'

'Why would I think you had? If you were upset about this, you could've had today off.'

'I had yesterday off, and look what happened.' Reece closed her eyes.

'You OK to finish out your shift?'

'Yes. I'd rather have something to do.'

'Then go cook. Meanwhile, if you've got something eating at you, screw what Rick Mardson tells you. You come to me.'

'All right. Thanks.'

The soup was a hit, so there was no point thinking it would've been better if she'd had everything she wanted at hand. Nobody here cared if the oregano was fresh. Why should she?

She only had to cook, serve and pick up her cheque.

She had no investment here. In fact, she'd probably made a mistake taking the apartment. She should move back to the hotel. Better, she should just toss her things into her car and move on. Nothing to keep her here. Nothing to keep her anywhere.

'Brody's arrived,' Linda-Gail called out. 'Ticket up, he and the doc are going for the soup.'

'Brody and the doctor,' Reece muttered. 'Isn't that perfect?' With rage just beginning to bubble, she ladled up two bowls, plated them with rolls and butter. And personally carried them out to the booth.

'Let me make this clear. I don't need a medical examination. I'm not sick. There's nothing wrong with my eyesight. I didn't fall asleep on the trail and dream I saw a woman being strangled to death.'

With the outrage of her words stinging the air, she strode back to the kitchen. She yanked off her apron, grabbed her jacket. 'My shift's over. I'm going upstairs.'

'Go right ahead.' Joanie placidly flipped a burger on the grill. 'You're on eleven to eight tomorrow.'

'I know my schedule.' She walked out the back, round the side, and stomped up the steps.

Inside the apartment, she went directly to her maps and guides. She'd find her way to the spot by herself. She pulled open the map that applied, then watched it flutter to the floor from her limp fingers.

It was covered with jagged red lines and splotches. The area across from the trail where she'd stood was circled dozens of times.

She hadn't done that, she hadn't. Still, she looked at her fingers as if expecting to see red smears on the tips. The map, pristine only the day before, now looked as if it had been scribbled on in some crazy code.

She hadn't done it. She couldn't have done it.

She dashed to the kitchen drawer. There, just where she'd put it, was her red marker. With trembling fingers, she pulled off the top, and saw the tip was dull and flattened. But she'd bought it only a few days before.

With great care she replaced the top, laid the marker back in the drawer. Then she scanned the apartment.

There was nothing out of place. She'd know. She'd know if a book had been moved an inch out of position, but everything was precisely how she'd left it that morning. When she'd locked the door behind her.

Checked the lock twice. Maybe three times.

She looked down at the map again. Had she done that? Sometime during the night, between the bad dreams and the shakes?

It didn't matter, she told herself. She'd been upset and she'd gotten the marker to be certain she didn't forget the exact spot where she'd seen the murder. It didn't make her crazy.

She refolded the map. It was nothing to worry about. But when she heard footsteps on the stairs, she stuffed it guiltily in her back pocket.

The knock was brisk. Certain it was Brody, she took a moment to be sure she was calm enough, then walked to the door to unlock it.

'You ready?'

'I changed my mind. I'll go by myself.'

'Fine. Do that.' But he nudged her back a step, then slammed the door behind him. 'I don't know why I bother. I didn't drag Doc down to take a look at you. Why the hell would I? It happens he comes in for lunch a few times a week, as you will have seen, and, if we happen to be in at the same time, we sometimes sit together. It's called being sociable. Happy?'

'No. Not especially.'

'Good because this is bound to get you going again. Rick's made some enquiries, so word's getting around. Doc asked me if I knew about it. Whether I'd have told him was up for debate until you served the soup. Damn good soup, by the way. You maniac.'

'I was in a psych ward for three months. Being called a maniac doesn't hurt my feelings.'

'Maybe you should've given it a few more weeks.'

She opened her mouth, shut it. Then walked to the day bed, sat. And laughed. Kept laughing as she pulled the tie out of her hair so it fell free down her back. 'Why is that comforting? Why the hell is that sort of rude, inappropriate response easier to hear than all the "there, there, it's all right now"? Maybe I am a maniac. Maybe I am just out of my mind.'

'Maybe you should stop feeling sorry for yourself.'

'I thought I had. I guess not.' She set the tie on a little table by the day bed. 'Are you still willing to take me out there?'

'My day's shot to hell anyway.'

'OK then.' She rose to retrieve her pack.

He stood by the door and watched her check the contents. Zip the pack. Unzip it, check inside again. Zip it. Unless he missed his guess, she struggled for a moment not to open it yet again.

When he opened the door, she went out, locked it. Then simply stood for a moment staring at the door.

'Go ahead. Check the lock. No point in obsessing over it after we leave.'

'Thanks.' She checked it, sent him a brief, apologetic look, then checked it again before she started down the stairs.

'It's an improvement,' she told him. 'It used to take me twenty minutes to get out of a room. And that was with a tranquilliser.' Before she got into his car, she checked the back seat. 'I'd rather take the time than take a pill. Don't you care why I was in a psych ward?'

'Are you going to tell me your life story now?'

'No. But I figure since I've pulled you in this far, you should know part of it.'

He pulled away from the kerb to start the drive out of town. 'I already know part of it. The sheriff did a background check on you.'

'He—' She broke off. 'I guess that would be a logical step. Nobody knows me, and suddenly I'm yelling murder.'

'Did they catch the guy who shot you?'

'No.' Automatically her hand came up to rub her chest. 'Twelve people. People I worked with or cooked for and cared about, all dead. I should've been dead, too. It's one of the things I think about. Why I lived and they didn't.'

'Luck of the draw. Why did they die?'

'Because the people who came in wanted it that way. For the fun of it. Thrill kills. They didn't get more than a couple of thousand. Most people use credit cards when they go out to dinner.' She stared at the mountains, so wild against the blue of the sky. 'I'd worked there since I was sixteen. I grew up in Maneo's. I loved it. I loved them.'

She could see it now, as it had been then. The bustle in the kitchen, the clatter outside the swinging door, the voices, the smells.

'It was my last night. They were giving me a little going-away party. It was supposed to be a surprise, so I was fooling around in the kitchen to give them time to set it up. There was screaming and gunfire and crashing. When I dream about it, I see the gun, and the dark grey hooded sweatshirt, that's all, then the pain erupts. Once in the chest, and the other bullet grazed my head.'

When she paused, he glanced towards her. 'Keep going.'

'I fell back into the closet. I'd been putting away cleaning supplies. The cops told me that later. I didn't know where I was.'

She rubbed her hand between her breasts again. 'I couldn't get my breath. This weight on my chest. The door was still open, just a few inches. I heard voices.' She lowered her hand. 'I thought only about being quiet, so they wouldn't kill me. My friend, my prep cook, fell on the other side of the door. Ginny Shanks. She'd just got engaged the month before.' Reece closed her eyes and let the rest come. 'I could see her bloody face through the crack of the door. She was crying, and she was begging. And our eyes met, just for a second. I think they did. Then I heard the gunshot, and her eyes changed. A fingersnap, and the life was just gone. Ginny was just on the other side of the door, and there was nothing I could do for her. For any of them.'

'How long were you in the hospital?'

'Six weeks, but I don't remember the first two at all. Then I didn't respond to therapy very well. Flashbacks and night terrors. Sleepwalking, bouts of hysteria, lethargy. I'd think I'd hear them coming for me, see that grey sweatshirt on strangers on the street. I checked myself into a psychiatric hospital, but I had to leave because I realised how easy it would be to stay. With pills I pretty much remained blank, and I'd been blank too long already.'

'So now you're just neurotic.'

'Claustrophobic, obsessive/compulsive, with paranoia and panic attacks. Crappy dreams, and I do sometimes wake up thinking it's all happening again, but I didn't imagine I saw those two people.'

He veered to the side of the road. 'We'll walk from here.'

She got out first and, bracing herself, pulled the map out of her pocket. 'I went to get this when I was angry, thinking you'd sicced the doctor on me.' She handed it to him. 'I don't remember marking it up, but I must've had a panic attack during the night, and I'm blocking it out.'

'Then why are you showing it to me?'

'You ought to know what you're dealing with.'

He studied the map briefly, then refolded it. 'I saw your face yesterday when you came running down the trail. You saw what you saw, and it's not right. A woman's dead, and somebody ought to give a damn about it.'

She closed her eyes a minute. 'Don't take this the wrong way, OK?' Stepping up, she wrapped her arms around him, pressed her lips lightly to his.

'What would be the wrong way to take that?'

'As anything other than sincere gratitude.' She swung her pack over her shoulder. 'Do you know the way?'

'Yeah, I know the way.'

As they stepped off the road, she gave him a quick glance. 'That's the first time I've kissed a man in two years.'

'No wonder you're crazy. How was it?'

'Comforting.'

He snorted. 'Some other time, Slim, maybe we'll go for something a little more interesting than comforting.'

They hiked through the trees to the river canyon and its tumble of rocks.

'There weren't any tracks, Reece, in any direction, but for Rick's going in and out. Look.' He crouched. 'See here? My tracks from this morning, and Rick's. Ground's pretty soft.'

'Well, they didn't fly in on the wings of a dove.'

'But if he knew anything about tracking, anything about hiking, he could've covered his tracks.'

'Why? Who'd look here for a dead woman no one saw him kill?'

'You saw him. And maybe he saw you right back.'

'He never looked around, never looked across.'

'You ran, didn't you? And left your stuff sitting on the rock. Maybe he caught a glimpse of you, or just saw your pack.'

'He saw me.' Her throat slapped shut on the idea of it.

'Maybe he did, maybe he didn't. Either way, he was careful. Smart and careful enough to take his time, cover up any sign.'

'He saw me. Why didn't I think of that before?'

'Can you see where you were from here?'

She walked out, closer to the river. 'There.' She pointed up, over. 'I stopped there. They were here. She was struggling, twisting under him. He rapped her head down hard, then put his hands round her throat.'

Brody studied the ground. 'Pretty clean. Could be, maybe, you bring in a team of crime-scene experts, they'd find a stray hair, but what's that going to prove? He's smart. He drags or carries her off, out of sight of the river, the canyon, then all he has to do is cover his tracks. If he had a car, he could've tossed the body in the trunk and driven somewhere else. Somewhere he could take his time to dig a hole deep enough so the animals wouldn't find her.'

'That's so cold.'

'Killing somebody takes ice or heat, depending. Getting away with it? Yeah, that takes cold blood. Seen enough?'

She nodded. 'More than.'

Back in the car, Reece felt ridiculously tired. She wanted a nap, a dim, quiet room, a soft blanket, locked doors.

When Brody started the car she closed her gritty eyes for just a moment. And slid off the edge of fatigue into sleep.

She slept quietly, Brody thought, not a sound, not a movement. Her head rested in that nook between the seat and the window, and her hands lay limp in her lap.

What the hell was he supposed to do with her now?

Since he wasn't entirely sure, he idled along, taking impulsive detours to extend the trip back to town.

He was sucked in now, and not just because he was a degree of separation away from witnessing a murder. She pulled at him. Not her weaknesses, but the strength she struggled to find to fight them. He had to respect that. Just as he had to acknowledge the low simmer of attraction.

So he drove while she slept, across the yellow grasses and washed-out green of the ubiquitous sage. Snow still swirled on the Tetons, adding another layer of might as they knocked against the sky. The Rockies were grander, he supposed, but these rough, magical mountains were primal.

He drove fast along the empty road across the sage flats towards Angel's Fist, and the stands of cottonwood and pine that bordered it. Reece moaned quietly in sleep. When Brody glanced at her, he saw she'd begun to quiver.

He stopped, then gave her arm a quick shake. 'Wake up.'

'No!' She came out of sleep like a runner off the starting block. When her fist shot out, he blocked it with the flat of his hand. 'Hit me,' he said mildly, 'I'll hit back.'

'What? What?' She stared blearily at her fist cupped firmly in his hand. 'I fell asleep. Did I fall asleep?'

'If you didn't, you gave a good imitation of it.'

'Did I hit you?'

'You gave it a shot. Don't try it again.'

'Check.' She willed her heartbeat to steady. 'Can I have my hand back?'

He opened his fingers and she drew her fist back and let it fall to her lap. 'You always wake up like you just heard the bell for Round Two?'

'I don't know. It's been a long time since I slept when anyone's been around. I guess I feel comfortable around you.'

'Comforting, comfortable.' That eyebrow winged up. 'Use words like that, I'm going to feel honour-bound to change your mind.'

She smiled a little. 'You don't . . . Oh! Oh, just look at them.'

Struck, she unhooked her seat belt, pushed open her door. The wind streamed over her as she stepped out of the car.

'It's all so *raw*, so stunning and scary. All this open, and there they are, the—I don't know—fortress of them taking over everything. It's like they just shoved their way up, straight out of the ground. I love the suddenness of them.' She walked to the front of the car, to lean back against the hood. 'I look at them every day, but it's not the same as being out here without buildings, without people.'

'I'm people.'

'You know what I mean. Out here, faced with them, you feel so utterly human.' She looked over, pleased he'd come to join her. 'I thought I'd pass through, pick up a little work, move on. And every morning I see them and can't think of any reason to leave.' She tipped her head back, closed her eyes and just breathed.

'You look like that sometimes when you're cooking.'

She opened her eyes again, the deep Spanish brown. 'I do?'

He planted his hands on the hood on either side of her.

'Brody.'

'Do you want to tell me you didn't figure this was coming?'

Her heart kicked, and maybe some of it was fear. But not all of it. 'I guess it slipped by me. Mostly slipped by me,' she corrected.

'If you're not interested, you'd better make it clear.'

'Of course I'm interested, it's just—whoa.'

He took her arms, lifted her right up to her toes. 'You'd better get your breath,' he warned. 'We're going for a dive.'

She couldn't get her breath, or her balance. His mouth wasn't patient or kind, didn't seduce or persuade. The sensation of being swept up, swept away, left her giddy and loose.

Even as she wondered if there'd be anything left of her when he was done, her arms locked round his neck. Her heart pounded against his, and she trembled. But her mouth was as avid as his.

He hitched her up by the hips until she sat on the hood. His hands streaked under the soft cotton of her sweater, closed over her breasts. They were rough and hard and direct. Brody found her eager response unexpected. 'Easy.' His hands weren't completely steady this time as he took her in his arms. 'Let's ease back a little.'

She let her head fall to his shoulder. 'OK. Right. We can't . . .'

'We did. We damn sure will again, but since we're not sixteen, it won't be in the middle of the road on the hood of a car.'

'No. Right. I'm not ready to . . . This isn't a good idea.'

'I'm not asking you to marry me and bear my children, Slim. It was a kiss, and a damn good idea. Sleeping together's an even better one.'

She pressed her hands to her temples. 'I can't think. Look at us, talking about sex. A woman's dead.'

'She's going to be dead whether or not we go to bed. If you need time to get your head around that, take a couple days.'

She stared at him, big and male and rugged, backed by the towering spread of the Tetons. 'I don't sleep with every man I'm attracted to.'

'Then let's get back. I want a beer.' He slid into the car.

She marched to the passenger door and slid inside the car. 'I don't even know why I like you,' she muttered. 'And while I'm grateful to you for believing me, for supporting me, I—'

'One has nothing to do with the other.' His voice was dangerously cold. 'Don't go there.'

'I . . .' She took a breath when he began to drive. 'That was insulting, you're right. It was insulting to both of us. I told you I couldn't think.' She stared at the mountains. 'This has been the strangest couple of days.'

'Tell me about it.'

'I want to talk to the sheriff. You could just drop me off there.'

'Suit yourself. What's for dinner tomorrow?'

'What?'

'You're feeding me.'

'Oh. I forgot. I don't know. I'll think of something.'

When he pulled over in front of the sheriff's office, she waited one beat, two, then grabbed her pack from the floor.

'Problem?'

'No. Well, I thought you'd kiss me goodbye.'

His lips twitched. 'Gee, Slim, are we going steady?'

'You're such an ass.' But she laughed. 'When you ask me to go steady, make sure to bring a ring. And tulips—they're my favourite.'

The sheriff's office smelt of stale coffee. There were two face-to-face metal desks where, Reece assumed, the deputies worked. Only one was occupied. Mop of dark hair, little goatee, cheerful hazel eyes, slight, youthful build. Denny Darwin, Reece remembered, who liked his eggs over hard and his bacon next to burnt.

He glanced up. 'Hey, Ms Gilmore.'

'Reece. I was hoping to speak to the sheriff if he's in.'

'Sure, he's back in his office. Just go ahead.'

'Thanks.' She walked through the outer office in the direction he had gestured. Down one end of a hall, across from two unoccupied cells, Rick Mardson's door stood open.

He sat behind an oak desk that looked as if it had been through several wars. Besides the computer and phone system, it held a couple of picture frames. On the old coatrack in the corner hung his hat and a faded brown barn jacket.

He rose. 'Come on in, Reece. I just called your place.'

'Have you got a minute?'

'Sure. Have a seat. Want some of the nastiest coffee in Wyoming?'

'I'll skip it, but thanks. I wondered if you had any news.'

'Well, on the good-news front, no missing persons in the area matched the description of the woman you reported.'

'No one's realised she's gone yet. It's only been a day.'

'That may be, and I'll check on that periodically.'

'You think I imagined it.'

He walked over to the door, shut it, then came back to his desk. There was nothing in his face but kindness and patience. 'I can only tell you what I know. Right now, I know every female in town is accounted for, and the visitors here are alive and well. And I know, because part of my job is to check things out, that you had a bad time a couple years back.'

'That doesn't have any bearing on this.'

'Perhaps it does. Now I want you to take time and think it all through.

It could be you saw people having an argument. Maybe things got physical. But you were some ways off, Reece, even with the field glasses. I want you to think if it's possible both those people walked away.'

'She was dead.'

'Now, seeing as you were up on the trail, you couldn't take her pulse, could you? Isn't it possible she got up and walked off with a few bruises, but alive?'

'She was dead. If she walked off, how do you explain the fact there were no tracks?'

When he spoke that same patience was in his tone. It was beginning to crawl up her spine like spiders. 'It was your first time on the trail. You were shocked and upset. It's a long river, Reece. Easy to mistake the spot when you got back with Brody.'

'I couldn't have been that far off.'

'Well, I've looked the best I can, but it's a lot of ground to cover. I went ahead and contacted the closest hospitals. No woman was treated who matched your description with trauma to the neck or head. I'll follow up on that again tomorrow.'

She got to her feet. 'You don't think I saw a thing.'

'You're wrong. I think you saw something that scared and upset you. But I can't find a single thing to support you witnessed a homicide. My advice is to let me follow through on this, and you've got my word I will.'

When she left, Mardson blew out a breath. He'd do all he could do, he thought, and that was all that could be asked of a man.

Now he was going home to have dinner with his wife and kids.

Chapter 6

BRODY GOT HIS BEER and tossed a frozen pizza in the oven. When he punched the button on his answering machine, it spat out a message from his agent. The book scheduled for early fall had snagged a very decent book-club deal. Which might call for a second beer with dinner.

Maybe, with a part of his take from it, he'd splurge on a new TV. Plasma. Hang it over the fireplace. It would be very sweet to stretch out on the couch and watch it.

But for now, he had work to make up—can't afford a plasma TV if you don't put in the time at the keyboard. Besides, he was looking forward to digging into his current work-in-progress before he called it a night.

Still, over a beer, waiting for his pizza, he could spare the time to find out more about Reece. He glanced around. His laptop was on the table. With another sip of his beer, he booted up. Googling her, he got enough hits to keep him busy, and interested.

He dug up an old article on up-and-coming Boston chefs that featured the then twenty-four-year-old Reece. Young, vibrant, *essential*, somehow, grinning into the camera while holding a big blue bowl and a shining silver whisk. The article gave her educational background—a year in Paris added a lot of polish—personalised with an anecdote about how she'd prepared five-course dinners for her dolls when she was a child.

He learned she was orphaned at fifteen, raised from that point by her maternal grandmother. She'd spoken fluent French and was apparently renowned for her Sunday brunches.

There was a splashy *Boston Globe* feature about her taking the position as head chef for a 'wildly popular hot spot known for its American fusion cuisine and convivial atmosphere'. The photograph was of a sophisticated-looking Reece wearing her hair up and posed in what would have been the stainless-steel glory of her new kitchen in a sexy black suit and mile-high seductress-red heels.

The date was three days before the report of the killings at Maneo's.

Reece filled her little bathtub with hot water and an indulgent squirt of drugstore bath foam. She'd eaten some cheese and crackers—now she was going to soak and start Brody's book which she'd bought at the mercantile. *Down Low*. Mac had liked it. She didn't want to think about reality, at least not for the next hour. She debated whether or not to close and lock the bathroom door, but the room was so small she'd never be able to handle being closed in that way.

The front door was locked, she reminded herself, and the back of a chair under the handle. She was perfectly safe. But after she slid into the tub she had to sit up twice, to see round the doorway into the living area. In case. She read for ten minutes before the growing jitters told her she'd had enough and she pulled the plug.

As she pulled on flannel trousers and a T-shirt, Joanie banged on the door. 'Open up,' she barked. I haven't got all night.'

On jellied knees Reece hurried across the room and, as quietly as she could manage, drew the chair away. 'Sorry, just a second!' She unlocked the door, unlatched the chain.

Joanie trooped in. 'I'm taking my break.' She walked to the front window, opened it a few inches, then took out a pack of Marlboro Lights. 'You gonna say I can't smoke in here?'

'No.' Reece carried over a tea saucer to serve as an ashtray. 'How's the crowd tonight?'

'Not bad. Lo's downstairs. He's worried about you.' She took a contemplative drag. 'Word's got around about what you saw on the trail yesterday.'

'Saw, or thought I saw?'

'Well, which is it?'

'I saw.'

'OK then. Linda-Gail wanted me to tell you she'd come up and stay the night, or you could go to her place.'

'She did? That's so sweet of her. But I'm all right.'

'Seeing as I'm your boss and your landlord, it's been my task today to field enquiries as to how you're doing, Mac, Carl, Doc, Bebe, Pete, Beck and so on, but most everyone was sincere in their concern. Thought you should know.'

'Joanie, the sheriff still can't find anything.'

'Some things take longer than others. Rick'll keep looking.'

'Yes, I suppose he will. But he doesn't really believe I saw what I said I saw. Why should anyone, really? If they do now, they'll think differently once word gets around—about what happened in Boston. And . . .' She trailed off, narrowing her eyes. 'I guess it already has.'

'Somebody murmured to somebody who murmured to somebody else. So, yeah, there's been some talk about how you were hurt.'

With her habitual quick jabs, Joanie stubbed out the cigarette. 'I know good stock when I see it. You'll hold up. You held up to worse.'

'I didn't.'

'Don't tell me you didn't,' Joanie snapped back. 'I'm standing here looking at you, aren't I? Bad things happen everywhere.' She stepped to the door. 'I have to get back down. You gonna put the chair under the doorknob again?'

Reece shrugged. 'Nothing gets by you,' she said.

Lo cruised into Angel's Fist in his black Ford with a Waylon Jennings CD wailing on the stereo. He'd been listening to Faith Hill, but even with her superior pipes, a guy just couldn't be riding around town with a girl singing in his pick-up.

He had his mind on a girl now. Actually on a couple, but he had plenty of room in his mind for females. He saw one of them in skinny jeans and a red sweatshirt standing on a stepladder painting the shutters on the little doll's house she rented a bright, sunny yellow.

He gunned the motor, waiting for her to turn and admire the way he looked in the muscular truck. When she didn't, he pulled over.

God knew he'd always had to work harder with this female for crumbs than he ever did with others for the whole damn cake.

'Hey, Linda-Gail!'

'Hey, yourself.' She kept right on painting.

'What are you doing?'

'Having myself a pedicure. What does it look like?'

He got out of the truck to saunter over. 'Got the day off?' He'd already snuck a look at the schedule and knew she did.

'That's right. You?'

'Got some people in, but they're going on a paddling tour today. You seen Reece?'

'No.' She slapped paint on wood hard enough to make him jump out of range.

'Watch it.'

Ornery woman, he thought. He didn't know why he kept coming back for more abuse. 'Listen, I just wondered how she was.'

'Your ma said to give her room, so I'm giving her room.' Still she sighed. 'I wish I knew, though. It's an awful thing.'

'Awful,' he repeated. 'Kind of exciting, though.'

'It is! We're sick, sick people, but damn, murder and all. Bebe thinks it was a couple of people who robbed a bank or something, then had a falling-out, so now he's got all the money.'

'Good a theory as any.'

Lowering her brush, she leaned on the ladder. 'But I think they were having this adulterous fling and ran away. Then she changed her mind and wanted to go back to her husband and kids, so he killed her in the heat of passion.'

'Sounds good, too. Weighted the body down, then crammed it into an old beaver lodge.'

'Oh, that's just *awful*, Lo. Worse than burying her out there.'

'Any way you slice it, he's long gone by now.'

'I guess. Doesn't make it any better for Reece.' She went back to painting. 'I guess you're going by to see her.'

'I thought I might, if you wanted to go with me.'

'Your ma told me not to pester Reece today. Besides, I've got this started. I need to finish it.'

'Take you half the day the way you're going.'

She looked down. 'I've got another brush, smart guy. You could do something useful instead of standing around posing.'

Damned if he wanted to paint stupid shutters, but he reached for the brush. 'Guess I could give you a hand. Maybe, if we get this done, we could drive out to the ranch. Nice day for a ride.'

Linda-Gail smiled. 'Maybe. It is a pretty nice day.'

Reece had dashed upstairs on her break to make the marinade for the pot-roast she'd settled on for dinner.

When her shift was over she zipped back. It had been a long time since she had prepared a serious, intimate meal. While the potatoes and carrots browned in the roast's juices, she opened a bottle of Cabernet to let it breathe. It had probably been silly, she thought, to buy the cloth napkins in their bright, paisley print, but they looked so festive tented on the white plates. And the candles were practical. The power might go out sometime, and her flashlight batteries might die.

She had slid the stuffed mushrooms into the oven in plenty of time before she heard footsteps on the stairs.

She let the initial panic go, crossed to the door. 'Brody?'

'You expecting someone else? What's for dinner?'

Smiling, she opened the door. 'Salmon croquettes and steamed asparagus with a side of polenta.'

His eyes narrowed as he stepped in. Then he took a good sniff of the air. 'Meat. Looks like you might want to put this away for another time.'

She took the wine he offered, a nice Pinot Grigio. He paid attention, she realised, even when he didn't seem to. 'Thanks. I've got Cabernet open, if you'd like a glass.'

'Wouldn't turn it down.' He took off his jacket, tossed it over the back of a chair.

She poured him a glass of wine. Then she took the roast out of the oven, set it on the stovetop. 'Ah, just like Mom used to make.'

'Really?'

'No. My mother could burn takeout.'

Amused, Reece set out a dish of olives. 'What does she do?'

'She's a psychiatrist. Private practice.'

'Oh.' She tried to ignore the automatic bump in her belly.

'And she macramés.'

'She what?'

'Makes things by tying rope into knots. I think she once macraméd a small studio apartment. Furnished. It's an obsession.'

'And your father?'

'My father likes to cook out on the grill, even in winter. He's a college professor. Romance languages. You having wine?'

'In a minute.' She pulled out the mushrooms, sprinkled them with Parmesan. Set them under the broiler. 'These would be better with fresh Parmesan, but I couldn't find any.'

'I'll probably be able to choke one or two down.'

Once they were done to her specification, were arranged on a plate, she set them on the counter between them, then raised her glass in a half-toast. 'This is the first meal I've cooked for anyone in two years.'

'You cook every day downstairs.'

She shook her head. 'I mean it's the first meal I've cooked for plea-sure. The other night doesn't count. That was a throw-it-together deal. I've missed doing this, and didn't realise just how much until tonight.'

'Glad to help.' He picked up a mushroom, popped it in his mouth. 'Good.'

She took one herself, bit in. Smiled. 'Yes, they are.'

While Reece served, Brody poured them both more wine. He'd noted the candles, the fancy napkins. New, he thought, since his last visit. And he'd noticed his book sitting on the tiny table by her day bed. The woman was settling in, he decided.

'I started your book. I like it.' She came round the counter to sit beside him. 'It's scary, and that's good. It takes my mind off my own nerves. I like Jack—he's such a screwup. I hope Leah can straighten him out.'

'Is that what women are supposed to do? Straighten men out?'

'People are supposed to straighten people out. If they care enough. She cares for him. So I hope they end up together.'

'Happily ever after doesn't win Pulitzers.'

She pursed her lips. 'Is that what you're after?'

'If it was, I'd still be working for the *Trib*. Cooking pot-roast over a diner in Wyoming isn't going to win you whatever the epicurean equiv-alent might be.'

'I thought I wanted that once, too. I'd rather cook pot-roast.' She paused a minute. 'How's that going for you?'

'I'd give you an award.' He cut another piece, followed with gener-ously buttered biscuit. 'Where'd you get these biscuits?'

'I made them.'

'Get out.' His disbelief was instant. 'Like with flour?'

'That would be one ingredient.' She passed him the bowl so he could take another. 'Let me guess what's in your larder. Frozen pizza, cans of chilli, maybe some hot dogs?'

'Keeps body and soul together.' He speared one of the tiny roasted potatoes. 'Going to straighten me out, Slim?'

'I'll feed you now and then, which works for both of us.'

'Do you ever write any of this stuff down? Recipes?'

'Sure. I was organised even before I went crazy. I've got recipes on my laptop. Why? You planning on trying your hand at buttermilk biscuits?'

'No. I just wondered why you haven't done a cookbook.'

'I used to think I might, eventually. Something hip and fun and skewed towards the urban dinner party and Sunday brunch crowd.'

'Eventually's a myth. You want to do something, do it. If you put a proposal together, I'll send it to my agent.'

'Why would you do that?'

He ate his last bite of meat. 'Damn good pot-roast. Now if you'd written a manuscript for a novel, the only way I'd read it would be if you held a gun to my head or slept with me.'

'Under those conditions, how many manuscripts have you sent to your agent?'

'That would be none. The subject's come up a few times, but I've managed to slip through loopholes.'

'Of course.' She shook her head. 'I'd offer you seconds, but you'll need room for dessert. So. Why don't you retire to the salon, enjoy your wine. I'm going to clear this up.'

'Fine, but the view's better from here. I saw a picture of you from a few years back. Article on the Internet,' he explained when she only stared at him.

'Why were you looking at articles on the Internet?'

'About you? Curiosity. Your hair was shorter.'

Reece took the plates to the sink. 'Yes. I haven't been able to handle a salon since . . .' She turned on the taps, squirted in washing-up liquid. 'So I've let it grow.'

'It's nice hair. You look good. You've got lucky genes.'

She swung round just as he pushed off the stool.

He laid his hands on the sink on either side of her, much as he'd done on the hood of his car. 'What's for dessert?'

'Apple brown betty with vanilla bean ice cream . . .'

His mouth captured hers, firm and strong. She tasted the wine on his tongue, heady and tempting. 'Oh boy,' she managed. 'It's like I have the circuits in my brain crossed. All sizzle and smoke.'

'Maybe you need to lie down.'

'I'd like to. Let me say first, I even washed the sheets, in case.'

His lips quirked. 'You washed the sheets.'

'Seemed like the thing to do. But . . . Would you just take a step back? I can't breathe right.'

He eased back. 'Better?'

'Yes and no.' He was so compelling, she thought. She stood by her initial impression of him. Not handsome, but so compellingly male. 'I want to go to bed with you, but I think I need to wait until I'm a little more sure of myself.'

'And of me.'

'It's one of the things I like about you. You get the point. It would be normal for you, but for me, being intimate again would be monumental. I guess that's a big weight on you.'

'Damn considerate. What the hell is apple brown betty?'

'Who? Oh. It's delicious. Go sit down and I'll prove it. You want coffee?'

'You don't have coffee.'

'Actually . . .' She picked up a Thermos she had on the counter. 'I got some from downstairs. Light, one sugar, right?'

'Yeah. Thanks.'

She fixed the dessert, served it in the living area. 'You haven't said anything at all about the murder. One of the sheriff's theories is that I mistook the spot, and she wasn't dead. Which is why no one's reported her missing.'

'And you disagree.'

'On every point. Maybe she's not important to anyone. Or was, well, from France.'

Brody smiled. 'Wherever she was from, odds are someone saw her. Getting gas, buying supplies, in a campground, in a motel. Could you describe her to an artist?'

'Like a police artist?'

'Angel's Fist doesn't run to that, but I was thinking of Doc. He does charcoal sketches.'

'I'd be willing to try, if you come with me.'

He'd already planned to go with her. 'What have you got to trade for my time? I'm thinking along the lines of something that goes with the bottle of white in your fridge.'

'I've got Sunday off. I'll take care of the menu.'

He took the first spoonful in his bowl. 'Where has this been all my life? I'll talk to Doc.'

'So how'd it go?' Linda-Gail set the tub of cleared dishes on the counter for Pete, then gave Reece an elbow bump.

'How'd what go?'

'Your date with Brody last night.'

Reece was grilling burgers for a table of after-school teenagers. 'I just fixed him dinner. A payback for a favour.'

'Just dinner.' Linda-Gail rolled her eyes over at Pete.

'She's in love with me.' Pete slid dishes into the sink.

'You bought candles,' Linda-Gail pointed out. 'And cloth napkins. *And* fancy wine.'

'Oh boy.' Reece didn't know whether to laugh or cringe. 'Are there no secrets in the Fist?'

'None I can't unearth,' Linda-Gail said. 'You want to go out for a beer later to toast your good deed?'

Reece smiled. 'You know what, I would.'

The bar food at Clancy's wasn't bad, at least not washed down with beer. But more important to Reece, she'd taken another step. She was sitting in a bar with a friend. A very strange bar, to her East Coast sensibilities. Mounted heads of bear, elk, moose and mule deer adorned the knotty pine panelling. They all stared out into the bar with what Reece thought of as a little shock, a little annoyance. The panelling looked as if it had soaked up a generation of smoke and beer fumes and the floors were scuffed and scarred. Part of the area, in front of a low stage, was sectioned off for dancing. Beside the bar, the bar stools were worn and shiny and behind it, the crowded display leaned heavily to whiskeys.

There were a couple of pool tables, and the sound of balls clacking carried through the music piped through speakers.

'Now that I'm plying you with alcohol, spill,' said Linda-Gail. 'Just how hot is Brody?'

If she was going to have a girlfriend, Reece decided, she was going to act like one herself. She leaned in. 'Combustible.'

'I *knew* it!' Linda-Gail banged a fist on the table. 'You can just tell. The eyes, the mouth. The mouth especially.'

'It is, it is. I must admit, I'm thinking about the rest.'

Eyes wide, Linda-Gail sat back. 'You have superhuman control. Is it learned or inherited?'

'It's what you call a by-product of abject fear. You've got the story on me by now.'

Linda-Gail sipped at her beer. 'Does that bother you?'

'I don't know. Sometimes it's a relief.'

'I didn't know whether to say anything about it or not. Especially after Joanie gave the bunch of us the what-for when Juanita started chattering. Juanita doesn't mean anything by it, she just can't keep her mouth shut.'

'It's all right.' And wasn't it amazing, to have the inimitable Joanie Parks as her champion? 'It's just not something I like to talk about.'

'I don't blame you.' Linda-Gail squeezed a hand over Reece's. 'So, we'll only talk about men and food and shoes. Just so we'll be on level ground, men-wise, I'm going to marry Lo.'

'Oh, oh, my God! This is great. I had no idea.'

'Neither does he. And I figure it's going to take some more time and effort to refine him into anything worth marrying. But I'm really good at projects.'

'Ah. Um, so you're in love with him.'

Her pretty face softened. 'I've loved him all my life. Well, since I was sixteen, and that's a long time. He loves me, too, but his way of dealing with that is to run in the opposite direction. I'm letting him get it out of his system.'

'Well, huh. That's unique and broad-minded, Linda-Gail.'

'A little more narrow-minded these days. Time's about up. Brody hasn't dated anyone in the Fist, in case you wonder. Word was he was seeing some lawyer type in Jackson on and off for a while, but nobody local.'

'I guess that's good to know. I'm not sure what's between us, really.'

Idly Reece toyed with the ends of her hair. 'Linda-Gail, where do you get your hair done?'

'When I'm in a hurry, or when I want to splurge?'

'I'm mulling the splurge.'

'Reece, you can't mull the splurge. You just take it. I know the perfect place. We can finagle Joanie into giving us the same day off next week.'

'OK, but I should tell you that the last time I tried to keep a salon date, I ran like a rabbit.'

'No problem,' Linda-Gail said. 'I'll bring some rope.'

As Reece broke into a grin, one of the local cowboys had sauntered up to the little stage, picked up a microphone and broken into a rendition of 'Ruby'.

'Live entertainment, too?' Reece asked.

'Depends on how you measure entertainment. Karaoke. That's Reuben Gates, works out at the Circle K with Lo.'

He had a deep, strong baritone, and was an obvious favourite with the crowd, who whistled and clapped. As he ended to enthusiastic applause, another man headed to the stage, a sweet, if thready, tenor with a ballad. Next, a blonde with a tin ear and a lot of self-deprecating humour, butchered a Dolly Parton classic.

Reece made it a full hour, and considered the evening an enormous success. Walking back to her apartment, she let herself in the door.

After locking the door, checking the knob, bracing the back of a chair under it, she went to wash.

In the doorway of her little bathroom, she froze. None of her toiletries were on the shelf by the sink. She squeezed her eyes shut, but when she reopened them, the shelf was still empty. She yanked open the mirrored medicine cabinet. It, too, was empty. With a whimper of distress she spun round. Her bed was neatly made, as she'd left it that morning. The kettle sat shining on the stove. But her duffle sat at the foot of the bed.

Her legs trembled as she crossed to it, and the whimper became a muffled cry as she yanked the zipper and found her clothes neatly packed inside. Everything she'd come with, all her things, carefully folded and ready to go.

Who would do such a thing?

She lowered herself to the side of the bed. And faced the truth. No one could. She'd done it herself. She must have done it. Some remnant from the worst of her breakdown kicking in. Telling her to run, to go, to move on. Why couldn't she remember?

Not the first time, she reminded herself, and dropped her head in her hands. Not nearly the first time she'd lost time, or couldn't quite recall doing something. But it had been months since she'd had these kinds of episodes.

Maybe she should take a hint. Pick up the duffle and go down, toss it in her car and drive. To anywhere. And if she did, *anywhere* would just be another place where she'd cease to be. She had a place here, an identity.

She put all her stuff away—the clothes, the toothbrush, the bottles, the shoes. She didn't run. Not today. Not tomorrow.

Chapter 7

DOC WALLACE SET OUT tea and coffee and sugar cookies among the framed family photographs of his parlour. Reece found herself charmed as they sat in front of the low glow of the fire. Her grandmother would have very much approved.

Doc passed her tea, poured Brody a cup of coffee. He picked up his sketch pad and a pencil. 'I've got to admit, this is exciting for me. It's like being on *Law and Order*, so I did a little research. Think of the shape of her face to begin with. Can you do that?'

'Yeah, I think I can.'

'Close your eyes a minute, get the picture in your mind.'

She did, and saw the woman. 'Oval, I guess. But a long, narrow oval. Ellipse?'

'That's good. On the thin side, then?'

'Yes. She wore her hair long, and the red cap pulled down low, but I got the sense of a long, narrow face.'

'How about her nose?'

'Her nose?' She drew a complete blank. 'God, I don't think I'm going to be very good at this.'

'Do the best you can.'

'I think . . . I think long and narrow, like her face. Not prominent. I noticed her mouth. Her mouth seemed hard to me.'

'Thin mouth?'

'I don't know, maybe. It was . . . mobile. And when she wasn't yelling, she was scowling, sneering. Her hair was past her shoulders, wavy, very dark. Her sunglasses fell off when he knocked her down, but it all happened so fast. I had the impression of big eyes . . . And make-up,' Reece said suddenly, putting down her cup. 'I think she wore a lot of make-up, red lipstick.'

'If you had to guess her age?'

'Oh boy. Ah, late thirties maybe. Give or take a decade,' Reece added and pressed her fingers to her eyes. 'Hell.'

'Just go with your first impression. Is this close?'

Reece edged forward when Doc turned the pad round. He was better than she'd assumed. 'OK. OK,' she murmured. 'I think her chin was a little more pointed. And, um, her eyes not that round, a little longer maybe.' She picked up her tea again. 'I think they were dark. I don't think her mouth was that wide. And her eyebrows were thinner, really arched. When he yanked her head, her cap came off. Did I forget that before? She had a wide forehead.'

'Take a breath,' Brody suggested.

'What?'

'Take a breath.'

'Right.' When she stopped to take one, she realised how hard her heart was pounding, that her hands were starting to tremble.

'How's this?'

Reece studied the sketch. It was closer. 'Yes. Yes, it's good. I can see her in it.'

'Let's see if we can refine it a bit. You eat one of those cookies, Reece, before Brody scarfs them all down.'

She nibbled on a cookie while Doc asked questions, finessed the shape of the woman's mouth, eyebrows. 'That's it.' Reece set her cup down with a rattle. 'That's really close. What I remember she looked like. What I—'

'Stop second-guessing yourself,' Brody ordered. 'If that's your impression of her, it's good enough.'

'Not from the Fist.' Doc looked up at Brody. 'Doesn't look like anyone I know, not offhand.'

'No. But if she passed through, someone saw her. We'll show it around.'

'Rick can fax copies to other town authorities.' Doc studied his own sketch. 'Park Service, too. She doesn't look familiar to me. I've treated just about everyone in the vicinity, including tourists and transients, one time or another.'

'We may never know who she was,' Reece said quietly.

'Slim, you want to take a shot at describing him for the Doc?' Brody caged another cookie.

'I didn't *see* him. Not really. Flashes of profile. His back, his hands, but he was wearing gloves. Cap, sunglasses, coat.'

'Any hair below the cap?' Doc asked.

'No. I don't think so. I didn't notice.'

'How about his jawline?'

'All I can think is he seemed hard. But I said that about her, didn't I?' She rubbed her eyes, tried to think. 'He hardly moved most of the time. I had the impression of control.'

Doc sketched idly. 'What about build?'

'Everything about him seems big now. Taller and broader than she was, certainly. I think he could've held her down, worn her out until he could reason with her. It seemed so deliberate, so cold.'

Doc held up his sketch pad. And Reece shuddered. This was a full-length image, back turned, face in one-quarter profile. Because it could have been so many men, fear balled ice in Reece's belly. 'Anonymous,' she commented. 'Still, I don't think he was young. I mean, say, early twenties. His body language was mature.'

'I'll make copies, post one in my office. Most everybody's through there.' Doc picked up the sketch of the woman again. 'I'll take copies down to the sheriff's office.'

'Thanks. A lot.'

'Like I said, it's a little like playing detective. Interesting change of pace.' Doc walked them to the door. When they were outside, Brody headed for his car.

'I'm just going to walk,' Reece told him. 'I want the air, and I've got a little time before my shift.'

'Fine. I'll walk up with you, and you can fix me lunch.'

She shook her head. 'You'll have to walk back again to get your car.'

'I'll walk off lunch. You do blackened chicken?'

'Can I do it, yes. But it's not on the menu.'

'So charge me extra. I feel like a blackened chicken sandwich on a kaiser, with onion rings. Feeling better?'

'I guess I am. Doc has a way of smoothing out the edges.' She dipped her hands into the pocket of her sweatshirt. 'I'd like to come over to your place tomorrow night, fix you dinner and stay the night.'

He walked a little further, stopped. 'OK. I'll wash the sheets.'

Brody's work-in-progress sucked him in for a straight six-hour stint.

When he surfaced from the driving rain and spring mud he'd tossed his characters into, he had a vague and nagging urge for a cigarette. He hadn't taken a long, deep drag for three years, but a good writing session often teased the urge back.

Maybe he'd go get a bag of crisps. Probably should make a sandwich.

It was the thought of food that reminded him Reece was due in a few hours. That made him remember the sheets in the washing machine.

'Hell.' He shoved away from the desk, headed downstairs. Once he had the sheets tumbling, he turned to the kitchen.

The breakfast dishes were in the sink. OK, so were last night's dishes. The local paper, and his daily copy of the *Chicago Tribune*—old habits die hard—were spread out on the table, along with notebooks, pens and pencils, a pile of mail. He pushed up the sleeves of his ratty favourite sweatshirt. 'Why do you put them in there in the first place?' he asked himself as he ran hot water in the sink. 'Every damn time, you have to pull them back out again.'

He washed, he rinsed, he got to work on the table. It occurred to him he'd never really shared a meal in the cabin. Beer and pretzels maybe, if Doc or Mac or Rick dropped over. He'd hosted a poker game a time or two. More beer, chips, cigars. There'd been wine and scrambled eggs at two a.m. with the delightful Gwen from L.A. who'd come to ski and had ended up in his bed one memorable January night.

He should straighten up the bedroom. He scrubbed a hand over his face, reminding himself to shave. She'd probably want candles, so he'd dig some out. . . .

'Wine. Damn it.'

He knew all he had was beer and a bottle of Jack Daniel's. Grumbling, he prepared to leave for town when inspiration struck. He called the liquor store. 'Hey, has Reece Gilmore been in there today? Yeah? What did she—Oh, OK. Thanks. I'm good, thanks. How you doing? Uh-huh.' Brody leaned a hip into the counter for a few minutes of conversation, but straightened back up. 'Did you recognise the woman? No. No, I can't say I thought she looked anything like Penelope Cruz. No, Jeff, I really don't think Penelope Cruz was in the area and got herself murdered. Sure, if I hear anything, I'll let you know. See you later.'

He remembered the sheets after he'd come up with a couple of white tapers and a jar candle someone had given him. Better than nothing, he thought. He took them and the dry sheets upstairs to the bedroom, looked out of the window. A couple of sailboats skimmed along the lake, their sails fat with wind. He recognised Carl's canoe near the north end. And there was a kid with a dog. The dog took a flying leap after a ball, and something sucked Brody's mind back into the book. He narrowed his eyes as the dog paddled back to shore, the ball gripped in his teeth.

But what if it wasn't a ball . . .

He left the tangle of sheets on the bed and strode into his office. He'd just get this one partial scene down. Thirty minutes tops.

Two hours later, Reece set one big box of supplies on the porch of Brody's cabin, knocked briskly, then walked back to her car for a second box.

She knocked again, louder this time. The lack of response had her frowning, and gingerly trying the door. She knew her instinctive worry that he'd drowned in the tub, fallen down the stairs or been murdered was ridiculous. But the house seemed so empty. It wasn't a place she really knew. She forced herself inside, called his name. And, when she heard floorboards creak overhead, she grabbed her chef's knife out of a box, gripped its handle with both hands.

He came scowling—alive and in one piece—to the top of the stairs. 'What? What time is it?'

Relief nearly sent her to her knees. 'About six. I knocked—'

'Six? Damn it. I, ah, got hung up.'

'It's OK, no problem. You want a rain check?'

'No.' His frown only deepened. 'How do I know when it's going to rain again? I need to . . . clean up.'

'I'll just get started on dinner. You take your time.'

'Good.' He paused. 'What were you going to do with the knife?'

She'd forgotten it was in her hands, and now looked down at it with embarrassment. 'I don't really know.'

'Maybe you could put it down so I don't get in the shower with the image of Norman Bates in my head?'

'Sure.' She turned to set it back in the box, and when she turned again, he was gone. She hauled in both boxes. And locked the doors. Satisfied, she put the wine in the refrigerator.

When Brody walked in thirty minutes later, the table was set with his plates and candles, along with dark blue napkins, wineglasses, and a little clear bowl of yellow miniature roses.

She turned, nerves and sorrow in her dark eyes. 'I thought I'd . . . Oh.'

She took a step back as he strode to her. He took her in his arms and kissed her. 'Hi,' he said, and released her.

'Hi. Ah, where am I again?'

He grinned. 'Where do you want to be?'

'I guess right here. I was about to do something. Oh yeah, I was going to make martinis.'

'No kidding?'

'You don't like martinis?'

'What's not to like?'

'I borrowed the glasses and shaker from Linda-Gail.'

He watched her measure and shake, toss the ice, pour, add olives. Then he studied the results in the glass she handed him.

She touched her glass to his, waited until he'd sipped.

'Damn good martini.' He sipped again, studying her over the rim. 'You're something.'

'Or other,' she agreed. 'Try this.'

She lifted a small dish where stuffed celery was arranged in some intricate geometric pattern. 'What's in it?'

'State secret, but primarily smoked Gouda and sun-dried tomatoes.'

Figuring the vodka would kill the taste, he gave it a shot and changed his position. 'Whatever the state secret might be, it does a hell of a lot more for celery than the peanut butter my mother used to dump on it.'

'I should hope so. You can sit down, enjoy.' She picked up her glass for another tiny sip.

He didn't sit. 'Have you given any more thought to putting a cookbook together?'

'Actually I spent some time on that last night after my shift.'

'Is that why you look tired?'

'I couldn't sleep, so fiddling with the proposal gave me something to do. I was thinking of *The Simple Gourmet* as a title.'

'It's OK.'

'You have better?'

'Let me think about it. Why couldn't you sleep?'

'How do I know?'

'Sex is a good sedative.'

'Maybe. Especially, for instance, if your partner's on the inadequate side. You can catch a quick nap during the act.'

'I can promise you won't sleep through it.'

She only smiled, and took another minute sip of her martini.

She wouldn't trust him to carve the pork roast, which was vaguely insulting. Brody decided not to complain, as the meat smelt incredible and he noted there was a serving of scalloped potatoes in his immediate future.

She drizzled hollandaise over tender asparagus, fragrant gravy over the slices of pork. Poured the Chenin Blanc.

'We ought to be able to work a deal, you and me,' Brody began when he cut into the pork.

'A deal?'

'Yeah, just a minute.' He sampled. 'Just as I figured. So, a deal. We'll barter. Sex for food.'

She lifted her brows. 'Interesting. However, I really think you're reaping the benefits on both sides of that deal.'

'You, too.' He tried the potatoes. 'My God, you should be canonised. *The Casual Gourmet.*'

'St Reece, the casual gourmet?'

'No, that's your title. *The Casual Gourmet.* It's not simple, which can be construed as ordinary. But you don't need to spend all day sweating over the stove to make it. Gourmet, the way people live, not just the way they entertain to impress.'

She sat back. 'That's a better title, and a better summary of the idea than mine. Damn it.'

'I'm a professional.'

'Eat your asparagus,' she ordered.

He ate, he drank, he watched her. And at some point, he simply lost the thread of the casual conversation. 'Reece?'

'Hmm.'

'The eyes grab me by the throat, but the rest of you? It looks really good in candlelight, too.'

She smiled at him, and let the glow of it warm her while they ate.

She insisted on clearing up. He'd expected that, as she was a woman who liked to put, and to keep, things in their place. He'd have laid odds she had that tendency before the violence in Boston. And in all likelihood, at this point, she *needed* things tidy. He dried off dishes, put them back in the cupboard. But he largely stayed out of her way.

Nerves were coming back, and she'd gone very quiet with them. He supposed now that the meal was over, sex had stumbled back into the room like an awkward guest. He considered just hauling her upstairs and into bed before she thought about it. There was an advantage to the technique but he rejected it in favour of a more subtle approach.

'Want to take a walk? Down to the lake, maybe?'

'That'd be nice. I haven't done that on this side yet.'

'There's light enough, but you'll need your jacket.'

'Right.' She took hers off the peg in the utility room. He moved in for his, then reached for the door.

Her nerves seemed to evaporate in the cool air.

'It's gorgeous out.' She breathed it in, earth and pine. 'I haven't been able to talk myself into a solo walk at night. I think about it though.' She pulled her jacket on as she walked.

'The sky's so big, so clear. I can see the Milky Way. I think that's the Milky Way. And both Dippers, which is about it for my constellation knowledge.'

'Don't look at me. I just see a bunch of stars, and a white, waning moon.'

'So make one up. You're in the business of making things up.'

He studied the star pattern. 'There's the Lonely Herman—or the Fat Man Standing on One Leg. Over to the west, there's the Goddess Sally, who guards over all fry cooks.'

'And here, all this time, I didn't know I had a patron goddess.'

'You're no fry cook.'

'Right now, I am. Besides, I want Sally for my own. Look how she shines in the water.'

Stars swam in the lake, a thousand lights sparkling on its dark plate. Moonlight cut a white swatch over the gleam.

'Sometimes I miss Boston so much it's an ache in the bones,' she told him. 'And I think I need to go back and find what I had there. My busy life, my busy friends. My apartment with the Chinese-red walls and sleek black dining-room table.'

'Chinese red?'

'I liked bold once.' She'd been bold once. 'Then I stand at a spot like this, and I think, I'm not Chinese red any more.'

'What does it matter? You make your place where you are, and use whatever colours you damn well please.'

'That's exactly what I told myself when I left.' They stood for a moment, side by side. 'When we were up on the trail that day, and I went on by, did you stay up there to make sure I got back safely?'

'It was a nice day. I didn't have anything else to do.'

'You were heading in my direction even before you heard me running back. You were being a nice guy.'

She lifted her hands to his face, rose up to her toes. And touched her lips to his. 'I'm afraid I'm going to screw this up. You should know that before we go back. But I'd like to go to bed with you anyway.'

'That's an excellent idea.'

'Maybe you should hold my hand in case I lose my nerve.'

'Sure.'

She didn't lose it all, but with every step the doubts crept closer. 'Maybe we should have another glass of wine first.'

'Had enough, thanks.' He kept her hand in his, kept walking.

'It might be best if we talked about where this is leading.'

'Right now it's leading up to my bedroom.'

'Yes, but . . .' It was no use baulking when he was already pulling her inside. 'Um, you need to lock the door.'

He turned the lock. 'There.'

'I really think we need to—'

He simply plucked her up and laid her over his shoulder.

There were too many conflicting currents running inside her to let her decide whether being carried through the house was romantic or mortifying. 'I'd just like to ask if you'd keep your expectations on the low side. I'm really out of practice—'

'You're talking too much.'

'It's going to get worse.' She squeezed her eyes shut as he started up the stairs. 'I can actually feel the babbling rising in my throat. Listen, listen, when we were outside, I could breathe, and I thought I could handle it. I'm just not sure. I don't know. Does the bedroom door have a lock?'

He booted it shut, then turned and locked the door. 'Better?'

'I don't know. Maybe. I know I'm being an idiot, but—'

'Knowing you're an idiot's the first step to recovery.' He dropped her on her feet by the bed. 'Now be quiet.'

'I just think if we—'

He closed her mouth with his, with heat, with hunger. All she could do was hold on. Part of her was falling apart. And part of her was falling away.

'I think I—'

'Need to be quiet,' he finished and kissed her again.

'I know. But would you turn out the lights?'

'I never turned them on.'

'Oh. Oh.' Now the silver starshine seemed too bright.

'Pretend I'm still holding your hand so you don't run away.'

But she felt his hands run up her body, over her breasts. Lovely little thrills. 'How many hands do you have?'

'Enough to get the job done. You ought to look at me. Look at me, Reece. That's the way. You know the first time I saw you?'

'In the diner.' Moonlight darkened his eyes. 'In Joanie's.'

'Yeah.' He unbuttoned her shirt. 'First time I saw you, I got that little snap in the blood. You know what I'm saying?'

'Yes. Yes. Brody, just—'

'Sometimes you act on it.' He nipped his way down her throat. 'Sometimes you don't, but you know when you feel it.'

'If it was dark . . . It'd be better if it was dark.'

He drew away the hand she'd lifted to cover the scar on her chest. 'We'll test that theory sometime.' He let his hands travel down her arms, sliding the shirt away. 'Look at me.'

Cat's eyes, she thought. And so watchful. She didn't feel safe staring into them, but the fear was somehow thrilling.

Then the fingers of his free hand snapped open the hook of her bra, and he was devouring her again, mouth to mouth, body to body. Everything about him was hard and strong and just a little rough. Hands along her skin, learning secrets she'd forgotten she had, causing delicious little lines of heat. Shy and avid, she fumbled at his shirt, and her breath caught, caught again and again, whenever he touched her.

Her arms tightened around him when he scooped her up, all but tossed her on the bed. When his mouth tore from hers to close over her breast, her heartbeat went to thunder. His weight pinned her, his mouth claimed her. Even through the silver haze of lust, panic began to crawl. She fought it, willing her mind to shut off, to let her body rule. But in the end they both betrayed her as her lungs simply shut down.

'I can't breathe. I can't. Wait, stop.'

He rolled aside to yank her up to sitting. 'You are breathing.' He gave her a little shake. 'Stop gasping for air.'

'OK. OK.' She knew she had to concentrate on each breath, on the physical act of inhaling slow and steady.

Mortified, she crossed her arms over her breasts. 'I'm sorry. I'm sorry. I'm sick of being a freak.'

'Then stop.'

'You really think it's so easy? You think I like sitting here naked and humiliated?'

'I don't know, do you?'

'You son of a bitch.'

'There you go, sweet-talking me again.' There was heat in her eyes, which he appreciated. But the shine came into them. 'You start crying, you're going to piss me off.'

'I'm not going to cry.' She knuckled a tear away.

He pushed her hair off her shoulders. 'Did I hurt you?'

'No. No, just a flare of claustrophobia, and so on and so forth.'

'Oh, if that's all, I can fix it.' He took her shoulders, pulling her down to him as he lay on his back. 'Just look at me.' He cupped a hand on the back of her head, drew her lips to his. 'Take it easy,' he murmured against her mouth.

'I feel clumsy. Brody—'

'No, you don't.' He let his hands wander, watched the flush come back into her cheeks. 'You feel smooth, a little on the slight side. But not clumsy. Kiss me again.'

She laid her lips on his and let go of the panic. His heart beat strong and steady against hers; his lips demanded that hers yield. Still when he lifted her hips, she started to protest, to pull away. But he held her, and his eyes trapped her, until, at last, she took and took.

Chapter 8

RATHER THAN A MERRY MONTH, May plagued Angel's Fist with a series of wicked storms that thundered over the mountains. But the days stretched longer, and in Reece's little valley the cottonwoods and willows hazed with green. Daffodils popped in cheerful yellow even when the wind and rain pelted them.

And on this monumental day, she was going to venture beyond the Fist.

'I can reschedule,' she told Joanie. 'If you're pressed—'

'Didn't say I was pressed.' Joanie poured pancake batter on the griddle.

'Yes, but with the weather breaking, you'll probably be swamped at lunch. I don't mind pitching in.'

'I handled this kitchen before you came along. You want to be useful? Top off Mac's coffee on your way out the door.'

She dragged her feet a little, but she grabbed the pot, moved to the counter where Mac sat and poured the coffee.

'Big plans?' he asked

'Yes. Sort of. Linda-Gail and I are going into Jackson.'

'Shopping spree, huh?'

'Probably some of that. I'm getting my hair cut.'

'Going all the way to Jackson for a haircut?' Fist loyalty had him frowning. 'We've got the Curry Comb right here in town.'

Reece passed him the sugar bowl. 'Sounds silly, doesn't it?'

'Get out.' Joanie delivered Mac's pancakes with the side of elk sausage herself.

'I'm leaving.' Reece picked up her bag, and the file folder with Doc's sketch, and sailed out.

There hadn't been a single hit on the sketch in the Fist. If the woman had been travelling through the area, odds were she'd swung into a bigger, flashier place like Jackson Hole.

Now, since she had a little time to spare and didn't want to spend it obsessing about her hair, Reece walked down to the sheriff's office.

It had been nearly a week since she'd asked Sheriff Mardson if he'd learned anything new. Of course, she'd been spending a lot of that week working, or in Brody's bed. But thanks to the distractions, Mardson couldn't accuse her of nagging him.

When she walked in, Hank O'Brian glanced over from Dispatch. He had a full black beard and a fondness for chicken-fried steak. 'How you doing there, Reece?'

'Good, thanks. Is the sheriff busy? I just wanted to—'

Even as she spoke, she heard the trill of laughter. Mardson walked out hand in hand with his wife.

That was sweet, Reece thought. The way people looked together when they *were* together. Mardson had an easy smile on his face. Debbie, a pretty, athletic-looking blonde with short tousled hair, wore snug jeans, cowboy boots and a red shirt under a denim jacket. A pendant at the end of a sparkling gold chain hung round her neck. A shining sun, Reece noted.

Debbie ran the outfitters, On the Trail, next door to the hotel, and was tight with Brenda, the hotel receptionist. Sunday afternoons, she brought her three girls into Joanie's for ice cream. She sent Reece a quick, friendly smile. 'Hi! I thought you were heading into Jackson Hole today.'

'Um, well, yeah. Later.'

'I ran into Linda-Gail yesterday. Getting your hair cut? It's so pretty— but it gets in the way at the grill, I bet. Still, men like long hair on a woman. Poor Rick,' she said with another laugh. 'I'm always having mine chopped off.'

'I like it just fine.' He leaned down to peck her cheek, flicked a finger at the ends of her hair. 'You're my sunlight.'

'Listen to him.' Smiling, Debbie bumped Rick, arm against arm. 'Sweet-talking. And after I came in to talk him into taking an hour off and taking a ride with me. Turned me down flat.'

'Something I can do for you, Reece?' Rick asked.

'I thought I'd just call in to see if you found out anything new.'

'Wish I could say I had. No missing person reports. And nobody recognises her. Not much more I can do.'

'No. Well, I know you've done what you could. I'm going to show the sketch around while I'm in Jackson.'

'I'm not going to tell you not to,' Rick said slowly. 'But you need to understand—and nothing against Doc—but that's a pretty rough sketch. Without more details, you're liable to end up chasing a lot of wild geese.'

'You're probably right.' Reece didn't miss the look of quiet pity on Debbie's face. 'I feel like I have to try at least.' She felt the heat rising up the back of her neck as she walked out. She knew there was speculation mixed in with the pity. Just how crazy was Reece Gilmore?

Screw it. Just screw it, she told herself. She wasn't going to pretend she hadn't seen what she'd seen, wasn't going to stuff the sketches in some drawer and forget about it.

And today she was going to town and getting her hair done.

God help her.

If Reece considered Angel's Fist a rough and interesting little diamond, Jackson was big and polished and faceted with its fashionable western flair and colourful neon. Shops and restaurants and galleries, wooden boardwalks. Streets busy with people stopping in town before visiting one of the great parks now that summer was nearly here. Beyond, white-frosted mountains stood in dazzling splendour.

It took Reece less than two minutes to understand that she'd made a better choice with Angel's Fist.

Too many people here, she thought. Too much going on. Hotels, motels, recreation centres, winter sports, summer sports, real-estate offices. She was barely inside the town limits when she wanted out.

'This is going to be fun!' Linda-Gail swung through traffic as if it were a carnival ride. 'We should do a serious splurge sometime at one of the day spas. They have *amazing* spas here. Holy cow, a parking place!'

They parked and walked a block.

'I think I need to go lie down.'

'You'll be fine. And if you get shaky. I've got a flask of apple martinis in my bag, just to take the edge off. Here we are.'

Reece didn't reach for the flask, though it was tempting, and in the time they waited for their stylists, she nearly baulked half a dozen times. But she learned something. It wasn't as bad as last time she tried. The walls didn't seem so close together, or the sounds so harsh. And when her stylist introduced himself, she didn't burst into tears and sprint for the door.

Serge had the slightest Slavonic accent, and a winning smile. 'Baby doll, let's get you a nice cup of tea. Nan! We need a cup of camomile. You just come with me.'

She went along like a puppy. He had her seated at his station, swathed in a mint-green cape, before her brain engaged again. 'I'm not sure I—'

'Gorgeous texture, and so thick! Very healthy. You take care of it.' He lifted her hair, let it fall, studied it. 'And what is it you do, my angel?'

'I'm a cook. I work with Linda-Gail. Is she going to be nearby?'

'She's fine. We don't see nearly enough of her in here.' And with that winning smile, he met Reece's eyes in the mirror. 'Trust me?' he said.

She'd forgotten the indulgence of it. Hands massaging her scalp, glossy magazines. She was getting highlights, because Serge wanted her to. Linda-Gail trotted up, her slathered hair covered with plastic.

'Vixen Red,' she announced. 'I'm going for it. I'm squeezing in a manicure. Want one?'

'No. No, I can't take any more.'

She actually drowsed over *Vogue* until it was time for the cut.

'So now, tell me about the man in your life.' Serge began to clip and snip. 'You must have one.'

'I guess I do.' My God, she had a man in her life. 'He's a writer. We're just really starting to be together.'

'Excitement. Discovery.'

A smile flickered over her face. 'Exactly. He's smart, self-reliant and likes my cooking. He masks this incredible patience under pithy comments. He doesn't treat me like I'm breakable. And . . . oh, I forgot this.' She leaned forward for the file. 'I wonder if you recognise this woman.'

Serge pocketed the scissors long enough to take the sketch and study it. 'I don't think she's been in my chair. I'd have talked her into shortening that hair. Does she belong to you?'

'In a way. Could I leave it here? Someone might recognise her.'

'Absolutely.'

Reece refocused on herself. 'Wow. That's, ah, that's a lot of hair falling off my head.'

'Not to worry.' He turned to admire the newly redheaded Linda-Gail. 'Look at you! Gorgeous!'

'I *love* it!' She spun a circle, showing off the bold red in her sassy new cut. 'I'm reinvented. Reece, what do you think?'

'It's wonderful. Linda-Gail, you look seriously amazing.'

'When we get back, I'm going to track down Lo and make him suffer.' Linda-Gail angled her head. 'I see where Serge is going here. Your face is more out there.'

'Damn right, frame those gorgeous eyes. All that weight's off your shoulders, your neck. Still, nice, long layers.'

Reece stared at the picture emerging in the mirror. I almost recognise that woman, she thought. I almost see me again. When her eyes filled, Serge lowered the scissors with alarm. 'You're upset. You don't like it.'

'No, no, I do like it. I do. It's been a long time since I looked in the mirror and saw something I did like.'

She wanted to show off. She'd had the most fantastic day, and looked the part. Of course she shouldn't have let Linda-Gail talk her into buying that delicious yellow shirt. Still, she'd given the salesclerk a copy of the sketch—as she had done in every store Linda-Gail had dragged her into.

She intended to go straight home, put the new shirt on, call Brody and see if he was interested in coming over for dinner. She'd found some lovely field greens in a market in Jackson, and some nice diver-harvested scallops, and saffron.

She all but danced up the steps to her apartment. Humming, she unlocked the door, told herself to wait until she'd put the bags on the counter to lock it again. Then waltzed to the bathroom just for another look a her happy self. And all the blood in her face drained with shock as she stared at the mirror.

The sketch was taped to it so that she stared at the face of a dead woman instead of her own. On the walls, the floor, written over and over with red marker bright as blood, was the single question.

IS THIS ME?

She sank down in the doorway, shivering.

Had to be home by now, Brody thought as he drove round the lake. How long did it take to have somebody whack at her hair anyway? She didn't answer the phone, and he felt ridiculous as he'd called four times in the last hour. He'd missed her. And that was even more ridiculous. He never missed anyone. He hadn't yet lowered himself to trying her cellphone.

He spotted her car in its habitual place, and going up her steps, banged with some impatience on her door.

'It's Brody,' he called out. 'Open up.'

It took her so long to answer, his scowl had turned into knitted-brow concern. 'Brody, sorry, I was lying down. I have a headache.'

He tried the knob. 'Open the door.'

'Really, I'm just going to sleep it off. I'll call you tomorrow.'

He didn't like the sound of her voice. 'Open the door, Reece.'

'Fine, fine, fine.' The lock turned, and she yanked it open. 'Do you have trouble understanding? I have a headache; I don't want company. I certainly don't feel like heating up the sheets.'

She was pale as wax. His gaze tracked over the bags on the counter. 'How long have you been back?'

'I don't know. Maybe an hour.'

Headache, his ass. He knew her well enough by now to be sure she could have severed a limb and she'd still have put her groceries away the minute she walked in the door. 'What happened?'

'Would you back *off*? I'm entitled to some privacy.'

'True,' he said. 'And I'll give you plenty as soon as you tell me what's going on. What did you do to your hands?' He grabbed one, terrified it was blood smearing her fingers. 'What the hell? Is this ink?'

She started to weep, silently. She made no sound at all.

'For God's sake, Reece, what is it?'

'I can't get it off. I can't get it off, and I don't remember doing it. I don't remember, and it won't come off.'

She didn't resist when he picked her up and carried her to the bed to rock her in his arms.

Portions of the walls and the floor were smeared where she'd gone at them, Brody could see, the wet towel now heaped in the bath. She'd torn the sketch off the mirror. Still the message was clear a dozen times over.

'I don't remember doing it.' She stood behind him.

He didn't turn. 'Where's the red marker?'

'I don't know. I must have put it away.' She crossed back into the kitchen, opened a drawer. 'It's not here.' On a spurt of desperation, she pawed through the contents of the drawer.

'Stop it.'

'It's not here. I must have taken it with me, thrown it away. I don't remember. Just like the other times.'

His eyes sharpened. 'What other times?'

'I think I'm going to be sick.'

'No, you're not.'

She slammed the drawer, her eyes red-rimmed from weeping. 'Don't tell me what I am, what I'm not.'

'You're not going to be sick,' he said walking over, 'because you haven't told me about the other times. Let's sit down.'

'I can't.'

'Fine, we'll stand up. Got any brandy?'

'I don't want any brandy.'

'I didn't ask what you wanted.' He opened cupboards until he found a small bottle, poured brandy into a juice glass. 'Knock it back, Slim.'

Reece took the glass, swallowed the brandy in one gulp. And shuddered. 'The sketch could be me. If I imagined it . . .'

'How do you figure? Ever been strangled?'

'So it took another form. Someone tried to kill me once, and I've spent the last two years waiting for someone to try again. There's a resemblance between me and the sketch.'

'In that you both have long, dark hair. Or you did.' Frowning a little, he reached out to touch the hair that fell above her shoulders now. 'It's not your face.'

'But I didn't see her very well.'

'But you did see her.'

'I don't *know*.'

'I do.' He opened her refrigerator and was pleasantly surprised to see she'd stocked his brand of beer. He took one out, popped the top. 'You saw those two people by the river.'

'How can you be sure? You didn't see them.'

'I saw you. What other things don't you remember?'

'I don't remember marking up my trail map. And I don't remember packing my clothes in my duffle. And there are other things, little things. I need to go back in the hospital.' She scrubbed her hands over her face, left them there. 'I'm not functioning.'

'That's crap.' Idly, he took a pull of beer, poked in the grocery bag. 'What're all these leaves and grasses?'

'Field greens.' She rubbed at the headache drilling into her temple. 'I was telling myself I need to go when I packed. I must have been telling myself that on the trail.'

'You saw a woman murdered on the trail. I had doubts about that at the time, but now—'

'You did?'

'It was marginally possible she walked out of there.'

'Are you listening to me? Did you see what I did in there?' She flung a hand towards the bathroom.

'What if you didn't?'

'Who the hell else?' she exploded. 'I'm unstable, Brody, for God's sake. I'm hallucinating murders and writing on walls.'

'What if you're not?' he repeated in the same implacable tone. 'Listen, I make a pretty decent living on what-ifs. What if you saw exactly what you said you saw?'

Her head hurt; her stomach was raw from churning. Since she was too tired to walk to a chair, she just sat on the floor. 'Maybe that's why I'm attracted to you. You're as crazy as I am.'

'You reported a murder, and word got around. What if the killer got that word—or, as we considered before, he saw you. He didn't get away clean, after all.'

'Because there was a witness,' she whispered.

'Yeah. But the witness has a history of psychological problems with their roots in violence. He can use that. Not everyone believes her anyway—new in town, a little shaky on her pins. Why not give her a little push? Chances are she breaks down, or she runs and has her breakdown somewhere else. Either way, her claims are likely to be dismissed.'

'But that's . . .'

'Crazy? No, it's not. It's smart, and very cool-headed.'

'So, instead of believing I'm a complete emotional and mental disaster, you want me to believe a killer is breaking into my apartment and trying to spook me.'

He took another pull of beer. 'It's a theory.'

'The first option is easier. Been there, after all, done that.'

'I bet it is. But you don't take the easy way.'

'That's a strange thing to say to someone who's been running away from everything, including herself, for the better part of a year.'

'I'm looking at a woman who survived. Everything she knew and cherished was taken, for no rhyme, no reason. She's been fighting her way back. I think she's one of the strongest people I've ever met.'

'I guess you don't get out much.'

He smiled a little. 'Get some things together; you'd better stay at my place tonight.'

'I can't take this in.'

'You will.' He poked in the grocery bag again. 'Would this be dinner?'

'Oh *hell*! The scallops!'

He knew she was all the way back when she leapt to the bag and dug down. 'Thank God I had them bagged with an ice pack.'

'I like scallops.'

'You haven't seen food you don't like.' Then she braced her hands on the counter and just closed her eyes. 'You won't let me fall apart. You just won't let me.'

'I told you once before, hysterical women annoy me.'

She looked at him. 'You held me while I cried. Annoying for you.'

'You were hurting. Just don't make a habit of it.'

'I love you. I'm in love with you.'

For ten full seconds he didn't speak. 'Hell. No good deed goes unpunished.'

She laughed, rich and full and long. 'Don't worry about it, Brody. You're not under obligation to reciprocate. But when you've gone through what I've been through, you learn not to take things for granted.'

He stared at her with the cautious respect a man shows a ticking bomb. 'You're mixing up trust, and a misplaced sense of gratitude, and the fact we've got heat.'

'My head may be screwed up, but my heart's fine. But if it scares you, I can call Linda-Gail and stay with her.'

'Just get what you need,' he said abruptly. 'Including whatever it takes to cook this stuff.'

You want some wine?' Brody asked.

'No, thanks.' Reece arranged dressed field greens, tossed with carrot curls, on small plates. 'Joanie'll have a fit when she sees that bathroom.'

'So paint it.'

Reece stabbed at her salad. 'I can't paint the tiles.'

'Mac's probably got some solvent or something. The place isn't a penthouse, Slim. Needed work anyway.'

'Brody, I lost time before. And had memory lapses. Not in more than a year, but I experienced both.'

'Doesn't mean you are now, does it? I've been around you a lot the last couple of weeks. I haven't seen you go into a fugue state or sleep-walk.' Since it was there, he ate the salad. 'Has anyone at Joanie's mentioned you did anything weird?'

'Joanie thought it was weird I needed okra to make minestrone.' She rose to put the finishing touches to the rest of the meal. 'After I got out of the hospital—the first time—my grandmother took me shopping. Later, I found this hideous brown sweater in my drawer, and I asked her where it came from. I could see something was wrong by the way she looked at me. I'd told her I had to buy it because it was bulletproof.'

She flipped the scallops with a flick of the wrist. 'And there were other incidents. I had night terrors where I could hear the gunshots, the screaming. I'd try to break down doors. I climbed out of the window one night. A neighbour found me on the sidewalk in a nightshirt. I didn't know where I was.' She laid a plate in front of Brody. 'That's when I checked myself into the hospital. This could be a relapse.'

'Which happens only when you're alone? I'm not buying. You haven't had an episode except in your apartment.'

'You're making me feel better. A couple of hours ago I was curled up on the floor whimpering. I was back at the bottom.'

'No, just slipped a few rungs. And you got up again.'

'I don't know what to do.'

'Right now, you should eat your scallops. They're pretty terrific.'

'OK.' She took a deliberate bite, and of course he was right. 'I had my hair cut and styled.'

'So noted.'

She cocked her head. 'Well, do you like it or not?'

'It's OK.'

'Oh, please stop.' She waved a hand. 'Must you be so effusive with your compliments?'

'I'm an effusive kind of guy.'

She flipped her fingers through it. 'I like it. If you don't, just say so.'

'If I didn't like it, I'd say I didn't. Or I'd say it was your business if you want to have crappy-looking hair all over your head.'

'That's exactly what you'd say,' she replied. 'Being with you has been really good for me. I've felt more like . . . I won't say *who I was*, because you can never go back. I've felt more like who I hoped I could be. But we both know it would be smarter, all round, for you and me to take a step back from each other.'

'Look, if this is about you thinking you're in love with me—'

'It's not. You should consider yourself lucky I'm in love with you. A lot of women would be put off by your cranky nature. But if I'm back-sliding, it's because I'm not a good bet for even the most casual of relationships.'

He picked up his beer, took a contemplative sip. 'If I back off, it says I can't handle the rough spots. Plus, I miss out on figuring it all out.' He took her hand across the table. 'I care about what happens to you.'

'I know you do.'

'Good. Then we don't have to analyse and dissect it all for the next hour and a half. We'll figure it out, Reece.'

And right at that moment, with his hand on hers, she believed him.

With the kitchen to rights, he tried the next step.

'Will you be OK here alone for an hour?'

'Why?'

'I thought I'd go get Rick and take a look at your place.'

'Don't.' She shook her head. 'He doesn't believe me about what I saw on the trail. He's done what his job says he has to do, and this morning I saw him, and Debbie and Hank. When I talked about showing the sketch around Jackson Hole, all I saw on their faces was pity.'

'If someone's been breaking into your place—'

'If they have, we'd never prove it.'

'Locks get picked, keys get copied. Where do you keep your keys?'

'In the inside pocket of my bag, or if I don't carry one, in my jacket pocket.'

'Where are the bag, the jacket when you're working?'

'In Joanie's office. She's got a copy of the key in her key cupboard thing on the wall in there.'

'Wouldn't be hard for anyone to slip into the office, make an impression of the key, have one made.'

'You think it's someone from the Fist?'

'Possible. Possible it's someone who was staying in the area and stayed on when it got out that you saw something.'

'But no one's recognised the woman. I guess I just assumed that if she wasn't from here, he wasn't.'

'Could be someone who comes in with some regularity. Who knew you were going to be gone most of the day today?'

'Who didn't?'

'Yeah, that's how it goes.' He started to scowl. 'You look wiped. Go to bed. I'm going to do a little work.'

'Oh.' Her gaze slid to the door. 'All right, maybe . . .'

'After I check the locks. Go on up to bed, Slim.'

It was silly to pretend she wasn't exhausted, so she got to her feet. 'Thanks for the shoulder, Brody.'

'You didn't use my shoulder.'

She leaned down, laid her lips on his. 'Yes, I did. A couple dozen times just tonight.'

Brody crouched in front of Reece's apartment door with a penlight and a magnifying glass. He felt a little ridiculous.

Though he considered being able to sleep on in the mornings one of the big perks of writing fiction, he'd got up early, when she had. And ignored her claims she could walk to the diner.

No problem at all, a couple of miles in the dark for a woman who may or may not have a homicidal stalker.

Now he was playing detective. Since he didn't have personal experience with breaking and entering, he couldn't be certain the lock hadn't been tampered with, but he couldn't see any signs.

He took out the key she'd given him, stared at it in the palm of his hand. He unlocked the door, stepped inside.

Light spilled through the windows to fall on the bare floors, the thirdhand furniture, the bright blue spread she'd bought for the narrow day bed. He unhooked her laptop, put it and her thumb drive into its case. She'd need another night, at least, away from this place.

Idly, he opened the drawer on the little desk Joanie must have had hauled up for her. In it he found two pencils snapped in half, a Magic Marker and a slim leather-bound book. Curious, he flipped it open.

The photo of an older woman sitting on a bench in a nicely tended garden had thick black Xs over the face. A couple in long bib aprons, a group holding glasses of champagne, a man in front of a big wall oven. Everyone had Xs over their faces.

In the last, Reece was standing in a large group of people. Maneo's, Brody concluded. Under each person, in small print, was the single word: DEAD. And under Reece: INSANE.

He slipped the book into the outside pocket of the laptop case. Though he hadn't intended to invade her privacy quite so deeply, Brody began to search the dresser drawers.

She didn't have much. The woman travelled light, he decided.

The kitchen drawers were another matter. It was all ruthlessly organised. But in the one cupboard he found a mortar and pestle, with the bowl filled to the brim with pills. He pulled it out, set it aside.

In the bathroom, in the medicine cabinet, all the bottles were lined up on the shelf. And empty. Little booby traps, Brody thought. Clever bastard. He studied the walls. Block printing again, with words overlapping. The detail of having them travel up from the floor onto the wall was good.

Brody got the digital camera he'd brought. He took pictures from every angle he could manage in the tiny room.

He'd just go down to Mac's, see if there was something he could use to get the marker off. No big deal. He'd pick up paint while he was there. In short order he was back in the bathroom, on hands and knees, scrubbing.

Reece turned the door handle gingerly. She hated that it wasn't locked. She hated the throat-closing fear that Brody was lying inside hurt, or worse. Why was he still here? She'd expected him to drop back in downstairs with her key long before her break.

'Brody?'

'Yeah. Back here.'

'You're OK?' She stopped, sniffed. 'What is that? Paint?'

He stepped out of the bathroom with a roller in his hand, paint specks in his hair. 'It ain't the perfumes of Araby.'

'You're painting the bathroom?'

'It's no big deal. You've got two feet of wall space.'

'A bit more than that.' Her voice was full of emotion. 'Thank you.' She walked over to take a look.

He'd already done the ceiling, and primed the walls. The colour was a pale, pale blue. None of the red letters or smears remained. Reece just leaned against him. 'I like the colour. I'll have to pay you back in food.'

'Works for me. But if you want the rest of this place painted, you're on your own. I forgot I hate to paint.'

She turned into him, nuzzled. 'I can finish it up after my shift.'

'I started, I finish.' He caught himself pressing his lips to the top of her head. But it was too late to stop the gesture. 'I didn't want you to have to see it again.'

'Could I bunk at your place tonight anyway?'

'Yeah, we wouldn't want you breathing in the fumes.'

'I'll need a few . . . You were going to grind something?'

'Huh?'

'You got out my mortar and pestle.'

And he cursed himself for leaving it out. 'Reece—'

'What've you got in here? It looks like . . . I don't take them. I just keep them, in case. I don't want you to think I—'

'I didn't put them there. They're booby traps.' He set the roller in the tray. 'He's setting traps for you, and you can't step into them.'

'What do you think he's saying with this?' She let pills sift through her fingers. '"Why don't you grind these up into a nice paste, spread it on toast and send yourself into oblivion"?'

'It doesn't matter what he's saying if you don't listen.'

'It does matter.' She whirled round. 'If I don't listen, I can't let him know he's not going to send me back to the doctors. I'm not going back into the dark because he's a killer and a son of a bitch.' She upended the bowl in the sink, then wrenched the water on. 'I don't need them.'

He thought of the photo book he'd tucked away. It wasn't protection she needed, he realised. It was faith. She needed someone to believe she was steady. 'There's something else. It's going to hit you a little harder than this.'

'What?'

Even as she glanced around, he crossed to the laptop, took out the little book. 'He did it to upset you. Don't let him win.'

She opened it. 'How could he do this? All they went through, and he crosses them out like they were nothing.'

'They're not, to him.'

'I would never have done this,' she said. 'No matter how far I fell. He made a mistake doing this, because this wasn't me.' She ran a finger over the blacked-out faces. 'I loved them. I'd never have tried to erase them.'

She went through every page, as Brody had done, then went back to the desk, laid the book down. 'I've got to get back down, finish my shift.' She pushed at her hair. 'I'll be fine.'

'I'll come down when I'm done.'

Pete sent her a wink when she walked into the kitchen.

'Brody painting upstairs?' Joanie said from the grill.

Reece paused in the act of washing her hands. 'How do you know these things?'

'Carl told Linda-Gail Brody was down to the mercantile and bought paint. Brody's car's still out front here. Two and two.'

'Yes, he's doing me a favour.'

'Better not be some crazy colour.'

'It's a very pale blue. Just the bathroom.'

Joanie piled steak on a long bun, flipped on eggs and began to build a hoagie. 'Nice having a man take on some of the chores. Don't recall Brody ever doing the same for any other woman round here. You recall him doing the same, Pete?'

'Can't say that I do.'

Joanie dumped an order of fries on the plate with the hoagie and added a scoop of coleslaw. 'Order up! Denny, how you doing?'

'Doing fine, Joanie.' The deputy stood at the counter. 'Sheriff wanted to see if Reece could come in for a few minutes.'

'Hell, Denny, the lunch rush is starting.'

'The sheriff wants me?' Reece looked over from sizzling chicken.

'He'd like it if you could come down for a couple of minutes. Thing is, they found a woman's body in the marshes in Moose Ponds. Sheriff's got, um, a picture he thought you should look at. See if she's the one you saw up over the river.'

'You go on,' Joanie said briskly.

'Yes.' Reece's voice was dull. 'I'll just finish this order.'

'I can finish the order. Pete, run upstairs and get Brody.'

'No. I'll be fine. Don't bother him.' Absently, Reece untied her apron. 'We'll just go now.'

Denny had brought the radio car, so the trip was quick. It didn't give Reece time to obsess. He walked her to the sheriff's office.

The door was open, and Rick was already coming round the desk to meet her. He took her arm, gently, led her to a chair.

'Kids came across the body. She matches your description. It's not an easy picture, but if you can look at it, that would be a big help.'

'Was she strangled?'

'There's some indication she might've been throttled some. You think you can look at the picture?'

'I can look at it.' She gripped her hands together in her lap to anchor herself while he took a file off his desk, sat in the other visitor's chair, then held out a photo. She looked, then looked away as her breath wheezed out. 'She's—Oh God.'

'I know it's hard. She was in the marsh for a day or two. Coroner's got to determine time of death and so on.'

'A day or two? But it's been weeks.'

'If she walked away with him that day, this could've happened later. Is this the woman you saw, Reece?'

She braced herself to look again. The face was so bruised, so swollen, with bloodless cuts all over it, down the throat. Whatever lived in the marsh had sampled the eyes as well.

Her hair was dark, long. Reece tried to superimpose her memory of the woman she'd seen over the ruined face of this one.

'I don't . . . Her face seems less narrow, and her hair seems shorter. I don't know.'

'You were a good distance away that day.'

'He didn't beat her. Her face—this face—someone beat her.'

Rick said nothing, then when Reece looked away again, he turned the photo face down. 'It could be he dragged her off, she came round, and they patched up for a while. Travelling round the area, maybe. Had another fight a couple weeks later. A man puts his hands round a woman's throat once, he could do it again. They've run her prints, but there's no record of them. They'll use dental, and they're running Missing Persons.'

Reece kept her eyes on his, level, steady. 'You didn't believe me before.'

'I had my doubts, I won't lie to you. That doesn't mean I didn't look into it, or that I'm not still doing just that.'

'All right. If they identify her, if I could see a picture of her before this was done to her, I think I could say yes or no with more certainty.'

'OK.' He laid a hand over hers and squeezed. 'I know this was hard for you. I appreciate you coming down. I'll drive you back home.'

Joanie asked no questions, and had given the stern word that she didn't want to hear any aimed in Reece's direction. The lunch crowd slowed, and when her shift was over, Reece drove to the mercantile. She owed Brody a meal for painting, and by God, she was paying her debt.

She arrowed to the grocery section, picked through hothouse tomatoes for chicken frangellico.

'Hey there, Reece.'

Tossing peppers in her basket, she frowned up at Lo.

'Saw your car out front. Listen, I just came in because I heard about the woman up near Moose Ponds. News like that doesn't stay under the lid,' he added when she only stared at him. 'Has to be rough on you.'

'A lot rougher on her, I'd say.' She headed over to the packaged chicken breasts.

'Can't be easy for you though. Seeing her again, even a picture of her. Having to go back in your head to the day you were on the trail. But at least you know they found her.'

'I don't know if it was the same woman I saw.'

'Sure it was. Had to be.' He trailed her over to the counter. 'Everybody's saying so.'

'Everybody doesn't know jack. Funny how it takes a dead body to make people decide I wasn't making the whole thing up. Gee, maybe Reece isn't crazy, after all.'

With more care than usual, Mac boxed her purchases and took her money. 'Nobody thinks you're crazy, Reece.'

She started for the door. 'Sure they do. Once a nutcase, always a nutcase. That's how it goes.'

The sound of the front door slamming shot Brody out of a tense scene between his central character and the man she has no choice but to trust.

He cursed, reached for his coffee only to discover he'd already finished it. His first thought was to go down for a refill, but he heard further slamming—cupboard doors?—and decided he'd rather stay out of the war zone and do without the caffeine.

He rubbed the stiffness out of the back of his neck, which he attributed to craning it in order to paint the bathroom ceiling. Then he closed his eyes, pushed himself back into the scene.

At some point he thought he heard either the front or the back door open, but he was in the zone and continued to write until it closed on him. Satisfied, he pushed away from his keyboard. Right now he deserved a cold beer, and headed down to get one. A cold beer and a hot meal.

The fact that nothing was simmering on the stove was a bit of a shock. Nothing cooking, and the back door wide open. He stepped over to the door.

Reece was sitting on the squat back porch with a bottle of wine. From the level in the bottle, he deduced she'd been sitting there for some time.

He sat down beside her. 'Having a party?'

'Sure.' She gestured sloppily with her glass. 'Big party. You can buy yourself a very decent bottle of wine around here.'

'Apparently.' She was quite drunk. 'Come on, Slim, you're toasted. Let's go on up so you can sleep it off.'

She got to her feet, swaying a little as the wine sloshed in her head as unsteadily as it did in her glass. 'I should've told Mardson that she was the woman I saw. I should've just said it was. So I'm going to go tell him.'

Clutching her stomach, she dashed to the bathroom.

She lay curled on her side in the bed, fallen into sleep. He put the silver insulated cup on the nightstand. He'd made her tea, and he'd go back down to make her soup.

It was just what you did when someone was sick.

He wondered how much of whatever poisons she'd had bottled up inside her she'd managed to reject along with the wine.

He should've expected her to blow at some point. She'd been handling herself pretty well, rocking back from each sucker punch, swallowing down the fear, the rage, the hurts. Sooner or later, they'd have to spill out. Being asked to look at pictures of a dead woman, today had been the day.

Lo had his hand up Linda-Gail's shirt. He flashed back to when they'd been sixteen and the situation had been remarkably similar.

Only this time they were in her little house instead of the old Ford pick-up his mother had helped him buy. There was a bedroom close by, though the couch would do just fine.

Her pretty breast—which he hadn't got a look at since that summer so long ago—was soft and warm in his hand. Her mouth, and he'd never forgotten her mouth, was just as sweet. And she was so miraculously curvy. Fuller than she'd been at sixteen, but in all the right places. But when that hand slid down to her jeans, hers clamped over it.

'Oh, now, honey.' He nibbled her throat. 'I just want—'

'Can't always get what you want, Lo.'

'You know I want you. I always have. You want me, too.' His lips made a lazy journey back to hers. 'Why do you want to tease me this way, sweetheart?'

'Don't call me sweetheart unless you mean it. And this isn't a tease. It's not going to be like that between you and me.'

'Like what? You're the one who said I should come over. You didn't scream for help when I kissed you.'

'I liked when you kissed me. I always did, Lo. But we're not kids any more.' Fussily, she smoothed her half-buttoned shirt. 'I've got higher standards.'

'Higher standards? You got me here just to stir me up. Got names for women like that.'

Her chin lifted. 'You think that, you'd better get out now.'

He shoved to his feet. 'What the hell do you want?'

'You figure it out.' She picked up his hat, tossed it to him. 'But you leave here and go hunt up one of those women and I hear about it, you won't get in the door again.'

'So I can't have you, or anybody else until you say different?'

'No, Lo, you can't have me or anybody else until you know the difference. One thing you do know is the way out the door.'

Furious, Lo stormed out. Women like her, he thought, women who used a man, played games, should be made to pay a price.

He slammed into his truck, sent one dark look back towards the house. She thought she knew him, thought she had him pegged.

She was dead wrong.

He went back to the river. There was no sign of what had happened there, and he was sure of that. He'd been careful. He was a careful man.

It should never have happened, of course. Would never have happened if he'd had a choice. Everything that he'd done since was because she'd *left* him no choice.

He could still hear her voice screaming if he let himself.

Threatening him, as if she'd had the right.

Her death had been her own doing. He felt no guilt over it. How could he have known someone would be on the trail, looking in that direction at that time, with field glasses? Even a careful man couldn't anticipate every quirk of fate.

Reece Gilmore. She should have been easy to handle. So easy to discredit, even to herself. But she wouldn't let it go, wouldn't crack and turn it loose.

There was too much at stake to allow some refugee from a padded room to ruin things for him. If he had to turn the pressure up, he'd turn it up. Whatever needed to be done to protect what he had, he'd do.

Reece Gilmore would have to go. One way or the other.

Chapter 9

REECE HAD BEEN hard put getting to work for the breakfast shift yesterday. Today, since she didn't have to be at Joanie's until two, she considered just futzing around Brody's cabin, doing some light housekeeping, some laundry. She could easily keep out of his way while he wrote.

She was already dressed and making the bed when he got out of the shower. 'Anything special you want for breakfast?'

'No. I'm just going to have some cereal.'

'Oh. All right.' She smoothed the spread and thought idly that a few throw pillows in primary colours would liven it up. 'I'm going to put together some soup for Joanie. You can have some at lunch, see if it passes the test. I can make a casserole or something easy to heat up for your supper. Oh, and I thought I might do some laundry. Is there anything you want washed?'

'Let's just back up.'

She gave him a puzzled smile. 'OK.'

'I don't need you to start planning breakfast, lunch, dinner or a midnight snack every morning.'

The smile dropped into a blink of surprise. 'Well . . .'

'And you're not here to do laundry and make beds and casseroles.'

'No,' she said slowly, 'but I'd like to be useful.'

'I don't want you fussing around the place. I can handle my own chores. I've been handling them for years.'

'Obviously I've misunderstood something. I thought you wanted me to cook.'

'That's different.'

'Different than, say, tossing our laundry in together. That being somehow symbolic of a level of relationship you don't want?'

'Maybe.'

She stepped back to the bed, yanked the spread down, tugged out the sheets. 'There, all better. Do you really think because I'm in love with you I'm trying to trap you into something by washing socks and making chicken and dumplings?' She strode to the door. 'You're an idiot, Brody, and you think entirely too much of your own worth. I'll just leave you to bask in the delusion of your own reflected glory.'

Reece grabbed only what was closest at hand, then shoved it into her car. She'd worry about the rest of her things—not that there was much—later.

She'd get some change and haul her laundry—only her laundry—to the crappy machines in the hotel's basement. It wasn't as if she hadn't done it before.

She aimed the car towards town, frowning at the way it handled. 'What now?' she muttered as the steering dragged. She gave the wheel one bad-tempered smack. Then, resigned, she detoured to Lynt's.

The garage doors were raised with an ageing truck up on the lift. Lynt came out from under it, a rangy forty in a chambray shirt with the sleeves rolled up to expose tough sinews.

He tipped back his oil-stained cap as Reece stepped out of the car. 'Got yourself some trouble?'

'Seems like it. The steering's funny.'

'Not surprised. You got your two back tyres next to flat.'

'Flat?' She turned to look. 'They were fine yesterday.'

'Could be you drove over something, got a slow leak.'

'I have a spare in the trunk.' Damn, was she going to have to replace two tyres?

'I'll get to it as soon as I finish these brake pads. Need a lift somewhere?'

'No. No. I could use the walk.' She got her laptop out. 'If I have to get new tyres, how much do you think?'

'Let's just worry about that when we have to worry about it.' He took her car key. 'I'll give you a call.'

'Thanks.' She hitched her bag on one shoulder, her laptop on the other. It was a nice day for a walk, she reminded herself in an attempt to chase away depression. And if she was in love with a jackass, she'd just have to start working on getting over it. She needed time by herself anyway to get serious about that cookbook. Not that she was going to pass that by Brody now. But she wanted to organise the recipes, take a stab at writing an introduction to them.

'A little lame,' she said aloud, 'but you have to start somewhere.'

'Hey! Hey!'

Reece jerked to a stop and saw Linda-Gail kneeling in her tiny yard with marigolds and pansies all around her.

'Too busy talking to yourself to talk to me?'

'Was I? I was going over something in my head. Too often it runs out of my mouth. They're so pretty. Your flowers.'

'Should've put the pansies in before.' She tipped the straw cowboy hat back on her head. 'They don't mind the cold. But with one thing and another. What are you doing over this way?'

'Flat tyre, or tyres. I had to take the car to Lynt.'

'Bummer. I figured you'd be hanging at Brody's today.'

'Clearly, he didn't. I seem to be getting in his way.'

'The hell with men. I booted Lo out the other night. He wouldn't keep his hands to himself. Want to plant pansies and curse Y-chromo-somes?'

'I really would, but I have things to do this morning.'

'Then we'll go to Clancy's after work tonight, drink a few beers and karaoke down-with-men songs.'

'I can get behind that. I'll see you at work.'

Reece walked home. She gathered up laundry, and detergent, and carried her little basket to the hotel.

'Hi, Brenda. Wash day. Can I get some change?'

'Sure, no problem.'

Reece put bills on the counter and Brenda counted out quarters. Because the elevator wasn't an option for her, Reece took the stairs.

'Seven times one is seven.' She hated the hotel basement. Hated it. 'Seven times two is fourteen.' She made it into the eights, then rushed out of the laundry area as the machine hummed.

Back home, she started her stock and made meatballs for the soup. She zipped back to the hotel, braved the basement to transfer her clothes from washer to dryer. Dashing back home again, she set up her laptop and began to toy with different approaches for an introduction to the cookbook.

When her kitchen timer went off, she headed out one more time.

Walking through the lobby, she tried the twelve times table—a tough one—as she hurried down.

She pulled open the dryer door and found nothing.

'Well, that's . . .' She opened the other dryer. It was empty. 'That's ridiculous. No one would steal my clothes.'

And why was her basket on top of the washer? Gingerly, she picked it up, then slowly opened the washer's lid.

Her clothes were there, wet and spun.

'I put them in the dryer.' She dug an unsteady hand in her pocket, found only the single coin she had left after plugging change into the machines. 'I put them in the dryer.' She tugged wet clothes free to heave them into the basket. A Magic Marker fell to the floor.

A red marker. Her red marker. Shaking now, Reece tossed it in with the clothes she now saw were stained with red.

Someone had done this to her, someone who wanted her to think she was losing it. Someone who could be there, watching her.

Her breath wheezed out as her head swivelled right and left. She bit off a moan, grabbed the basket and ran.

At the desk, Brenda gaped at her. 'What? Who? Are you OK?'

'My clothes. They put my clothes in the washing machine.'

'But, Reece, you put them in.' Brenda spoke slowly, as to a slow-witted child. 'Remember? You went down to wash clothes.'

'After! I put them in the dryer, but they were back in the washer. You saw me come back to put them in the dryer.'

'Well . . . sure, I saw you come back, go down.'

'I put them in. Who went down there?'

'Look, just calm down. I didn't see anyone but you.'

'Maybe you went down.'

Shock blew across Brenda's face. 'Reece, why would I do that? Get a hold of yourself. If you need quarters—'

'I don't need anything.'

Rage and panic pounded through her, shortened her breath as she rushed down the street with her basket of wet clothes.

Get home, was all she could think. Lock the door.

At the beep of a horn, she stumbled, and, whirling round, watched her own car slide into its place near her steps.

Lynt got out. 'Didn't mean to startle you. Ah, tyres were just real low. I put air in them.'

She managed a nod. 'Oh. Thanks. Thank you.'

'And, ah, I was going to check your spare for you. But . . .'

'Is there something wrong with the spare?'

'The thing is it's kind of buried in there.'

'I don't know what you mean.' She set the basket on the steps, crossed over. 'I don't have anything in there.'

When he hesitated, she took the key, popped the trunk.

The smell came first. Garbage just going over. The trunk was full of it—coffee grounds, wet, stained papers, empty cans.

'I wasn't sure what you wanted me to do.'

'I didn't do this.' She stepped back. 'I didn't. Did you?'

"Course not, Reece. I found it like this.'

'Somebody *did* this. Someone's doing this to me. Someone—'

'I don't like shouting outside my place.' Joanie came out the back of the building. 'What's going on here? What's all this?' She wrinkled her nose as she peered into the trunk.

'I didn't do this,' Reece began.

'Well, I sure as hell didn't. Went to get her spare,' Lynt said. 'She's got some crazy idea I dumped garbage in here.'

'She's just upset. Wouldn't you be?' Joanie said mildly. 'Bunch of asinine kids most likely. Lynt, I got rubber gloves in the back room. Give me a hand cleaning this out.'

'I'll do it.' Reece's words jerked out. 'I'm sorry, Lynt—'

'Go upstairs,' Joanie ordered her. 'Go on. I'll be up in a minute. Don't argue with me.'

Reece dragged up the basket. 'Lynt, I'll get your money.'

'No charge.' He waved it away. 'It was nothing but air.'

When Joanie stepped inside the apartment, Reece was sitting on the day bed, the basket of wet laundry at her feet.

Joanie frowned at the clothes. 'You didn't use the dryer?'

'I did. I know I did. But they were in the washer.'

'What the hell's all over them?'

'Ink. Red ink. Someone put my red marker in the machine.'

Joanie puffed up her cheeks. She went over, got a saucer out of Reece's cupboard. She lit up a cigarette, sat on the bed beside Reece. 'I'm going to have a cigarette, and you're going to tell me what's going on.'

'I don't know what's going on. But I know I didn't put those clothes in the washer. I know I didn't put that garbage in my trunk, but it's there. I didn't write all over the bathroom.'

'My bathroom?' Joanie popped up, went to have a look. 'I don't see anything written in here.'

'Brody painted over it. I didn't do those things.'

'Look at me. Look me in the eyes here.' Joanie studied her face. 'Have you been taking drugs? Prescribed or otherwise?'

'No, nothing but sleeping pills.'

'Why would anyone do any of that?'

'To make me think I'm crazy. To make me crazy, which doesn't take much of a push. Because I saw what I saw.'

'They found a body—'

'Wasn't her,' Reece's voice began to rise and pitch. 'Wasn't the same. It wasn't her, and—'

'Stop that.' Joanie's voice snapped out like a slap. 'I'm not talking to you unless you calm down.'

'You try to be calm when someone's doing things to you.'

'How long has this been going on?'

'Almost since I got back from seeing that woman killed.'

'You ought to be talking to the sheriff.'

'Why?' Reece dragged her hands through her hair. 'You think that pile of garbage in my trunk has fingerprints on it?'

'All the same, Reece.'

'Yes. Yes, I'll tell the sheriff.'

'Fine. Brody know about all this?'

'Yes, except for what happened today, yes.'

'Pull yourself together and come on down. Prime rib's the special tonight.'

Reece stirred herself. 'Prime rib of what?'

'Buffalo. Maybe you got a way to fancy that up.'

'As a matter of fact . . .'

'Then get down and do it. I've only got two hands.'

Brody had just wanted her to back up. Isn't that exactly what he'd said? But she overreacted, as women always did.

A man was entitled to a little breathing room in his own house, wasn't he? A little solitude? Without a woman fussing?

He was entitled to frozen pizza if he wanted it. It just so happened he didn't. He wanted a good, hot meal. He'd eaten at Angel Food before she came along, he thought as he went out to his car.

When he pulled up at Joanie's, Joanie herself came out. 'I was just coming over to see you,' she said.

'About what? Reece is—'

She told him quickly. 'Said she'd call the sheriff, but she hasn't. That was nasty, that garbage in her trunk.'

'It's all been nasty. I need to talk to her now.'

'She can have ten, if she wants. Go round to the back.'

He did as Joanie suggested, then brushed right by Pete and took Reece's arm. 'Outside.'

'I'm busy.'

'It'll wait.' He hauled her straight out of the door. 'Why didn't you call me when all this crap happened today?'

'As usual, word travels,' she said sourly. 'And I didn't feel like calling. I don't need a hero to ride to the rescue. I need to do my job.'

'I'll wait and drive you back. We'll see Rick in the morning.'

'I don't want anyone waiting for me, and I don't need you to go to the sheriff with me. I don't need a baby sitter or pity any more than you need me to make your bed and do your laundry. And it's not time for my break.'

When she turned towards the door, he took her arm, pulled her round again. 'Damn it, Reece.' He sighed, gave up. 'Damn it,' he said quietly now. 'Come home.'

She stared at him, then she shut her eyes. 'That was a sneaky punch.' And it took her breath away. 'I think we'd both better take a little time thinking about what that means, and if it's what we both want. Maybe we'll talk tomorrow.'

'I'll sleep in my office, or down on the couch.'

'I'm not coming to your place so you can protect me. If it turns out it's more than that, we'll see what happens. You'd better figure it out before we talk again.'

She left him, baffled and edgy, to go back to the grill.

Clancy's was hopping with locals mixing and mingling with the tourists who'd sprinkled into the area to fish or hike. Reuben had the mike and was doing a soulful version of Keith Urban's 'You'll Think of Me'. A group of cowboys had flirted a couple of town girls into a game of pool. Two couples from back East were hoisting drinks and snapping pictures of themselves against the backdrop of sheep's heads and elk.

At the bar, his boot propped on the rail, Lo brooded into his bottle of Big Horn.

'He looks like he's suffering.'

At Reece's comment, Linda-Gail shrugged. 'Not enough. He's going to have to come hat in hand. I've been hung up on that stupid cowboy most of my life, and I've given him enough time to finish riding the range. I'm ready to start building the rest of my life. Want another beer?'

'No, I'm fine.'

Linda-Gail signalled for one as the two women from back East took over the stage with 'I Feel Like a Woman'. 'What about you?'

'I can't imagine not wanting Brody. He came into the kitchen tonight, dragged me out the back.'

'What? What? How did I miss this? What happened?'

'He wanted me to go home with him.'

'And you're here listening to bad karaoke because?'

Reece's jaw set. 'I won't go back until I know he wants me.'

Linda-Gail set down her fresh beer. 'I'm lost.'

'I want a lover on equal terms. I don't want to feel like a guest in that cabin. I'm so pissed off I'm in love with him.'

With a mournful look, Linda-Gail tapped her glass to Reece's. 'Right there with you.' Then she glanced towards the bar and noted that Lo was telling his troubles to one of the waitresses. 'Let's dance.'

Reece blinked. 'What?'

'Let's go over, see if a couple of those fly-fishing types want to take a turn on the dance floor.'

The fly-fishing types were half-drunk. 'I don't think so.'

'Well, I'm going over and pick me one out of the pack.' Linda-Gail shoved back. 'How do I look?'

'A little dangerous just now.

'That's perfect.' Linda-Gail glided into Lo's line of sight, braced her palms on the men's table, leaned over.

Reece couldn't hear what was being said. She didn't have to. The men were grinning; Lo looked murderous. Then Linda-Gail led one of the men to the floor, put her hands on his shoulders. And danced with her hips.

The two left behind whooped. One of them shouted, 'Go for it, Chuck!'

And Chuck planted his hands on Linda-Gail's ass.

Lo slapped his Big Horn back on the bar and strode onto the dance floor.

Chuck shoved Lo; Lo shoved Chuck. Linda-Gail put her full hundred and twenty pounds into it and shoved them both.

When Chuck's friends pushed up from the table, the small herd of cowboys playing pool stepped forward. Lo was one of their own.

She was going to be in the middle of a bar fight, Reece thought with full amazement. Caught in a melee in a karaoke bar in Wyoming. Unless she managed to grab Linda-Gail and run.

She glanced to the exit. And saw, moving through the noisy, surged-to-its-feet crowd, a man wearing an orange hunter's cap.

Her breath hitched and tore. She lurched up, knocking her beer to the floor, where the glass shattered with a sound like a gunshot. She stumbled, shoving into one of the cowboys, and sent him bumping hard into one of the fishermen.

Fists flew. Onstage, the women screamed and clutched at each other. Bodies thudded against table and bar. Glassware and bottles crashed and shattered. An elbow caught Reece along the cheekbone and sent her sprawling to the floor.

Reeking of beer and smoke, holding an ice pack to her throbbing cheek, Reece sat in the sheriff's office. If she'd been more humiliated in her life, her brain wouldn't allow the previous incident to surface.

'Last thing I expected was to pull you out of a bar fight.'

'It wasn't in my plans for the evening. And I wasn't fighting.'

'You pushed Jud Horst into one Robert Gavin, inciting the incident. You threw your beer.'

'No, I didn't! I knocked it over when I tried to get up from the table and I slipped into Jud.'

'You were drinking,' Rick continued.

'A half a beer. Of course I was drinking. So was everyone else. I panicked, OK. I saw . . .'

'You saw?'

'I saw a man in an orange hat in the back of the crowd.'

Rick's weary, annoyed expression sharpened. 'You saw the man you previously saw by the river?'

'I don't know. I couldn't see that well. I got up. I wanted to get away. I wanted to see him better.'

'Which was it?'

'Both,' she snapped. 'I was scared. I slipped. That's all.'

He let out a windy sigh. He'd been pulled out of bed by a screaming call from one of Clancy's waitresses. Now he had property damage, bodily injuries, possible charges to wade through.

'Min Hobalt claims you struck her.'

'I didn't hit anyone.' Had she? 'I was trying to get clear. I got jabbed in the face, I was seeing stars. I *fell* into a table. *I've* got bruises over most of my body.'

He puffed out a breath. 'Who swung first?'

'I don't know. The guy they called Chuck gave Lo a little shove; Lo gave him one back. Then I saw . . . I saw the hat.'

'You saw the hat.'

'Yes, yes, I know a lot of men wear those hats. But I was jumpy because I could see a fight coming, saw the hat and freaked out. Big surprise. Charge me with inciting a riot, or whatever you want.'

'Nobody's going to lock you away.' Rick rubbed his face. 'The thing is, you've got a habit of stirring things up. You had some trouble down at the hotel laundry today?'

'I . . .' Of course he knew about it. Brenda was tight as spandex with Debbie.

'That was different. Someone played a joke on me.' While he waited, brows lifted, Reece contemplated telling him the truth. 'It was nothing. Do you interrogate everyone who has words with the hotel's desk clerk, or is it just me?'

His face hardened. 'I've got a job to do, Reece. Now I've got to sort through this mess. You want Doc to look at that cheek?'

'No.' She got to her feet. 'I didn't start what happened tonight. I just got caught in it.' She turned for the door.

'You've got a habit of getting caught in things. And if you jump and swing every time you see orange, we have a problem.'

She just kept going. She wanted to burn off her anger and humiliation in private.

But first, she noted, she'd have to get through Brody.

He was sitting in the outer office, legs stretched out, eyes half closed. She tried to simply go round him.

'Hold on there, Slim.' He got lazily to his feet. 'Let's have a look at that face.'

'Nothing to see.'

He got to the door first, closed his hand round the handle, then just leaned on it. 'You smell like the barroom floor.'

'I spent some time on it tonight. Will you excuse me?'

He opened the door. 'Let's not go through the ridiculous routine about you walking home alone. I'm driving.'

She didn't bother to argue. 'Fine. What are you doing here?'

'Linda-Gail called me in case you needed somebody to post bail.' He pulled open the passenger-side door. 'You sure keep life interesting.'

'I didn't *do* anything.'

'You stick with that.'

She stewed until he'd skirted the hood and climbed behind the wheel. 'You think this is funny?'

'It has classic farce elements. Yeah, I think it's funny. OK, Slim, your place or mine?'

'Mine. You can consider your Good Samaritan duties at an end.'

He started to drive, tapping his fingers against the steering wheel. 'Damn it, I was lying awake cursing you when your partner in crime called. I think about you.' Resentment rippled in his voice. 'You get in my way.'

'As this is the second time you've popped up tonight, I'd say you're in my way. You wanted me to back up, back off, I did. Your whim changes, Brody, that's not my problem.'

'I felt squeezed.' He pulled up behind her car. 'And you said you loved me.'

'I didn't ask you to love me back. I'm tired, Brody. If you want to hash this through, it'll have to be some other time.'

'Wait. Damn it.' He sat back, his expression pained and frustrated. 'I was out of line this morning. I'm sorry.'

She said nothing for a moment. 'Ow. I bet that hurt you as much as my face hurts me.' She touched his arm, then reached for the door.

'Will you wait? Listen.'

At the ensuing silence, she said, 'I'm listening.'

'OK. Before you said you didn't want me to take care of you. That's fine. The thought of wanting to take care of you is scaring the hell out of me. But I want to be with you. There's no one else I want to be with. Can we get back to that?'

She pushed open her door, then stopped. Looked at him. Life was so terrifyingly short. Who knew that better than she did? 'That's all I was looking for. Do you want to come up?'

'Yeah.' He waited while she walked round the car, then held his hand out for hers. 'Come here a minute.' Leaning down, he brushed his lips gently over her bruised cheek. 'Ouch.'

'I'm not going to be very good company. All I want is a hot bath, a bottle of aspirin and a soft bed.'

'You don't have a soft bed.'

'I'll compensate.' She unlocked the door.

As she opened it, he pulled her back, shifted his body in front of hers. 'What's that sound? Stay right here.'

Of course she couldn't, and eased in behind him. 'In the bathroom,' she whispered. 'The door's closed. I never close the door. There's water running. Oh God, it's coming under the door.'

He shoved the door open so more water sloshed out. Inside, the bath overflowed as the water poured from the tap.

'Oh God, Joanie's. Downstairs. The diner.'

Joanie came with the keys, and a Shop-Vac. Her eyes grim, she pushed the vac at Reece. 'Go up, suck up that water. When you're done, bring it down here.'

'Joanie, I'm so sorry—'

'Just be quiet and do what I told you.'

Joanie unlocked the door, stepped in, flipped on the lights.

Water streamed through the ceiling of the north corner. The plasterboard had buckled under the weight and split like bad fruit. Below it two booths were soaked. 'Son of a bitching bastard.'

'She's not responsible,' Brody began, but Joanie only jabbed a finger towards him, her eyes on the damage.

'I'm going to need some fans in here, dry things out. Some plastic to put up over that hole in the ceiling before the health inspector shuts me down. You want to be helpful, drag out that big standing fan in the storeroom. Then you can go back to my place. I got a roll of plastic out in my shed. A staple gun.'

Brody glanced at the ceiling. 'Stepladder.'

'That, too.'

Reece wept as she worked. It was all a mess. Ruined floor, ruined ceiling and God only knew what else was ruined.

She emptied the tank of the vacuum, started it again.

She glanced up miserably when Joanie came through the door.

'How bad is it?'

'Bad enough. Fixable.'

'I'll pay—'

'I got insurance, don't I? Skin me for premiums every month.'

Reece stared at the floor as she worked. 'I know how this looks, but I didn't leave the water on. I didn't even—'

'I know damn well you didn't.'

Reece jerked her head up. 'You do?'

'You never forget a goddamn thing. Didn't I just use my key to open that stupid door? You said somebody's been screwing with you. Now they're screwing with me. And I am *pissed*. But that floor's going to have to come up. We fix what has to be fixed, then we figure out the rest.'

'**S**he believed me. I didn't even have to try to explain.'

It was after three when Reece stowed the last of her things in the back of Brody's car and climbed in.

'Joanie's a smart woman. She sees through most crap.'

'Whoever this is, he didn't have to do this to her.' As he drove, she looked out at the dark surface of the lake. Her life felt like that tonight. Too dark to see what lay under it.

'If she'd fired you, kicked you out, odds were you'd leave town. It's a smart move.'

'Following that logic, you'd be the next on his list. I'm not exactly anyone's good luck charm, Brody.'

'I don't believe in luck.' He pulled up at his cabin.

From the back of the car he took the hefty box of her kitchen tools, slid the strap of her laptop case over his shoulder. He left the second box and the duffle for her.

Inside, he set the box on the floor. 'I'm not putting this stuff away.' He took the other box from her, set it down. 'Go on up and take a shower.'

'I think a bath.' She managed a smile. 'Pretty bad.'

'Not if you like stale beer and smoke.'

She went up, ran the bath hot. Sinking into it, she scooted straight up when Brody walked in.

'Aspirin,' he said. He set the bottle, a glass of water on the lip of the bath, then walked out.

When she came out wearing a baggy grey T-shirt with red stains and a pair of loose flannel trousers, he was standing by the window. He turned, cocked his head. 'Nice outfit.'

'I don't have a lot left.'

'Well. You can put what you do have left in there.' He jerked a thumb at his dresser. 'I cleaned out a couple of drawers.'

'Oh.'

'It's not a marriage proposal.'

'Check. I'll do it tomorrow. I'm really tired. I'm sorry, Brody, but did you—'

'Yes. The doors are locked.'

'OK.' She slipped into bed and sighed at the sheer relief.

Moments later, the lights switched off, the mattress dipped. Then his body was warm against hers, and his arm draped round her waist.

She took his hand and fell asleep, too exhausted to dream.

Chapter 10

BRODY DROVE REECE to Joanie's at six sharp. The lights were on in the diner, a hard shine against the dark. A vile green dumpster sat at the kerb, already half loaded with plasterboard and debris.

The sight of it had Reece's shoulders going tight. Insurance was all well and good, but what about the deductible? Behind a curtain of plastic, she could see men on ladders. The place smelt of coffee and wet.

'You're not on until eleven today,' Joanie said.

'I'm working off my part of this. Argue,' Reece added, 'and I'll move to Jackson Hole. You'll not only be shy a couple of booths but a cook.'

'These boys've been at this an hour already. Go rustle up a couple of cattleman's breakfasts. Eggs sunny side.'

Reece served them herself, at the counter. The regular early birds were already dribbling in, and the always sleepy morning guy shuffled in to wash dishes.

No one complained, but the mess held as top topic of conversation. When speculative looks were sent her way, Reece told herself it was no less than she could expect.

She was making salsa when Linda-Gail came to the back of the diner. 'Oh, Reece, honey, your poor face. You must be so mad at me.'

'I was.' Reece chopped and considered trying out a little bruschetta on the lunch crowd. 'Then I looked at the big picture and decided it wasn't your fault. Well, not completely.'

'Really? I feel like such an ass.'

'You were an ass. But that only contributed to the general mayhem. Between Clancy's and the mess here, people are going to have something to talk about for a week.'

'Linda-Gail Case, I believe I'm paying you.' Joanie walked in. 'Rick's out front, Reece, wants to talk to you.'

'I guess we'd best have this conversation out front. People'll just talk about me more if we go behind closed doors.'

Joanie nodded, approval in her eyes. 'Good for you.'

Reece left her apron on. Rick was loitering by the counter. 'Reece. Why don't we go sit in the back?'

'Out here's fine. Table five's empty. Linda-Gail,' Reece called. 'Would you bring the sheriff some coffee?'

She led the way and sat down. 'Is Min pressing charges?'

'No. On some rethinking, witness consensus is that Clancy's was a series of lamebrain actions by a number of people.'

'Me included.'

'Well.' He smiled, just a little round the edges. 'You do seem to draw responses. Now.' He paused, looked towards the plastic. 'Why don't you tell me about this one?'

'After I left your office, Brody drove me back here. We went upstairs and I heard water running. When we went in, the bathroom door was closed. Water leaking under it. Someone had turned the water on in the bath, plugged it up. It flooded.'

'Someone?'

'It wasn't me. I wasn't there. You know I wasn't there because you know I was at Clancy's, then at your office.'

'From what I can see, the water was running for some time.'

'I didn't turn it on. After my shift, I couldn't have been upstairs for more than three minutes. I changed my shoes and . . .'

'And?'

Checked the locks, the windows. 'Nothing. I changed my shoes, and I went back down to meet Linda-Gail.'

'Did you go in the bathroom?'

'I used the bathroom. I had no reason to turn the bath on.'

He glanced up as Linda-Gail brought his coffee. 'Linda-Gail, you didn't go upstairs before you and Reece went to Clancy's?' Rick asked.

'Well, no. Reece couldn't have been but a few minutes.'

'Thanks, Linda-Gail. I'll let you know if I need anything else.'

'Why would I turn the water on?' Reece demanded. 'It wouldn't be natural to run a bath when you had no intention of taking one, then walk out. Someone's been in my apartment. This isn't the first time.'

Rick levelled his gaze at her. 'First I'm hearing about it.'

'It started right after I saw the murder,' Reece began. She told him: the map, the bathroom, finding her things packed. The pills, the photograph album.

He took notes. 'Why didn't you report these incidents?'

'Because I knew you'd think just what you're thinking now. That I either did them or I imagined them.'

'You don't have a window into my head, Reece.' His voice warned her his patience was at a low ebb. 'Have you noticed anyone loitering?'

'Half the town loiters here at some point.'

'Who has access to your key?'

'I keep it with me. There's a spare in Joanie's office.'

'You had trouble, had words with anyone in town?'

'Not until I clocked Min at Clancy's last night.'

He gave that faint smile. 'I think we can rule her out.'

'He must have seen me on the trail. The man by the river.'

Rick drew a breath, sat back. 'Saw you, at that distance?'

'Not me. He must have seen there was someone. It wouldn't take any effort to find out it was me, not after the whole town knew about it. So he's trying to discredit me as a witness.'

Rick closed his notebook.

'What are you going to do?' Reece demanded.

'I'm going to look into it. Next time something happens tell me about it. I can't help you if I don't know you've got trouble.'

'All right. Have they identified the woman? The body?'

'Haven't matched dental records yet. She's still a Jane Doe.' He pushed to his feet. 'You got a place to stay while these repairs are going on?'

'I'm at Brody's.'

'I'll be in touch.'

Rick walked up to Reece's apartment. The door was wide open. Rock pumped out along with the sound of hammer on chisel.

Inside, Brody was on his knees in the bathroom, painfully from the looks of it, chipping up the ancient linoleum.

'Not your usual line of work,' Rick called out.

'Change of pace.' Brody sat back on his heels.

Rick hunkered down. 'Subflooring's trashed.'

'So I'm told.'

'You should've come to me with these incidents with Reece before this, Brody.'

'Her choice. Understandable. I can look at your face and see you're not leaning towards believing her.'

'I'm not leaning any particular way. Hard to investigate if I don't know. See you painted over what was done in here.'

'Took pictures first. I'll get you copies.'

'That's a start. None of these incidents happened at your place, or while you were with her?'

'Not so far.' Brody went back to chipping.

'I can't see any signs of forced entry.'

'He's got a key. I'm going to see the lock is changed.'

'You do that.'

'Brody, she's got it in her head the man she says she saw by the river's doing this.'

'I put it in her head.'

'Now why the hell did you go and do that?'

'It makes sense to me. Play on her weaknesses, scare her, make her doubt herself. Make sure everyone else doubts her, too. It's smart, and it's clean. Doesn't mean he won't harm her.'

And that, Brody thought, was why she wasn't going anywhere alone. 'It seems to me it's escalating,' he continued. 'She wasn't isolated this time. Joanie got hit, too. Because it's not working. Reece is sticking.'

Rick shook his head. 'Why don't you drop those pictures you took of the bathroom off to me when you get the chance? And maybe write me up your version of the events and incidents. Get me dates and times best as you can.'

'Yeah, I can do that.'

'You got a serious thing happening? You two?'

'We've got a thing happening.'

'When you've got feelings for a woman, it tends to shade things. Be best not to let that colour your statement.'

'She's not crazy, Rick. Hell, she doesn't even hit eccentric in some areas.'

'And in others?'

'Sure, she rings the bell. Who doesn't? People here used to think I was strange because I write about murder, don't shoot mammals and can't name the top ten songs on the country music chart.'

Rick smiled his little smile. 'Brody, people still think you're strange.'

Linda-Gail wasn't quite sure what to do. As far as she could remember, she'd never screwed up so completely with a man—and there'd never been a man who'd mattered as much as Lo.

He wasn't answering her calls. She wanted to be pissed off at him, but instead felt sad and a little scared. And confused.

She'd planned it all out, spent days and nights calculating how to bring Lo to heel, when it suited her. It was time for both of them to settle down. Together.

As she drove out towards the ranch, with the sage flats ripening to bloom around her, she was determined to tell him just that.

What had she been thinking, sashaying up with that stupid guy right in front of Lo's face? Make him a little jealous. It seemed like the thing to do at the time. The problem was, it had worked too well.

She'd only been dancing, for heaven's sake.

She tapped her fingers on the wheel in time with Kenny Chesney, pushed her little car to eighty. Time to give that brainless cowboy a piece of her mind for causing a ruckus over nothing.

She slowed as she approached the big open gate with its wrought-iron *K* wrapped in a circle. She passed a corral, the bunkhouse, the main house sprawling in every direction. Guests could belly up to the bar there at night, then slide into a feather bed no cowboy had ever found at the end of the trail.

She parked at the stables, flipped down the vanity mirror to finger-fluff her hair. As she got out of the car, the cowboy giving a riding lesson tapped the brim of his hat.

'Hey there, Harley.' She fixed a bright smile on her face.

'Linda-Gail, how ya doing?' Harley raised an eyebrow. 'Lo's back in the tack room. Pretty pissy, too.'

'Good. I'm feeling the same.'

Linda-Gail swung into the stable, smelling the strong odour of horses and hay, the sweet scent of grain and leather. Stiffening her spine she walked back into the tack room.

He had Toby Keith on the CD player and his hat tipped back on his head as he worked saddle soap into leather. His jeans were faded and snug. His denim shirt was rolled up to the elbows. His face looked sulky and ridiculously handsome despite the puffy bottom lip and the bruising around his eye.

'Lo.' The sight of him drowned the leading edge of her temper.

His head came up. 'What do you want? I'm working.'

'I can see that. I'm sorry about your eye.'

He kept his gaze on hers for one long, humming moment.

'I am sorry,' she said. 'Still, it's not like it's the first time you've ever had a fist in the eye. I was just dancing.'

He rubbed leather, kept his silence.

'That's it? You're not going to speak to me? How many times have I been in Clancy's when you've been dancing with somebody?'

'That's different.'

'What's different about it? I dance with somebody and it's OK for you to start a brawl. But you can dance and whatever with anyone you like and I'm not supposed to think anything of it.'

'Doesn't mean anything.'

'So you say. And I say I can dance with whoever I want and you've got no right to cause trouble.'

'Fine. You can bet I won't from here on. So if that's it—'

'Don't you dismiss me, William Butler. Why'd you start that fight?'

'I didn't. He did.'

'You got in his face.'

'He had his hands on your ass!' Lo threw down his rag and surged to his feet. 'You let him paw you, in public.'

'I wouldn't have let him if you hadn't been such a jerk. I've waited long enough for you to grow the hell up and be a man.'

Danger shot into his eyes. 'I am a man.' He grabbed her arm and yanked her forward. 'And I'm the only man who's going to put his hands on you. Got that?'

'What gives you the right?' Tears started in her eyes.

'I'm taking the right. Next time you let some other guy handle you, he's going to have more than a bloody nose.'

'What do you care who handles me?' she shouted. 'What do you care? If you can't say it to my face and mean it, right now, I'm walking, Lo.'

'You're not going anywhere.'

'Then say it.' Tears tracked down her cheeks. 'Look at me and say it, and I'll know if you mean it.'

'I'm so damn mad at you, Linda-Gail.'

'I know you mean that.'

'I love you. Is that what you need to hear? I love you. Probably always have.'

'Yeah, that's what I need to hear. I've been waiting my whole life to hear it.'

His hands stroked her arms. 'I never could get over you.' He pulled her close. 'I wanted to. A lot.'

'You think you can get the rest of the night off? And come on home with me? And get me all stirred up, and make love with me till sunrise?'

His smile spread, slow. 'Only till sunrise?'

'This time,' she said and kissed him again.

He was good. Linda-Gail imagined he would be—and she'd been imagining since she was old enough to understand what men and women did together in the dark. 'Where did you learn all that?' she said.

'I've been studying on it for some time.' He spoke lazily, eyes closed, his head resting on her belly. 'So I could perfect the matter before I got to you.'

'Good job. Now you have to marry me, Lo.'

'I have to . . .' His head came up. 'What?'

Shock, she thought, but that she'd expected. 'I'm not another one of your women, Lo. I'm the only woman from here on out. If all you want is what we just had, you say so. No hard feelings. But I can promise you, you won't get me here again.'

He pushed up until he was sitting. 'You want to get married?'

'I want a home and a family. I've loved you as long as I can remember. If you don't love me enough to start a life with me, I need to know it.'

For a time he said nothing, only stared over her head. 'I'm twenty-eight years old,' he began.

'You think that makes you too young to settle down and—'

'Just be quiet, and let someone else talk for a change. I'm twenty-eight years old,' he repeated. 'I got a good job, and I got money put by. Not a lot, but you could do worse.' He looked at her now. 'Why don't you marry me, Linda-Gail?'

Tim McGraw was crooning on the jukebox, with one of the carpenters in an off-key duet while Reece juggled orders in the lunch rush. It was almost normal, as long as she didn't think beyond the moment. Elk burger, rare, white bean soup, meat-loaf sandwich, chicken sub. Slice, dice, scoop, man the grill.

She could do it in her sleep. Routine was good. There was nothing wrong with clinging to routine between crises.

She plated the meat-loaf san, the burger, their sides, and turned. 'Orders up.'

And saw Debbie Mardson sliding onto a stool at the counter.

Debbie pursed her lips, touched her own cheek and said, 'You poor thing.'

'Probably looks worse than it is.'

'I hope so. Min Hobalt said you pack a hell of a punch.'

'I didn't—'

'She was joking.' Debbie held up both hands. 'Soup smells good. Maybe I could get a cup of that and a side salad.' She glanced around, conspiratorially. 'Your dressing.'

'Sure. Coming right up.'

She made out the ticket herself, put it in line.

Twenty minutes later when the rush had settled, Debbie was still there.

'Boy, I thought getting dinner on the table most nights was a challenge. How do you keep it all straight?'

'It gets to be routine.'

'Feeding three kids and a man is more routine than I can handle some days. Can you take a break? Buy you a cup of coffee?'

'I don't drink coffee. But I can take a break.'

She grabbed a bottle of water before she came out to sit at the counter. It felt good to get off her feet. She felt wilted and sweaty beside Debbie's white shirt and pink cardigan.

'Amazing soup. I don't suppose you'd part with the recipe?'

'I'm thinking about parting with a lot of them. And maybe doing a cookbook.'

'Really?' Debbie swung on her stool, so her rose quartz bangles danced. 'That's so interesting. We'd have two famous writers in the Fist. Seems like you and Brody have an awful lot in common.'

Reece sipped her water. 'You think?'

'Well, you're both from back East, and creative. No wonder you two hooked up so fast.'

'Did we?'

'A lot of women around here had their eye on him, but he didn't do a lot of eyeing back. Until you.' Debbie beamed a smile. 'It seemed, at first, you were just passing through. We get a lot of that. Now, I guess you're settling in.'

'I like it here. Bar fights notwithstanding.'

'It's a good town. People look after each other.' She inclined her head towards the plastic tarp. 'Something like that happened in the city, Joanie'd have to shut down for a week.'

'Lucky break.'

'I'm sorry.' She patted Reece's arm. 'You probably don't want to think about it. It's all getting fixed up. Be the better for it, too, when it's done.'

'I didn't turn the water on,' Reece said flatly. 'I do feel bad that whoever's messing with me took it out on Joanie.'

'She's got a bigger heart than she lets on. Listen, I didn't mean to make it sound like you'd caused her trouble.' Debbie gave Reece's arm another pat. 'I think maybe you should try aromatherapy. When I'm stressed, nothing smooths me out like lavender oil.'

'I'll put that on the list. The next time a murderer floods my apartment, I'll smooth out with lavender oil.' Reece pushed off the stool. 'Debbie, I appreciate the attempt to be friendly. I've got to get back to work.'

She stewed about it for the rest of her shift, and was still stewing when she left the diner. Since Brody had insisted on driving her in that morning, she didn't have her car.

She could use the walk, she thought. It was warm enough to leave her jacket unbuttoned, breezy enough to smell the water, the woods and the grass that was beginning to green.

She missed the green, the lushness of it on lawns and in parks. The stately old trees, the zipping traffic. The anonymity of a thriving city. What was she doing here, flipping elk burgers, defending herself to Wyoming's version of a soccer mom, worrying about the death of a woman she didn't even know?

When the car slowed beside her, the light tap of the horn made her jump. She scowled at Brody through the open window. 'What are you doing?'

'Driving around looking for hot women to pick up. You're close enough. Get in.'

'I don't want you breaking up your day to drive me back and forth to work.'

'Good, because I didn't. Break up my day.' He unhooked his seat belt to lean over and open the passenger door himself. 'Get in. You can snarl just as well in here as out there.'

'I'm not snarling.' But she got in. 'I'm serious, Brody.'

'I like changing my routine. Buckle up, Slim. I had an excellent day. And it ain't over yet.'

He drove out of the Fist to the bloom of the flats. He stopped where they'd had their first kiss.

Silent, she reached out, touched her hand to his before climbing out.

She stood where the world was a carpet of colour guarded by silver and blue peaks, gilded by the sun that sat low in the west.

Pinks and blues, vibrant reds and purples, sunny yellows spiked and spread among the soft green of sage. And where the flats blurred into marsh was a dreamy green ribbon of cottonwood and willow. 'Worth seeing?' he asked.

'I've never seen anything like it. Is that larkspur?'

'Yeah, and stonecrop, harebells, bitterbrush, scarlet gilia.' He took a blanket out of the back of the car, tossed it to her. 'Spread that out. I've got wine in the cooler. We'll watch the sun set.'

'Brody?'

He hefted out the cooler, glanced her way. 'Yeah?'

'We need to go over your excellent day point by point, so you can have more of them.' She spread out the blanket, sat on it, then saw he had not only wine but cheese and bread and fat purple grapes. 'Wow. I didn't expect to end my day with a picnic.'

'You won't. You're going to end it having sweaty sex. This is a prelude.'

She took the wine. 'So far, I like it.'

They ate and drank and watched the sun slide behind the mountains until their edges went from silver to fire-red.

Chapter 11

FROM THE SHADOWS of the trees, in the light from the three-quarter moon, he watched the house. It was too early for sleep, he knew. He could wait them out.

He had several plans to suit whatever opportunity presented itself. Instead of running, she appeared to be heeling in, so he'd adjusted. He could work with that. He might have preferred it otherwise, but his life was full of half-realised preferences. The realised ones he damn well meant to keep intact.

When the bedroom light came on, he watched Reece cross to the door in Brody's shirt, say something over her shoulder.

So he adjusted his plans to opportunity.

'Water,' Reece repeated. 'I'm about to die of thirst.'

'The shower has water, so I'm told.'

'I'm not getting into the shower with you—that's a path to perdition, and I need to hydrate. I can throw something simple together while you get yours.'

'As in food?'

'I'll do a stir-fry. Bread and cheese won't hold you.'

He scowled instantly. 'You said food, not vegetables.'

'You'll like it.' She wished she had some water chestnuts, but what could you do.

Rolling up the sleeves of his shirt, she walked to the kitchen. She switched on the light and went for the water first. Standing with one hand braced on the refrigerator, she gulped it down straight from the bottle.

When she lowered it, a faint tapping had her glancing to the window over the sink.

Shoulders covered in a black jacket, head covered with an orange cap. Sunglasses black as the night hiding most of his face.

On a hitching gasp, she stumbled back as the bottle dropped and water glugged out on the floor. The image was gone. She stood frozen in place, trying to gather her senses.

And saw the doorknob move right, move left.

Now she screamed, leaping forward to grab the chef's knife from the counter. She kept screaming, gripping the knife with both hands even as she backed up.

When the door flew open, she ran.

Brody had his head under the spray when he heard the bathroom door slam open. Idly, he pulled back the curtain. Reece held a big knife and had her back pressed to the door.

'He's in the house. In the back door, in the kitchen.'

'Stay here.' Brody shut off the water, grabbed a towel.

'He's in the house.'

With one snap, Brody wrapped the towel round his waist. 'Give me the knife, Reece.' He had to prise it out of her hands. 'Get behind me. We're going to the bedroom. When I'm sure it's clear, lock yourself in and call nine-one-one. Understand me?'

'Yes. Don't go.' Gripping his arm, she darted glances at the door. 'Stay in there with me. Don't go down there. Don't go down.'

'You'll be fine.' He nudged her behind him, shoved the door open quickly. 'Did he come after you?'

'No. I don't know. No. He was just there, and I grabbed the knife and ran.'

'Stay close.' He moved to the bedroom, locked the door, searched under the bed, in the closet. Setting down the knife, he yanked on his jeans. 'Call the cops, Reece.'

'Please. He could have a gun. Please don't leave.'

'I'll be back.' He left the knife where it was, took his baseball bat out of the closet. 'Lock the door. Make the call.'

Alone, Reece stared at the door. She leapt onto the bed, crawling over it to the phone.

'Nine-one-one. What's the nature of your emergency?'

'Help. We need help. He's here.'

'What kind of—Reece? Is this Reece Gilmore? It's Hank. What's going on? Are you hurt?'

'Brody's. Brody's cabin. He killed her. He's here. Hurry.'

'Stay on the line. I'm sending someone. Just hang on.'

A crash from downstairs had her choking out a scream. Gunfire? Was that gunfire? Was it real or in her head?

Sobbing, she dropped the phone and picked up the knife.

She hadn't locked the door. If she locked it, Brody would be trapped on one side, she on the other. He could die.

Ginny had died while she did nothing.

Through the dull buzzing in her head, she heard footsteps on the stairs.

This time they'd find her, and they'd finish it.

'Reece. It's OK. It's Brody. Unlock the door.'

'Brody.' She yanked open the door and stared at him. Swayed.

'It's OK.' He took the knife out of her hand. 'He's gone.'

Dots flashed in front of her eyes, black and white. Even as the edges went red, he propelled her to a chair, shoved her head between her knees. 'Cut it out. Cut it out and breathe.'

His voice sliced through the dizziness. 'I heard . . .'

'I slipped. There was water on the kitchen floor. Knocked over a chair. Keep breathing.'

'You're not shot.' Slowly, she lifted her head. 'I wasn't sure what was real, where I was. Did you see him?'

'No. Cowardly bastard took off. That's what you need to remember.' He took her face firmly in his hands. 'He's a coward.'

He heard the sirens. 'There's the cavalry. Get some clothes.'

Dressed, she came down to find the back door open, with the floodlights on. She could hear the mutter of voices. Seeking solace in order, she started coffee, then mopped the floor.

She had cups, milk and sugar on the table when Brody came in with Denny. 'Coffee, Deputy?'

'Wouldn't mind it. You up to giving a statement, Reece?'

'Yes. It's coffee regular, isn't it?'

'Yeah.' Denny took a seat at the table, took out his pad. 'Can you tell me what happened?'

'I came downstairs to make dinner. Brody was in the shower.' She poured the coffee and told him. 'It was dark, and the kitchen light reflected on the glass. I didn't see him clearly.'

'Height? Weight? Colouring?'

She squeezed her eyes shut. He'd seemed huge to her, impossibly huge. How could she see through the haze of her own fear? 'White, clean-shaven. I'm not sure. It was quick.'

'Did he say anything?'

'No.' She jumped at the sound of a car pulling up.

'That's probably the sheriff,' Denny said. 'Hank contacted him. I'll just go on out, fill him in.'

She sat with her hands in her lap when Denny went out. 'It's pitiful, isn't it? He was standing right there, but I can't tell you what he looked like. He knows just how to play me. They won't believe me, Brody. I'm an hysterical woman, with delusions. You and Denny, you didn't find anything outside?'

'No. He's careful.'

She took a breath. 'When I was upstairs alone, I thought I heard gunshots. I got everything tangled up.'

'Give yourself a break, Reece. You snapped back.' Brody glanced over, signalled at the knock on the back door.

Rick came in, removed his hat. 'Evening. Heard you had some trouble.'

'Breaking and entering and harassment,' Brody told him.

'Maybe I could get a cup of that coffee. I asked Denny to take one more look round.' He paused while Reece poured another cup. 'Reece, why don't you show me where you were standing when you saw someone—at the window, is that right?'

'I was here.' She moved to the refrigerator. 'I heard a sound and looked over.'

'Kitchen light glares on the window glass. You go closer?'

'I . . . no. He stepped back, then I saw the doorknob turn. I grabbed a knife, then the door opened, and he was standing just outside. I turned and ran.'

'Uh-huh. Brody, you were in the shower?'

'That's right.'

'How about the door there? Locked? Unlocked?'

'It was locked.'

'OK.' Rick opened the back door, squatted to examine the lock, the jamb. 'Was he wearing gloves?'

'He—' Reece forced her mind back. 'Yes. Black gloves.'

'Any other details about him?'

'I'm sorry.'

Rick straightened. 'Well, let's take it back some. You were home here, Brody, until what time?'

'I left about six thirty, quarter to seven, I'd say.'

'Went and picked Reece up at Joanie's, came back here.'

'No, we drove out to the flats.'

'Blooming out there. So you took a drive.'

'Watched the sunset, got back here about eight thirty, nine.'

Rick glanced over when Denny came in, shook his head. 'OK then. I'd say you've had all the excitement you're going to have for tonight. I can swing by tomorrow, see what I see in the light of day. You go on back, Denny, file the report. Brody, why don't you walk me out?'

'All right.' He looked at Reece. 'I'll be back in a minute.'

They went out the front. Rick took a look up at the star-flooded sky, hooked his thumbs in his pockets. 'I'm going to lay this out for you, Brody. There's no sign that door was forced.'

'He picked the lock, had a dupe key. He's done it before. He had to be watching the house.'

'For what? To play bogeyman? If he was going to do anything, he'd have done it when he had her alone. If he existed.'

'Just wait one damn minute.'

'No, you wait one damn minute. I'm a tolerant man, Brody, but I'm not stupid. You've got a woman with a history of emotional disorder who claims she sees the same man she claimed to see kill some woman *only* she's seen. And this happens at the exact moment there's no one to verify it. There's no sign anyone's been here. Just like there was no sign anyone was killed by the river, no sign anyone broke into her apartment, or messed with her laundry. You're sleeping with her, so you want to believe her. Nothing's so alluring as a damsel in distress.'

'What crap. Total crap. Since you've got that badge, you've got a responsibility to protect and serve.'

'To protect and serve this town. I've done about all I can for Reece Gilmore. I can't waste time and manpower chasing her demons. She's a nice woman who caught a big, bad break, and she's going to have to get over it.'

'I thought better of you, Rick.'

'At this point, Brody,' Rick said wearily as he pulled open the door of his truck, 'I can say the same right back at you.' He climbed in, slammed the door. 'You care about that woman, get her some help.'

When Brody stomped back in Reece was at the stove, sautéing chicken and garlic in a skillet.

'Screw that.' Brody pulled a beer out of the refrigerator.

'Thanks for taking my side.' She shook the pan, added the vegetables. 'I didn't have to hear the conversation to know he doesn't believe me, and I've moved up from town cuckoo to town nuisance.' Her eyes stung. 'I know you believe me, and knowing that is a lifeline.'

Reece went back to Joanie's for the second half of a split shift. She walked into the kitchen in time to see Linda-Gail slam a tub of dirty dishes next to Pete.

'Uh-oh. Trouble in paradise,' Pete said out of the corner of his mouth.

'Don't mutter around me,' Linda-Gail snapped. 'I'm not deaf.'

'Going to be unemployed you keep slamming things around.'

Linda-Gail rounded on Joanie. 'I wouldn't be slamming things around if your son wasn't a liar and a cheat.'

Joanie continued to grill steak and onions. 'My boy may be a lot of things not so complimentary, but I've never known him to be either of those. Mind yourself, Linda-Gail.'

'Did he or did he not tell me he had to stay at the ranch last night helping out with a colicky mare? And was that or was that not a big, fat lie as Reuben was in here fifteen minutes ago asking me how I enjoyed the movie Lo took me to last night?'

'Could be Reuben was mistaken. Could be a lot of things.'

Linda-Gail lifted her chin. 'He said he loved me, Joanie.' Her voice cracked, just a little. 'He said he was ready to build a life with me. Men are no damn good for anything.'

She stalked out, leaving Joanie sighing. While Reece felt a tightly clenched fist in her belly. Where had Lo been last night and why had he lied about it?

'Are you going to stand there daydreaming,' Joanie demanded, 'or take over this grill? I've got office work waiting, and I've got to pay for all this damn paint.'

'Sorry.' Reece grabbed an apron, headed to the sink to wash her hands. 'The yellow paint looks good. Cheerful.'

'New and cheerful costs.'

There'd been a three-man crew painting after closing, Reece recalled, but what had those men been doing before? 'So, when did the painting start, exactly?'

'Eleven. You'd think Reuben would be too tired to flap his lips in here today after working till three in the morning.'

Casually now, Reece warned herself. Very casual. Just making conversation. 'Is that when they came in, eleven?'

'Didn't I just say so? Reuben and Brenda. Her brother Dean had something else to do, she said.'

Reece began to cook, and as she cooked she tried to imagine Reuben or Lo or Dean behind sunglasses and an orange hat, outside Brody's kitchen window.

After work, Reece snagged a ride home with Pete.

'I appreciate you taking me to Brody's.'

'Not far, no problem.'

'Pete, what do you suppose Lo was up to last night?'

'Some woman's skirt.'

'I guess if that's so, he's had his share of trouble with women. Now Reuben, you don't see him with women, at least not right and left.'

'He gets around. He's just got the sense to be discreet.' Pete slanted his gaze to Reece. 'Had himself a red-hot fling last winter with a snow bunny. Kept it quiet, but it ain't easy slipping in and out of a woman's hotel room without somebody noticing. That Brenda's got a nose for that sort of thing. Even if, as I heard, he came in through the basement entrance.'

'The hotel basement,' Reece murmured.

'Word got out altogether when they had a hell of a row.'

'What did she look like, the woman?'

'Good-looking brunette, as I recall. About ten years older than Reuben's what I heard. Called him up at the ranch for weeks after, crying, yelling. Reuben, he confessed to me one night over a few beers how the experience put him clean off married women.'

They were already turning towards Brody's. 'I guess Brenda's brother, Dean, had a hot date last night?'

'Or a poker game.' Pete clucked his tongue. 'That boy's got ten dollars in his pocket, he's going to stake himself to Texas Hold 'Em with it.' He stopped his truck in front of the cabin. 'Heard you had some doings out here.'

'I guess everyone's heard by now.'

'Don't you let it get you down, Reece.'

She turned to him. 'How come you don't think I'm crazy?'

'Hell, everybody is, to some extent or other. But you say somebody was prowling around out here, I figure there was.'

'Thanks.' She opened the door, smiled. 'Thanks, Pete.'

'Nothing to it.'

There was to her. Maybe the cops didn't believe her, but Pete did. And Brody, Linda-Gail, Joanie. She had people on her side. And another angle to pursue.

She found Brody on the back porch, drinking a Coke and reading a paperback.

He glanced up. As he was obviously pleased with what he saw, a smile flitted at the corners of his mouth. 'How'd it go today?'

'From bad to better. Pete gave me a run-down on the romantic lives of a couple of guys in town.'

'Been quite busy.'

'And then some. Lo lied to Linda-Gail about his whereabouts last night. Damn it, I like him, and my friend's in love with him. But isn't it, traditionally, the least likely who's the killer? Isn't that how it works?'

'In fiction, and in good fiction only if it makes sense. Lo plays it pretty loose with the ladies, Slim, but he doesn't choke them to death.'

'And if one threatened him in some way, pushed him until he snapped?' She crouched by Brody's chair. 'Reuben had a hot affair with a violent ending last winter. He didn't start painting at Joanie's last night until eleven. And Brenda's brother didn't show at all.'

'So you've decided on a suspect list?'

'I have to start somewhere. Fight back.'

'And, what, work your way through every man in the Fist?'

'I can cross some off. Anyone over, say, sixty-five, under twenty. Anyone with a beard or moustache, considerably over or under average height and weight. I know he might not be in the Fist—'

'Yeah, I think he is.'

'Why?'

'You didn't hear a car last night. How'd he get away?'

'Walked?'

'Maybe had a car far enough away not to be noticed. But, if this is someone from outside, he'd have to get your routine. Somebody would notice. And nobody's stayed at the hotel for more than a week since April. Some of the cabins have rented, but not for long lengths.'

'You've done some research.'

'One of my things. So, going with that reasoning, he's one of us.'

She sat down at the kitchen table with her laptop. The list came first. Along with names, she keyed in basics she knew.

William (Lo) Butler, late twenties. Knows the area well. (Could the couple by the river have come there on horseback?) Cowboy type, womaniser. Easy access to Joanie's keys. Violent streak when riled, as demonstrated at Clancy's.

It seemed so cold, she thought. She continued with Reuben.

Early to mid-thirties, she supposed. *Employed at Circle K Guest Ranch. Good with his hands. Pick-up—with gun rack. In town at least once a week. Previous affair (possibly victim).*

She continued on, listing names, information, then stopped with a twinge of guilt as she thought of Doc Wallace. He hit the top of her age barrier, but he was robust. He hiked, fished and was welcome everywhere. And wouldn't a man who healed know how to kill?

Then there was Mac Drubber, Dean, Liquor Store Jeff, the stalwart sheriff, accommodating Lynt, and more. The idea of listing them all, men she knew, made her feel a little ill.

Across the lake, Lo knocked on Linda-Gail's door.

When it opened, he held out a single pink rose and said, 'Hey, baby.'

Linda-Gail fisted a hand on her hip. 'What do you want?'

'You.' He made a grab for her with his free hand, but she stepped back and gave the door a boot that nearly slammed it. He caught it on the shoulder, butted it open again. 'Damn, what's the problem?'

'I don't take flowers from liars. So get your boots walking.'

'What the hell are you talking about?' This time he kicked the door when she swung it. 'Cut that out. I put in fourteen hours today so I could get tonight off and see you.'

'Is that so? Seems unfair when you had to work extra last night, too. With a colicky horse.' She saw his wince, and her eyes narrowed. 'You lying son of a bitch. You may have been rolling in the hay, but it wasn't with any damn horse.'

'It wasn't like that. Just hold on.'

'How could you lie to me like that?' She swung on her heel. 'I told you I wouldn't be one of the herd for you, Lo.'

'You're not. You couldn't be. Hell, you never were. Linda-Gail. Honey. It's not anything like what you think.'

'Then what is it, Lo? You didn't lie to me?'

He shoved back his hat. 'Well, yeah, I did, but—'

'Get out.'

He tossed the rose, then his hat, aside. 'I'm not leaving like this. Yeah, I lied, but I had a good reason to.'

'Oh? What's her name?'

Frustration hardened on his face into cold anger. 'If I'm ready to move on, I break it off. I don't two-time anyone. Why would I start with you when you're the one who matters?'

'I don't know.' Her eyes filled. 'I wish I did.'

'I wasn't with another woman, Linda-Gail. I swear it. If you love me, you need to trust me on this one thing.'

'Trust gets earned, William.' Furious with them, she dashed the tears away. 'Tell me where you were.'

'I can't. Not yet. I had something I needed to do. I'll tell you Saturday night.'

She sniffled. 'What's Saturday night got to do with it?'

'I can't tell you that, either, but I want a Saturday night date with you.' He smiled, slow and utterly charming. 'I love you, Linda-Gail. It's getting so I like saying it.'

Getting up early every day changed Brody's perspective. He saw more sunrises, and some of them were worth the trouble of prising his eyes open. He got more work done. In his office now, with coffee, he went to his desk. Picking up the thumb drive Reece had given him, he booted up. There were two documents, one headed CB, the other LIST.

'Cookbook thing,' he mumbled, and opened that first, started reading the text she had headed as intro. 'Not bad,' he decided. She'd woven in little bits about time, equipment, lifestyles. Kept it all light, accessible.

After the introduction, she'd included a basic summary of the tone of the book, then recipes. Topping each were chef's hats, from one to four. Degree of difficulty, he noted. 'Clever girl, aren't you, Slim?'

He considered for a moment, then composed a quick email to his agent. And attached Reece's file.

He closed it, opened her list. He edited in some comments of his own. She couldn't have known, for instance, that Deputy Denny had got his heart broken by a girl who'd worked as a maid at the hotel who'd strung him along for six months, then blown out of town with a biker the previous autumn.

He copied the updated file, and the cookbook data to his machine. It was still shy of eight in the morning.

Nothing left to do but go to work.

He broke at eleven, when his phone rang and his agent asked if he had time to talk. 'Yeah, I got a few minutes. What did you think?'

He wandered into Joanie's, leaned on the counter. Reece had her hair bundled up, and the heat from the grill had her face flushed. She looked soft, he thought.

'You can be among the first to sample our new and experimental paninis.'

'Paninis. At Joanie's.'

'*Et tu*, Brody? You'd think I was cooking snails and calf brains—which I can do, and deliciously.'

'I'll take the panini. I read your list.'

'Oh.' She got him the toasted sandwich and a Coke. 'What did you think?'

'Pretty thorough. I added some bits. I already found out Reuben, Lynt and Dean were in a poker game in Clancy's back room. After ten Reuben knocked off to head to Joanie's. Dean and Lynt were in it until one in the morning. Dean lost eighty bucks.'

'Well, three down.'

'My agent liked your cookbook proposal.'

'What? *What?*'

Brody took a bite of the panini. 'Damn good sandwich,' he said. 'Needs to talk to you directly.'

'But it's not ready.'

'Then why'd you give it to me?'

'I just . . . I thought, if you felt like it, you could glance over it. That's all. Give me pointers.'

'I thought it was good, so I asked my agent for her opinion. Being a bright individual, she agrees with me. Anyway, you probably want to talk to her tomorrow.'

'I'm nervous.'

'Sure.' He drank the Coke, took another bite of his panini. 'Why'd you put paninis on Joanie's menu today?'

'Because they're good, fun, fast. Add a little variety.'

'Are you going to give me another one?'

Grinning, she passed one over, and the cellphone in her pocket rang. 'Nobody calls me.' Reece dug it out. 'Hello?'

'Reece Gilmore?'

'Yes.'

'It's Serge. I made you beautiful in Jackson.'

'Oh, yes. Serge. Um, how are you?'

'Absolutely fine, and hoping you and Linda-Gail will come back to visit me. Meanwhile, I called about the picture you left.'

'The sketch? You recognised her?'

'I just hired a new shampoo girl who thinks she does. She's starting Monday. You want her information?'

'Yes. Wait!' She found a pad, a pen. 'OK.' She wrote it down, name, address, phone number. 'Thank you, Serge, thanks so much. As soon as I can possibly manage it, Linda-Gail and I are coming in for the works.'

Chapter 12

MARLIE MATTHEWS LIVED on the ground floor of a two-level wooden box of furnished apartments off Highway 89. Inside its little cement court-yard gated with wrought iron, a towheaded boy of about four was riding a red tricycle in wide, determined circles. Through an open window on the first floor came a baby's long, furious wails.

The minute they started across the courtyard, a small, wiry woman with sleek dark hair stepped through sliding glass doors. 'Help you?'

'I hope so.' Reece tried an easy, open smile. 'We're looking for Marlie Matthews.'

All it took was a crook of the woman's finger to have the small boy aiming his little bike in her direction. 'What for?'

'She may know someone we're looking for. Serge from the Hair Corral called me. I'm Reece Gilmore. This is Brody.'

'Oh, well, I'm Marlie.'

Upstairs, the baby stopped crying, and someone began to sing in crooning Spanish. 'I guess you can come in for a minute.' Marlie said. 'Rory, you stay where I can see you.'

The living room was whistle clean, though on the sparse side with its two-seater sofa and single chair. A corner had been fashioned into a play area with a little table and chair and a plastic tub of toys.

'You can go ahead and sit down,' Marlie told them.

'I left a sketch at the salon a few weeks ago,' Reece began. 'Serge said you might have recognised the woman.'

'Maybe. I can't say for certain sure. It's just that when I saw the draw-ing, I thought, what's Deena's picture doing here?'

'Deena?'

'Deena Black.'

'A friend of yours?' Brody said casually.

'Not exactly. She used to live upstairs where Lupe does now.'

'Used to?' Brody repeated.

'Yeah, she left. A month or so ago.'

'Moved out?' Reece asked.

'Sort of. She took her clothes, but left some kitchen stuff, magazines, that kind of thing. Said she didn't want it, just junk anyhow.'

'She told you that?'

'Me? No.' Marlie thinned her lips. 'We weren't actually on what you'd call speaking terms by that time. But she left a note for the super, took her clothes, got on her bike and blew.'

'Bike?' Brody repeated.

'She drove a Harley. Fitted her, I guess, 'cause she brought a lot of biker types home while she lived here. Worked in a bar called the Rendezvous. Deena used to tell me, when we were still talking, that I'd make money there.'

'She lived alone?' Reece prodded.

'Yeah, but she had *company* most every night until six, eight months ago. Sorry if she's a friend of yours, but that's the way it was.'

'What changed?'

'Pretty sure there was a man—a particular one. She'd light out for a day, sometimes two. Told me she had a fish on the line. He bought her stuff, new leather jacket, a necklace, lingerie. Then I guess they had a falling-out.'

'Why do you think that?'

'Well, she came roaring in here early one morning. I was getting Rory in the car to take him to preschool. She was cursing a streak. I told her to take it down. We had a round out in the parking lot. Got right up in my face, said nobody pushes her around. Nobody screws with her. And he—must've been the guy she was seeing—was going to pay. When she was done with him, she'd be moving on to better.'

'Is that the last time you saw her?' Brody asked.

'No, I guess I saw her around a couple more times. Avoided her, to tell the truth. Heard her bike a few times. Last time it was the middle of the damn night. Woke me up. Next day the super told me she'd split.' Suddenly Marlie frowned. 'Are you cops or something? She in trouble?'

'We're not cops,' Reece replied. 'But I think there may have been trouble. Do you know if the super's home?'

'He mostly is.'

He was. Jacob Mecklanburg was a tall, lean seventy with a dapper white moustache. His apartment was crammed with books.

'Deena Black. High maintenance,' he said with a shake of his head. 'Not a happy woman, the sort that blames everyone else for the fact her life isn't what she imagined it would be.'

Reece took the sketch from her bag. 'Is this Deena?'

Mecklanburg studied the sketch. 'Strong resemblance. I'd say it was her, or a close relation. Why are you looking for her?'

'She's missing,' Brody said before Reece could speak. 'Would she have been seeing someone the last several months?'

'I believe so. But she stopped . . . entertaining here oh, some time before the holidays last year.'

'Did you ever see him, the man she was involved with?'

Mecklanburg paused a moment in thought. 'I'd have to say Deena went out to meet him. As far as I know, he never came round here.'

Reece didn't know what she was expecting. The music was harsh, gritty rock that pumped out over the stage, where a woman with purple hair wore a red G-string and platform heels. Smoke curled blue over a stage-side table where a couple of hefty guys with generously tattooed arms sucked down bottled beer.

There were a lot of tables but only a few of them were occupied. Since it seemed the thing to do, Reece sat at the bar and said nothing while Brody ordered them Coors on draught.

The bartender had a russet-coloured moustache that hung to either side of his chin. And a head as bald as a peeled melon. 'Seen Deena lately?' Brady asked him.

The man swiped at spilt foam with his rag. 'Nope.'

'Quit?'

'Musta. Stopped showing up.'

'When?'

'While back. Whatsit to ya?'

'She's my sister.' Reece sent out a big smile. 'Well, half-sister. We're on our way to Vegas, and I thought we could hook up with her for a day or two.' She glanced at Brody and noted he'd simply lifted that single eyebrow in an expression she recognised as surprised amusement. 'We went by her place, and they said this is where she worked. Just wanted to say hey, you know?'

'Can't help you.'

'Oh well.' Reece picked up her beer, frowned at it. 'It's not like we're tight or anything. I just figured since we were so close and all we'd touch base with her. Maybe somebody knows where she went.'

'Didn't tell me. Left me short a dancer.'

'Typical.' Reece shrugged. 'I guess we wasted our time,' she said to Brody. 'Maybe she took off with that guy she was seeing.'

There was a snort from the waitress as she dumped a tray of glasses and bottles. 'Not likely.'

'Sorry?'

'Had a bust-up. Big, bad one. You remember, Joe?'

The bartender shrugged.

Reece rolled her eyes. 'But she made out this was serious. What the hell was his name?'

'Never told me,' the waitress replied. 'Two beers and bumps, Joe. Bud and the house whiskey.'

Reece bided her time as the waitress gathered the order, clipped over to the table nearest the stage. She came back with another tray of empties.

Reece tried a smile. 'Couldn't have been that serious then.'

'Huh?'

'Deena and this guy. Guess it wasn't much of anything.'

'Got to be, you ask me. Her side, anyway.'

'Really?' Reece took a small sip of beer. 'Deena liked to bag 'em, but she wasn't into tagging 'em.'

With a grin, the waitress leaned over the bar, pulled out a pack of Virginia Slims. 'Good one. Joe, I'm taking a break.'

'I'm Reece.' She offered a smile again. 'Nice to meet you. Maybe Deena mentioned me.'

'No, not that I remember. I'm Jade.' She pulled a matchbook out of the pocket of her abbreviated shorts, struck flame. 'Said this guy had some class. Don't see how, since she met him in here.'

'Oh.' Reece struggled to keep her voice casual. 'You saw him then.'

'Might've. Wasn't a regular, 'cause she'da pointed him out when he came back. Did buy her stuff though. Showed off this necklace. Said it was eighteen-carat gold. Had a moon on it, said it was like mother-of-pearl, and that the sparkles in the chain were real diamonds.'

'Diamonds? No joke.'

'Probably weren't, but she said they were. She took to wearing it all the time, said there was more where that came from. He called her his dark side of the moon, she said.'

'Maybe he knows where she is. Do you think someone else who works here might know him? Maybe one of the other dancers'

'Deena wasn't one to share, if you get me. Wasn't a biker.'

'Oh?'

'She said it was time she got one who had a straight job. They busted up, then she took off. Greener pastures, I expect.'

'I guess you're right.'

Brody didn't speak until they were back in his car. 'Here's a whole new side to you, Slim. You can sit in a titty bar and lie with absolute believability.'

'It just seemed the most direct route. I don't know if it did any good though.'

'Sure it did. All information points to her disappearance, which coordinates with what you saw by the river. She was involved with a man in deep enough to spend money on her. They broke up, and she pushed. He pushed back—and pushed back too hard.'

'She may have been after what she was after, but she didn't deserve to die that way. I think—' Abruptly she pulled up short. 'Is that Lo? Is that Lo's truck, Brody?'

He looked round just in time to see the back of a black pick-up turn a corner. 'I don't know. Didn't see enough of it.'

'I think it was Lo. Why would he be in Jackson?'

'People come to Jackson for a lot of reasons. It doesn't mean he followed us, Slim. It'd be a hell of a trick tailing us on the stretch of road from the Fist. Are you sure it was him?'

'Not absolutely.' And there was nothing she could do about it. 'So, what now? How many jewellery stores in Jackson?'

'I'm afraid we're going to find out.'

Too many, was Brody's opinion after the first hour. He'd never understood the need for people to hang metal and stone all over their bodies. He was, however, relieved that the back-of-his-mind fear that Reece would surrender to the need to *browse* wasn't realised. His respect was such that he stopped along their walking route, pulled her up against him and kissed her enthusiastically.

'Nice. Why?'

'Because you're a sensible woman. This business could take twice as long, but we're moving on.'

'True.' She slipped her hand into his as they headed for the next shop. 'I also try to be an honest woman, so I should tell you I can't afford to buy anything. And I'm out of the habit.'

'You *were* browsing.'

'I'd rather have a set of new cookware. Anyway, this place looks like a possibility. Upscale.' Reece scanned the window. 'The real deal. If Deena was telling it straight about the eighteen carats and the diamonds.'

It was, Brody noted on entering, a bit rarefied. A woman with luxuriant auburn hair sat at a table studying sparklers on black velvet while she sipped from a thimble-sized cup. The man across from her spoke in hushed tones.

Another woman in stylish red came from behind a counter. 'Welcome to Delvechio's. Is there anything you'd like me to show you?'

'Actually, we're looking for a specific piece,' Reece began. 'A moon pendant in mother-of-pearl. Diamonds spaced along the chain.'

'We had something along those lines a few months ago. Lovely piece. It may be possible to design something similar for you.'

'You sold it?'

The woman smiled. 'I don't believe I sold it personally, but it was sold.'

'You'd have a record of the purchase?'

The smile shifted down several notches. 'Perhaps you'd like to speak with Mr Delvechio. He's with a client now.' She gestured towards the customer. 'Would you like some coffee, tea, espresso?'

Before they could answer, the redhead rose. With a light laugh she leaned over and gave Delvechio—a distinguished type with pewter hair and horn-rims—a peck on both cheeks.

'They're perfect, Marco. You knew I couldn't resist.'

'I only had to see them to think of you. Enjoy.'

'I certainly will.'

The clerk in red hurried over to scoop up the sparkles. Delvechio turned to Reece and Brody. 'A mother-of-pearl moon pendant on a gold chain, with diamond accents?'

'Yes,' Reece said, impressed. 'Exactly.'

'Very specific.'

'A woman named Deena Black had one. She's missing. We'd like to find the person who bought it for her.'

'I see,' Delvechio said. 'Are you with the police?'

'No, we're interested parties.'

'We had several pieces last year designed with moons, stars, suns, planets. Our Universe of Gems theme. They sold quite well for the holidays. I'm afraid I wouldn't be able to give you client information, not unless you're with the police and in possession of a warrant.'

'How about when it was sold, and for how much?'

Delvechio raised his eyebrows. 'I couldn't say when, with absolute certainty. A piece as you describe would have been priced at around three thousand dollars.'

'Whoever gave it to her knows what happened to her,' Reece insisted.

'If that's so, you should contact the police. I can't tell you any more under the circumstances. If you'll excuse me.'

He left them to go into the back. He went to his computer, called up data, nodded. His memory was excellent, and no less honed than his client loyalty. Picking up the phone, he made a call.

'**T**hree thousand dollars isn't chump change,' Brody commented on the drive back.

Reece continued to frown out of the window. The shadows were long as the sun eased towards the far west with the mountains holding on to every drop of fading light. 'So who on the list could spend three thousand dollars without it being noticed?'

'I'd say any one of them could have it tucked away.'

'Dark side of the moon.' Reece turned to him. 'It wants to click in my head with something. Did I see the necklace when he strangled her? I can't remember.'

'In fiction land we could go to the cops and they'd get the warrant. Unfortunately, in this world of probable cause, even if we nailed down who bought the necklace, it's no proof he gave it to her. Certainly none that he killed her.'

Logically, he was right, but Reece was growing weary of logic. 'Then what the hell are we doing, Brody?'

'Gathering information. We have more than we did yesterday. And we'll find somebody who knows something else.'

The Saturday crowd kept Reece busy while she imagined, even now, Brody picking through the Internet, gathering information on Deena Black. But knowing where and when she was born, where she went to school, if she had a criminal record wouldn't point the way to her killer.

Older men often fell for younger, inappropriate women. Reece tried to imagine Doc Wallace or Mac Drubber with a woman like Deena Black. Just as someone young, still impressionable like Denny, might fall—or someone used to getting his way, like Lo. Maybe they should bypass Sheriff Mardson—as for all she knew, really, he could be a killer—and dump all they knew in the lap of the Jackson police.

'Talking to yourself again.'

She jumped a little, glancing over. 'Probably, Linda-Gail.'

'When it's your break, can you take a look at something?'

'Sure, what?'

'This dress I ordered online. I just want your opinion.'

'All right, as soon as I—'

Joanie moved in, took over the grill. 'Make it quick.'

'Thanks, Joanie.' Linda-Gail grabbed Reece's arm and hustled her out to Joanie's office. She snagged the dress from the back of the door, then held it against her. 'What do you think?'

It was short and strapless in a tender, spring leaf green. Reece imagined when Linda-Gail filled it, it would be a knockout.

'It's great. Should be fabulous with your hair.'

'Really? Now if it doesn't fit, I'll kill myself. Saturday night date with Lo. He said to wear something wow.'

There was a jump in Reece's belly. 'Where are you going?'

'He won't say. Really secretive about it. I wish I could've got back to Jackson for touch-up, but I had to colour my hair myself.'

'It's fine. It's good. Linda-Gail—'

'It's an ultimatum night. He's got to explain why he lied to me. He knows it's on the line.'

'Linda-Gail, don't go.'

'What? What are you talking about?'

'Just wait. Don't go off with him anywhere until you know what's going on.'

'I'm going off with him to find out what's going on.' She hung the dress on the door again. 'He swore it wasn't another woman, and I believe him.'

'What if he was involved before? Seriously involved.'

'Lo? Serious?' She huffed out a laugh. 'Not a chance. He hasn't been serious about anyone ever.' Her pretty face went tight with determination. 'Not the way he is with me, and the way he's going to stay. What's got into you? I thought you liked him.'

'I do. But he wasn't honest with you. Just call me on my cell. When you get where you're going, and after he explains.'

'Come on, Reece.'

'Just do me that favour. I'll be worrying if you don't.'

'OK, fine. But I'm going to feel pretty stupid.'

At his computer, Brody was making some progress. He knew Deena Black had some slaps for soliciting, one for disturbing the peace, two for assault. The second assault had earned her three months in county. Not a sterling citizen. Still, she'd been a looker in her way. He had an ID photo now, on screen.

'The bad girl,' he said aloud. 'Who likes it that way.'

According to data he found, she had a mother in Oklahoma. There was always the possibility Deena had kept in touch, and told her the name of the man she was involved with.

So how to play it? An old friend of Deena's trying to catch up? A Wyoming cop trying to track down known associates?

Before he could make a decision, his phone rang.

The familiar voice had him relaxing. The unusual but interesting request had him considering. Ten minutes later, he was walking out of the house, then driving out of town.

He glanced at Angel Food as he passed. If this panned out, he hoped to have a resolution for Reece in a couple of hours.

Everything started now. And there would be no going back. The timing would have to be perfect, but it could be done.

The cabin was the right place for this first step, quiet and secluded. No one would come there looking for them. Just as no one had ever come there looking for Deena. He'd have hours to make certain he'd covered all the tracks. And he'd put things right again. Back again. The way they should be.

'All right, Lo, I want to know where we're going.'

'That's for me to know.'

Linda-Gail tried a narrow stare, but he didn't crack.

It wasn't the way to Jackson Hole. She'd secretly hoped he was taking her to a fancy dinner somewhere she could show off her new dress. But he hadn't gone that way. In fact—

'If you think I'm going to sit around some campfire in this dress, you're crazier than I ever gave you credit for.'

'We're not going camping. And that dress sure is a killer.' He shot her a quick, heated look. 'I hope whatever you got on under it's just as lethal.'

'You're not going to see what's under it, this keeps up.'

'Wanna bet?' He gave her a smug grin, made the next turn.

She saw where he was going now, and went to silent fume. 'You might as well turn this truck right round and take me back home.'

'If you still feel that way in ten minutes, I will.'

He pulled up at the cabin. Nerves threatened, but he steeled himself. He'd come too far to back down now.

Since Linda-Gail didn't budge, he got out, came round and opened her door. It was probably the way it should have been anyway, he decided, since he was duded up in his best suit.

'Just come on inside, honey, don't be stubborn,' he cajoled her. 'Otherwise, I'm just going to cart you in anyway.'

'Fine. I'm going to call Reece and ask her to come get me.'

'I don't think you're going to be calling anybody,' Lo muttered, and pulled her towards the cabin. 'We weren't supposed to get here this soon, but you were all fired up to leave. I wanted it to be dusk when we got here.'

'Well, it's not.' She stalked inside, pulling out her phone. Then she was too stunned to do anything but stare.

For the third time in ten minutes, Reece checked her watch. Why didn't Linda-Gail call?

Five more minutes, she vowed, and she was calling. No matter how crazy it sounded, Reece was going to demand to know her where-abouts. And she'd make sure Lo understood she knew.

'Looking at the time isn't going to make it go any faster. You're on till ten regardless.' Joanie ladled up stew from the pot. 'I'm already a wait-ress short.'

'It's just Linda-Gail said she'd call me, and she hasn't.'

'I expect she's too busy. Wheedled Saturday night off, didn't she? Her and my boy ganging up on me. Everything's sunshine, roses and moon-beams from where they're standing. Well, in here, it's stew and fried steak, so get that order up.'

'What? What did you say?'

'I said get that order up.'

'Sunshine and moonbeams. Oh, oh, God! I remember.' Reece got the order up. ' I'll be back in a minute.'

There was a table in front of the fireplace. On the table was a white cloth, on the cloth a blue vase with pink roses. There were candles and pretty dishes. On a stand beside the table in a silver bucket, rested a bottle of champagne.

And when Lo picked up a remote and pressed PLAY, Wynona Judd sang a ballad, very softly.

'What is all this?' a confused Linda-Gail asked.

'It's a Saturday night date.' Lo slipped off the shawl she wore round her shoulders. He hurried round the room lighting candles. 'I thought it would be darker, but that's OK.'

'That's OK,' she repeated, dazed. 'Lo, it's so pretty.'

The mounted head of a bighorn sheep didn't detract. Even the lamp with a bear climbing a tree forming its pole only made it all sweeter. Lo crouched to light kindling in the fireplace.

'Does your ma know about this?'

'Sure. She doesn't rent this one out much. I had to ask her to fix dinner. She wasn't too happy about it.' He rose from the hearth and turned. 'What do you think about me opening that champagne?'

And my, didn't he look handsome? she thought. All that pretty sun-streaked hair, that nice, lean body all done up in a grey suit. 'I think that'd be just fine.'

She wandered over to the table, brushed her fingertips over velvety petals. 'You bought me pink rosebuds once before.'

'Your sixteenth birthday. Been some time between deliveries.'

'I guess. I guess we needed it. You set this all up?'

'Wasn't that much. The trick was to do it on the QT.' He gave her a wink as he started on the champagne. 'Try to do anything special around here, everybody knows. Had to go clean into Jackson for those roses. Ma's the only one who knows we're here. I nearly told her the rest, but . . .'

'The rest?'

When the cork popped, he let out a little whoop of delight. 'Sounds good, doesn't it? Fancy.'

'What rest?'

'She, ah . . . You got a few things back in the bedroom. In case you wanted to stay over.'

'You went into my house, into my *things*?'

'No. Ma did. Don't get riled already.' He handed her a glass. 'Should we have a toast? To surprises, and lots of them?'

Her eyes were narrowed, but she tapped her glass to his. 'This is all beautiful, Lo, but we have issues to deal with.'

'Maybe we could relax, have some dinner, then—'

'Lo, I need to know why you lied to me. I really want to sit at that pretty table, drinking champagne and having you serve me dinner, but I can't. Not till I know.'

'I had this planned out different, but OK.' In truth, he didn't think his nerves would stay in check all through dinner. 'You have to come in the bedroom.'

'I'm not going in that bedroom with you.'

'I'm not going to try to get you naked. Linda-Gail, give me some credit, will you? Just come on in for a minute.'

She set the champagne down. 'This better be good.'

There were more candles he'd yet to light, and more flowers on the dresser. A single rose lay on the pillow. Her heart so yearned that she had to harden it.

'It's pretty and it's romantic. And it won't work, Lo.'

'That's your special rose. You need to take your rose there. Please,' he said when she didn't move. 'Do that one thing.'

On a windy sigh, she crossed over, snatched up the rose. 'There, are you . . .' As she turned, the ribbon tied to the stem swung, and what was looped through it shot sparks. 'Oh my God.'

'Now maybe you'll be quiet for a minute.' Smug, he drew the ring off the ribbon. 'I went out to buy this the evening I said I was working. I wanted to give it to you when it was special.'

Her heart was actually fluttering. 'You lied so you could go out and buy this?'

'That's right.'

'You did this, all this, for me?' She looked at the sparkle of the diamond in a gold band. 'I love it, I do. But there's a problem.'

'What? What now?'

She smiled. 'You haven't asked me yet. Not officially.'

'You're going to have to marry me, Linda-Gail, and save me from wasting my life on wild women. You do that,' he continued when she choked out a laugh, 'I'll work hard to make you happy.'

'I'll do that.' She held out her hand for the ring, 'and I'll make you happy right back.'

The minute the ring was on her finger, she jumped into his arms. When his mouth met hers, she thought she heard a car on the road outside. But she was too busy to care.

Her apron flapping round her legs, Reece flew down the street. She burst through the door of On the Trail.

'The necklace.'

Debbie turned from showing a couple of customers a selection of backpacks. 'Reece.' Her gaze registered faintly amused annoyance. 'I'll be right with you.'

'You have a necklace.'

'Excuse me,' Debbie said to the customers, 'just one minute.' With her business smile in place, she gripped Reece's arm. 'I'm busy here, Reece.'

'A sun on a gold chain. From Delvechio's in Jackson.'

'Very good, you win today's trivia contest. Now go away.'

Reece turned in, all but nose to nose. 'Who gave it to you?'

'Rick did, of course. What is *wrong* with you?'

'You're his sunlight,' Reece murmured. 'I heard him say that. That's the opposite of the dark side of the moon.'

Debbie backed up a step. 'I want you out.'

'Where is he? Where's the sheriff? Where?'

'In Moose, he has a meeting tonight.'

Sympathy welled up inside Reece. 'I'm sorry. I'm really sorry.'

As she hurried back to the diner, Reece pulled her cellphone out of her pocket. Then cursed when Brody's answering machine picked up on the fourth ring. 'Damn it. Call me back, soon as you can. I'm going to try your cell.'

But that, too, switched to voicemail.

Frustrated, she jammed the phone back in her pocket.

Brody spotted Lo's truck when he passed Joanie's cabin. He hated the fact that his first thought was that he knew the location of one of the suspects. All he could hope was in the next hour, he'd know who Reece

Angels Fall | 337

had seen by the river. He wanted it over for her.

He thought about maybe taking her away for a couple of days until the bulk of the dust settled. She'd have to give statements, answer questions. Be the centre of attention for a while. Rough on her, but she'd get through it.

And once she had, they'd have to get started on some pretty serious business of their own. He was buying that damn cabin from Joanie. Reece Gilmore was staying put. With him. He could bribe her with a set of fancy pots. The idea made him smile.

He turned onto the quiet, secluded drive, winding among the pines, and parked in front of the cabin.

Rick came out on the porch. His eyes grave, he walked down the steps. 'Thanks for coming, Brody. Let's go on inside.'

Chapter 13

BRODY WALKED INTO the kitchen at the Mardson cabin.

'Got fresh coffee,' Rick told him, and poured out a mug.

'Thanks. State cops aren't here yet?'

'On their way. Might as well go in and sit down.'

'You didn't want to get into details over the phone.'

'Touchy business.' Rick stirred in the sugar and cream Brody took in his coffee. 'I hardly know what to think.'

He led the way to the living room, sat in the wingback chair as Brody settled on the rusty red-and-grey checks of the sofa. 'I appreciate you coming out here like this, so we can keep this quiet for now.'

'No problem. I should tell you we're pretty confident we've identified the victim. Deena Black, out of Jackson.'

Rick leaned forward in his chair. 'How'd you come by that?'

'So, we were right.' Brody drank his coffee. 'We followed a tip, on the sketch, tracked her name down in Jackson.'

'Lowering to have to admit a couple of civilians got there about the same time I did.' Rick shook his head, laid his hands on his knees. 'First off, I owe Reece a big apology. I never did believe her. I've got to take the weight of that.'

'But you believe her now.'

Rick sat back, set his own coffee aside. 'I do. I did think she might've seen something when I got that wire alert on the Jane Doe. But she wouldn't identify her.'

'Was it Deena Black?'

'No, turns out it was a runaway from Tucson. They got the two men who picked her up hitching. That's something anyway.'

'So, Reece was right about that, too.'

'I'd say she was right about a lot of things. Took me out at the knees when the state boys got in touch with me.' Rick looked off. 'Lot I should've done, could've done. I asked you to come out here and talk about this, Brody, because I felt you should know first. You stuck by Reece through this.'

'She knew what she saw.' Brody's vision blurred briefly.

'Yeah, she did. Couldn't shake her off it. Damn shame.'

'She ought to be here, too.' Brody took another swallow of coffee. Fatigue was falling over him like a fog.

'She will be.'

'Give me some details before . . .' Was that his voice, slurred like a drunk's? When the room spun, a quick spurt of knowledge had him push to his feet. 'Son of a bitch.'

'Nothing else I can do.' When Brody fell, Rick looked down at him with sincere regret. 'Not a damn thing I can do but this.'

Reece called Brody's home phone and his cell half a dozen times each. It was getting dark now. She wanted to hear his voice, wanted to tell him what she knew. 'I have to go, Joanie.'

'This here's what we call the dinner rush. You're what we call the cook.'

'I can't reach Brody. It's important.' She took off her apron. 'I'm sorry. I'm really sorry. I have to find him.' She bolted out with Joanie's curses racing behind her. The sun was already behind the peaks.

She cursed herself because Brody's insistence she not drive to and from work alone now meant she had to hike to the cabin. She did the first mile at a steady jog, searching through the gloom for the light he should switch on at dusk.

He went out for some beer, she told herself. Or he was in the shower.

He was fine, wherever he was. Just fine.

She was panicking over nothing.

Sunshine and the dark side of the moon. Rick Mardson had bought both those necklaces, one for his wife, one for his lover.

He'd been having an affair with Deena. And he killed her.

She slowed, catching her breath. And ran again with her heart stumbling in her chest, finally hitting the hardpack of Brody's short drive.

His car wasn't beside hers. And the cabin was dark.

She fumbled out the key he'd given her, then had to stand with her head pressed against the door. 'Six times one is six,' she began, fighting the key into the lock. 'Six times two is twelve.' She locked the door behind her.

'Not here. But he'll be back in just a minute. Maybe he left a note. Except he never leaves notes.'

The kitchen first, she decided. She turned on lights as she went, chasing away the dark. There was an open bag of pretzels on the counter. She looked in the refrigerator, saw a supply of beer, of Cokes.

'So he went out for something else, that's all.' She grabbed the kitchen phone to try his cell again.

And heard a car pull up.

'Oh God, thank God.' She ran out of the kitchen to the front door. 'Brody.' She yanked the door open, and there was his big, burly SUV. 'Brody?' she called again. 'I need to talk to you.'

At the sound behind her, she whirled, saw the blur of a fist.

When she came to, she found her arms pinned behind her.

'Only tapped you,' Rick said. 'Quickest way, that's all.'

She struggled, a mad moment of wild panic and denial.

'You're cuffed,' he said calmly as he drove Brody's car. 'Padded your wrists good. You'll have a bruise on your jaw, but there'd have been a struggle.'

'Where's Brody? Where are you taking me?'

'You wanted to talk to Brody. I'm taking you to Brody.'

'Is he . . .?'

'He's all right. I kept a supply of those sleeping pills of yours. Gave him enough to put him out for a couple of hours. He's a friend of mine, Reece. It didn't have to be this way. I'm going to make this as quick as I can.'

He made the turn towards his cabin. 'The more you scream and kick, the more I'll hurt Brody. Is that what you want?'

'No.'

He stopped the car, got out and came round for her. 'I can hurt you, too, if I have to,' he warned her, quickstepping her to the cabin. 'It's your choice.'

He gave her a light shove inside before locking the door, turning on the light.

Brody was tied to a kitchen chair, his chin slumped on his chest.

Reece fell on her knees beside him. 'Oh God, Brody.'

'He's a little drugged is all. Should be coming out of it soon enough. When he does, we're getting this done.'

'Done?' She shoved herself round, and hated that she was on her knees in front of him. 'Do you think because you got away with killing once, you can kill both of us and no one will know?'

'You talked him into driving out this way, hiking down to where you said you saw the killing. You drugged him. Bottle's going to be in your pocket when we find you. You snapped, drugged him so he wouldn't see it coming. You shot him, then shot yourself. Your prints'll be on the gun Joanie keeps in her desk drawer, and your behaviour gives it plausibility.'

'That's just crap. I've already called the state police and told them about Deena Black.'

'No, you didn't. I'm going to take those cuffs off you. If you try to run, I'll put a bullet in Brody.'

'I won't run. Do you think I'd just leave him?'

He rose, a patient, cautious man. Taking out his key, he uncuffed her. 'You sit right there. Rub the circulation back into your wrists. Do it now.'

Her arms trembled as she rubbed her wrists. 'I said we called and reported to the state police.'

'You'd've done that, Brody would've said so when he came out here.' Going to the table, he picked up the plastic cup of water and the pill he'd set out. 'Want you to take this.'

'No.'

'It's one of yours, for anxiety. I want them to find drugs in your system. You're going to take it, Reece, or I'm going to force it down your throat.'

She took the glass, the pill.

Satisfied, he sat. 'We'll give that a few minutes. I'm sorry it's come to this, but I've got to protect my family.'

'Were you protecting them when you slept with Deena?'

His face tightened, but he nodded. 'I made a mistake. A human mistake. I love my wife, my kids. Nothing's more important. But there are needs, that's all. Two, three times a year I took care of those needs. None of it ever touched my family.'

'You took care of them with Deena Black.'

'It was supposed to be just one night. Just sex, that's all. Things a man needs but doesn't want his wife doing. One night, but I couldn't stop. For a while I guess I thought it was love. And that I could have them both.'

'The dark and the light,' Reece said.

'That's right.' He smiled. 'I gave Deena all I could. She kept wanting more. She wanted me to leave Debbie, leave my kids. I was never going to do that. We had a terrible fight, and you could say I woke up from a long, dark dream.'

'But she wouldn't let you break it off.' Wake up, Brody, she thought desperately. Wake up and tell me what to do.

'She wanted ten thousand or she'd tell my wife. She said I'd better find it. How you feeling? Calmer?'

'I saw you, by the river. I saw you kill her.'

'I was just going to reason with her. I used to bring her here when I was in that long, dark dream. But when she came again, I couldn't talk to her here. Maybe you should have two pills.'

'You took her down to the river.'

'Wanted to walk, that's all. Never planned it. I told her maybe I could finance her, if she left Wyoming. Said she wasn't settling for crumbs. Wanted the whole cake. I could take it out of the money we had for the kids. I don't know why I told her we'd put money by for our kids, for their college. She wanted it. Not ten now, she said, but twenty-five, or I'd end up with nothing.

'I called her a whore, because that's what she was. And she came at me. When I pushed her down, she came at me again, screaming. She was going to tell Debbie every dirty little thing we'd ever done. I couldn't even hear her any more. It was like wasps buzzing in my head. But my hands were round her throat, and I kept squeezing, squeezing, until the buzzing stopped.'

'You didn't have any choice.' Reece's voice was absolutely calm. 'She pushed you to it. She attacked you, threatened you. You had to protect yourself, your family.'

'Yes, I did. She wasn't even real. She was only a dream.'

'I understand. If I'd understood all this before, I'd have let it go.'

'Guess one of those pills was enough, after all. Now, move away from him. It's time I woke him up.'

'If you do this, you don't deserve your wife and children.'

'Once it's done, they'll never have to know.' He crossed to her, grabbed the collar of her shirt and dragged her away from Brody.

As he turned back, Brody pumped his legs, rising up, chair and all. He swung his body hard into Rick's and sent them both sprawling. 'Run!' he shouted at Reece. 'Run.'

She ran, terrified and blind, following the order as if a switch had been flicked inside her. Spitting out the pill she'd cheeked, she yanked open the front door. She heard the crash, the curses, the crack of wood as she flew outside.

And she ran with a scream shrieking in her head when she heard the gunshot.

'**D**id you hear that?' Linda-Gail pushed up on her elbow in bed. 'I heard a shot.' She poked Lo in the side. 'I heard somebody shooting.'

'Now who'd think you'd ever hear somebody shooting in the back-woods of Wyoming?' He pulled her back down.

'No . . . Did you hear *that*? Is that someone shouting?'

'I don't hear anything but my own heart begging yours for a little more sugar. Now come on, honey, let's—' Lo broke off at the crash out-side the cabin. 'Stay right here.'

He strode buck naked out of the bedroom. When Reece burst in, he could only cross his hands over his privates.

'He's got Brody. He's got Brody. He's going to kill him.'

'What, what? What?'

'Help. You have to help.'

'Reece?' Linda-Gail came out, a sheet wrapped around herself.

No time, Reece thought. Brody could already be dying. She spotted the rifle in a display case. 'Is that loaded?'

'That's my granddaddy's Henry rifle. Just a damn minute,' Lo began, but Reece rushed to the case. She found it locked, spun, grabbed the bear pole lamp and shattered the glass.

'Call for help. Call the state police!' Reece yanked the rifle out. Leaving them gaping, she streaked for the door.

Reece prayed the rifle was loaded. That she could figure out how to work it. That she wouldn't have to.

But she wouldn't lie helpless this time, while someone she loved was taken from her. Not ever again.

She heard Rick shouting her name, and forced back the tears. Brody hadn't stopped him. Circle round, she decided. She could do that. He wouldn't expect her to come back to fight.

'No place I can't find you,' Rick shouted. 'This is my land, I can track you as easy as walk down the street in the Fist. You want me to finish Brody now? Want a bullet in his head while you hide like you did back in Boston? Think you can live through that again?'

In front of the cabin, he dragged a bleeding Brody to his knees. And pressed the gun to his temple. 'Call her back.'

'No.' Brody's heart squeezed as the barrel pressed hard against his temple. 'Think about it, Rick. Is that what you'd do if it was your woman's life on the line? She's it for me, so pull the trigger if you have to. But that's your service revolver you're holding, not Joanie's gun.'

'I'll make it work. You call her back. Now.'

'You hear me, Reece?' Brody shouted. 'Keep running.'

Rick kicked him down on the arm where a bullet was lodged. 'I've got no choice,' he said, but now his face ran with sweat. 'I'm sorry.' He lifted the gun.

Struggling not to shake, Reece brought the rifle to her shoulder. She sucked in a breath and pulled the trigger.

It sounded like a bomb. As the recoil slammed into her, she fell, landing flat on her back. The shot from the revolver flew over her head. When she scrambled up, she saw Brody and Rick struggling on the ground, the gun gripped in each of their hands.

'Stop it.' She rushed forward. 'Stop it. Stop it.' Pressed the barrel of the rifle to Rick's head. 'Stop it.'

'Hold on, Slim,' Brody panted out. He shifted to get a better grip on the gun. Rick rolled into Reece, knocking her down as he yanked it clear. As he turned it towards his own temple, Brody ploughed his fist into Rick's face.

'It won't be that easy,' he told him, and crawled over to retrieve the gun that had fallen out of Rick's hands. 'Point that thing somewhere else,' he told Reece.

Lo and Linda-Gail, in jeans and a trailing sheet, rushed over. 'What in the hell is going on?' Lo demanded. 'Brody, you shot?'

'Yeah.' Brody pressed a hand to his arm, studied the palm that came away wet and red before he looked up at Reece. 'Something else we've got in common now.'

Rick covered his face with his hands and wept.

At dawn, Reece helped Brody out of the car. 'You could've stayed in the hospital for the day. A couple of days.'

'Did you see that nurse? She had a face like a bulldog. Scary.'

'Then you're going to do what you're told. You can have the bed or the sofa.'

'Where will you be?'

'In the kitchen. You're not having coffee.'

'Slim, I may just be off coffee for life.'

Her lips trembled, but she firmed them. 'I'm making you some tea, and some soft scrambled eggs. Bed or couch?'

'I want to sit in the kitchen and watch you cook for me. It'll take my mind off my pain.'

'You wouldn't have pain if you'd take the drugs.'

'I think I'm off drugs for life, too.' Brody let out a long breath when she eased him into a chair at the table. 'Hell of a night. Reece?' he said when she kept her back turned.

'Yeah.' She put on water for tea, got out a skillet.

'You figured it out before I did. I'm the mystery writer, but the cook figured it out first. I walked right into it.' He'd never forget, never, swimming through the drugs and hearing her voice, that marrow-deep terror. 'My walking into it might've got you killed.'

'You walked into it, Brody, because he was your friend.'

She got out the butter, sliced off a hunk for the skillet. She broke eggs, whisked them with a little fresh dill and pepper.

'If he'd managed to scare you off, Slim, he'd have got away with it.'

'If you hadn't believed me, that probably would have happened.' She set his plate of eggs in front of him. Then touched his face. 'I'd have gone under without you, Brody. I'd have gone under if he'd killed you. So'—she bent down, touched her lips to his—'thanks for staying alive. Eat your eggs.'

She turned to finish making his tea.

'One question. Why don't you push?'

'Push what?'

'Me. We've just been through a near-death experience together; you probably heard me say something about being ready to die for you. But you don't push.'

'I don't want what I have to push out of you, so this is fine.' She set his tea on the table, then frowned at the knock on the front door. 'Already. We're going to have a lot of visitors.'

'No, I need to get that.' He grabbed her hand before she could turn from the table. 'I'm expecting something.'

'You're supposed to rest.'

'I can walk to my own damn door. And drink that prissy tea yourself. I'll wash down the eggs with a Coke.'

She shook her head as he walked out, but decided to indulge him. Taking down a glass, she filled it with ice, got a Coke.

He came back carrying a load of tulips in the cradle of his good arm. 'You never said what colour, so I got all of them.'

'Wow.'

'Favourite flower, right? You want them or not?'

'I certainly do.' Her smile was luminous as she took them, as she buried her face in them. 'They're so pretty and simple and sweet. Like a rainbow after a really bad storm.'

'Hell of a storm, Slim. I'd say you deserve a rainbow.'

'We both do.' She lifted her head to grin at him. 'So, are you asking me to go steady?'

When he said nothing, her heart began a slow, steady thud.

'I'm going to be buying the cabin,' he told her.

'You are?'

'As soon as I talk Joanie into it. I'm going to add on to it some. Office, deck. I see two chairs on that deck. I see tulips outside—spring, right?'

'They would be.'

'You can cook at the diner, run your own kitchen, write cook-books—whatever suits you. But you're going to have to stay, and sooner or later, we're going to make it legal.'

'Are we?'

'You love me or not?'

'Yes. Yes, I do.'

'I love you right back. How about that?'

With two quick whooshes, her breath came in and out. 'How about that?'

He curled a hand round the back of her neck, bringing her towards him, taking her lips with his as the tulips glowed between them. 'I'm where I want to be. Are you?'

'Exactly where.' Everything inside her settled when she looked into his eyes. 'Exactly where I want to be.'

'So. Want to sit on the deck with me one of these days? Look out at the lake, see the mountains swimming in it?'

'I really do, Brody.' She pressed her cheek to his. 'I really do.'

'We're going to make that happen, you and me.' He drew back. 'For right now, why don't you do something about those flowers? Then get another fork. We ought to share these eggs.'

So the morning bloomed bright with hints of summer that would stretch through to fall. And they sat at the kitchen table, a vase of rain-bow tulips on the counter, eating scrambled eggs that had gone cold.

Nora Roberts

Born into a family of readers, American novelist Nora Roberts has never known a time that she wasn't devouring stories or making them up. With dozens of best sellers under her belt, she is now one of today's most popular authors, but how long did it take her to get her first novel, *Irish Thoroughbred*, published? 'It took me about a year and a half, and that's a relatively short time—although it doesn't seem like it when you're waiting to hear. But when the new romance publisher, Silhouette, opened in 1980, looking for new American writers, I was right there.'

Since those early days, Nora has achieved enormous success, becoming the first author ever to be chosen for the Romance Writers of America's Hall of Fame and the recipient of almost every award given in recognition of excellence in romance writing. However, she also enjoys writing mysteries, or a blend of both genres, and, in addition, she writes futuristic novels about police work under the pen name J. D. Robb. She has been known to complete six or more books in a year, so what gives her the inspiration to write so much?

'I don't count on inspiration. I think it's overrated. Wait for it and you can be waiting a *long* time. I believe in storytelling, in being driven to tell the story. I really love the process of writing and, so far, I don't have a problem with coming up with ideas. I also have a fast pace, a lot of discipline. If you add those three things together, you can produce a lot of books.' Has she ever doubted herself or her talent? 'You always have doubts. I think a complacent writer can easily become a sloppy one. I never know how the book I'm working on will turn out, because I've never written that book before. So I worry over each one.'

Early in her career, as the divorced mother of two young sons, Jason and Dan, Nora Roberts worked her writing in between the children's pre-school needs, and then, when they were both in full-time education, she moulded her schedule around their weekly timetables, as well as settling down to her typewriter in the evenings after they were in bed, and during weekends. Even now, with her sons grown up and no longer living at home, she still keeps up her prolific output—the only difference is that these days she's using a laptop to draft and redraft her books.

Nora has lived on the same hilltop in western Maryland for more than thirty years—and it's a haven she loves. When she first arrived there, alone with her children, she knew at once that she'd found the perfect spot. 'I realised I was home,' she explains. 'Sometimes you just recognise it.'

Since she began writing her stories down in notebooks twenty-six years ago, Nora's career has taken her all over the world, but she always returns to that hilltop to imagine and create her novels. It was there, shortly after her writing career started to take off, that she hired a local carpenter to build some shelves in her bedroom. In the manner of all good stories, the carpenter, Bruce Wilder, later became her second husband in 1985. 'He came and just never left,' Nora jokes. In fact, she turned down his marriage proposals several times, before slowly allowing him into her life.

Nora Roberts is proud of her success and the genre that has made her rich and famous. She feels that her novels are so popular because they stir the emotions of readers, especially women, and let them celebrate falling in love again. 'The romance novel at its core celebrates that rush of emotions you have when you are falling in love, and it's a lovely thing to relive those feelings through a book.'

With such a busy and varied writing schedule, it seems hard to believe that Nora still finds time to enjoy books by other authors. 'I don't know how anyone can write if they don't love to read. Books have always been an important part of my life. I still read right across the board. My all-time fave is Mary Stewart. I just love her work. I read all the books by my pals in romance. And I read mystery, horror, science fiction, and so on.'

Finally, as the author of more than 100 *New York Times* best sellers, and with over 280 million copies of her books in print, does Nora ever have any thoughts of closing her laptop for the last time and retiring? 'No, I'm not planning to retire. What would I retire from? A lot of people say they're going to retire and write a book. I'm already there!'

Anne Jenkins

Frangipani
Célestine Hitiura Vaite

If you're looking for a wise pair of ears and some good advice, then the best person to go to on the sunbaked island of Tahiti is Materena Mahi. She's a champion professional cleaner, wife of Pito and mother of two handsome sons and a clever daughter, Leilani.

But right now, Leilani doesn't seem to need her mother's ears or advice. In fact, she doesn't seem to need her mother at all . . .

The day you came to me

WHEN A WOMAN doesn't collect her man's pay she gets zero francs because her man goes to the bar with his colleagues to celebrate the end of the week and you know how it is, eh? A drink for *les copains*! Then he comes home with empty pockets, but he's very happy. He tells his woman stories that don't stand straight to make her laugh, but she doesn't feel like laughing at all. She's cranky and she just wants her man to shut up. Finally he falls asleep. He wakes up with a sore head and says that he'd like some slices of roast beef and lemonade.

Well, Materena is *fiu* of all this!

She's not asking Pito to give her all his pay. She just wants a few thousand francs that's all. Just enough for food, gas, kerosene, washing powder and bits and pieces for their son. That is why it is imperative that Materena collects Pito's pay, to which she believes she's absolutely entitled. She's Pito's cook, cleaner, listener, lover and she's the mother of his son. It's not as if she does nothing all day.

Materena asks Pito if she could collect his pay with sugar in her voice and tenderness in her smile.

'Don't even think about it woman,' Pito snaps, flicking a page of last week's newspaper. He tells Materena about his colleague whose woman collects his pay, and how all the others mock him. 'Who's the man and who's the woman between you and your woman? Who's the noodle? Who wears the pants? Who wears the dress?' they taunt him. Pito doesn't want the same thing to happen to him. When you have no respect at work and the colleagues mock you both behind your back and to your face, your life is hell. You don't get invited to the bar on Friday afternoon.

On Thursday night, Materena combs her hair wild style, rubs coconut oil on her body, sprinkles perfume behind her ears and attacks Pito with caresses just as he's about to drift off to sleep. Pito opens his eyes and chuckles. And while Pito is busy satisfying Materena, she's busy thinking about collecting Pito's pay, filling her *garde manger*, painting the house, buying a new oven. The future and not just tomorrow.

Materena moans with pleasure because Pito sure knows what he's doing. She loves him so much right now. She adores him. He's the king of the sexy loving. 'Pito, I love you!'

With a grunt, his nipples harden, Pito sows his seeds.

After the romance, Materena lovingly strokes Pito's hair as he falls asleep, his head nested on Materena's chest. Materena hurries to ask Pito about his pay before he falls unconscious. 'Pito *chéri* . . . You're so wonderful . . . your muscles are so big . . . can I collect your pay?'

Pito's answer is a tired whisper. '*Non.*'

That con! Materena yells in her head. He only says *oui* when it suits him! Well, sweet water is over. Materena lifts Pito's head off her chest and plonks it on his pillow.

The following Thursday Materena (one hand around nine-month-old baby Tamatoa sitting on her hip and the other stirring the breadfruit stew) asks Pito, who's just walked into the house, about his pay.

'Are you going to leave off about that pay?' Pito growls.

'*Non!*' Materena's answer is loud and clear.

'You want the colleagues to laugh at me?' Pito professes again how he sure doesn't want the colleagues to say behind his back: 'Between Pito and his woman, who's the noodle? Who's the boss? Who slaves by the machine five days a week? Pito or his half?'

Materena, who didn't even have enough money to buy a can of tomatoes for the stew, explodes, 'Ah! It's your mates who decide these days? It's not you? It's your mates who wash your clothes, who cook your food? It's your mates who open their legs when you need?'

Pito gives Materena a cranky look and stomps out of the house.

'Pito?' Materena calls out rushing to him. 'You're not eating?'

But he's gone.

Materena and Pito have a miserable week. There's no yelling—no drama. Pito doesn't talk to Materena and he sleeps on the sofa.

Four times Materena says, 'Pito . . .' and waits for him to say a word, but he's lost his tongue.

Days pass. A week . . . Gradually things get back to normal. Pito sleeps in the bed again. He agrees with Materena that it's hot. He smiles. He rakes the leaves. Materena forgets about his pay. Materena smiles.

Then Materena finds out she's pregnant. She cries her eyes out because she's happy but at the same time she's devastated. Another child, with the pay situation still the same! Materena can't believe what's happening. *Aue, eh* . . . eh well, the baby is conceived, she tells herself. Welcome into my womb and into my life. Now, Materena decides, she will simply have to collect Pito's pay.

Materena is very nervous as she opens the office door. She's wearing her old faded brown dress. She wants to make the right impression.

'*Iaorana.*' Materena does her *air de pitié* to the young woman at the reception.

'*Iaorana.*' The woman's greeting is polite and professional. A bit abrupt too because, so Materena understands, the woman doesn't know who she is and maybe she's mistaking Materena for someone who's here to sell something to eat. So Materena reveals her identity (I'm with Pito Tehana, he works here, we live in Faa'a behind the petrol station, we have a ten-month-old son, he's with my mother today for a few hours etc., etc., etc.) and how are you today?

Minutes later Materena knows that Josephine has a *tane* and a fifteen-month-old son. She lives with her *tane's* parents. Josephine's mother-in-law is a bitch woman. Josephine's father is a postman. Josephine's mother died a long time ago, she fell out of a tree.

Finally there is a silence and Materena can explain her delicate situation. Josephine understands immediately. '*Aue, oui*, of course,' she says. 'There's food to put on the table . . . there's bills to pay. No problems.'

She gives Materena the envelope with Pito's name written on it and Pito's pay in it and asks Materena to sign her name in full in a black book—the-picking-up-pay procedure. After the procedure, Materena opens the envelope and takes Pito's pay out. Then she puts back one thousand francs. There, that should be enough for Pito to buy himself three beers at the bar tonight.

Less than two hours later Materena is in her house feeling very happy as she puts away the cans of corned beef, the packets of rice, the washing powder, and the chocolate biscuits for Pito. The family-size can of Milo that was on special and . . . what else did Materena get? Ah, mosquito coils, two cans of salmon for Pito, a litre of Faragui red wine for Pito, soap, aluminium foil, shaving cream for Pito. Materena's arms are sore from carrying the shopping bags, but she's not complaining. It hurts more walking home from the Chinese store carrying just one can. After putting away all the goodies, Materena steps back to admire her pantry stacked to the maximum. Nothing compares to a pantry that is stacked to the maximum. Materena hopes Pito is going to be very happy about the salmon, the chocolate biscuits . . . and the baby inside her belly.

At midnight, Materena is still waiting for Pito to come home.

He's absent the whole weekend and by Wednesday he's still missing. To explain things to the relatives who ask where Pito is hiding, Materena invents a story about Pito looking after his sick mother. Six relatives, including Materena's mother, say, 'Ah that's nice of Pito to be with his mama when she's sick. I didn't know he was like that.'

Pito makes a brief appearance one Friday morning very early to inform Materena he's leaving her, and she can keep his sofa, but he's taking his shorts, his shirts and his thongs. Materena, half-awake, wants to shout, 'Stay! I'm pregnant and I love you! I'm never going to pick up your pay again! I swear it on top of my grandmother's grave!' But she just looks at Pito from under her eyelashes as he turns round and leaves.

She remembers herself with him in the shower and they're embracing like they're under the rain. She pushes the soap away with her foot. The last thing she needs right now is to slip on the soap and crack her head open.

She's with Pito under the frangipani tree behind the bank and he rips her sexy black underpants with his teeth.

Pito busts a wall to install a shutter so that more light and fresh air come in the bedroom. Materena passes him the nails. He doesn't know what he's doing and she tells him what she thinks. He gets cranky and yells at her. She yells back at him.

Pito is gone now, and Materena walks to the kitchen to get her broom. She starts sweeping long sad strokes.

She doesn't know what else to do.

Some women like to keep the sex of their baby in the dark until the midwife shouts, 'It's a boy!' or 'It's a girl!' Other women, like Materena, want to know right from the start if they're talking to a son or a daughter. Holding a needle attached to a thread above her bellybutton, Materena waits for the verdict. After a while the needle starts to move. Clockwise one time, in a tiny circle, a big circle, another and bigger circle. Tears fall out of Materena's eyes. It's a girl! Materena is going to have a daughter! What a responsibility! Materena isn't saying that a boy isn't a responsibility. A child, no matter the sex, is a responsibility. From the day the child is conceived till the day the child leaves home you're responsible for its wellbeing. Actually, you feel responsible until you die. Even then it's not guaranteed the children are going to stop needing you and leave you alone. A child is a gift for eternity.

Materena lovingly rubs her belly, thinking of her daughter. First she sees a little girl with plaits who looks like her when she was little. Next she sees a confident and strong woman with a degree, a good job, a driver's licence, a briefcase—a school teacher, a professor, a *somebody*.

She realises that children don't always fulfil their mother's dream but Materena will definitely aim to raise a woman who knows what she wants and makes it happen. When you're this way, it means you believe in yourself, which is not a bad way to be when you're a woman. Materena is determined her daughter will never worry that she's not good enough. She will know that she is, end of argument.

As the days go by Materena talks to her daughter in her womb. And how are you today, girl? You're comfortable? It's Mamie here talking to you . . . Materena talks about Tahiti to give her unborn baby girl a general idea of her soon-to-be home. That place is the scorching sun at midday, the heavy and still humidity before the rain. Materena describes to her the sweet smell of flowers as they are opening up early in the morning, the aroma of coffee brewing in kitchens, and fresh bread being baked at the bakery nearby. She talks about the bright colours everywhere you look; the red and orange hibiscus edges, the yellow *monettes*—'They make the gardens so pretty, little one, you're going to like them!'—the white Tiare Tahiti flowers people wear behind their ears, the right one meaning 'I'm free', the left one 'Sorry, I'm taken.'

She points out the trees planted to mark the day a child comes into the world, the day someone we love goes away, a day people will talk about in one hundred years. Frangipani, kava, mape, tamarind, lime, orange, star fruit, quenettes, the list is endless because the soil here is so fertile. You throw a seed and it grows. But the tree Materena prefers, she confides to her unborn daughter, is by far the breadfruit, because it is beautiful with its large green leaves; strong too, and what's more, it is a tree that feeds—always there for you when money is low.

'Our island is so beautiful, girl, it's paradise,' Materena gushes, listing off all the things that people come here to see—the mountains, the white-sanded beaches, rivers, waterfalls . . . 'But I've never been to these places,' she admits. 'Why? Well, because I love it so much here.'

And as she continues the baby's guided tour, Materena sees her place with new eyes herself. Faa'a PK 5—behind a petrol station, not far from the Chinese store, the church, the cemetery and the international airport. It is mismatched painted fibro-cement shacks, church bells calling out the faithful on Sunday morning, the endless narrow paths leading to relatives, quilts adorning walls, nappy cloths drying on clothes lines, and someone in the neighbourhood raking brown leaves.

Here is also women talking stories by the side of the road, barefoot children chasing chickens or flying kites, babies falling asleep at their mother's breast, men gathered outside the Chinese store counting the few cars driving past.

'It's our ways, our island,' Materena says, with a tender pat for her belly, and keeps on talking. About the weather today, what she ate this morning, who the baby's father is, what happened with him three days ago, how she met him, the two years she waited for him when he went away for military service in France, and how he never sent her a parcel, not even a postcard. She talks about the baby's family—the brother is Tamatoa, the grandmother is Loana, the other grandmother is Mama Roti, and the uncles are . . . And the aunties are . . . One by one, Materena tells her unborn daughter who is who in the family, who is nice, who is not so nice, who is dead.

When baby Tamatoa has his nap Materena talks to her unborn daughter about herself. Well, for a start she likes to broom. When she's cranky she brooms (rapidly), when she's sad she brooms (slowly), when she's lost she brooms (half rapidly and half slowly). The result is the same though. The floor is clean and Materena is happy. She's also happy when the *garde manger* is full, when she gets a little compliment about her cooking; love, respect, a bit of rain now and then.

She's sad when people and animals die, someone she loves yells at her, money is low. She likes to listen to people talk and she doesn't mind raking the leaves.

She left school at fourteen years old and has been working ever since. She's sold peanuts and lemonade at a football stadium, washed dishes in a restaurant, made sandwiches at a snackbar, where she met Pito, cleaned houses, and now she's a housewife.

She doesn't have a coconut tree in her hand that's for sure. She's not lazy. And she's very proud to have been born a woman because women are the strongest creatures on Earth. Her favourite cousin is Rita. Her favourite colour is blue. Her favourite singer is Gabilou. And she used to have a dog.

Materena keeps on talking cheerfully as she makes her son's bottle. He wakes up minutes later. 'Your brother is awake,' she says out loud, walking to his room to get him. '*Oh la la*, he's so cranky today! Can you hear him?' By the time Materena opens the door, Tamatoa, sitting upright, is yelling his head off.

'What's the matter with you today?' she asks, thinking that the whole neighbourhood must be wondering what she's doing to her baby for him to yell like this. Materena picks him up and gently pats him on the bottom. 'Good baby,' she says, and he buries his head on his mother's chest and starts to sob.

'But, *chéri*,' Materena whispers. 'It's not like you to cry like this. What's wrong?' The baby, now whimpering, lifts his beautiful sad eyes to his mother and suddenly she thinks she understands the situation.

She squeezes her baby tight. 'I forbid you to cry for him, you hear? I forbid you. I'm all that you need.' And for the first time since Pito has left, Materena bursts into tears, her head falling on her son's shoulder, her heart beating with profound sorrow.

Even if your heart feels like it is being crucified you still have to wave to relatives. Materena, on her way to visit her mother from the Chinese store, carrying a bottle of cooking oil and a crucified heart, waves to her cousin Tapeta on the other side of the road. Tapeta waves back and hurries to cross the road as fast as her big pregnant belly allows her, all the while calling out, '*Iaorana* Cousin! I need to ask you something!'

The two cousins embrace, gently tapping each other on the shoulder.

'How's baby?' asks Materena.

'Oh, *bébé* Rose is fine,' Tapeta replies, rubbing her enormous belly. 'But she is getting heavy.'

'Eh, eh,' Materena smiles, eyeing her cousin's belly, thinking, how is that baby ever going to come out?

Tapeta, mistaking Materena's smile for a smile of envy, chuckles. 'Eh! Don't you get clucky on me now! You've got to wait until Tamatoa is two years old to get pregnant again, you don't want your children to be too close. Don't do what I've done three times!'

Materena laughs a faint laugh, and she's just about to excuse herself when Tapeta takes her hand and leads her to the shade of a mango tree near the petrol station. She needs to ask something. 'I need some advice, but first I have to tell you the full story. You know I had a brother?'

'*Oui, oui*, he died before you were born.'

'Correct, five years before I was born, and you know on which island he's buried?'

Aue, Materena thinks. She knows it's an island far away but which one is it? 'Raiatea?' Materena says, hesitantly.

'Apataki!'

'Ah, *oui*! Apataki . . . I don't know why I said Raiatea.'

'Well, you forgot where my mother is from that's all. Now, I hope you remember where she's buried.'

Yes, this Materena remembers. Tapeta's mother is buried in the Faa'a cemetery, in the Mahi burial plot, underneath her husband, one grave up from Mama Jose's grave and one grave down from Papa Penu's grave. When it comes to the people buried in the Faa'a cemetery, Materena knows all the details.

Tapeta gives Materena a big smile of gratitude, her eyes getting tearier by the second, and asks, 'You know how my brother died, eh?'

Materena, hoping she's remembering correctly, tells Tapeta that her brother died in his sleep.

Tapeta confirms this with a sad nod. 'Eh, *oui*,' she sighs. 'Three months old. One day he was alive and the next . . . eh-eh, poor Mama.' Tapeta talks about how her mother carried the memory of her beautiful son in her heart right till the day she died. 'She could never love me like she loved him,' Tapeta says, her head down.

'Cousin.' Materena takes Tapeta's hand in hers. 'Don't think about stories like that when you're pregnant, it's not good.'

'I know, but bloody Mama came into my dream last night! I've been calling out to Mama for years but she never came. She just bloody ignored me. And then last night, just like that, she decides to visit me. She comes into my dream to tell me she wants to be next to her son.'

'*Aue*.' Materena has goose bumps.

'She says this to me,' Tapeta continues, shaking her head with disbelief. 'But she doesn't give me instructions. It's up to me to guess who has to be moved! Who do I dig out, eh? Mama? Private as she was? I don't think she's going to be too happy having people going through her bones. I move my brother then? But he's already been moved once.'

'Really? Your brother has already been moved?'

'Ah, you didn't know?' Tapeta informs Materena that her parents were in Makatea working in the nickel mine when her brother died, so the boy was buried there. But two years later, when Reri and Julien returned to Apataki, Reri took her son along even though it was, at the time, against the law that says you can't move a dead body for fifty years. The mama furiously dug the little coffin out in the middle of the night, all the while muttering, 'I'm not leaving my son behind.'

Years later, the husband decided to come back to Tahiti and Reri was prepared to do the same thing but he said, 'What for? We're going home to Apataki soon. Your island is my island.'

God decided otherwise.

'I understand that Mama wants to be next to her son,' Tapeta tells Materena. 'She only had him for three months when he was alive, so it's normal she wants him for hundreds of years dead. I understand.'

Silent tears roll down Materena's cheeks. Materena also understands but it doesn't mean she knows whom Tapeta should move. Ah, it's a shame Auntie Reri wasn't more specific in the dream. What about Uncle Julien?

'Have you asked your father for advice?' Materena asks.

'He's a man,' Tapeta snorts. 'You don't talk about babies to men. You talk about the gas bottle and the lawn, not babies.'

Materena sighs a long sad sigh. She would probably have laughed at Tapeta's comment if her man hadn't abandoned her with one son born and one daughter on the way. She would have said, 'Ah, you're right, cousin, men are hopeless with babies. All they know is how to make them, eh?' Materena and Tapeta would have had a good chuckle. But right now, Materena is crying.

'Cousin?' Tapeta looks at Materena closely. 'Ah well, it's a sad story, I'm sorry I told you but don't worry, I'm going to see Mama at the cemetery today and ask her to give me a few more details next time.'

One step forward

PITO HAS BEEN GONE for eighteen days now. It's time to get up and move on. To give herself strength Materena thinks about Auntie Antoinette, the mother of Rita, Materena's favourite cousin. Antoinette fell on the ground and cried her eyes out when her husband went to get the newspaper and didn't come back for days. But when Antoinette's sister, Mama George, saw him at the market with another woman (they were holding hands and kissing like crazy people) and told the whole population, Antoinette stopped crying. She shoved all of her ex-husband's things (*chemises*, shaving brush, ties, thongs, shorts etc.) into a box and left it by the side of road with a note saying, 'Free, please take.' The box was gone within seconds. She then painted the doors in her house blue, took the white curtains her ex-husband had insisted on down and replaced them with colourful curtains as her sister Teresia had told her to do years ago. Antoinette got up after her fall and moved on with her life.

Materena intends to do this, but she's not having 'father unknown' written on her daughter's birth certificate. That's the only reason Materena has to see Pito. She doesn't care if there's another woman.

Materena admits to her daughter in the womb that she's a bit worried about being a single mother. When she smells Pito's pillow her heart aches, it is a crucifix for her. But women are real strong creatures, she assures the baby, they can survive anything. So her man has abandoned her and their baby son Tamatoa, and, yes, she's heartbroken. But it doesn't mean she's going to lie on the ground for days and days. It's time to get up and march on.

The previous week Materena had been prepared to go and see Pito at his work to say sorry, and ask him to come home, kiss him and hold him tight. She got all dressed up. But a voice inside her head shouted, 'Materena, don't you dare do that! If Pito loves you he'll come back. Let him show you what he really feels for you.' To resist the temptation Materena raked the leaves. She needed to do that, there were yellow breadfruit leaves all over the place, and no dignified Tahitian would have leaves rotting away in the garden. Leaves must be raked and then burned, which is exactly what Materena did. The smoke did her good, it was like she was burning the past, moving on. After that, she planted a tamarind tree, she marked the day, the day when she got up and walked.

'Men . . . they're such *cons*,' Materena says to her daughter. But she is determined not to turn into a man-hater. Materena certainly hopes that she and Pito will remain friends. It's important for the children.

That is what she told Pito's best friend, Ati, when he came to visit yesterday after having been away for a month in the islands. He's the only person who knows that Pito has left (and for a question of pay). Ati was so cranky with Pito. When he visited her he said, 'Materena, Pito is blind, he doesn't know what he's got.' Then Ati took Materena in his arms and held her tight. A bit too tight, Materena thought.

Before Ati left, he told Materena that he was going to visit her again later on in the evening but Materena told him it was better that he didn't. She didn't want people to start talking. She had to tell the family about Pito and everything first.

Aue, Materena says to her baby. She can't keep lying to the family that Pito is looking after his sick mama. Sooner or later the relatives are going to put two and two together, smell the rat, hold meetings outside the Chinese store and whisper to each other. Materena is well aware of this. She's not Tahitian for nothing.

Oh, it's not as if her relatives are after a juicy story because they're so bored. But they want to know where they stand. They're getting a bit sick of calling out to Materena to see if Pito's mama is fine, not counting the fact that they're by now very concerned for Mama Roti.

It's time to inform the population, starting with her mother, although Materena suspects her mother already knows the situation. Loana has been round a few times lately with boxes of food. She's slept over twice.

Well, anyway, it's time to tell the truth. But first Materena is going to put Pito's Akim comics in the bin along with his toothbrush and his old things. Then she's going to move the sofa to where the wardrobe is, and move the wardrobe to where the sofa is. No need to change the curtains, they're already colourful. Materena would never have white curtains, they get dirty too easily.

But first of all, she must see Pito. Baby Tamatoa is with Loana. Materena checks herself in front of the mirror one more time. Yes, she tells herself, she looks fine . . . She looks closer into the mirror. But! She's really blossoming!

OK, off she goes.

She swirls out of the house, closes the door, and marches off ahead and . . . Is that Mama Roti under the mango tree next to the petrol station? In a coat? But *oui*! And she's talking to Mama George and Auntie Stella and a few of Materena's other aunties. No doubt they're asking her if she's feeling better. And no doubt Mama Roti is telling them that she doesn't know what they're going on about.

Oh la la, Materena is just about to turn around and run back inside the house when Mama George spots her. 'Materena!'

Now Mama Roti also starts calling out to Materena, so Materena keeps on walking to face the music.

'*Iaorana*, Aunties,' Materena sings, kissing each of them.

Now the ex-mother-in-law. '*Iaorana*, Mama Roti. You're fine?'

Mama Roti does her *air de pitié* and moans that *oui*, she's fine, but yesterday she thought she was going to die. She had a forty-degree temperature, and she was so cold. Luckily her son Pito was looking after his poor dying mama. He cooked her soups, he buttered her bread, checked her temperature in the middle of the night.

'Ah, *oui*?' Materena says, thinking that Pito is so nice.

'*Oui*,' Mama Roti confirms, looking for a moment like she's about to cry. She gives more information about how Pito looked after her so tenderly . . . ah, bless the day he was conceived etc., etc. . . . 'OK, *au revoir*,' Mama Roti says suddenly to Materena's aunties in the middle of her praises for her son. Then, grabbing Materena by the shoulder, 'I need to ask you to do something for me, girl, let's go inside the house.'

Materena and Mama Roti go inside the house and sit on the sofa.

'How's Pito?' Materena asks.

'Oh, he's fine, I told him to stop worrying about me and to go back to you and his son but he said, "Mama, you gave birth to me, I'm staying here until you feel better."'

'Ah . . . and . . .' But Materena is not going to ask Mama Roti if Pito has told her about their fight. 'Why do you need to talk to me?' Materena asks.

'*Aue*,' Mama Roti moans. 'Men sometimes. Nothing in the coconut.'

Here's the reason why Mama Roti needs Materena.

There's a confrontation planned this afternoon between the Tehanas and the Piris, and Pito is getting ready to defend the honour of the family. *Aue*, Mama Roti laments, she has done all she could to stop her son from going to the confrontation. She cried, she begged, she yelled, and Pito yelled back. So Mama Roti got out of her sick bed and hopped in the truck to come to talk to Materena. She counts on Materena to stop Pito from going to the confrontation.

'Eh, girl?' she says. 'Come do your tricks on my son.'

Mama Roti cries silent tears. It's not enough for Pito that his father broke his back at a confrontation, that he couldn't play football any more. When Mama Roti met Frank Tehana he was a football star. Months later she was pregnant and her man was in hospital for an operation on his back. From that day on till the day he died, Frank complained about his back every day driving Mama Roti crazy . . . *Aue*, eh . . .

Materena joins Mama Roti in her desperation. She knows all about confrontations. A confrontation is when two enemy families meet in the dark and hit out at each other until the last man falls. A confrontation usually happens because one person from one family said something nasty (or did something nasty) to a person from the other family and before you know it cousins and uncles from both families are involved and next thing, there's a confrontation. Anyone can participate, there's no age limit. But most of the participants are young. The older men have better things to do.

Anything can happen in a confrontation. Well, firstly, you can die and, secondly, you can get paralysed for life. And while the men are at war, the women stay at home and pray. Materena gets up. 'Mama Roti, let's go and save Pito.'

Pito is pumping his muscles when Materena walks in. Eyes meet eyes . . . Materena wants to run to her man, hold him tight and kiss him hard. It's strange but when you haven't seen your man for a while he somehow improves. Materena has always found Pito handsome but today she finds him irresistible. Looking at the expression in

Pito's eyes he seems to be thinking the same about Materena too.

'Pito.' This is Mama Roti talking in between two long sighs. 'I went to get Materena like I told you.'

Pito ignores his mother to ask Materena where Tamatoa is.

'He's with Mamie.'

'Ah . . . and he's fine?' Pito says.

'He's going to have a new tooth soon, at the front.'

'Ah, *oui*!' Pito exclaims smiling. Then to his mother he says, 'Mama, can I speak to my woman in private?'

My woman? Materena thinks to herself. Does this mean reconciliation? He's not cranky with me any more?

As soon as Mama Roti leaves the living room, Pito walks to Materena and Materena walks to Pito, and next minute they're jumping on each other. In the middle of all the heat and the passion Materena urges Pito not to go to the confrontation and Pito explains that he has to because his family needs him.

'I'm your family now Pito,' Materena says. 'Me and your son . . . and I'm pregnant . . . It's a girl . . . I did the needle test.' It all rushes out.

The first time Pito found out he was going to be a father he stood still like a coconut tree and said nothing. He does the same today. That's just the way Pito reacts to this kind of news.

'Come home, eh?' continues Materena. She promises Pito to cook him chicken curry and to give him a massage if he comes now.

But their conversation is interrupted by a car tooting and men's voices calling out, 'Cousin! You're ready!'

In a flash Mama Roti comes out of her hiding spot, shrieking, 'Pito! You stay right where you are.' She holds on to him just to make sure.

Two young men come to the door, and Materena vaguely recognises them. The young men's faces are covered with green and red stripes and they are dressed in a khaki military uniform

'*Iaorana*, Mama Roti,' Pito's cousins say together.

'*Iaorana* what?' By now Mama Roti is firing angry sparkles from her eyes to her nephews. She yells at them that they look stupid with all that war paint on their face. 'You've got nothing else better to do, eh?' With giant strides she's at the door, grabbing one of her nephews by the hair. 'Mama Roti *aita* . . .' he shouts. She grabs the other nephew by the hair. 'Pito . . . control your mama,' the nephew shrieks. Pito heads for the door but not before his mama catches him. The more Pito tries to unlock himself from his mother's mad embrace the tighter Mama Roti holds onto her son. In the end the cousins come to Pito's rescue. It's three against one. Mama Roti has zero chance.

'Materena!' Mama Roti shouts as Pito slips between her fingers. 'Help me!' But Materena is still immobile like a statue. She's thinking.

She hears the car driving away and Mama Roti's angry yell, 'Pito! If you get paralysed, don't you come running crying to me!'

After a while Mama Roti stomps inside the house and gives Materena a cranky look. 'I didn't see you try to stop my son,' she says. 'If my son comes back in a wheelchair, you better look after him . . . Eh, well, I don't know what you're going to do but I'm going to pray.'

Materena nods and sets off to the nearest gendarmerie without a word. When you can't talk people you love out of doing stupid things you've got to swallow your pride and appeal to the gendarmes for help because praying is not enough. Before she knows it, she's standing and smiling at the front desk where a young gendarme is typing a letter.

He lifts his head and, beaming with delight, asks her how he can be of assistance. Materena quickly realises she's dealing with a gendarme who's new to Tahiti. He doesn't have that look gendarmes who are not new to Tahiti have (frown and cranky eyes). But then again Materena understands how extremely rare it is to see Tahitians walk into the gendarmerie office of their own free will—what's more, relaxed and smiling. Tahitians are usually dragged in kicking and cursing by French people. The young gendarme must be relieved to be dealing with a smiling Tahitian. Still smiling, he waits for Materena to let him know how he can be of assistance and so she tells him the whole story about the confrontation.

The gendarme, smiling a bit less, asks Materena if she knows what kind of weapons the fighters would be using. Any guns?

'Non,' Materena reassures the gendarme. 'In Tahiti people only use thick pieces of wood and machetes to fight. They don't shoot each other. They just hit each other's limbs.'

The gendarme thanks Materena for the information and promises to look into the matter. A very proud Materena walks out of the gendarmerie. She can't believe her audacity! Her courage! The warriors are going to be surprised to see the gendarmes. They'll run all over the place like chickens without a head.

That's what happened all right, so Pito informs Materena next morning as he walks into the house with his haggard face and puffy eyes, casually picking up his son as if he's only been away for ten minutes.

Yesterday, he explains, right in the middle of the confrontation, gendarmes crept from behind the bushes yelling, and surprised the warriors with batonettes and tear gas. All the warriors ran back to their vehicles of transportation (cars, bicycles, trucks, vespas) except for

Pito. He was still in shock over the news Materena had told him. That he was going to be a father again and the baby was a girl. A girl! What was he going to do with a daughter?

So he stood still and the gendarmes grabbed him and shoved him in the police wagon, direction the police station, where he spent the night in a stinky prison cell, sleeping on a concrete floor. But all is OK, Pito goes on, the gendarmes didn't take his fingerprints so he doesn't have a police record. He's not a criminal, and he's not going to lose his job.

Anyway, Pito was released half an hour ago and he caught the truck straight to Faa'a. Materena, relieved to see him in one piece, cooks her man an omelette.

A written contract

THE NEWSPAPER IS ON the kitchen table, opened to page seventeen. The ad is below the winning numbers of last week's *tombola*. It's in a square with a postal box address in capital letters. It's an ad for a position as a cleaner. Materena, six months pregnant, has decided to apply for it. She feels it's time to get back into the workforce.

'There's going to be a tough battle,' says Loana, who's come to help Materena write the letter. 'The whole island has seen that ad.' Meaning Materena won't be battling *just* against the relatives.

That's the problem when an ad is in the newspapers and not taped to the front window of the Chinese store. What's more, the ad is below the winning numbers of last week's *tombola*. There's going to be a tough battle all right; but then again, Materena points out to her mother, the position is not just for a cleaner, it's for a *professional* cleaner.

'Where's the difference?' asks Loana. 'A cleaner is a cleaner. She cleans, she scrubs, she mops. Professional doesn't mean anything Materena! It's just a word.'

Materena nods in agreement, but in her mind there's a big difference between a cleaner and a professional cleaner. She's not going to start an argument with her mother about the meaning of the word professional though. She didn't ask her mother over to argue. She asked her mother over to help her write the letter of application.

That's what Madame Colette Dumonnier wants. She wants a letter, a reference, an interview. She wants a professional cleaner for two years, and there will be a contract.

This is highly unusual. Most French women don't have contracts with their cleaner. They hire and fire as they wish. And cleaners don't mind a loose agreement. They're free to walk out of the door the day the boss starts to be too bitchy, the day they decide they're *fiu* of cleaning houses, and anyway they prefer to clean hotel rooms and meet tourists.

All right, back to the letter. Materena rubs her hands together. She's never written a letter in her life, but it doesn't mean she can't begin today. In her opinion, writing is like talking, except that she has to worry about spelling mistakes. Materena bought a dictionary today to make sure her letter is perfect. She also bought a felt pen and nice writing paper.

'Dear Madame Colette Dumonnier?' Materena asks.

Loana gives her approval with a sharp nod and watches her daughter write it down. 'Now, first sentence: I'm a cleaner.'

Materena grimaces and tells her mother that it is such a weak first line. Why should she tell Madame Colette she's a cleaner? If she's applying for the position as a cleaner it is because she is a cleaner, *non*? Why tell Madame Colette Dumonnier what she already knows?

'Materena,' Loana snaps. 'How many letters have you written?'

'Mamie . . .'

'*Non*, just tell me.'

'Zero?'

'I've written three letters in my life, OK?'

Oui, true, Materena thinks, but they weren't letters to a potential boss, they were letters to a potential lover. It's different. But Materena doesn't say this to her mother, it is only going to make her cranky.

'And what do you want to say in the first line?' asks Loana.

'I don't know.'

'Well, what about, How are you today?' Loana says.

Non. It doesn't sound professional.

'What about, I hope all is well with you?' suggests Loana, seeing Materena's reaction. Materena isn't happy with this suggestion either.

'My name is Materena. I'm responding to an ad in the *Journal*?'

Materena puts her pen down and thanks her mother for all her wonderful ideas. Loana gets up. 'If my ideas are so wonderful, how come you're not writing them down? *Aue*, you write your letter yourself. I've got plants to water.'

By nine o'clock that night Materena is still searching for her first line.

The first line in a letter is as important as the first line in a story. In Materena's experience as a listener, when people tell her stories, the first line can make her think, 'I can't wait to hear the rest of the story' or 'What am I going to cook for dinner tonight?' Then again, Materena knows many stories that start with a weak line only to become wonderful stories later on. You never know with stories.

But when you're writing a letter for a job you really want, you've got to instantly win the person reading it. When you're writing a letter for a job you really want you've got to be prepared to spend hours and hours on it. Materena wants that job. She can clean with her eyes closed and she doesn't mind the two-year contract. A two-year contract means she won't get fired the day she goes into labour. It means Madame Colette Dumonnier understands that when a woman has a baby, she can't work for at least two weeks because she's got to recuperate from the birth and take care of all the Tahitian Welcome into the World rituals. Madame Colette Dumonnier is also going to understand that Materena will be taking her newborn to work for a few months.

If Madame Colette Dumonnier understands all of this, Materena really doesn't mind having a two-year contract with that woman.

Pito lets Materena collect his pay these days, but when your man lets you collect his pay, he expects to eat what he likes to eat. He expects to have razor blades available when he shaves. He expects, expects, expects. And when you buy yourself a tiny little thing like a pair of cheap plastic earrings, you worry he's going to be cranky at you, he's going to ask you how much the earrings cost etc, etc. It's quite nerve-racking spoiling yourself even a little with the money your man lets you have. Well, anyway, for Materena it is. She'd like to be able to buy things without feeling guilty; lavender-scented soaps, a two-sided vinyl tablecloth reduced by fifty per cent and so forth.

Work is health, that song says. No work, eat stones.

OK, then, first line. The first line has to make Madame Colette Dumonnier exclaim, 'I don't need to interview twenty-five people, I've found my professional cleaner!' Materena thinks and thinks . . . She's thinking so much she gives herself a headache. You stupid, she tells herself as she gets up. She grabs the broom. She's got to do something with her hands to help her think clearly . . .

It is twenty to one in the morning when, finally, the line Materena has been searching for comes into her mind. 'I've been cleaning houses since I was eight years old to help my mother.' That first line, the magical line, unleashes the rest of the letter. Materena writes away furiously.

She writes that people can eat off her mother's floor. She says how the cleaning of a house always starts from the top and not the bottom, how a professional cleaner must be able to keep secrets because she's bound to see things, find things, hear things, things that don't concern anyone else but the boss. She writes that she's six months pregnant and all is well with her and the baby.

Once she's satisfied with her words Materena checks on the spelling and writes a clean copy. And another. And another. Until she's finally happy her letter is as perfect as she can possibly make it.

Next morning, Materena kisses the envelope before posting it with the words, 'OK, letter, off you go. Good luck.'

The waiting begins . . . One day, two days, four. A whole week. Each day when the postman approaches, Materena's heart starts to go *thump thump* with hope. When the postman walks past her house, Materena's heart goes *thump thump* with dejection.

By the second week Materena is sure Madame Colette Dumonnier threw her letter in the bin the second she read it because it was so stupid. She didn't care that you could eat off Materena's mother's floor.

Loana says, 'It's God's plan for you not to work at that house.'

This isn't making Materena feel any better. She's thinking, if I can't even get an interview for a cleaning job, what am I good for?

Just as Materena is about to give up on Madame Colette Dumonnier, the postman slides a letter under the door. Materena shrieks with delight, does a little dance with her son, smells the letter, waves it in the air, puts it on the kitchen table and looks at it.

What if Madame Colette Dumonnier has written to say, 'Thank you but no thank you'? *Ouh*, that is the last time Materena is applying for a job in writing! She much prefers the usual system. You stand in a line with all the applicants, you talk to the woman who wants a cleaner, you get told on the spot if you have the job or not. There's no waiting in agony. Materena has applied for a position as a cleaner three times that way and she was successful three times. For some reason French women like the look of her. They like the fact that she dresses like a cleaner. She doesn't wear short dresses and make-up. She doesn't look like a cleaner who steals rich husbands.

One of Materena's bosses went back to her country, one boss moved to another island and the other cried when Materena resigned so that she could be a full-time mother.

Materena opens the envelope, sighing with anxiety.

Inside is a two-page letter. Materena wonders what Madame Colette Dumonnier has to tell her. She glances at the messy writing, the words crossed with a line, the spelling mistakes, the exclamation marks. She reads that Madame Colette Dumonnier has been in Tahiti for six months and she still doesn't understand this island! The last time Madame Colette Dumonnier needed a plumber she had to wait four days! Many people here shouldn't be holding a driver's licence! she continues. Not many people here wear shoes! The cemeteries are rather splendid! Many people here go to church! Women here have a lot of children! Men here drink a lot! The sound of the ukulele is rather nice! The mosquitoes here are very vicious! It is very hot here!

Anyway, she also writes that Materena was the only person who responded to the ad. And since Madame Colette Dumonnier is only days from going into labour with her first child, Materena's got the job. Congratulations. The address is . . . See you on Monday.

There won't be any contract as Madame Colette Dumonnier is not sure she'll last that long in this strange island.

Materena's baby was expected to arrive in this world two weeks ago but she doesn't want to come out of her mother's belly yet. Materena isn't too worried. Some babies arrive before the due date like Tapeta's daughter Rose, some babies arrive right on time like Madame Colette's son Marc, and some babies arrive after the due date.

Loana doesn't feel too happy about her granddaughter's delayed arrival. She makes Materena promise to go and see the doctor to check all is fine with the baby. 'You don't want the baby to be strangled by the umbilical cord,' she says.

The next day Materena goes to see her doctor because a promise to her mother is sacred.

He's very busy, says the doctor's secretary. The best he can do is to see Materena in four days. Adopting a pitiful air, Materena explains how she's very worried about the umbilical cord strangling her baby.

The doctor's secretary sighs. 'Well, how about tomorrow morning at seven o'clock? Dr Marshall is very busy.'

This is more suitable for Materena. 'Eh, eh, *merci beaucoup*,' she says.

At seven o'clock in the morning precisely, on Wednesday, July 26, Materena is in the doctor's waiting room with Loana, who has Materena's suitcase for the hospital just in case there's going to be an emergency. Loana also has with her the coconut for Materena to drink from, to make the baby slide out with ease.

At twenty past nine, Dr Marshall is finally free to see Materena. He takes her pulse, listens to her heartbeat and to the baby's heartbeat, reads Materena's medical card, does some calculations. Then he looks into Materena's eyes and tells her that they are going to activate the birth.

Well, doctors know best. But she does ask her doctor if there will be a problem with the umbilical cord strangling her baby. Dr Marshall says. '*Non*, I'm not anticipating any problems.'

Loana thinks they are going to the hospital in the ambulance and when she finds out that there is no ambulance, she gets cranky. 'And how are we supposed to go to the hospital? On foot?'

After two trucks and forty stairs to the maternity ward, Materena, with her mother carrying the suitcase, rings the labour room's buzzer, and the nurse tells her to wait in the corridor. It is about eleven o'clock. To make the minutes go faster Materena and Loana talk. They talk and talk, and meanwhile the minutes turn into hours.

At two o'clock Loana says out loud, 'Eh, well, we could die in this hospital and no one would come!'

At half past two, Loana rushes over to the nurse wheeling a mother and her newborn out of the labour room. 'Nurse?' she says. 'My daughter has been here since twelve o'clock, she's here to have her birth activated and she hasn't eaten anything since this morning.'

'It's not our fault everybody decided to give birth today!' The nurse snaps. 'They all went to the same party or what?' And off she hurries.

Not long after, another nurse walks out of the labour room but this time with an empty wheelchair. Smiling, the nurse says, 'You'll be next.'

An excited Loana hurries to the telephone to call the family; Pito at work, Mama Roti at her cousin's, Cousin Rita who is looking after Tamatoa, an auntie and another auntie, and a few favourite cousins.

Little by little the relatives arrive and get comfortable on the bench and on the ground and they joke around to make the pregnant woman laugh, to give her strength before going into the labour room. But when the minutes turn into another hour, everybody gets tired of joking around. Mama Roti and her cousin get the cards out.

Another hour passes and another, and at about five thirty Pito takes off with one of his cousins to get some breadsticks and cheese for the family. 'And you, *chérie*?' Pito asks Materena. 'You want something?'

'*Oui*, please.' Materena wants a packet of Twisties, the green ones.

'The green ones?' says Pito, puzzled.

'*Oui*, the chicken flavoured ones, you see? Not the red packet.'

As soon as he disappears, a nurse walks out of the labour room with a notepad and calls out, 'Materena Mahi!'

The relatives start to cry, wishing Materena good luck. Loana runs to get Pito, hoping to catch him in time, as Materena follows the nurse into the labour room. She is made to lie down on the bed. Materena takes a deep breath, trying to distract herself by remembering all the traditional Tahitian rules about giving birth.

First rule: no shouting as you push the baby into the world, because when you shout, the baby inside gets frightened and it's not wise to be born frightened. It's enough that one second the baby is in his mama's belly and it's dark and comfortable and warm, and next minute he's in this strange place he doesn't know. And the light is hurting his eyes, he can't breathe and it's cold.

Second rule: no crying out loud as you push the baby into the world, because when you cry out loud, the baby about to be born gets all sad and it's not wise to be born sad. The baby is going to be a crying-for-no-reason baby, and then that baby is going to grow into a crying-for-no-reason person. And when you're a crying-for-no-reason person and you're a woman, life is just going to be one misery after the next. One little pain, and that's it, you'll cry your eyes out. It's much better for you to be a woman who only cries for big pains.

Third rule: no cursing and screaming words of insult as you push your baby into the world, because when you curse and scream words of insult the baby inside gets all cranky and it's not wise to be born cranky. That baby is going to be a cranky-for-no-reason baby and then that baby is going to grow into a cranky-for-no-reason person.

Materena is trying to remember all these rules while a nurse, all smiling and friendly, puts a drip into her arm. For a long while after the drip is inserted nothing happens and Materena is starting to get really bored until, at last, she gets a contraction. She's so happy! At least something is happening. The next contraction is a bit more painful but it is still comfortable. Within an hour the contractions are so painful Materena is moaning, 'Aue! When is this going to stop!'

Three times she calls out to the nurse that she is ready to push and three times the nurse says, 'You've got a long way to go yet,' and poor Materena is left all alone to deal with her suffering.

'Aue!' Materena yells. By now, Materena is in too much pain to follow the traditional Tahitian rules. She falls back on the bed moaning with a fist shoved in her mouth as another contraction comes on and goes on and on and on. Materena feels like eating her hand. Her whole body tenses, her legs tremble, until at last the contraction eases up and Materena sighs with relief, even knowing that everything is going to start up all over again in less than thirty seconds.

'She's having a baby girl,' Materena hears a woman say. 'Girls hurt their mother from the day they come into the world. It's like that.'

The curtain is suddenly pulled open, and a big mama midwife, smiling and introducing herself as Mary, walks in and closes the curtain behind her. She checks how everything is going and is very pleased to inform Materena that it is time to push. Grinding her teeth, Materena pushes and pushes but nothing is coming out.

'Push!' Mary the midwife commands.

'That's what I'm doing!' Materena growls.

She pushes and pushes, she pushes and yells her head off for twenty excruciating minutes. But still nothing comes out.

The curtain is pulled open, and what a relief for Materena to see Auntie Stella, long regarded as the best midwife on the island.

'Auntie Stella,' Materena cries. 'My baby doesn't want to come out.'

Stella kisses Materena's forehead and tells her to be strong. Then she begins her inspection and concludes that the only way for the baby to come out is for Materena to push standing up. Let gravity help. Stella frees Materena of the tube and helps her get out of bed.

At that precise moment, Pito walks in, red-eyed, with Materena's packet of Twisties.

'But!' Stella exclaims. 'You've smoked paka or what? Unbelievable! All you men are the same!' Materena is in too much pain to say anything. She feels like all her insides are going to fall out. But she can't believe Pito bought her the red packet of Twisties when she asked for the green one.

'Come here,' Stella orders Pito. 'Make yourself useful, hold her good!'

Pito puts the packet of Twisties on the bed and holds Materena good.

'Mary . . . quick, grab a pillow and put it on the floor here,' Stella goes on with her orders. And to Materena she adds, 'Next contraction, I want you to push real hard. Don't stop until I tell you, OK?'

They all wait for the next contraction as Materena begs her baby to please come out. Then it comes, and Materena pushes with all her heart and soul and her baby daughter makes her entrance into the world upside-down, with her mother's hands underneath her head in case the baby falls, but there's no need. Stella has it all under control.

Leilani Loana Rita Imelda comes into the world the week her cousin Rose is baptised and the week her older brother falls off the table and breaks his arm. She comes into the world frowning and with her eyes wide open.

Auntie Stella, relieved that all is well, laughs and says, 'Oh, but we have a thinker here. We have a professor.' Then, to Mary, 'What's the time?'

It's twenty-nine past eight precisely.

And Materena cries out with joy, 'Welcome into the world, girl!' There and then she feels that magical bond mothers feel when they see their child for the very first time.

'Eh, well, that's one very lucky baby,' Stella says as she cuts the cord.

'Look at your daughter,' Materena tells Pito. 'Look how beautiful she is.' Perhaps the paka is affecting Pito's vision but he really can't see what Materena is seeing.

Over the next few days Materena tries very hard to breastfeed her daughter, but there's a problem with her breasts. In the end, the hungry crying baby girl is offered a bottle and drinks it all in one go. After that first bottle, Leilani seals her lips real tight whenever Materena's nipple comes near her mouth.

Materena is so devastated. For her, breastfeeding is the reward that comes after the pain of the birth. Breastfeeding is what makes the mother and child get close, bond. She tells her mother that.

Loana's reply is a reprimand. 'Stop talking nonsense. It's not breast-feeding that makes a mother and her child bond. It's everyday life.'

The everyday life Tahitian style begins with the Welcome into the World rituals. So, here is Materena, accompanied by her mother, intro-ducing *bébé* Leilani to her relatives, and everyone has something *gentil* to say about Loana's granddaughter who came into the world upside-down. That she has beautiful eyes, long legs, a wide nose, the only kind of nose to have when you're a woman. Then it's off to the cemetery to introduce the little one to the dead.

After that all Materena wants to do is rest, but she catches the truck to Punauiaa instead to meet her mother-in-law so that she can intro-duce Pito's daughter to the family. And what a pain Mama Roti is! Mama Roti is hopeless at introducing newborns. Instead of talking about her newborn granddaughter, she talks about herself. 'Eh, Uncle, come and look at Pito's daughter!' Then next minute. 'Uncle, I've got to do some tests for my eyesight tomorrow. My doctor is saying I'm going blind!' Materena is so annoyed, even more annoyed to hear one of Mama Roti's cousins comment on how Leilani is so small, that *her* granddaughter was so much bigger when she was born—3.9 kilos. You don't make comparisons when a baby is being introduced to you! You just give compliments!

That day Mama Roti gives Materena a lime tree to be Leilani's tree, but Materena already chose Leilani's tree, a beautiful frangipani, to be planted after the baptism next week along with Leilani's placenta. Materena also chose Leilani's baptism robe and the godparents (Ati and his girlfriend Marieta, who left him two weeks later to marry a legionnaire).

The night before the baptism, Materena cuddles her baby all night long because Leilani is crying non-stop. It's always like that before a baptism. The baby cries because the devil is cranky at the thought of losing another soul and so he makes the baby cry. But it could be that Materena is really stressed tonight and her baby can feel it. Materena is stressed because her daughter's baptism is heading towards a night of drinking and Materena doesn't want that. Just looking at Pito and his cousins drinking and joking around is making her heart twitch in a knot. Materena doesn't mind drinking at weddings, but at baptisms, come on, where's the civilisation? Why do we have to drink every time there's something to celebrate?

Materena is so annoyed, but for her daughter's sake (it's enough that Leilani has to deal with the devil) she settles down. She wraps her baby tight in a cloth, holds her close to her heart and recites prayers. Never carry baby with its head over your shoulder looking out into darkness because the devil is lurking around. Hold baby tight with its head buried in your chest. Hold baby tight, and love your baby with all your *mana,* the power within you.

The encyclopedia

THE BATHROOM IS SCRUBBED every day in Materena's house because Materena can't stand her bathroom dirty. She's scrubbing, scrubbing really hard and wishing her twelve-year-old daughter, also scrubbing, would stop talking, but when your daughter helps you with the house-work you don't criticise. You just smile and nod, you answer her questions, or you say nothing because you don't know what to say.

'Mamie?' Leilani taps her mother's hand. 'Did you hear me?' She's waiting for her mother to explain why it doesn't snow in Tahiti, and once again, Materena will have to say that she doesn't know.

This is happening more and more these days. Let's just say that Materena can't keep up with Leilani's complicated questions. Who started the French Revolution? What's the medical term for the neck? There's a limit to what Materena knows. People can't know everything.

Aue, Materena was much more comfortable with her daughter's questions when they weren't complicated: Who invented the broom?

(A woman.) Is it true that eating charcoal makes the teeth white? (Absolutely not—brushing your teeth every day with toothpaste makes them white.) Who invented the rake? (A woman.) What time does the first star appear? (The first star appears at quarter past six.) Is God a woman or a man? (God is everything that is beautiful.)

Leilani used to say how clever her mother was, but these days Leilani doesn't say this any more. 'Girl,' Materena sighs. 'I don't know why it doesn't snow in Tahiti. Ask me about the ancestors, the old days, cleaning tricks, budgeting, who's who in the family album and at the cemetery, plants, words of wisdom Tahitian style, traditions. Don't ask me why it doesn't snow in Tahiti. Ask your teacher.'

'I do but Madame always says, "That's not what this lesson is about Leilani."' Leilani drops her scrubbing brush and stomps out of the bathroom complaining that she doesn't know anybody who can answer her questions, and that all she gets is 'Be quiet Leilani.'

Aue! Materena feels so guilty now. My poor girl, Materena thinks.

Materena finds Leilani reading yesterday's newspapers at the kitchen table. 'Girl? You want to get yourself an ice block at the Chinese store?'

'*Non*, I'm fine.'

'You're sure, *chérie*?' Materena kisses the top of Leilani's head.

'I'm just having a rest. I'll come and help you again in a minute, OK?'

'*Non*, just relax.' And with this Materena escapes to her bathroom and locks the door. Ah, what peace. Materena can sure do with a few minutes of silence.

A few minutes later. 'Mamie?' It's Leilani knocking at the door.

'*Oui*,' Materena chuckles, thinking, already?

'There's someone at the door.'

'Who is it?' Materena opens the door, scrubbing brush in hand.

'It's a woman with a briefcase. She said, "Is your mother home?"'

'Eh, *hia*.' Materena is annoyed. That woman at the door is here to sell her something like perfumes or to talk about religion, and Materena is in the mood for neither. 'Couldn't you say I was asleep?' Materena puts her scrubbing brush down, and rearranges her chignon and her *pareu*. 'People should know we're Catholics around here and that we've got no money,' she says, walking to the door. 'You only have to look at the houses.'

'Good afternoon,' Materena greets the French woman, who can't be more than twenty years old and who looks a bit like a Gipsy with her floral dress, sandals and loose hair.

'Oh, good afternoon, Madame,' the young woman says with a rather strange yet beautiful accent.

'Are you from France, girl?' Materena asks.

'*Oui*, from Marseilles. Have you been there?' the young woman asks Materena eagerly.

'Girl, I've never been out of Tahiti in my whole life,' Materena laughs.

'Where's Marseilles?' asks Leilani.

'It is in the south of France . . . I could show you on a map.'

Before Materena has the chance to tell the young woman not to worry about it and to go on with her mission, Leilani gives her consent. In a flash an encyclopedia comes out of the woman's briefcase as she explains that she always has an encyclopedia with her to show people what the encyclopedia set looks like. And it's just by chance she has volume 6 E–F with her.

'You sell encyclopedias?' Materena asks.

In one breath the young woman confirms that she is selling encyclopedias, and there's a promotion (a twenty per cent reduction). She loves encyclopedias, she's had an encyclopedia set since she was eight years old, she's on holidays in Tahiti (one of the most beautiful countries in the world), she arrived two days ago.

Ouf, that's a lot to spill in one go, Materena thinks. But how nice to say that Tahiti is one of the most beautiful countries in the world. 'Come inside the house,' Materena says. 'Let's sit at the kitchen table.' The young woman doesn't need to be asked twice. She's in the house before Materena can ask her (politely) to take her shoes off. It isn't a Tahitian custom to take your shoes off before walking into a house, but it's nice when you do, that way you don't bring dirt into the house.

Well, anyway, it's too late for Materena to tell that woman about shoes and everything. But for Leilani it isn't. 'You can't come in the house with your shoes on,' she says, her eyes widening in stupefaction. 'You're going to put dirt on Mamie's carpet.'

The young woman, her face red with embarrassment, hurries back outside. She takes her shoes off and neatly places them next to the row of thongs by the door. 'I'm very sorry,' she says. 'I've just arrived, you see. I'm not aware of this country's customs as yet.' Walking in, she adds, 'Oh, it's so lovely here.'

'It's comfortable, girl,' Materena smiles, relieved her house is very clean today. Materena's house is always clean, but today it really shines. 'Oh,' the woman exclaims, stopping right in front of the pot plant placed in the middle of the living room. 'Is this a real plant?' she asks, stroking the leaves. Before Materena can say, '*Of course it's a real plant!*' the woman enquires if it is a Tahitian custom to place a pot plant in the middle of the living room.

'Well,' Materena replies, '*oui* and *non*. In Tahiti, we believe that—'

'It's to hide the missing carpet square.' Here, Leilani has informed the visitor. And right before her mother's horrified eyes, she lifts the pot so that the visitor can see for herself, and explains that everybody does this in Tahiti. They use pot plants to hide missing carpet squares, holes in walls, anything.

'I see,' the woman nods. 'It's a very intelligent way of doing things.' She walks to the wall to admire a quilt pinned to the wall. '*Magnifique!* Whoever made that quilt is talented. This quilt is truly a piece of art.'

'My mother made that quilt when I got married,' Materena says.

'Mamie is going to be wrapped in that quilt in her coffin,' Leilani adds.

Materena gives her daughter a quick cranky look. You don't tell strangers stories that only concern the family! The woman looks to Materena. 'Is this a custom in Tahiti?'

'An old custom, girl. Not many people are wrapped in quilts when they're dead these days but I want to be wrapped in a quilt my mother made just for me because you know, once you're linked with your mother through the umbilical cord you're linked for the eternity.'

'These are such beautiful words, Madame . . .'

Materena cackles, thinking this girl has got to be the best seller she's ever met in her life. She is now looking at the framed photographs below the quilt, and Materena doesn't mind. If photographs are on the wall it means it's fine for people to look at them, you don't need permission. You only need permission to look through a photo album.

'This is my beautiful oldest son, Tamatoa, at his confirmation,' Materena tells the interested visitor. 'He's playing football at the moment with his father and uncle. And this is my youngest son, Moana, at his confirmation. He's also playing football with his father and uncle at the moment This is my husband and me when we got married six months ago . . . with our beautiful children.'

'Is it the custom to marry late in Tahiti?'

'Oh, *oui* and *non*,' replies Materena. 'In Tahiti we believe that it's unwise to marry before—'

'Men don't like to get married in Tahiti. They always give women excuses and they're lazy.'

'And this is a school award Leilani got when she was ten years old,' Materena says, ignoring Leilani's last comment. 'For a story she wrote.'

'Do you like to write?' asks the woman, smiling at Leilani.

'Oh, *oui* she loves to write!' Materena exclaims. 'She's always writing that one. She writes, she reads, she's very intelligent. All my children are intelligent, and to think that I'm just a professional cleaner.'

'Oh, you're a cleaner!'

'I am a professional cleaner,' Materena corrects. Because there *is* a difference.

'I admire professional cleaners!' The woman exclaims. 'My mother is a professional cleaner, I believe professional cleaners ought to be decorated!' Materena looks at the young woman with little eyes. What's this? she thinks. It's to make me buy an encyclopedia set?

'I admire professional cleaners too,' says Leilani. 'It's so hard to clean. Last time I helped Mamie clean Madame Colette's house, I was so tired. I had to sleep in the truck on the way home.'

'You didn't help me,' Materena hurries to add. 'When you told me you wanted to be a cleaner, I had to show you how hard cleaning is.' She explains to the French woman that it is definitely not her plan for her daughter to become a cleaner. In fact she's always pushed her daughter to get a job that has nothing to do with a broom and a scrubbing brush.

'You are a clever woman,' the encyclopedia woman says. 'May I show you the encyclopedia?'

'Sure. What's your name by the way, girl?'

'Chantal.'

'Ah, what a beautiful name. OK, then, Chantal, you and Leilani make yourself comfortable, I'm going to make us a lemonade.'

'And what is your name, Madame?' Chantal asks.

'Materena.'

'You have a beautiful name too, and,' turning to Leilani, Chantal adds, 'your name is lovely as well.'

Leilani informs the visitor that she was called after a Hawaiian ancestor, Leilani Bodie. 'She was very serious. She was a medicine woman.'

'Oh . . . well you might become a medicine woman too.'

'I don't think so. I don't like sick people.'

'We never know!' Chantal exclaims as she sits at the kitchen table.

'May I ask you a few questions?' Materena, cutting the lemons for the lemonade, hears Leilani ask. Chantal invites Leilani to ask her as many questions as she wants. She's in no hurry at all. Materena cackles. Chantal, you have no idea what you've just got yourself into.

'Why doesn't it snow in Tahiti?' Chantal repeats Leilani's question. 'That is a very intelligent question and the answer is that Tahiti is too close to the equator.' Next minute, Leilani is getting a free geography lesson.

Now Leilani would like to know what is the medical term for the neck. Easy, the French woman quickly draws a human body, and next minute, Leilani is getting a free biology lesson.

And who started the French Revolution?

Easy . . .

And do fish sleep?

On and on and on Chantal shares her knowledge with a delighted Leilani, the knowledge she insists she got after years of reading encyclopedias and other books of interest.

The main salt in the sea is the same as the salt people put on their food. Its chemical name is sodium chloride.

Plants make much of their food from water, carbon dioxide and sunlight. This process, called photosynthesis, produces oxygen.

The human body has more than six hundred muscles, which together make up more than forty per cent of the body's weight.

Fingernails grow four times as fast as toenails.

By the time Materena is signing her name at the bottom of the form binding her to thirty-six repayments for the encyclopedias, Chantal looks very drained.

She earned her commission that's for sure.

Materena's deal with the children is: read the encyclopedias and you won't have to lift a finger around the house. But Leilani is the only one who has taken up Materena's offer. You won't see Leilani with a scrubbing brush these days. She's too busy reading her encyclopedias, which she has personally covered so that they won't get dirty.

Materena is certainly pleased with her daughter's fondness for the encyclopedias but she really wishes her sons were fond of them too. So far, Tamatoa has opened one single page to see what the word *sex* had to say. He was so disappointed he shoved the book back in the bookcase. As for Moana, he makes an effort now and then to read the encyclopedia, but Materena knows it is only to make her happy.

Presently the boys are doing pumps outside, right in front of their father and Uncle Ati, comfortable in a chair with a beer in hand, and counting from one to ten. When Pito and Ati get to ten, the boys have a quick rest, enough for Papi and Uncle to take a couple of sips.

Materena peeps outside from behind the curtains and shakes her head with disapproval, but what is bothering her more now is to watch her youngest son crumple on the ground as soon as his set of ten pumps is finished. My poor baby, Materena thinks.

Moana is red in the face, sweating and suffering, not keeping up at all with his older brother who, to make matters worse, decides to clap his hands together as he lifts his body up. Tamatoa just has to show off that he's unbeatable.

Aue, Materena can't bear to watch. 'Pito!' she calls. 'I want the boys inside the house for a bit of reading.'

Pito glances to Ati and shakes his head. 'What did I tell you,' he says. 'She's obsessed with her encyclopedias.'

'Well,' Ati says. 'We've got to see beyond our noses.'

'*Merci*, Ati.' Materena smiles a sweet smile to her husband's best friend, who smiles back, winking.

'Come on boys, chop-chop, on your feet.'

'Mamie,' Tamatoa protests. 'I just want to be strong.'

'Me too,' Moana follows.

The training continues. Materena can't believe her eyes! Where's the respect for the mother! It's like I'm invisible, Materena yells in her head. Well, if it's so important for Tamatoa and Moana to be strong, they can start making their own bed, wash their own clothes, and cook.

'So you want to be strong?' Materena asks her boys the next day when they are arm wrestling at the kitchen table.

'Yeah,' Tamatoa replies, looking at his mother straight in the eye, and flattening his brother's arm on the table.

'And you?' Materena asks Moana, who's rubbing his arm.

He nods, grimacing a little.

So far, so good. Now to Materena's mission, but first here's a packet of Delta Cream biscuits to make sure the boys don't run off. They're into those biscuits in a flash, and so Materena begins. She better because the biscuits are disappearing fast and once they're gone, she'll be talking to the chairs. 'Boys, the world has changed. Women are doing lots of things they didn't do in my day, like drive trucks. So men have to change too.' Materena informs her sons that women of today are only interested in men who know how to do women's things like iron, fold clothes, sweep, make the bed, cook . . . Men who know nothing about these things can't get a woman. 'And I'm telling both of you,' says Materena in a *seriouso* voice, 'As soon as you're men, you have to look after yourselves. Mama Roti gave me a man who couldn't cook, couldn't do zero, and I'm not going to do this to my daughters-in-law.'

'Mamie.' Tamatoa is up. 'I've got things to do.'

'Tamatoa! I haven't finished!' But Tamatoa walks away because the last person he fears in this world is his mother.

Moana stays because the person he loves the most in this world is his mother. 'Mamie,' he says, taking his mother's hand. 'I'll listen to you . . . so women like when men cook?'

'Oh, *oui!*' she exclaims. 'You want me to teach you how to cook?'

'OK.'

Later, in front of the *garde manger*, Moana gets his first cooking lesson. 'A good cook,' Materena tells him, 'can cook anything with whatever is in the *garde manger*, but always make sure to have cans of tomatoes and coconut milk, onions and rice in your *garde manger*.'

And to Tamatoa, standing at the fridge snorting, Materena says, 'As for you, you can change your own bed from now on. You're going to be fourteen years old soon and I sure don't want to be changing your bed sheets by then.'

On the subject of cleaners

IN THE MAHI FAMILY cleaning is one of the best jobs to have. Cleaning houses helps you to be independent (you don't have to rely on your man's pay so much) and, what's more, you're your own boss. You walk into a house, you clean, you get out. There are no papers to sign.

The only downside is that when you're sick and you can't go to work you don't get paid. But the boss still gets her house cleaned because you've sent a cousin to replace you for the day. The boss is happy, the cousin is happy, and even you're happy because you didn't let your boss down. Your conscience is clear.

It's impossible to count on the fingers how many Mahi women are cleaners. But one thing's for sure, Materena is the champion cleaner of all. She's the only cleaner in the family who's been cleaning the same house, the house of Madame Colette Dumonnier, for over twelve years. And that is no small achievement considering that there are more women willing to clean houses than there are women willing to pay for that service.

So, that's why Materena is always the relative that young women thinking of a career as a professional cleaner go to see.

Not only does Materena know all the tricks of the cleaning trade but she also knows what makes a boss really happy, so happy that even if another cleaner came tomorrow to propose her services for thirty per cent less pay, the boss would say, 'I've already got a cleaner, thank you.'

In Materena's mind, cleaning is not just about cleaning, because anyone can clean. Not just anyone can be trusted and keep secrets, however. You see, a cleaner is bound to see things, and find things— things that she might be tempted to take, or that are so bizarre she'd want to tell the whole population about it.

With Materena, no matter how much the relatives ask her questions about her boss, the boss's family, the boss's husband, the boss's house, she only has one answer to give: 'It's not your onions.'

Other relatives aren't so discreet.

One relative, not long ago, told the whole population about how her boss was having an affair with a man she called her architect. Apparently, as soon as the boss's husband left for work, the lover appeared to pick up the boss. The boss would say to her cleaner, 'I have a meeting with my architect, I will be back at three o'clock.' But one morning the relative (who was already suspecting her boss's story) saw her boss and the architect kissing like crazy in the car, and she said to the whole population (right outside the church), 'My architect my eye! We kiss our architect in the car, eh?'

Another relative told the whole population about her boss going into hospital to have an abortion.

Another relative told the whole population about her boss writing a very mean letter to her mother.

You're never going to hear these kinds of secrets coming out of Materena's mouth about her boss. She's taking every single secret about her boss and her family to the grave. Still, she agrees that some information about the boss can be passed on to the whole population.

Like a relative passed on the information about how her boss only ate soups. Soup after soup, soup day and night. Worse than Mama George. And another relative passed on the information about how her boss hated living in Tahiti, she hated the heat, the mosquitoes, she was always begging her husband to go home where they belonged.

Another relative talked about her two bosses who were sisters. Their house was always clean and always tidy, and most of the time the sisters would ask their cleaner to join them around the piano and sing.

Now, there's no harm passing that kind of information to the whole population. But still you're never going to get any information out of Materena about her boss (and family, house etc.) because when Materena cleans, she cleans, she doesn't snoop around looking for secrets. She only does this with her children.

Materena really takes pride in her work. She's the only cleaner in the family who gets Christmas and birthday presents from her boss.

That's another reason why young women thinking of a career as a professional cleaner come to see Auntie Materena, and this is what Materena tells these young women, the future cleaners of Tahiti.

Firstly, if the young woman has only just left school, because she was too bored there, Materena tells her to forget about a career in cleaning because there's too many cleaners as it is. Go back to school, get your degree. But if the young woman has left school a long time ago and she's got a couple of children and a man who doesn't have a job, or a man who's tight with his money, well this is what Materena says:

Always start from the top and work your way down to the bottom.

Look for chances to show your boss you're more than a cleaner. For example, remind her that the food in her fridge is about to go out of date, or if you see that one of your boss's plants is not doing too well, find out why. The plant may need shade and your boss has planted it in full sun. Tell your boss about it.

Grab every single opportunity to show your boss that you're honest. Let's say you find a banknote in your boss's husband's shirt, well don't you go slipping that banknote in your wallet. Slip that banknote in an envelope instead and write a short note to explain the situation.

Always remember that your boss is just another woman and that she's got feelings. If you find a love letter in your boss's husband's trousers, don't you go showing it to your boss. Flush the love letter down the toilet instead. When Materena gets to that rule, the nieces always ask her if she has ever done this and Materena always says, 'Of course not!'

All in all . . . When it comes to being a professional cleaner, Materena is unbeatable. That is why she's always pushed her daughter to see beyond the scrubbing brush and the broom. 'Don't you dare be a cleaner like me.' Materena said this to her daughter many times, and it seems Leilani understood her mother's message.

Today she told her mother what she'd like to do when she finishes school. She'd like to be a pilot. Materena said, 'And why not? We're not living next to the airport for nothing.' But deep down Materena thinks, I hope Leilani isn't going to be a pilot. Planes are so dangerous.

Leilani would also like to be a psychiatrist. Materena said, 'Ah, that's nice.' But deep down Materena thinks, She's not going to have a lot of business in Tahiti—we talk to a favourite cousin or to the priest. Tahitians who pour their troubles out to a psychiatrist don't exist.

Leilani would also like to be a *mutoi* (she's going to see the worst in people as a cop, thinks Materena), and a *militaire* (what about the war?). Leilani wants to be so many things. Ideas keep on coming into her mind and she can't decide, unlike her younger brother Moana whose mind is set on becoming a chef.

Then Leilani asked her mother if she always wanted to be a cleaner. She was very shocked to hear her mother exclaim, 'Of course not!'

'How come you're a cleaner then?' asked Leilani, puzzled.

Materena didn't feel like replying to this question. Instead she went to get the washing off the line, and she thought about how it wasn't her plan to be scrubbing and sweeping for years and years and years.

But at least it pays the bills.

Anne Marie Javouhey is the Catholic girls' school facing the magnificent cathedral in Papeete. It's hidden behind a high concrete wall with an iron-grilled gate. Although the school looks like a prison, it is not. It is the best school in Tahiti. In this school, young girls are trained to become independent, free women, and although it costs much more than the Catholic school in Faa'a, Materena doesn't care. Her cousin Tapeta's daughter, Rose, attends Anne Marie Javouhey. The whole family is on a constant breadfruit diet so that Rose gets her chance to become somebody. That is what her mother wishes for, with all her heart and soul.

Tapeta complains to Materena that every now and then Rose puts on airs like she's a rich little daddy's girl and Tapeta just slaps her daughter back to reality. And when Rose gets teased at school about her plain dress, thongs and woven pandanus bag, Tapeta tells her that she can do with a bit of suffering. In Tapeta's opinion, people need a bit of suffering to become better people.

Tapeta is determined her daughter will always work hard at school so that she will not be poor when she grows up. She wants her to get a top job that pays big money, or marry a man who has a top job that pays big money. And then Rose will be able to pay her hardworking mother back and perhaps take her to Rome, too. It is Tapeta's dream to see the Popes' graves.

The last time Materena saw Tapeta she asked her how Rose was doing at school. 'She's not first,' Tapeta said, 'but she's not last.' Materena found out that Rose had been on the waiting list for Anne Marie Javouhey ever since she was in primary school. Tapeta would visit Anne Marie Javouhey four times a year to remind the headmistress or the headmistress's secretary that her daughter deserved a chance just as any other woman's daughter. Tapeta also reminded the headmistress or the headmistress's secretary that she always paid her bills. And Tapeta's daughter Rose got in.

Today, at two thirty, Materena has an appointment with the headmistress at Anne Marie Javouhey.

It is now two fifteen and Materena is waiting inside the cathedral. She is wearing a white missionary dress that falls right near her ankles, wanting to make the right impression. In her pandanus bag Materena has Leilani's exceptional school reports. Materena thought about wearing her gold necklace with the gold Virgin Mary pendant but that necklace, blessed by the archbishop himself, is reserved for special occasions like baptisms, communions and confirmations. Not that she needs such a necklace to prove to the headmistress that she regularly goes to Mass. Tapeta did say that the only two things the headmistress cares about are: You can pay. Your daughter is not going to jump over the wall to go meet boys lurking on the other side.

At twenty-five past two, Materena walks into the college. The woman at the front desk is busy putting a letter into an envelope. Materena, standing straight and tall, waits for the front-desk woman to acknowledge her presence. The woman, after half a second glance at Materena, opens a drawer, gets a stamp, licks it, rubs it on the envelope, closes the envelope, places it in an office basket, and buttons up her crocheted white jumper. She does all of these things very slowly and Materena would like to shake that rude woman a little.

At last the front-desk woman lifts her eyes to Materena and looks at her. 'May I help you?'

Smiling a polite smile, Materena replies, 'Good afternoon. I have an appointment with the headmistress at two thirty today.'

'What is it in regards to?'

Smiling still, Materena says, 'It is in regards to my daughter Leilani.'

The front-desk woman gives Materena a blank look.

'I'm here to enrol my daughter Leilani.'

The front-desk woman sighs and painfully reaches out to a thick book. 'Name please, school details and contact details.' After writing the information down, the front-desk woman tells Materena that she will be advised should a place become available. But Materena is not leaving before showing off Leilani's school reports.

'You can see . . .'

The woman is not interested in the reports that Materena is almost shoving in front of her face. 'That won't be necessary, Madame.' She goes back to her envelope ritual and completely ignores Materena.

'Thank you.' Materena walks out, smiling. But once outside the school, the smile drops off, and, twenty metres later, Materena loudly tells the front-desk woman off.

Well, at least Leilani has her name in on the waiting list and that is a start. To celebrate, Materena buys a watermelon at the market.

Mother and daughter, in the kitchen, are now enjoying the sweet watermelon together. The boys are outside flying their kites.

'Girl,' Materena says. 'I did something today. I went to Anne Marie Javouhey College and put your name on the waiting list.'

Leilani widens her eyes. 'And the money? It's expensive!'

'Eh, money we can always find.' Materena smiles to her daughter. 'The money is not your concern, girl. You just keep working good at school, OK?'

'I promise, I swear!'

Ah, Materena feels so happy. She's at the stove stirring the stew with Moana carefully watching when Pito, in the company of Ati, walks in.

'Something smells good, woman!' Pito is in a happy mood. He pinches Materena on the bottom and, turning to his son, he says, 'What are you doing in the bloody kitchen again? You're always skulking around in here these days. Go and play outside.'

'Pito.' Materena brushes Moana's shoulder to show him not to worry about anything. 'We're not going to start again.'

She's getting sick of having to defend Moana's ambition to be a chef. His older brother, Tamatoa, doesn't get teased at all for his ambition to be a body builder, but poor Moana cops it all the time. When Materena bought Moana a ceramic bowl last week, Pito shrieked, 'A bowl! What's next? An apron? I'm not having my son wearing an apron!'

But today, Pito chuckles and messes Moana's hair. This is as good as him saying, 'Oh, all right, then, stay in the bloody kitchen.'

Materena laughs with relief and invites Ati to stay for dinner. Without waiting for him to accept the invitation she gets another plate. The fact is that Ati always stays for dinner when he visits around dinner time, but Materena doesn't necessarily always invite him to stay.

'So,' she says, winking to Ati. 'What have you two been up to?'

But here's Leilani charging into the kitchen. 'Papi! Guess what? I'm going to Anne Marie Javouhey College. Mamie went to see today!'

Materena looks over at Pito. She expects him to say something like, 'What a good mother you are.' Instead he says, 'I'm not sure about that.'

Materena, thinking he's making allusion to the money, exclaims, 'I will sell my body if I have to! I will find the money!'

Pito gets a beer from the fridge, 'Ah, *hia*, relax. I wasn't talking about the money. I just don't like Catholic schools.'

'I went to a Catholic school and there's nothing wrong with me!' Well, Materena feels she's a bit of a martyr sometimes because when you're Catholic, you're not supposed to enjoy yourself. You're supposed to think about all the people in the world who are suffering. 'I'm a good and caring person and it's very good to be that way.'

'Catholic girls,' Pito says, smirking. 'They're . . .' He looks over to Ati who starts chuckling. And the men go on drinking their beer.

'What?' Materena would like to be informed. 'What about Catholic girls?'

Pito and Ati just look at each other and smirk.

Typical men, Materena thinks. '*Aue bof!*' she says waving a hand in the air. 'Anyway, for me, Catholic girls are really nice girls.'

Standing in front of the intimidating iron gates a few months later, Materena rearranges her daughter's immaculate plaits and says, 'Show respect to the nuns, girl. Don't get into trouble.' As she straightens Leilani's long brown dress, Materena adds, 'You're very lucky you can go to this school for free. I'm very proud of you getting that scholarship. Be good, OK? Don't talk back to the nuns.'

Then to her son, whom Materena is taking to the hospital for his plaster to get taken off, Materena asks, 'Tamatoa, say something nice to your sister.'

'Your school looks like a prison,' he says.

All right, time to walk in.

The place is swarming with girls running all over the place. They all eye Tamatoa (the only male around) and giggle into their books. The two nuns on duty don't seem like they're in control. But it's madness here this Monday morning!

Meanwhile, as Tamatoa is shaking his head and telling his mother how the girls here are so ugly, they walk in the office for the formalities. The headmistress, a large black woman with the most beautiful teeth Materena has ever seen, officially welcomes Leilani into the school and introduces her to another young girl, a small cute brown girl with hazel eyes, freckles, crooked teeth and flaming red hair.

'Vahine,' the headmistress says, 'this is Leilani. Say good morning.'

'Good morning,' the young girl smiles, blushing in front of Tamatoa looking at her up and down.

'Good morning,' Leilani says.

'Go on, girls,' the headmistress says. 'Off to class.'

Materena thanks the headmistress profusely and follows her daughter and her daughter's new friend outside. She watches them walk away. She hears them say, 'You like pancakes? So do I! You believe in aliens? So do I!'

Into womanhood

A GIRL IS OFFICIALLY A WOMAN the day she has her period. Tears fall out of the mama's eyes when she welcomes her daughter into womanhood. *Aue!* I can't believe you're a woman! It only seems like yesterday that I was pushing you into the world! I'm still the boss!

After the crying, the lamentations and the embrace, traditionally mother and daughter sit at the kitchen table for the Welcome into Womanhood talk, beginning with the rules that are passed on from generation to generation, from mother to daughter and on and on. The mama talks, keeping in mind that the purpose of the Welcome into Womanhood talk is to enlighten the new woman, pass on her experience so that her daughter's life will be a bit easier.

Cleaning tricks may be revealed, secrets that are not meant for the grave, recipes that fill the stomach and take less than ten minutes to prepare, advice on curtains, plants, men, life in general. It generally starts with: *Don't wash your hair during your period, otherwise the blood is going to turn into ice and you're going to be mad. Don't touch plants, trees or flowers during your period otherwise they're going to die. Make sure to rest. You lose litres of blood when you have your period . . .* The daughter is supposed to listen dutifully and nod. Comments are not required.

But Materena is not going to give her daughter, who became a woman about ten minutes ago, the traditional Welcome into Womanhood talk. She's going to do it the new way. Let's move on to the new century! So what is she going to say?

'Mamie?' Leilani is waiting for her mother to begin talking. 'Are you dreaming?'

'I'm thinking, girl.'

'And my Kotex?'

'Don't panic, I'm going to get you a packet of Kotex at the Chinese store soon.' Materena wipes the corner of her eyes.

'Mamie,' Leilani says, cackling, as she affectionately takes her mother's hand in hers. 'Stop crying.'

'I'm not crying because I'm sad, I'm crying because I'm moved, I'm happy.' Materena smiles through her tears. 'Just give me one minute.'

'Toilet paper is really uncomfortable.'

'*Aue!* Is that all you can think about? Your Kotex? I use toilet paper and it's not uncomfortable for me. Let me think a little . . .'

There's a silence until finally Materena is ready.

'I admire you.' There, Materena spoke.

'*Merci*, Mamie! I admire you too.'

'Ah, *oui?*' Materena feels honoured. 'And why do you admire me?'

'I admire you for lots of reasons . . . but shouldn't you be the one telling me why you admire me?'

'*Oui*, of course . . . sorry, this is *your* day . . . Well, I admire you because . . .' And Materena lists the reasons.

Because her daughter can point to north just like that, name all the countries on the atlas, she can write pages and pages without checking the spelling in the dictionary, give the medical word for every part of the body. Read books thicker than the Bible. Not eat for two days to raise money for the starving children of Africa. Materena admires how her daughter is courageous enough to tell anyone jumping in front of her at the Chinese store, 'Excuse me but I think I was before you.' Or yell at people for throwing rubbish out of their car window. She can speak four languages (French, English, Spanish and a bit of Tahitian). Ask strangers questions.

Materena finally finishes. That's enough compliments for today.

'Now,' she continues. 'I'm not going to tell you not to wash your hair during your period otherwise the blood is going to turn into ice because—well, I was right, you're laughing. Let's calm ourselves, OK? I didn't invent this talk. See what happens when you read too many books? You don't believe in Tahitian ways any more! Stop, you're making me laugh! I know it sounds stupid . . . Let me continue.' Materena takes a deep breath. You're not supposed to be laughing during the Welcome into Womanhood talk. You're supposed to be serious. 'Be proud to have been born a woman,' Materena says.

'*Oui*,' Leilani sighs.

'Don't you sigh on me!' Materena talks about how it's important for mothers to tell their daughters to be proud to have been born a woman. Being born a woman doesn't mean you have to be the one stuck with the cooking and the cleaning and looking after the children for the rest of your life. Women can do anything. Being a woman also means you add something magical and special to this world.

'Oh,' Leilani shakes her head, 'women do have a harder life. You can't deny that.'

'I don't deny it,' Materena says. 'But why do you think God gave us all these hardships, eh? It's not because he knows we're capable?'

'Mamie, I don't want to talk about God today, please.'

'All right . . . no God today . . .' Materena knows that Leilani is a bit cranky with God at the moment because He's allowing children in Africa to starve, He's making people die young, He's doing many things Leilani doesn't approve of. And plus God doesn't make any sense for Leilani. She finds it easier to believe in the existence of aliens.

'Now,' Materena says, smiling. 'Always believe in yourself, OK?'

'I will.'

'If you don't believe in yourself, you're not going to be able to take that step forward you need to take to be a truly happy person. It's all in here.' Materena places a hand on her heart. 'And in here.' The hand goes to the head. 'Remember, only you can make it happen. You follow me?'

'I follow you, Mamie.'

'Know what you want and make it happen.'

'*Oui.*'

'Mamie is always going to be here for you, remember that.'

'I'll remember.'

'Keep on working hard at school, don't get distracted. Get your papers—degrees—and then get a good job. When a woman has a good job, she doesn't have to rely on anyone, you understand?'

'I understand.'

'Don't be a nobody like me.'

'I don't think you're a nobody, Mamie.'

Materena smiles, and pats her daughter's hand. 'You're so intelligent.'

'You're intelligent. You are *very* intelligent.'

'*Merci*, girl,' Materena cackles.

'It's a fact.' Leilani takes her mother's hand. 'You also can have a new exciting future. All you need is to know what you want.'

'I know what I want!'

'And what do you want?' asks Leilani, interested.

'I want . . .' Materena stops talking to look at her daughter closely. 'Why am I talking about myself?' she chuckles. 'Today is not my day . . . Last thing, don't you dare make me a grandmother before I'm forty,' she says, trying to lighten up the conversation.

'I'm not interested in boys.'

'We all say that but when the hormones—'

'Mamie, I'll tell you, don't worry.'

'Promise?'

'Promise.'

'You tell me and I'll get you the contraceptive pill *illico presto*, OK?'

'The pill? My boyfriend will be wearing a condom.'

'Oh, I don't know any Tahitian man who wears a condom.'

'Well, my boyfriend will. No condom—no sexy loving.'

Materena widens her eyes. She can't believe the conversation she's having with her daughter today! Well, this is what happens when you don't follow the tradition, you pay the price.

OK, it's time to move away from the subject of boys and condoms. 'I really believe you're capable of doing whatever you want with your life,' Materena says.

There's no response from Leilani.

'Leilani? Did you hear what I've just told you?'

Leilani comes out of her reverie to reveal that she's never noticed her mother's breasts were so small.

'Eh? Why are you talking about my breasts?'

'Did you always have small breasts, Mamie?'

'Well, *oui*! Mamie Loana has small breasts. I've got the size of my breasts from her.'

'Am I going to have small breasts too?' Leilani asks, clearly worried.

Materena glances at her daughter's chest. At fourteen years old, Leilani still doesn't need to wear a bra but she wears one anyway. 'Maybe,' she replies. 'But I can't say . . . Anyway, you're clever, you have long legs, beautiful eyes and beautiful teeth, you can't have everything . . . Now let's go back to the Welcome into Womanhood talk . . . why are you sighing? You want your Kotex?'

Materena gets up. She understands that young girls are too embarrassed to buy pads at the Chinese store. There are always a lot of relatives at the Chinese store and when they see the pads wrapped in newspaper for privacy, the whole population knows you've got your period, the whole population can say, 'Here's one who's not going to wash her hair for the next four days.'

Sitting at the kitchen table with the transistor in front of her hours later, Materena is ready to record the Welcome to Womanhood talk. This is the talk her mother gave her twenty-four years ago, the talk Materena now feels she should have given her daughter, if only to follow the tradition that certain things should be passed from mother to daughter and on and on. Certain things such as good habits, family stories, the everyday life. Well, Materena is just about to do this—on a tape, so that Leilani can listen to it over and over again. It's quarter past eleven and everyone is asleep, the perfect time for a recording session.

Materena presses the RECORD button:

Curtains don't just stop the rays of sunshine and the eyes of the curious coming into the house. They uplift the soul of a woman too, but to do that they've got to be colourful and pretty. Never cut cost with your curtains, Leilani.

Breadfruit fills the stomach, is nice to eat, and can be cooked in many different ways; barbecued, baked, in the stew. Plant a breadfruit tree if you don't have one growing where you live. You won't regret it.

Clothes are hung first thing in the morning and taken off at least half an hour before it gets dark otherwise they will be damp. Clothes are folded as soon as they are taken off the line otherwise they will be creased. Babies' clothes are never washed with adults' clothes. Shirts are hung way down but trousers are hung way up. Sheets need four pegs. Bras and underpants are hung in the house, not on the clothes line for the whole population to admire.

Lemon squeezed on the dishes gets rid of odours, like fish, garlic and onions. Dirty dishes left by the sink overnight attract cockroaches.

Only buy two-sided tablecloths, that way you'll have two tablecloths for the price of one. Only buy dresses that can be taken down.

Tidy your house before going to bed because when the first thing you see in the morning is *bordel*, you get cranky.

Always put the soap back in the soap holder. When it's on the ground somebody might step on it one day and crack his head open.

When you visit somebody, stop five metres away from the house and call out. Don't walk into the house in case that somebody is doing something you don't want to see or something you don't need to see. Call but don't call like somebody died, call with a normal voice. If nobody answers your call after the third call it means nobody's home or maybe the relative you want to see doesn't want to see you.

To get rid of unwanted guests without hurting their feelings, broom around their feet.

Don't eat in front of people if you can't share.

When someone tells you a secret for the grave, it means you have to take that secret with you to the grave. Reveal a secret for the grave and your tongue will swell and suffocate you.

Don't visit people at eating times unless you've been invited.

Show respect to old people.

Never say anything to a bad mouth because everything you say is going to be used against you later on.

Don't get married before you have at least one child with your man. When there are no children, everything is easy, everybody wants to get married. Once there are children, everything changes.

Check the woman who raised the man you want as your husband. Men like to say to their sons, 'How's the mama? A big pork chop? That's your girlfriend in twenty years.' Well, girl, check your boyfriend's mama, see how she raised her son. Was she still changing her son's bed sheets after he turned fourteen years old?

It is taboo, forbidden, to fall in love with a cousin, remember that. Your family is not going to speak to you, attend your children's baptism, communion, confirmation etc. Your name will no longer mean anything, and your children will be born deformed.

Don't fall in love with a man from an enemy family either. You'll be caught between your family and his family, torn this way, torn that way. Your life will be nothing but misery.

Forget about falling in love with a man from another religion. There's always going to be an argument about this and that, God, the Virgin Mary, where the children are going to be baptised.

Avoid foreigners at all cost. Foreigners always go back to their country and they don't always ask the woman to follow. If your foreigner by some miracle asks you to follow him back to his country, you better make sure your passport is always valid so that you can come home to your mother's funeral. Foreigners eat raw fish with salad dressing.

Stay away from typical Tahitian men. A typical Tahitian man will make you earn your wedding ring. Expect to wait years for a typical Tahitian man to commit. One day he'll tell you: 'Oui, I'm ready to marry you.' The next day: 'Non, I can't marry you yet, maybe next year.'

A typical Tahitian man must have three nocturnal meetings a week at least with his mates. They drink, listen to music, smoke and laugh.

If you're depressed, lost, crying, your typical Tahitian man pretends he can't see your suffering. He walks straight past you.

A typical Tahitian man holds his baby as if it were a pack of taro cards. He's proud to show off the baby to his mates but when the baby becomes a child and starts asking questions, he says, 'You can't see I'm busy, eh? Go see your mama.'

A typical Tahitian man believes that it is beneath his dignity to show his woman affection. You ask a typical Tahitian man, 'Am I beautiful, chéri?' He answers, 'You're not ugly.'

Enough about men. Now to make a fruit tree produce you bash it around with a stick and say, 'You're going to give me a fruit or what? Eh? You ungrateful tree! I water you, I give you fertiliser and all you give me is a great big zero!'

When somebody gives you something in a bowl, give the bowl back as soon as possible, and give it back with something in it.

Never visit a woman who's just given birth looking your best.

You can put up a two-metre high fence around your house if you want to. But a two-metre high fence is like saying to the relatives, 'I don't want anything to do with you lot.' So, next time you're going to be in the shit up to here, you can cry until midnight for the relatives to come and save you. It's fair. It's the Tahitian way. You're in or you're out.

Soups are always better the next day. So are stews.

A man with missing teeth means he's been in a fight. A woman with missing teeth means her man beat her. If a man ever knocks out any of your beautiful teeth I'll cut his balls.

It's better to put a bandage over a black eye and have people think you've just had an operation on your eye than reveal your black eye and have people believe a man beat you. If a man ever gives you a black eye I'll cut his balls.

When we die it doesn't mean that we don't exist any more. True, we are buried, we become a skeleton then we become soil but all that we have left behind is still there. Whenever people talk about us, well, we come alive again.

A dead man's last wishes are law and must be followed.

Don't start thinking you know more than I do.

Materena presses the stop button, puts the tape in an envelope, writes Leilani a note and slips the envelope under Leilani's bedroom door. Then she switches the lights off and goes to bed.

Secrets for the grave

THERE ARE SECRETS that can never be told. They are called secrets for the grave. And there are secrets that can be told one day, it's just a question of waiting for the right moment. They are called secrets, pure and simple. With the secrets for the grave, we promise never to reveal them on the head of somebody we love and who is dead, we promise before God, and above all we promise to the person who trusted us with her secret. These kinds of secrets die with us.

With the secrets pure and simple, we don't promise anybody never to tell. We just wait for the right time to spill the bucket. Sometimes though, it happens that secrets come out into the open at the wrong time. This happened to Materena when her mother told her the truth about her dog. Materena's dog was named Prince and Materena loved him so much. But one sunny morning he ran away. For years Materena was so confused. She kept thinking, What did I do to Prince for him to go and abandon me like that?

Years later her mother told her the truth. It just slipped out. Materena had been going on about Prince and all that, how she couldn't believe he had abandoned her, and Loana said, 'Aue! Prince didn't abandon you. Stop going on about him. Your cousin Richard sold Prince to some Chinese people, they wanted to eat your dog.'

When secrets come out at the wrong time people can be hurt. That's why Materena is going to reveal a few secrets to her daughter today. Leilani is drinking her chicken soup with ginger Materena has made just for her. And plus, nobody else is home. Today is a good day to say a few more things to the new woman.

'Girl?' Materena begins, as she sits at the kitchen table, facing Leilani. 'I have a few things to tell you.'

'A few things?' asks Leilani. 'Like what?'

'Like secrets.'

'Secrets about who?'

'About you. But these are not secrets for the grave.'

'Oh, a secret is a secret,' says Leilani, shrugging.

Materena explains the two types of secret to her daughter.

Leilani listens attentively, then says, 'Go on then, spill the bucket.'

Materena takes a deep breath and begins:

Her first secret is about how she lied that her French father had died in the Second World War, defending his country. Materena explains to Leilani that she was just too young that day she asked about her French grandfather to know the truth. That he'd left after military service in Tahiti. That Materena had never met him.

Leilani cackles, 'Oh, Mamie, I've known the truth for years.' Leilani explains to her mother that it was impossible for her grandfather to have died in the Second World War. She'd done some calculations and concluded that Tom was about eleven years old (the same age as Materena's mother) when the Second World War broke out.

And now Materena is really embarrassed. 'Ah,' she says. 'Ah . . . I didn't think you were going to do some calculations.'

'Mamie,' Leilani laughs, enjoying herself. 'Have you forgotten that I have a scientific mind? People with scientific minds always question things. They never assume. What's your next secret?' she asks, cheekily.

First Materena would like her daughter to promise that she won't get cranky because it's quite a big secret. Leilani promises. So Materena tells her daughter about that pink bicycle which Mama Roti had given her for her seventh birthday. But first, let's have a bit of recapitulation.

That day Mama Roti couldn't stop raving how the pink bicycle had cost her the eyes of her head. Mama Roti was so happy her grand-daughter loved the bicycle more than she loved the quilt her other grandmother had made working day and night for a whole week. But Materena was not happy at all about that bicycle. In her opinion, you just don't give vehicles to other people's children. Materena really believes you should see the parents and ask them if it's OK with them for you to give their child a vehicle. But even back then Mama Roti never asked Materena what she thought about her ideas. Here she was, clapping her hands at Leilani riding that bicycle, and every time she fell, she yelled, 'Watch out for your brand new bicycle!'

The second Leilani fell and split her chin open Materena understood God was giving her a sign, and so she decided to make that bicycle disappear. That night Materena wrapped the bicycle in a bed sheet and hid it on top of a wardrobe at her mother's house. Her mother said, 'My eyes didn't see what you've just put on top of the wardrobe.' Leilani cried for days when Materena told her somebody had stolen her bicycle.

Right now, Leilani is laughing. 'Mamie,' she says. 'I've known the truth for years!' Leilani explains to her mother that the day she saw that thing wrapped in a bed sheet on top of the wardrobe she knew straight away it was her bicycle. She could see the shape of the handlebars.

So she got a chair, climbed on top of it, grabbed her bicycle, and started to ride it in her grandmother's garden. When Loana saw Leilani she said, 'It's best you don't tell your mother about that bike.'

'I rode my bicycle in Mamie Loana's garden for years,' says Leilani, clearly enjoying watching her mother's eyes popping out of her head. 'You're not the only person with secrets you know,' she cackles.

'What other secrets have you got for me?' Materena asks, shaking her head with disbelief.

'OK, do you remember how I used to go to school with four slices of banana cake to eat at recreation?'

Materena nods. *Oui,* she remembers the two years Leilani went to school with four slices of banana cake to eat at recreation. She was always making banana cakes. She couldn't keep up with Leilani's growing appetite. Then one day Leilani said, 'I don't need four slices of cake any more. One is enough. I think I've stopped growing.'

'What about those slices of banana cake?' Materena asks. 'Don't you dare tell me you were chucking them in the bin?'

'Me, chuck food in the bin?' Leilani exclaims. 'I would never ever chuck food in the bin! I gave those slices of cake to a girl who had nothing to eat.'

'Oh, *chérie*.' Materena smiles. 'Oh . . . that was so nice of you to do that. But how come that girl stopped eating my banana cake?'

'She backstabbed me,' Leilani says. 'She told everyone in our classroom I was a show-off.' Leilani continues about how she confronted that girl and told her, 'You idiot. Don't you know never to bite the hand that feeds you?' From that day on, Leilani stopped feeding that girl.

'Just like that?' Materena asks. 'No second chance?'

'You know me, Mamie. People are nice to me and I'm nice back. People are mean to me and I'm mean back . . . This chicken soup is delicious! I'm going to have some more.'

As soon as Leilani is back at the table, she asks her mother if she could ask her a question. 'It's a bit private though,' she adds.

'Well, ask your question and I'll tell you if I can answer it or not.'

'I'm just curious. I don't want you to think I'm being disrespectful.'

What is her question, Materena asks herself. She is now very curious. 'Come on, scientific mind,' she smiles. 'I'm waiting.'

'OK.' Leilani puts the spoon down. 'How was I conceived?'

Materena can't believe Leilani's question. The conception of a baby is a very private affair. Well, you have the right to know if you were conceived in a bed, on a rock, on the kitchen table, in the bathroom. But how? None of your business!

'Leilani, the hormones have already started kicking or what?'

'Oh, Mamie! You're the one always talking about the hormones!'

Materena shakes her head and laughs.

'Mamie, was I an accident?'

Materena stops laughing.

Was Leilani an accident? Well, most babies are accidents aren't they? Materena asks herself. The only person Materena knows who fell pregnant because she decided to was Madame Colette. Twice Madame Colette said to her husband, 'Jules, I'm ovulating, I'll see you in bed.' But all the other women Materena knows (cousins, aunties and herself) fell pregnant because they didn't think. Materena's three children were accidents. The first accident took place under a tree, the second in bed, and the third on the kitchen table. But the moment Materena discovered her children's existence, she welcomed them into her womb and into her life, as if she had planned them.

'You were not an accident,' Materena says, firmly.

'Oh,' Leilani shrugs. 'It's just that I always thought I was an accident.' She now wants to keep talking about secrets—the ones she won't be taking to her grave.

'Don't tell me you have secrets to take to the grave,' says Materena.

'Mamie, every woman in the world has secrets to take to the grave.' Leilani says this with her very serious woman voice.

And now Materena is worried. Leilani is far too young to have secrets for the grave entrusted to her because it is a huge responsibility, a heavy weight on the conscience.

'How many secrets for the grave have you got so far?' Materena asks.

'Oh, about four.'

'And who are they about?'

'I can't tell you.'

'Are they about me?'

'I can't tell you.'

'That means they're about me. Come on girl,' Materena pleads, smiling. 'You know me. I'm very good at keeping secrets. I've got about two hundred and fifty secrets in my head.'

'Who told everybody that I got my period?'

'Eh?' Materena didn't expect that question. 'Everyone?' she says, 'Who do you take me for? The coconut radio? I only told two people.'

'Didn't I specifically ask you to keep the news of my period secret?'

'I only told two people!' Materena really can't understand why her daughter is making such a fuss.

'It doesn't matter if you've only told my secret to two people.' Leilani is cranky. 'What is important is that you didn't respect my secret.'

Materena is about to defend herself, to explain that when your daughter has her period for the first time, you, the mother, are *allowed* to share your joy, the news with the family . . . But she doesn't want to get into an argument with Leilani. What Materena wants is for her daughter to reveal one of her secrets for the grave. The one which is about her. But there's no way Leilani is spilling the bucket.

What else can you expect from someone who writes in a diary?

These days when Materena talks to her daughter she's got to lift her head because Leilani's grown by at least six centimetres since her fifteenth birthday, that girl! It means Leilani's dresses, although still fine at the top, are far too short and need to be taken down. This is what Materena is planning to do today.

Materena carefully lays out Leilani's dresses (seven in total: five brown, one yellow, one white) on her bed. Now all Materena needs to begin is the mannequin. 'Leilani! I need you!'

'In a minute,' Leilani calls. 'I'm changing a light bulb.'

'Make sure the light is switched off!'

'*Oui*, I know!'

All right, here's the mannequin now. With a resigned sigh, Leilani slips into one of her too-short dresses. This particular dress, brown with thick straps, a zip at the back and pockets at the front, is way above Leilani's knees. On her knees, and with one expert hand, Materena undoes the stitches at the bottom of the dress, lets the dress fall down below Leilani's knees, and marks the dress's new length with a pin.

'Everybody is going to know my dresses have been taken down,' Leilani says.

'And so? At least you've got something to put on your body.'

'Why do you keep buying brown dresses?'

'Because they're easy to wash.'

OK, next dress. Still sighing, Leilani slips into another dress, this one white with thick straps, a zip at the back and pockets at the front. It doesn't need to be taken down too much. Two to three centimetres should suffice.

'I look like a nun in this dress,' Leilani points out.

'Ah, *non*, not at all,' says Materena. 'You're very pretty in this dress, you look respectable.'

OK, next dress. 'Why can't I get a new dress?' Leilani asks, slipping into another brown dress with a zip at the back but no pockets at the front.

'Leilani . . . you know about our finances. I'm still paying your encyclopedia off . . . and I'm also paying for that window your big brother broke at school, and plus your little brother wants an electric mixer.'

OK, next dress. 'Vahine got a new dress because she got ten out of twenty in the history test,' Leilani says as she slips into another brown dress with thick straps but with huge yellow buttons at the front. 'I got nineteen out of twenty . . .' Materena shakes her head.

Now, it's not as if Leilani's excellent schoolwork is never rewarded. Materena often treats her daughter to an ice cream when they're in town or she buys the kids a family-size container of ice cream. And yes, Materena was very proud when Leilani got nineteen out of twenty for her history test. The teacher wrote *Fantastique!* on Leilani's test sheet.

'Yesterday my maths teacher told me I had a brain for mathematics,' continues Leilani. 'And, my French teacher told me I was very gifted with compositions.'

'I already know this. Your teachers told me.'

'My science teacher told me it's a pleasure to teach me.'

'This was yesterday too?' Materena asks, suspecting that Leilani is starting to invent. At the last parents' and teachers' interview, Madame Bellard complained to Materena about Leilani being a very challenging student to teach. According to Madame Bellard, Leilani is a typical scientist. She questions and questions and questions until everything makes sense, everything is proven. 'I'm not a professor at a university,' Madame Bellard told Materena. 'This is a high school and I'm just a high school teacher.' So, it's very unlikely for Madame Bellard to have told Leilani that she was such a pleasure to teach.

OK, next dress. 'You know Mamie . . . I won't be able to wear any of these dresses once I have breasts.' This is Leilani's declaration and Materena bursts out laughing. That Leilani, she thinks. She will stop at nothing to get a new dress. But! It makes sense what Leilani is saying. Once Leilani is going to start having breasts, she's not going to fit into any of her dresses. Materena could be wasting her time taking down all these dresses today because Leilani's breasts have already popped out a tiny bit. It's only a matter of time before they erupt.

Sitting in the back of Auntie Rita's car on the way to town the next day, Leilani can't stop grinning with delight. She's getting a new dress today and Rita, being an expert with fabric, is going to help her and Materena, who's not an expert with fabric.

'And I get to choose the dress, OK?' Leilani says.

Materena glances at her daughter for a second, then goes back to discussing fabric with her cousin.

'I wouldn't mind a dress with thin straps,' Leilani says. 'I used to have dresses with thin straps when I was little,' she sighs with nostalgia.

Rita glances at her niece in the rear mirror and smiles. 'Ah,' she says. 'I would give anything to be able to wear a dress with thin straps.' Rita can't wear that kind of dress. Her arms are too fat.

Materena puts a comforting arm on her cousin's shoulder. 'Cousin, your beauty is on the inside and that's more important than the beauty from the outside.'

'What do you mean to say here?' Rita asks. 'That I'm not beautiful on the outside?'

'But, *non*!' Materena exclaims in protest. 'Rita . . .'

Rita chuckles. *Ouf* . . . luckily she is in a good mood today.

Anyway, they're in town now and after driving around for twenty minutes looking for a free parking spot, Rita scores one at last. Rita can't stand paying for parking spots. She'd pay thousands of francs for an ornament but there's no way she'd pay hundreds of francs for a parking spot. It's against her nature. That free parking spot puts her in an even better mood. OK . . . let's go and get that dress.

First stop is a little shop where dresses don't cost the eyes of the head, dresses that are on sale prices all year round. Ah! And what does Materena see hanging at the back? A dress that has not only been reduced by fifty per cent but that is so beautiful. Feel the fabric! And check out the large pockets! In Materena's opinion, women can always do with large pockets. You can put all sorts of things in large pockets: money for the truck, pens, sandwiches, bottles of lemonade.

'Go and try that dress on, girl. I can't wait to see you in it. You're going to look so beautiful.' Then, looking at Rita, she adds, 'Eh, Rita?'

Rita looks at her niece and sees the desperation in her eyes. She smiles with compassion. Yes, she knows how it is when your mother chooses the dress you're going to wear.

'The pockets aren't ripped?' Rita asks Materena. She explains that when a dress is on sale it is usually because there's something wrong with it.

Materena checks the pockets. No, they're not ripped.

'And the zip?' Rita asks. 'It's not stuck?' Materena checks the zip. *Non*, it's not stuck, it works perfectly. Rita feels the fabric and grimaces. 'That's cheap fabric,' she says, shaking her head with regret. 'That dress is going to tear in the washing machine like that.' She clicks her fingers.

'Ah, you think?' Materena asks. 'And if I wash it by hand?'

Rita feels the fabric again and looks up to the ceiling for a moment, as if deep in thought. 'Three washes. After that the fabric is going to tear. But you decide, it's your money.'

Materena hangs the dress back on the rack.

Next shop. Next dress . . . and Materena is so excited. She can't believe her luck today! She just loves the red dots on that dress.

Again, Auntie Rita steps in. 'Cousin, the fabric . . .' But there's only so much Rita can say about fabric and she's running out of ideas. It's Leilani's turn now to tell Materena what's wrong with the dress she's just taken off the rack.

'I don't like that dress,' Leilani says.

'What don't you like?' Materena asks.

'Everything, Mamie,' Leilani says, trying to keep her sweet voice. 'The shape, the size, the colour.'

'What's wrong with the colour? Yellow is a beautiful colour.'

'Mamie . . .'

Next shop. Materena doesn't want to go into the next shop. She doesn't like the shopkeeper, who always looks at you like you're going to steal something.

Next shop. No, clothes in that shop cost the eyes of the head. Next shop. No, that shop looks too high-class.

'Come on, let's go in,' Rita says.

'Ah, *non*, cousin,' Materena says. 'That shop is for rich people.'

'Well, I'm going to look inside,' Rita announces. 'You can wait outside.' Rita and Leilani walk in while Materena stands outside. Every time Leilani waves her mother to come in, Materena waves her away.

Here's Leilani taking a lacy black dress off the rack. Facing her mother, she puts it in front of her and shakes her shoulders. Materena widens her eyes, meaning: Stop it, hurry up and put that dress back on the rack before the shopkeeper sees you!

Grinning, Leilani puts the dress back on the rack. Then she takes another one. This time it's a very long white dress with frills, which Leilani puts in front of her, bowing before her mother.

But what's this? Materena asks herself. It's to try to get me into that shop? Materena gets her purse from inside her pandanus bag. OK, there's five thousand franc bills, one five hundred franc bill, lots of coins . . . total (approximate) is seven thousand francs. She looks down at her thongs, cursing herself for not wearing her shoes today. Well, anyway, her thongs are clean, she scrubbed them last night. We're going to eat breadfruit today, tomorrow and the day after, Materena tells herself as she walks into the shop, trying to muster all her dignity.

Here's Leilani holding a folded blue dress with thin straps, asking her mother if she can try it on.

'Why not?' Materena says. 'But let me feel the fabric first.'

Materena discreetly checks out the price tag as she feels the fabric. Oh, what a relief! The price is quite reasonable. There must be something wrong with it. Materena asks Rita to feel the fabric.

'Top quality,' Rita declares.

All right, then. Leilani hurries into the changing room.

'So?' Materena discreetly calls out from behind the curtains.

'This is the dress I want, Mamie!' Leilani calls back.

'Can I look?'

Materena is just thinking of walking into the changing room when Leilani pulls the curtains open in one theatrical movement, then rolls her *derrière*, one hand on her hip, before marching out of the room. You would think she was on the podium for the Miss Tahiti contest. Materena calls out to Rita to come and see. Rita appears in a flash.

Her face lights up, '*Aue!* Boys are going to fall on their knees for you.'

But Materena is not sharing Rita's emotion. Frowning, Materena asks Leilani, 'It's not a bit too short?'

'*Non*,' Leilani replies. 'This is the normal length.'

'Eh, stop . . . I wasn't born in the last rain . . . Bend over.'

Leilani bends over.

'Eh, here,' Materena says. 'I saw your *culotte*. That dress is just too short. It's shorter than all the dresses you have at home.'

'No, it's not!' Then pleading with Auntie Rita with her eyes, Leilani asks her what she thinks.

Aue, poor Auntie Rita, stuck between the tomato and the lettuce again, between the daughter and the mother. Is the dress a bit too short? she asks herself. Well, yes, but when you've got nice legs, you might as well show them off. 'Not necessarily,' she says.

'You see,' Leilani says. 'This dress is fine. *Please*, Mamie.'

Please, Mamie, Materena thinks. That girl only says please when she needs me to open my purse. What is a young clever girl going to get wearing a dress so short?

She's going to get a lot of attention from boys, boys who've only seen her in long dresses with thick straps, pockets, and huge buttons.

'I've taken my decision,' Materena says. 'And my decision is that the dress is too short.' She goes on about how a dress like this is only going to cause trouble with boys.

'But I don't want to cause trouble!' Leilani's voice is no longer a whisper. 'I just want to wear that dress for me!'

Materena turns to Rita and asks, 'What do you think?'

And this is Rita's answer: 'Even if your daughter wears a sack of potato, boys are going to look at her because she's got slim legs.'

This answer comes out of Rita's mouth in one go. But she's not the mother of the young girl. She doesn't have to worry about certain things like Materena has to. And if Materena doesn't buy that dress, her daughter is going to do her long face. *Aue!* Imagine having the money to buy your daughter a new dress every week. What a nightmare!

'Mamie?' Leilani pleads. 'You know me. Do I look at boys? *Non*. Never. I will go to university . . . I will become a professor . . .'

But she will stop at nothing that one! Materena yells in her head. And she's going to be a professor now? Last month Leilani said she was going to be a social worker. She keeps changing her mind.

'You're going to be a professor now?' asks Materena. Leilani nods, her hands clasped in prayer, miming, *Please*, Mamie.

Eh, eh, Materena remembers back to when she was fifteen years old and the fashion was for shirt-dresses with a picture of a fruit on the front. When you scratched the picture of the fruit you could smell its scent. There was one with a picture of an apple, one with a picture of a pineapple, there were many choices and everybody had a shirt-dress like that, except for Materena. Then, one day her mother said, 'All right, let's go and get that shirt-dress you've been talking about.'

But when Loana saw the shirt-dress in the shop, she looked at the price tag and did her horrified eyes. 'This dress costs the eyes of the head!' she said. 'What am I paying all that money for? And is this a dress or a shirt for when you sleep? It's way below the knees.'

'It's a shirt!' Materena said, with all her heart and soul.

Loana shook her head and mumbled. 'All that money for you to look like an old woman.'

Eh, well, times sure have changed.

'All right, then,' Materena sighs, smiling to her daughter. 'Hurry up, go and put your dress on the counter before I change my mind.'

We're a different generation

THERE'S A BOUM, a party, this Saturday, three houses away from where Leilani's best friend Vahine lives. Vahine has been invited and so has Leilani, and of course Leilani is expecting her mother to say, 'Yes, of course you can go to the boum.'

Leilani has it all planned, so she tells her mother. She'll be wearing her new dress (it has already made one of the nuns so cranky she sent Leilani home to get changed). She'll be picked up at around six thirty by Vahine's mother, she and Vahine will be picked up at around eleven o'clock from the boum, she'll sleep at Vahine's house and then she will be dropped home on Sunday before nine o'clock, for Mass.

Materena cackles. 'Why? Are you going to Mass this Sunday?'

Leilani has stopped going to Mass for months.

'Maybe,' Leilani whispers sweetly. 'So? Can I go to the boum? I'm nearly sixteen years old.'

'Leilani, your birthday is in nine months. You've got plenty of time to go to boums when you're older.'

'Mamie!' Leilani follows her mother, stomping her foot along the way. 'You were young once, you used to go to *boums*.'

Materena informs her daughter that actually she didn't go to *boums* at Leilani's age. She went to baptisms, weddings and funerals.

'Oh . . .' Leilani searches for the right word to say. 'Oh . . .'

Leilani, elbows on the kitchen table, is admiring her mother sewing buttons on Tamatoa's shirt. 'You're such a good sewer.' Leilani is still on her mission to persuade her mother to let her go to the *boum* this Saturday. She moans that she's hopeless with sewing, she's not patient enough, whereas her mother is so talented with sewing—with everything she does, actually.

'*Merci, chérie*,' says Materena, smiling. She doesn't mind the compliment, even if there's another agenda behind it. However, Materena feels it's important to remind Leilani that she's offered to teach her to sew on several occasions.

'Oh.' Leilani waves a hand. 'Sewing is not really important for our new generation because we care about other things.'

'What, for example?' Materena asks, very interested.

'Well . . .' Leilani looks into her mother's eyes. 'The death penalty. The starving children in Africa. The laws. Empowering women. The alarming birth rate in Tahiti and in the world. Our generation has so many issues to worry about, Mamie.'

'Ah, I see,' Materena nods, knowingly. 'And are you saying that the women of the old generation had nothing to worry about?'

'Of course I'm not!' The women of Materena's generation paved the way for the women of her new generation. They said no to arranged marriages, no to work without pay. They said less sewing, please.

Materena bursts out laughing. And that is when Leilani attacks her mother with her request about the *boum*.

Materena stops laughing. 'Girl . . . sometimes children have to accept their mother's decision.' Then, smiling, Materena adds that she has her reasons for not letting Leilani go to the *boum*.

'What are they?' Leilani insists.

Materena shakes her head with disbelief. Her generation wouldn't dare ask their mother to justify their decision. What mamas said was the law. Well, anyway, this is the new generation and so Materena explains the situation which all has to do with danger.

'Danger?' The situation is still not clear for Leilani. 'What do you mean? What's so dangerous about dancing?' Before Materena has the chance to explain that the danger she's talking about has got nothing to do with dancing, Leilani is passionately defending the art of dancing, this wonderful art that is part of Tahitian culture. She's raving about the *Arioi*, the professional dancers from a long time ago, who travelled from one island to the next to entertain the people and bring peace.

How does my daughter know about the *Arioi*? I've never told her about the *Arioi*. 'The *Arioi*, eh?' Materena says. 'And did the person who told you about them also mention how the *Arioi* were forbidden to have children, they had to kill their babies, all they were allowed to do was dance? Love was forbidden. Family was forbidden.'

'All right, you win,' Leilani says. 'At least we both agree that dancing is not dangerous.'

'Of course dancing is not dangerous! I've never said that! When I said danger I meant boys and girls, they drink, they do stupid things . . .'

'Mamie, you know I'm allergic to alcohol.' Leilani reminds her. Materena keeps on nodding as Leilani talks about how young girls of today aren't interested in getting drunk anyway. They're more interested in celebrating their youth with dancing. 'Please, Mamie,' Leilani begs. 'And plus, no boys will pay attention to me, I have a flat chest.'

Aue, Materena thinks. If I say *oui* and something bad happens to my girl, I'm never going to forgive myself. Ah, here's Pito, coming home from his walkabout. He's jovial, of course, and whistling a happy tune.

'Ask Papi,' she says.

Before Leilani has a chance to put her request forward Tamatoa is in the kitchen. 'Papi!' Tamatoa asks, smiling. 'Can I borrow your nice shirt for Saturday?'

'What's happening on Saturday?'

'I'm going to a *boum*.'

'Ah, and can I go with you?' Pito chuckles. 'Yeah, all right, you can borrow my shirt but you better bring it back with all the buttons.'

'*Merci*, Papi!'

'Where's the *boum*?' Materena asks.

'It's near Vahine's house.'

'Did she invite you too!' Leilani shrieks.

'*Oui*, and so?' Tamatoa doesn't see what the problem is.

'You've been invited to the *boum* too?' Pito asks Leilani.

'Well, *oui*, Papi. She's *my* friend.'

'Ah, OK . . . you two have fun.'

By the time Materena arrives home after Mass with her youngest son, her eldest son is on the sofa telling his father he got lucky, and Pito is very delighted. Here he is, shaking his son's hand. Welcoming him into manhood. Telling the new man that of course he doesn't mind that a girl ripped three buttons off this *chemise* to get to his son.

As for Leilani, she's in bed. She tells her mother the *boum* was so boring. The music was way too loud. She couldn't talk to anyone.

To Materena's great relief Leilani growing breasts hasn't turned her into a boy admirer, contrary to what her cousin Tapeta told her to expect. The day Tapeta's daughter Rose started getting breasts, she started smiling to boys, giving them the you're-a-nice-looking-boy-you look. Tapeta is even more worried now that Rose got herself a weekend job at the Airport Café, because, in Tapeta's experience, the Airport Café is filled with boys who are after only one thing. If Tapeta didn't need the money, she'd tie her daughter to a tree until she finishes school.

Well, Leilani getting breasts hasn't turned her into a boy admirer. They have just made her even more outspoken. For example, Leilani told her father he was starting to look a bit yellow and that was because all his alcohol consumption was poisoning his blood. Pito laughed his head off, but then he went to check himself in front of the mirror. Materena had a good chuckle.

Then last week, on the way home from Euromarche, a woman was smoking in the truck. People have been smoking in the truck for centuries and people who don't smoke just bear it. Nobody wants to have a fight in a truck because of a cigarette. That day, Leilani, looking at that woman (and she was not little), coughed and waved her hand in front of her face. Then she read (and not in a low voice) the announcement written next to the tariff. *It is forbidden to drink, smoke, and eat sandwiches in the truck*. And she went on again with her coughing. Materena discreetly tapped her daughter to be quiet. It wasn't in her plan to fight a big woman that day.

Ah, one more example: yesterday, Materena and Leilani met Cousin Giselle at the Chinese store, who told them about taking Isidore Louis Junior to the doctor last week. He had a skin disease that looked like chicken pox, but it was something else Giselle couldn't remember the name of. The doctor gave him some antibiotic and a cream. And now Giselle's three children have that skin disease!

Next thing, Leilani was asking her auntie why didn't she ask her doctor if her son's skin disease was contagious. If she had done so, she might have been able to prevent the contagion. 'Girl,' Giselle said, 'the doctor should have told me. It wasn't up to me to ask.'

Materena dragged Leilani away before she angered Giselle more. But this didn't stop her from talking about it later on at home. Leilani was so cranky with her Auntie Giselle, her doctor, and everyone who doesn't think. 'Are we stupid or what?' she exclaimed.

'Who's we?' Materena asked.

'We, us, Tahitian people.' Leilani went on with her comments about how it's so stupid that a mother doesn't ask her doctor if her child's skin disease is contagious. It's so stupid that we let a woman smoke in the truck when it is clearly forbidden. That a woman covers her bruised eye with a bandage instead of leaving her husband. It's so stupid . . .

Materena went outside to water the plants. She needed time to think.

Anyway, Materena can do with a no-comment day today, and so she isn't going to ask Leilani to come with her to her favourite shop, Ah Kiong. That Chinese store wouldn't survive without women like Materena, Tahitian women, Tahitian women without a husband, Tahitian women with too many children, Tahitian women who don't mind that their towels don't dry the skin very well. Ah Kiong has been Materena's favourite place to spend her hard-earned money for five years now. Nothing there costs the eyes of the head.

The moment Materena announces that she's off to Ah Kiong, Leilani, up and marching towards her room to get her shoes, tells her mother to wait. She's going to town too.

'Eh!' Materena calls out. 'I'm going to that shop you don't like!'

'*Oui*, I know!' Leilani calls back. Leilani is ready and smiling. These days, Leilani smiles so rarely that Materena melts. Leilani is so pretty when she smiles. So, smiling back, Materena nods to her daughter the signal—OK, then, girlfriend, let's go.

They sit side by side in the truck, which is packed. Facing Materena and Leilani is a very young woman with a newborn baby sucking on her breast. Materena gives her daughter the 'you better not say anything about this' look. Saying something to a woman breastfeeding is asking for trouble, you're going to get your eyes scratched out. Plus a woman breastfeeding is a beautiful thing to see.

Materena looks tenderly at that baby sucking at his mama's breast and thinking how the father must be a *popa'a*, a foreigner, because that is one very pink baby.

Very soon, the young mother notices Materena. A smile follows, another smile, a word, and next minute she's pouring her heart out to Materena about how she's on her way to talk to her man, the father of that little one. She's going to tell him that the baby is his and that the reason he looks *popa'a* is because she's got an American ancestor. She's also going to warn her ex-boyfriend that if he doesn't recognise their baby, her grandmother is going to curse him. He's going to die of a horrible disease. His left leg is going to swell on him. He's going to get a horrible punishment if her son ends up having 'father unknown' on his birth certificate.

Well, she's here at her ex-boyfriend's house now, she says. But before she steps down from the truck, she wants to show Materena her baby's birthmark. Off comes the baby's nappy. Pointing to a tiny dot under one of the baby boy's private parts, she informs Materena that his father has the same dot and at the same place. So there. The young girl steps down from the truck with her head held up high.

Leilani, looking at her mother, shakes her head and asks, 'Why do people always tell you their stories? It's amazing!' Materena tells her daughter that everyone is born with a gift and hers is to listen to people telling her stories. Leilani takes her mother's hand. Materena squeezes it with all her heart and soul. The last time Leilani held her mother's hand in public, she was ten years old.

They walk into Materena's favourite shop in a very good mood. It's a real Ali Baba cave here, with every single shelf packed with cheap things. First, though, Materena leaves her pandanus bag at the counter (as always) and ignores Leilani's comment, 'Mamie, stop acting like you're a thief.' Materena has good reasons to leave her bag at the counter. When you walk around the shop with a bag, you can be sure you're going to be followed by one of the shop assistants.

Ah, and what does Materena see out there? Stuffed on one of the shelves? Reduced by fifty per cent? Towels! She's going to grab five. You can always do with extra towels. Materena rubs a towel on her face—it's so soft. Is this silk by any chance? She checks the label. Ah, she knew it. Polyester. Still, it's very soft. Here, she's going to buy two more.

Right then, Materena notices a young Tahitian man wearing a beanie with a ripped T-shirt, and trousers falling down his *derrière*, looking like he's waiting for an opportunity to sneak the purse he's looking at under his shirt. The shop assistant, eyeing him with suspicious eyes, seems to be thinking the same. Materena turns to Leilani, who's staring at a young French woman wearing an immaculate office outfit with gold shoes and a silver handbag, who's admiring ornaments, and whispers, 'Check that man there. He sure looks like he's waiting for an opportunity to sneak the purse under his shirt eh?'

Leilani looks at the man, and whispers back, 'Here you go assuming again.' In Leilani's mind, the French woman looks more like a suspect. She just doesn't fit the criteria of this shop's customers.

Materena tells Leilani that the French woman is probably buying her cleaner a gift.

'How do you know this?' asks Leilani. 'That man may also be buying his cleaner a gift. Just because he's Tahitian doesn't mean he's a thief.'

'I didn't say he was a thief, I said he looked like a thief.'

'Where's the difference?'

Aue . . . Materena is not interested to have an argument. She goes on with her shopping, feeling . . . well, a bit ashamed. She'd be the first to tell people, don't judge an orange by its peel, and here she was judging an orange by its peel. *Pardon*, Materena says in her head.

She calls out to Leilani to ask her opinion about some ornaments to put in the garden, when the shop owner yells, 'Somebody stole all the sunglasses!' and runs over to lock the door.

She's onto the young Tahitian man real quick, who takes his shirt off at her request. He takes his beanie off. He takes his trousers off. No sunglasses are found.

'Will you be checking that French woman too?' asks Leilani. But the French woman has already checked herself out.

Later, Materena and Leilani are walking to the snackbar not far from the trucks for Materena to buy Leilani a lemonade. Meanwhile, Leilani is going off at those French people giving Tahitian people a bad reputation, making them look stupid.

'We can't even look around in stores without being suspected of stealing! French doctors don't tell us anything! French priests order us around! And look at . . . But do you see what I see?'

Materena looks to where Leilani is pointing. She can't believe her eyes! Sitting on a bench, the *popa'a* woman is taking a pair of sunglasses out of her silver bag and putting them on the Tahitian man's nose. And they're laughing their heads off, those two!

Unbelievable! I knew he wasn't innocent! Materena yells in her head.

For the first time in weeks, Leilani is speechless.

Materena walks to the cathedral in Papeete. She needs to talk to somebody. And not to her mother, who's only going to say, 'I don't understand, girl, you were not like that when you were Leilani's age. Don't worry, it's the new generation.' Not to Cousin Rita who's only going to say, 'It's normal, it's the hormones.' Not to Pito who's going to say . . . nothing. Pito is deaf when it suits him. He's definitely deaf when she talks to him about problems. Problems regarding his daughter? Let's not talk about it. As far as Pito is concerned, his daughter is fine. It's Materena who has a problem. She takes things too seriously.

Materena walks into the cathedral, crosses herself, and looks around. She counts four women. Four women who, just like Materena, need somebody to talk to or perhaps they have something to ask. She's not surprised to find no men. The church for men is the bar.

Materena takes a seat right by the door opposite the statue of the Virgin Mary Understanding Woman, and cries her eyes out, all the while pouring out her problem to Virgin Mary Understanding Woman, who understands all kind of trouble.

Aue, Virgin Mary, moans Materena in her head. Give me strength. Materena reminds the Virgin Mary how she's not the kind to annoy her about the littlest trouble. She's here today because . . . she's *that* close from throwing her daughter into the street! She needs help; it's not natural for a mother to want to throw her daughter into the street. It's more natural for a mother to love her daughter no matter what.

Aue, Virgin Mary, that girl, she's going to see where not respecting your mother takes you. It takes you into the street that's where!

Well, Leilani is never really going to have to live in the street. A relative is bound to rescue her and then Materena is going to get a bad name. When you throw your children out, it means you're weak, you're a bad mother. 'Shame on you,' the relatives are going to say.

Oh, here's a well-dressed Chinese woman with very high-heeled shoes, holding about ten shopping bags, walking into the cathedral. What has she got to ask Virgin Mary? Materena wonders. The Chinese woman sits in the front row, makes a fanning movement with the palm of her hand and Materena understands that she's here because it's nice and cool. But some people, she thinks. You don't go in the church to cool down!

Anyway, about Leilani. Is she supposed to be my cross to bear in this life? she asks the Virgin Mary. Was she born to give me miseries? My boys don't give me half as much trouble.

These days, Materena can't say anything to Leilani without Leilani finding the little beast. For example, when Materena says that the reason Rita can't lose weight is because of her problems with hormones, Leilani says, 'Auntie Rita eats too much.'

When Materena complains of her hands being so used up because of all the cleaning they do, and dares tell Her Highness that she wouldn't mind another job because cleaning is so lonely sometimes, Her Highness says, 'Get another job. Don't just complain about it. Make a change. Take control of your life!'

So, the Chinese woman has had enough of cooling herself. She's off. Materena goes back to her misery.

Ah, what misery when your daughter thinks she knows better than you do. You're always on the defensive, on edge, and you can't relax.

Materena smiles a faint smile to a middle-aged woman walking into the cathedral. The middle-aged woman also smiles a faint smile and sits right in front of Materena.

And now she's crying her heart out.

Fifteen minutes later she is still crying. Everyone else has left the cathedral except for Materena, who is asking herself if she should reach out to the woman. Because sometimes crying to the statue of the Virgin Mary Understanding Woman is not enough. You've got to cry to a woman in the flesh.

'Girlfriend?' Materena says quietly. 'Can I help you?'

The woman turns to Materena and holds onto Materena's hand. She tells Materena her name and how, ten minutes ago, she nearly died. She was walking to the market when a concrete beam fell off a construction site and crashed on the concrete path, missing Vairua by only two centimetres, maybe one. A woman on the other side of the road called out to her, 'Eh, girlfriend! You OK?'

Vairua called back, '*Oui*, I'm fine! Thank you for asking.' But she was not fine at all. She was in shock. She stared at the concrete beam and saw herself crushed underneath it. Then she stepped over the beam and kept on walking, all the while visualising her wake. She saw herself in an open coffin, dressed in a long white frilly robe, and there's a crowd of people crying and shaking their head.

Vairua's mother shoves her fist in her mouth for that daughter gone before her. Vairua's youngest son openly sobs on his mother's bare feet until his older brother pulls him away and says, 'Mamie wouldn't want us to cry like babies.' As for the daughter . . . she is not here.

'My daughter was not at my wake,' Vairua cries on Materena's hand. And the reason Vairua's daughter wasn't at her mother's wake, so Vairua tells Materena, was because she kicked her out of the house six years ago. And the daughter never came back. Vairua just wouldn't accept her daughter becoming a Protestant. She expects her children whom she raised in the Catholic faith to remain Catholic till the day they die. Shaking her head with sorrow, she looks into Materena's eyes. 'We used to be so close, my daughter and I,' she says, 'and now she doesn't even come to my wake.'

Vairua talks about the curse that makes all mothers believe that the fruit *has* to fall near the tree.

Catholic mothers must have Catholic children.

Hardworking mothers must have hardworking children.

Giving mothers must have giving children.

And on and on and on . . .

Smiling through her tears Materena admits that it is a curse. 'You know, girlfriend,' she says, 'when we think about it, it takes courage for a fruit to fall far from his tree.'

'True,' the woman who nearly died today replies, 'but life is easier for everyone when we just fall back to our roots.'

It's quiet here at the cemetery this morning. Materena can sure do with a few moments on her own weeding her grandmother's grave, but she bumps into Mama Teta, on her way home from her husband's grave.

Auntie and niece hug each other tight. 'Are you all right girl?' Mama Teta asks. 'I've never seen you with *cernes* under your eyes before.'

'Oh, I have problems with my daughter.' Materena's eyes fill with tears. After meeting that woman in the cathedral last week, Materena has been very easy-going with Leilani. She stopped expecting her daughter to be like her. When Leilani didn't thank her mother for the cup of Milo she made her, Materena didn't say anything about it. She has been trying really hard to keep her cool but last night she borrowed a pen from her daughter and said, 'Thank you,' and Leilani got cranky. 'Mamie,' she said, 'I don't care, it's only a pen!'

'So what if it's only a pen!' Materena shouted. 'I can't say thank you? What? Do I have to be like you? Ungrateful?' And Leilani shouted again, 'It's only a pen!'

Next minute, Materena and Leilani were shouting at each other, and Pito told them both to shut up. 'You two are driving me crazy!'

'Do you want to do a little *parau-parau*, girl?' Mama Teta asks.

'I'm trying so hard to be a good mother Mama Teta,' says Materena, her voice trembling. 'I don't know what to do any more.' She goes on about how she really can't wait for Leilani to get married and leave.

'Girl,' says Mama Teta. 'I've got bad news for you, nobody is getting married these days. Come, we sit in the shade and I'm going to tell you what happened to me last Saturday.'

Saturday morning and what a beautiful morning it was. It's a good day to get married, and Mama Teta, yawning, forces herself to get out of bed. She starts the day with her usual *café*, grabs her cosmetic bag out of the fridge and heads for the bathroom.

The first thing she does is check in the mirror for the grey hairs that have grown during the past twenty-three days since her last bridal driving job. No bride wants her chauffeur to look like she's on the age pension. She plucks her eyebrows, blow-dries her hair, cream on the face, blue eyeshadow, eyeliner, mascara, lipstick; the hair goes up in a neat chignon, and plastic white flowers go into the chignon. There, finished.

OK, now the suit, zip, buttons, shoes. All right, time to go.

Mama Teta hops in the bridal car, all decorated with plastic red roses. She reverses out of the driveway and recites a little prayer for all the lunatic drivers not to be on the road at the same time as she is, and drivers without a driver's licence, and drunk drivers, and drivers with poor eyesight, and stressed-out mothers, and cranky gendarmes.

Ouh, it's so dangerous on the roads. No wonder Mama Teta hardly drives these days. She's glad today's bride doesn't live too far away.

Ah, here's the house of the bride's parents. Mama Teta parks the car and she can smell roasted pig, there's party in the air. She slowly gets out of the car, and waits for a family member to come and greet her. But nobody is coming out of the house and so Mama Teta walks to the house, calling out, 'The chauffeur of the bride is here!'

Finally a middle-aged woman, all done up, comes to the door.

'*Aue . . . aue*,' she says. 'There's a bit of a problem.'

Mama Teta smiles. 'There always a bit of a problem at the last minute. I'll go and wait in the car, OK?'

The middle-aged woman, looks to the crowd outside, which has doubled in size in less than a minute. '*Non*, it's best you wait in the house, I don't want anybody to know there's a bit of a problem.' And so Mama Teta walks into the house and is greeted by a crying bride in the living room. There's a man dressed in his funeral and wedding suit (the papi) standing by the crying bride, looking lost. The bride is getting cold feet. She's going on and on about how she doesn't want to get married. And the middle-aged woman, who Mama Teta met at the door and who must be the mama, is going on and on about all the food, and all the relatives, saying how so many caught the boat from Raiatea to Tahiti especially for the marriage.

'Think, girl,' the mama says. 'It's normal to be nervous.'

'Ma,' the bride says behind her tears. 'I'm not nervous, OK? I just don't want to marry that . . . that . . .' Ten heads go on nodding. 'I'm not nervous!'

The poor mama turns to the papi and pleads, 'Say something to your daughter, you!'

Mama Teta checks the time on her watch. The bride is always late, that's the tradition, but she can't be too late, otherwise the priest might get cranky and walk off.

The papi is still beside his daughter, not saying anything, and so the mama is off again. 'All right, I'm sick of the comedy. You'—she pokes the bride's chest—'are going to get fixed up, get your behind into the bridal car, and then you're going to walk into the church and say "I do"!'

'Non!'

'Ah, oui, you are, my dear! I made a personal loan for your wedding.' The mama points a finger to herself. 'You hear? I signed some papers and so you're going to get married.' The mama is now shouting.

The daughter looks into her mother's eyes. 'You really want me to get married to somebody who's sleeping around, somebody who doesn't respect me? He's sleeping around, you hear?'

Mama Teta looks at the ceiling. This has never happened in her bridal car chauffeur's career. The room is suddenly silent. Aue, she feels so sorry for the young woman.

As for the mama of the bride, she must be feeling weak in the knees because her husband has to support her. He says, 'Listen girl . . . What Teri'i has done doesn't mean he doesn't love you . . . all men do that . . . it's just for fun, it's the heat, we forget ourselves.'

Oh my God, Mama Teta thinks, what a stupid man he is.

'Excuse me? All men? We forget ourselves?' This is the wife talking and she's not leaning on her husband any more.

The husband's face goes pale and he has to undo the top button on his shirt because the words he has just said are now choking him.

'All men you say?' The wife looks at her husband like she's about to devour him raw. 'I've had suspicions all my life, so tell me now, when you say all men, it means you too, eh?' She pushes him. 'Eh? Why are you pale, why are you sweating?'

'Angelica,' he says.

'Don't Angelica me, get out, get out, get out.' She pushes him again.

The daughter makes one desperate attempt to bring the attention back to her. She gets up and insists they all go to the church for her to get married. But her mother pins her back to the couch with the verdict: there is to be no wedding today.

'But what about the personal loan you made?' the daughter asks, with big sorry eyes for all the drama.

'Everything is off—your marriage, my marriage—and we're going to celebrate our freedom.' Then, looking at her ex-husband. 'Get out of my house before I call my cousins.'

Mama Teta drives the father to his cousin's house. The onlookers peer in trying to see where the bride is. And she's thinking, Mama Teta, that she's definitely getting too old for this kind of business.

'Ah, non alors,' Materena says, half laughing. 'Does this mean my daughter is going to be living with me until she's thirty years old?'

'Why don't you stop trying so hard?' Mama Teta says. 'Just give your daughter some space, that may be all she needs at the moment.'

When a child is born in Tahiti, his placenta is buried under a tree and the child and the tree grow together. A healthy tree means a healthy child, just as a sick tree means a sick child. When a child's tree is sick, the mother takes the sick child to the doctor.

But Tepua cannot do this. She gave her baby girl away for adoption to a French couple and she has no idea where her daughter lives except that she is somewhere in France. What irony too that after years of praying for children to stop coming her way, Tepua would get her wish after her sixth child was born, the one she'll never get to raise.

Relatives have told Tepua that her baby girl is not completely lost. One day she will return, they say, because the calling of a mother is louder than the calling of a land. This is a comfort to Tepua but she would give anything to see her child grow right in front of her eyes.

Tepua's sixth child is named Moea, and although that name is sure to have been changed to a *popa'a* name, she will always be Moea around here. Moea is sick—her tree has spoken.

The news of this misfortune was on the coconut radio two days ago. And yesterday afternoon Tepua's ten-year-old son came to see Materena. 'Auntie Materena, Mamie wants to know if you can come to the house tomorrow at one o'clock for a prayer for my sister Moea.'

Materena replied immediately. '*Oui!* Your mama can count on me.'

The boy ticked his Auntie Materena's name and said, 'Now, I'm going to call Auntie Georgette.'

This morning, after Mass, Loma made a big song and dance because she's not one of the ten women requested for the prayer at Tepua's house when Georgette, who's not even a woman, is. Someone reminded Loma that until she starts saying good words about people instead of backstabbing them she will never be invited to special occasions.

The ten very special women are now sitting in a circle round the sick tree. Tepua thanks them all for coming. They all say that it is an honour to be present. The prayer begins. The women, eyes fervently closed, sing for the little girl and her tree.

The prayer goes on for an hour until Tepua calls for a break, and the women go inside the house. Materena and Rita, with slices of chocolate cake preciously wrapped in a tissue, go and stand in the kitchen by the louvres. As they look out to the tree through the four missing louvres, they sigh and shake their head. 'I'm sure Moea is going to get better from today,' Rita whispers. 'There's nothing like women's power. There's eleven women here today and we're all giving that tree all the love and the power within us because . . .'

But here is Georgette, running from her car to the tree with a bucket.

Georgette's on her knees now, furiously spreading what looks like dirt round the tree.

Materena and Rita press their faces to the gap between the louvres.

'What is that Georgette doing?' asks Rita.

Georgette jumps to her feet. She's looking down at the tree and scratching herself between the legs.

'But! Georgette is scratching her balls!'

'*Shussh*, Rita.' Rita is all red in the face from trying to keep the laughter inside. But Georgette must have heard Rita's laughter for she swings round. She sees Materena and Rita and waves and then, walking her feminine walk, Georgette walks to the house.

Minutes later, the prayers continue in the living room. The women fervently beg the Virgin Mary Understanding Woman to take away whatever Moea's sickness is. For two long hours.

Every now and then Materena stops thinking about her niece to think about her daughter. Following Mama Teta's advice at the cemetery four days ago, Materena has been giving her daughter space, but first she explained the situation. 'Girl,' she said to Leilani, at her desk doing her homework, 'you've been very mean to me lately, it's like you hate me, but I'm not going to hate you back because I love you, so I'm just going to give you space, but if you need me, you know where I am.' Leilani nodded a vague nod—yeah whatever—and Materena left the room, crying her eyes out. Since then, mother and daughter have been avoiding each other.

When the ten women very special to Tepua leave, they are all red-eyed and exhausted. As they walk back to Rita's car, Rita says to Materena that praying with all your heart and soul is draining. 'I gave all my love to that baby girl.'

'Me too.' Materena is aching all over. 'I gave her all my love.'

'And I gave her all the power within me.' Rita gets into her car.

'Cousin, I'll walk,' says Materena.

'*Non*, I'll drive you . . . I don't want you passing out on the highway.'

The cousins remain silent except for frequent sighings of sadness and they both jump with surprise when the back door opens and in sneaks Georgette. 'I have a confession to make.'

'Ah, *oui alors*,' says Rita. 'What were you doing with that bucket?'

Georgette confesses that all she did was put a bit of fertiliser around the tree. Materena and Rita, stunned, say in unison, 'Fertiliser?'

Georgette hurries to explain that it's not that she doesn't believe in prayers but she thought it could just be that the tree needed a bit of fertiliser. She's been thinking about this since yesterday.

'Jeez Georgette,' Rita says. 'Too much fertiliser can be fatal! What got into your head? I thought it was just dirt you put around the tree! Georgette, you stupid man!'

Materena tenderly reaches out for Georgette's hand. It must hurt Georgette when people refer to her as a man when she is, in her head, in her heart, in the way she dresses, a woman. A woman who is always so willing to help out because she was born with a big giving heart. But she shouldn't have tampered with Tepua's daughter's tree. All women have got to know their limit. 'Cousin,' Materena says, worried, 'do you know a bit about fertilisers?'

Georgette swears that she followed the instructions religiously.

On the coconut radio news three days later, it is confirmed that Moea has been cured from her illness. Her tree is beautiful and healthy again. Some say this is the result of the prayers to the Virgin Mary Understanding Woman at Tepua's house. Others say Madame Pietre took her adopted daughter to the doctor because that is what mothers do.

A long time ago

MATERENA FELL IN LOVE with Pito a long time ago but she still remembers those distant days, when her mind would be all over the place. She once forgot about a chicken cooking in the oven, despite her mother reminding her about it before leaving for a family meeting. Materena was in the clouds, she was in love.

Now, almost twenty years later, she's in bed and Pito is snoring next to her. Materena puts her head under her pillow, but she can still hear it.

'Pito! I can't sleep!' Growling, Pito rolls onto his side.

Materena closes her eyes, enjoying the silence. Then her mind starts ticking away about this and that: tomorrow night's dinner, Moana who's just turned fifteen and who left school two months ago for an apprenticeship at the five-star international Beachcomber Hotel's restaurant as a chef, Tamatoa enlisting for military service in France, how she needs to buy new thongs. Suddenly a thought pops into her head. Is there a boy on her daughter's horizon? Lately Leilani has been so nice (but *so* nice! Which makes a welcome change!). And she's got that look, that special look girls get when there's a boy on the horizon.

Aue, girl, eh, Materena thinks, don't pay attention to boys, work hard at school, you're almost there. Get your degree and then you can look around as much as you like. Pick the best one of the lot.

The following morning, Saturday, Materena is on a mission.

'Girl? Do you have a boyfriend?'

'*Non!*' Leilani laughs that little laugh that says, yes.

'Girl,' Materena says very seriously, 'you can tell me if you have a boyfriend. I'm not going to get cranky, because it's normal.'

'There's no boyfriend.'

OK, then, since Leilani refuses to share the news, Materena is going to have to turn into a spy. Here is that diary on the desk, wide open. Materena, hands on her broom, ready to start brooming in case Leilani appears out of nowhere, begins to read.

'Eh?' she says out loud. 'What's this? This is not writing!' There's a rectangle followed by a sun, another rectangle, a flower, a circle, a star, a square, and an exclamation mark.

OK, another way for a mother to find out secrets about her children is to listen to them talk to their friends. Materena, washing basket on her hip, strolls to the clothes line. Leilani and Vahine are lying on the grass. Materena puts the basket on the ground and hangs the sheet first to hide behind, all the while pretending she's looking for pegs.

'Girlfriend, you're sure we're not going to die with your invention?'

'*Non*, girlfriend, it's great for sweating.'

Materena peeps from behind the bed sheet. Leilani and Vahine are wrapping plastic sheets round their waists. If Materena understands the situation correctly, the plastic sheets, combined with the heat of the sun, are supposed to make the girls melt. But what is there to melt? They're so skinny as they are.

'Mamie!' Leilani calls out sweetly. 'Are you going to be long?'

Materena calls back that she's going to be as long as she has to because clothes should always be hung properly and not in a hurry.

After a while, the girls start talking loud and clear, like they want the whole population to hear their conversation. They're talking in a foreign language which is definitely not English. It sounds more like a made-up secret code language. And they're laughing their heads off.

Materena knows very well the girls are talking in a secret code because they suspect her to be listening—as if she's got nothing else better to do in her life. Materena hurries up with her job. The secret code language is getting on her nerves.

Every now and then she hears Vahine languidly pronounce the name of Materena's eldest son Tamatoa. Vahine is in love with Tamatoa and the less he's interested in her, the more she wants him. It's complicated.

Well, anyway, there are no more clothes to hang. Materena marches back to the house. 'Eh,' she says. 'I'm not a spy, you know, and keep your laughter down, Moana is asleep. Some people work at nights.'

The girls are still outside hours later and Materena is getting worried. Sun goes to the head. Sweating too much is not good for the health.

'Eh, girls!' she calls out from the shutter. 'You don't think you're brown enough? You don't think you've sweated enough?'

'We're nearly finished,' the girls call back.

All right, then. Materena gets the ironing board and the iron out to iron Moana's uniform. But first it's time to wake him up.

'It's twelve thirty, *chéri*,' Materena says, caressing her son's hair.

Moana nods, sits on his bed yawning and stretching himself.

'When are you going to start having day shifts?' asks Materena. She feels so sorry for Moana. 'I'm going to complain to the hotel.'

'Mamie . . . I'm learning a lot of things at the hotel for when I have my restaurant.' After kissing his mother on her forehead, Moana goes to have his shower, while Materena finishes ironing his uniform.

'What are Leilani and Vahine doing?' Moana, out of the shower with his towel wrapped round his waist, asks.

'It's to lose weight,' Materena says shaking her head.

'Lose weight? They're perfect as they are, they're beautiful . . .' Moana's voice trails off and looking at his eyes it seems to Materena that Moana is admiring his sister's best friend. Materena says nothing.

Ah, and here's her eldest son all sweaty from his ten-kilometre run and his workout at his friend's gym. He's in preparation for military service. Tamatoa gives his mother a quick kiss on the forehead, looks out of the shutter, shakes his head with disbelief and asks, 'What are these two crazy *nenettes* doing?'

'It's to lose weight,' Materena says, cackling. She adds with a wink how Vahine is so pretty, she's like a porcelain doll, and plus she's so nice. For a rich girl, Materena means. Looking at Vahine you wouldn't know that her French father is a director of a company.

'*Bof*,' Tamatoa shrugs. 'When I look at girls, I don't care if they're rich or if they're poor. I care more about what they look like, and that one is just too skinny.' Then, doing his loud papa voice, Tamatoa calls out to his sister and her friend that boys don't like skinny girls, they like girls with flesh, girls they can hold on to.

Vahine, sitting right up, turns to Tamatoa and listens attentively.

'Boys don't like skinny girls!' he shouts.

Five days a week, here at the kitchen table, Mama George and Loma gossip about what they've seen with their own two eyes or heard with their own two ears by the side of the road or outside the Chinese store. On Sundays, they gossip about what they've seen with their own two eyes and heard with their own two ears outside the church, after and before Mass. And on Saturdays, confession day, Mama George and Loma talk about each relative who was in the confessional box for more than ten minutes. Since only the priest can hear confessions, all Mama George and Loma can do is sit at the back of the church and time how long a relative has been in the confessional box.

Now, when a woman is in the confessional box for more than ten minutes, Mama George and Loma declare she's been up to no good. If the woman has a man she's seeing another man, and if she doesn't have a man she's seeing a married man. And a young girl in the confessional box for more than ten minutes means there's a boy on the horizon. It doesn't take ten minutes to confess you've talked bad about your mama, you borrowed something from her without her permission. Sins like these are fine with the priest. He tells you, don't do this again and sends you off with his absolution, and a little smile. However, sins of the flesh, lust, young girls sneaking out of the shutter in the middle of the night to meet a lover, make the priest cranky like you wouldn't believe. His absolution comes at a price: a ten-minute sermon.

The mother of a young girl confessing sins of the flesh must be immediately informed of the situation. It's the rule and the regulation, according to Loma and Mama George.

Materena, about to cross the road on her way to visit her mother, has some information coming her way. 'Materena cousin! Materena cousin!'

This is the distinctive high-pitched voice of big mouth Cousin Loma, and Materena hurries to cross the road.

Loma also hurries to cross the road. 'Materena cousin!'

Materena quickens her steps, still pretending oblivion.

Loma starts to run. 'Materena cousin!' She's now in front of Materena.

'Eh, Loma!' Materena exclaims, surprised. 'Where are you off to?'

'Didn't you hear me call out to you?' Loma asks, puffing.

'*Non*,' Materena replies innocently. 'I was thinking about . . .'

But Loma is not interested in knowing what Materena was thinking. She's more interested in delivering information about Leilani's recent fourteen-minute visit to the confessional box and waiting for a reaction.

This is Materena's reaction from the inside: *What?* Fourteen minutes in the confessional box! My girl tells the priest everything and she tells me zero! Is my girl still a virgin? Who's the boy on the horizon?

This is Materena's reaction from the outside: she sighs, 'Cousin, you don't have *anything* better to do than time people in the confessional?'

'Yes, I do!' Loma exclaims before stomping away.

Materena can now do two things. She can go home and question her daughter or she can go ahead and visit her mother.

Materena finds her mother in the garden pulling weeds.

'Eh, *chérie*!' Loana exclaims with joy. Loana is always happy when her daughter visits, even if the last time they saw each other was yesterday.

'Let me help you weed,' Materena says.

'Oh, *non*! The last time you helped me weed you pulled out my good grass. Just sit next to me and talk, my ears are opened.'

'Leilani was in the confessional box for fourteen minutes,' Materena says, making herself comfortable on the grass. 'Loma told me.'

'Ah, *oui*?' Loana says, cackling. She tells her daughter that being in the confessional box for more than ten minutes doesn't necessarily mean there's a confession happening. Sometimes people just want to talk to the priest because he's got time to listen.

'I've got time to listen to my daughter!' Materena exclaims. 'I always want to listen . . . You know me, Mamie, I love to listen to people . . . It's Leilani who doesn't want to tell me anything. I know we've had problems in the past but we're friends again. She can tell me anything.'

'Well,' says Loana. 'Lie next to your daughter in her bed and patiently wait until she talks to you.'

'Leilani?' Materena says absently as she's chopping onions later on. 'Did you go to confession today?'

'What?' Leilani turns to face her mother. 'Are you crazy? I was with Rose. *She* was in the confessional box. I was waiting for her outside. Father Arthur would be the last to know about my affairs!'

'Don't talk about Father Arthur like that!' Materena is cranky now. 'He's a very nice priest.' All right, she thinks, but what was Rose doing in the confessional box for more than fourteen minutes? Should I tell Cousin Tapeta about this?

Eh, it's not my onions, Materena decides.

Much later, comfortable in her daughter's bed, Materena looks around. Leilani's desk is a mess, there's paper everywhere (scrunched, torn, flat), pens, chewing-gum wrappers. Materena wonders how her daughter does her homework in these conditions. And what is that glass doing in the bookcase? And a packet of noodle soup! And what's with all these stones everywhere? Is Leilani collecting them?

Aue, the poor plant in the corner is dying. When was the last time

Leilani watered it? Materena makes a mental note to save it tomorrow.

Ah, Materena really loves Leilani's words of wisdom on the walls:

When you feel down, think of something that makes you happy.
To die with a clear conscience is the only way to leave this world.
Don't eat in front of people if you can't share.
Show respect to all people.
KNOW WHAT YOU WANT AND MAKE IT HAPPEN.

Materena told Leilani all of these words of wisdom.

But the following words of wisdom come from the books Leilani has read or heard from other people (relatives and strangers):

Why worry about your beard when your head is about to be taken?
The truth is in the pudding.
A man in love mistakes a harelip for a dimple.

Materena hasn't read that one before, it must be new . . .

Sex is the poor man's opera . . .

Materena hasn't read that one either. Very interested she reads on.

Kisses are like almonds.
Love makes all hard hearts gentle.
First prize is finding someone to be passionately in love with you for a lifetime.

Ah . . . here's Leilani.

'Oh,' she says, seeing her mother on the bed. 'You're here.' She ties the towel round her body tighter.

'I just felt like resting my legs on your bed. That's OK with you, *chérie*?' Materena hurries to add that her feet are clean.

'Of course it's OK, *mi casa es tu casa*.' Leilani is looking for something to wear tonight in bed, and meanwhile, water from her long wet hair is dripping on the floor. Materena tightens her lips before she starts going on about how hair shouldn't be washed at night.

Leilani has found an oversize T-shirt. She slips into it, dries her hair with the towel, drops it on the floor, wipes her feet on it. Materena is looking but she's not saying anything although she really wants to. What's a towel, she thinks, compared to your daughter telling you secrets.

'You're all right, Mamie?' Leilani asks, walking to her desk.

'I'm fine, girl, no problems, and I'm not here to start a fight.'

Leilani smiles as she sits at her desk. She grabs her schoolbag from under the desk, takes copybooks, books and pencil case out, and attacks her homework. She begins to write, and furiously too. Materena has never seen anyone write so fast in her life.

Ten minutes later. 'You're all right, Mamie?'

'I'm fine, *chérie*.'

Twenty minutes later. 'Mamie? Is there anything you want to tell me?'

'*Non*.'

Patiently Materena waits for Leilani to start a conversation. It's quite boring. waiting. Just as Materena is about to fall asleep, finally Leilani says the magic words. 'Mamie, can you help me?'

'Sure! No problems, tell me everything.' Materena, excited, sits up.

Leilani needs help with the family genealogical tree.

'Ah,' Materena says, disappointed. 'I know my ancestors, but only from my mother's side.'

'That's all right, Mamie.' Leilani passes a thick textbook for her mother to lean on, along with paper and a pen. 'Thanks,' she says.

Materena starts writing Leilani's name at the bottom of the page, links it to her name, alongside Pito's name, up to Loana's name, the daughter of Kika Mahi *née* Raufaki from Rangiroa and of Apoto Mahi from Tahiti . . . on and on.

'Your great-grandmother was born with twelve toes,' Materena says.

'Ah, really?' Leilani doesn't sound too interested.

But for Materena this is an interesting detail. 'You know what her nickname was?' she asks.

'Just write it down,' Leilani says.

'Ah, *oui*?' OK then, and so Materena writes her grandmother's nick-name—*Twelve toes*. Now, next ancestor.

'Your great-great-grandfather was the Chief of Faa'a. He signed the Protectorate paper to France before the King of Tahiti. He gave Tahiti to the French people.'

'Really!' Leilani exclaims.

'Eh, *oui*.' It's not really something Materena is proud of but she understands her ancestor was under a lot of pressure being a chief. 'You want me to write this information?' she asks.

'Absolutely. Write everything.'

Aue, Materena thinks, it's like I'm Leilani's secretary but it's good to help your kids with their school projects. So, applying herself writing and reading out loud what she's writing, Materena resumes her task.

There was an ancestor who had a red beard.

Materena looks up. No reaction from Leilani.

An ancestor who was a Filipino sailor.

No reaction.

An ancestor who used to be a slave before she escaped and came to Tahiti. She was black, sixteen years old, her name was Josephina.

'Josephina . . . a beautiful name,' Leilani says. 'What a brave girl.'

Then there were Leilani Lexter and Leilani Bodie from Hawaii whom Leilani already knows about, an English ancestor by the name of Williams—he's the last ancestor on the list and Materena's hand hurts.

'Finished! I'm not complaining but my hand really hurts. Can I do anything else for you?'

'*Non*, it's OK.'

All right then . . . 'You know,' Materena says, 'when I was your age, I used to sneak out of the shutter in the night to go and meet your father.' Materena can't believe her ears. What on earth made her confess this?

'Sneak out of the shutter!' Leilani shrieks, with a smirk on her face. 'In the night! Where did you two naughties meet?'

Materena tells Leilani where, and adds that Pito brought a quilt along and laid the quilt underneath the frangipani tree behind the bank. Leilani is getting very interested in the story. She particularly wants to know what her parents did on that quilt.

'Well,' Materena says. 'We talked, we did chitchat.'

'And what else did you do?'

'Well, we kissed . . .' Materena can feel the top of her head burning.

'And what else did you do?'

'We caressed . . . and there was the moon and the stars and the gentle breeze and the sweet perfume of the frangipani flowers and . . .'

Leilani bursts out laughing and Materena doesn't need to say more. It's clear what happened: sexy loving. Sexy loving always happens when there's chitchat, kisses and caresses under the frangipani tree.

'Do your homework,' Materena says, quietly leaving the room.

And now, in the kitchen drinking lemonade, Materena thinks about how she used to tell her mother everything. But by the time Materena was sixteen years old she was telling her mother nothing because . . . Because there was a boy on the horizon of course!

Loana didn't ask Materena why she'd stopped telling her everything until the day before Materena gave birth to her first child. 'Why didn't you tell me you had a boyfriend?' Loana said. 'I would have told you about contraception. But now it's too late, you're about to give birth.' When the mothers don't know what's going on they can't help.

Materena walks back to Leilani's bedroom.

'You've got something else to confess?' Leilani asks, cackling.

'*Non*, it's not about that,' Materena says. 'Leilani . . . I just want you to know that you can tell me anything OK? I'm not going to ask you any questions. With whom, where, etc. OK?' Materena is a bit uncomfortable saying what she really means but she's sure Leilani understands. She wishes Leilani would stop laughing. 'Leilani! Stop laughing!'

'I just can't imagine you and Papi doing . . .' She can't say the word. 'And are you still doing . . . ?' She still can't say that word.

'*Aue!*' Materena exclaims. 'Do your homework.' And off she goes to iron. She switches the radio on to keep her company, tuning it to Radio Tefana, to listen to Ati's love songs programme.

One son leaves, another son arrives

TAMATOA IS LEAVING next week, three months ahead of his scheduled departure date, and Materena is panicking—so much to do in such a short time!

Buy gifts to help her eldest son remember his island. Organise a photo album of the family for Tamatoa to flick through whenever he feels homesick. A new suitcase! Install the telephone, that's what you do when one of your children is on the other side of the planet.

After much running around, draining the emergency account and borrowing a bit of money from her mother, Materena has everything under control. All she needs now is for her son to grant her a few minutes of his time. 'I need you. I have to tell you about the rules.'

Tamatoa has just come home from training. 'Not now,' he says.

'Now?' Materena says as Tamatoa walks out of the shower.

'I've got to get dressed first.'

'Now?' Materena says as Tamatoa walks out of his bedroom. His hair is oiled and he reeks of perfume.

'Later,' he says as he flees the house.

'What's with the perfume?' Materena calls out. 'What time are you coming home? What are you going to eat tonight?'

Tamatoa doesn't come home that night, nor the next day, or the day after. Materena starts to get worried. People don't disappear for four days before they're about to do something they've always wanted to do in their life: catch a plane. Pito tells Materena not to worry because it's the tradition to go out drinking with your *copains* before you leave for military service. You drink, you say goodbye, you have fun.

Materena is still worried. 'I'm calling the gendarmes,' she tells Pito and starts dialling. Pito snatches the phone from Materena.

'Relax, woman!'

Materena snatches the phone back. 'I'm calling the gendarmes!'

Pito pulls the cord out of its socket. 'Tamatoa is just out drinking!'

Materena plugs the cord back in. 'What if my son is in danger? Get out of my way, Pito. Get out of my way, I'm going to hit you with that telephone! It's my telephone, give me my telephone back! Pito you . . .'

'Are you two going to stop?' This is Leilani speaking. 'He's with Vahine.' Leilani explains how Vahine came to school this morning and told her that . . . well . . . that all is great with Tamatoa.

'And her parents?' asks Materena. 'They don't mind?'

'They're at a conference in Hawaii. Vahine's grandmother is looking after Vahine.'

'Ah, my boy is with a girl,' cackles Pito, smiling away. He's all happy.

Although Materena is relieved to know her son is not in danger it doesn't mean she's happy. When is Tamatoa going to pack the suitcase? And what is going to happen to Vahine when Tamatoa leaves? Materena knows how hard it is when the boy you love leaves on military service. Just thinking about it makes her even crankier with Pito.

Tamatoa comes home the morning before departure day as if nothing was amiss. He kisses his younger brother, busy marinating chicken thighs, and he kisses his mother, also in the kitchen, helping out the cook.

'What's with all the food?' he asks.

'But it's for your farewell party!' says Materena. 'Your brother has been busy for two days for you.'

'My brother, eh,' Tamatoa says giving him a little punch on the arm. 'I hope you're going to cook my favourite dish, chicken curry.'

'Of course I will,' says Moana, grating coconut.

Materena looks at her youngest son, so touched by all the cooking he's doing for his brother, and she sure hopes Tamatoa doesn't forget to thank him properly. In the meantime, Materena would like Tamatoa to confess about his whereabouts. 'Where have you been?' she asks.

'Somewhere.'

'You must like skinny girls now.'

'Eh? What are you going on about?'

'Is she your girlfriend or just a body for your pleasure?'

'Mamie . . . it's not like in your days, OK?'

'*Aue*,' Materena sighs. 'Sit down while I tell you about the rules.'

'The rules? What are you going on about?'

'The rules when you're a visitor, you big silly!'

'In a minute,' Tamatoa says.

In a minute turns into many hours later . . . The house is packed with relatives who have come for the farewell ritual but right this moment, Materena has her son all to herself in his bedroom. He's crying silent tears and just looking at him is breaking Materena's heart, but she's not going to tell her son not to cry, that's he's a man. Crying is good for the soul, just as laughing is. You've got to release. If only Tamatoa also cried when he was not drunk.

Anyway, here are the rules, which must be followed when you are on foreign soil and your family is on the other side of the planet:

First rule: No fighting with the locals, you don't want to upset the wrong family. What if it's the Mafia? And plus it's not nice to fight.

Second rule: No rendezvous in a girl's bedroom, even if she tells you that her parents are fine with her having boys in their house. It's more likely that the girl's parents don't know anything about it, and all you're going to get is a a thick piece of wood smashed across your back.

Third rule: Never arrive with empty hands at a dinner. Show your gratitude for the invitation.

Tamatoa nods, meaning that he's registering the information.

Fourth rule (still about being a guest at dinner): Leave a bit of food on your plate to show the host you're too full to have another serving. If there's nothing left on your plate and the host can't serve you more food, because there's no more food in the cooking pot, she's going to be very embarrassed. She's going to assume you're still hungry. Eat the food even if you don't like the taste of it and it looks bizarre.

'Don't you make anyone think that I didn't raise you proper.'

Another nod from Tamatoa, as he puts his arms round his mother.

'You're a number one mamie,' he sniffs.

Aue, Materena thinks, it's so nice when the children make such confessions, even if they are drunk. She puts her arm round her son and is about to go on with the rules when the door of the bedroom swings open. It's Pito, also drunk.

'Son,' he says, jovial. 'Come outside with the men.'

And like he's done many times before, Tamatoa abandons his mother for his father's company.

The airport is packed. Tamatoa is the grandson of Loana, the relative who never says anything bad about anybody, and the son of Materena, the relative who is nice to everybody. By the time he's walking through customs, he has about one hundred shell necklaces round his neck. He's less drunk than he was four hours ago (Materena made him stand under a cold shower for thirty minutes) but he still looks like he's falling asleep. According to Pito, speaking from experience, catching a plane drunk is better than catching a plane sober. First of all you don't get scared, and secondly you sleep and so the time goes faster.

There's crying all over the place. The grandmothers are crying, the aunties and the cousins are crying, the sister is crying, the brother is crying. The sister's girlfriend (alias Tamatoa's secret lover) is wailing and digging her long fingernails into Moana's arm. Moana takes it on. Anything to help his brother's ex-girlfriend.

But everybody knows that the woman suffering the most is the mother. *Aue*, Materena needs to hold onto someone, her legs are weak, she's going to faint in a minute. Here's Ati on her left. No, not him, the relatives will gossip about how she held her husband's best mate instead of her husband, even if he was closer to her than her husband who is hiding behind a pillar metres away.

Here's Cousin Mori on her right. *Oui*, he'll do.

Mori puts an arm round Materena and says, 'One son leaves, another son arrives, eh?'

Materena doesn't understand. She lifts her crying eyes to her cousin. 'What are you saying?'

'Your son leaves, your daughter brings home a boyfriend,' says Mori.

'What boyfriend?' asks Materena.

'But Leilani's boyfriend, the one with the motorbike.'

'Boyfriend?' Materena says again. 'Motorbike?'

'Ah,' Mori says, realising that once again in his life he didn't look where he was walking. He quickly moves back to the subject of Materena's son. What a fine man he's going to be that one . . .

In the days after Tamatoa left on military service, Materena moped around the house with her broom like a lost soul, brooming sad long strokes here and there. She did feel a bit better when her son called to let her know that he had arrived in France and all was well, all was fantastic. He sounded so happy and that was a real comfort to Materena. But it still felt like her heart was being crucified.

She got lots of embraces from Pito, Moana and Leilani.

Pito's hug was a quick embrace. He tapped Materena on the shoulder and said, 'OK, Mama, we stop crying.'

Moana's embrace was tender and cuddly. Materena felt like a teddy bear in her son's arms. He said, 'Mamie, we're all sad.'

Leilani's embrace was strong and positive. She said, 'Mamie . . . we're the strongest creatures on earth, don't forget.'

Nobody who saw Materena by the side of the road waiting for the truck to go to work dared call out a happy greeting. A nod that is polite and full of compassion is much more appropriate in such situations. Even Loma, the cousin voted most insensitive by the family, made sure to remain low-key.

Also nobody has been visiting Materena except for Loana, who came by to cry along and to say, 'Girl, you've got other children to look after. Get up and walk.'

But Materena wasn't ready to do this yet. She had to cry for a little bit longer and remember those days when Tamatoa was a sweet little boy before he turned into a cheeky boy and later on a hoodlum.

It is only after a week that Materena starts to feel better. She realises that military service is good for young men. It keeps them out of trouble. OK, then, time to get on with the day. First on Materena's list is to find out about that boy who has a motorbike.

No more believing Leilani's stories that she spends two hours after school comforting Vahine because Tamatoa has left to do his military service in France instead of doing it in Tahiti and marrying her.

Materena marches to her daughter's bedroom. After two knocks, she walks in, just as Leilani is shoving something under her shirt.

'I've heard you've got a boyfriend and that he's got a motorbike.'

Leilani's response is an exclamation. 'Who told you!'

Ah ha, Materena thinks. 'I just hope that you're protecting yourself. You don't want to fall pregnant with the wrong boy, a boy who's using you for his pleasure. Not counting the diseases and everything.'

An angel must be passing through because it's very quiet.

'So?' Materena says to break the silence. 'Who's the boy on the horizon?'

The silence continues until Leilani turns to her mother, patiently waiting. She confirms that there is a boy on the horizon and he does have a motorbike but she can't really call him a boyfriend.

'Ah, *oui?*' And why not? Materena asks herself. He's a married man?

Leilani informs her mother that she doesn't really want to be his girlfriend and she's trying very hard to resist him but it's so difficult.

'Ah, *oui?*' And now Materena is really worried. And why does Leilani have to resist that boy? He's like thirty? He's a cousin? He's a foreigner? He's a Protestant? 'And why do you have to resist him?'

Leilani sighs. 'I know I shouldn't,' she says. 'I mean, resist him . . . He's got everything on my list.'

List? Materena is intrigued. 'What list? What's this?'

Leilani puts a hand under her shirt, fumbles for a few seconds with her bra and now she's holding a folded piece of paper. 'Here. Read.'

My boyfriend must be a reader like me.

Materena glances at her daughter for a quick second.

My boyfriend must not be an alcoholic. One beer or two per day is fine, but not ten.

My boyfriend must be a nice person.

Materena nods. She agrees. One hundred per cent.

Being handsome is definitely optional.

Materena reads on, agreeing over and over again. 'That boy,' she asks just to make sure. 'He's like on your list?'

Leilani nods, her eyes twinkling with delight.

But what is there to resist? Materena asks in her head.

'Where does he live?' She asks out of interest.

Leilani casually replies that the boy lives in Punaauia PK 18.

'Punaauia PK 18!' Materena is exclaiming, because it costs millions to live there. The houses have access to the white sanded beach and electrical gates. Then at PK 21, where Pito's family is from, you've got the fibro shacks.

'Oh, Mamie, you're impossible. So what if he lives in Punaauia PK 18? He's not a king.'

'I know that . . . but tell me, why do you have to resist that boy?'

The news is that he's too nice.

'Eh? What?' Materena asks, confused. 'That's the reason?'

Leilani confirms this with a slow nod. 'Sometimes I wonder if it's just an act to get into my *culotte*,' she continues.

Materena bursts out laughing. 'One minute you're telling me nothing and next minute you're telling me everything!'

'But how can I tell if he's being nice because he is nice or if he's being nice because he wants to get into my *culotte*?'

Materena looks up to the ceiling. 'Let me think a little.'

'Was Papi really nice to you at the beginning?' Leilani asks.

'*Non*, he was like he is today.'

'And you still went with him!' Leilani can't believe her ears.

'What do you want,' says Materena shrugging her shoulders. 'Love is like that. You can't explain. What's the boy's name?'

'Hotu Viriatu.' And before Materena can say anything about this piece of information, Leilani advises her mother that he's Catholic, he's not from an enemy family, and he's not a cousin.

He's just Hotu Viriatu: twenty-two, handsome, smart and nice.

'You're nice too,' says Materena. 'Nice people often attract each other.'

'He's had five girlfriends.'

'Five,' calmly repeats Materena. Five! She yells in her head, but he's worse than Ati that one!

'Is this a lot?' asks Leilani.

'Oh . . . it depends.' These days Materena is very careful of what she says to Leilani. Leilani goes on about Hotu's ex-girlfriends. Hotu was last year's Miss Tahiti's boyfriend!

And before her there was the champion rower from Hawaii! And before her there was one of the President of Tahiti's nieces!

Before Materena has the chance to say that Hotu might have exaggerated a little bit, Leilani informs her mother that she didn't find out about these women from Hotu, but from his mother.

'Ah, because you met the mama?' Materena is so surprised. It is unusual for the mama to want to meet her son's girlfriend so soon! Materena met her mother-in-law when she was pregnant with her first child with Pito. 'Hotu's mama invited you to her house to talk?' Materena asks.

'*Non*, she just walked past the restaurant and saw us.' Leilani adds that Hotu ducked under the table but it was too late. His mother had seen him. So she came in and made herself comfortable at the table. She looked at Leilani up and down. She talked about this and that, Hotu's famous girlfriends whose photos are hung in the living room.

Now, Materena understands that when a girlfriend becomes an ex-girlfriend it doesn't mean you put all her photos in the bin. But putting them up in your living room? 'Hotu's mother sounds like a bizarre woman,' she says, getting up. 'What does she look like?'

'A Christmas tree,' laughs Leilani. 'Mamie, she's got so much jewellery, it's ridiculous and you know what they say about people who wear a lot of jewellery,' she goes on.

'*Non*.' Materena doesn't know anyone who wears a lot of jewellery.

'They have a low self-esteem,' Leilani informs her mother. 'They're not confident. That's why you are confident, because you don't wear any jewellery except for your wedding ring.'

'Ah.' Materena agrees with a nod, although in her mind, people wear a lot of jewellery because they can afford to buy a lot of jewellery.

'She's Tahitian, she's brown as us, but she speaks like she was born into the French aristocracy,' says Leilani. 'She has a French accent, Mamie!'

'Ah.' Anyway, let's go back to Hotu's ex-girlfriends, Materena would like to know who broke up with who.

'He did.'

'He did, eh?' Materena says, shaking her head. Now she can see the type. He sounds like Monsieur Casanova that one.

'Mamie, he had to go back to France, you know,' explains Leilani. 'To finish his studies.'

'What does he do?' Materena can't believe she forgot to ask this very important question.

Well, he's a dentist. Leilani explains that at the moment he's working with a dentist in town but he will be opening his own practice soon.

'A dentist!' exclaims Materena. 'How old was he when he finished school? Twelve?'

'Seventeen like I will be when I finish school.' Leilani goes on about how it's the normal age to finish school when you don't repeat classes. 'And Hotu didn't become a dentist for the money,' stresses Leilani.

'Ah, *oui?*' Materena can't help being a bit sceptical.

Leilani continues about Hotu's mission as a dentist: to educate people on the importance of looking after their teeth (because bad teeth affect health), and to donate several hours of his time each month to poor people who can't afford a dentist and who badly need one. That's why Hotu is taking lessons to perfect his Tahitian. He wants to be able to speak to people who can't express themselves in the French language.

'Ah, his Tahitian is not really good?' Materena asks.

'Oh, he's like me you know. He gets by . . . he's like many of us. He's so wonderful,' Leilani sighs. 'He really wants to give something back to the world having had such a fortunate childhood. But I don't think it's the right time for me to be with him.'

'All right, then. Forget about that boy, OK? Work hard at school. Get your degrees and a good job. Then, if the dentist is still free, and you still feel strongly about him, don't resist him any more. But he sounds to me like a real nice person.'

Now, Materena knows a lot of things about the everyday life but she has no idea how it feels to love someone you have to resist. She's never had to resist physical attraction. When she met Pito and fell in love with him, she didn't stop to think if he was a good catch. She just ran to him with open arms. Since then, she' s never looked at another man. Oh, Materena is not saying that when a good-looking man walks her way, she closes her eyes. She looks, she admires the body, but that's it.

Materena has resisted a lot of things in her life, like telling her mother-in-law off to her face, hitting Pito on the head with the steel frying pan he gave her for one of her birthdays, slapping her big-mouth Cousin Loma across the face . . . Let's just say that Materena knows very well how hard resisting can be, and resisting physical attraction must be even harder. If Materena was in such a situation she'd avoid being in the whereabouts of the man.

But her daughter's plan of action is very different. In fact, Materena doesn't really believe that Leilani is doing much resisting these days.

Leilani is coming home later and later, and since Materena knows that the reason for her daughter's lateness has got nothing to do with Leilani comforting her crying friend, she doesn't need to ask, 'How's Vahine? Is she still crying over Tamatoa?'. Materena only has to ask one question, 'Did you resist today?' That is the question Materena asks the very next day, the question she asks every day from then on.

And these are the answers Materena gets.

'We just talked.'

'I wasn't with him, I was with Vahine.'

'The truck ran out of petrol.'

Ah, here's Leilani coming home now, five minutes later than yesterday. 'So girl?' Materena asks. 'Did you resist today?'

'Stop asking me that question!' Leilani exclaims with a faint smirk.

And Materena understands all that there is to understand.

If your daughter is thirty years old when she first gets a boyfriend, the relatives say, 'Ah, finally! About time! It's a miracle!' If your daughter is in her twenties, the relatives don't say much. But when she's not even seventeen years old, the relatives talk about it for days and days. They say, somebody has got fire up her arse!

Oh, they don't say these very words to the mother. Say these very words to any mother and you'll get a slap across the face, so the relatives just interrogate the mother. 'I heard your beautiful daughter has got a boyfriend. And who is he? How old is he? Has he got a job?'

Materena, about to go to the Chinese store, braces herself for the upcoming interrogation. She can't hide for ever. Plus, she much prefers to be interrogated on her way to the Chinese store, outside the Chinese store, inside the Chinese store, anywhere but in the whereabouts of her house. Because when the relatives are in the whereabouts of your house, they trick you. Before you know it, they're inside your house. And before you know it, they're sitting on the sofa in your living room.

Now, Materena could just ignore the questions fired at her. She could say, 'It's none of your onions.' But the trouble with relatives is that, if they don't get informed, they invent. They believe every word the big-mouth relative of the family—Cousin Loma, the one and only—says.

Aue . . . might as well give the population what the population wants. Following is the information Materena is prepared to share. Yes, her daughter has a boyfriend and Materena prefers this to her daughter being at the mercy of different boys who are only after one thing. True, her daughter's boyfriend is older than Leilani, but only about six years.

Leilani's boyfriend. His name is Hotu Viriatu (he's Catholic, he's not from an enemy family and he's not a cousin). He's very charming. He won Materena over in one second with that beautiful smile of his. His teeth are so white! What about the body! *Ouf!* What a fine specimen.

He came to visit last night but at least he called first to warn of his arrival. Materena had plenty of time to hide the parts of the walls that had paint peeling off. She ignored Leilani and Pito making fun of her. Monsieur Dentist arrived not on his motorbike but in the silver BMW his father bought him. Pito asked Hotu to take him for a drive in his BMW. 'Eh,' Pito said, 'take the old man for a drive, OK?'

'Pito!' Materena said under her breath. She was so embarrassed!

'Sure,' Hotu said. 'I'll take you for a drive.'

'You can fix my teeth too, eh?' Pito said, winking at Materena.

Nevertheless, despite that embarrassment it was fun last night. After the drive, Hotu talked to Materena about what a fine girl Leilani is. 'She is so smart,' he said, 'and I know where she gets her beauty from.' Immediately after this lovely compliment, Pito decided to challenge Hotu to an arm-wrestling competition.

Pito won.

Of course Hotu let Pito win because he knows it's a good idea to let the father of the house win. He's not stupid, Leilani's boyfriend.

When he left, Pito tapped Leilani on the shoulder and said, 'Eh, your boyfriend is too skinny. Tell him to eat a bit more.'

As for Materena, she said, 'What a nice boy!'

OK, who's going to be the first relative to be asking Materena about her daughter's boyfriend? Ah, and who does Materena see in the distance running towards her? Cousin Loma in flesh and bones.

'All is fine?' Materena casually asks, as she greets Cousin Loma.

'*Oui! Oui! Oui!* All is fine!' Loma is so excited today. 'So! Leilani has a boyfriend! I saw them yesterday and he's got a BMW?'

'Well, you saw him so you know,' Materena says.

'I can't believe he's a *popa'a!*'

'Eh, what?' Materena says. 'What are you going on about?'

'Ah, he's not a *popa'a?*' Loma asks, confused. 'He's so white.'

'Lots of Tahitians are white!'

Loma does her I'm-not-so-sure-about-that look. When you're a Tahitian, you're brown, you're not white. 'Maybe there's a white ancestor in his family,' Loma goes on.

'Eh, Loma. We all have white ancestors, OK. If you want to see pure Tahitians go back to the first century.'

Materena didn't even see that Hotu was white. When he walked into the house all she saw was a good-looking young man with combed hair and cut fingernails. She also saw his crisp ironed trousers and shirt, and the white shoes he didn't take off before walking into the house. That Loma, Materena thinks. She needs glasses. 'His name is Hotu Viriatu, does that name sound *popa'a* to you?' she asks.

'Ah, *non*, that name sounds very Tahitian . . . And how many sisters and brothers has he got?'

'One sister.'

'He's not Tahitian.' Loma does her I'm-not-impressed look.

'Eh, Loma,' Materena snaps. 'Must we have ten children to be Tahitian these days? I have three children, does this mean I'm not Tahitian?'

Ah, here's Cousin Giselle. Materena can sure do with a break from Cousin Loma's stupid questions, and presently Cousin Giselle with her big pregnant belly and her tribe of three children is hurrying over.

'So, Leilani has a boyfriend?' Giselle asks.

'Eh, *oui*, what do you want, that's life.'

'*Aue*, love eh,' Giselle sighs. 'It's so wonderful.'

'Love?' Materena cackles. 'You mean to say passion, cousin.' Materena tells Giselle about that kiss Leilani and Hotu gave each other outside the house before he left. Materena didn't mean to look, of course, she was just putting rubbish in the bin. That kiss just went on and on and on and on.

'*Oh la la!*' Giselle exclaims. 'Somebody has got fire up her . . . And he's a *popa'a*?' Again Materena rectifies the situation to Giselle. Then it's Auntie Stella's turn to be enlightened, and another auntie, and another cousin, and another cousin, and another cousin, and three mamas.

Well, they're all very pleased that Leilani's boyfriend is a local and not a foreigner like Rose's Australian boyfriend, because foreigners always go back to their country and they don't necessarily ask the woman to follow. Sometimes, of course, this is not a bad thing.

Anyway, he's a local. What is his family name? His family name is Viriatu, he's Catholic, he's not from an enemy family, and there's no connection whatsoever. And . . . has he got a job? He's a dentist.

'*Ouh!*' The relatives are so happy for Leilani. 'Lucky girl,' they say.

'Lucky us!' they shout. 'He can fix our teeth for free!'

And where did they meet? the relatives want to know. Ah, that's another story. They met in the truck and usually Hotu never catches the truck since he has a motorbike and a car. But one morning he was driving his motorbike to work and it broke down. And so Hotu caught the truck. It was Papa Lucky-Luke's truck, the truck locals never catch because Papa Lucky-Luke's a slow driver and he doesn't play music.

That's the truck Leilani always catches, that way she can read on her way to school or write things down in her little notebook.

So, anyway, Papa Lucky-Luke's truck stopped and Hotu hopped in. Leilani didn't even look up, she was so busy writing. This went on for minutes until Hotu, who'd been staring at Leilani, felt it was the right moment to say something.

'Are you writing your memoirs?'

Leilani looked up. 'Pardon?'

'Are you writing your memoirs?' he said.

She laughed, he laughed, they looked into each other's eyes, and as we say, the rest is History with a capital H.

The relatives agree that it's an unusual way for two people to meet. In the family people meet at the Chinese store, the snackbar, the church, the nightclub, they meet at the airport as it happened with Rose and Matt. Matt was ordering a coffee at the Airport Café, while waiting for the check-in line for the plane to Australia to be less busy. He'd been on a three-week visit to Tahiti, surfing. At the Airport Café, Matt and Rose met, and Matt didn't catch his plane.

All right, then, now that the population has been informed about Leilani's boyfriend the population can go on with their chores.

Getting serious

WHAT CAN A MOTHER DO, Materena says to Cousin Rita, when her daughter is in love and all is new and wonderful? She can't compare, she can't preach, especially when she had a baby at nineteen years old.

She just has to accept the situation that her daughter wants to live with her boyfriend because she wants to be with him twenty-four hours a day, seven days a week. *Oui*, it's the big love between those two.

Materena dropped her broom when Leilani said, 'Guess what we did this weekend?' Materena thought Leilani and Hotu were spending the weekend at Hotu's parents' weekender in Vairao. Instead they rowed from Tahiti to Moorea together.

Materena dropped her broom when Leilani told her, 'Guess where Hotu and I slept in Moorea?' Materena guessed Leilani and Hotu stayed at the Club Med. But Leilani and Hotu slept on the beach under the stars like in the old days.

And two weeks ago (Leilani's bedroom was half opened) Materena saw Leilani and Hotu sitting on the floor holding each other by the chin and singing, 'I hold you, you hold me by the goatee beard, the first one who laughs gets a slap.' This is an old Tahitian nursery rhyme. Materena went on spying. After half a minute, Hotu burst out laughing and said, 'You're crazy, I'm marrying you.'

But last week, in the middle of the night, Leilani shouted, 'Not until I have a job!' Pito, watching TV, and Materena, ironing sheets, looked up, and waited for the continuation. But there was no continuation.

Then, three days ago, Materena heard Leilani shriek, 'I can't go on, it's hurting me!' And then Materena heard Hotu say, 'Just a little bit more . . . come on you can do it.' Poor Leilani was moaning like she was in real pain! What is going on in that room? Materena asked herself. Some kind of torture? After two seconds of reflection, Materena's mind was made up. She stomped over and put her hand on the doorknob, took a big breath then changed her mind when she heard Leilani tell Hotu that she'd had no idea how weak her belly muscles were, and how she'll definitely aim to do fifty sit-ups every day from now on. Ah, Materena thought. Well, anyway, what can a mother do when her daughter wants to be with her boyfriend twenty-four hours a day?

She can tell her daughter to wait a little, have fun, go to the cinema, plan your future, finish school, you only have three months left. But the daughter is most likely to say, 'It's my life, you had a baby at nineteen years old. And it's not as if I'm leaving school.'

Aue, Materena sighs. She's sure all of this is Hotu's idea. He thinks he owns Leilani just because she tattooed his initials on her hand two days ago. When Materena saw that tattoo, she went mad. She yelled at Leilani, and they had their first big argument in two years.

Aue, Materena sighs again. Children, eh . . . they give you tears. One son leaves for another country, another son says he's going to Bora-Bora to be chef at a hotel there, and now it's the daughter's turn to leave. My children, thinks Materena, can't wait to leave me!

Aue, Materena is so sad but she can't go on doing her long face with her cousin visiting and sitting right next to her at the kitchen table.

'So, cousin?' Materena says. 'Work is fine?'

'Cousin,' Rita replies. 'You can be sad. I understand. I'm not here for you to make me laugh.' She puts a hand over Materena's hand. 'It's a shock when the daughter leaves the house.' Rita knows what's she's talking about. When she left her mama's house at the age of thirty-one, her mama was inconsolable for three whole weeks. 'Has Leilani packed her bags yet?' she asks.

'*Non*, not yet. They're going to find a house first.'

'Ah.' Rita caresses her cousin's hand. 'Be strong, eh, cousin? Don't watch the packing of the bags. Go in the kitchen, OK?'

'*Oui*,' Materena says, wiping her eyes with the back of her hands. 'I just hope Leilani is going to choose the house she's going to live in. She's the one who's going to be in it most of the time . . .'

'True,' Rita nods in agreement. 'I hope too that there aren't too many doors in the house. I should have told Leilani about the doors. Doors are bad. Doors suck energy,' she says to Materena's sceptical look.

'Doors . . .' Materena says vaguely. 'What kind of doors? Opened doors, closed doors, doors that keep banging shut and you get cranky?'

'Doors, full stop!' Rita shouts crankily. 'It's not complicated!' Then, quickly remembering the situation, Rita goes back to doing her air of compassion. 'At least Leilani is not moving to another country.'

'Well, I just hope Leilani isn't going to let Hotu take her to the other side of the island. It's a very long way when you want to see the family.'

'Cousin,' Rita says cackling. 'Have you seen Tahiti on a map of the world? It's a dot . . . to go around the island takes less than an hour.'

Materena gives her cousin an angry look. 'In a car, Rita, *oui*, but I don't have a car . . . If I want to see my daughter for five minutes, I have to be in a truck for two hours.'

'Oh,' Rita hurries to say. 'I'm sure Leilani is not going to go and live on the other side of the island. She doesn't need to hide.'

'You know what Pito said when Leilani told him she was moving out with Hotu?' Materena asks.

Before Rita has time to guess, Materena tells her what Pito said. He said that he's going to put the TV in Leilani's room because he wants to watch it in peace without Materena brooming in the living room. But there's no way Materena is going to let Pito lock himself in Leilani's room with his TV and his beer. 'My children's bedrooms are not for TV,' Materena says to Rita. 'Leilani wants to come home, no problem, her bedroom is here waiting for her.'

Rita nods. And talking about Materena's daughter, here's the girl in question, coming through the door, all smiling and happy, announcing that she and Hotu have found the perfect house! And the rent is cheap!

'Oh, when the rent is cheap,' Materena snarls, 'there's something wrong.'

'And how do you know this?' Leilani laughs. 'You've never rented a house in your whole life, Mamie.' Then, sitting next to Auntie Rita, she asks, 'Auntie Rita, tell me, when the rent is cheap, does it mean there's something wrong?'

Oh la la . . . poor Auntie Rita. Stuck between the lettuce and the tomato yet again. 'Not necessarily,' she says.

'I hope there's not a hacked tree in the garden,' Materena says. And before her daughter gets the chance to inform her mother, the auntie asks if the house faces north because you've got to have the morning rays of sunshine filtering into the house through the louvres.

'Ah, *oui*, Auntie!' Leilani exclaims. And here she is demonstrating with her hands which part of the house faces where, and Materena, who still doesn't know where north is, shakes her head, thinking, Here's Leilani going on again with her geography. Like it's more impor-tant than to know that when there's a hacked tree in the garden, it means someone fell off that tree and died.

'Your house?' Materena asks Leilani, who's still going on about north and all that. 'It's not built on top of a sacred site?'

Leilani stops talking to give her mother a funny look, then looks back to her Auntie Rita, who says, 'I hope there's not too many doors girl, doors are bad, they suck the energy out.'

'There's no doors,' Leilani says.

'No doors?' Materena and Rita say together. 'What do you mean?

Well, there are no doors in Leilani and Hotu's house.

'How do you lock the house?' Rita asks. No doors? What is this house? A cave?

Well there is a door, the door to get in and out of the house, but then once you're in the house itself there's no doors.

'So what do you have?' Materena asks. 'Curtains?'

'*Non*,' Leilani replies, 'just empty space. You walk in the house and there's the living room, the bathroom, the kitchen and the bedroom.'

Materena and Rita look at each other.

'Then,' Leilani continues, 'you go outside and there's the verandah with the table to eat and here's the view right in front of your eyes. The view of the ocean.'

'You can see the ocean from your house?' Rita exclaims. She's so excited she hugs her niece and congratulates her. 'You're so lucky girl,' she says.

But Materena is not sharing her cousin's opinion. When a house has got views it means the house is on the top of a hill, and you know what that means, eh? You've got to get the telephone connected because the relatives aren't going to walk all the way up the hill only to find out that there's nobody home. They're going to want to go to the telephone booth and ring to make sure someone is going to be in. You're never going to have unexpected relatives visiting.

Now, sometimes that is not a bad thing. But don't forget that when a house is on top of a hill, it also means it's a long way from the main road. You're not going to be able to decide at six o'clock what you're going to cook and then stroll to the Chinese store, minutes before it closes, to get the ingredients. You're going to have to run. And if you're pregnant, you're still going to have to run. And if you have a baby in the pram, you're still going to have to run. Good luck to you on your way back to your house with all the shopping bags.

Materena tells all of this to her daughter.

'*Oh la la,*' Leilani says. 'So what?'

'There's a breadfruit tree in the garden at least?' Materena asks.

With a breadfruit tree nearby, when there's no money in the bank and no money in the can, no worries. Just climb that tree and get a breadfruit, and eat it barbecued, baked, in the stew, fried, with jam.

So, there's a breadfruit in the garden at least?

Non, there's no breadfruit and this doesn't bother Leilani at all because she doesn't really like breadfruit and Hotu doesn't either.

Well, anyway, Materena asks if it's possible to see that house on top of a hill, which has a view but not one single breadfruit tree.

Within minutes, the three women are on their way, with Leilani in the front of the car to give Rita directions.

'Turn left here.' Rita turns left and they're now heading for the road that takes you to the top of the mountain. Materena shakes her head with disbelief. It's one thing to be living on top of a hill but another thing to be living on top of a mountain. 'Turn right,' Leilani says.

Rita turns right and glances to Materena through the rear mirror. They haven't even done one kilometre so it means . . .

'Keep going . . . keep going . . . turn left . . . and here's the house.'

Rita switches the engine off and comments on the house. 'The house looks a bit abandoned,' she says. 'But it's very cute. All it needs is a good coat of paint. Look at that frangipani tree! It's so beautiful! It must be over one hundred years old! What do you think, cousin?'

Materena admits that the house is very cute and that the frangipani is very beautiful and she's now looking at the view. This is a very beautiful view, she thinks, it's a shame the airport is in the way, but still. And there's the green house on the corner before you get to the airport and a bit further the Chinese store and a bit further the petrol station.

Well, she didn't go too far that one, Materena smiles with relief. 'How much is it going to cost Hotu for you two to live here?' she calls.

'I'm paying the rent, Mamie.'

Materena turns around. 'But, how are you going to pay the rent?'

'I've got a budget book and a job,' a proud Leilani announces. She informs her mother and auntie that she will be working every afternoon after school in the pet shop in Papeete. She will also be working two Saturdays a month. This will give her enough money to pay the rent.

Now, when a woman and a man move in together, when they share the roof, the bed, the kitchen table, it means they're getting serious. Only time will tell how long these two will last but it doesn't mean the family can't guess, the family can't bet. 'Who's saying six months? Four months? Two months?'

The word in Materena's neighbourhood is that Hotu will pack his bags in three weeks because his girlfriend can't cook or iron. Her mother never taught her these things deliberately. But when you are the daughter of a professional cleaner you're ahead of everyone else in the cleaning department. And when you've seen your mother cook over a thousand meals, cooking isn't witchcraft. And when you're a man who's lived five years away from home, you're ahead of all the men who've never left a home run by a woman (first the mother then the woman).

OK, Leilani and Hotu's house is not as clean and tidy as it should be and the meals aren't as delectable as they could be but when passion is new, who cares about such things? According to Leilani and Hotu's neighbour, it's the big love between Leilani and Hotu. The neighbour sees the young couple chase each other in the garden and fall on the grass and embrace; she sees the young lovebirds sleep on the roof for a bit of romance under the stars and the moon . . . Though, there have been some arguments, and big ones too. Ah yes, the neighbour confirmed to Materena that objects have occasionally been flying out of the house through the door. And another time, it was in the afternoon, so the neighbour also dutifully repeats to Materena, Hotu and Leilani were outside on the mat reading. One minute they were hugging and next minute they were yelling at each other.

Well, that yelling is reassuring Materena. When a woman yells, it means she's not lying low taking shit. And Materena is relieved her daughter is paying the rent. When a woman pays, she has rights.

Still Materena feels lonely with Leilani no longer living at home. She spends her nights cleaning, going through the photo albums, listening to the radio and getting cranky at that talkback DJ who, really, has zero listening skills. He sure loves the sound of his own voice.

Tapeta's grandchild is definitely a boy. The sex of Rose's baby wasn't revealed using the needle test because Rose doesn't believe that a needle hanging over a woman's navel can predict what the sex of the baby is.

'Come on,' Rose said to her mother. 'What's this? Witchcraft? If the needle swings left to right, the baby is a boy, if the needle moves in a circle, the baby is a girl?' *Non*, Rose wasn't interested in doing the needle test, but she's one hundred per cent sure that her baby is a boy. She saw him in her dream. She saw her son. And Rose's son is going to be called Duke because his father, who called yesterday from Australia, wants his son to be named after Duke Kahanamoku.

That's why Tapeta is going to town today to buy a book about that man Duke Kahanamoku. And it just happens that Materena and Leilani are also going to the bookshop in Papeete. The three met by the side of the road to wait for the truck, and that is how Materena and Leilani got to hear about the story of Rose's baby's name being Duke.

'Duke?' Materena asks. 'Who's that man? He's a singer?'

'*Aue, non!*' Tapeta says. 'He was a surfer. A Hawaiian surfer. But he was not just any kind of surfer. He was legendary. He was the best.'

'Was? He's dead this Duke?'

'*Oui*, he's dead.'

'I thought Rose was going to call the baby Manutahi,' Leilani says.

'Well, now it's Duke,' Tapeta says, a little annoyed. She would have much preferred that name Manutahi. He's an ancestor and we know who that man was.

'*Aue!*' she laments about how none of this would have happened if Rose had married a local. She goes on, blaming herself for Rose falling in love with a foreigner . . . but she doesn't blame herself for Rose getting married instead of finishing school. Rose got married in Australia while visiting her boyfriend who had been kicked out of Tahiti for having an expired visa.

'*Aue*,' Tapeta says, brushing Leilani's fingers. 'Don't you leave school for a boyfriend.' Tapeta explains how it's OK to leave school to look after your sick mother, but it's stupid to leave school for a husband. 'Don't you leave school,' Tapeta repeats.

'I won't, Auntie.'

'And what are you going to do when you finish?' Tapeta asks. 'I hope you're going to go to university. Your mamie will be very proud. So?

Why don't you become a schoolteacher? They earn a lot of money.'

'Auntie!' Leilani exclaims. 'I'm not just interested in the money you know!' Leilani stresses that her plan is to get a job where she can make a difference in this world. But she doesn't know what that job is yet, she's still searching. Until then, she plans to take on any job to pay the rent.

Auntie Tapeta slowly nods. 'Well,' she sighs. 'As long as you have your *baccalaureate* you're going to be fine. It's one big key in your pocket already.'

'That's what I've told her,' Materena says.

Words that cut

MATERENA IS WATERING the garden when she notices Leilani's birth tree, her frangipani, has brown leaves and its flowers are on the ground.

Aue! Virgin Mary Understanding Woman! Have pity on me! Materena drops the hose and runs inside her house to call . . . Call who? The emergency ward at the hospital? Hotu's mother? She has no idea where Leilani is. She could be anywhere!

It's Sunday morning, six o'clock. All right, then, Materena is going to run up that hill. She rushes out of the front door, falling on her daughter just as she steps out of the house.

'You're here!' Materena exclaims. '*Aue*, I got so scared, I thought . . .' Materena stops talking. Something is not right. What's all this trembling Leilani is doing? 'Girl? What happened? What's going on?'

Once inside the house Leilani bursts into tears on her mother, and all Materena can do is hold her daughter tighter and repeat, 'It's all right, girl, cry . . . You want Mamie to make you a cordial?'

'*Oui*,' Leilani hiccups.

Materena makes the cordial and sits next to her daughter, putting a loving arm around her. 'What happened, girl?'

'Mamie,' Leilani sniffs, a hand gripping on her glass. 'My heart feels like it's being crucified.'

'Cry, girl,' Materena says. 'Crying is good, let it all out. Cry.'

As Leilani lets it all out, 'Girl,' Materena says anxious now. 'Did somebody die?'

'Me.' Crying even more, Leilani buries her head in her hands.

Ah, Materena is relieved. It's only a story about love. And she patiently waits for Leilani to start talking. Minutes pass.

OK, Leilani drinks her cordial, good. More minutes pass.

Leilani wipes her eyes with the back of her hands, good. She starts talking. And here's the story.

Yesterday afternoon at four o'clock Leilani wanted to have Hotu's baby. By four twenty the same day Leilani wanted to kill Hotu.

They were at his parents' house so Hotu could replace two light bulbs because Hotu's father is away and Hotu's mother can't change light bulbs. As Hotu was screwing the new light bulbs in, his mother said, 'Why don't you two stay for dinner? I'm all alone tonight.'

But first Constance wanted to have a Scotch on ice on the verandah.

So they all went to sit on the verandah overlooking the white sanded beach, and Constance started talking about her cleaner, whom she suspected of stealing food out of the freezer. 'Nobody steals from me,' Constance spat, 'especially not a cleaner.'

At that precise moment, Leilani excused herself to go to the bathroom. She can't stand Constance's stories about her cleaner being a thief. Every time Leilani is here, all Constance wants to do is put her cleaner down. And of course, this really annoys Leilani, knowing many cleaners, including her own mother.

The bathroom is located at the front of the mansion, but Leilani didn't get to the bathroom, she stopped instead in the living room to look at those damned photos of Hotu's famous ex-girlfriends. She thought, Why is Constance keeping them? What is she trying to tell me? This is the last time I'm coming here.

At that precise moment, Leilani heard Constance tell her son, 'I've never said anything to you about your choice of girlfriends . . .'

Leilani moved closer to the verandah and listened, even though her mother had told her many times never to listen to people talk when they don't know you're listening. It's not proper, Materena has always said, it's not proper and you might hear words that are going to cut you.

'You are a fool.' (Constance speaking.)

'Maman, that's enough.' (Hotu speaking.)

'Do you realise what you are doing?' (Constance speaking.) 'That girl already has your initials tattooed on her hand. Next, she'll get herself pregnant. She is a nothing, her family live in a fibro shack.'

'It's a house.' (Hotu speaking.)

'It's a fibro shack,' (Constance correcting) 'with pot plants to hide holes in the walls.'

Hotu cackled.

'Already she has her whole family getting you to fix their teeth for free!' (Constance exclaiming.)

What! (Leilani exclaiming in her head.) Hotu didn't tell me!

'What!' (Hotu laughing.) 'I've only seen her grandmother, Mama Roti.'

Mama Roti! (Leilani exclaiming in her head.) How could you do this to me?

(Constance sniggering.) 'The daughter of a cleaner. Oh, I'm sorry, a *professional* cleaner. Because there is a big difference.' (Constance being sarcastic.)

Hotu laughed. His mother joined in.

'Stop talking about that.' (Hotu speaking.) 'Leilani will be here soon.'

Leilani tiptoed to the other side of the living room, crouching down and feeling like vomiting. She appealed to God to give her strength. God? I know I haven't been to Mass lately but give me a hand. In case you've forgotten me, I'm Materena's daughter.

Soon after, Leilani felt much better. Hotu was talking about plants by the time she sat down next to him.

'Those ones will never pick up, Maman,' Hotu said, stroking Leilani on the arm. 'You need plants that tolerate salt.'

This was what Leilani wanted to do to Hotu: bite his arm off and punch him in the face. But instead she turned to him, winked, and whispered in his ear, 'I need my ration. I want to be on top of you.'

Five minutes later they were riding home, having declined Constance's invitation for dinner.

Fifteen minutes later, Leilani was on top of Hotu.

This morning, Leilani got up at five thirty and wrote Hotu the following very short letter: *I don't love you any more. When I look at you it's like I'm looking at a tree. My Uncle Mori will get all my stuff this afternoon.*

Then she sneaked out of the house and walked down the hill, stopping several times to ask herself, Am I overreacting? But how dare he let his mother mock my mother! Leilani kept on walking.

And now she's here.

'I can't believe that Mama Roti!' Materena exclaims. 'What a nerve!' Materena made it clear to Pito and their relatives that they were not, under any circumstance, to ask Hotu to fix their teeth for free.

'Mamie?' says Leilani, cranky now. 'Have you been listening to me?'

'*Oui*, of course. Girl, people have been making fun of professional cleaners for centuries, I'm used to it you know.'

'Well.' Leilani grinds her teeth. 'I don't like it.'

'Sure, I see what you're saying, but people always mock mother-in-laws, you know, like I mock Mama Roti and Papi mocks my mother.'

'*Oui*, but there's mocking and there's mocking!' Leilani explains that it's OK for her mother to mock Mama Roti about being so rude because she *is* so rude. It's OK for her father to mock Mamie Loana for being a bit of a martyr because she *is* a bit of a martyr.

'Eh, oh,' Materena interrupts. 'Be careful what you say. My mother is not a martyr.' Materena stops. She's not in the mood to fight about her mother today. '*Chérie*,' she continues tenderly. 'Don't leave Hotu just because he laughed about me, OK? Leave him because you don't want to settle down too young or because he's too demanding, but don't leave because he mocked me behind my back. You know . . . I can tell you now. It really annoyed me to see Hotu walk into my house with his shoes on.'

'Lots of people do that when they're wearing shoes and not thongs.' Leilani gives her mother a cranky look.

'He chews his food for such a long time.'

'That's the proper way to eat.'

The proper way, Materena thinks. Well, maybe it is, but it's still very annoying for her to watch Hotu eat. So many times she nearly shouted to him, 'But swallow!' Well, anyway, it's obvious to Materena that now is not the right moment to criticise Hotu because Leilani is still in love with him. The mama can only criticise her daughter's boyfriend or husband when he's completely out of the picture. As far as Materena is concerned, Hotu is not completely out of the picture yet.

Ah, a motorbike is arriving right now, and there's only one person Materena knows who owns a motorbike. Leilani springs to her feet and instructs her mother to tell Hotu that she's not here.

'Girl, he knows you're here. Where else could you have gone?'

'I don't want to see him.'

'You've got to explain the situation.'

'Why?'

'Why? So he knows never to make fun of cleaners ever again, that's why . . . Stay right where you are, I'm going to tell him to come inside the house.' Materena opens the door.

Here's Hotu without his helmet, without his shoes, and with so much suffering and anger in his eyes. *Aue*, Materena thinks. She hopes he's not here to make a scene. She hopes she's not going to have to use the steel frying pan to put some sense into Hotu's head.

'Eh, Hotu!' Materena says. She leans over to greet him as she always does, with a kiss on each cheek. But he puts his arms round her and squeezes her tight.

After a while Hotu gently pulls away and asks to speak to Leilani.

'Come inside,' Materena says.

Non, he prefers to stay outside. OK then, and so Materena goes and gets Leilani, in her bedroom now, on her bed. 'Leilani, get up, hurry up, it's an order.' Although Materena is semi-happy that it's over between Leilani and Hotu (if it is really over) she feels Hotu needs to know what he's done. 'When I look at you it's like I'm looking at a tree,' is, in Materena's opinion, not a proper separation line. It's too cruel. 'Get up.'

'Fine.' Leilani gets out of bed and stomps to the door, with Materena following just in case Hotu decides to do something horrible like put his big strong hands round Leilani's small neck.

'Are you out of your fucking mind?' says Hotu.

'What do you mean am I out of my fucking mind? It's you who's out of your fucking mind!'

'What the fuck did I *do*? What's this note?' Hotu fumbles in the pocket of his jeans and reads it to Leilani. 'Is this a game?' On and on the two of them go, and Materena can't believe the language! Their voices are rising by the second and soon there's going to be a crowd.

'Children,' Materena says softly. 'Come inside the house.'

But Hotu is too busy screaming about how much effort he's put into chasing Leilani. With all the other girls, they chased him. 'Doesn't this show you anything?' he screams.

He goes on about how much he loves Leilani, how he was going to tattoo her initials on his hand, propose . . .

Heads are shaking with disbelief in the crowd, meaning, Leilani, you're such a coconut head breaking up with someone like him. Plus he's a dentist!

'Are you finished with your monologue?' Leilani interrupts.

'JUST TELL ME WHAT I'VE DONE!'

All eyes are now on Leilani.

So here it is, for Hotu, for the crowd, for the whole world to hear. 'YOU MOCKED MY MOTHER!'

'Excuse me?' Hotu sounds very surprised to hear this.

Is this the reason? Relatives gathered in the crowd ask each other. Everyone was expecting something bad, something cruel like Hotu slept with another woman.

'I mocked your mother?' Hotu asks, his eyes on Materena. And for the first time since knowing Hotu, Materena can now see that he *is* white. Actually, he's quite pale. It must be the shock.

'I mocked your mother?' Hotu asks again. 'You've mocked my mother ever since you met her. It's almost a full-time job for you.'

Hotu repeats (word for word) all the things Leilani has said to him about his mother. He even assumes Leilani's facial mannerisms and gestures perfectly as he says: 'I'm sorry but your mother really looks like a Christmas tree with all that jewellery she wears. She's obviously not allergic to gold. She's only allergic to work.'

'Your mother can't change light bulbs! What *can* she do?'

'Why does your mother speak as if she were French? Is she ashamed to be Tahitian?'

'Oh, your mother's cleaner resigned? Well, I'm not surprised! Who wants to work for a woman like your mother? I'm sorry, but there's something wrong with people who put other people down to get a kick. Who will be carrying her coffin when she dies?'

'Your mother only likes people if they've got a lot of money. I'm not surprised she closes her eyes on your father's infidelities. As long as she has his chequebook she doesn't care.'

Eyes are popping out of people's heads, and everyone is waiting for Hotu to go on with all that Leilani has said about his mother (especially the bit about her being a wronged woman) but he stops talking to look at Leilani, now very pale herself.

'Well,' she says after a while, and clearly embarrassed. 'You mocked my mother too, so we're equal.'

Leilani repeats (word for word) all the things Hotu has said (to her) about her mother: 'Your mother is constantly sweeping. I feel sorry for the broom! It never gets a minute of rest in that house.' Then Leilani looks at Hotu fiercely in the eye.

He cracks up laughing. She cracks up laughing too.

'Come on,' Hotu says. 'Let's have a coffee at home and talk.'

Leilani doesn't need to be persuaded, though she says, 'All right, but only to talk.' After a quick kiss for her mother, she's on that bike holding her boyfriend tight. And nobody is surprised.

Every day there's a couple separating in the neighbourhood, there's a woman throwing all of her man's clothes out of the window with the words, 'It's finished!' Then, a few hours later, that same woman is picking clothes off the ground and calling, '*Chéri!*' And life continues, eh?

Well, it's the same with Hotu and Leilani. Life continues. Hotu is extra nice to Materena and Leilani does not speak to Hotu's mother.

Leilani is so in love with her man that the day after finding out she'd passed her *baccalaureate* exam, she walked across the road from Hotu's surgery to Dr Bernard's surgery to persuade the sixty-five-year-old doctor looking for an assistant/receptionist that she was fit to carry out such duties. Leilani passionately sang her assistant/receptionist attributes. 'I can write very fast, I have an excellent memory, and I never assume anything. I can take secrets to the grave and I scored twenty out of twenty in biology and chemistry tests in my *baccalaureate*. I'm ready to start on Monday.'

Dr Bernard must have been impressed with Leilani's speech because he just said, 'Well, I'll see you on Monday, then.'

So now Leilani and Hotu work across the road from one another. They can wave to one another ten times a day. They can go to work together on the motorbike, have lunch together on a bench in the park . . . love each other till death do them part.

This morning, on her way home from the frame shop with Leilani's *baccalaureate* certificate, Materena stops outside Dr Bernard's surgery to look at her daughter. Just now Leilani is hanging onto every word Dr Bernard is telling her. She's nodding in agreement, in between scribbling the doctor's words. Just being a perfect assistant/receptionist and an overqualified one at that. And Materena cannot help feeling a twinge of disappointment, but then she reminds herself that we don't own our children's lives, and Leilani only intends to be an overqualified assistant/receptionist for one year.

Sighing, she keeps on walking, with her daughter's well-earned *baccalaureate* facing the public, for anyone interested to see.

At the drive-in cinema

THE MOVIE TONIGHT at the drive-in cinema is a love movie, and Materena loves movies about love. But the movie is not the reason why Materena is here at the drive-in cinema. She's here to help Mama Teta raise money for the church and they're going to do this selling roasted *mape* fruit.

It's against the law to sell things to eat at the drive-in cinema. There's a snackbar for the customers to buy packets of crisps, Coca-Cola etc. But as Mama Teta said to Materena this morning, it's for the church they're going to sell *mape*, so it's fine. With the church in a story there's no law, because when the church needs money, it's to do good deeds, and when you help the church do good deeds you get help from above.

Mama Teta's car is now three cars away from the ticket office. She hangs her rosary beads on the rear-view mirror. And Materena, half laughing, says, 'And what's this for, Mama Teta? So they don't suspect we've got about sixty bags of *mape* hidden at the back of the car?'

'*Shusssh!*' Mama Teta replies. And to the young man at the ticket office, she says, smiling, 'I hope the movie is good!' Then Mama Teta drives away. But, unlike the other cars circling around the parking lot looking for the best parking spot, she parks at the first spot she sees. The parking is not an issue since Mama Teta won't be watching the movie, being too busy selling *mape*, hopefully the whole lot. Materena reaches for her pandanus bag out of the back.

Mama Teta snatches Materena's hands off the bag. 'You can't go selling the *mape* right now, girl!' She explains that they have to wait for the movie to start, for the lights to be switched off.

'Mama Teta,' Materena says. 'When people are watching a movie, they don't want somebody annoying them with *mape*.'

But Mama Teta insists that the operation be carried out in darkness. 'There's a security guard, girl,' she says. 'He's mean, he patrols with a torch and a baton. He used to be in the army.' Then, almost whispering, she continues, 'If he catches you . . .'

A story follows, about the mean security guard catching a woman, a good innocent woman, selling *mape* to the people inside the cars watching the movie because she needed the money to feed her children. And the good woman begged the security guard to close his eyes on her illegal act but he called the gendarmerie and two gendarmes took the good innocent woman into their office for interrogation. They took her fingerprints, and that meant she's got a criminal record.

Materena sighs. She's getting Mama Teta's message all right, which is: You don't think you could, by any chance, sell the *mape*, all the *mape*, by yourself? The fact is that Mama Teta is afraid of gendarmes.

'Mama Teta, I'm going to do the selling, you just stay in the car,' Materena says.

'*Non*, I'm going to do the selling too . . . but my legs . . . *Aue*, they hurt a little tonight, I don't know why.' Mama Teta puts a hand on Materena's hand. 'It's OK with you if you sell the *mape* . . . all the *mape*?'

'Of course it's OK,' Materena replies. As soon as the movie begins, Materena is off on her mission.

She walks past the cars, her eyes looking for people of her age, because in her opinion, people of her age have a conscience about the church. Well, she doesn't see many young people at the church on

Sundays, but people of her age, ah yes, lots. Materena looks for those people, and at the same time follows the movie—without sound.

She stops at a car to ask an old woman if she would like some *mape*. 'It's to raise money for the St Joseph's Church,' she explains. The old woman wants to see the official paper signed by the priest. 'How do I know you're not lying?' she asks.

'Well, the priest didn't give me any papers,' Materena says.

Well, no official paper means no *mape*.

'OK, thank you,' Materena says. But some people! she thinks.

In the movie, the actor and the actress are now smiling at each other.

'*Mape*? Delicious *mape* cooked today.'

Materena sells two packets, and moves on to other people of her age.

Materena sells one packet.

The woman in the car asks if the *mape* are hard. She says that she likes her *mape* hard and not soggy, she can't eat soggy *mape*.

'The *mape* are very hard,' Materena says. 'We don't sell soggy *mape*.' She sells five packets. One packet. Two packets.

A young French woman is now asking Materena what *mape* is.

'It's very delicious,' Materena says.

'But what is it?' The French woman turns the light in the car on and asks to see the *mape*.

'Is it a vegetable? A fruit?'

'The *mape* tree is very tall, it takes years to grow,' Materena says.

'Oh, that's very interesting, but is it a vegetable or a fruit?'

'It's a fruit.'

'And is it in its natural state?' the French woman asks.

'Eh?'

'Did you pick the fruit off the tree and put it straight in a packet?'

'You have to cook it.'

'How long did the process of cooking take?'

'Natalie!' This is her man speaking. 'Just give that woman her money and get a packet of whatever it is called.' But the woman says that she wants to know what she is eating because she's wary of food poisoning.

'Our *mape* is not poisonous,' Materena interrupts. 'We've been eating *mape* for hundreds of years. If *mape* were poisonous, there'd be no Tahitians left in Tahiti today and I wouldn't be selling you *mape* right this moment to raise money for the church.'

'Oh, it's for the church, I'm sorry.' The French woman hurries to get a banknote from her bag. 'I admire you.'

She gives Materena the money and Materena gives the woman the packet of *mape*. And goes on with her mission.

She has a lot of luck tonight, selling *mape*. It seems everybody wants to eat *mape*. But suddenly, a torch illuminates Materena and a man is walking towards her.

Hei! It's the bloody security guard! Materena shrieks to herself. She runs this way and she runs that way. The security guard is getting closer and closer, and poor Materena has got a stitch.

'Halt!' The security guard yells.

Materena has got to do something about the evidence real quick because when there's no evidence, there's no crime. OK, the *mape* have been discarded under a truck and now Materena can start running again. But here, she recognises Hotu's car five spaces up. Saved!

Materena starts to run towards the BMW with the intention to sneak in and hide but . . . just a minute . . . Yes, that's Hotu at the wheel and he's kissing the woman sitting on the other seat. But that woman Hotu is kissing has got very very short hair. Materena's daughter has very very long hair. What's going on around here? Materena is so shocked she stops running. *Aue* . . .

But what should Materena do now? Should she go and tell Hotu off? It's not really her onions what Hotu does when he's not with Leilani . . . Or is it? Like father, like son! *Eh, eh*, my Leilani, Materena thinks.

Aue! Is this what happens when a couple spends too much time together? Materena wonders. The man gets bored? He needs a change? Since they've met, Hotu can't go anywhere without Leilani following, and here is Hotu now in *flagrant delit*. Materena is so confused. The last time she spoke to Leilani and Hotu's neighbour (alias Materena's spy) she said it was still the big love on top of the hill.

A hand grabs Materena's wrist, making her jump with fright. Ah, it's only the security guard. He's saying how he's seen Materena sell *mape* and he wants her to follow him into the office, but Materena is not going anywhere. Right now she really doesn't care that she broke the law. Right now she's more concerned about what her son-in-law is doing behind her daughter's back.

'Eh,' Materena says to the security guard. 'Let go of my wrist . . . See that couple there? In the BMW?' The security guard looks up and now he's chuckling away. He switches his torch off. And now both Materena and the security guard are watching the couple half illuminated by the light from the screen.

Ah . . . the mistress has flattened her seat and Hotu is . . . *Oh la la*, it's the full passion.

Now what is that security guard trying to do? Materena just felt his hand on her back. Is he *crazy*? She takes a step to the side. The security guard also takes another step to the side. Meanwhile in the BMW Hotu is doing his trousers up.

And what is that security guard doing?

Well he's trying to kiss Materena on the cheek. 'Eh!' She shrieks. 'Are you crazy?' She takes another step to the side, and the security guard follows, all the while going on about how Materena has lured him here to watch that couple and so it must mean she's interested.

What? Materena has to slap him across the face to bring him back to reality. She also has to make a quick dash to the BMW and, before you know it, she's in the car on the back seat, surprising Hotu and that woman, who turns round.

'*Chérie!*' Materena exclaims, all happy and relieved to see her darling sweet daughter. 'You had a haircut today?'

Women have better ears

ATI IS HERE to pick up Pito for a bit of fishing, but Pito is not home.

'He's out,' Materena informs Ati.

'Ah,' says Ati, still standing at the door, looking like he wants to come inside the house, but Materena is not inviting him in. She doesn't need the whole neighbourhood to start gossiping. There are enough stories of wives getting on with their husband's best friends going around. Not only that but Materena really has nothing to say to Ati. They have nothing in common. But Ati just won't go away.

'How's your speedboat?' asks Materena finally. Ati's speedboat just popped into her mind.

'Looking good, I'm thinking of having it painted blue.'

'Ah . . . blue is a nice colour . . . ' What now, Materena wonders, but to look into Ati's brown eyes and feel a bit strange. Ati's brown eyes are always getting him into trouble with women . . . And, anyway, it's not really wise to look into your husband's best friend's eyes for too long.

Just as Materena is about to tell Ati that she was actually on her way to her mother's house, Leilani appears. 'Eh, Leilani!' Materena calls out, glad her daughter is visiting.

Ati will simply have to leave now, but Leilani tells her uncle how happy she is to see him because there's something she'd like to talk to him about—something really important.

'Come in the house, Ati,' says Materena. What else can she do? Let Ati and Leilani talk outside? *Non*, it's not done.

'Tonton,' Leilani fires away as soon as she's at the kitchen table. 'I'm really annoyed with that DJ you work with at Radio Tefana.' To prove her point Leilani does her little cranky eyes at her uncle.

He takes a sip of his lemonade as Leilani talks about Radio Tefana, the radio that supports Independence, and also the radio that hires stupid people.

'I'm not talking about you,' Leilani says. 'I'm talking about the other DJ. He's so . . .' Leilani shakes her head with anger.

'I'm not a DJ,' says Ati. 'I just play love songs. Tihoti is the DJ.'

'Tihoti, *oui*, I'm talking about him, what is his last name?'

'Why?'

'Because I'm actually thinking about lodging a complaint, and I'm also thinking of sending an article to *Les Nouvelles*. That big mouth has got to be stopped!'

'Since when do you listen to Radio Tefana?' Materena asks. This is news to her. Leilani's first experience with Radio Tefana was four years ago. She'd called to give her opinion about all those people who call Radio Tefana to moan about the past, those days when they were called uneducated, ignorant savages. 'Moan, moan,' Leilani said. 'Let's move forward!' In Leilani's world, people would light a candle instead of cursing the darkness. Anyway, Leilani called the radio and was cut off halfway through her speech to make way for a Bob Marley song. Since then she's vowed to have nothing to do with that radio—ever.

However, Leilani hears a lot about that stupid man in the waiting room at the surgery. She hears the shocking degrading things he says on air about women, laughing his head off. He says that when he's stuck in the traffic he looks at women and rates them from one to ten beers. A no-beer woman means that she's very beautiful and that he could sleep with her sober. A ten-beer woman means that she's one ugly woman and that he could only sleep with her if he was very drunk.

He says that after a woman has a couple of kids, she's ruined. A woman with something in her head is dangerous. A woman who talks too much is a bore. A woman with cracked hands is a turn-off. A woman with saggy *titis* reminds him of a cow.

Materena's jaw drops. 'I'm going to punch that man in the face!'

'You're not the only one who feels that way,' Leilani says, 'but we need to do more than that, we must get him off the air.'

She goes on about how talkback radio DJs are in a powerful situation and should do something constructive with it such as uplift people, educate them, reassure, entertain, but stupid jokes are not necessary.

'My role at the surgery,' Leilani continues, 'is also about giving people, women especially, hope, to let them know that they're still beautiful women even with cracked hands or a breast lost to cancer. I can't have someone like that man ruin all my good work. Is he actually aware that more women listen to the radio than men?'

'Really?' Materena asks, interested.

'Absolutely.' The love-song DJ nods in agreement. 'It's true, the people who call me to request a love song are mostly women.'

'But, of course!' Leilani exclaims. 'It's proven that men watch TV and women listen to the radio.'

'How come?' Materena is getting very interested with the discussion.

'Well, because men sit on the couch whereas women are busy running around cleaning or whatever and they need music to make those chores less boring. Tonton, do you know what your radio needs?'

Before Ati has the chance to reply, Leilani shouts, 'A woman!'

'A woman,' Ati repeats.

'What's wrong with my idea?' Leilani snaps, her eyes firing bullets.

'*Rien*,' he hurries to say. 'It's just I never thought about that before.'

'Well, start thinking, Tonton. I'm surprised that idiot is still alive, even more surprised that he still has a job. Who is he? The son of the boss? It's not acceptable any more, Tonton, to say degrading words about women, you know. Imagine that the stuff that idiot says ON AIR is about your mother? Or your sister, Mamie, me, your goddaughter!'

Silence falls as Ati, deep in thought, nods a slow nod.

'So?' Materena tells Ati, half serious, half laughing. 'When are we going to hear a woman's voice on your radio, eh?'

'Women have better ears anyway,' Leilani says.

'Ah, true, women have better ears,' Materena confirms.

'Women would bring so much to Radio Tefana,' Leilani continues.

'You've got to do something, Tonton.'

'You've got to do something, Ati.'

Poor Tonton Ati . . . he looks like he's having trouble swallowing his spit. He must be regretting setting a foot in this house today, in which live two women rebelling for the same cause.

The whole population is talking about Mama Teta's new business. Well, all the relatives at least. Ninety-nine per cent of them are saying, 'That one, when is she going to stop thinking about businesses?

When you're her age you're supposed to just grow old peacefully!'

But Materena believes in dreams. 'Bon courage,' she tells Mama Teta outside the church.

'Maururu, girl,' Mama Teta says, affectionately tapping her niece's hand. 'Luckily, we women know that word.'

'And what is your new business going to be?' Materena asks with interest. Nobody has bothered asking Mama Teta this. As soon as the relatives heard the words 'new business' they shrieked, 'What? A new business at your age!' And so Mama Teta told them nothing.

'A nursing home.'

Materena nods. 'And it's going to be at your house?'

'Oui, at my house,' Mama Teta confirms. 'Oh, I know that my house isn't a four-star hotel but it's a house. There's a roof.' Her nursing home, she insists, is not going to be like the nursing home where the old people sit on their bed waiting for the night to come because they've got nothing to do. Her nursing home (Mama Teta's voice rises with excitement) is going to be a place for friendship and fun. Her old people will play cards, grow their own vegetables, bake their own bread, do talk-talk, laugh and share experiences.

'Your nursing home sounds like a good place!' Materena exclaims.

Cackling, Mama Teta thanks her for the kind words about her new business, but admits that selling it to her son Johno was another story. Johno works at the Socredo Bank; he knows a bit about finance.

Here's what Johno said. Mama Teta uses her fingers to tick them off:

1) 'But you've already got a business Ma.'

'You mean my bridal-car driving business?' Mama Teta asked. 'Bof, I'm going to stop that business. Nobody is getting married any more, that kind of business is way too slow; plus, my eyes are going a bit funny on me and you need good eyes to be a driver.'

2) 'Your house is not a good location for a nursing home. You can see the cemetery.'

'And so?' Mama Teta didn't see where the problem was.

'Ma, think a little eh?' He went on about how the cemetery was going to make the old people sad because it was going to remind them of their death.

Mama Teta shrugged. 'Eh, Johno, old people don't go around thinking they're immortal, it's up to the young people to think that.'

3) 'Do you want my honest opinion?' Johno asked before he left.

'Oh, you know, give me your opinion, don't give me your opinion, I'm still going to do my new business.'

'Well, if it's what you want,' Johno said this like he didn't believe his mama's new business idea was going to become a reality, 'but you know it's hard work looking after old people.'

He went on about other unimportant things meant to discourage Mama Teta, but what happened was the opposite. Mama Teta was even more excited about her idea. She believes in herself. After all, she passed her driver's test at the age of fifty-six years old when most women think their life is over. She overcame her fear of running a child over and learned not to worry so much about all the gendarmes roaming around the island. She passed her driving test with flying colours, and became a bridal car driver.

But Mama Teta is now ready for a change. 'Looking after old people is less stressing than driving on the road, especially these days,' she tells Materena. Mama Teta informs her that she feels very positive about her new business idea because whenever she thinks about it, she gets all happy inside. And this means she's on the right track. 'Eh, things change, girl, and life is short. We've got to do what we love.'

That's what Mama Teta told Johno too, and this is what Johno said before he left: 'You're going to have a lot to do in the house.'

Smiling with delight, Mama Teta asked, 'Are you telling me that your bank is going to lend me the money?'

'It's not my bank, it's not my decision.'

'Well, see what you can do, OK?'

And last week, Johno was pleased to advise his mother that he'd throw a couple of hundred thousand francs into her venture, enough to repaint the house and fix it up a little. 'I can get the rest of the money from the government,' Mama Teta tells Materena.

Two days later, the whole population is talking about how Mama Teta changed all the curtains in her house. 'But, she's serious that one,' the relatives say. 'And at her age! It certainly makes you think.'

Materena agrees with this one hundred per cent. Right now, Mama Teta is an inspiration for Materena.

Tonight Materena feels like going out and why not? She'll be forty years old next Wednesday. Isn't it about time she experiences dancing in a nightclub?

How about at the famous Zizou Bar?

The house is clean and tidy, she doesn't feel tired, and all her children are away. Tamatoa is in France (Materena snorts; she has not had a phone call for nearly three weeks), Leilani is with her boyfriend in Moorea for a romantic weekend, and even Moana is doing a bit of romance tonight after work with a mystery girl.

So Materena is going out to the Zizou Bar where her mother and father met. Materena has always wanted to have a quick look inside that bar but she's never had the courage. The same as she never had the courage to search for her father. She didn't have the courage because . . . well, because, she thought, he's not going to want to know me. I'm just a cleaner. Well, anyway, that's an old story.

At the Zizou Bar, French *militaires* and local girls meet and dance.

People say that the girls who dance the night away at the Zizou Bar wouldn't be dancing one single dance at the local bar because they're not good-looking enough for the local men. At the Zizou Bar, those girls are queens because the *militaires* are prepared to dance with anyone as long as it is a woman and she's Tahitian.

Tonight Materena is going to see all of this for herself, and she's expecting Pito to escort her.

'I'm not putting my feet in that bloody bar.' Pito doesn't even take his eyes away from the TV.

Materena immediately guesses the reason. She gives Pito the death look. 'Ah, it's OK for you to have a wife who has a *popa'a* father and it's OK for you to have children who have a *popa'a* grandfather, but it's not OK for you to put your feet in the Zizou Bar!' Pito lifts his eyes to Materena for a second and says nothing.

Materena furiously rearranges things around the living room and goes on about how she will just have to go to the Zizou Bar by herself.

'Eh!' Pito is cranky now. 'Leave me alone with that Zizou Bar story, OK? I don't force you to come to my bar so don't force me to go to yours!'

'You don't want me at your bar full stop. You want to be with your *copains* and . . .' OK, that's enough about Pito and bars, thinks Materena. 'Well, I'm going to go out with Cousin Lily,' she says. 'Cousin Lily knows about bars and everything.'

Pito tells Materena that it is a very bad idea to go out with Lily because Lily is trouble. It's best to go out with Rita instead.

Materena immediately gets the picture. 'You know lots of men wink at Rita when she's walking around in Papeete, it's not just Lily who can be trouble.'

Pito nods distantly, concentrating on the TV screen again. Materena is going to call Rita to escort her, but just as she's about to dial Rita's number, something occurs to her, and she marches back to the sofa where Pito is sitting still like a statue. 'What's this about Lily being trouble, eh? And me? You don't think I can be trouble?' Before Pito has the chance to comment, Materena is dialling Rita's number again.

But Rita is not picking up the phone. '*Ah hia hia*,' Materena says to herself. 'Eh, well, maybe it was a silly idea for me to go to that bar.'

Later on, when Materena goes to get some cooking oil, she meets Cousin Mori outside the Chinese store. The two cousins greet each other with the usual Tahitian kisses on both cheeks. Cousin Mori doesn't smell of beer and his eyes aren't red from smoking *paka*. So Materena is going to have a quick chitchat with him, but first she is going to admire the painting Of the Virgin Understanding Woman on the bonnet of Mori's car. 'Eh, eh,' she says. 'She's so beautiful Virgin Mary.' Cousin Mori agrees.

OK, now time for a quick chitchat about this and about that, about how Materena wanted to go to the Zizou Bar but Pito didn't want to escort her. 'I don't want to be at the Zizou Bar on my own,' Materena says. 'It's going to look like I'm after an adventure.' Mori nods knowingly and proposes to be Materena's chauffeur and bodyguard.

'You don't mind to be seen at the Zizou Bar?' Materena asks.

Mori, shrugging with indifference, replies, 'Beer tastes the same in all bars and there's going to be girls at the Zizou Bar, *non?*'

So here they are now on their way to the Zizou Bar and Materena reminds Mori that he is not to start a fight at the Zizou Bar because some *militaires* are special *militaires*, they're legionnaires, and they carry knives. They're trained to kill in the event of an attack.

Mori, bopping to a Bob Marley song, laughs.

Materena glances at Mori. He's all dressed up and his hair is twisted into a heavy plait. He reeks of perfume.

'And your car?' she says.

'*Oh la la!*' Mori smacks the wheel. 'Everybody is always asking me about my car! What's the problem with my car?'

Materena wants to say, 'The problem with your car is that it's always breaking down.' Instead, she says, 'There's enough petrol?'

There is and so Materena looks out of the window and hums to the no woman no cry song, all the while thinking that she's done very well taking some extra francs with her for a taxi in case Mori's car breaks down. Or in case Mori drinks too much although he did swear not to. She's also done very well wearing a dress that falls down to her knees.

Mori parks his car right in front of the Zizou Bar. He explains that it will be easier for him to check on his car during the night.

'OK, fine, fine, let's go in.'

The bouncer politely greets the middle-aged woman dressed like she's off to church, but no way is he letting the big thug in. Looking into Mori's eyes the bouncer says solemnly, 'Policy, mate.'

Mori, his fists clenched and a mean look on his face, says, 'Mate . . . are you telling me that I can't get in because I'm not a *popa'a* but you're going to let my cousin in because she's a woman, even though she's a Tahitian? Is this what you're telling me, eh? You want me to start a riot? You want my family to smash this bloody bar down?' After Mori has paid his way in and got his hand stamped, the bouncer opens the door and wishes the two cousins a very pleasant night.

The Zizou Bar is packed and Materena can see within one second that the story about only ugly Tahitian girls dancing at the Zizou Bar is an absolute myth. The girls here tonight are stunning!

Materena reminds Mori that he's her bodyguard tonight and that he'd better not disappear on her. 'I'm not paying for your two glasses of beer for you to go drinking with another woman,' she says. They head for the bar and Mori gets his beer, then they sit at a table away from the dance floor. Materena, sipping her water, looks around.

She feels strange . . . All those *popa'a* men, those *militaires*, those young men flirting with the young women. The romance in the dark. Materena watches the couples dancing away on the dance floor, smiling the smile of love. Was it like this when Loana was dancing with Tom? When they were young? Tears well in Materena's eyes, as Mori finishes his beer and gets up to buy his second.

There's a woman sitting on her *popa'a* lover's knee and they're passionately kissing. There's drunken laughter all around. Mori is now talking to a woman standing against the wall. Well, as long as they're only talking, Materena thinks, but Mori better not disappear.

Five minutes later, while Materena is busy looking at the couples dancing, Mori and the mysterious beauty make a quick exit and not long after, three *militaires* sit down at Materena's table. They ask her if she'd like a dance, if she'd like to go for a little walk.

Materena's answer is firm. 'Thank you, but my cousin, the big tall man over there with the Rasta hairstyle . . .' she says looking over to where Mori was standing seconds ago. 'My cousin,' she continues, smiling at her *militaire* friends, 'he's going to be back soon.'

Materena thinks that those *militaires* must be pretty desperate because she knows very well she looks like a middle-aged woman dressed like she's going to clean someone's house.

'You are so beautiful,' one slurs. 'Are you happy?'

'My eldest son is in France.' Materena is trying to divert the conversation. 'He's in the army.'

'I love older women.' This *militaire* is drunk too.

'My youngest son is a chef at the Beachcomber.'

'I think I'm in love with you.' Another drunk *militaire*.

OK, that's it, Materena is going outside to see what's going on with Mori. But there's no sign of Mori. She asks the bouncer if he saw her cousin. He shrugs, 'It's not my business what people do outside the bar.'

So Materena walks up and down the street, calling out, 'Mori! Mori? Mori?' In the end, she gets into Mori's car and waits, muttering about how Mori is going to get it. Bodyguards don't just go walkabout!

But here is a taxi pulling up in front of Mori's car. Materena is inside that taxi in a flash. 'How much for you to drive me to Faa'a?'

The driver turns around and checks his passenger. 'For you . . . half price.'

Materena gives the taxi driver a smile of gratitude and to prove to him that she indeed appreciates the special price, she asks him questions about his family, if he's got a wife, children.

'I've got four children,' he says, 'but I'm not with my wife any more.'

'Oh, really? That's sad, but maybe it was for the best, eh.'

'I've got a new wife and my new wife, she . . .' the taxi driver glances at Materena. 'My new wife, she likes sex, not like my old wife.'

Materena is tempted to say, 'Well, that's because she's a new wife,' but she just nods.

'You're married?' the taxi driver asks.

Materena says that she is and that she's been with her husband for more than twenty years now.

'Ah, you must like sex!'

Materena wants to tell that man off, but thinking about the special price, she giggles uncomfortably and looks out of the window.

But the taxi driver is very interested to talk about sex to Materena. He gives Materena hints that he's a great lover and very soon he's proposing to take Materena to a hotel for a quiet drink.

Materena stays silent, thinking: I can't believe what I'm hearing! Can't he see I'm a respectable middle-aged woman? Luckily the taxi driver is a little skinny man. With one slap, Materena could make him fly all the way to France.

'So?' The taxi driver switches the light on. 'We go to the hotel?'

Materena quickly reads the driver's identity card hanging from the rear view mirror. 'Listen, Justin Ah-Kan, number fifteen. People don't call me mad Materena for nothing, OK?'

The light goes off and Materena ponders if she's going to have enough money to pay the taxi fare, considering that Justin is not going to be giving her a special price. Plus, he's driving so slowly now. He slows down at the orange light instead of accelerating as trucks do, and stops for the red light. Materena, annoyed, looks at the Suzuki car pulling up next to them. The couple inside the car are kissing, full on the lips, and it seems to Materena that she's recognising Ati. She hurries to wind the window down and hesitantly calls out, 'Ati? Is that you?'

The kissing ceases abruptly and Ati, shocked, exclaims, 'Materena? What are you doing in a taxi at this time of night?'

'Can you drive me home?' Next minute, Materena is in her husband's best friend's car telling him all about her mission and how Mori disappeared on her. Ati listens, but his girlfriend doesn't seem to care about Materena's mission, she cares more about kissing Ati on the neck.

'Can you stop!' Ati says to his girlfriend.

Materena hurries to say that she doesn't mind all the kissing but now Ati is dropping the girlfriend at her door.

'Good night, I'll call you tomorrow.' Ati speeds away, firing questions at Materena about her night. Materena wonders if Ati is interrogating her so that he can report the answers back to Pito. Is Ati playing spy?

'Ati, I've had lots of men interested in me tonight,' Materena wants Pito to know this, 'but I'm only interested in one person.'

'I know what you mean. I'm also only interested in one person.'

'You!' Materena laughs. 'You think women are like tyres.'

'That's because I can't have the woman I love.'

Materena guesses that Ati is referring to the woman he lost to a legionnaire many years ago. She puts a hand on Ati's shoulder. 'Ati, you can't go on mourning that woman you lost to a legionnaire.'

'That bitch! I'm not talking about her!' Speaking softly, Ati goes on about how he's talking about another woman. A woman he has loved for years. She is the only woman Ati wants.

'Well, go get her!' Materena says. 'What are you waiting for?'

But the woman Ati loves is married, so he tells Materena. All Materena can say is that another woman is sure to come Ati's way one day. Ati laughs a faint laughter.

'Did you know I'm living by myself now?' Ati says.

'What?' That has got to be the news of the century. Materena can't believe Pito didn't tell her about it. 'And your mama? She's fine?'

'Oh, she cried, she threw herself on the ground, but I wasn't going to live with her for the rest of my life.'

'Ah, true,' Materena agrees, thinking, Well, you're forty-two years old after all.

'I've got a flat in Papeete. You should come and see it one day,' Ati says, smiling.

'Of course,' Materena says, thinking, What's this?

'You want a coffee at the airport? I've got a proposition for you.'

Usually, whenever Ati has a proposition to make, Materena laughs, and says, 'Ati, you're never going to convert me, OK? You know very well what I feel about Independence. I'm half French, and I can't change this.' But, tonight, Materena would like to find out what his proposition is. She herself has a proposition for Ati . . . her only connection to Radio Tefana. So Materena tells her husband's best friend that coffee at the airport sounds like a very good idea.

'So,' Materena says, stirring her coffee. 'What's your proposition?'

'You know that I've always liked you.' Ati looks deeply into Materena's eyes.

'*Oui*, I know, you like me because I'm the wife of your best friend.'

'*Non*, I like you because of you.'

Materena smiles and takes a sip of her coffee, thinking how she should have gone home instead of accepting Ati's invitation, but she has an idea and it's really important that she talks about it with him.

'I like you a lot,' Ati repeats, this time sounding so serious.

'Enough to help me with anything?' Materena asks.

'Anything you want, just ask me.'

'Well,' Materena begins. 'I've got an idea and it's about . . .' Materena's voice trails off. She's a bit embarrassed to talk about her idea to start a talkback radio show aimed at women. Ati might think she's trying to big-note herself. He might laugh and say, 'This is your idea? I thought it was something interesting.'

'So?' Ati asks, putting a hand on Materena's. 'What is your idea?'

'I can't tell you about it now,' Materena says, taking her hand away. 'Maybe after my fortieth birthday.'

'What's happening after your birthday?'

'Who knows.'

'Am I in your idea?'

'Indirectly, *oui*,' Materena smiles, but when Ati puts his hand on hers again, she hurries to add, 'but it's not what you think.' She feels Ati better know this now. She doesn't want to lead him onto the wrong path, so she takes her hand away again. 'I love Pito, you know that.'

'*Salaud*,' Ati cackles. 'I'm jealous.'

'But are you still going to be there for me when I'm going to need you?' Materena asks. She doesn't know yet how strongly she feels about her idea, but tomorrow might be a different story.

'Materena,' says Ati, keeping both hands in his pockets. 'I've known you for more than twenty years. You're like a best friend for me.'

Impossible is not French

THE BIRTHDAY GIRL is about to blow the candles out on her triple chocolate cake. But first she's got to make her wish, eh? Everyone standing around the kitchen table is waiting, and there are so many wishes Materena could make tonight, on her fortieth birthday.

She looks round at all the people who are part of her life, thinking, I can't believe I'm forty years old! *Merde,* life goes fast.

Now, about that wish, what is it going to be?

Well, Materena wishes for Cousin Rita to fulfil her dream of falling pregnant. She wishes for her mother to fulfil her wish of having her son and her grandchildren live in Tahiti. She wishes for Moana to get his wish of buying a restaurant.

She also wishes for: Ati to meet a very nice woman, Pito to get promoted, Vahine to forget about Tamatoa and move on with her life.

When it comes to wishing, Materena is never out of ideas. She wishes for Tamatoa to remember it's her birthday tonight, she wishes for Leilani to find out what she'd like to do with her life soon, she's been Dr Bernard's assistant/receptionist for nearly two years now . . . She wishes for . . .

'Come on, Materena,' Pito says. 'How hard is it to make a wish?'

Materena blows out her candles.

'Joyeux anniversaire!'

They're all singing the birthday song now, making Materena cry. The next fifteen minutes are spent kissing the birthday girl, and the next hour is spent teasing the birthday girl who is, as of now, entitled to the title "Mama". The day you turn forty, you become a mama. Welcome into the respectable clan of hardworking mothers!

'Non, thank you,' Materena tells everyone, her husband especially. 'I'm Materena full stop. When you are a mama, the next thing you are a *meme*, an old woman only good for raking the leaves and minding the grandchildren. I'm not ready for that yet!' As far as Materena is concerned, turning forty is not about turning into a mama, it's about . . . it's about something else. But first things first . . . Materena best mingle with her guests and thank everyone for coming.

She thanks Moana for his wonderful effort with the menu. He's been in the kitchen since seven o'clock this morning with his helper, Vahine, mixing ingredients, stuffing chickens, stirring soups, chopping onions, tomatoes and cayenne, marinating fish. '*Merci, chéri*,' she says, hugging him tight. 'I'm sure your restaurant is going to become a reality.'

Moana hugs his mother tighter and thanks her for believing in him.

She thanks Ati for coming to her birthday party even though he had a very important political meeting to attend tonight, and he says, 'Don't forget to tell me about your idea.'

'*Maururu*, Ati,' Materena says.

She thanks Leilani for all the decorations, and tells her that she's sure she's going to know what she wants to do in her life very soon.

Leilani hugs her mother and whispers in her ear, 'I'll have a talk with you later.'

'OK,' Materena whispers back.

Materena thanks Vahine for having been so kind to spend the whole day helping Moana in the kitchen, and tells her that one day she will meet the man who truly deserves her. Vahine squeezes Materena tight and says, 'I think I've already found him.'

On and on Materena thanks her guests and tells them what they'd like to hear.

Now, let the party begin!

By two o'clock in the morning, everyone has gone home or fallen asleep. Hotu was the first to leave and Vahine was the first to fall asleep in her ex-boyfriend's bed, next to Moana's bed.

The only people left are Materena and her daughter, both slouched at the kitchen table. '*Ouf*,' Materena sighs. 'That was a good party.'

Leilani confirms this.

'So, how's Dr Bernard?' Materena asks. 'He's still your hero?'

'Oh, *oui*!' Leilani exclaims. 'I love that man.'

'What did he do this time?'

The last time Materena asked this question, she found out that Dr Bernard spent twenty minutes teaching X (Leilani never reveals the identity of Dr Bernard's patients. X is for women patients and Y for men) about the many contraception methods that her boyfriend wouldn't find out about. Dr Bernard said to X, 'You're the one who will be carrying his child. *You* decide when.'

Materena also found out that Dr Bernard cried tears of anger when he received the results from the laboratory for Y, diagnosed with leukaemia. But then he was on the phone making one phone call after another to colleagues, and Leilani heard him say, angrily, 'Don't you dare tell me nothing can be done! Until proven otherwise, there's hope!'

He spoke softly to little Y, about to receive an immunisation shot. 'This is going to hurt a little bit, but you need this shot my boy, to protect yourself from all those nasty germs. Do you understand me?'

So what did Dr Bernard do and say this time? Materena is still waiting for Leilani to tell her.

But Leilani asks, 'Mamie, do you sometimes wonder what your purpose in life is?'

Oh la la, Materena thinks. I'm too tired for an intellectual discussion. Nevertheless, she begins by saying that people don't just have one purpose in life, and that purposes can be as simple as helping a child cross the road. Making someone sad smile. Listening to someone's story. According to Materena, a person's purpose in life should be about making a difference, and the opportunity to do so comes to us every single day. There, Materena hopes this answers Leilani's question.

Well, Leilani is nodding in agreement. 'You know, Mamie,' she says, 'one of Dr Bernard's patients told me that when we don't fulfil our purpose in life, we make ourselves heavy in the coffin on the way to the cemetery because we're so angry with ourselves.' She sighs. 'I don't want to be heavy in the coffin.'

'Oh, Leilani! Don't talk about death on my birthday!' Materena chuckles to lighten up the atmosphere a bit.

'Mamie . . .' Leilani's voice trails off. 'Imagine you're young.'

'Eh ho,' Materena smiles. 'What do you mean, I *am* young.'

Leilani smiles along. 'You're right, you are still young.' She goes on about how these days, with all the progress in medicine, being forty years old is nothing. 'Now that all your children have grown up, you are free to do whatever you want, Mamie.'

'Whatever I want,' Materena murmurs. 'That would be nice . . .'

'Mamie, the sky is the limit for you. Do you remember how I used to draw you three times taller than anyone else in my drawings?'

'Oh, *oui*,' Materena laughs.

'You're still three times taller than anyone else for me, but you know, Mamie . . .' Cringing, Leilani confesses that there was a time when she was a bit embarrassed about her mother being a cleaner, but that was a long time ago when she was an adolescent.

'Ah,' Materena says, smiling. 'Back when you hated me.'

'I've never hated you, Mamie, I was just *contraire* that's all. And I'm so thankful you're still here today so I can tell you how much I admire you, and love you, and how sorry I am for all the grief I've given you.'

Materena looks her daughter in the eyes. 'Don't cry on your birthday!' Leilani pinches her on the arm. 'Today is a new day for you! You are forty years old, you are free!'

'Girl, what is this?' Materena smiles through her tears. 'Are you on a mission or something?' But the telephone starts ringing before she can finish, and Materena is up in a flash. She hears the click noise, meaning the call is from overseas.

'Ah,' she says out loud. 'It's my son finally remembering to call his mamie. I thought it was impossible.'

'Impossible is not French, Mamie.' Tamatoa's voice is getting deeper every time he calls. He can't talk for long he says, but just wanted to wish his mother a happy birthday 'and may all your wishes come true.'

Walking back to the kitchen, Materena chuckles. May all your wishes come true . . . What wishes?

As she has done for the past twenty years, Madame Colette has bought Materena a birthday present.

'Oh, Colette,' Materena says. 'You didn't have to.'

'Open your present!' Colette says, all excited.

Materena eagerly opens her birthday present even if she already knows what it is. 'Colette!' And yes, it's another box of chocolates.

Materena thanks her boss profusely. Colette invites her to sit at the table while she makes some coffee. That has been the ritual for the past twenty years—but only on Materena's birthday. On the other days of the year, Materena jumps into her chores straight away; Colette has already left for her office by the time Materena arrives. But on Materena's birthday, Materena has coffee and chocolate and a ten-minute chat with her friend.

'So,' Colette is saying, pouring fresh coffee into the cups. 'How does it feel to be forty years old?' Colette will be forty years old in five months, so she's very interested.

'Oh, I feel the same, Colette,' Materena replies.

'Really?' Taking a quick sip she adds, 'No midlife crisis?'

'Midlife crisis? Colette, what are you talking about?' Colette explains. A midlife crisis is like feeling lost. Midlife crises are like wanting more. 'Ah.' Materena nods in agreement. 'That . . . well . . . '

Colette is waiting, but the words are stuck in Materena's throat. How do you tell your boss you don't want to clean her house any more? You want to do something else with your life. Here, Materena is going to take a sip of her coffee. This should give her more time to think.

Materena drinks her whole coffee and she still can't tell Colette what she's rehearsed since three o'clock this morning, straight after Leilani left. Words were flying out of Materena's mouth then in the comfort of her kitchen. She was going to say, 'Colette, here's the situation. After twenty years as a professional cleaner I feel—'

Colette interrupts Materena's train of thought. 'Materena . . . we've known each other for twenty years . . . you shouldn't have to weigh your words when speaking to me.'

'OK, then, Colette, here's the situation. After twenty years as a professional cleaner I feel like a change.'

'A change?' Colette asks, sounding worried. 'What do you mean?' Before Materena has the chance to explain what she means, Colette, speaking with her I'm-so-stressed voice, is telling Materena that she can't abandon her, not now, not with all that mountain of work she has at the office. Not now with the children still living at home. Not now with Colette so close to being promoted to company director. Not now.

'I need you Materena,' Colette says, as she puts a hand on Materena's hand. 'I'll be lost without you.'

Aue this conversation is so hard for Materena. She loves Colette but sometimes you've got to love yourself more. 'Colette,' Materena says. 'I've been cleaning houses for more than twenty years, and I *choose* to do something else with my life now.'

On air with Materena

THE WORD IS THAT everybody who can help Materena is to meet at Loana's house at six thirty tonight. But please arrive before six thirty so that Rita can go through a few things with everyone.

By six o'clock, Loana's house is crowded with relatives, and so is her verandah and garden. Rita is standing on a chair, microphone in hand, addressing the audience, beginning with words of gratitude because today is a big day for her favourite cousin.

So here's the plan, Rita goes on. As soon as Materena starts on air at her new job on Radio Tefana, relatives are to take turns calling the radio on Auntie Loana's telephone to speak to Materena. But don't give out your last name. It's important that the director of the radio doesn't know that the reason his radio is being inundated with calls is because Materena has a lot of relatives who like her. Just give out your first name, but you're free to invent a last name if you want. No problems.

'Everybody is following me?' Rita shouts into the microphone.

'*Oui!*' Everybody is so excited. It's like a spy game. 'What name are you going to give?' they ask one another.

'People! Are you listening?' Rita continues with the plan's objective, which is of course to help Materena get her idea approved by the director of the radio, who unfortunately is not a relative otherwise nobody would be needed today. But at least he granted Materena one night's trial (with Ati's good word) to see how people all over Tahiti will respond to her programme about women sharing stories with other women on the island. Inspiring, interesting stories worth listening to, stories that will make women listen and call Radio Tefana.

'So call and say something interesting!' Rita shouts brandishing a fist.

'*Oui* . . .' This time the answer is hesitant. Something interesting? the relatives ask each other. Like what? Nothing interesting ever happens.

Meanwhile, Rita is looking at the crowd trying to find someone who has an interesting story. Ah, yes, Giselle. 'You, Giselle!' Rita calls out into the microphone. 'You've got an interesting story. You've given birth in a car three times!'

'Do you think it was interesting for me?' Giselle calls to Rita. 'It was only interesting the first time!'

All right, then . . . Rita needs another example. Ah, yes, Auntie Tapeta. 'Auntie Tapeta!' she calls out. 'You've got an interesting story. Your daughter meets an Australian in Tahiti, he gets kicked out of Tahiti when his visa expires, your daughter visits him in Australia and marries him so that her darling boyfriend can live here.'

'Do you think it's interesting for me?' Tapeta is cranky. 'Imagine you have a daughter, eh? She's so clever but then she falls in love with an Australian surfer, she leaves school to visit him in his country, she marries him (not even in the church!), then she falls pregnant. And is leaving Tahiti for good with her husband (because he can't get a work visa) and your granddaughter (who's not even ten weeks old!).

Aue, Rita thinks. The poor grandmother. There are no words to describe. It's one thing to say farewell to a daughter you've raised, another to say farewell to a granddaughter (Rose's baby was a girl; they called her Taina-Duke) you might not see again. All right . . . she needs another example, but she's running out of time. Let's leave it all to destiny.

'Auntie Loana?' she calls out, looking inside the living room. Ah, she's next to the telephone, ready to dial as soon as Ati, presenting

Materena tonight, says, 'Call now!' It has been agreed that the person who will make the first call to Radio Tefana will be Loana, since Materena is her daughter and this is her telephone.

For the moment they're just going to switch the radio on.

'Georgette!' Rita calls. 'You're on!' Georgette, professional dancer, transvestite and DJ, has brought her hi-fi system to propel Materena's voice into the living room, the garden and beyond. A reggae song is playing and a few relatives decide to do a little dance. Another song comes on, a *tamure*, and it's party time on the verandah.

'People!' Rita calls out. 'Think about your interesting story!'

'Rita sure loves that microphone,' says a relative.

A roar of excitement greets Ati opening Materena's programme. All the relatives are so excited because soon they're going to hear Materena's voice blast from the speakers.

'Silence!' Rita herself is very excited but there's a need to calm the crowd a little.

Meanwhile, back in the Radio Tefana studio, Materena, facing Ati, is breathing deep breaths to relax. She's so nervous. Ati is waving one arm in front of her. 'I have in the studio with me a very charming woman,' he says. 'How are you, Materena?'

'Oh, I'm fine, and you, Ati?' Materena grimaces, eyeing all the people behind the glass window staring at her. They rehearsed that line yesterday afternoon, as well as speaking in front of the microphone (not too close—Ati showed Materena how).

'Materena will be doing a special edition on radio tonight,' Ati continues. 'But before we go on, I must say Materena that tonight is quite hot, don't you think?'

'Ah, *oui*, Ati, you're quite right about that.' Ati did explain to her yesterday how they'd do a bit of chitchat before beginning the programme to give Materena time to relax and the audience a chance to warm up to that woman they've never heard about before.

'All I can say is,' Ati cackles, winking at Materena, 'I hope it's going to rain soon.'

'Oh, me too,' cackles Materena. 'Rain is very good for the . . .' And for some reason Materena's mind goes blank mid-sentence. For the life of her she can't remember what she's supposed to say now. And here's Ati miming words at her, looking a bit worried.

Back in Loana's house, relatives are shrieking, 'The plants, Materena. Rain is very good for the plants. *Aue!* Materena wake up!'

At the Beachcomber Hotel, Moana, outside the kitchen with one arm around his secret girlfriend, Vahine, is speaking to his mother in his mind: Mamie, the plants . . . the rain is very good for the plants.

In a house behind the petrol station, Pito, the receiver against the radio so that Tamatoa, in a phone booth outside a bar in Paris, can hear his mother doing her cinema on the radio, is saying out loud: 'The plants, Materena! What's wrong with you?'

In a house on top of a hill, Leilani, her head resting on her boyfriend's shoulder, her radio tuned to Radio Tefana for the first time ever, is doing telepathy with her mother: Mamie, say whatever comes to you . . . You always say interesting words anyway . . . Free your mind and the rest will follow . . .

'Rain,' says Materena, 'is very good for a woman's soul.' This sentence just spilled out of her mouth.

'What?' her relatives shout in despair. 'The plants, Materena!'

'You know, Ati,' Materena continues, not intimidated any more by the microphone, and the people staring at her from behind the glass window, 'people always say rain is good for the plants and that is true, but rain, especially when it sprinkles, is music to a woman's ears and warms the soul.' Totally at ease now, Materena continues to praise the rain. When it splatters on the tin roof, it makes you feel a bit melancholic, and takes you back to some happy days, or to those black years you've had but survived because you're a woman and surviving is not a foreign word to women from anywhere in the world. Watching rain is magic. It calms the anxious spirit and the tormented soul. It gives women hope. It reminds us how strong we are. Determined. Courageous. Understanding. And with so much love to give.

Rain is a miracle. Just like a woman is.

'You know, Ati,' says Materena, thinking, I hope I'm not raving on too much. Ati's eyes are popping out of his head. 'I'm so proud to have been born a woman. And as a proud woman I'm calling on all the women listening right now to share their stories on the radio for other women to learn something and be inspired. Every single woman has something to say. A story. A story about mistakes, obstacles overcome, discoveries, a story. A story that will help another woman take a step forward. A story that will warn another woman before she takes a step backwards. A story to reassure all of us that we're not all alone . . .'

'CALL NOW—84 27 17!' Ati, jubilant and showing Materena his thumb up, shouts into the microphone.

Back in Loana's house, an hour later, nobody can get through to the bloody radio. It's engaged all the time and it's making Loana very cranky. 'How many lines does that stupid radio have!' she exclaims. Some relatives have walked to the public phone thinking that there must be something wrong with Auntie Loana's telephone. Other relatives are quite happy just listening to all these lucky women who have managed to get through to Materena.

One woman talks about visualising her children in a tunnel of light whenever she knows they're driving at night, to help guide them safely home.

Another woman told the story of being abandoned by her mother.

Yet another woman told about how she loves her mother with all her heart and soul, and she'll always remember the day she had a splinter in her foot and her mother took it out with a razor blade. She remembers shouting out in pain and her mother telling her, What do you want, eh? It's hurting—we're always hurting us women, it's like that, it's life, we're born to suffer. We suffer but we don't cry. We have to be strong in life. When you fall, well, get up, go to work, clean the house, go and do something with your hands! And so? Do you think God is going to ask men to give birth? Do you think it's a man who transformed himself into a breadfruit tree to feed his family? Let's keep our tears for someone we love who died. Yes, then, it's worth crying.'

There are all kinds of stories on Radio Tefana tonight—funny, sad, unbelievable, frightening, inspiring. It sure beats watching TV.

A woman gave birth in the bathroom while she was showering to be clean for the hospital but she didn't make it. She didn't make it six times actually. Her six sons just wanted to come into the world with their mother under the shower.

A woman left her husband for true love with another woman. Another woman confessed how she's always wanted to be a detective.

A woman calls to tell Materena and all the women listening that her husband uprooted a tree she's planted just because it was dying. He didn't even try to save that tree, he just got the machete out. The woman is sure that when her turn to die comes, her husband will turn the machine off without remorse.

After Materena talked about her garden, a woman called to ask Materena for some help with *her* garden. Materena was more than pleased to share all that she knew about cuttings with that stranger.

One woman gave her man a black eye because he said her mother had a pitiful air and so she threw a mango at her man and gave him a pitiful air. He told his friends that he'd been involved in a fight . . .

Within a week of Materena being on air, she receives a contract from Radio Tefana. Screaming with joy and crying her eyes out, she grips onto that piece of paper, and hugs Leilani, embracing her daughter and her new life.

The day after Materena receives her contract in the mail Leilani invites her for lunch in town to celebrate the wonderful event and also because Leilani has an announcement to make.

'A good announcement or a bad one?' Materena asks.

'I'll meet you at Chez Patrick at twelve o'clock.'

By twelve thirty, Materena is still waiting and looking very much like she's been stood up. She's drunk all the water in the carafe and eaten all the olives on the plate, and she's getting crankier by the second.

This announcement of Leilani's better be important, she growls in her head. Meanwhile, the waiters (four in total) are busy taking dishes to tables, and none of them notices Materena's discreet wave. She'd like more olives, if possible. She only ate a little piece of bread this morning, saving herself for the restaurant food, but the waiters are so preoccupied, she understands. *Oh la la*, and plus it's so hot in here. But the nets on the ceiling are nice, they give the restaurant a bit of a Tahitian atmosphere. Materena makes a mental note to tell Moana about the nets. He might be interested about this idea when he opens his own restaurant.

Materena wonders what Leilani's announcement is about. Could it be a marriage announcement? Leilani and Hotu are still madly in love (so their neighbour is always kind enough to report to Materena).

She hopes Leilani hasn't forgotten the rendezvous. Leilani could be having lunch in the park with her boyfriend now as they've been doing for the past two years, leaving her poor mamie stuck in this restaurant.

Ah, finally! Here she is! The mad mood of Materena disappears in a flash. Firstly because she's going to be eating soon and secondly because Leilani is her daughter.

'Mamie!' Leilani calls out, walking in. 'I'm so sorry! We had an emergency at the surgery, a kid fell off his bike. Eight stitches!'

All heads turn to Materena's daughter. She's young, she's loud, and she has long legs and a beautiful face.

Leilani gives her mother a big embrace, falls on her chair, calls out to one of the waiters. '*Ouh-ouh!* Excuse me!' The waiter promptly attends to Leilani. 'Could we have more olives, please?' she says, flashing her white teeth. 'And some water, too, that would be great, *merci*.' Then turning to her mother she asks, 'So? What do you feel like eating?'

'What's the announcement?' Materena is too curious to wait.

'Let's eat first, Mamie.' Leilani is already looking at the menu.

'Is it a good announcement or a bad one?' When it comes to announcements Materena is very impatient. Never tell her you've got a surprise for her either. She'll hound you until you crack and then she'll be cranky at you for telling her about her surprise.

'I think I'll have fish. The grilled *mahi-mahi* with salad,' Leilani says.
'Me too.'

The grilled *mahi-mahi* rates ten out of ten with both Materena and Leilani. Their only criticism is that the portion is too small. But at least there was lots of bread and Materena isn't famished any more.

'So?' she says picking at a tomato. 'What's the announcement?'

Leilani fills her glass with water along with her mother's. 'A toast to you, Mamie,' she says. 'You are the most inspiring woman I know.'

Aue . . . what pride. Materena raises her glass, her other hand on her chest. 'Tchin-tchin.'

Mother and daughter gently knock their glasses together. 'So? The announcement?' asks Materena.

'Mamie, I'm leaving.'

'Pardon?' Materena wasn't expecting that kind of announcement. 'Leaving . . . Leaving what? Your job? Your boyfriend?'

'I'm leaving Tahiti.'

'To go where?'

'Mamie.' Leilani places a hand on her mother's hand. 'You know how you always tell me that things happen for a reason?'

'Things happen for a reason sometimes, not all the time.' Materena replies. 'What happened to you?'

Leilani recapitulates: She's called after Leilani Bodie, a medicinal woman. Biology and chemistry were her favourite subjects at school. She met a boy with whom she could explore these subjects. She got a job at a doctor's surgery facing her boyfriend's surgery. Under the guidance of the wonderful Dr Bernard, Leilani grew very fond of dealing with people in need, and helping them.

Leilani now has all five of her left-hand fingers down and she gives her mother the see-what-I-mean look.

'And . . .' Materena says.

'Mamie, I've found my purpose in life!'

'To be . . .'

'To be a doctor!'

'A doctor!'

'*Oui!*' Leilani takes her mother's hands and squeezes them tight, grinning. She goes on about how watching Dr Bernard made her realise how fulfilling life as a doctor can be. 'Doctors don't just write prescriptions and sign death certificates,' says Leilani. 'They investigate, they repair, prevent, nurture, educate, warn, help, love . . . Being a doctor, a good doctor, is a mission, not just a job. It's a purpose in life, you know, Mamie . . . It is mine.'

Materena is very happy her daughter has found her purpose in life, but . . . 'How long does it take to become a doctor?'

'Seven years.'

'Seven years! That's so long.'

'Mamie, I don't want to be forty like you and realise I should have done what I wanted a long time ago.' Leilani continues about how she's never seen her mother so happy since she got that job at the radio. 'Look at you, you're radiant, you're beautiful, you're so happy.'

'I was happy before.'

'You're the one who's always pushed me to know what I want and to make it happen.' Materena nods in agreement. But seven years . . .

'What about Hotu?' she asks. 'What does he say about it?'

Leilani confesses he's very upset but he understands that this is what she wants to do. The same as she understands that he won't be following her to university in France having already spent five years of his life there pursuing his own studies.

Materena looks down at her salad, thinking that young people today are so understanding. 'It's finished between you two, then?' she asks, even sadder now. Despite his annoying habits like chewing food for such a long time, Materena has grown very fond of Hotu over the past three years. He's like family. And he's such a good man. Three times Materena has looked at him thinking, what a wonderful father he's going to be for my daughter's children.

Leilani informs her mother that it is indeed finished.

'Aren't you sad?' Materena asks, looking at Hotu's initials tattooed on Leilani's hand.

'Of course I'm sad. Mamie, we both cried, Hotu and me. But there's no other solution than to go our own way.' Leilani explains that Hotu's life plan is to enjoy his work, continue to rediscover his island and start a family. And she refuses to ask him to consider altering his plans.

'I thought it was you he loved,' Materena says, wishing Leilani had not made her announcement in this crowded restaurant.

'He hasn't asked me to change my plan,' Leilani snaps. 'This is the best proof of his love for me.'

'What about his initials tattooed on your hand?' asks Materena.

'I'm keeping them . . .' Leilani's voice trails off. She looks away for a second and adds that he'll always be a part of her life.

Materena looks down at her salad again. Tears are falling into the lettuce. 'Seven years,' she whispers, sadly.

'Why are you sad? What would you have preferred? That I left you for a man?'

'Leilani, stop.'

'Please be happy for me,' Leilani pleads, her voice breaking up. 'I will be leaving all the people I love behind . . . if you think this is easy for me to do, it's not, *merde*. Mamie, it'd be easier for me to go on doing what I'm doing, but you showed me the way . . . Please say you're happy for me.' Leilani bursts into tears.

Materena is on her feet. Mother and daughter fall into each other's arms. 'I'm happy,' Materena cries, 'but I can't help it if I'm sad.' Materena goes on about how it's like that when you're a mother. Sometimes you cry but deep down you're happy.

She goes on agreeing with her daughter that it makes sense that she wishes to give something back to the world, having had such a fortunate childhood.

Before she walks through customs, Leilani, struggling with her shell necklaces, turns round to look at all the people who have come to wish her well in her journey.

She sees her father hiding behind a pillar. Auntie Rita is rocking her adopted three-month-old baby girl to sleep.

Moana and Vahine are holding hands.

Grandmothers Mamie Loana and Mama Roti are competing to cry the most tears. There's Mama Teta, Giselle and another auntie and more mamas. Nieces and nephews are yawning because they're not allowed to run around and because everybody is crying. It's so boring.

Leilani sees the man who will always be her inspiration in her journey as a doctor—Dr Bernard.

Her ex-mother-in-law, the one and only Constance, is all made up and the only one not crying.

She sees the man of her life and her heart feels like it's being crucified. She wants to run out to him and say, 'Come with me, I beg you.' But like that song says: If you love somebody, set them free. Sometimes, people who are so meant for each other don't meet at the right time.

She sees her mother presently, holding onto Uncle Ati, and Leilani bursts into tears. She walks to her mother, arms opened, for one more of her legendary hug-and-kisses. 'I will miss you, Mamie.'

'Go on,' Materena says, smiling through her crying and holding her daughter tight. '*Faaitoito*, girl, be strong. We're not women for nothing, eh? Bless the day you came into my life.'

Célestine Hitiura Vaite

The daughter of a Tahitian mother and a French father, who went back to his country after military service, Célestine grew up in a large extended family in Tahiti, where everyone was a relative or related somehow. 'I'm from the Mai family. My ancestor was Chief of Faa'a and one of the people to sign the French Protectorate. I grew up in Faa'a exactly where *Frangipani* is situated. We lived in a fibro shack behind a petrol station next to the international airport and not far from the Chinese store and the cemetery. My mum said recently, "I can't believe you put our fibro shacks in your books!"'

When she was growing up, Célestine loved to listen to stories about the old days, about Tahitian traditions, legends, customs and social etiquette. She was also an excellent student, winning a scholarship to one of Papeetes's most prestigious girls' schools, where she absorbed the French classics: Balzac, Flaubert, Zola and Maupassant. 'Books do change lives. They changed mine. I did not grow up in a family of readers. Tahitians are oral people—we do *parau parau*, talk talk. For my eighth birthday, my godmother gave me my first book, *Les Aventures D'Olivier Twist*—I wanted a Barbie doll! I read it to please her but very soon I was hooked on words. Reading was like being told a story except that I was in control. When I wanted to stop reading to go and play with my cousins, I just closed the book. However, interrupting an auntie telling me a story was, let me tell you, out of the question!'

At sixteen, Célestine fell in love with an Australian surfer. 'When I first met Michael, I had to pick my heart up off the ground. He was in Tahiti on a three-month working visa, shaping and spray-painting surfboards at a factory not far from where I lived. He was twenty-two and a sexy spunk!' After they were married, Célestine and Michael went to live in Australia and by the time she was twenty-two they had two children.

Despite her happy new life, Célestine reveals that she occasionally became homesick and would find a secluded spot in the sand dunes behind their home and cry. Pregnant with her third child, and overcome with nostalgia, she started a collection of short stories: *The Electricity Man*, *Leaving* and *The First Day Here*. Within weeks these stories about ordinary Tahitian people overcoming everyday obstacles were published in various literary journals. This led to Célestine creating Materena Mahi and her first novel, *Breadfruit*, so called because 'it is the food of the Tahitian people and represents for me the strength of women and the beauty of my island.' *Frangipani* is her second novel about Materena and she is currently working on a third, *Tiare*.

Célestine now has four children and, remaining true to her roots, they all follow the Tahitian tradition of every person having a birth tree. 'My eldest two children's birth trees are in my mother's garden in Faa'a, on their ancestors' fertile soil. The trees are huge, healthy and beautiful. The minute I get home, I caress those Tahiti trees and cry. The two youngests' birth trees are in our garden in Ulladulla, facing the Tasman Sea. They are gum trees; tough trees that tolerate salt sprays, wind and drought. We nearly lost them a few years ago during a bush fire and I remember thinking, "Take the house, take the cars, but not my sons' trees."'

So is the character of Materena Mahi based on her own mother? 'Materena is part my mother, part me. I also take one bit from this auntie and another bit from this cousin. My mother's very proud of my success but she's over the moon about my involvement with literacy programmes back home. I've made it my life's mission to blast the literacy rate in French Polynesia to the sky, and I will!'

Will *Tiare* be the final chapter for Materena and the characters created in *Breadfruit* and *Frangipani*? 'People ask me if there's one more book about Materena on the horizon, one more, just one. There isn't. I love Materena to bits, she's a wonderful and fun woman to be with until the early hours of the morning, but she has fulfilled her purpose now. It is time for her to go. She can finally put her broom to rest.'

Jane Eastgate